A STOUT CORD
and a
GOOD DROP

A STOUT CORD
and a
GOOD DROP

A Novel of the Founding of Montana

James M. Gaitis

TWODOT®

GUILFORD, CONNECTICUT
HELENA, MONTANA
AN IMPRINT OF THE GLOBE PEQUOT PRESS

A · TWODOT® · BOOK

Copyright © 2007 by James M. Gaitis

Text design: Lisa Reneson

Library of Congress Cataloging-in-Publication Data
Gaitis, James.
 A stout cord and a good drop : a novel of the founding of Montana / James M. Gaitis.
— 1st ed.
    p. cm.
 ISBN-13: 978-0-7627-4314-8
 ISBN-10: 0-7627-4314-X
 1. Montana—History—Fiction. 2. Gold mines and mining—Fiction. I. Title.
 PS3607.A36S76 2006
 813'.6—dc22

                                                    2006011883

Manufactured in the United States of America
First Globe Pequot Edition/First Printing

For my parents, in gratitude for their enduring patience

CONTENTS

A NOTE TO THE READER

The following tale has the merit of being rooted in fact, and in this sense it is historical. The story as written here, however, as being told by five youthful narrators (only two of which actually lived during and witnessed some of the events portrayed), is presented in fictional form, with all the license necessary for fiction writing having been self-granted to the author.

In depicting those occurrences that are critical to the development and outcome of the history, I have done my best to remain accurate. The existing written accounts of those early days, though, are incomplete and contradictory and contain the usual biases. A critical, and somewhat judicial, analysis was thus often required in order to derive the best interpretation of who did what, when, why, and to whom. In all such cases, I have sought to objectively and fairly make the most honest judgments possible, given the unique circumstances and conditions in which the players lived and acted.

The subject matter of the novel occurred more than 135 years before this work was first published. The novel is in no way intended to comment, whether directly or by inference, on people, institutions, or organizations living or existing at a later time.

"It has been commonly said in Montana that the Vigilante organization and the Masonic fraternity were practically synonymous. The true situation was probably more correctly expressed by Cornelius Hedges, second grand master of Masons in Montana, when he said that while it was by no means true that every Vigilante was a Mason it might be true without serious derivation from exact fact that every Mason in those days was a Vigilante."

—*Montana, The Land and the People,*
by Robert George Raymer,
The Lewis Publishing Company, 1930

BOOK I

WILL PEARSON

CHAPTER 1

If nothing else, the remote mining settlement of Bannack City was singularly busy on that cool, early October day in the year of 1862. We had come off the trail and straight into the center of Bannack and were now stopped again at the end of the long line of wagons. And Father saw the anxiousness in my eyes. "Get down if you want," he said. "But stay close." Then he and Mother sat patient and still while the wagon master, Bastrum, made his way back, easing from wagon to wagon with a casual air of indifference and accomplishment, having agreed along the way to change our destination and bring us to the gold strike at Grasshopper Creek, and having done so, too, albeit a month late with two new graves to mark the trail.

When he finally made his way to the back of the line, Bastrum said, "This is it, Pearson. Bannack City in all her glory, as promised."

And Father said nothing in return and instead continued to survey the mining hamlet with a look filled with weariness and maybe even frustration.

Then Bastrum offered his services to guide us on to Walla Walla for $50 more.

"I don't think so," Father answered. "We'll try our luck here.

1

Thanks just the same." So Bastrum pulled his mare back and moved on to the next wagon.

All around us the modest foundations of Bannack City declared the place to be nothing more than a ramshackle assortment of hastily thrown together structures, some little more than tents or mud huts with a billboard out front to identify what was supposed to be inside, be it a saloon, or bakery, or smithy. And the townspeople invariably were dressed in work clothes, with not a polished boot nor a piece of broadcloth in sight. And all along the main thoroughfare, the Indians about the town lazed indolently, looking like vagrant thieves in their throwaway white man's hats and clothes. So that there appeared to be very little of prosperity or anything else to our new home.

From where our wagon stood, as we waited our turn to pull out of line, we could see that an immense amount of labor was occurring all along the creek and up against the autumn brown hillsides where the miners fought with the hard rocky ground and the rushing creek water that pulled ceaselessly at their legs and arms. And in the town itself, the activity was just as vigorous, with banjo music emanating from one tent saloon, and mixed shouts of anger and laughter from another, and the ring of iron against iron hammering out rhythmically from a half-completed log building across the street. There was the smell, too, of burning wood and baking bread and roasting meat, and of a tar pit that smoldered somewhere unseen.

Against the unexpected tide of our wagons, an endless disorderly traffic of mules and wagons and oxen and pedestrians struggled—transporting logs and whipsawed lumber, tools and crated boxes, and sacks of food and wares—along and across the town's main street. As though, with an intent attitude toward construction and commerce, the citizens of Bannack had all but forgotten that they were all but alone in the world, their little would-be town isolated from the next outpost of humanity by hundreds of rolling and vacant miles.

The townspeople only slowly began to intercept members of our train. Then more came, drawn gradually and inexorably like steel to a magnet, off the creek and out of the buildings and away from their work to swarm about us all like frenzied ants, asking for news, particularly concerning the war between the North and South, and for mail, and newspapers, and other sundries that any one of us might be willing to sell them.

Bastrum had said, "Give them nothing, and sell them nothing 'til you understand the new prices." But we had nothing to give them anyway other than the details of what we knew of the great battles that had taken place at Shiloh and Seven Pines and Manassas and a dozen other places; and we had even less to sell, having been longer on the trail than we had expected and thus having eaten and used much of what we had hoped to keep for our first winter in the West. Father nonetheless allowed, and out of politeness even prolonged, their conversations, so that along with much chaff we thereby came to know that there was only one stable in midconstruction in Bannack City, and that land along the main street surveyed in plots of 50 by 100 feet, and that two new strikes had occurred along Grasshopper Creek in the past week, and that a dance was held every Saturday night. So I knew that we were staying before Father even said it, because one other stable was not enough competition to scare him off and move us on. And I saw, too, that Mother had already known it without having to pass a word with Father.

That was on the first day of our arrival at Bannack City, which was situated in an obscure cleft of the great Stony Mountains that was then part of the Dakota Territory and soon would fall within the Idaho Territory and then the territory of Montana, and long after that within the full-fledged state of the same name; and Father had no mind to let the day pass without getting settled in and started at making a living and a home. There were already the beginnings of that one stable in town, right there on the main street where everything else seemed to be located under some western myopic and linear concept of convenience—the hotel and saloon and gunsmith and bakeries and dry goods store, all in various stages of completion and strung out along the thoroughfare. But that didn't seem to bother Father much, seeing as how there soon would be two or more of just about everything else sitting on that dusty avenue. And he didn't as much as blink when the man told him the town had all been claimed and that it would cost him $300 for the lot and half-built cabin and the remaining logs, which sat together on the main street near where the freight route rose out of the little valley. Instead, he counted it out twice in gold coin until it equaled $300, never showing how much it hurt—when I knew it was close to half of what we had left after paying for the wagon supplies and Bastrum before ever driving out onto that battered track they had the nerve to call a road but which was really nothing more than a rutted and worn trail. Then came $50 more for the whipsawed lumber and half as much again for the extra logs Father had to buy because the hills around Bannack had been almost stripped clean of timber in order to build the town and the sluices you could see the miners running along the creek. And $5 a day more to pay a man to help us raise the rafters for the stables and set the posts for the corral, with the man working as hard and as fast and as long as he could just so he could buy enough more of food and supplies to stake another claim and go back to turning that creek inside out looking for more of the gold that some were bringing back in full canteens and which others hadn't even seen except in the hands of another man.

That was all there was to it: eight days of blisters and splinters and a lot of sweating (and some cursing too by the man who had helped) and a half hour more for me to paint the sign that said PEARSON STABLES & FARRIER. And then we were part of it, integral and resident to Bannack City, which was destined, Father said, to become another Salt Lake or San Francisco before it was over. And part, too, of something even greater, entailing all there was of Montana before they ever saw that it had to bear that name, with Bannack City and Grasshopper Creek and the hills and valleys and canyons being nothing more than the foreground for the great drama of wilderness that performed daily on its own terms beneath the forested and granite-chiseled mountains that rose everywhere in the distance, behind and around and above. At the time, it was hard for me to see it the way Father did, to see how the place could justify calling itself a city or ever expect to become one, not with the town being nothing more than a one-street affair, with the buildings all made of thatch or poles and bark or hastily cut and notched and chinked logs with incongruous plank and Athenian facades that showed the townsfolk knew it was just a barn-board hamlet but didn't want anybody who might be passing through to think it.

On the day we finished building the stables and corral, snow fell high up on the mountains to the west and north. It was cold, and when the snow stopped and the clouds came off the peaks, seemingly dissolving into the crisp, clear air, you could almost taste the winter that was to come. Father got his first bit of business that day, too. And it was as fine a piece of work as I had ever seen.

We were sitting underneath the stable eaves oiling tack, just like we used to do on Monday mornings in St. Louis, when a wagon pulled up with all sorts of shovels and picks and traps slung over its sides. The driver set its brake and then silently stared down at us, like we were supposed to be waiting for him to arrive. "Morning," Father finally said, and when the man on the wagon still said nothing, Father added, "Can we help you?"

"Ya'll open fer business here?" the man asked curtly, and when he spoke his lips curled inward and the white whiskers of his wiry beard covered his mouth such that it appeared he had no teeth at all and maybe even no lips. "Yer new in Bannack, ain't ya."

"We are, indeed," Father said as he rose and came up to the wagon. "Open and new."

The man said his horses needed shoeing, which was plain to see since they didn't have any shoes on them at all and their hooves were too long and one was split wide open and growing outward. "How much fer the lot of em?" the old man asked with that same mannerism that caused his whole face to scrunch up with every word he spoke. "An' keep in mind I ain't sure I can afford one of 'em let alone the whole team." Father quoted a price that was double what he had charged in St. Louis, and I thought he had overstepped it. But the old man said, "That'll do," and so we took the horses out of the traces one by one and Father began to shoe them in his best form.

All the while the old man talked and chewed at a wad of something and then spat, always aiming for the same area in the dirt and then mumbling "sorry" like he hadn't meant to or couldn't help spitting that juice that came out in a brilliant green quid, like the insides of a caterpillar, all thick and slimy and ambiguous. He had a dog with him, too; it looked like it had been in the same places as the old man, each just as ragged and dirty and matted as the other.

He talked a lot about prospecting and gold mining, and Father mostly listened and asked an occasional question while he worked deftly at the horses. During a moment of quiet, I asked what the dog's name was and the old man matter-of-factly said, "Rat."

It was a man's prerogative to name his dog, so I said nothing. Then the old man started idly talking about his dog, as if to himself. He recalled how he'd been a prospector out West in California just a few years after the rush in '49, and how he'd just about given it up when he met an Irishman in Sacramento who claimed to know geology and who had some ideas about how there was an undiscovered lode up the Feather River. "I was pretty much played out by then," the old man said as Father moved to another hoof. "So I joined up with that Irishman and we laid our plans. Went to work fer wages at a placer down the crick, and in a few months we had us enough to buy an outfit, and we pulled out and went to the feeders off the Feather River an' started lookin' fer that lode. An' everywhere that little Irishman went, these two dogs of his followed along. A big wolfish dog, gentle as a kitten, an' a little dog, floppy ears, big feet," saying this while he bent and scratched at Rat's mangy head.

The old man said how the Irishman was right about the gold and that after a month or so, they knew they had a find and that they'd be needing more supplies and materials to build them a real mine and get at the vein. "So I loaded up my possibles," he said, "an' left my partner in our little cabin in the pines and headed back down."

Father was what you might call proper, and so I thought he might make some kind of comment when the old man described in some detail how he had met up with a young Spanish girl down in the town where he was getting the supplies and how he got sidetracked and was running two weeks late before he started back up to the mining claim and the Irishman. But Father just kept on with the shoeing and never even looked up, and the old man continued on as before. "Wound my way up that mountain and back down into the canyon, an' when I got there, there weren't no one round outside that cabin; an' Max, that was my partner's name, didn't come outta the cabin or up from the crick when I yelled. So I took the load off the mules an' sat down under a tree an' smoked me a cigar an' drank a little of the whiskey I'd brought back fer the both of us. An' I sat there thinkin' 'bout that girl, and then thinkin' 'bout that gold me an' Max was findin', an' I couldn't decide what to do. I can't tell ya how pretty she was. Long black hair. Black eyes. Smooth skin.

"I must've been real tired from ridin' that mule—took me three days—so I sort of took a nap beneath that tree. When I woke, it was gettin' dark an' there still weren't no sign of Max. So I walked over to the cabin an' decided I'd fix up some beans an' wait fer Max to get back from wherever he was. I found that big dog lyin' right there inside the door, all bloated an smellin' of death and flies all over 'im. An' Max was there too, an' he was just as dead, lyin' on the cot an' covered with more of them flies. But the other one, that little dog, was still alive, eatin' on one of Max's leather boots when I walked in.

"Weren't the first dead man I'd seen; weren't even the first one I'd found. But I wasn't none too happy 'bout it. Max was a good man, as they go. Shared his food; even shared his dreams. An' that's more than most are willin' to do. An' I felt kinda lonely there with them bodies, an' I pulled 'em outside an' gassed 'em an' went back in to get a shovel to dig a grave. That's when I saw what happened. There were claw marks on the box where the food was locked up to keep out the bears, an' scratches on the door where that poor dog finally couldn't even claw no

more. An' I got mad. 'Cause it seemed like Max died without even
thinkin' 'bout either of them dogs; and here they were the best two dogs
in the world with the big one not eatin' the small one when he could've
to stay alive, an' the little one not eatin' either of 'em once they were
dead an' it would have been all right to do it. The best two dogs in the
world, an' Max never gave 'em a chance to make it on their own. Just
closed that door on 'em an' died with the dogs sittin' there hungry an'
thirsty an' cryin'."

The old man shook his head as if the recollection of it all were
somewhat painful. And then he said, "I buried 'em together. Put the two
of 'em together in a grave, an' covered 'em with limestone an' dirt, an' I
carved a marker on a stone to say MAX O'KEEFE AND A DOG, 'cause that
big dog weren't his no more than the mountains an' the trees, even if they
did die together. An' I took that little dog with me, an' I named him Rat,
'cause he managed to survive only by scratchin' it out when there weren't
no other way. Just like a rat would do. An' I'll tell ya this much: fer all
these years we've been together since, ole Rat here ain't never gone into
no cabin with me less'n there's a way fer him to get back out."

Father finished his work and got up. He smiled at the old man
just as the old man stopped talking. We'd had dogs before ourselves,
mostly strays that would come and set up in the stables. And Mother
always would go about talking Father into letting me keep and feed
them as long as they were willing to keep clear of the horses. But I
wasn't allowed to bring any of them West with us because Father had
said they would just impede us when we didn't even know what it was
we might encounter. And I believe it had hurt him as much as me
when we pulled out of St. Louis in that wagon and one of the strays
followed behind until Father fired off the shotgun and turned him
back. Because in the end it was usually Father who tended to them,
bringing table scraps and corn bread with him into the stable when he
thought Mother and I weren't looking, and feeding the strays by hand
when he just as easily could have dropped the food scraps in the dirt
and soiled hay.

We walked out into the sunlight with the last horse in tow, and Father said, "I'd like to get Will here a dog for company one of these days. Expect one'll show up, and then we'll have us one."

The old man shot a perfect stream of his green quid into the dust. "Wouldn't go bettin' on it," he said. "Them Shoshones think a dog's a delicacy. Seen 'em roastin' on spits in the middle of the trail. No, sir, a stray dog don't last long in these parts."

I hated the Indians for it and might have even said so, except the next thing I knew the old man was offering Rat to us. Father smiled and shook his head. "That's right kind of you, friend. But I couldn't allow it; a man's dog's a special thing."

The old man had Rat on his back by then, and one of Rat's legs was akickin' uncontrollably at the air. "Truth is," he said, "I'm headin' into the high country to set some trap lines, an' ole Rat's got too many years on 'im to be up there with all them wolves and cats runnin' around. Like as not, I'd lose 'im before the new year. Be the best thing fer 'im to be stayin' here. Long as you promise to feed 'im an keep 'im outta the rain. He don't like lightnin' an' thunder."

"All right then; we'll keep him," Father said. And as if on cue, Rat came up to us and rolled onto his back to expose his underside, which was every bit as mangy as his top.

When we got back out front, Father noticed something about the old man's wagon, and he moved under it to look more closely. "You're going to lose this wheel here any minute," he said to the old man. "Got three spokes cracked clean through, and the hub's split."

"Know it," the old man said. "Wheelwright ain't got any in stock though. Says it won't be fer another week before them Mormon freighters bring in his order up from Salt Lake. An' I can't chance another week if I'm gonna get my traps out. Just got to chance it an' hope fer the best."

Our wagon was sitting out there right next to his, and it would have been an oversight to not notice that the wheels on ours and his were exactly the same. And I guess now I'm glad that it was Father and not me that pointed it out, but at the time I wished it had been me because we'd got Rat and it only seemed fitting. "Guess I could sell you one of mine," Father said. "What does the wheelwright charge?"

The old man shook his head and came over and patted Father on the back. "I couldn't let you do it," he said. "Being without yer wagon fer a week or better."

Father smiled then. "I've got no use for that wagon in the next week. How much are they?"

"Fifteen dollars," the old man answered. "But I won't take it from ya fer less than $25." Father said no to that, but the old man insisted, saying he was flush with dust anyway; so they weighed it out on the new scale Father had bought in St. Louis, the $25, plus the price of the shoeing, almost three ounces of flaky gold at $18 an ounce, which is what Bastrum had said was the price in Bannack for the assay out of the Dakota lode. And it sure was shiny and clean to the eye.

The old man drove off with his horses all neatly trimmed and shod and the wagon no longer lurching like it had when he pulled up, and the sky now perfectly clear of the clouds that had vaporized into the nothingness of the ether, and Rat sitting at our side like he'd always been a part of the family. And I could tell Father was pleased, not so much with having made some money off the shoeing (and the wagon wheel, too, once he bought another) as by the fact that his hands had seen work again and we had had a neighborly exchange.

Two or three days later, we went over to the wheelwright's and Father asked him when he thought his shipment of wheels would be in. The man just looked at him quizzically. "I'm not expecting no shipment here," the man said. "Make my own wheels from scratch up." Father didn't have anything to say to that so he asked him to make him a front wheel and gave him the dimensions. "It'll be $20, up front," the wheelwright said.

Father pulled out the wide-mouth flask into which he had placed the old man's gold. And when he poured the contents out unto the little scale on the counter, the wheelwright looked at him and frowned.

"You're new in town, ain't ya?" he said. And when Father said he was, the wheelwright asked him where the gold dust had come from. So Father told him about the old man, and the wheelwright said, "Well, you've been taken, my friend. What you got there is mostly sand an' galvanized copper. By the looks of it, I'd say it's a quarter gold, at best. Ain't nobody in town that's gonna take that for payment for nothin'."

So after you counted the cost of the cabin and the logs and the whipsawed lumber and labor to build the stables and the corral, together with the $20 for the new wheel, we were less about three-fourths of what we had started with. And short, too, of sixteen horseshoes and the nails it took to set them. And we had Rat, who proved to own a much greater appetite than one would have thought his size allowed.

CHAPTER 2

Over the next few weeks we learned a lot about living in the wilderness, much of it stemming from that one experience involving what Mother called the fool's gold, the colloquial name of which grated on Father like a whetstone on a dull knife. The first thing Father came to know was that there was no law in town. We searched it out that very afternoon the wheelwright discovered our loss and were told by the tattooed proprietor at Skinner's Saloon that there was no such thing in Bannack City. "We ain't go no law department here," he said with a peculiar grin. "What we got's a miners' committee. You got a problem, you can be sure the committee'll handle it."

Father wasn't one to go against the flow, so he asked where he might find the committee, only to be queried as to whether he'd staked a claim in the district. "Pretty much need to be a miner if you're wantin' somethin' from the committee," Skinner said as he poured drinks for a couple of dirty miners who had walked in and up to the bar.

Skinner's was really nothing more than a large cabin with a dirt floor and a long, crudely constructed bar running along one wall, together with a bunch of roughly hewn tables and chairs spread about, all camouflaged out front with that same Greek-revival facade behind which half the town coyly hid. Nothing to adorn the walls, no etched nor leaded mirror to reflect the dark, weathered visages of the hard men who sat at or stood by the bar and who found it necessary and even proper to carry their pistols and shotguns with them into the saloon, the guns no doubt primed and readied for firing; in fact, nothing at all to distinguish the place other than the rank odor of sweat and cheap liquor and cheaper tobacco.

At the time, I knew little of the impulse of working men to gather together and drink intoxicants and smoke tobacco and gamble and lie out of all proportion to their general means. That, and the rain that had begun to fall, however, were apparently enough that afternoon to crowd the bar and fill two full tables with monte players and other gamblers who readily won and lost the soft, golden fruit of their labors on the turn of a card or role of the dice.

Someone from one of the tables asked Father if he'd been robbed, and someone else asked more generally why he needed the law, but Father didn't answer them. "Guess there's no judge here either," he said instead to Skinner, who paused without answering and then suddenly drew a pistol from underneath the bar and shot it into the wall with great effect. Several of the patrons began to hoot and whoop, and a number of them drew their pistols and shot them into the wall, too, or into the roof. And then they returned to their cards and dice.

"This here's the only law you need to know about," Skinner said after the demonstration cooled, hefting his pistol in his hand and half exposing the tattooed woman beneath his sleeve. "Least ways in my place it is."

Father bought a drink from Skinner for a quarter dollar and was paying him with some of the dust he had purchased at the assay office when we heard the clatter of hooves on the boardwalk outside. And then a man entered the saloon; he was strong limbed with light hair and a rather gallant look about him with his Union greatcoat and white cavalry hat suggesting experience, if not authority. With an air of stubborn indifference, he led behind him a fine-looking sable mare, as if bringing a horse into a saloon was in no way out of the ordinary. He came up to the bar so that the horse almost knocked me aside. "Forty rod," he stated in a loud emphatic voice, and then he slammed his fist down on the bar as if to punctuate his order.

Skinner bit at the inside of his cheek and shook his head. Then he slowly reached down under the bar where he had just replaced the pistol, all the while keeping his eye directly on the man. But he only brought out a rag with which he wiped at the counter, sending the tattooed lady dancing in and out from underneath his cuff. "I done told you before, George," he finally said, calmly and without irritation. "I ain't servin' you if you bring that goddamn horse in here."

George Ives, the horseman, motionlessly dropped the reins, which he had been holding behind his back. "Look for yourself now, Cyrus," he said. "I didn't bring her in; followed me in all by herself. Fact is, I tied her up outside and told her to stay put, but she said, 'I'm the one doin' the work and I'm thirsty,' and she untied herself and came in after me." And then he exploded in a wild, self-congratulatory laugh and slapped Father hard against the back, spilling his drink. Father looked a bit stunned until everyone started to laugh, and he joined them; and I wanted to also but could only muster something less.

They all talked awhile longer, and it was as though George Ives's horse was just one of the crowd. The conversation centered mostly on the old man who had finessed the free shoeing and wagon wheel out of Father. Ives found it all to be a fine joke. He seemed to know all about the old man, whom he referred to only as Old Man Sessions. Ives claimed the old man had carried his cache of bogus gold with him wherever he went, throughout the mining camps for two years now, and had managed to make half a living off it just by moving from one place to the next, preying, as George Ives put it, on "porkeaters" who'd come from out East and who didn't know a nugget from a pebble. "Won't come back neither since he knows that stealin' from a man's bad enough, but hurtin' his pride's even worse," he said. "An you'd never find him if you went lookin'; not with three days lead and him with two years practice.

Otherwise, I'd take ole Sally here, once she's through gettin' her drink that is, and go out with you lookin' for him." To which Father said he was much obliged.

So we learned that much—that there was no ordinary law in Bannack City. And we also learned why, from no less a worldly source than Carlon Bishop, who, as the local shipping agent of the Mormon freighter Shelton, took and oversaw the ultimate delivery of orders placed for shipment out of Salt Lake City. "You've got no use for law-men here," he told us as we stood at the counter of the new freight office while Father reviewed the price lists of items available for order and delivery. "This place has all the makings of another Nevada City without having to push it along in that direction."

So Father asked, "Why's that? What happened there that makes peace and order so undesirable in Bannack?"

"I'd say you ain't never heard of Henry Plummer, mister," Carlon Bishop said while he wrote the order Father was already placing in antic-ipation of a busy spring. "Or road agents neither. Well, Nevada City thought they needed the law there too, so they got them some in the form of a man named Henry Plummer. Fastest gun west of the divide. A charmer, too. Ladies' man. Professional gambler. Best miner in the ter-ritory. And a Democrat politician to boot. And before he was through, he'd shot him a score of good men and ruined the reputation of as many good women and burnt down the whole town and broke clean out of jail twice. Now that's what you end up with when you go tryin' to get law. Nothin' but trouble in a big, big way." He was fairly wound up by then, and Father didn't seem to care to continue the implausible thrust of the conversation, so I didn't remind the man that he had failed to enlighten us as to what road agents were and where they might be found.

That was the first rumor we heard of Henry Plummer, but in no way the last. The approach of the winter season that year was foretold by more than the browning of the grasses and the turned leaves of the cottonwood and alder and the swift organized flight of the geese and ducks and cranes high overhead. We were witness, as well, to a steady influx of immigrants, together with a wave of latecomers to the strike at Grasshopper Creek. Among the confused and burdensome baggage they drew with them were the hearsay and convoluted and ever-exaggerating histories of the entire region, most of it associated somehow with the uncompromising struggle to isolate and exhume vast treasures of gold and silver, interlaced with tales of notorious and famous men (and for that matter, several women, too) including that of Henry Plummer who, by some accounts, was capable of single-handedly terrorizing the entire West, or, as conversely told by others, was the model of all that was good and true.

I believed some of it, I admit. Maybe even a lot of it, because it wasn't just the men telling the men, but also the women in town exchanging facts (as they called them) among themselves and thereby with Mother, with the new boys and young men telling me as well. So that there was this form of mitigating corroboration that you couldn't just totally ignore. But I never believed all of it, not with the anecdotes themselves being so numerous and diverse that if you took them all as gospel truth they described, in collage, a man that was at once an incarnation of all that could ever be good and evil: the Savior and Lucifer combined, with a penchant both for the highest forms of grace and the most lascivious degree of vice, indiscriminate and impalpable, at once thief and protector, chivalric and whoring, misanthropic and charitable, far past the plausible capacity of any single human being. Besides, it was not as though this Henry Plummer alone had distinguished himself by notoriety; there were many others described with approbation or acclaim within the rumor mill. It was only that Henry Plummer stood out above the rest, supposedly being some each of desperado and lawman in an untamed frontier that recognized that a man could be one or the other, but not both. So I believed some of it, at least; and the more I learned about men in general in the year and so many months that followed, the less I trusted to believe in any man, woman, or child.

~~~~

Father, at that time, came to be the most changed in our family by what I thought to be the meager loss of sixteen horseshoes and a wagon wheel. He took to wearing his army revolver in a holster at his side and kept the Henry rifle in a saddle holster, ready and loaded at the door. He also took up mining. At first, Mother was against it. "You have more than enough to do here," she said, "without digging in the ground for treasures like a mad fool."

And there was that word again, bothering Father even more when it was Mother that was using it. But that didn't stop him from resisting her, explaining that it wasn't for the money, not for the gold dust hidden randomly in the gravel that lay beneath the creek bed and up against the canyon ledges and spurs: "It's this miners' committee of theirs, Nadine. It's plain these miners are only serving themselves by that organization; there's no protection for us here unless I become one of them, so that if and when the time comes, this committee of theirs will give us the same dispensation as it gives to all of them."

And it was true. The miners' committee didn't seem to operate by any particular rule except that miners be protected, not only from each other but from anyone else that dared to interfere with their peculiar lifestyle of toil and debauch. So with Mother's reluctant agreement Father paid another one hundred of our dollars for a claim that had never been more than slightly panned—$100 for 100 feet of creek from canyon ledge to canyon ledge—and I found myself responsible at least every third day for tending the stables and business alone while Father satisfied the district's rule that an unworked claim was free to be jumped by any man who saw fit to do it.

He didn't know what he was doing, of course. There was far more to it than digging a hole in the rock and silt and picking out handfuls of nuggets or dust. And Mother showed no appreciation after his first few efforts when he brought home some glistening rocks that, other than being modestly pretty to look at when they were wet, were perfectly and utterly without any worth. Then one day he brought home an ounce of dust, $18 worth by Bannack City standards, and on another, twice that much, and Mother finally let it be known that perhaps this mining was for the best after all. In the meanwhile, I eased into my own new-found responsibilities, dealing with men who wanted to stable a horse or a mule, purchasing and receiving hay from the cutters up on Horse Prairie, on the same terms as Father would offer on any other day. And some of them who before had called me "Boy" or "Son" now addressed me as Will and even shook my hand or slapped my back in appreciation for a subtle witticism I might offer for their consideration.

~~~

In the weeks that followed, there was an increasing number of trans-gressions of almost every type. Horse thieving in particular seemed to be a common occupation; and while it is certain that much of it could be attributed to the Crows and Bannocks and Flatheads and Shoshones, it was just as clear that white-skinned people, also, were relieving right-ful owners of their stock. To these thefts I attributed the shootings of several Indians, two of whom died and another who might have but didn't. It also became more of a risk to travel the roads and trails from Bannack to Spanish Fork and Hell Gate and Salt Lake City. And while the assumption prevailed that organized bands of marauding men—those same road agents that Carlon Bishop had warned us of—were waylaying travelers for their purses and canteens filled with dust, I sus-pected that the increase in criminal activity was merely proportionate to the increase in traffic upon the roads.

There were also a variety of more petty altercations on the street, in the saloons, at the dance hall, anywhere that man's spleen and endless vexations might be vented freely and aloud. Mostly, these ended in newly formed or rekindled friendships, professedly of eternal and unseverable duration, consummated by the shake of bloodied hands. Only rarely did the unseen thrust of a knife or flight of a derringer ball, neither of which were generally enough to kill but always sufficient to debilitate or maim, bring the quarrel to a close.

These disturbances greatly agitated Father, and I silently attributed to their collective advent the fact that I twice chanced upon him practicing the quick draw with his pistol within the darkness of the closed stables where he would not be noticed. Then, maybe two days later, on an afternoon that held no promise of being any different than any other, with the midday flow of traffic modest, and the placers still being heavily worked in appreciation of the mild November weather, and the saloons reasonably suspended in quiet anticipation of the evening's celebrations, and the sky a bright even blue that made you glad that you were there with the world as wide and open as it could ever be, two men rode down into Bannack City carrying an object rolled up in a blanket and slung over a mule. They came up Main Street and into the quiet with that wide blue sky above them, and it would have been obvious that it was a body that they brought, even if that arm had not slipped out and jostled with each plodding step that mule lazily took. They rode up the freight road to the cemetery since there wasn't any undertaker, and no preacher either, and a slow but growing stream of townsfolk trailed behind them.

Mother and I had gone to Mrs. Gibson's and we missed it entirely. But Father didn't; he was among the crowd. When he returned later, his pants and hands dirtied from the newly turned earth, he told us that it was none other than George Guy, whom I knew to say hello to and to whom Father and several others had given sums of money to purchase certain items at Salt Lake City, where Guy had been headed with his team and wagon.

That was not enough for Mother though. She had learned long ago of the tendency men harbored to limit the permitted flow of information to their womenfolk, and she as quickly had denied its application to her. "Well, what happened to him, Walt?" she asked in a tone that insisted on fact and not evasion. And then voicing her greatest fear, she added, "Was it Indians?"

Father drew a deep breath and looked down at me at the slightest angle with an expressionless gaze, like he couldn't bear to answer her but could still talk to me. "I don't know, Nadine," he said. "He's been murdered; that much is clear. They found him down at Red Creek. He'd been robbed and that team of his is gone, but he wasn't scalped so I couldn't say." He didn't offer anything else, and he left it to our imagination to picture how it had been done and what the wounds might look like up close.

Mother stood there, as if she were waiting for something more. And when he continued to stand motionless, staring at me like she wasn't even there, she asked, "How much did you give him, Walter?"

"One hundred dollars," the answer came back in a confessing monotone.

"One hundred dollars!" Mother exclaimed. And then she said, "Oh, Walter. We hardly have that much all told."

"It was in gold dust, Nada, from the claim," Father said, again in that tone that was expressionless and vacant. "I'd been saving it on the side." And then, when she said nothing else and instead just stared and waited for the rest, he said, "It was for Christmas, Nada. All right. It was for something special for you for Christmas; and now it's gone." And when he went to the drawer where he kept the boxes of pistol and rifle caps and balls and drew them out, I knew he was going to join the other men in looking for the killers of George Guy.

There was never any suggestion that I might go with him and the other men, that I could be of some help with the horses, perhaps, or something even more mundane in comparison to the real nature of their business. I knew him that well, at least; so I never even asked, never even proposed that I could cook their meals or set the picket line for the horses or reload their guns. Which left us, me and Mother, with nothing else to do than just stand there as he packed his bedroll in silence and stuffed some flour and salted pork and dried beans and his cooking gear into a leather sack and then put on his hat and moved toward the door. I offered to saddle and bridle his horse, and Mother began to arrange for the food, but he said no, he'd do it himself.

He allowed us only to go out to the stables with him, to be able to say good-bye to him, I suppose, in the sanctity of the outdoors rather than through the hard finality of an opening and closing door. Hank Crawford and Harry Phleger, and the two men who had found George Guy, and some others were already there, waiting. Their conversations were muffled even as we approached and seemed to fall in volume and increase in ambiguity as we came nearer. Then Father was atop his horse, and then they moved off down the street and up the freight road until the dull sounds of rubbing leather and the stamp of hooves in the dust dissipated and the silence reemerged.

We ate our evening meal that night in the same empty silence, broken only by the courtesy of an offer or a thanks. And that night, after I had tended to the stables and Mother had cleaned and put away the dishes, it almost seemed natural that there would be but the two of us alone in the narrow confinement of the one-room cabin.

He didn't return the next morning either, and that made sense, too, because it was a good distance to where they had found George Guy on the route southward, and they would have to be cautious, and Hank Crawford, who was leading the search, seemed slow in everything he did. And then there would be the difficulties in transporting prisoners, or bodies maybe, if it came to that. So we went about our separate chores, turning every now and then to see if he were coming up the street or down off the freight road, listening for the sound of the horses and mules, the squeak of leather and the stamp of hooves.

At the table that evening, the same oppressive silence returned, with Mother breaking it only by offering me more of the meat or bread and me thanking her without looking too directly into her eyes. And then suddenly he was there in the doorway and Mother was standing, and we knew instantly that they had not found the killers, because he was already shaking his head and telling it as he came through the door and dropped the bedroll and took off his hat. "We didn't get 'em, Nada. We did all we could, but the signs are just too confused. Hank wanted to keep after it, but we finally convinced him it was a waste of time."

Then he was in the cabin and the door was closed, and then he was sitting down at the table with his head buried in his hands. "Old George's wagon was still there," he said without looking up. "So we brought that back anyway. But there's no telling what happened out there, not with the trail being four days old and four days worn by wind and traffic. We did all we could, and that's the end of it."

But a week later, Henry Plummer himself arrived in Bannack City. He rode straight up to the stables on a large bay gelding with a handsome packhorse behind and dismounted with a fluid, effortless motion that showed he knew horses well. He approached the gate in an even, casual stroll, taking the time to stoop and gently pat Rat along the head and back. And I could see beneath his mud-spattered artillery greatcoat that his clothes were finely made—linen shirt, silk tie, felt hat no worse for sunshine or rain. And while I did not as yet know that he was Henry Plummer, there was something about him that told me he wasn't just another novice miner or merchant aiming to make his riches fast in the gold town boom. He wore a revolver in a scabbard at his hip; a shotgun with a bolted stock lay loosely across his saddle.

"Good morning, my young friend," he said with a calm, peaceful, genuine smile and an elegant voice. "Are you in charge of this establishment?"

"Yes, sir," I said. "This here's Pearson's Stables and I'm Will Pearson."

He looked around, perhaps for a price listing, but more likely, I thought, for an adult. "And may I ask what the going rate is for two horses, brushed and bedded?"

Now the rate had been $1 a day, but then Father had commented one evening on how there were so many people with horses and mules moving into town that it seemed traffic could bear an increase. So now it was a $1.50 a day and 50 cents more to have them groomed.

"That will be fine, just fine," he said. "I would like to board them until I tell you otherwise." All the while the gelding stood iron still, not moving 1 inch from the moment he had been dismounted. "And if you please, you will need to keep him separate all the time."

He paid in dust for three days in advance, trusting my application of the scales when few others had, and then he told me he would return with the horses after he had an opportunity to unpack them at the new Goodrich Hotel, erected out of timbers and fronted with clapboard, down the street, next to Skinner's.

"What name should I put them under?" I asked.

"Henry Plummer," he said. "Two *m*'s."

~~~

There were plenty of miners in Bannack City who knew Henry Plummer from the Oro Fino mines on the other side of the mountains, and even some from California where Henry Plummer had been sheriff at Nevada City. It was thus logical that his name would be bandied about when talk arose, as it often did, about the posse's failure to catch George Guy's killers. And since Crawford had led the posse, it was Crawford's name, and Henry Plummer's, that came up again, and again, in the conversations in the saloons and in the broken discussions that occurred while sluices were being built and gravel shoveled and the creek mined.

Father reacted poorly to it, to the suggestion that repeatedly could be heard on the street, along the creek, in the stores, and in the shops, that perhaps they would have found George Guy's killers if Henry Plummer had been along on the search. And perhaps it didn't help when Henry Plummer took to visiting our neighbors and us as well. There was no fanfare to it; he just came over to the stables early one morning, all neat and shaved as if he'd been up for hours and had already been to the barber and had himself a bath. "I just wanted to introduce myself, Mr. Pearson," he said. "And to offer to you and Mrs. Pearson my services if you might ever be in need. I have prior experience as a law officer and very much feel it is every citizen's duty to do his part."

It didn't seem much to me then, Henry Plummer's being neighborly and all, and it didn't bother Mother any either, because he had said "madam" to her and had taken his hat off completely. And he always was clean shaved, with his shirts starched and pressed, and a neat black tie to close the collar, such that Mother said he seemed every bit the gentleman and that she had no doubt that the stories she had heard were nothing more than the fabrications of people who had nothing better to do than bear malicious jealousies against a man like Mr. Plummer. Father didn't like Mother's attitude much, but he held it back, saying nothing of it to her.

In the end, the competition that had arisen between Hank Crawford and Henry Plummer, sometimes manifesting itself subtly and on other occasions in much more blatant form, had a particularly polarizing effect, with half the town now siding with Crawford and as many just as ardently revering Henry Plummer, who furthered his cause by courting the womenfolk who, while having no formal vote in matters, nonetheless carried great powers of persuasion in the doings of Bannack City. It got so that Henry Plummer and Hank Crawford seemed to be the focal point of every conversation in Bannack, until one day Plummer accosted Hank Crawford in the street and insisted he wished to be his friend. And when Hank Crawford finally shook hands, though somewhat reluctantly and without feeling, the public debate subsided.

Through the final month of 1862 there was little hardship occasioned by inclement weather. Which perhaps was unfortunate, since the mild conditions engendered an unhindered restlessness; the violence increased, dispatching itself with greater viciousness and intensity. You would hear a noise as you worked or slept, a gunshot or a crash or an angry word, and you would know that something else had occurred, somewhere. And on occasion you might not even react to it at all, going on, instead, with your task or sleep and not bothering with what almost came to seem commonplace. But there were times when you could not avoid it, as was the case when I watched through the rear stable door as George Ives and George Carrhart, who were said to be the best of friends, took shots at each other from 30 feet apart. The one would discharge his revolver and you could tell how close the ball came to the other by the way the other would suddenly move away in one direction, showing more that he had heard the ball whiz by than that there was any chance of its being dodged. And then the other would fire back with the same result, each intentionally missing the other by inches and the other trying all the while to not move.

In the long run, it was Carrhart that showed he had less nerve for the game, or maybe less trust in Ives than Ives had in him. Because the two of them were not being playful about it. Ives was calling Carrhart by every profane name he could think of, and Carrhart was returning it to him, until Ives finally fired two shots in sequence, the first hitting at Carrhart's feet and Carrhart diving for the ground when he saw that Ives had changed the rules and maybe his intent as well. And when Ives saw Carrhart facedown in the dirt, Ives spat and swore at him again, and then Carrhart rose and shot Ives in the back, or more accurately in the side of his back so that the ball passed clean through Ives's flesh and raised up some dust in the street before him. And the remarkable thing about it wasn't that Ives merely grabbed his side and turned and swore at Carrhart again and then marched off, but that two days later the two men had reconciled and resumed their joint living arrangement.

Father had been at the claim all that day, and Mother had joined Mrs. Ball and Mrs. Waddam for a washing outing at the creek. When I told them about it at the dinner table that evening, Father wanted to know more. "You're saying they weren't trying to hit each other? Is that what you're saying?"

"Least ways it looked that way," I answered, "since when the one who was shooting missed, he seemed as happy about it as the one he was shooting at."

"I'm not sure which is worse," Father said, shaking his head. "Trying to kill each other in broad daylight in the middle of town, or trying to miss and taking the chance that someone else will catch a stray ball through a window or open door."

There was a dance scheduled at the Roundhouse for Christmas Eve, and it was understood that anyone who cared for society was expected to attend. Father recognized the event as an important outlet for Mother, the dance being one of very few opportunities for her to be freed from our smallish and poorly ventilated cabin. He thus encouraged her every preparation. She made herself up in her most presentable attire, her Sunday-best fully pleated, with the bottom hoop perfectly in place; and she attended to our appearances as well, with our collars starched and ties pressed and boots blackened and polished. "Now you promise me, Walter," she insisted before we left the house that evening, "there will be no imbibing by either of you," looking sternly over to me as if to say, "Yes, I know, you are soon to be sixteen, so you can call yourself a man and act like a man and can even be a man, but I am still your mother and am not to be denied."

It delighted Mother when Father offered to take us in the wagon so that she need not worry about her dress; and she said she felt "such the lady" as Father drove the wagon the entire third of a mile from our stables across the creek ford to the large log building at which the dance was to be held. We arrived early, and that pleased Mother also. Father paid out the $5, times three, in dust from his claim and then directed me to take the wagon back home, at which I protested and he insisted.

Mother was at the height of her anticipation when I returned. She seemed to be in the throes of a need to see everything at once; her eyes darted from one side of the great room to the other, cataloging who was there, what they wore, to whom they spoke. "There's the Waddams, Walt. I was afraid they might not come," I heard her say. "Wilson has had quite a battle with the mountain fever." And then she moved on to another subject. "Who is that man in the flannel shirt without a tie?" and, "One would hope they'd make it warmer in here before the dancing starts." And it soon became apparent which aspects of the party met with, or without, Mother's approval.

The Roundhouse was spacious by Bannack City standards. A puncheon floor had been laid reasonably smoothly such that the place was as good as was available to hold a dance. In Bannack's earliest days, the building had served as a diminutive fortress by which the discoverers of Grasshopper Creek planned to defend themselves from Indian attacks that never came. Now it was a sort of community hall where the townspeople gathered on occasion to dance and celebrate their frontier camaraderie. And it served its function well. There were plenty of chairs along the walls upon which to take your rest, and a large wood stove in one of the corners from which a generous amount of heat emitted. And while there was no supper provided in the formal sense, there was enough of punch and pies and other sundry pastries and meats to more than make a meal. There was a sufficiency of everything, in fact, except the female gender, of which there was a known and notable imbalance. The attending women thus proved to be in such great demand that particular evening that a great discourtesy resulted, for they were hardly ever afforded a respite from their efforts. And Henry Plummer diplomatically shared a set with every one of them, even with the younger girls of ten and twelve modest years of age, who equally delighted in his company, Plummer executing with a suave and debonair precision every step and turn and spin and bow of each waltz, polka, and reel. Such that matters quickly escalated to the point that, amongst several of the men, there grew a feeling that Plummer was usurping the limited number of females.

You had only to watch to see that the women themselves sought Henry Plummer out and, having done so, that they easily fell victim to the attraction of his lithe posture and steel grey eyes, to the chivalric sweep of his courtly bow. Hank Crawford thus commented that the womenfolk weren't safe with Henry Plummer about and drew a general laugh with the remark. And while he meant it as a gesture of conciliatory humor, others agreed literally upon the sentiment. Among these was Jack Cleveland, whom I thought to be not only a traveling companion but also a friend of Plummer's. He had been there all evening, from the moment they opened the doors, eating the food and drinking from the bowl that was filled and refilled with rum punch. And with each dance, at which the women totally avoided him or politely turned him down, Cleveland had become more drunk and belligerent. Finally, he expressed his own outrage at Henry Plummer's monopolization of the womenfolk, harshly threatening that he would take care of Plummer when the occasion arose and generally libeling Plummer by obscure references to the past. Until some of Plummer's and Cleveland's mutual friends, Bill Graves and Cy Skinner included, roughly removed Cleveland from the hall. The music seemed to pick up again, and the dancers regained the center stage. The women slowed and tired, and Buz Caven and Mrs. Caven entertained the spent dancers and wallflowers with the recitation of several lighthearted poems and ditties, and the ball closed with a wonderful quadrille in which everyone participated, many of the men pairing in order to not lose out.

~~~

By the advent of the New Year, the stable had established itself as a perfectly viable Bannack City enterprise. The purchase from the cutters of a large quantity of hay had proved to be a particularly profitable investment, and Father's decision to offer out for rent teams of horses and mules was symptomatic of the local shortage in riding stock. It was emphasized to me that I was always to ask exactly who the renter was, and where he was going, and when he might return, and, if possible, to extract some form of guarantee securing the animals' value. And I grew to appreciate the reasons for Father's extraordinary concern, and to seek sufficient assurances before I permitted the horses to escape my sight.

The new year also brought with it a great snowfall lasting for three gloriously idle days, blanketing the countryside and the town site and the higher mountains with a pristine brilliance that covered over, seemed almost to forgive, the ugly scars of the gold rush: the endless stumps where great trees once stood, the torn and pitted creek, the eroding wheel ruts, all of it healed over and falsely rejuvenated by the temporary whiteness of the storm. And its aura of purity and newness was so refreshing and absolute that it invigorated a new sensation of goodwill and utter peacefulness amid new hopes and aspirations for the coming year. You could see it in the street where the exchange of a greeting was warmer and heartier than before and infer it from the sounds emanating from the saloon, just as vociferous and drunken as before but without the intimidating inflections and innuendoes of violence and anger. It brought out the child in almost every one of us, with snowballs mercilessly aimed at the back of best friends' heads, and humorously dressed figures made of snow appearing almost everywhere they might be seen. And it lasted the entirety of a week, at the end of which two miners I had seen before, but did not know, approached Father for the purpose of renting horses, together with the tack to hitch them to a wagon.

Father knew them both and trusted them, it seemed, implicitly. So his conversation with the men was born solely out of curiosity. "Where you boys heading?" he asked. "Looks like there's an awful lot of snow in the high country for prospecting just now."

"We're goin' lookin' for George Evans, Walt," one of them answered. "Been gone two days now. Went out to bring in his horses from the prairie and never come back."

When they returned the horses the next day they were carrying with them the grim remainder of George Evans's bloodied clothes, but nothing else.

Some of the townspeople suspected Charlie Reeves and Bill Graves perpetrated the crime, but the more accepted rumor spoke against Jack Cleveland. Cleveland was reportedly seen out near Horse Prairie at about the time of George Evans's disappearance and afterwards was said to be possessed of quantities of gold far beyond his own lazy capacity and limited means. He seemed a dirty, ill-tempered, hateful man, prone to swearing at and threatening anyone or anything that stood in what might be considered to be his way, be it man, horse, or even Rat, whom he had kicked at and maltreated more than once. At the dinner table one night soon thereafter, I thus expressed my opinion that Jack Cleveland had killed Evans. Father reacted instantly.

"You know nothing of Jack Cleveland," he said harshly, "except what you've heard from others."

"I've heard and seen some of Jack Cleveland," I said.

"What have you seen that tells you he's murdered someone?"

"I've heard him say he would kill Henry Plummer someday. He said so at the ball. I thought you heard him too."

"Saying he'd kill a man that's still living don't give rise to blame him for murdering one that's dead. Especially if the living one is Henry Plummer. Now you better be taking care who you're accusing of murder around here, or you'll find yourself having to answer to him directly. You hear?"

"Yes, Father," I answered respectfully, as though I had been corrected; but in truth I felt only unreasonably chastised. And from the corner of my eye, I saw Mother looking up, coldly and with reserved disagreement, at Father as he looked angrily at me.

~~~~~

From the front porch of the stables, you could sit in the daylight and watch the Bannack traffic move along the main street, which always seemed crowded with people and loads of logs and lumber and tethered horses and wagons of every size and design. And through the month of January, it was generally a particularly muddy scene, the hard clays of summer having proved capable of turning to a greasy puddinglike substance as quickly as the snow might melt or the rain fall. I could work, or in my idleness sit, with it all in front of me and watch the drama of the strike at Grasshopper Creek play itself out with Main Street as the center stage. Skinner's Saloon and the Goodrich Hotel and Peabody's and Allen & Arnold's Smithy and Granville Stuart's butcher shop were all there before me, such that I could see and hear much of what was reported, or experienced, at those establishments: of new color being found in some formerly unprospected bar, of new rules to govern the district, a fight here and gunfire there, all made incomplete and thereby mysterious by the obscuring facades of the buildings and the unseen acts and unheard conversations taking place behind their walls. And I could, as well, watch the town grow by the constant accretion of human beings, the white folk who brought with them the makings of their dreams slung over weary mules and into creaking wagons, and the Indians who had all but lost their hopes in the past and now were left only to make migrant camps on the edges of the town so that they could be nearer to the menial, laborious jobs the white folk offered to them.

During the nights it was much the same, although in the darkness it was the sound rather than the sights that pronounced and emphasized the constant acts of determination and treachery and meanness that made Bannack City what it was. And yet, according to Father's view, one could draw only limited conclusions from what was seen and heard, that is unless the seeing or the hearing was entirely unclouded by physical barrier and psychological bias, such that no room for question might exist regarding what had actually transpired.

So Father said it meant nothing when I told him how I had seen Henry Plummer enter the Goodrich Hotel on the bitter January morning on which Jack Cleveland died, had seen him walk casually across the street in his neat attire as if the day were no different from any other, and that there was no relevance in the fact that I had watched a while later when Jack Cleveland came up the street talking angrily to himself, as if he were already drunk, and stumbled through the doorway of the Goodrich Hotel as though he did not know the threshold through which he passed most every day. And when I told Father I had heard the shots just minutes later, first one, then a second from a different gun, and then two more from the latter in close succession, he said it did not matter.

So I did not tell him how I had watched as the curious poured into the hotel, drawn by the macabre desire to observe the workings of man against his fellow man, and how Hank Crawford had carried the yet conscious and profusely bleeding Cleveland out and over to his own cabin where he closed the door behind him, nor the fact that I had seen

Henry Plummer leave soon thereafter, with George Ives and Bill Graves and Charley Reeves leading him away and he looking no different in any way than when he had arrived. Nor did I tell him that I had heard it said on the street by one person that Plummer had gunned down Cleveland just for the practice it entailed, and, by another, who claimed to have seen the shooting, that Plummer had come to the aid of a miner accosted by Jack Cleveland and that Plummer had drawn and fired only after being shot at first. So maybe it was logical that I could not know exactly what had occurred, despite my being witness to so much. In my heart of hearts though, I knew somehow, felt confidant in the proposition, that Henry Plummer was innocent of any criminal act in the shooting at the Goodrich Hotel.

No one made much of it, at first. Henry Plummer was by then a known commodity for more than several reasons. He had joined the mining community by buying up unwanted claims that had been all but placered out and had commenced excavating and mill stamping the rock beneath the gravels when few others would. He had intervened in any number of altercations and was said to have mended and healed the worst of torn relationships. Amongst certain circles of the women, he was a favorite. And he was knowledgeable of the rules employed by mining districts and their various committees. All in all, he was uniquely respectable and at the same time equally imposing; all of which imbued him with an aspect of power that was obvious and undeniable.

Jack Cleveland died that night on a feather bolster in Hank Crawford's cabin. Crawford took the initiative the next day to bury him in the town cemetery at his own expense and over the objections of some who argued that Boot Hill was a more suitable place for Jack Cleveland's last repose. Crawford placed the blanket-wrapped body in a white pine casket he purchased from a carpenter and loaded it in a wagon and drove it down the street past the stables and up the freight road to where the growing cemetery overlooked the town, with only a few of his friends, including Father, joining Crawford in the procession. And I would guess that Crawford presided over the burial too, said something fitting over the grave (being as how there wasn't a preacher within 200 miles), and set the wooden marker that I saw afterwards, when I had my own reasons for being there.

Father, by that time, had become closely acquainted with Hank Crawford, both because each were Masons and because they had purchased several claims together, each taking equal time away from their personal business to work the placers and recover the gold. From these efforts they realized some meaningful gains. But they seemed haunted by the fact that certain others, Henry Plummer included, could start up or revive a claim just when they did and almost instantly begin to remove five, ten times as much gold as did they. Father called it luck, but I knew better.

I didn't care much for Hank Crawford. Not that he was a bad man or ill intentioned. It was just that he had that form of weakling capacity to politick himself out of risks and into undeserved positions. Had he been back East, he easily could have been a merchant to the army, or a banker in a conservative investment house, or even a local legislator or a justice of the peace. But he wasn't out East, he was West, and there in Bannack City his lack of fortitude was something that he could not as easily hide.

The old tension between Crawford and Henry Plummer resurrected itself immediately after Jack Cleveland's death. I saw it in Crawford's face when he came over to do business with Father; the strain gave a pasty luster to his skin and hinted of a nervous hesitation when he spoke. Father conjectured that it no doubt was because Plummer was afraid of what Cleveland had told Hank Crawford about Plummer's past before Cleveland died, and because Crawford was afraid of what Plummer might do about it to keep the information quiet. And Hank Crawford spoke to Father more than once about their jointly asking for a miners' court to try Henry Plummer for Jack Cleveland's murder.

Maybe it was because I was finally beginning to feel that my time had come, that the time was ripe for me to assert myself and not be quieted. Or maybe I just could no longer be told that I had to feel something other than what was deep inside. So I made it my cause to dissuade Father from the course on which Crawford tried to set him. When direct observation as to Henry Plummer's probable innocence failed, I succumbed to other devices. I argued my case to Mother. "I know, Will," she said. "I know Mr. Plummer's innocent, too." And she told Father of her opinion without letting it be known that we had talked. I laid the groundwork with other miners of influence, speaking my mind openly to Archie Gibson, who owned the boardinghouse two buildings down, and subtly reminding others that Henry Plummer had averted violence when others sought only to invite it. Amongst my peers I as much as lied, misrepresenting the sentiments expressed by others in the hope that my acquaintances would repeat their stories to their fathers who would pass them further on, all such that a majority at least partly of my making would form against prosecuting Henry Plummer on the account of Jack Cleveland's death.

CHAPTER 3

O nly a few days, five or six at the most, had passed since Jack Cleveland's death. And once again, Bannack seemed ready to move on and forget about the past. The revelry renewed itself, and two new saloons opened, and miners and merchants alike already began to lay their plans for the New Year. But for me, it wasn't that easy, and while I worked in the stables cleaning the bedding and grooming the horses, my mind ruminated over all that had transpired. The hardest thing to figure was Father: how distant and changed he had become, and how difficult it now was to talk with him. So when he came into the stables that afternoon, I thought it best to simply avoid him, until he came up to where I was working and said, "How would you like a break from here? I need some things delivered upcreek to Wiley's Bar."

I answered that I'd rather stay in town, but he ignored me. "Get your gear ready," he said. "You'll need to stay overnight at Wiley's, so bring a bedroll."

It was in the afternoon before Father managed to shoe up Wiley's horses and mule and then send me over to Chrisman's to fill Wiley's order, so that while it might not have been a necessity for me to spend the night at the camps when Father first made the suggestion, it became a fact by the time I left. And to compound it all, the creek was up and the trail, which Wiley's mule stubbornly insisted on following, crossed through enough mud and pooled water to ensure the going was slow. I arrived far too late into the evening to enjoy one of Wiley's famed venison stews.

Wiley's Bar had achieved some notoriety the previous year. Wiley and his partner Lester Freeman had pitched their shovels into a sandy beach along the creek and in a single day pulled out $100 in dust. In two months they had fifteen pounds worth, and they brought it into Bannack in a leather sack and promptly lost it all to a monte sharp named Benfield, who then lost most of it to someone else. There were some who said that Wiley and Freeman didn't even blink when it happened, that they finished their bottle and laughed it off and headed back up the creek for more.

Thing was, there wasn't any more, at least not after one or two days' work; and the word went out that Wiley's Bar no longer could make the rifle, and that the claim was no longer worth the paper on which it was recorded. Even Freeman believed that it was so, and when Wiley wouldn't agree to abandon it altogether, Freeman gave up his own share, leaving Wiley alone, throughout December, fighting the ice and lack of water and not finding enough of anything by which he might buy a meal or hire the labor he needed to help him with the sluice and rocker.

Then an early January rain came and in one sudden flush of torrent and melted snow, the creek went out. There was only one miner that didn't come into Bannack for the four days it rained, and that miner was Tom Wiley. And they joked for hours at a time, at Skinner's and the Goodrich and even at the stables, at how all that water wasn't rain but rather old Tom Wiley's tears, shed over what he'd had and lost.

That is until Wiley came down, only after the rains had backed off and froze and the creek had receded. Straight up Main Street he came, sitting on that mule and his eyes as wide and unblinking as they could be and a grin from ear to ear that told you either he'd gone crazy or was just glad to be done with all that precipitation. And he rode straight up to Skinner's and pulled out a little beaker filled with the cleanest gold dust ever seen in Bannack.

"Where'd you get that dust?" someone asked him.

"Outta my bar," Wiley answered.

And someone said, "Thought that bar was played out."

And Wiley answered, "Got me a new one now."

Because that's the way it was. You couldn't ever really know where the old creek bed had been from one decade to the last, let alone century after century. And all Wiley did in the rain is what most others preferred be done in the sunlight, which was to rechannel that water that was flash flooding anyway into a new direction, and uncover the gold that lay 2 or 3 feet beneath the gravel.

When Wiley went back up to his claim that second time, he still had some of his dust left in that beaker. And he took Freeman with him, saying that the claim wasn't worth half to him what Freeman made up in companionship, and that he figured it was a fair price to pay Freeman for his time. And he even told Freeman he could call it Freeman's Bar if he preferred. But Freeman had said, "No, sir. I'd rather have a Wiley's Bar that moves about to suit Tom Wiley's need than a Freeman's Bar that's set in one place and gettin' smaller by the day."

It was the third location for Wiley's Bar that Tom Wiley and Lester Freeman were working on when I arrived at their camp. I could see it in the moonlight: the small windlass and the rockers and the sluice squared and dark against the grey rock. They were asleep when I rode up, having risen before the sun and eaten in the dark and having worked against the heavy sands and gravel and the cold water for twelve backbreaking hours and then having eaten again in the recurrent dark that, alone of all the elements, saved them from themselves.

~~~~~

There were horses, saddled and unbridled alike, everywhere outside the stables upon my return the next morning. The unlikely number of men loitering around the horses was just an intimation of what was going on inside. And when I saw that Henry Plummer was the central and unwilling focus of the proceedings, my immediate thought was that Father had deceived and manipulated me; he had sent me out, far upcreek on a contrived errand, and then had conspired with Hank Crawford to call a miners' meeting right there in the stables for the sole purpose of indicting and convicting Henry Plummer of Jack Cleveland's murder. Then I saw that Charley Reeves and Gus Moore and Bill Mitchell, who were all seated on a bench in the corner, were also plainly under arrest and had been bound around the wrists, and so I knew something else had happened while I was away.

All of the horses had been removed from the stables, and there were seventy or eighty men inside. Some sat up in the rafters or on the stall doors; others lined the walls and crowded anywhere there might be room—against a closed door or leaning into the tack hung on the walls. And it looked as though most, if not all, had brought their firearms with them. There was the noise of assembled men who have not satisfied their purposes: a low indecipherable rumbling of anxious intermingled conversation, and the raised voices of invective and disagreement, volatility, impatience. Half of them, at least, were drunk or moving in that direction, and, as I worked my way through the crowd, the smell of their whiskey was as obvious as that of the mixture of tobacco smoke and horse dung that hung in the air, stagnant and pervasive. And there was the stifling odor of kerosene lamps burning, despite the fact that it was light outside. All such that the atmosphere inside the stables—the smell of men and their vices—as well as the artificial yellow light was nauseating and putrid.

A workbench had been cleaned off and moved into the middle of the room, and Henry Plummer was sitting at it with his hat off and his hands tied in front. Next to him stood George Copely, leaning with one hand on the table and his other smartly holding his lapel in a contrived oratorical pose. A moment earlier I had seen Copely across the room talking with Hank Crawford in veiled voices, with Father standing between them saying nothing.

Copely, I knew, purported to be a lawyer of some former accomplishment back East. But you could never really tell since scores of Bannack's population claimed status through aristocratic titles, be it doctor or lawyer or colonel or senator, all of which instantly accorded varying degrees of credibility and respect to their otherwise unestablished reputations. Now Copely was saying something, as if to the crowd in general, but he could not be heard above the din, so he picked up Father's hand sledge and hammered it onto the anvil. And the crowd quieted completely. "I set a motion before the committee," he stated with great flourish, "that testimony be taken here and now for the purpose of determining whether Henry Plummer is guilty of the murder of Jack Cleveland." The crowd revived in a dissonant uproar indicating both agreement and dissension at once. And then Hank Crawford moved to the bench and beat upon the anvil with the sledge, and the crowd quieted again. "The motion is seconded," he said loudly.

It had all the appearance of a mob, of an impassioned manifestation of uncontrolled fear and ignorance, and the only thing I could think was that they were going to hang Henry Plummer and those other men right there in our stable with Mother presumably next door and not only hearing it but knowing full well what would most satisfy Crawford and many of the others, including Father. Henry Plummer stood up. "Let us make sure of our agreement, first, George," he said, familiarly; and the crowd remained hushed, instantly mesmerized and interested by the casual tone of Henry Plummer's voice, and the precision of his diction. "These men and I surrendered to the authority of the committee with the understanding that any trial will be to a jury impaneled by the miners' committee. Am I correct in assuming, George, that our compact will be fully honored?"

There was a general indication of agreement amid the crowd, if only in approval of the way Henry Plummer had spoken the words. Crawford and Copely conferred between themselves for a moment. Then Copely moved toward the center of the room as though the two men had agreed that Plummer would as much as be ignored. But before Copely could complete his maneuver, Plummer spoke again, this time after struggling atop the bench with his hands tied and then standing again so he rose above all of the men inside the stables except those that sat on the beams and rafters. "John Higgins," he called out. "There you are, John. Come up here if you please, sir."

In the direction in which Henry Plummer's stare was focused, a tall, simple-looking man had become the center of attention. Several of the men nearest to him were whooping and laughing and slapping him on the back and pushing him forward while he resisted his involvement in the proceedings.

Copely could see he was losing control, and so he tried to stop Henry Plummer. "Stay where you're at, Higgins," he stated loudly and firmly. "This is no way to run a trial. The prosecution will put on its witnesses first, and then the accused can follow."

"You're wrong, George," Henry Plummer said. "This is the way we run a trial to a miners' committee. Before we go trying a man, and wasting the time to do it, we let the miners themselves decide whether there's any reason do be trying him at all." Which brought a loud expression of approval from a vast majority of those present.

"Come up here, John," Henry Plummer said again. "I believe these good miners have agreed that a preliminary determination is warranted. Let us ascertain whether there is reason to try me for any crime. And if so, whether our agreement, in which you joined, John Higgins, will be honorably acknowledged."

This drew another generally favorable reaction of approval from the miners. By the thrust of a dozen hands, John Higgins was moved involuntarily through the crowd until he emerged from the throng into the opening where the bench and Henry Plummer stood.

"Now," Henry Plummer said. And then he paused, slowly turning atop the bench so that he caught the eye of many of the men standing below him. "Why don't you tell us all why I have been brought before this august body? Who sent you and your deputies after me?" The use of the word "deputies" invoked a laugh from some directions; some took Henry Plummer to be speaking sarcastically since, with the lack of a sheriff or marshal, any deputizing of someone would have been without authority or basis. "Come on, John; tell these good miners why I have been arrested."

"Well, you know why, Henry," John Higgins said.

"Well, no, I don't, John. None of you think I had anything to do with the shooting of those Bannocks, and the old Frenchman, up on Yankee Flat last night; now, do you? There's a dozen men in this stable that will swear I was over at Skinner's at the time, and that I was among those that heard the shots being fired."

"Come on now, Henry. It's Jack Cleveland you're here for. Quit pulling me along. You know why you're here; we talked about it before you agreed to come in with us." Henry Plummer, standing erect atop the bench like a statue, said nothing. "There's some that believe you murdered Jack Cleveland. That's why you're here."

"Well, you don't have any reason to believe that. Do you, John? You personally, I mean, by your own observation, have no reason to believe that; now do you?"

"Some of the boys say . . ."

"Whoa up there, John," Henry Plummer interrupted. "I'm not asking you what others might be saying; I'm asking what you know about it yourself."

There was a long pause and, when Henry Plummer remained silent, Higgins said, "I don't know anything about it, Henry."

"I thought as much, John," Henry Plummer said, almost apologizing for Higgins, who stood before him like a timid schoolboy awaiting punishment or a lengthy assignment. "You were just acting as the law when you and the other boys came out looking for me and these other men here."

"Well, that's right, Henry. Hank here, and George Copely, told me they needed help about that papoose getting shot along with the old chief and the Frenchman, too. And seeing how I was there, I pitched in.

I figured someone has to put a stop to that kind of killing right here in the middle of the district."

"But that had nothing to do with me, John. You said so yourself. What made you include me as being wanted along with ole Charley and the others there. It wasn't your idea, was it, John?"

Higgins looked up at Crawford and then down at the floor. "Hank Crawford told me to bring you in," he finally said in a muffled voice. "For murdering Jack Cleveland."

"All right, John. I think we all understand," Henry Plummer said.

As John Higgins moved back to his place in the crowd, he was enveloped in an absolute silence that was broken only by the shuffling of feet and other restless movement. It was as though the inertia of the proceeding had been completely averted, suspended in a sudden lack of certainty. And George Copely knew as much, saw that he had lost control and was on the verge of failing entirely in his office. He moved over to the bench on which Henry Plummer continued to stand, and the effect was not favorable to George Copely, with Copely standing below Henry Plummer, like a powerless tormentor, and Henry Plummer standing atop the bench and emphasizing through exaggerated gestures that he had been bound with rope for no apparent reason. "Gentlemen," George Copely finally said. "This is no way to hold a trial. Let us start from the beginning and do this in an orderly fashion."

"I can agree with you there, George," Henry Plummer said before the crowd could respond to Copely's plea. "Let us start from the beginning. And as most of us have agreed, the beginning would be for the committee to determine whether there even is any reason to waste time on a trial when all these miners could be out working or sleeping or socializing according to their own desires. And that's what I'm doing, George, trying to assist this committee in making that determination. And I welcome you to assist me in that endeavor, if you please."

Here, almost the entire gathering roared with approval, stamping their feet, discharging their pistols in reckless disregard of those posted in the rafters, pulling down on their bottles as though in salutation to

Henry Plummer. Henry Plummer saw that he had gained the advantage and he moved to maintain it. "Now where's Jeff Perkins? Is Jeff here?"

"I'm here, Henry," a voice from the rear spoke out. "But I wish I wasn't all of a sudden."

Laughter rolled, muffled and random, through the crowd. Then, Henry Plummer said, "Well, come up here, Jeff; we've got a question or two for you." So Jeff Perkins moved out into the center of the room and took his turn before the bench.

"Hello, Jeff," Henry Plummer said, moving to shake Jeff Perkin's hand as if his own hands were not tied, and then shrugging his shoulders as he looked down at his bound wrists. "We'll make it easy for you here, Jeff. Why don't you tell us about what you saw or didn't see on the day in question. Tell it any way you want. All we're interested in here is the truth, and to see if we can save ourselves some time."

"Okay, Henry," Jeff Perkins said. "You mean from the beginnin'."

"Yes. It would be of some help. And turn around here. You don't need to be telling me; tell the boys here. I already know what happened. Tell them."

Jeff Perkins turned and faced the gallery of men to give his statement. There were some amongst the crowd who didn't care, the likes of Copely and Father and Skinner and Bill Graves who had their minds made up for or against before the proceedings even began. But there were others, also: men like Paddy Sky and Andy Brown and Buz Caven to whom justice meant everything in a mining camp. They needed to hear the words themselves, so that they might judge as best they could.

"Guess there really ain't that much to tell," Jeff Perkins began. "Some of you here know how I borrowed money from Jack Cleveland at the faro table at the Goodrich last November. And I have to say I don't think he would have given it to me if he hadn't rightly figured he'd win it back from me right then and there. And there are plenty of you out there that knows I paid it back as soon as I could sluice out enough dust to cover the debt. But that wasn't the end of it even though I thought it was, because Jack Cleveland come into the Goodrich the

mornin' you're all botherin' with here as stiff as a plank and told me if
I didn't pay him back right then, I'd be in the ground by sundown. 'I
done paid you already,' I told him; but he wasn't there to listen to reason. 'I want it now,' he said back, and when I told him I'd paid him once
and I wasn't about to pay him twice, he pulled his pistol and stuck it
right up in my face.

"Henry Plummer was there that mornin'. Guess you all know
that much. I'm not sure why he was there, but he wasn't drinkin' like
Jack Cleveland was; I know that. Maybe he was just warmin' up at the
stove. Anyway, when Cleveland stuck his pistol up in my face, Henry
stepped over and told Cleveland to back off, that I'd paid my debt, and
that was that.

"Half the town's heard Jack Cleveland claim he'd take Henry
Plummer when the time came, but I never thought it'd amount to any-
thin'. But I swear before Henry finished speakin' on my behalf, Jack
Cleveland turned that pistol away from me and shot it straight at Henry
here. I can still see the rest of it in my mind like it just happened. Jack
Cleveland turnin' that pistol away from me and aimin' it at Henry
Plummer and pullin' that trigger without a thought. And missin' him
somehow at 10 feet, and then Henry drawin' so fast that you really
couldn't see it and firin' back and hittin' Cleveland right in the shoulder.
That was when Cleveland made his biggest mistake when he should have
just laid there on the floor and bled some and lived. He brought that
pistol of his back up, and Henry shot twice, and it was over." Then Jeff
Perkins stopped talking and stood motionless.

"Cut him loose, George," a voice from the rafters broke the
silence that had followed. "Plummer ain't done nothin'." And then
from elsewhere in the crowd George Ives repeated, "Yeah, Copely. Cut
him loose."

But George Copely's nature, if not his training, was adversarial,
and he was not inclined to abdicate his role without some form of
rebuttal and counterthrust. So he said loudly as Jeff Perkins began to
move back to his original place among the miners, "Hold on there, Jeff,"

stopping him in his tracks, drawing him back involuntarily. "Now Jeff," George Copely said. "I want you to tell us who else saw Jack Cleveland shoot at Henry Plummer first. Tell us their names."

"Can't tell you any names, George, 'cause the only ones there were Henry and me and Cleveland. Gad had been there but a minute before; but he went into the back room and missed everything but the cleaning up. And I guess Buck was there too. Buck Stinson, I mean. But he was sleepin' in the barber's chair when Jack showed up. Like he always does, with that barber's cape pulled over his head. So he never heard the talkin' and didn't even wake up til the shootin' started. And even then he didn't see nothin'. Ole Buck got so excited and tangled up in that cape that he ended up fallin' down to the floor. Ain't that right, Buck?" Jeff Perkins yelled over to where Buck Stinson was standing in the crowd.

And Buck Stinson yelled back, "That's the truth, boys. When you hear shots like that comin' out of a dream, best thing's to drop to the ground and hope when you wake up, it was a dream and you ain't got no holes in you. 'Cept when I finally got untangled, first thing I saw was Jack Cleveland with a hole in him and a smokin' pistol in his hand."

Copely was about to ask Stinson a question, but Stinson was a close friend of Henry Plummer's, and Copely probably thought better of it. He turned back to Jeff Perkins, instead. "So I guess we just have to take your word for it then, is that it, Jeff?"

"Well, come to think of it, there was one other fella there, George. But he was just stoppin' over for the night on his way to Cottonwood. He saw the shootin'; but he didn't wait around to see if Jack Cleveland would make it or not."

"Then it's as I said, Jeff. Isn't it? What you're saying is that we have no choice here but to take your word?"

"I guess that's right, George. Mine and Henry's."

"Well, let me ask you something else, Jeff. You've come to be a rather close friend of Henry Plummer's, haven't you?"

"I guess you'd say we're friends," Jeff Perkins said. And he suddenly seemed embarrassed and made restless by Copely's implication that he was lying on behalf of Henry Plummer. "Least I like to think we are."

"Well, you're not just trying to help out a friend here, are you, Jeff? I mean, how do we know you saw what you claim? How do we know you were even there? After all. Jack Cleveland's dead. It doesn't matter much anymore. Does it, Jeff?"

"I've done told you I was there, George. Henry can tell you that."

George Copely laughed lightly, as did some of the crowd; and Jeff Perkins looked around, puzzled by what could be humorous in what he had said. "Well, I'm not much interested in what Henry Plummer has to say about it. He's standing here accused of murder, Jeff; and I'd pretty much expect him to swear on a Bible to anything that will save his neck. And here you are, maybe one of his best friends in the territory, telling us just what Henry Plummer would like for us to hear. I'll tell you this, Jeff. Cleveland did a lot of talking to Hank Crawford while he was lying there dying in Hank's cabin. And the one thing Cleveland made clear was that Henry Plummer shot him down in cold blood, with no warning and no remorse."

That was what spurred me forward. Some of anger, I guess, and maybe some of plain disgust. Because I now knew what had happened, and I knew also that George Copely would never let it go on his own volition. So I pushed through the crowd impulsively, in somewhat of a fit; and as I stepped next to Jeff Perkins and turned my face to the miners, I said, "I know. I know he was there. I saw Jeff Perkins go into the Goodrich before the shots were fired and saw him leave after; and I heard him say immediately afterwards how Henry Plummer fired in self-defense; and I heard the shots go off just like Jeff Perkins says: one, and then three from a different pistol. And I'm one of those that's heard Jack Cleveland threaten to kill Henry Plummer. And my father's heard it, too."

I was shaking some as I spoke. And I must have gotten carried away at that point, because I continued when it would have been best for me to stop. "And I saw the stranger come out of the Goodrich right after the shooting, and I heard him say how Jack Cleveland had drawn and fired first." My voice quavered some as I said it. And that's when I saw Father; his face came out of the crowd at me with an icy, emotionless, repudiating stare.

It's hard to say whether my statement caused it, but as soon as I spoke, several other miners also confirmed that they, too, had heard the stranger say how Cleveland had started the shooting. Then the crowd surged forward, and in another moment the cords around Henry Plummer's wrists were cut. There was a tumult of premature celebration, and some confusion, too, with pistols being discharged and bottles passed; and, still, Henry Plummer stood above the crowd on Father's bench. The noise was finally broken by the ringing hammering of the sledge upon the anvil, and there was Buck Stinson, the barber, atop the bench standing side by side with Henry Plummer. "Move that the charge of murder against Henry Plummer be dropped," he yelled out.

And someone far back yelled "Seconded."

"In favor?" Stinson invoked the vote, and an uproarious affirmation was expressed. "Against?" drawing only a murmur of discontent. So Henry Plummer stepped down, and I watched with some admiration as he moved discreetly through the crowd, shaking hands and yet refraining from reveling too greatly in the glory of his victory.

~~~

Matters were not so easily resolved when it came to the other three, who were accused of the wanton shooting of two Bannocks and the old Frenchman who had come to their aid. It was already far too late into the day to treat with them, and the call that had been sent out throughout the region for potential jurors was only then being answered by a steady trickle of men coming in from their camps and ranches to at least observe the trial that would begin in the morning. In the meanwhile, the accused men would be incarcerated in the Goodrich Hotel, where the accommodations far exceeded the comforts of their own shacks and drafty cabins, and then they would be brought to the

Roundhouse where the trial would be conducted to better suit the inevitable crowd.

I as much as expected that when the light of morning dawned over the mountains, the townspeople would find that Charley Reeves and Bill Mitchell and Gus Moore would long be departed from the scene. It was not that the men appointed to guard them could not be trusted; they were chosen for their sincerity and their standing in the district. It was rather that it had become evident during Henry Plummer's hearing that the crowd was rife with supporters of the accused, and that they, to a number, were constituted from the most aggressive and reckless sector of the population—those who resolved every dispute through the discharge of a firearm or the wielding of a knife. Mother called them ruffians and, in a rare descent into her Irish lineage, even referred to them as hooligans; but I was coming to know them for what they were—which to me meant mostly they were nothing more than most other men, and nothing less either, being not much different from those who chose more subtle means to accomplish their purposes and satisfy even the most hidden and innocuous of their desires. But the prisoners were still there when the sun rose, and they probably would have been there even without the guard since the snows in the elevations were so deep that they had only made it to Rattlesnake Creek in their original attempt to escape, before the drifts brought them to a halt and Henry Plummer negotiated for a fair trial.

The saloons and restaurants and the bakery all were opened early and, even in the ambiguity of the dawning light, the town was enlivened with the sort of activity one would normally attribute to the closing of the workday and the advent of the evening's hard-earned recreation. The street filled prematurely with pedestrians and horsemen alike, lending to the appearance that Bannack City was in celebration of a uniformly recognized holiday. And everywhere, the topic was that of the proceedings to be held that day, and of the implications of the senseless shootings and the rampage of crime and violence that seemed to have taken hold.

Father had yet to speak a word to me. After I had offered my statement in defense of Henry Plummer, he had walked right by me without as much as an acknowledgment. And in the morning, having been separated through the brief night by only the curtain that defined Mother and Father's area from the rest of the cabin, it was the same; we sat at the same table and ate the same food and drank the same scalding coffee without any indication that we were even aware of the other's presence. Mother saw it, of course. She did not know how to mollify it, though, without the benefit of knowing what had happened between us. And so she didn't even try, not being willing to risk the worsening of the situation. "Will they hang them, Walter?" she asked instead.

Her question brought him out of a deep thought, and by its frankness caught him by surprise. "I don't know what we'll do, Nadine," he said quietly.

"Well, shouldn't they bring the men before the territorial government? They have judges, don't they, Walter?"

"We can't do that, Nadine. It's not practical. And not safe, either. There's no one in their right mind that would take the chance to haul these kind of men 200 miles over those mountains just so some lawyer and judge who have never even been to Bannack can find some reason to let them off. We have to try them here, now. To put a stop to it all before it's too late."

"Well, can't they get a judge to come here then? Someone could go and get him."

"And where would we keep the prisoners in the meantime? There's not even a jail here, Nada. You know that. And what's the difference whether we bring in a judge from over the mountains or we have one of our own act as judge?"

"I thought it was more complicated than that, Walter," she said. "The way the law works and all. I didn't mean to interfere." There was nowhere for her to go then, in her rebuke. No other room, once the curtain had been drawn open, to withdraw into, not even enough of occupation in the cubicle of log walls and plank roof by which she might actually divert her attention. She had tried to assure herself that it was "they" and not "us"—not "we"—that stood to prosecute and finally judge and convict and execute others. And she had failed completely, because what she attributed to Father was attributable to her as well; she could not evade the "us" she sought to avoid, which to me meant "them." She turned to her feather duster and redusted what was already clean.

It devolved upon me, as punishment I suppose, to mind the stables while Father again participated in the proceedings to be held this time across the creek on Yankee Flat. So I didn't actually see what followed, and in the long run could only piece it together, to understand it and what it meant. When you heard it all told by the different voices of Bannack, it seemed that three factions ultimately revealed themselves that day; and there, of course, were extremists on either end of the spectrum within each group. You almost could have strung them along a contin-uum: at the one end were the prosecutors and detractors of the accused, made up mostly of the merchant class and comprised mostly of Masonic brothers and Republicans; and at the other end, the defenders and cohorts of Reeves and Moore and Mitchell, being mostly Southerners and Democrats; and in between, the general populace, diverse in their perspective, and nowhere as extreme as those to their left and right.

The funny thing about it was that the winners that day lost what they in truth wanted, and then later lost what they had won, while the losers simultaneously lost, although not nearly as badly as they might have, and then later won back what they had been deprived of in defeat. So that, under the miner's unique form of logic, by winning you lost and by losing you won, and no one comes out ahead or behind, the sta-tus quo being fully preserved by the conundrum.

It was a system for remedying social ills that evolved via great philosophical debate and practical trial and error, and it worked like this: First, they dropped the charges against Mitchell for lack of evi-dence, but only after they banished him from the district. Then, they wrangled over everything else: whether they should try the two remain-ing men to a jury or to the entire mining district, and whether they ought to be permitted lawyers and if so whom, and who was trustworthy and unbiased enough to sit on the jury. After which, the miners, through the artifice of a panel of twelve duly sworn jurors, tried and found Charley Reeves and Gus Moore guilty of murder. And then, in what all the posturing and blandishments and maneuvering was really all about, the friends of Reeves and Moore prevailed upon the jury, who feared mostly and deeply for their lives, to banish the guilty (along with the innocent Mitchell) from the district rather than hang them, but only after the snows had melted and passage thereby made safe. And when, a month and more later, Charley Reeves and Gus Moore and Bill Mitchell still remained in Bannack City, a reconvened and reconstituted miners' committee voted back their citizenship and residence. Which, in the end, made it just as I say, with the winners losing and the losers winning and the status quo, which entailed a particularly arbitrary brand of violence and vice, more entrenched than ever.

What was not, and never could have been, preserved was peace between Henry Plummer and Hank Crawford. Because there was something about Henry Plummer that caused him to bring things to a conclusion, and because Hank Crawford was just petty enough to be unable to let things be. Besides, Crawford had a way of doing things wrongly, even when they seemed like the right thing to do. And Father somehow managed to get himself right into the middle of it all, without hardly any effort. The confluence of which, of the convergence of Henry Plummer's determination and Hank Crawford's miscalculations and Father's misfortunes, brought Henry Plummer to the stables looking for Hank Crawford a few days after the trial. He came up to the porch and I thought how even his spurs rang out with his own special brand of confidence.

"Morning, Will," he said, easily and with a cordial, familiar inflection. "Hank Crawford been around today?"

I wanted to ask Henry Plummer a dozen questions, things concerning bravery and shooting and California; but I was afraid, somehow, that he might rebuff me. "They're out back," I said. "In the stables."

I followed him back because that made the odds even, fairer, less confrontational. And his spurs were like the snare drums of a well-paraded army, perfect in their cadence and authoritative in their ring. Crawford and Father were too preoccupied to hear us coming until we were through the door. They were standing at the bench doing something together, and it was not until they heard us and turned that we could see that they were adding up figures and dividing between themselves the money and dust that was stacked and measured before them. You could see their surprise to have Plummer there at the very place where they had tried to hang him. Crawford looked plainly frightened, and so it was Father that spoke first. "You've come for your horse, I suppose," he said.

"Yes," Henry Plummer said. "That's one reason." And Crawford looked at him dumbly. "I'm also here for my revolvers and my shotgun. I understand they are in your possession, Crawford."

"I don't know anything about your weapons, Plummer," Crawford said.

"I was told you have them."

"By who? It's a lie. Who told you that?" Crawford said.

"George Copely told me that, Crawford. Not ten minutes ago. A double action army and a navy colt, and a sawed shotgun bolted at the stock."

I saw Crawford give Father a surprised and implicating look, and then he caught himself. "I don't have them," he said.

"Well, where are they? I want them back. If you'll just tell me where they're at, I will retrieve them myself."

Crawford stood absolutely quiet, and then, when he finally must have concluded that the silence would not save him, he said, "I'm out $200 between burying Jack Cleveland and paying the deputies and putting those murderers up at the Goodrich and feeding them. I thought those guns were theirs. I sold 'em to recover my costs."

It came so fast that all I saw was the impact when his fist struck Hank Crawford in the face, sending Crawford falling heavily backwards and into the hay. And then the same thing a second time when Henry Plummer's boot flashed and kicked away the pistol Crawford drew as he lay.

"You've got twenty-four hours to return my firearms," Henry Plummer said. "And not a minute more." And when Father told Henry Plummer that the charge for stabling his horse during the pendency of his hearing and incarceration would be $2 a day for a total of $4, Henry Plummer gave him a rigid and otherwise expressionless stare and then walked out, leading his horse after I saddled and bridled it for him.

After that, it was only a matter of time. Not measured by the twenty-four hours that Henry Plummer had accorded Crawford, because Crawford complied, as I knew he would. At twice the price he had received, he bought back Henry Plummer's revolvers and shotgun and then turned them over to Father, who delivered them to me with the instruction to find Plummer immediately and return his weapons to him. But measured, instead, by the infinite opportunity of inevitability. Since that's what it was, inevitable. As sure as the melting of the snow in the spring and of the blossoms that surely follow, it was preordained that the conflict between Henry Plummer and Hank Crawford would resolve itself in one final culmination.

I watched for it, early in the morning and late into the night, and listened for it, through the watchfulness of James O'Flaherty and a half dozen other friends. Then one evening, after dark had draped itself over the canyon as it did on cloudy moonless nights, James discreetly came calling for me and drew me outside where Father and Mother would not hear. He was visibly excited. "Henry Plummer's at the butcher's," he said breathlessly. And then he looked at me as though I should have understood.

"What of it?" I said.

"He's at Crawford's, not Stuart's. In the dark. Outside the window, I mean."

"That's not Henry Plummer's way," I whispered back. "He's not one to slink around in alleys and shoot under cover of dark. You must be mistaken, James. It's someone else."

And when we moved closer, I could see that it in fact was not Henry Plummer at all, but just a drunken miner slouched in his stupor against the wall. "Damn it, James," I said. "This ain't no game."

~~~

Toward the end of March the spring winds came warmly out of the west, and the accumulation of snow and ice that had gradually converted the landscape into a frozen tableau now rapidly melted off; and then it began to rain. The creeks swelled with water and in some places flooded and overflowed; placers that had been frozen into the ground leaned and fell and were carried off, and mine shafts submerged and eroded into the waters that carried them downstream. In the higher country, slopes washed out and avalanched whatever tree or rock or bush that might be pulled along. The sod roofs of thrown-together cabins and wickiups dripped and then oozed and then failed completely; and the ground, which in many places had frost heaved up a half of a foot or more, thawed and turned into a dismal muddy slop.

The mire of Bannack City and its environs brought whatever remained of human activity to a halt, the street being impassable with the mud at times axle deep, and Grasshopper Creek a torrent of churning water that was so rapid and silted that you could not stand against the water long enough to shovel or pan. And the roads that led to other places—to Spanish Fork and Walla Walla and South Pass—were even worse for their isolation and undeveloped nature. And as if the mud, which seemed capable of sucking you in and then holding as firmly as a leghold trap, were not in and of itself enough, it arrived at a time when both the overwintered spirit and the financial resources of the populace of Bannack were almost totally exhausted.

A restless and irritable anxiety prevailed, and as the days lengthened, it found more time and means to outwardly exhibit itself in Father's character and demeanor. Mother attributed his disposition to the long winter and its aftermath. "He just has cabin fever," she said.

"He'll be his old self once things dry out and the days lengthen." But I knew better and therefore did not foolishly expend my hopes on his resurrection. James O'Flaherty, whose father and brother had aligned themselves in Henry Plummer's camp, compensated more than adequately for the sudden lack of information from Father, who no longer conducted his business with Hank Crawford in the stables where I might chance to observe them. From James I could measure the increasing animosity between Plummer and Crawford, like you might gauge the building of steam on a railway engine, or the rising temperature of a wood-burning stove.

James understood my interest well enough, and he felt obliged to offer his own speculations as to the meaning of each new encounter and exchange between the two men. But all he ever saw was the moment and by this narrow vision failed totally to see the trend that would lead to the final resolution. So that when Plummer and Crawford were observed to be exchanging verbal hostilities, James announced that "they wouldn't last another day without a gunfight" and then never saw the contradiction when, two days later, Plummer was heard to offer Crawford a truce, and James proclaimed that "the battle's over between 'em." In the meanwhile, the last snows melted and the ground solidified some, and primarily by the indisputable evidence of the productivity of Henry Plummer's ingeniously designed stamp mill, the creek exploded with a fervor of hard-rock mining activity unrivaled by the prior year.

What also came, in close succession, were three more events that helped Father to step over the brink into an abyss from which he could never, ever extricate himself. The first of which was the theft of Father's prize stallion, Falstaff, in the middle of the night. "You would think he'd been married to that horse," Mother said when Father reacted badly by taking on a drunk and then wandering through the town with his shotgun slung across his shoulder.

Then, Buck Stinson and a posse rode out of Bannack after a band of Shoshones—seeking revenge on behalf of a large train of miners that had been massacred down on the Snake River on their way to

Bannack—to which Father said, "Good riddance," and then was infuri-
ated when they not only managed to return, but to carry back with them
two scalps, one of which had previously adorned the head of Old Snag,
who was revered by the most Christian element of Bannack as a kindly
old man. Not that Father cared much about the Indians, because he
didn't. What set him off was that Skinner then hung those scalps up
over his bar, as if to say this saloon's for the hard lot only, knowing full
well that a family man's wife would not tolerate such barbarity.

And then, lastly, in the second week of April, some of the best citizens of Bannack City, James Stuart and John Vanderbilt and Jim York
included, set off on a prospecting expedition to Colter's Hell, followed
but a few days later by a second group that included Tom Cover and
Louis Simmons. So that in one week's time, a goodly portion of Hank
Crawford's most vocal supporters had left Bannack City, and its troubles, far behind. And Father could do nothing for any of it: not for the
loss of Falstaff, the likes of which was never seen again to Father's way
of thinking; nor for those bloody scalps that hung there, prominently,
for as long as Skinner ran the place; nor for his missing out on the
Yellowstone foray, for which Father should have been thankful, but
never was.

So there was all that, and then there were other reasons, as well,
that explained how and why he stumbled and fell over that edge of the
abyss that was to prove deeper and darker than he could have known.
But in the end, he had no one and nothing to blame for what was to follow thereafter, except himself and hundreds of other men just like him.

CHAPTER 4

T he first I ever heard of Electa Bryan was on the day that Henry Plummer and Hank Crawford renewed their feud for the final time. By then, I had almost acceded to James's most recently expressed viewpoint that the anticipated confrontation between Henry Plummer and Hank Crawford would never come to pass.

So when I heard mention of Electa Bryan, of the existence of a lady whom Henry Plummer intended to marry and bring to Bannack City, it was as though a freshet of renewal flowed through me. And then, within the hour, I heard tell of a rumor spread by Hank Crawford that Henry Plummer had been cavorting with a Bannock squaw, and I became indignant, and after some investigation I chose to bring the word directly to him.

I found Henry Plummer at Peabody's, where he was sitting at a table drawing up mining deeds and assignments. Several other men watched while they drank whiskey and made bets on the flip of a gold coin. One of these was speaking as he played along. "I know you're gonna make that claim start workin' agin, Henry, but I shore don't see how. I've panned it an' picked it an' ain't found nothin' to speak of since that first month. But my belly tells me as soon as I sign it over an' take your money, it'll start showin' dust like sand on a beach."

Henry Plummer smiled. "I'll still let you out of it, Emmett, if you'd like. I certainly don't want anyone thinking I'm cheating them."

"Too late for that, Henry," Emmet Johnson said with a sort of gleaming smile. "Got me some plans. Goin' to Eureka an' get me a dance partner. B'sides, you're payin' twice what it's worth to me. So you go right along an' make it worth ten times what you paid and I'll still be no worse for it."

Then Henry Plummer saw me at the door. "Hello, Will," he spoke out, interrupting one of the other men who had started to speak. And then he said, "Come on in here. I'd like you to meet some of the boys. This here is Emmet Johnson. You may know him," he said with a wink, "as Crazy Legs Johnson. Does a jig that would make you swear his legs must be detached at the hip as well as the knee. And this is Ned Ray and Tex Crowley. And you know Buck." And each of then received me cordially, in their own ways, with their own twist on a nod, or a slap, or a smile, or a wave.

It was by then my practice to address him as "Henry." That had come a couple of weeks after the trial, after he had recovered his horse and revolvers and shotgun, when I had run into him crossing the street and had said, "Excuse me, Mr. Plummer" and he had said, "Henry; please, call me Henry."

So when I said, "I need to tell you something, Henry," it was not in any way out of disrespect.

"Well, all right, Will," he said. "What is it?" And when he saw me look over, unsure, at the other men, he said, "It's okay, Will. These men are all friends of mine."

So I told it. "It's Hank Crawford. He's telling stories about you and that squaw, Catherine. Says you've been visiting her at night up on Yankee Flat. He's been saying she's your squaw now."

Anger came to Henry Plummer in a way different than in other men; it didn't boil up red and steaming, nor did it show itself in instant, uncontrollable violence. Instead, it was as though Henry Plummer summoned anger and retribution from out of dormancy so that he might

use their power to suit his will. I saw it in his eyes as I stood there waiting for him to speak—a sudden, determined look, drawing on something deep within, requiring satisfaction. "Is that so," he finally said.
"And you yourself heard him say this?"

"I didn't hear it directly. But James O'Flaherty says he did, and
Dave Mueller says his pa did, and Web Warner heard it over at
Chrisman's. And they're my best sources, so to speak, so I know it's fact."

"Well, then," he said, shaking his head and looking down at the
mining assignment on the table in front of him, "something will need
to be done about it."

Which I guess explains why some would later say that I caused
what was to follow, but I don't think that was the case. He would have
heard the rumor elsewhere, from another direction, and then he would
have acted without any help from me. I only made it happen sooner,
only hurried matters along.

The two things I always figured were that Father would ultimately
regret his association with Hank Crawford and that Crawford would die
at the hand of Henry Plummer. Henry Plummer's quickness with a gun,
after all, was no longer merely the subject of distant hearsay and rumor;
his dexterity had been observed and the results recounted—in the
saloons, at the placers, in daydreamt recollections—ten score times with
admirations and regrets. And Father's shrewdness at selecting financial
dealings and business partners was, to put it mildly, largely unproved
and subject to a reasonable modicum of doubt. I thus thought it more
likely that Henry Plummer would kill Hank Crawford, as many said was
now his right, and I believed that in the aftermath, Father would be
forced, to his disadvantage, to partition and dissolve his former partnership interests with Crawford in order to satisfy the demands of
Crawford's sole heir and brother who had, but a week prior, arrived in
Bannack.

When Henry Plummer intercepted Crawford in the street that
afternoon and demanded that he draw, no one was surprised; nor was it
unexpected when Crawford sheepishly declined. And when Henry

Plummer offered him certain advantages in a duel that Plummer proposed take place the next morning, Crawford would have nothing to do with it, and these refusals marked him as a coward in the eyes of a majority of the mining population of Bannack City.

Both men were as visible as ever over the next few days, each presumably knowing that their sudden absence would imply fear if not outright concession. But they were seldom alone; each was frequently surrounded by a coterie of heavily armed and grim-faced men. Only, when it came to Henry Plummer and his partisans, you could see that Plummer commanded a clear and recognized authority over them, like an officer of high rank amongst his adjutants and orderlies, whereas Hank Crawford seemed almost to be furtively hiding behind his sympathetic companions. It began in a way that was somewhat humorous, with Crawford surrounded by his escort suddenly crossing the street the morning after Henry Plummer's challenge, navigating the entire span with a seriousness that seemed out of proportion to what was involved. That Henry Plummer was traversing the street alone at that very moment spoke more to the diminutive size of Bannack than to the oddities of circumstance; and the fact that not a man amongst them responded when Henry Plummer called Crawford a coward and a woman spoke volumes more.

There were minor fights and exchanges of words and even gunfire, although misdirected and ineffective, between the two factions, within the next several days. And when James told me that his older brother had heard Crawford say that he or Henry Plummer had to die in order for it to end, I laughed. "Then Hank Crawford's as good as dead," I said to James.

The next day began no differently than it would have on any other bright cloudless gift of a midspring morning: The bear grass and paintweed and mountain lilies and sedges were all in glorious stages of bloom and growth, sprinkling the canyon ledges and hills with a gentle waving spread of color; and the bluebirds and flickers and ravens were active with song and flight; and the sky was depthless, and the mountains in the distance strong and clear. Redtail hawks plied the rising thermals, effortlessly casting in the air in search of mice and voles and grouse on which to feed. And the breeze drew down the creek lightly, carrying the scent of the fresh flowing water like the sweet fragrance of a bouquet delivered to a waiting lady, and then moved east in search of the rising heat. There was the tranquility of renewal—of the grasses greening and the earth warming, of continuity and promise and change. And it was all shattered by the blast of a shotgun in the center of the town, and again by a second explosive discharge from the other barrel, followed by shouts and the sounds of boots and spurs along the boardwalk.

By the time I reached Henry Plummer, there were already half a dozen other men around him. There was blood spattered on a nearby wagon, and Henry Plummer's own unfired shotgun lay in the dirt of the hoofprinted, track-imbedded street where he had dropped it. And he stood in the middle of them all, ashen almost to a ghostly white and wincing from the pain, but standing motionless nonetheless. A hateful look I had never seen before was in his eyes.

"Who done it, Henry?" someone asked in an excited voice.

"Yeah, who was it?"

Henry Plummer looked toward the butcher's. "It was that son of a bitch Crawford," he said, short of breath. "He shot me from behind. Not 30 feet away. He shot me and I called him a coward and a dog . . . and the son of a bitch shot me again."

"Where'd he go?" Buck Stinson asked in a cold, patternless voice. And the crowd expressed a general intention to go after Hank Crawford.

"No," Henry Plummer said, and now he was doubled over. "Not now. Get me over to Doc Glick's."

Several of us helped him slowly across the street, avoiding with great care his right arm, which pulsed a steady flow of blood as it dangled loosely at his side. When we were almost to the cabin that Doc Glick utilized both as his visiting office and his home, Henry Plummer suddenly stopped, and I thought he had lost his strength. But he turned to Buck Stinson and said, "You find Crawford and tell him fifteen days. In fifteen days he and I will duel. Whether he likes it or not."

By evening, the word was out that the ball had entered the elbow from the rear as Henry Plummer leaned on a wagon wheel, and had traveled far into the bone of the arm, breaking and shattering it all along its path. Some said that Doc Glick had already amputated the arm, but others claimed that Henry Plummer would rather die than lose a limb. And by the next day the town generally understood that Henry Plummer had refused the amputation and was now in a great physical struggle for survival.

Hank Crawford never waited to learn whether Henry Plummer would live. Two days after the shooting, in a secret meeting, he conveyed his entire partnership interest to Father at bargain prices; he disposed of his other possessions in similar fashion and then fled Bannack City in the middle of the night, heading west, some said. But most figured it would be back East, where, despite the war, the environs would be generally less threatening to Crawford.

And then a most unnatural calm fell over Bannack City.

In two weeks time, Henry Plummer emerged from his cabin, where he had been tended by Doc Glick and an assistant under the good doctor's employ. I thought him to look worn and much aged by his ordeal and wondered how long it took a man to recover from such a great fatigue. And I wondered, as well, what it did deep down, whether the memory of the pain lingered forever, somewhere, in some dark shadow of reflection waiting to play the tormentor again, at a moment's notice. But if it did, Henry Plummer didn't show it, would not allow for it to show itself other than superficially. He was, by all accounts, at the very apex of his spirits.

Father and Hank Crawford's other most ardent supporters— Walter Dance and Harry Phleger and Bill Roe—laid low at Henry Plummer's reappearance. The warming weather had brought new droves of migrants to Bannack City, and with them came even more violence and crime. Chrisman's was robbed by a drunk who passed out only two buildings down and whom they let off only because they had no place to put him. The Rattlesnake Ranch, up north of Bannack, lost an entire team to thieves in the night. And George Carrhart took a stray bullet in the belly at Skinner's during a shoot-out between Dick Sapp and George Benfield, who Sapp claimed was dealing from under the deck. I could hear from the stables as Carrhart screamed aloud before he finally succumbed, and I watched as they carried him out to be buried on the hill.

The apparent unmanageability of the situation finally caused the miners to raise a call for the formal election of mining district officers. And Henry Plummer's name was foremost among those mentioned for sheriff. So Father backed away from it, tending instead to his own mining claims, which had virtually doubled in size with Crawford's departure, and managing the stables and the new stable hand he had hired out of what I knew was distrust for me but for reasons he characterized in business terms of increased volume and competition. At the same time Henry Plummer won a landslide victory and was elected sheriff of not only Bannack City and Grasshopper Creek but also the surrounding mining districts and feeder creeks and drainages, and the outlying settlements and hamlets in which many of the miners lived.

Being the sheriff of Bannack City didn't pay much—a pittance each for summoning witnesses and travel and not much more for serving warrants and attending trials. And that seemed to inspire Mother. "I think very highly of Mr. Plummer for taking the job, especially after all that's happened," she said at the evening meal.

"He's got his reasons," Father had answered.

"Well, what are they, Walter? I don't see what comes out of it other than a little respect from the community."

"I'll tell you what comes out of it, Nadine. Corrupt power. Another goddamn copperhead Democrat. A common murderer for a lawman. A rebel sympathizer and a traitor to his country. Right when that's just what the Union doesn't need. What Bannack City doesn't need. More power to the corrupt. And that's what a man like Henry Plummer thrives on. The power to manipulate things and people to suit

himself, to attain his own objectives. It's no different than those spine-
less politicians fighting the president back East. Without their rank and
their fancy carriages, they're nothing. But you give them a title or an
office and it takes no time before they're suddenly set up in bigger
houses and riding the best horses and wearing tailored clothes and uniforms and living the life of royalty. And in the end they always come up
rich. You wait and see, Nadine. Time will show it."

It wasn't even worth it for me to try and rebut him anymore, not
worth the humiliation and intimidation that was sure to follow. So I
didn't even bother to note that Henry Plummer was already rich, both
in terms of the value of his mines—which, even exclusive of the new
and fabulous Richardson claim in which Henry Plummer owned a quarter interest, could only be valued by tens of thousands of dollars—and
by the number and dedication of his friends and admirers.

And Father knew as much, out of envy reminded himself ad nau-
seam that while he had gained significant wealth from his own quartz-
crushing operation, sometimes returning as much as $50 a day, Henry
Plummer was easily bringing in fivefold that much. And knowing, also,
that of all the officers elected that day, Henry Plummer's margin of victory was the most impressive. In a way, it even might have been said that
Henry Plummer spoke more for the community than Judge Burchett,
who also won by a significant majority, although not as great as Henry
Plummer's.

The only amenity granted to Henry Plummer as sheriff was a box
of an office in the back of Chrisman's store; and for the first three days
after he assumed his responsibilities, Henry Plummer holed up there,
receiving visitors one at a time. I could see Chrisman's clearly from the
stables. And it was also plainly viewable from O'Flaherty's mechanical
bakery, in front of which James and I and our peers passed a great deal
of time jousting for our own rank and dominance. So I could watch the
comings and goings of Henry Plummer's back-room office; and I could
not but wonder at the diversity of the character of the men separately
entering and then departing. Some of them certainly fell within a sphere

of respectability that fostered the speculation that the new sheriff was interviewing potential candidates for deputy posts. But others, the likes of Cy Skinner and Buck Stinson and Ned Ray, were of such a violent and volatile disposition that by reasonable estimation they fell more closely into the category known provincially as roughs.

What I didn't understand was how much compromise and moderation and even hypocrisy would be involved in anything that so much as touched upon the political and politic. At least it could be said that the end result of the interviews was the product of intuitive calculation on the part of Henry Plummer, for each of the newly appointed lawmen maintained at least one preeminence, be it absolute proficiency with a firearm or a horse, or with the application of a persuasive and mollifying word, the usefulness of which strongly justified his selection for the post. And while no one seemed totally pleased by the ultimate deputy selections, no one was fully dissatisfied with them either, so broad was the spectrum from which the men had been chosen.

Having satisfied this first and foremost obligation to the public, Henry Plummer made it known that in a week's time he would depart for a destination on the Sun River, west of Fort Benton, where he would marry Electa Bryan. In the meanwhile, he invited dialogue with anyone who wished it, whether on topics of law enforcement or assaying silver or on matters of even less import. And within a handful of days, he had charmed all but the most conservative segment of Bannack City society, Father and Harry Phleger latterly included.

Henry Plummer, alone in Bannack City, was thus of both worlds. He could, without any semblance of compromise or condescension, spend his morning amongst businessmen discussing further potentialities for commerce and finance and then spend his afternoon in the company of the rowdier element competing in displays of horsemanship and shooting and then spend his evening at a gaming table at which any sort might play, interacting with the others in each instance in an almost dominating way and on whatever level they maintained. Not that any one of them wholly accepted it; there was and had to be a certain degree of resentment and distrust with which any particular crowd viewed Henry Plummer's association with its adversaries. But there was a certain form of harmony to it, also, that resulted from his collaborations; aside from his good company and conversation, each faction enjoyed a form of moderating protection through their relationship with him. And this, for the while, held the mining district together at a time when it otherwise would have disintegrated into chaos. So that the miners tolerated the merchants who grossly overcharged for their commodities and wares; and they both, to some degree, accepted the roughs who provided something of a labor force and who reveled in the disturbance of the community's quiet; and the roughs in turn acquiesced in a self-imposed restraint on the impulsiveness that drove them to live it all in a more reckless and wanton manner. This was Henry Plummer's contribution; and there were few who saw it clearly, or admitted to it even if they did.

You could hear the steely ring of his spurs along the boardwalks—that confident and drumlike roll of a regimental snare—and you would know instantly, without even seeing him, that it was Henry Plummer's slow, cool, decided gait. And with a marked admiration, I watched how he engaged in amiable and genuine conversation with everyone he encountered, how he almost effortlessly could establish himself as being integral to and compatible with any situation or setting. Concurrently, he somehow managed his many mining interests in full compliance with the district rules, employing no fewer than half a dozen men, each of whom reportedly was handsomely compensated for his loyalty and efforts. And daily, Bannack City and its environs grew at a phenomenal and uncontrolled rate until, by the first of June, the population had doubled from its New Year's high.

There were still only the two stables in town on the day of Henry Plummer's departure, and two butchers; but there were three of almost everything else—blacksmiths and bakeries and hotels—and five full-time saloons whose doors only closed in deference to an occasional miners' court proceeding. And they were all gaily alive with the continuing freshness of springtime activity as Henry Plummer mounted his horse and turned to head down the street and out of Bannack. And it was almost as if the populace came out to send him off; all along the railing and porches and walkways men and women waved or voiced some friendly or playful sentiment as he passed by, and even the Indians in town watched him with a sort of knowing empathy as he gracefully sat astride his horse.

When he saw me, he stopped so that he might pass a word. "Morning, Will," he said with a wide smile.

And I said, "Morning, Henry," back to him, proudly in front of what seemed the entire town.

"I wonder if you might do me a favor, Will," he said quietly. And when I readily and faithfully acknowledged that I would, he said, "Watch things for me. I don't mean I want you to do anything if something goes wrong, other than to report it to one of the deputies. But I'd like for you to just sort of look out. Like you've done for me before." And after I repeated gladly that I would, he said, "Thank you, Will. You're a good man. I knew I could count on you." Then we shook hands and he pulled his horse back and headed up the hillside and away from Bannack. And it seemed to me, as he diminished and slipped from my view, that he was very much like a heralded knight, departing on some solitary and selfless epic from which only providence would determine whether he would eventually return. And when he was gone, a lonely and empty sensation enveloped me, and I leaned down to Rat and scratched underneath his plump and well-fed underbelly.

BOOK II

JOSEPH SWIFT

CHAPTER 1

Every morning she would stroll out into the yard and dutifully spread the seed for the laying hens, taking care to dispense it widely so that they might not battle over it unnecessarily. And then she would move on to the next chore without any intimation of impatience or expectation. At first, her seeming indifference was not obvious, because it was still too early in the spring then to even hope, with the rivers choked with broken floes of ice, and the mountain passes drifted over and still shrouded in snow, and the days still shortened by the premature fall of night and the tardy rising of the sun. But by the advent of June, the promise was at risk of being unfulfilled.

I found myself looking west, across the banks of the swollen Sun River, toward the mountains I could not even see from James Vail's missionary farm. And that is when I saw how she would move about the farmyard, hanging out the wash, conversing happily with her sister and the children, tending gently to the stock, never once pausing to gaze out over the walls to at least wonder at the slow and tedious passage of time.

I suppose she always knew that he would come and so she never bothered to expend her emotion and energy on worrying when that moment might arrive. And her humility was such that she never would

69

have told you so, never would have said, "He will be here," and thereby suggest that her foresight was any greater than the norm. So, instead, out of pride no doubt, or if not that then at least out of respect and responsibility, she performed her chores with an abject patience that instilled and implied calm and reassurance.

Francis Thompson had returned from his overwinter in California, and he observed her behavior also. He had brought back with him strange tales of Henry Plummer, and he shared them with James and Martha when he thought Electa and the children and I were out of range of hearing. But I caught some of it nonetheless, and the description of Henry Plummer as outlaw and desperado was enough to stimulate and excite my imagination.

We were so greatly removed from civilization. For me, that isolation meant much time spent in speculation on what was transpiring in the world at the time: of the hurried conferences between great field generals, batteries of artillery working all around them with frenetic regularity to clear and load and fire. Of sounds generated a thousand miles away, the rail yards' screeching, squealing sounds of steel, the almost windlike whispered swish of a gentle ocean reef. And it was these things, the distant possibilities of culture, the proud and diffident demeanor of the young finished women at the dance of their coming out, that I compared to the reality of the wild ruggedness of the setting in which I lived, with the barren crudities of the gold towns just a few days' journey to the west where the resolution of a dispute was achieved by the sudden draw and discharge of revolvers. Francis Thompson's talk thus only fed my already strained impatience, and I began to worry that Henry Plummer might not return, that he might be dead or have had a change of heart or be lying that moment in a dark jail cell somewhere such that I might never realize the chance to see him again and decide for myself what he was all about.

Electa heard the words also, directly from Martha and Francis, who both sought to dissuade her from her intent to marry Henry Plummer immediately upon his arrival. And she ignored them, admonishing

Francis, who had never even met Henry Plummer, and reminding Martha how much a gentleman Henry Plummer had been the previous fall, when he and Jack Cleveland had courted her with an intense rivalry.

"I love him, and I shall marry him and devote myself to him," I heard Electa say the first time they confronted her. Martha only struggled that much harder against that very result. And by week's end Martha had succeeded enough in creating doubt or hesitation that Electa was finally saying that she would, at least, delay the ceremony a sufficient amount of time to allow Henry Plummer to prove himself.

It was Francis who first espied Henry Plummer's approach from up the Mullan Road, noting how boldly and gracefully he forded the flooding river on his handsome horse when other riders had been turned back at the crossing or had been widely detoured. And when Francis called out to Electa to announce Henry Plummer's arrival, I detected a note of disappointment in his voice.

Henry Plummer rode up to the gate and then passed through, wet to the hip, his fine horse at a proud, disciplined trot; and James and Martha greeted him in the same manner they greeted every visitor, with an air of superiority and aloofness. Then Henry Plummer's eye turned to Electa, and it was as though he became unconscious of all else. He tipped his hat and bowed his head in a dignified, respectful acknowledgment, and then he lithely dismounted. Walking over to her, he took her hand and kissed the back of it and said, "Miss Electa," saying it not as greeting, but as something more, as an exclamation of long-awaited reunion, as a pronouncement of something profound and of great and overwhelming significance. And then he said, "Just to see you again is the fulfillment of my greatest hope."

So I could not help but be impressed, just as I had been the previous fall when he had accepted and then performed with dedication the task of guarding the Vail farm in exchange for nothing more than meals and a place to sleep. Jack Cleveland, who had accompanied him, had been another story altogether; his conduct had been so coarse and demeaning that even Electa, who usually was most condescending, found it difficult to conceal her contempt. Francis Thompson also was taken with Henry Plummer; that much was obvious. He had expected a disreputable ruffian deserving of disrespect and instead had encountered not only a gentleman but an almost stately individual who spoke with an educated precision and displayed aristocratic manners extremely unlikely in that remote, uncivilized corner of the territory.

The Vails allowed Henry Plummer the courtesy only of a bath and a shave and a change of clothes before Martha called us all into the great room for dinner. He was the last to walk into the room, and each of us admired how marblelike his smooth, square jaw and slick, sandy hair looked, and of how unconscious he seemed to be of his fine, commanding features.

With a gesture of her hand, Martha showed us each to our seat. "Won't you sit here, Mr. Plummer. Here, between Mr. Vail and me," she said as she pulled back a chair and as much as placed him in it. And then, after the side meat of salted pork and the potatoes and bread and peas had been portioned out and a prayer of thanks offered, her inquisition began in earnest. "Now I'm sure you won't mind our asking a few questions, Mr. Plummer—may I call you Henry—a few questions concerning your desire to marry our Electa."

To which Electa objected. "Martha! Please," she said in a flustered voice. "Henry has just arrived. Let us give him a little peace."

"It's all right, Electa," Henry Plummer said. "I really do not mind. After all, is it not customary for the suitor to justify himself to the family of the bride?"

"Well then, Henry," Martha continued, "won't you tell us how you intend to support Electa. To provide for her, I mean. One cannot just assume that good fortune will come one's way. I hope you don't mind my asking, but I am Electa's older sister, and it falls on me to ask the proper questions."

I thought her question to be particularly unfair, especially since James and Martha were not exactly prospering themselves. They were owed compensation for a year's worth of work, and for the last three months had been rationing much of their supplies, including those that we were consuming at that moment.

But Henry Plummer was not troubled by her inquiry. "No, one cannot," he said in a way that connoted real agreement. "Indeed, one cannot assume anything in this day and age. In my case, however, good fortune has already come. I have been blessed with extravagant fortune, far more than any man could hope for. As of today, I own five mines outright and fractional interests in half a dozen more."

"We know you're a prospector, Henry," Martha interrupted. "But those are only mines you're talking about. Or what do you call them? Claims, isn't it? I mean, you can't know they'll be worth anything until they've been worked. What I was asking was how you can be sure you'll be able to support Electa in a reasonable fashion."

Henry Plummer smiled and shook his head. "I'm sorry, Martha. I wasn't being clear. You misunderstand. These are all proven mines— mines that are currently producing in paying quantities."

Martha knew nothing of gold mining, and James knew even less; and the conversation had therefore taken a difficult turn. "Well, what are they worth, then, Mr. Plummer?" she finally asked in frustration. "Perhaps you'll tell us that."

Henry Plummer paused before he responded, and when I looked at Electa from the corner of my eye, it seemed to me that she had turned a pale, bloodless color; she had abandoned any pretense of eating. "I would not want to overstate it," he finally said. And Martha's head came back some, as though she were about to be vindicated. And then Henry Plummer said, "Twenty thousand dollars, at least."

His estimate caused Martha involuntarily to draw a deep breath.

"You see," he explained, "You can never really know exactly how much there is until it runs out. But to date, I've extracted over $4,000 worth of dust and nuggets and mill stamp at $18 an ounce. On the day before I left, my interests returned $200 to me. So I would say, conservatively, $20,000. Although, you understand, I expect to do much better." This last statement was made with great humility and deference, as though he could understand how the stated amount of worth might not be sufficient in the eyes of James and Martha Vail.

There suddenly appeared to be nothing left to say. James and Francis must have been overwhelmed by the fact that Henry Plummer had accumulated such great wealth in so short a period of time, and I am sure they felt suddenly insecure and inadequate before both Martha and Electa, and perhaps even before the children. But Martha was more aggressive and less intimidated, intent as she was on doing everything in her power to preserve Electa for herself. So she said, "Well, what about Electa's safety? I understand these mining towns are rough places. Some say they're lawless."

"We have law in Bannack City now," Henry Plummer answered with a modest smile. And when Martha asked, almost out of desperation, whether the law was effective, whether it would serve to keep the peace and provide a place where women and children could live reasonably and comfortably, Henry Plummer said, "That remains to be seen. You see, Martha, I was elected sheriff just two weeks ago. It will take some time before one can judge what my influence upon the place will be."

And that was the end of it. Because there was nothing left that she or James or Francis could even hope or want to argue against, such that anything else that afterwards came to light—be it Jack Cleveland's death at Henry Plummer's hand or the admitted fact that Henry had been convicted, although wrongly, and then finally pardoned for the murder of a man in California—only served to corroborate the fact that Henry Plummer was a man of great fortitude and dignity who inevitably would succeed in society and business and even politics should he so desire.

The days that followed seemed to me to be the most wonderfully idle ever lived by man. The sun rose brilliantly each morning such that the dawn warmed into a gentle bath of light, forming soft and billowing clouds, in and out of which the sun wove to provide warmth and then, by its momentary absence, a most desirable cooling. The blossoms were of a greater number than ever before or since, and there were birds on the wing and antelope afoot in graceful herds that circled fluidly upon the plains. And even the cottonwood and birch leafed out more heavily, spreading great canopies over meadows more filled with lupine and lilies than seemed possible, than reality would ever allow. And in the midst of this most pleasant similitude of life and living, Henry and Electa strolled arm in arm and rode abreast and talked of simple things to share. And not one of us, neither James nor Martha nor Francis nor I, thought anything other than that the world was not good enough for Henry Plummer and Electa Bryan, that they together transcended it without effort or intent, and that this seemingly divine offering of paradise failed to do them justice.

～～～

I knew it wouldn't last forever; nothing does. But I wanted it to be prolonged for as long as might be possible; and thus, although it meant that I would have to continue to wait to be paid by the Vails, I was gladdened by the news that the sternwheeler due at Fort Benton apparently had been delayed. For the Reverend Reed was to be on that boat, and it was he, as Indian Agent for the government, who was to pay the Vails for their efforts in running the experimental farm. And it was he, also, who Martha insisted would conduct the marriage ceremony. And since it was that same steamboat that was to deliver to Francis the supplies with which he intended to open up a general store somewhere in the region, we all waited and passed the time together to our mutual enjoyment, until Henry Plummer could wait no more. "I must get back," he said one evening after we had returned from a three-day excursion to the Great Falls of the Missouri River. "It is not right of me to assume the responsibilities of sheriff and then neglect them so readily."

Electa sat next to him on the settee, as she could for hours, content to rest her hand upon his forearm and stare into his sea-grey eyes in admiring devotion. "But I thought you had deputies for just that reason, Henry; so you would not have to be everywhere at once."

"Yes, that's true, Electa," he said. "But the deputies are just that, deputations. It is my duty to make the final decisions and to administer them. We must find someone else to perform the service, Electa. I can wait no longer."

Martha's objection to the marriage being performed by one of the fathers from the St. Peter's Mission was so strenuous that a compromise of sorts was struck. And the next morning I accompanied Henry in a hurried ride down the Mullan Road, past the Great Falls again, and on to Fort Benton. The fort, at that time, was under the charge of Andrew Dawson, an irascible fur trader whose bearing seemed to blame everyone he encountered for the leg he himself had mangled a few years back by negligently falling through a trapdoor in one of the fort's storehouses. He had come to Fort Benton in 1854, at a time when a road west connecting waterway to waterway was no more than a reminiscence of Jefferson's failed aspiration, and he had watched the isolated fur trading post evolve into a way station of ever greater importance to road builders and engineers and miners and travelers until, with the simultaneous arrival and docking of the freight- and passenger-laden sternwheelers *Chippewa* and *Key West,* it became the world's innermost port.

He was outside the gates of the fort when we arrived, leaning on his crutch as he shouted angry directions at laborers who were struggling to move several awkward mackinaw boats toward the river. "Work together, damn you," he yelled. "You, Saxton, wait for the others. Now together, you lazy sons. One, two, pull." And then he swore volubly when several of the men fell and the rope went slack.

There were hundreds of large bales of buffalo robes and sacks of buffalo tongue stacked everywhere, representing the remnants of many hundreds of the huge woolly beasts. And the few Blackfeet who lingered to watch the white men struggle with the boats looked pleased by the trades they had made in exchange for the buffalo hides and meat; in particular, they showed great pride and possessiveness toward the rifles and steel knives held closely at their sides and for the tin and iron pots that so greatly pleased their women. When the laborers finally succeeded in aligning one mackinaw with the river's bank, Dawson, who never stopped working to direct and encourage his men, parceled out more orders to keep them moving. "Norwood, take three men and start loading that boat; and tie them hides down good. You over there. Watch that hull. Move it. Move it."

It was a rather remarkable, if not somewhat forlorn place, with the fort built on a long, desolate stretch of bottom along the river and not another building in sight, and the land rising up all around into sharp cutting buttes and rolling uplands to the north and a flat, endless plateau to the west. And the fort itself looking from the outside like nothing more than four squared walls of mud-plastered adobe brick guarded by two diagonally opposing bastions, until you went inside and saw the bakery and blacksmith and carpenter and cooper shops and the trade offices and retail shops all active with clerks and craftsmen attending to the needs of a variety of settlers and prospectors.

When the guard at the gate asked us our business, Henry let it be known that he wished to speak to Dawson. And then we waited while the work proceeded apace. Dawson, who went by "Major," finally acknowledged us with a nod, and then he hobbled over to where we stood. "You asking for me?" he said, as if he were offended by our very presence. He looked first at Henry Plummer and then he recognized me. "Hello, Joseph," he said. And now his tone softened some. "I trust your employers are doing well. And Miss Electa?"

"She's fine, Major. Everyone is doing just fine. We're checking on the *Shreveport*. Any word yet?"

"We finally got some word, all right." And from the way he said it, I could not help but wonder whether the *Shreveport* had suffered a fate similar to that of the *Chippewa*, which had been blown up far downriver two years back when a drunk dropped a candle into a stream of spilled alcohol.

"This here's Henry Plummer," I said. "Henry's sheriff at Bannack City. You might have heard of him."

Dawson scratched at the stubble on his chin. "Seems like I have at that," he said. "Can't think what it was though."

"Pleased to meet you, Major Dawson," Henry said as he extended his hand. "When's she due in, Major? The *Shreveport*, I mean."

"She ain't due in. She's stuck in low water at Cow Island," Dawson answered. And then he turned to me as he said, "And you know what that means."

"Guess it means they got 150 miles by trail to bring up the freight and passengers."

"Well, that too," Dawson said. "But it's worse than that. The *Shreveport's* got less draft than any of the rest of 'em, which means we ain't gettin' a single steamboat to Fort Benton all year. Not one. Don't matter much to me one way or the other. The trade's still here as long as those Blackfeet and Piegans keep bringin' in buffalo robes; they can always be taken downriver by mackinaw or keelboat. But it'll be tough on the fur company, and worse on LaBarge. They stuck their necks way out on freight contracts. It'll cost 'em a fortune to bring it all up the trail in wagons."

"Have you an estimate on when the passengers from the steamboat might arrive at your fort, Major?" Henry asked.

And I could see that Dawson was taken aback by the clarity of Henry Plummer's speech. "Got no idea at all. Ain't but a few wagons downriver, an' I'd guess the fur company'll rent 'em out first for freightin', seein' how that's where they're gonna lose their money. Them passengers are the least of their worries for now. I wouldn't even want to guess if and when the freight'll come up. Or what they'll do with it once it does."

So Henry said, "Thank you for your time, Major. That is what we needed to know. Let's tend to the horses, Joseph; it's a long way back." And then he said, "Thank you, Major. I imagine we will meet again." And they shook hands in a formal, official sort of way.

Once the facts relating to the *Shreveport* and the riverboat traffic in general had been relayed to Martha, she was left with no choice but to agree that Father Menetry from the St. Peter's Mission would marry Electa Bryan to Henry Plummer, which he did at the Sun River on the twentieth day of June in the year 1863.

Before departing from Fort Benton, Henry had bartered with some Piegans for a choice cut of buffalo hump, and Martha baked it ingeniously, with a delicate sprinkling of sage and ground gingerroot, and together with her corn bread and huckleberry pie, it made for a marvelous wedding feast. In honor of the occasion, James condescended to the opening of several bottles of brandy that he had saved for medicinal purposes. A glass would empty and there'd be a laugh and James would rise and refill it and all the other glasses, and not long after another glass would empty and there'd be laughter again and he would start anew. And we would have continued in that fashion late into the night had Henry not finally excused himself and Electa with a sudden and sobering reaffirmation that they would be leaving in the morning. And when they had left the room, an immediate and vacant silence prevailed that almost stupefied the four of us who remained, wounded and dizzied by the prospect of their departure.

The cancellation of steamboat traffic to Fort Benton was a sore blow for the scattered population of settlers in the area, and for each of us, also, since we now knew that the Reverend Reed's arrival was indefinitely delayed and that the supplies of the experimental farm and those ordered by Francis might not be delivered at all. So that all our plans and occupations failed contemporaneously. "What shall we do, James?" Martha finally said as we sat drinking the brandy.

"I don't know, Martha. We can't just leave. We can't pack up tomorrow and pull out of here and leave our duties and charges unattended."

"Well, we can plan on leaving," Martha said. And now she had put her glass of brandy aside and had turned to face James directly. "This is no way to live, being dependent on a river that can't even flow enough water to float a barge. This isn't what they told us it would be like, James. No one let on that the boats might not be able to come in. We'll starve here with no supplies and the Blackfeet being so protective of their precious heathen hunting grounds. We have every right to leave. We must give the Reverend Reed due notice and then depart at its expiration. We have no responsibility to these Indians. They couldn't care less whether we come or go as long as someone is around to answer to their begging."

"Now, Martha . . . ," James began.

But before James or I could appease her, Francis said, "I think Martha's right, James. I can't stay here indefinitely either. You know I've got plans to open a store. Sooner or later LaBarge will get me my order; I've got a solid commitment in writing. In the meanwhile, I'll still be able to buy supplies at Benton or from Salt Lake."

"Nor can I," I added. "You can't even pay me for last year, let alone for the next."

And the next morning, as we watched Henry and Electa depart for Bannack City in the ambulance wagon they borrowed from the farm, with the happy couple sitting closely side by side and Henry's horse following behind, untethered, at a royal trot, each of us knew that we would follow after them as soon as circumstance allowed.

For me this meant just a matter of days. Because James and Martha Vail were particularly responsible, and when they saw they could no longer keep me, their first concern was that I be compensated for my services. There was no money, and they knew I was right in refusing to accept a portion of the gold dust that Henry had left for them; it was the Reverend Reed and the United States government that owed me payment and not them. So they gave to me the entire three-hitch team of oxen that were to have plowed the cultivated fields, which were already growing over with native flora as they lay fallow and neglected. And Francis and I soon followed on the heels of Henry and Electa, toward the gold diggings at Grasshopper Creek.

CHAPTER 2

Once you came to accept the frontier truism that any road or trail or blaze was better than none at all, the route they called the Mullan Road was one you could appreciate above the rest. Constructed and improved over four years' time by the strength and will of driven men through some of the roughest country on the continent, the road was carved in a northland country so secluded and filled with hostile Blackfeet and Crow that the work parties had labored under a constant military guard beneath an open and lonely sky with storms that formed and descended from out of nothingness and the freezes early and the snows deep. Until, in the end, after an expenditure of a quarter million dollars and four lives, the route stretched over 600 miles, connecting the inland port at Fort Benton with that at Wallula. The Mullan Road, some said, was a marvel of engineering, and, except over the bridges that had been formed out of native timbers to cross the countless streams and creeks and ravines along the way, its width was wide enough to accommodate wagon traffic from both directions at once.

This was the route that Henry Plummer had taken on both occasions to reach Fort Benton and the Sun River farm, and it was the avenue on which he and Electa traveled toward Bannack City. Francis also had taken the Mullan Road any number of times and lastly that prior September on his journey to California. We had heard much of it from travelers who would often stop and camp at the Vail farm, just two days out from Fort Benton by wagon. So I envisioned it to be a great and easy thoroughfare, like the plank roads back East—well maintained and suitable for a Sunday outing in a buckboard or surrey in your best attire. And that was almost the case, at least at first, as we forded the now receding Sun River, with Francis before me in his chariotlike cart and me driving my oxen from astride my mare; and we followed the road across the river bottoms where the American Fur Company grazed its ever-increasing herd of cattle and horses.

But in the days to come, I would realize that the Mullan Road was unlike any I had traveled before or had even imagined. I had come all the way to Fort Benton from back East on a steamboat loaded with scores of people, and so I never experienced the great western wilderness except by watching from the railing as the varied scenes of Mandan Indian villages and grazing buffalo and distant prairie fires passed by like so many oil paintings set upon easels conveyed past you in a row. Whereas with the road you had to walk or ride to struggle through and over the wilderness of prairie and foothill and mountain and forest with nothing to stand between you and it, nothing by which you might think, "It is over there and I here." But it wasn't just the isolation and the unavoidable immersion into it that brought home how remote and primal it was. It was the night that made the real difference, the utter darkness that brought the real wild close, by which it folded itself around you. Because if you had just gone out into it in the day, you still could have taken comfort in the fact that, by nightfall, you would be under shelter and behind wall and that it would all be beyond you, the wind and the sounds and the violent mystery all blocked out by a man-made barrier. When the night began to fall on us that first evening, after we had worked so hard to make the distance to the Dearborn and then had crossed it with great effort on the hand-pull ferry that Mullan's party had left behind, with the clouds closing in and the real night subsuming and enveloping, it was then that the loneliness and the inhibition of being in the wild transformed into anxiety and fear.

On the third day out, with the Red Tail Divide behind us and having followed the washed out Mullan Road up the Little Prickly Pear, we rode deep into the foothills of the great mountains. There, at a point where a trail crossed the road, Francis pointed out the fresh track of Indian ponies. And not much later I began to hear unmistakable sounds of stealth moving just beyond sight through the trees. "Probably just a bear," Francis said quietly. And the prospect brought me little comfort as I thought of the grizzly hides I had seen at Fort Benton, brought in by trappers who had expended the time and effort to skin and haul the hides only because no one otherwise would have believed them of the grizzlies' great heads and jaws and the 4-inch claws as sharp as eagles' talons.

And so it was a great relief when we departed from the Mullan Road and came down out of the forested mountains and ultimately reached Cottonwood even though it was not much of a town, but rather an odd assortment of rough plank buildings and rougher log structures. As Francis searched for a room to rent for the night, I stood and watched. There was a wild rush of activity up and down the road that ran straight through the settlement, and a flow of wagons and pack trains and horsemen, all loaded down with tools and lumber and precious food stocks and panes of glass. And the men (there being very few females among them) all seemed to be hurrying about their business. Across the street, a shack-turned-saloon was abustle with fiddle music and the loud and excited exchange of called dances and shuffled boots.

"No luck," Francis said when he finally reappeared. The tune of the fiddle flowed out into the air and then faded as the door was closed by someone inside. "The whole place is full up. There's been a new strike east of Bannack. Alder Gulch they're calling it. And they say it's big."

I had entertained great hopes for a bath and a hot meal and a bed. And an even greater weariness descended over me as he said the words.

"Guess we move on," Francis said with his usual determination.

I wanted to protest and sought for an argument for staying anyway when two men came up to us. They had been standing nearby, smoking cigars and staring at my oxen; and it hadn't really bothered me because the single street was full of men drinking and talking and working to load or repack wagons and mules, and these seemed no more imposing than the rest. One of them was better attired than the other; he was clean shaven and wore a fine suit of light wool. The other was dressed in grease-blackened buckskin and heavy boots, with a revolver tucked into his shirt. Yet it was the latter that spoke. "Them your ox?" he asked Francis.

Francis said nothing and instead pointed over to me.

"They yours?" the man asked.

"Sure they are," I said. "Something wrong with their being on the street?"

"What'll you sell 'em for?" he asked. And I stood there looking at him while he picked at his teeth with a splinter of wood.

I had an idea what they were worth based on what James had owed me. But I knew better than to say it. So, even though I really did not want them, I said, "I wasn't planning on selling 'em."

The other man stepped forward at that moment. "Will you take $100?" he asked. And before I could reject his offer, before I could say "Go to hell, I won't be cheated," he said, "Apiece, of course; $600 for the lot."

"I was figuring on getting at least a thousand in Aspen Gulch," I said.

He said, "Seven hundred, take it or leave it," and when I hemmed and hawed just long enough, the buyer threw in a night's stay in town, and we agreed.

Francis and I waited in the street until the men returned with the money, and I counted it out twice before I turned the oxen over to them. "And where will we be staying?" I asked.

The buyer, whose name was Grant, pointed over to the long,

narrow log building that served as a hotel and said, "Over there. Room five. That's my room when I'm here. It's yours for tonight."

I couldn't figure it out, but I went along with it anyway. And I had good reason for not understanding it all, seeing as how, at that moment, I was only nineteen years of age and had never seen let alone touched $700. So I asked, "What are you going to do with 'em, Mr. Grant?"

"Fatten 'em up and butcher 'em," he said. And I didn't understand that either, how the economics worked out that you could buy an ox for that much money and then be willing to eat it.

We got our bath and went down to the saloon and ordered up some steaks and paid a ransom price of $2 each for our meals. So then I knew what was happening in Bannack City and at this new strike some were calling Alder or Aspen and others the Fairweather District and still others Varina or Virginia City. I knew that in the short span of time since Henry Plummer had left Bannack to come to the Sun River farm, gold had been struck again and the fever had spread and it was a boomtown like they said it was in California in '49. And if the fever got big enough, if it brought in enough new prospectors and merchants, and if there were enough of that gold and silver buried in the ground, Grant would be able to charge $3 or maybe even $5 or maybe even more for every steak and potato he sold. And Francis saw it too.

"You got as much money as I do now, Joseph," he said. "And you handled yourself pretty nicely in getting it, too. What do you say we make a partnership out of it and see what we can do about getting our share of this here gold strike?" And we toasted to it over shots of whiskey, for which we paid dearly.

Later, among the crowd at the bar, a man started talking so loudly about the new gold rush that we couldn't help but overhear him from our table. Thereafter, he commanded the attention of everyone in the establishment as he offered his version of the strike. "I've known Bill Fairweather for years now," he said boastfully, "an' I've always knowed he'd be the one to strike it. An' you know why? 'Cause he always brought an Irishman with him wherever he went. So when I heard he was joinin'

James Stuart an the rest of 'em on that prospectin' expedition to Colter's
Hell, an' that Irishman Barney Hughes was with 'em, I knew they'd find
'em the mother of all lodes."

"I thought you said this Fairweather didn't make it out with the
expedition," someone close to the bar said.

"That's right. That's what I said. Didn't make no difference to him
and that Irishman, though. Only mattered that they were involved. No,
sir. An' I'll bet he knew it from the beginnin'. So's everthin' that got
throw'd at him and the other stragglers—first no horses and then those
Crows stealin' 'bout everthin' they had—didn't make no matter no how."

"What'd you say they was gettin'?" someone else asked.

"First pan was $3 even. An' the next was even better. No matter
where they tried. Upstream, down, upslope, on the banks, in the bars.
The whole place covered with dust. I'm tellin' ya there's good claims for
20 mile in both directions."

Francis was taking it in with great interest. And when the miner
paused, Francis spoke up from our table. "You say there's still prospects
left? Aren't they all claimed?"

"Been seven weeks since the discovery. Five since the stampede. If
it was a normal find in a place with lots of miners nearby, I'd say yeah.
But there just ain't that many folks around. At first it was only miners
from Bannack and Spanish Fork, and Hell Gate, an' there's plenty of 'em
that abandoned some pretty good mines, at least down on the Grasshopper, just to look for somethin' better. Then they started tricklin' in
from Salt Lake an' Walla Walla. One or two with good horses even made
it in from Portland already. It's a stampede all right." The miner gave a
knowing shake of his head, like he'd seen it before and could definitely
identify it when he saw it again.

Five weeks was almost to the day how long Henry Plummer had
been gone from Bannack City. And I thought that either he had missed
it by a day or two, or that he had known and had left anyway so as to
not keep Electa waiting any longer. So I said, "You say you've just come
from this Alder Gulch?"

"Left three days back," the miner said.

"Meet anyone on the road?"

"Young fella, the road's full of anyones." And the saloon burst into laughter.

"Well, I didn't mean just anyone. I meant Henry Plummer. He's sheriff in Bannack City. You didn't happen to see him, did you?"

"Why you askin'?" the man said; and he looked at us suspiciously, like we suddenly were some kind of threat.

"We're friends of Henry's," I said. "We were at his wedding a few days ago. Up the Sun River. I was just wondering if he and his bride made it in to Bannack."

"That so. Guess you'd know his bride's name then, wouldn't you."

"Her name's Electa. Electa Bryan. That was her maiden name, I mean. Light brown hair. Blue eyes."

The miner eased up then. "Fact is I did see 'em. Had a pretty long talk with 'em, too; tellin' him about Dillingham an' the trial an all. Set 'em off somethin' fierce."

There were others in the saloon that knew some of the story. "I heard they let the killers off even though everyone knew they did the shootin'," one of them said.

"That ain't the way it went," the miner answered. "There were witnesses all right. The question was which ones did it, an' why. Seems that Deputy Gallagher got the pistols all switched around and reloaded after it happened so that everybody had a different idea who did the shootin'. An' it came out at the trial that one of 'em, ain't sure if it was Stinson or Forbes or that Haze Lyons, tole Dillingham about some plans they'd made to rob Wash Stapleton. Guess they figured Dillingham was a deputy an' they were deputies, too, so they could count on Dillingham to keep it quiet an' stay clear. But he didn't do it; he warned ole Wash. So they shot Dillingham right there in the street in Nevada City, just down the road from Virginia City, with half a dozen people seein' it happen."

"Mister," Francis said. "You're acting like this Alder Gulch is a great metropolis or something. You telling us there's towns where there wasn't even a cabin six weeks ago?"

"Guess that's exactly what I'm tellin' ya. Virginia City's the townsite at the new diggins. Or one of 'em. There's a town springin' up at every bend in the Gulch. There's some that wanted it to be called Varina, but ole Bissell wouldn't sign the townsite an' survey papers lest they called it somethin' other than after Jeff Davis's wife. So they compromised on Virginia, like that was a name both the North an' the South could claim."

"So where is this place, this Virginia City?" Francis asked.

"Seventy mile east of Bannack."

"And what's Henry Plummer's interest there?"

"Well, I guess it falls within his territory, seein' how his deputies is runnin' things. Or at least they were." And someone else told him to finish telling about Dillingham.

The miner smiled like he knew a good joke. "Well, they called a miners' meeting as soon as the word got out that Dillingham was dead. We decided on a miners' trial, with everyone gettin' to vote on the question of guilt, an' Doc Bissell an' Doc Steele an' Doc Ruter agreed to act as judges.

"Took two days, but in the end it came out that Haze Lyons an' Stinson were guilty as charged; an' it was determined that hangin' was too good for 'em but it would have to do."

"What about the third one?" one of the men behind the bar asked.

"You mean Charley Forbes. If you knew Charley, you wouldn't even ask. Best talker I've ever seen. All he had to do was stand up and talk for himself for an hour or so an' by the time he was done, there weren't a miner in that whole town that wouldn't a given Charley Forbes everythin' he had just to say they were his friend and knew him. Nope. Forbes got off clean."

"So they just hung the two of 'em?" the other asked.

"Not exactly. Almost hung 'em, anyway. Had a gallows rigged up right in the middle of town an' everythin'. X Beidler had already dug the graves. I ain't sure what happened, to tell it plain. That speech that Charley Forbes made got everyone goin', I guess. Got everyone feelin' kind of sentimental and weepy. An' there were some women around, too. An when they took to cryin' over the idea of hangin' Lyons an' Stinson there in their new town, a lot of folks had a bit of change of heart, an' some said there'd been a miscount the first time around. An ole H. P. Smith, who was actin' as lawyer, jumped on that gush of emotion an' played it for all it was worth. By the time he was through, he had most of the rest of us who weren't already cryin' feelin' so bad for those boys that we couldn't see through the tears. So they took the vote again, an' this time the yeas were separated to the right, an' the nays to the left, an accordin' to the count anyway, there were plenty more on the left than on the right."

"So they let the murderers go. Is that what you're saying?"

"Well, I figured we let the guilty party go when we acquitted Charley Forbes since the facts suggested he was the one that shot the ball that killed Dillingham."

"What about this Henry Plummer?" the other asked. "If he's the sheriff, how come he wasn't there keeping the peace?"

"Actually," the miner said, "we had to elect a sheriff when we formed the committee. Fella named Todd's the sheriff in Nevada City, although most of the boys consider Henry Plummer to be the law in the Gulch. An' Henry weren't there only because he had left to bring his bride back, just like this fella over here says. Otherwise, he'd a been there. Besides, it was just one of those things you got to expect in a minin' town. Can't blame it on Henry Plummer no more than you could blame him for the rain."

The saloon was filled with other travelers, and the miner soon eased into obscurity as the crowd milled about. There was a freightman from Salt Lake City who was traveling as far as Hell Gate before he returned home, and Francis managed to place an order with him for those sorts of things that typically ran short—salt and flour and tobacco, nails and shovels and picks—to be delivered to him in Bannack. And there was a man who claimed he had been with Hooker's Sixth Corps at Fredericksburg. He spoke as if he were in a daze as he told a small crowd of the stone wall behind which the rebels had lined up as far as a man could see to shoot at the oncoming Union troops, and of an open, barren field upon which great numbers of dying Union soldiers had lain and moaned and bled amongst the dead while the Union generals ordered charge after useless charge into the murderous volleys of musket fire and the rain of cannon grapeshot. "Even the crickets stopped that first night," he said. "And there was no sound at all of the wind. All there was, was that smell of the blood and burnt powder and burnt flesh and the cries of men you knew but couldn't get up to help for fear of losing what was left of you to a sharpshooter's ball."

He quickly drew a crowd of listeners, most of whom were at least a half year behind on developments in the war. And to each question he answered with slow dreamlike answers, as though he were suspended between two worlds, the unreal stygian world of battle and the earthly reality of living existence. "So what happened in the end?" one of the onlookers asked.

"They kept shooting. And we kept being ordered up. And they kept knocking us down."

"I mean in the end. How did the battle end?"

"There ain't no end," the soldier said in a dreamy voice. "There's just breaks between the fighting. That's all. Everyone stops shooting for a while and they pick up the dead and bury them in pits and everyone moves some, across a river or down a valley, and some pickets somewhere exchange some shots and then it starts up again." And somehow in the air you could almost hear it, the cries and shouts and screams, the unheeded orders amid the roar and flash of the cannon, the panic and frustration and glory; and you could almost taste it in your mouth, the acrid taste of gunpowder and the salted stickiness of blood.

After a while, Francis stood up. He motioned me to follow him over to a table where the miner sat drinking alone. "So you know Henry Plummer," Francis said to him. "I mean personally."

"Shore do."

Francis stuck out his hand and said, "Francis Thompson. Glad to know any friend of Henry Plummer's."

And the miner answered, "Jeff Perkins. Sit down an' have a drink."

~~~

It turned out that Jeff Perkins had come all that way just for supplies. "Bannack's sold out," he said. So we joined up with him in the morning and helped him load his wagon before we all set off together on the road to Bannack City. In exchange for which he agreed to haul some supplies for us, which we purchased at exorbitant prices from a store owned by John Grant, the man who had bought the oxen.

The previous night Francis and I had held a long debate regarding what our plans should be. I very much wanted to try the new placers in the Gulch, but Francis argued against it. "There's plenty of ways to make money at a gold strike," he said. "And finding the gold yourself is the hardest of all. Look at Jeff Perkins," he said. "And Grant. They know the strike does something besides just produce gold and wealth for miners. It creates need, demand. It keeps bringing in people, brings 'em in long after the diggings are dry. And all those people need to eat and build and wear clothes and have some recreation. So selling things is a lot surer than looking for metal in places that look no different than any other stream or creek. So that's one way we can be sure of getting rich when others can only hope. Another is to do what Henry did. I'm talking about the way he waited for winter to come, for all these miners who found gold and proved their claims only to go wild by it, to blow everything they've dug out on gambling and women or whatever. And then all Henry had to do was have enough money of his own to buy them out, as desperate as they were, for pennies on the dollar. And we don't even have to wait for it either. Perkins says there's plenty of abandoned claims in Bannack that have been left by miners who want more when they should be happy with what they've got. That can't work forever. You can't keep finding more and more. That kind of thing can't last forever."

"Nothing does," I said. So we agreed that Bannack City was the place for us.

Jeff Perkins made for good company upon the road that led south. As we rode, he described in detail much of the history of Grasshopper Creek and Alder Gulch. So we learned of how Henry Plummer alone had artfully avoided the trial on the issue of Jack Cleveland's death when the following day two other men, with lawyers to aid them, could not do well enough to prevail on as critical an issue as whether they should be tried to a jury or to the entire town. "Henry's sure a talker," Perkins said. "I'd put 'em right up there with ole Charley Forbes."

That night Perkins proposed a watch, and I thoroughly agreed, if only because there had been a band of Shoshones lingering at Cottonwood, and I knew they could not be trusted. But that wasn't Perkins's only reason for precaution, as I saw the next day when we reached the fork in the road, leading southwest to Bannack and southeast to Alder Gulch, and Jeff raised his shotgun to his hip and motioned us to do the same when he saw three riders approaching in the distance.

"What is it?" Francis asked. "Who are they?"

"Don't know yet," Perkins answered. "Can't see their faces from this distance."

"Well, what are you afraid of then? They're white men. That much is clear."

"I ain't afraid of nothin'. Now keep quiet."

The riders came up the road from Bannack at a gallop that slowed to a trot when they neared, and then finally to a walk when they saw our drawn weapons. And they raised theirs. And then Perkins recognized them and relaxed his shotgun. "Mornin', Dan," he said. "Wayman. Where you boys headed?"

One of them said, "Alder Gulch."

And Jeff Perkins said, "You're gettin' a little quick with those guns, ain't you?"

"Been two robberies along the lower route in the last two days," the one named Wayman said. "Two men been shot."

And after they had rode on, Perkins said, "Can't be too careful. Ain't nothin' safe around here lest you make it that way yourself."

"What about Henry Plummer?" I said. "And his deputies. It'll be better now that Henry's back."

And our companion just smiled and cracked the reins and said, "Get up," to his mules.

CHAPTER 3

There had been only one man hanged in the eastern Idaho Territory before Henry Plummer was made sheriff in Bannack. And that hanging had been up at American Fork, near Hell Gate, and a goodly distance from where gold was first panned by John White along a creek he named Grasshopper due to an infestation of that particular insect. The hanging occurred when a posse caught up with some horse thieves who had stopped in American Fork just long enough to pull in some tobacco and whiskey money by dealing a monte bank with a questionable deck. The posse had shot one of them right there at the table with his cards froze in one hand and his pistol in the other as he died; then, in an unlikely moment of calm reason, they set a second free for lack of evidence and then peremptorily tried and hanged the third. Soon after, American Fork became known to many as Hangtown, a term that carried a derisive or boastful or just plain ignominious meaning, depending on one's point of view. That had been back when Bannack was still nascent and disorganized, before Henry Plummer ever crossed over the divide from California.

Granville Stuart was telling us about the hanging as Francis and I examined the Bannack City store that Stuart and his brother James had

94

bought from Jim Bozeman the prior fall and now were offering for sale. "Right handsome young man we hung that day," he said, almost as an afterthought to the story. "Though he didn't seem to have much of an interest in living. Funny thing. He didn't say a single word throughout his trial, not in his own defense anyway. And when he knew he was going to die, all he asked for was time to write a letter to his family. It was a mighty good letter, too, full of contrition. After that there were some that started feeling sorry for him, so we got him a stout cord and gave him a good drop off a big pine there on the edge of town. Neck snapped like a twig under foot."

Since our arrival several weeks back, we had heard plenty of talk of hanging in Bannack City. A rash of robberies and shootings had spread like a prairie fire throughout both the Grasshopper and Alder Gulch regions, and some were clamoring for Henry Plummer to bring to bear a more immediate and decisive form of justice. Henry had tried to placate them by constructing a jail, which he located directly behind Chrisman's, near the bank of the creek, and which he financed through private donations. But that failed to appease the populace in the main; it took money to guard and feed prisoners. And toward what end? The tiny jail could not serve as a penitentiary; and the jurisdiction of the miners' court would not be recognized by the territorial government, which would refuse to receive prisoners convicted in Bannack City. So that every time a robbery or almost any other form of crime was committed, the cry went out to hang the perpetrator and be done with him, once and for all.

And now suddenly there was the real prospect that a man would be hanged in Bannack within a matter of days.

"I've never seen a man hanged," I said to Granville Stuart as we walked around back so that he could show us the corners of the property. The phrase "snapped like a twig" repeated in my mind, and it chilled me somehow up beneath my skull, made me twist and crane my neck uneasily.

From behind the building you could see the miners steadily working the water out of the new ditch that had been constructed at great expense to bring more water to the placer operations. "Hanging's not exactly the way I'd want to die," I said as I watched them shovel the gravel and dirt into sluices where the water washed out the lighter sediments.

"Depends on what you mean by that," Granville Stuart said. He seemed to convey an easy form of confidence, engendered, I assumed, from his hard years in the West. "Strictly in terms of dying, it's as fast a way as any I know. At least when it's done right, that is. It's those few minutes beforehand that's the tough part. It's the knowing what's about to happen—and not knowing what comes next—and all those faces staring up at you knowing too, but not stopping it anyway. Better'n being eaten by a bear while you're half alive, one chunk at a time, like Bill Paterson; better'n laying there half dead while a Shoshone yanks back your head and removes your scalp, like they did to John Burnett and Buffalo Joe down on the Salmon River. Yes, sir," he said, and I could see he was enjoying himself, "there's plenty of ways to die that're worse than hanging."

Francis and I had already decided in favor of buying the Stuart place, figuring it was well situated, and having confirmed, upon examination, that Virginia City and Alder Gulch were too frantic and crowded for our tastes. Besides, we both liked the looks of Bannack and relished the thought of operating out of a building that stood across from the thriving saloons and the Goodrich and next to Chrisman's store and the new bakery and cafe and billiard hall. We could make our own profits off the Alder Gulch miners from a base of operations working out of Bannack, which, if nothing else, was a much more central point to receive freight deliveries from Walla Walla to the west, and Salt Lake to the south, and Fort Benton to the east. But we had not informed the Stuart brothers of our intention.

This second meeting with Granville Stuart was an effort to negotiate a lower price. Francis had taken the lead and was getting nowhere. "Now, how much did you say you were asking, Granville? Was it $200? Is that your best price? Seems a bit on the high end of the market."

"There's only that one price," Granville Stuart said.

"Well, is that as low as you'll go? You wouldn't want to miss out on a sale just because you overpriced it."

"Won't go any lower and won't go any higher. Like I said: there's only that one price."

"What if I were to say we'd pay you cash for it today?"

"I'd say that'd be $200 in clean Gulch gold, or 60 cents on the dollar in greenbacks. Either way."

I thought Francis's tactics were too forward and simplistic, lacking entirely in finesse and stratagem. So I asked Granville Stuart what he thought would happen at the trial that was about to commence in only an hour's time.

"Not much to it really. Since everyone already knows he did it. Won't use up much time at all."

"Do you think they'll hang him?"

"Probably." Granville Stuart nodded as he pointed to a second stake. "Old Man Kealey had a lot of friends in these parts. And here he gives this Horen fellow a break and makes him into a partner and what does he get in return? Shot in the middle of the night in his own doorway. They'll hang him all right. And for good cause, too."

I knew it would be a spectacle. Because there was something in men that caused them to want to be there at the death, particularly when it came by hanging. "Aren't you going to stay around till it's over?" I asked. "The hanging, I mean."

Granville Stuart shook his head. "James left yesterday. He's getting pretty restless for some work. And I'm leaving as soon as I'm done with you boys."

He and James were in the process of moving to Virginia City, where Granville had contracted to build a blacksmithy and where James and Walter Dance intended to operate a store. James, who had headed the ill-fated expedition to the Yellowstone, had been more or less convalescing for the last few weeks. His party had been ambushed by Crows on the banks of the Yellowstone River, near Pompey's Pillar. Five members of the expedition had died either as a result of injuries inflicted by the Crow renegades, or by their own gunshots when it became clear that their wounds would not allow them to flee with their companions. The survivors, among them George Ives and Sam Hauser and Henry Greer and James Stuart, had crawled into Bannack looking like so many bedraggled hermits, only to find that the other members of their party who had never reached the rendezvous point had struck color at a place called Alder Gulch and that a rush was fully under way.

"Aren't you worried about your investment here?" I asked him. "I mean leaving this place empty like that?"

And Granville Stuart smiled with a sort of knowing grin and said, "I'm guessing we don't need to worry much about that." And when I asked why not, he said, "I'm guessing you two boys are going to pay $200 for this place before that trial even has a chance to start up."

It took all of two seconds for him to sign the deed, which James had already executed before he left, and another half hour to locate the district recorder, who was required to acknowledge the signatures and the transaction. With that, Granville Stuart mounted the seat of his lumber wagon and drove off, up the freight road northeast, on the road to Virginia City and Alder Gulch.

Francis and I hurried down the dusty street to where Peter Horen was to be tried by a miners' court for the murder of Lawrence Kealey. The street was crowded with men, mostly miners who reckoned that a good murder trial—in which they and any citizen were entitled to par-ticipate—was a fine form of entertainment worthy of neglecting their claims for a day or two. Many of them were gathered outside of Skinner's Saloon, which Skinner himself had started calling the Elkhorn after the huge elk antlers he had purchased from a Pikes Peaker named Clark and which he had hung high up on the facade. And many more of the public had congregated in front of the Goodrich, where we had spent a good portion of our time lately, play-ing cards and socializing with some of the newly arrived dance-hall girls. Most of the men in the street were midway into a drunk, and the proprietors inside were doing a splendid business filling flasks and bottles and pitchers with whiskey and beer. As we walked along the uneven boardwalk, we could hear them debate the merits of the case, wagging their cigars when they made a point, spitting when they disagreed, and some even taking bets on questions of guilt and punishment. "I'm figurin' he's secesh, an' I ain't votin' in favor of no Reb sympathizer," one said. And a second answered, "I wasn't too keen on ole Kealey, myself, the cheap son of a bitch."

"Seems Granville was right," Francis said as we crossed the street. "They might as well take a vote on it now and save some time."

They had decided to hold the trial outdoors beneath the bright August sun, no doubt counting on the warm breeze to clear out the inevitable cigar smoke and the unpleasant odor of unwashed men. Someone had pulled some tables and chairs out of the nearest business establishments and into the street to accommodate Judge Burchett and the prosecutor Copely and to better view the testimony and demeanor of the accused.

It was a fine scene for a warm summer's day, with the miners congregating in the street of the boomtown hamlet, surrounded by the industry of their effort in the form of new log buildings and signs and businesses, and the sagebrush and scrubland rising up to the north and south to define the narrow valley in which they stood. And as I looked about me, I thought how fortunate I was to be there at all—friend to Henry Plummer and Francis Thompson, and well off, with every prospect for improvement in the time to come. I sat down next to Francis on a stump in the shade of the Goodrich and prepared to watch them try Peter Horen.

The prisoner was seated in a chair that had been set out alone, with only his hands tied as restraint. I had seen him about town several times, and even then I had perceived something worthy of distrust in his sallow complexion and black narrow eyes. As I looked at him, I wondered how Henry Plummer had caught him, whether there had been shooting, and how he had recaptured Horen after his escape. Then I realized not only that I had not seen Henry all day, but that he was not in the crowd. I thought perhaps he shunned trials in favor of more important duties. And, in fact, we had heard the prior night of a robbery on the stage road above the Rattlesnake station, and that a yoke of oxen were missing out on Horse Prairie, where a good number of ranches and businesses were doing business.

Judge Burchett stood up and surveyed the mass of people in front of him; he took a deep drink from a bottle and then, after apparently concluding that everything was ready, banged a hammer on an iron plate that he had brought with him and placed upon the desk. He looked out, authoritatively, over the crowd, and glared at it until it slowly contained itself. "Gentlemen," he said. "The honorable miners' court, Judge B. B. Burchett presiding, of the mining district of Grasshopper, Bannack City, territory of Idaho, these *United* States, is now in session. George Copely for the prosecution. Smith Ball acting as secretary to the court. Are you ready, Mr. Copely?"

George Copely had been off to the side, talking with the stable owner Pearson and several other of the better-dressed men in attendance. At Judge Burchett's beckoning, he strutted up to the desk behind which the judge sat. Copely was a tall man with a small round head and long thin neck, the combination of which made him look very awkward, like a disproportionate scarecrow. Like the pictures I had seen of Lincoln: long bony legs, big hands. Copely had donned a suit despite the summer heat; the clothes hung off him loosely and fit him very poorly. And his mannerisms struck me as odd and overly practiced. "Ready, your honor," he said in a slow resonant voice, with an unnatural affectation. "People versus Peter Horen. The charge is the murder of one Lawrence Kealey."

Judge Burchett turned a hard stare toward the accused. "How say you, Mr. Horen? Guilty of this charge of murder? Or innocent?"

Peter Horen was known to be financially destitute and apparently was friendless as well. He thus was not a Southerner, for they stuck together without exception; nor was he of the hard-cut Republican class of which Copely and his cohorts were members. Horen had no money to hire one of the several self-proclaimed lawyers in Bannack; and no one had purchased one for him. He found himself providing his own defense in a process that was almost devoid of rules. "Innocent, judge," he blurted out. "I'm innocent." Clumsily, with his hands tied and interconnected, he tried to remove his hair from out of his eyes as he spoke the words.

"Proceed, Mr. Copely."

Copely strolled up to Peter Horen and, in a tone filled with contempt, said, "State your name, please."

"You just said my name," Peter Horen sneered. "Get on with it." He looked out uncomfortably across the crowd, so full of so many unsympathetic faces that had spread into a semicircle around the desk and chairs.

"Maybe he forgot it, Copely," someone shouted. "Just like he don't remember murderin' Kealey." And several of the lowest class of miners laughed and whooped and whistled.

"For the record, sir," Copely said sternly. "State your name."

Peter Horen stated his name.

"And your place of residence."

"Why does that matter?"

Another voice came out of the crowd. "What matters is that you answer the damned questions, Horen. Or we hang you now, no questions asked." A greater volume of laughter from the crowd.

Horen answered, "Marysville," which was downcreek from Bannack by several miles.

"You ever been charged with murder before, Mr. Horen?"

"No, sir. I have not."

"Well, tell us what crimes you have been charged with."

Which confused Peter Horen some. "No," he said. "I mean there ain't none."

There followed a long string of prefatory questions concerning Horen's past, all posed in such a way that a positive answer would implicate bad character in Horen, at least. And then even more questions of a similar nature.

"We know you and Kealey were partners. Was there a mining dispute?"

"There weren't no dispute," Horen answered. "An' anyone who says so is lyin'."

"Did you owe him money?"

"No, sir."

"Did Kealey have much money?"

"Not that I know of."

"Was there a grudge between you?"

Copely asked each question more quickly than the last, so that the questions were almost piling into each other. And Horen was finding it easy to defend himself, and it may be that he had concluded that if he answered every question in the negative he'd be safe. "No," he answered the last question before it was fully stated.

More easy questions followed in rapid succession. And then suddenly, like a dart, Copely asked, stated, in an angry tone: "You killed Lawrence Kealey," and then, after emphasizing the word "killed" so heavily that it sounded like he had completed his question, he paused; and Horen said, almost shouted, "No," just as Copely finished by saying, asking, "in self-defense?"

Before Horen could correct himself, Copely asked, "Then why did you kill Lawrence Kealey?"

And as Horen struggled to say something, anything, Copely asked, "What is your defense to this charge, Mr. Horen? You certainly have not told us that." And then he walked away from Horen with his hands behind his back and shaking his head as if out of disgust.

Horen was breathing heavily, almost panting. It was happening too fast for him. Copely could see that Horen had totally lost his composure; the accused man's face had flushed with splashes of crimson red, with a wild pitiful twitch at the corners of his mouth. So Copely waited into the silence, and waited, and then finally said, "We're waiting for an answer, sir. These miners are busy men. It takes hard work to earn an honest living."

There was a complaint from the back of the crowd regarding the reasonableness of the line of questioning, but for the most part the crowd had fallen behind Copely. "Hey, George," someone in the crowd yelled. "Ask him why he's got Henry Plummer auctionin' off his claims for him. Ask him why he's plannin' on leavin' town." But everyone knew the answer to the first question; Henry was the best appraiser and auctioneer in Bannack, and he knew the most people. And plenty of miners were selling claims and were on the go, to and from Bannack. It wasn't the kind of question Copely wanted to ask; it could be interpreted as reflecting negatively on Henry Plummer, who was immensely popular. So Copely propounded a different question that had been suggested by another miner.

"The committee would like to know, Mr. Horen, whether you were attacked in any way by Mr. Kealey on the night in question." And the entire crowd erupted in laughter and hooted at the thought of Old Man Kealey attacking anyone.

Horen mumbled, "No."

With great theatrics, Copely stared up into the clouds, and we were to believe that each time he smiled to himself with wry and deliberate affectation, he perceived more clearly how definitively he had proved Horen's guilt. "Judge," he finally said. "I could go on with this witness for hours; but I think we have enough. No further questions for the accused."

The crowd was then allowed to ask Horen questions, but they had no real impact.

And when Judge Burchett asked Horen whether he had anything to offer in his own defense, all Horen said was, "I'm innocent, judge. I didn't do it."

There was a fifteen-minute break while the better part of the crowd, together with the judiciary in the form of Judge Burchett, and the prosecutor's office in the form of George Copely, refreshed themselves with liquor and cigars. Some conducted business in the time available, negotiating the sale of some stock in the new Ditch Company, others hiring out labor. All the while, Buck Stinson and Ned Ray stood guard over Horen. Then Judge Burchett, who seemed to be slightly taken by the heat, called the trial back to order. In the next half hour, Copely paraded four witnesses before the crowd, including Madame Dumont, who was held in great reverence in Bannack City and who had caused a great disappointment by her recent announcement that she would be moving her business to Alder Gulch. Each of the witnesses had heard the shooting and had seen Horen fleeing toward Yankee Flat. Two of them swore that when they got to the body, which lay lifeless across the cabin threshold, there was no sign of a pistol or knife or any other weapon that would suggest that Lawrence Kealey had been armed before he died. Madame Dumont wept when she offered her statement, and then George Copely delicately led her away through the crowd of men, who removed their caps, or nodded, or bowed slightly, or said, "Madame Dumont," or "ma'am," as she passed by.

One could see that Horen understood what was happening. He had started out looking righteously indignant and defiant and determined enough to fend for himself. But he had slowly faded as a little more of breath and hope and resolve were knocked out of him with each turn the proceeding took. His mouth had continued to twitch at the corners, and his eyes stared wide open, unblinking, like a wild and caged animal.

He missed George Copely's closing statement altogether, did not hear a word of it, seemed entranced by the clouds moving across the hills that rimmed the creek. When he heard Copely move for a verdict, the stunned, almost awestruck look upon his face showed he plainly could not believe that it was over, that there was nothing more that would be said. There was then, in essence, a voice vote. A loud roar, in which Francis and I both joined, went up in favor of a verdict of guilty, with only a modest vote for acquittal. And Horen was so clearly guilty of the crime, that all I could think was that there were those in the crowd who would always vote for acquittal, for whatever reason.

Now Judge Burchett was standing with the hammer in his hand, ready to quiet the crowd again if necessary. "The court will entertain a motion on sentencing," he said, looking over to Copely.

"Move that Peter Horen, who has been found guilty, in a court of law, for the murder of Lawrence Kealey, be executed by hanging."

From out of the crowd came several cries advocating banishment as the appropriate punishment; and I assumed the proponents were the same as those who had voted for acquittal. And when Judge Burchett called for the vote, a vast majority of us voiced a preference for the noose.

There was a moment during which silence utterly prevailed, and then a miner yelled, "Here's to justice served." And he drank deeply from a bottle before a comrade took it from him and followed suit. Several revolvers were fired, and a shotgun, and the crowd began to celebrate in a dozen different ways, some dancing, others exchanging toasts, until it was halted by the banging of the carpenter's hammer upon the iron plate.

"Where's Sheriff Plummer?" Judge Burchett asked. "Is Henry Plummer here?"

And I was about to state that he was not, when I heard Henry's smooth, daunting voice. "Over here, Judge," he said. And everyone to a man turned to watch Henry Plummer coolly rise off a rail in front of Chrisman's and walk across the street and come up to Judge Burchett.

Judge Burchett looked at Henry Plummer with great seriousness. "Sheriff. May I assume you will carry out the sentence of this court?"

And Henry said, "I will do my duty, sir. If the court will allow me the remainder of this day to construct an appropriate gallows."

And Judge Burchett said, "So be it. The sentence of this court shall be carried out at eight o'clock on the morrow at a place to be designated by Sheriff Plummer. You may remove the prisoner, Sheriff."

~~~

That night we took our evening meal with Henry and Electa. Francis had protested to Henry, saying we'd become somewhat of a nuisance at mealtime. But Henry would have none of it. "I can't pay you for helping with the gallows," he said. "At least I can feed you. Electa is delighted to have you. I have already warned her that you will be joining us. Besides," he said with a reaffirming smile, "you know how she enjoys showing off her cooking."

It was true that Electa prepared a fine table, as was it indisputable that she would be pleased to see us, just as she always was. What Henry would not admit, but what we nonetheless knew full well, was that Electa was suffering from an intense loneliness, as well as a depression that together had all but overpowered her within the first month of her residence in Bannack City.

Poor Electa. She had dallied her youthful existence on the illusion of a dream, perpetrating both innocence and hope, ever since a journey long ago. Her father, still alive then, still there to hold the motherless family together by little more than sheer willful exertion, had taken them all with him on a pilgrimage of necessity to the great cities of Ohio where he might find the medicine that could cure him of an illness that would not relent. And there she had seen the ladies of Ohio, so dignified and beautiful and so closely attended by husbands of obvious wealth and philanthropy. And she, who could read and reread her Dickens novels forever, and those of Collins as well, saw that these were the same women as those portrayed on the printed page—so admirable, so devoted to charitable pursuits and worthy causes. Then she knew that her dream was palpable. So Electa waited, waited for opportunity and chance to present themselves to her.

When Martha had told her of the experimental farm, she said, "I will go too." Not because she saw it as the utter fulfillment of her vision, although it had elements of charity and benevolence to it, but because she had to have change for there to be any chance for opportunity. And she gave herself to it, to the Indians who were heathen and to whom Christ and his teachings must be brought, and to the farm animals that she could always love, and to the fertile earth and the growing crop, all beneath the great spreading horizon and the yawning winds and the countless stars. Until the passage of time and the isolation began to disprove her fantasy.

When Henry Plummer came that fall, she was more than ready for him, receptive to him; and his dispassionate, almost ambivalent descriptions of how rich he could be should he so desire revitalized what was left to her fading youth, of the illusion that Dickens and Collins brought to life. And she said, "Yes. I will marry you," and she loved him with all the dedication and sincerity that woman can offer. What she had never considered, what all the time spent idly in fascination had not allowed for, was the possibility, however remote, that she might have such great wealth at her disposal and be joined with such a man, and yet that there might be a place in God's creation that could be so inhospitable and repugnant to charitable goodwill that there would be no opportunity for her there at all. Bannack City was such a place for Electa Plummer.

She did not see it as such instantly, on the day of her arrival when she and Henry drove down off the freight road and past the cemetery and into the defile with broad smiles on their faces and the sun in their blond hair and she saw the crude shacks and the hard men. Nor on the second day which she spent arranging their possessions as best she could in the cramped one-room cabin, across the floor of which Henry had stretched and pegged cow hides to cover and hold down the dirt. But by the end of a week's time, she saw it for what it was: no church at which to worship, no schoolhouse where she might teach, in fact hardly any women or children at all with whom she might interact.

And then, little by little, the utter desolation of the place pulled her down. What beauty there had been, and there had been much indeed in terms of peaceful solitude and nature, had been reduced to its antithesis as the miners frantically turned the earth inside out and defiled the land to satisfy their needs: the trees all cut and formed into ugly buildings and other devices to expedite the task of separating the gold from the gravel and sand and rock; every deer and antelope and rabbit and bird shot instantly upon sight to eat or trade to the merchants who goaded the miners on with more and more amenities; the arrival of the whores and their welcoming into the community; and the abject gambling and swearing and drinking and only God knows what else into all hours of the night and throughout the Sabbath. All this in the midst of the quietude of God's creation. Such that she came to see the diggings and the mines along the Grasshopper, the regurgitated tailrace thrown up in great heaps, and the muddy erosion and the barren denuded slopes as something akin to the very gates of hell. And then she found she could not avoid the rank odors of the sewerless streets and the camps and the manure and the urine of the stock that collected in the alleys and all along the edge of Yankee Flat.

We, of course, saw things differently than Electa. But we resolved to give support to both her and Henry. That night, at dinner, we did everything in our power to lighten her mood, playing whist and cribbage with them for hours when neither of us really enjoyed the games. But her mood was even lower than when we had seen her last, and it was clear she was dwelling on something specific; twice, she almost spoke her mind, but ultimately refrained.

It was Francis, not me, who made the mistake of alluding to the hanging to take place in the morning, and then she held it back no more. "Will there be a minister there?" she asked. "To give him a final blessing? To guide him in a last prayer? To say something afterwards, over the grave?"

"I'm afraid not, Electa," Henry answered. "He asked for a priest. But Burchett said, 'No; it would take a week for a priest.' Besides. Horen has already escaped once. Give him enough time and he'll do it again. I'm sorry, Electa. He will have to do without."

"And will you be the one to hang him, Henry?"

"You know I will, Electa. It's my responsibility. I have no choice."

"Well, I think it's barbarous," she said. And I could see the water in her eyes. Henry put down his cards and sighed. We played more at the games, but Electa's heart wasn't in it, and no matter how hard Henry tried, he could not make her smile. He reached into a corner where a bottle of amber brandy stood. And then he saw her looking at him, silent but still conveying the words through her moist eyes—you promised, you promised not to—and he withdrew his arm. And then I knew she was about to cry. "This whole place is godless," she said in choked words; and she rose, only to remember that there was nowhere in the little cabin for her to go. So she walked over to the door and leaned into it and buried her face in her hands. And the sound of her heaving sobs was almost too much for me to bear.

The morning brought the first sunless day we had known since we came to Bannack City. Grey overcasting clouds had moved in late in the night, and they amplified the repeating morning songs of birds that you could not see but only hear. Yet it would not rain; there was no roll of thunder, nothing of a breeze, and the cloud cover was too high and hazy.

We had built the new gallows—posts and beam and nothing more—behind the jail so that Horen could be brought easily to the site. It stood in full view of Bannack City. A crowd of us stood there waiting, watching as Buck Stinson and Ned Ray brought the prisoner out of the jail. They had tied his hands behind his back, and he seemed unable to walk, though he did not resist; so they half carried him and half dragged him to where the citizens of Bannack stood ready to see justice done. Many of the same people who had watched the trial were there now, to see it to the end. Skinner was there, and Judge Burchett and the prosecutor Copely and his friend Pearson, and scores of other miners and businessmen, but not a single women, nor child. We watched as Horen stood beneath the gallows, the same wild, caged look in his eyes as toward the end of the trial, looking desperately for the help that would not come. And then someone threw the rope over the beam and someone else placed a tall rectangular box beneath it and he panicked. He tried to run, but only stumbled on the rocks and fell forward to the ground, into a thorny bush that tore his face and arms so that when they hauled him back to his feet, the blood ran into his eyes and mouth.

"Someone help me. Please," he cried out. "I'm innocent. Oh God. Please, help me."

It was Henry Plummer who confirmed the action of the noose before he directed Ned Ray to tie back the rope and set the distance for the drop. Then Henry set the noose around Horen's neck and tightened it, and then Ned Ray and Buz Caven lifted Horen atop the packing crate where he stood teetering as they tightened the rope again, looking fear struck into the faces of the crowd, which remained silent and watchful.

"Have you anything to say, Mr. Horen?" Henry Plummer said, almost too calmly.

And Horen cried out a last time, "I'm innocent. You've got the wrong man."

Henry Plummer looked at Ned Ray, who stood next to the crate, and said, "Do your duty, Deputy."

Ned Ray spit a stream of tobacco juice and then kicked the box away. But not hard enough. The box fell sideways and Horen caught it with his foot such that the rope went taut and yet the box still half supported Horen who visibly choked as he leaned uncontrollably off the edge. It was a horrid sight, the man's eyes bulging and his mouth wide open and his face turning a brilliant red and a gurgling sound emanating from somewhere deep in his throat.

Ned Ray, who had jumped back after he struck the box, did not know what to do. "Damn it, Ned," Henry shouted as he ran up to the hanging man and with his hands pulled the crate free and clear. And then there was nothing to do but stand there and watch as Peter Horen strangled to death, kicking and then jerking and then finally motionless at the end of the rope that still swung the body after he was dead, swinging in a slow even arc over the barren ground, marking time long after life had departed from him.

CHAPTER 4

We had been on the road to the Alder Gulch openings for over two hours, and Henry had been talking almost the whole while. His words seemed to be directed inward, as though he were discussing matters with himself. And even though we were riding abreast, I did not feel as though he were speaking to me.

"Fascinating," he said. "The tricks that time and circumstance play. You can count on neither. Neither time, nor circumstance. One day I am sheriff in a small mining district. In a one-street town. My mines are producing. My enemies are all dead or far away or sufficiently in check. Everything is neat and compact and contained. I ride out to retrieve Electa. And everything is as I would want it to be. Only, when I return, the place is totally transformed. With an entirely different set of rules in place. And ten times the distance from one end to the other." And then he seemingly was reminded that I was there. "Mark my words, Joseph. I have seen it before. Bring too many men together in any one place and they will diverge and factionalize and bring upon themselves the worst of everything they can contrive."

I thought he was worrying over Electa, who had cried again just a few hours earlier as he rode off, with me for company, to perform some duties in Virginia City. "Why do it then, Henry?" I asked. "Why don't you just work your mines and enjoy your money? Why don't you just be sheriff in Bannack, and leave it at that?"

"It's not that easy, Joseph. You don't understand that yet, but you will. When a man knows he's suited for something, he can't just leave it alone. It's not natural. I've seen it before. You know it somehow; somehow there's a suggestion or the proof that you have a certain ability. It eats away at you, pushes you forward so that you can't sleep or eat for thinking on it. There's something inside a man that drives him, something animal and instinctive that makes you act just so you can quit fighting it; just so you'll know someone else inferior will not step in to fill the void. Just to prove what something inside has told you all along."

Once you got past the sluices and the sight of the ditches and windlasses, the shafts and tailings and all the other paraphernalia and scars that marked the Grasshopper diggings, beyond the sounds of the men shouting and the stamp mills beating down upon the quartz lead rock, the open country resumed its former pristine state. You could follow the road down into a gully, and the narrowness and detail of the isolated, arid world contained therein would envelope you—where water flowed in a tumbling rush perhaps ten days a year and the cacti thrived and the rocks had been worn by ten days' water for 10,000 years—and you would want to dismount and sit there in the quiet where no one could see or disturb you. And then you would crest a hill and the entirety of the real world would spread out before you, with nothing in motion but the clouds and the few birds that flew beneath them. And in every direction you could see the foothills rising up and, behind them, real mountains and the beginnings of real forests, dark green and blue far up the slopes. Then the road would drop down again, bringing you back into the crevasses in the bare and worn rock, reminding you that the earth was not yet finished forming, that there were more changes ahead than you could ever know.

My mind wandered as we rode. I thought of Philadelphia, and how little I missed the crowds of people and the belching smokestacks and the slaughter yards where the bellows and cries of the animals were muffled by their own crowded mass. And then I thought back to Bannack, and I wondered what would become of it. I could remember Philadelphia changing, evolving with the increase in railroad traffic and the improvement of the roads and the influx of immigrants from Europe. And I knew there was much in the way of change ahead for Bannack City as well. And Henry's reflections caused me to think on what was happening even as we rode silently along the road that had become hard packed with so much recent use; of the fact that a weekly pony express service between Bannack and Fort Bridger had begun, so that what once took months or weeks now took days; of the hanging of Peter Horen, and the cries for greater and harsher enforcement of the laws; of the United States Marshal D. S. Payne, who had come to Bannack to request that the community nominate one of their own to be deputy marshal for the eastern portion of the Idaho Territory; and of the rumor that N. P. Langford's Union League had, to a man, nominated Henry Plummer despite the fact that Henry was known to associate with some individuals who were antiwar and whom the Union League saw as traitors to the nation. And I thought, "He already knows. He knows that change is coming for him, personally. That he will be deputy marshal; that someday they'll make the land east of the divide into its own territory, and then someday a state. He knows it, and knows he will be a part of it all. That he will be important and famous. That his responsibilities will take him far and wide. He knows it, and he has not told Electa." The road turned down again, back into the shadows, and I wished that I were alone, that I could dismount and sit there for a long while, just me and the cacti and the worn and timeless rock.

Bill Bunton and Frank Parish's Rattlesnake Ranch was only 15 miles northeast of Bannack, and it was thus only midmorning when we came up to the signpost that I had seen when Francis and I first came to Bannack and, then again, on our trips to Virginia City and Benton and back. On those occasions the sign had still been there, shot full of holes and splintered from the times the ranch hands and Bunton's rowdy friends had spent practicing at it as a target; but now the sign was gone, with only the post remaining. The ranch, which served as a way station for travelers and as a pasturage for horses that were grazed on the prairie, was totally isolated from any neighbors; so the men who worked for Bunton and Parish practiced with their revolvers and raced the horses, which were none the worse for the exercise. And the ranch hands disturbed no one by doing it, which was more than you could say for the raucous recreation in Bannack City that could keep half the town awake throughout the night.

Bunton was already outside, standing on the porch when we rode up, and when he saw that it was Henry Plummer, he relaxed the shotgun he had been holding at the ready. "Get on in here, Henry," he said as Henry swung off his horse and motioned for me to follow. "Breakfast is just up. There's biscuits an' gravy an' bacon. An' hot coffee. Get on in here." He slapped Henry on the back with cordial familiarity. "Who's your young friend here? Come on in here, young fella," he said to me. And he cracked his hand on my back also. He kept smiling at me as we walked in, and I figured it was because I was still young and yet, at six-foot-three, every bit as tall as him.

Inside there was the smell of greasy bacon and burnt coffee and cigars. Frank Parish came out and said hello to Henry, followed by Parish's squaw, who easily exceeded Parish in weight by eighty pounds. Two other men were asleep on straw mattresses in the corner, and another four sat around the table eating and exchanging barbs and passing a bottle. I believe Henry had it in mind to join them, when a loud knock came at the door. "Yeah," Bunton yelled out; and when the door did not open, he picked the shotgun back up and walked over and swung the door open. It had been hung on strong heavy hinges, and it moved easily, noiselessly. You noticed things like that. Hinges. And doorknobs. And real glass windows rather than the waxed or oiled paper most were forced to use for panes.

Through the opening I could see a neat, well-dressed man, and behind him a wagon.

When Henry heard him say something about being robbed, he walked over to the door and took the man by the arm and led him back off the porch. They talked for a while and then the man drove his wagon off toward Bannack, and Henry came back inside.

"What was that all about?" Parish asked as he poured us some coffee.

Henry shrugged his shoulders. "Name's Webster. Claims someone removed a bedroll from his wagon up near Dempsey's. Lost a good buffalo robe and some clothes. I told him I'd watch out for it, but that he shouldn't count on seeing it again." And then he looked up at me and said, "Best we'd be moving, Joseph. Why don't you water up the horses; and get Meiklejohn there to bring out some of the good hay. Without the mold on it."

Bunton nodded to a boy who had just come up to the table, and the boy immediately went out to the horses, and I followed. The boy pitched out some hay from one of the bins and then looked down the road to where you could still see Webster driving his wagon toward Bannack, the dust from the packed road trailing up and off the wagon as though it were moving at a breakneck speed. "You know Henry Plummer?" he asked. And when I said I did, he just nodded his head affirmatively, like it was a good thing.

Back on the road, Henry was silent, thoughtful. He had declined Bunton's offer of a meal, and he and Bunton and Parish had talked a bit and then we had moved on. "You going to look for that bedroll and robe?" I asked.

"Don't think so," he answered

"I didn't think you would. Your time's more valuable than that."

"Might be, Joseph. Might be. But the fact is there's no reason to go looking for it. It was right there at the Rattlesnake. Didn't you see it, all laid out by the fireplace with the robe on top?"

"And you knew it all along? While Webster was standing there in the door?"

And when I looked at him, waiting for an explanation, I could see that he was listening to me, and yet thinking of something else. As though he had already spent enough of his time and resources on Webster and even now was moving on to the next subject or issue that would have some meaning for him at some time, somehow. He finally turned to face me as we rode. "If I told Webster it was there," he said, "that he could take it, he'd figure he'd retrieved it all by himself, with all those men there not doing anything to stop him. Next time around he'd think he could do the same thing again, when he next needed to; and he'd end up with a hole in him. This way no one gets hurt and no one's worse off. We'll get it on the way back. Bunton said he'd hold it for me. I've known Bill a long time. He's good for his word. This is the best way. And it'll be worth at least one new vote next time an election comes along."

All day long we passed travelers on the road. Some were heading toward Bannack or further south, toward Salt Lake or Denver or belatedly down the wagon trail to South Pass, trying to beat winter on their way back to civilization. But mostly it was slower traffic that we were passing, heading in the same direction as us, toward what some had proclaimed to be the richest gold strike the world had ever seen. It was as if all of Salt Lake City and Denver were emptying toward Alder Gulch; and everyone we passed seemed to be made anxious by the fact that they were one or two days out from the new gold camps. Henry stopped and talked with most of them, introduced himself or casually conversed with them in a way that masked his real purpose of gathering news and making himself known. And by and large they welcomed his friendly approach and, when we departed ways, asked him to do what he could to keep the road safe for honest law-abiding citizens.

We stayed the night at the Cottonwood Ranch—another way station located near the Stinkingwater—where we slept on the floor amid half a dozen other travelers who were glad to have available the comfort of a real roof and the safety of a closed and locked door. Among them was a man named James Williams, an apparently emotionless sort with expressionless and deeply set blue eyes and unruly black hair and heavy, sloping shoulders. With his round wide face and broad nose he looked part Indian or maybe Asian, except for those blue eyes that looked through everything they saw, and his skin, which was pallid, and his accent, which was decidedly Northern. And while he seemed to take some interest in Henry Plummer, he spoke little, making it difficult to even speculate on the quality of his character.

Henry also must have seen something in the way the man carried himself. There was a strain between the two men, a mental tension that was inexplicable and yet real and extant. "Do you know him?" I asked as we rode out in the predawn of the morning, toward the gold diggings that some at Dempsey's Cottonwood had called the Stinking Water Mines after the nearby river of that name.

"I've heard some about him," Henry answered. "That's all."

Henry seemed thoughtful, reticent. And while I did not want to disturb him, I wanted to know more. "Who is he? He looks dishonest to me."

"Name's Williams. James Williams. Calls himself captain, but he's just another of those that have to have a title to make themselves sound like they should be bossing and leading others around. Came up from Pikes Peak last month leading a train of wagons. I've heard some say he fought as a sergeant in the border wars down in Kansas. Abolitionist." Henry Plummer stopped talking for a minute. And then he said, "They had a way of not taking prisoners in those fights. Lot of men surrendered or were taken by the other side after getting hurt, but somehow they never were seen or heard of again." He took a deep, involuntary breath. "That's all I know about the man, Joseph. But I don't mind telling you it's my belief that when a man goes calling himself captain or colonel or doctor or whatever, when he's not one, he's bound to create trouble for someone down the road. It's bad enough when they make too much out of a title when they're legitimate."

We rode for a while, and then he broke the silence. "A title won't make a man," he said. "It might help him along for a while. Might even make his whole life just the way he wants it. But in the end, maybe after a year, or maybe after a century, someone will look at it closely enough to see him for what he is or was. That's the way it's always been, I suppose. And that's probably the way it will always be. I wouldn't expect men will change that much over time. They'll just get more subtle."

Within an hour, we dropped down along the banks of the Stinkingwater, and the sure signs of mining settlements began to show: the rotting, fly-ridden carcasses of dead and abandoned stock and the piles of rusting cans where camps had been. Wickiups and shacks and tents where men were still living were scattered everywhere along the way. And where the Gulch itself emptied into the river, we began to see leaking flumes and discarded tailrace everywhere, and sunken shafts where men were already excavating down into the earth in search of quartz leads and bedrock. We climbed up the road that followed the course of the stream, past the newly forming district of Laurin, and then across the small, level, grassy plain on the east bank of the Alder to where Nevada City had sprung up.

It seemed as we rode through Nevada City that every other man and woman knew enough of Henry Plummer at least to recognize who he was when they heard someone else say his name. They greeted him in various ways, a nod or tipped hat, a word of salutation, and, infrequently, a rigid acknowledgment.

There were already several new cabins in place, and a cafe that was bristling with business, and a hurdy gurdy from which music and laughter emanated. And more buildings were in progress—a doctor's office and residence, stables, saloons—all in testament to the sudden birth of the settlement. And I thought back to my visit just two weeks prior, when we had found Jotham McKenzie on the road with a badly broken leg caught in a wagon wheel, when the town had been only half its present size.

A mile beyond Nevada City, we came to Central City, and it was even less of a town, having only one completed log building and nothing even resembling planned streets or a business district. But it had a substantial mining population also, and the creek at that point had already been churned into a gravel and waste pit of dramatic proportion; so they called it a city too, urban and developed as it was in its own remorse-less way.

Henry had a smile on his face as we moved through the settlement, and then he laughed outright. "You find something funny about this place, Henry?" I asked. "I think it's a mess."

"I know I've told you a little about my being sheriff in Nevada City, California, a few years back. I was just thinking of that Nevada City compared to the one we just passed through. The Nevada City in California was a big place. Ten thousand people, maybe more. Just the same as this one in a lot of ways though. Would you believe that the whole town burned down in a fire, and yet when I tried to enforce the new fire ordinance afterwards, they resisted in every way they could? One day I was sheriff and a member of the executive committee and a Democratic candidate for the state assembly, and the next day every damned merchant in town in violation of the fire ordinance was after my neck. One can only hope that this Nevada City is a little more sane than the last."

We followed the road up a modest incline and then around a bend to where Daylight Creek tumbled rapidly into the Alder. And there, at the confluence, sat Virginia City.

Here, at the discovery site, the people had been the most indus-trious and the most sensible. About 400 yards off and away from the gold-bearing creek bed a town had been platted, and a great number of buildings were in various stages of construction. In silence, we rode up the main avenue, which had been named Wallace Street. Business was being conducted all along the thoroughfare out of tents and half-completed cabins with tarps for roofs. There were one-room saloons and a variety of places where mining tools and sundries were being sold. In iron and tin shops, metalworkers were shaping instruments and devices to meet the miners' needs. And at some of the construction sites, placards had been set out to let the public know what the struc-ture would be upon completion, warning prospective competitors that the advantage had been gained: Rank's adobe drugstore, to be opened in but a few weeks; Saurbier's Saloon, which was being constructed out of native stone; Simpson's Dress Shop; Dance & Stuart's General Store. We turned where a sign demarked Spencer Street but on which there was nothing but a few tents and hovels, and then back left and west at Cover Street, and then left and back south onto busy Jackson Street, noting all along the way where home and business sites had been staked and claimed. We turned left and east onto Idaho, and then on Broadway, and then back on Wallace where Tom Luce had already opened a mechanical bakery, the wondrous smells of the ovens even at that moment wafting in the air. And then we stopped and Henry looked about, over his shoulder to the town site he had just surveyed. "Quite a place, isn't it, Joseph. For being nothing but alders and cottonwood just two months ago. Makes you wonder what will be here in a year. Or in five years."

"Might be nothing here at all," I said. "If the gold runs out." But in my thoughts I knew better. In a year, in five years? A new territory, at least. Maybe statehood. And who could say, depending on the outcome of the war. Because it was like Lincoln said, and everyone knew it, whether they cared or not. If the South could secede, quit the Union just as easily as join it, then so could others in the future. And still others that as yet were not even states, or even territories. Things were funny that way; someone you knew today might tomorrow be almost anything. One day a drifter or a laborer with nothing but a horse and saddle and gun, and the next day a traitor to his country, a congressman, a senator in one country or another. So when Henry said, "A year, or in five years," I knew that he was wondering just what the future might hold for him.

The miners' meeting that had prompted Henry Plummer's trip to Virginia City was to commence at noon, and while it was still two hours shy of that time, a crowd had already begun to gather outside Luce's Bakery where the proceedings would be held if the weather allowed. Henry had come to Virginia City informally, at the request of a large contingent of miners, many of whom had departed from

Bannack in the first few days of the stampede in early June; they had delivered to Henry a lengthy description of a recent Virginia City miners' meeting that had commenced regularly enough but then had digressed into a melee of violence in which one man had been shot and killed and several others injured. It had all tamed down in the end, enough so for the day's business to be conducted and an impromptu dance to be held afterwards right there in the street. But now another meeting had been scheduled, and Judge Bissell, who reluctantly chaired the gatherings, was concerned that a sensitive issue regarding the correct location of certain claim boundaries at the midstream of the creek would catalyze a free-for-all of intolerable proportions. So Henry Plummer had been sent for, not to act as lawman, because he had deputies there to watch over things in his absence, but to act as a mediator in the dispute. He explained his purpose to me as we watched from a distance while the men congregated. And then he said, "You can help me with this, Joseph. Just watch and listen for my cue. And play along."

Someone recognized Henry and called him over, and we dismounted and hitched our horses to a post. For the most part, the men had split themselves into two groups in which they had been holding earnest and heated discussions amongst themselves. A number from each contingent now hastily approached Henry, angrily jousting for position and priority. But Henry only said, "Gentlemen. Good morning." And then he said, "I think it would be best for us to wait for Judge Bissell and the appointed hour." So that thereafter it was understood that any conversation with him was to be limited to matters unrelated to the day's committee business. Some asked for Electa's well-being and some who had not seen him since he left for the Sun River congratulated him or ribbed him over his new marital status. But mostly they sought news from Bannack: of whether their claims had been jumped due to their failure to satisfy the representation work requirements, of freight shipment schedules and the safety and condition of the road, or of the hanging of Peter Horen.

The miners obviously came from extraordinarily diverse origins; there were Southerners and Northerners, Irishmen and Dutchmen, dandies and roughs, Pikes Peakers and Californians. They all had some knowledge of Henry Plummer, and their degree of familiarity or friendliness toward him seemed to be proportionate to what distance they had traveled to reach the Alder mines, so that those from Bannack acted almost like brothers toward him, whereas the Pikes Peakers, in particular, seemed distant and guarded.

"Boys, this is Joseph Swift," Henry repeated over the noise of the crowd. "He and a partner have opened a general store in the old Stuart building in Bannack. Joseph here was a groomsman at my wedding back at Sun River."

Judge Bissell was both late and inebriated when he arrived. He directed that a desk be brought out from the bakery for his convenience and comfort, and then he called the meeting to order. "We will begin," he said in a slur, "by welcoming Henry Plummer, who's traveled to the district to assist us in resolving this most difficult matter of boundaries." To which a round of cheers, and a few derogating remarks, were offered in response. "With no further ado, I turn the meeting temporarily to your hands, Sheriff."

Henry thanked Judge Bissell, who I later learned was not really a judge at all by former practice or training, but who still had insisted that since that was his new office, he should be addressed as such at all times thereafter. And then Henry asked that a representative from each faction of disputants explain the crisis in detail. There was a delay while the designees were selected out of the midst of angry argumentative huddles, and two men finally stepped forward to introduce themselves. Henry apparently knew them both, and I thought it logical that the miners would choose someone who knew Henry Plummer as well.

The first to speak was a bearded, heavy-set man with clumsy stumps for legs and an ugly scar that cut a pale thin line from his left eye into his beard. "Hullo, Henry," he said.

And Henry replied, "Afternoon, Frazier. Which side of this you on?"

"I'm on the west side, if that's what you're askin'. And that's the right side, too, so to speak." He spat tobacco juice into the dust-laden street. "The side that should win this here fight."

"I'm not here to see anyone win or lose anything," Henry Plummer said. "Only to try and help you all decide how to work it out without having to have a miners' trial. Now, just tell us how your boys see it. As plain as you can."

Frazier Haily shuffled his feet some and looked back at his supporters and then began. "The fire's what caused all the confusion, Henry. No one knows how it got to goin', but it probably started upstream where those boys had been stackin' all those logs and burnin' wood. By the time it'd moved down into the Gulch where our claims are, it was a hot one; and it was windy and that got the sparks flyin' everywhere and that's what kept it goin'. Every tree and bush and tent burst into flame, and everythin' else that wasn't got outta there ended up burnt: sluices an' flumes, lumber, braces, tools, pretty much everythin'. Well, naturally, it burnt up the stakes that'd been set to mark the outside borders of the claims. And since you couldn't stake the creek itself, those were the only stakes you could use to measure out into the crick to see where one claim stops and the other begins. And then, to make things worse, we got that early snow and then it melted and flash flooded the creek and took out what was left of the stakes, and then it got warm again and dried the creek back up so that the banks ain't nowhere near where they used to be, especially where there'd been bars in the past. What I'm tryin' to say, Henry, is that the middle ain't where the middle was."

Henry had been shaking his head judiciously all the while Frazier Haily explained the situation, nodding to show he understood the facts. When Haily finished with his account, Henry simply said, "I see. And what is it you propose will resolve the situation?"

"We think," he said, and then he looked back to his supporters again, as if to emphasize who the "we" in his statement were, "that the claims ought to be restaked and recorded on where the midpoint of the creek is today."

Immediately, the opposition voiced its dissapproval; and someone from the side of the gallery actually fired off a pistol.

Henry drew his revolver and then looked at it as if he were examining it for defects and then placed it back in its holster. "Now I'm not going to ask who fired off that shot," he said to the group in general. "But I can tell you one thing: when I hear pistol shots, I assume they're being fired at me. And all that leaves me with is to shoot back first, and if he's still talking, to ask questions later." There was some laughter, but no more shots. "All right, Frazier. I understand."

The second man to speak was Paddy Sky; his men owned claims to the east side of the Gulch. "And as far as we're concerned, Henry, we're on the right side," Paddy Sky said.

"Well, I figured as much, Paddy. Or we wouldn't be here. Tell me how you think the problem ought to be worked out."

"As you can guess," Paddy Sky answered, and he, too, looked back into the crowd for reassurance, "we don't agree with Haily and his boys. Not one bit. In the first place, it ain't the truth to say those stakes all got burnt up. Some of 'em may have gotten charred a bit, but the fact is that after the fire someone took the liberty of pulling most of 'em out. And I still can't figure how the recorder managed to spill coffee all over our records so that we can't look at them either. All I know is that Haily's boys want the center of the crick because they're on the steep side, the side that's got less sand on it. If we move the line to the new middle of the creek, they'll be gaining more of the bars and the creek bed. And everybody who's swung a pick in the Gulch knows that's where the gold is. Twenty foot down to the bed. Maybe it don't sound like much. But a foot or two difference along the bed could mean tens, maybe even hundreds, of thousands of dollars difference. You can see that. We think the way to do it is to find the last known stake upstream and downstream and draw as straight a line as possible between 'em. We're only talking about a quarter mile. It's the only fair way, Henry. You can see that."

Henry smiled. "I haven't really seen anything yet, Paddy. I don't even know what the claims look like up close. What I don't understand is how you boys ended up with claims on either side of the creek. Whose idea was that?"

"We had a bit of a disagreement on who made the claims first," Paddy Sky said. "So we agreed to compromise. We drew cards and split it the way we told you."

"Well, why can't you compromise now?" Henry asked. "After all, you've done it before."

"Well, hell, Henry," Paddy Sky answered. "We won the draw of the card. We're not about to give it back to 'em now."

"I see," Henry said. "If that's the way it's going to be, we had better go down and take a look."

We went down to Alder Creek, all forty or fifty of us, and Henry let Frazier Haily and Paddy Sky show us in their own terms how they thought the creek had changed and how the claims boundaries originally had been staked. When they were done, Henry looked over at me. "Boys," he said, "I haven't explained to you why I brought Joseph here with me. I already heard something about your problem, and I thought maybe Joseph could be of some help. You see, Joseph served as LaBarge's navigator in the past. Knows water better than anyone I've ever met. I figured he'd be of some use when it came to you boys making your choices here. You done looking at the way she lies, Joseph?"

And, in what I thought to be a quick and prompt reply, I said, "Not just yet, Henry. Give me another minute." Which I spent walking up and down the creek bank staring mindlessly at the water.

In the meantime, some of the miners were becoming impatient, and I wondered how Henry could ever get them to agree on anything. They began to push for an answer. "What do you think, Henry?" "We're right, ain't we, Henry?" "It should be the new midpoint, shouldn't it?"

Henry stood up on a large boulder, and the men quieted some. "That's not the way I'm going to do this," he said. "I'm not the judge here. Judge Bissell is." He looked around, perhaps hoping that Judge Bissell would confirm the point; but the judge was nowhere in sight. "And I'm not about to get half of you mad at me by telling you the other half is right and you're wrong."

There was some mumbling and complaining in the crowd. "I tole you he wouldn't be no help," one miner said.

But Henry Plummer wasn't through. "Now wait just a minute. I didn't say I wouldn't help. I'm just telling you that you boys are going to have to work this out yourselves if you want to avoid a trial. I'll tell you what we'll do."

He had known all along what he was going to do. I could see that now. So when he pulled Haily's faction aside, and then motioned me to go with them, I knew enough to be careful with what I said. He looked over their heads, assured himself that the others could not hear. "Now you men listen," he said. "It looks to me like you're on the wrong side of the argument. But let me see what the navigator here says." And then he turned to me. "It looks to me, Joseph, like the legal midpoint's been moved the way Paddy says, westward. Is that the way you're looking at it?"

Every one of the faces in the crowd now looked over at me. But it didn't bother me at all. I was a good liar and always had been. "That's right, Henry." And then I used the big word I had thought of a few minutes earlier. "When they flood and dry up quick like that—avulsion it's called—it usually moves the banks more to the inside than to the outside of the curve. And you fellows here are mostly on the outside. Looks to me like those other miners have got the better argument."

There was some disagreement, but mostly there was just disappointment. Then Henry spoke again. "Now I'll tell you what I think you all should do. If I were you, I'd join all these claims together with even shares like you should've done in the first place and call it a settled dispute. Now that's what I'd do. You boys can do what you want. But you won't get as good as that out of a miners' court."

"How we gonna do that unless they agree, Henry? Why will they agree to that?"

"You just leave that to me. Give me a minute with them." And they said all right, they'd try it.

I thought that was easy enough, but I had not yet seen where it would lead. Not until Henry drew the second group together and surprised me by telling them that, in his opinion, they were on the losing side of the argument. And then my mind went blank and I could not remember what I had told the first group. Was it that it had shifted further from or into the curve?

"What's your opinion on it, Joseph?" he asked me in front of the miners. "Which way do you think the midstream has moved?"

And when I could not remember, I guessed. "Away from the bends." And when Henry frowned, I added, "They always move away from the curve, to the outside bank, I mean, when you're dealing with avulsion."

Henry did them the favor of suggesting his compromise, and the men generally were anxious to agree. So Henry went back to the first group, to bring them what they thought was the answer to their proposed settlement but which the second group intended to be their own offer of compromise.

No one even bothered to disturb Judge Bissell from the drunken slumber into which he had fallen. Instead, the recorder was located and the new partnership and shares confirmed as a matter of record. And Henry Plummer was the man of the hour. And he received their compliments and thanks in an almost humble, and certainly obsequious, fashion.

CHAPTER 5

Henry had reluctantly agreed to remain in the Gulch and assay some silver leads upcreek at Summit for a modest fee; and there was a matter involving some missing stock out by George Ives's new ranch near Wisconsin Creek that required some investigation by the sheriff. So I had come back to Bannack on my own after making several brief business calls on local Virginia City merchants whom Francis thought we should befriend and propose to resupply when their inventories fell short. The trip back had been uneventful, although I feared for my safety as I traveled the notorious road alone. You would be riding along almost unconsciously, lost in the self-satisfaction of just being there, in the great frontier, and suddenly riders would approach from the opposite direction or come at a trot from behind. And all you could do was to be sure that your revolver was primed and your hand readied as you waited to see whether they might be highwaymen intent on waylaying you along the road. And then they would pass by with a tip of the hat or a reassuring word and you would feel the drain of energy as your nerves slowly eased.

I stayed the night at Dempsey's, and Dempsey himself paid for a fine steak cooked by his man Brown, and I was happy to share a bunk in the back room rather than sleep on the hard ground along the road. And then the next morning and into the afternoon, I rode steadily until I reached the Rattlesnake Ranch, where I refreshed myself and rested my horse long enough to become better acquainted with Bunton, who insisted I join him in watching his men and a number of Bannack citizens race horses for prize money around a well-marked 3-mile course. He primarily seemed interested in Henry Plummer, and in my relationship with him. And he said to me as I was leaving, "You watch out for Henry now. You hear? Henry's got more friends than anyone in these parts. But he's got himself some enemies, too. You can bet they don't have a mind to always be on the short end of things. We all need to keep an eye out."

At both Dempsey's and Bunton's, I had been treated well, the influence of Henry Plummer evident in the courtesies I received. And I could not help but wonder whether my known affiliation with him might not have brought me safely along the road. Now I found myself sitting in the large cabin the Vails had rented down on Yankee Flat, with the familiar faces of James and Martha and their children returned into my life and Francis agreeing, while I listened, that he and I would indeed be interested in boarding at the Vail cabin. And with that, as if by some magic distortion of time and space, we were suddenly all together again. Except for the fact that Electa, beautiful and innocent and endearing Electa, was about to leave us all.

To me it was utterly beyond belief that Electa would determine in two months of her marriage to Henry Plummer that she had been mistaken, that she did not love him or did not love him enough to stay with him there in Bannack. Perhaps in a year or more, she might reasonably have come to that conclusion. But not so quickly, not within the span of two short months, sixty fleeting days. And she had not been feeling well for the past two weeks, and Henry had seemed particularly deferential to her needs. So I suspected the explanation was that she was with Henry Plummer's child. As did Francis. But that was not the sort of thing you made inquiries about; the acknowledgment of a pregnancy would, after all, carry certain implications which, while entirely moral and appropriate within wedlock, were not mentionable in conjunction with a lady's name. Still, there was no other plausible explanation for Electa's sudden announcement that she would be leaving Bannack on the next of the infrequent stages that passed through on the way to Salt Lake City. And since Henry and Martha constantly reiterated that Electa would be back by the beginning of next summer, we were all made to know that the separation was only temporary.

Electa and Henry Plummer were still very much in love. That much was clear to anyone who saw them together. And while the demands placed upon him were great, often taking him away on trips to Alder Gulch and places in between for several days at a time, his occasional absence was something Electa could learn to tolerate. That was especially the case now that Martha and James and the children had come to Bannack City to reside, at least until normalized river traffic might alter their intentions. But there were no doctors in Bannack that had meaningful experience with the special needs of a woman with child; and the combination of the lack of a hospital and the cruelty of the harsh mountain winters would make it all but impossible for Electa to seek expert assistance in the final months before birth should she be so in need. Electa presumably brought these considerations to Henry's attention and announced what logically followed: she must leave in order to ensure that the child was brought safely into the world, and then they would reunite as soon as circumstances allowed.

That was the conclusion that Francis and I drew after discussing the matter at great length. Francis suggested initially that the hanging might have been too much for her, or the lack of a church too heathen, or her isolation too great. And in response to each such proposition, I had noted that her life at Sun River had not differed greatly, not with the Indians killing each other for the sport of it and the missions so distant and the isolation so absolute. And the neither of us ever once considered what appeared to be the absurd possibility that Henry had somehow dishonored or disappointed Electa. Which left only this one last possibility, that Electa would, after the passage of another seven or eight months, make Henry Plummer a father by the birth of a virile boy or a blonde and blue-eyed baby girl.

Not that the reasonableness underlying Electa's decision made it any easier for Henry Plummer. He was clearly saddened by the prospect of Electa's departure and had argued vehemently and loudly against it. But in the end Electa had prevailed, and Henry had accepted it stoically.

"Are you sure she will not change her mind?" I asked Martha as we discussed Henry and Electa's dilemma. "They seem to be ideal for each other. And Henry needs her here with him."

And Martha, who had been overjoyed at being reunited with her sister, and then had cried, long and implacably, over the news of her pending departure, only said, "Yes" in a staid and resigned monotone. "Yes. I am more than sure."

No one, not even Electa, suggested that Henry should accompany her to her new destination. In view of his meteoric rise to prominence, a sudden and lengthy abdication of his responsibilities and prospects was not a realistic choice.

From thereon afterwards, there was a marked change in Henry Plummer. Whereas he had previously vaguely promised to Electa to refrain from the gambling and the drinking that characterized the after-hours activity of the mining community, he now took the commitment entirely to heart. He might go into the saloons and dance halls and the new billiard hall, as was his duty, but he would not drink or gamble there, no matter how strenuously his friends urged him on. It was as though he had aged, matured instantly at the moment in time when he learned not only that Electa was leaving, but also the unpublicized reasons why. He seemed calmer, if that were possible, and more inclined to involve himself in the political scene that was slowly emerging. Some members of the secretive Mason sect were even courting him to join the lodge they were forming at that time.

I hoped he wouldn't do it. Because I thought the Masons to be a particularly dangerous element, a threat to a free society. You never knew exactly how they communicated, nor even when it was occurring. There were, no doubt, passwords. And it was as probable that there were secret signs, and perhaps even an agreed fashion by which to wear an item of clothing or to tip a hat in salutation. But you could not know. All that was definite was that they were organized and organizing, such that by the close of 1862, they had had enough time to determine who among the citizens of Bannack were lodge members, and to arrange between themselves enough to begin to form their own lodge, and to meet regularly at secretly appointed times and places, and even to begin to bury their own right there in the cemetery above Bannack.

No one ever explained the Masons to me; so I was left to imagine what they did. And, from what I could tell, what they did mostly was to meet, primarily under secretive conditions, and usually after dark. The consequence of which was that you never knew how many of them there really were, or what they might have decided in one of their ritual meetings. And by these petty and arcane maneuverings, they sought and managed somehow to gain strength and to arrogate power to themselves. Through their own ignorance and fear, the Masons imposed ignorance on others, such that they—the others—too, would be required to reckon with the unknown.

In those ways the Masons reflected the current martial attitude by which the Union government, under Lincoln's heavy-handed administration, ruled the nation: suspending such fundamental liberties as a free press and habeas corpus, incarcerating legislators and executing men who conscientiously objected to the war, all in the name of maintaining a form of government that those in power, in reality, were at that time actually subverting. So I hoped that Henry would not go that far, would not feel the need to ingratiate himself into the narrow-minded secret society of the Masons in order to maintain his status in the gold camps along the Alder and Grasshopper Creeks.

And apparently he either did not think the Masons were indispensable to his future success, or he was unwilling to so compromise his principles and character. Although he genuinely befriended many of their number, he accorded them no special dispensations or attentions.

There was one particular member of the local Masonic brotherhood who took some umbrage at Henry's disinterest in joining the sect,
especially after a substantial number of the other local Masons strongly
advocated Henry's candidacy. I saw him often in town where he sold a
good portion of the lumber that he and his partners milled at a site up
Godfrey's Canyon where there still was a sufficient amount of saw timber to cut and rip and plane. His name was Langford, and he was a
rather manipulative sort who seemed incapable of achieving his objectives despite his endless contrivances. Will Pearson, who worked up the
street at the stables when he wasn't working the claim he had legally
jumped, described to me one day how Langford and another Mason
named Crawford had attempted to fix the trial of Charles Reeves and
Augustus Moore. Crawford had conspired to appoint Langford to an
impaneled jury that had been promised to the accused men by an inept
posse who could find no other way to make their arrest.

Langford, who together with Crawford and the prosecutor Copely
and Judge Hoyt, had already determined the men were guilty of murder
and should be hanged; and when Langford got himself elected foreman
of the jury, Langford and Crawford and Copely and Hoyt, who all happened to be Masons, presumed the case was won before it was even
tried. What they had not contemplated was that the remainder of the
jury, who were selected as being amongst the most weak minded of the
entire community, would vote their conscience rather than another
man's expectations. "Didn't work out the way Crawford and his cronies
planned it," Will Pearson told me with obvious satisfaction. "When it
came to coming to a verdict, Langford was the only one of the twelve
who voted for a death sentence for Moore and Reeves. And the funny
thing about it was that I overheard him talking to Crawford and my
father and Copely before the jury even voted, and all he kept saying was
that he could talk the dumb sons of bitches into anything he wanted.
'No doubt about it'."

Langford was also president of the local Union League and, as
such, maintained a perfectly stalwart stance with respect to everything

pertaining to the war. He was aggravated by the presence in the territory
of so many Southern men and advocated the capture and execution of
those who twice tore down the national flag that had been hoisted high
over Nevada City during the July Fourth celebration. Initially, he was
almost entirely alone in the vehemence of his sentiments, and so he
bided his time, making acquaintances when he could with others like
himself who were arriving in increasing numbers to the Alder diggings
and, particularly, in and around Nevada City, where a second Union
League office was established.

I could tell that Henry viewed Langford as an extremist. There
were times when Langford could not be avoided, but Henry always kept
him at a distance. Henry, instead, aligned himself politically and in a
most subtle manner with Colonel Sam McLean, who had been one of
the first arrivals at Grasshopper Creek, having made the rush to the
Grasshopper while in route to Oro Fino with a large group of Pikes
Peakers that included amongst their number Wash Stapleton, Doc
Glick, Judge Bissell, and H. P. Smith. McLean was a whiskey drinker by
inclination, and a portly one at that; but what he was most admired for
by a majority of the miners in Bannack City, and then also in Virginia
City, was his middle-of-the-road Democratic politics that encouraged a
conciliatory approach to the divisive issues that formed the political
landscape.

It was not so much that the mining camps were filled with rebel
supporters, as it was that they were populated by sympathizers. I had
come to see the miners as free spirits, living their lives as they deemed
fit, and living it hard, indeed. They were not particularly amenable to a
centralized form of government such as that which ruled out of
Washington City; that form of federalism was insensitive toward, and
ignorant of, the unique needs, wants, and demands of the local populace. The miners wanted to be left alone to do their work and take their
chances and enjoy the fruits of their good fortune. And that is exactly
how Sam McLean believed the government should serve the mining settlements; and he let his opinions be known wherever the occasion arose.

I never did figure who was using the other more—Henry Plummer using Sam McLean, or McLean, Plummer. And perhaps it didn't matter since they were like minded on most things that mattered to them. Maybe it was simply that they saw each other as a conduit through which they might achieve their own objectives, or maybe even more. Maybe being at parity, with only the slightest of desires to be the first amongst equals.

All I knew for sure was that Sam McLean promoted Henry Plummer with consistency and frequency. I heard McLean often times intermingle Henry's name and reputation with the best interests of Bannack City. And word came to me that McLean spread the same advice not only throughout Alder Gulch but, first and foremost, in Virginia City. Founded by Bill Fairweather's decidedly pro-South contingent of friends and fellow adventurers, Virginia City was, of all the towns along the Gulch, the only place where the names of Jeff Davis and Bobby Lee were openly mentioned in admiration in the saloons and restaurants and during the long workdays along the creek. And there, also, could be heard the name of Henry Plummer: lawman, miner, horseman, and friend to the prospectors of Bannack and Virginia City. And a fine shot with a revolver too, and a gentleman as well, if that made any difference.

Francis, in contrast, was the antithesis of Sam McLean, meaning that McLean was a politician while Francis was merely politic. In this respect Francis, alone, was an anomaly amongst the men I knew and observed in the gold camps. The rest of them, including those I counted as my friends, all seemed driven by dual fevers that measured a man both by his political views and his progress toward achieving one or another form of traditional accumulation, be it quantified in gold or revenues or power. But not so with Francis Thompson; he was perfectly apolitical, going easily with the flow. And while just as impulsive, to be sure, and just as driven as other men, his only wants, nevertheless, seemed to be limited to undirected and unrestrained activity of almost any sort. If he were busy and on the go, and generally accepted by those around him, he seemed contented and gratified. And when his inertia expired and he found himself static and alone, for however brief the moment, he instantly devolved into an irascible and intolerable personality utterly devoid of patience.

In some ways, this worked well between us. In the first six weeks of our residence in Bannack City, he made the trip to the Sun River and Fort Benton three separate times, on each occasion returning with inventory and supplies by which our store became very much of a success. But his need was not limited only to action and travel; it encompassed interaction as well. Francis Thompson befriended every person he encountered and, his disposition being outgoing and his capacity to socialize with other men being somewhat high, he was well received by almost every class of men, wherever they might meet and whatever their objectives and politics might have been.

At the conclusion of one such journey to Fort Benton, Francis was very much enthused by certain of the travelers he had encountered on the road. "The quality of the men coming to the mines is outstanding," he had said as he described his trip. "I met the most interesting group in Cottonwood, Joseph. There was a freighter out of Lewiston named Magruder. An excellent fellow with plenty of money to start with and plans that you can bet will come to fruition. Would you believe he took only five men with him to handle six double tandem wagons all the way to Cottonwood?

"The only problem this Magruder had was that he only generally knew where they were going, and that once he left the Mullan Road, he was going to need a lot more help. So Magruder makes arrangements with a second group he meets in Cottonwood headed by this doctor out of Yale—Howard's his name—and a little red-haired fellow who, I can tell you from personal observation, can cook better than any woman you've ever met, including Martha Vail. And these boys, together with a giant Dutchman named Wagner and a younger fellow named Marshland and a couple others, ties up with me, being as how I'm the only one there that knows the way to Bannack.

"Now that's the way you do business, Joseph. Magruder took to me kindly, and he's agreed that we will be his first source when he has a special order that he can't fill himself. And he says he'll send whatever business he can our way. And this Doc Howard. Why he's a gentleman from the day one. We've made ourselves some good friends on this trip, Joseph. You can count on that."

In Bannack City and around the placers and mining operations both at Grasshopper Creek and Alder Gulch, Francis ingratiated himself into almost every circle and faction of men. He could engage a crowd of strangers with a humorous story, or on an issue of great intellectual interest, and then suddenly depart, leaving his victims to wonder at who he was and where he had gone. He drank, sometimes discreetly and sometimes in a rather reckless fashion, in the saloons, and gambled at the tables. Read what books he could locate, danced with those women who were available at the given time. He was so inclined toward this endless flush of hyperactivity, in fact, that he often seemed to pass himself by, his velocity overwhelming his own recollection of when he had been where with whom.

Francis tried to keep it all straight by maintaining a journal in which he recorded his activities and observations. But that was an undertaking for which he understandably had little time, and he often made his entries late and then even later supplemented what he had written down. On those occasions when I got to read what he had recorded, I often noticed the incongruities between the dates when I knew him to have been in one place, but at which he had located himself as being somewhere else. And once or twice he would recount how he would depart from a friend as he began a journey, only to meet that same person inexplicably at the place of his destination. So that Francis's journal read very much like Francis's personality; it raced wildly in all directions at once and left you wondering just where he was at, and from where he would next be coming.

There were only two things that Francis always tried to avoid, and one of those pleased me and the other left me very much to my own devices. He rarely declared his politics and just as rarely worked. "I bring in the business," he would say when my look suggested displeasure at the latest prospect of being left alone to run the store. And it was true, and I therefore seldom objected when he rode out on some illogical errand that might take him down the street or over the 70 miles to Virginia City.

Above all, he was kind to the Vails and seemed outwardly to support and admire Henry Plummer, and that is what mattered to me most. Because I thought Henry, of all the men in that portion of the territory, to be made for greatness and distinction. And when the crude Salt Lake stage rolled out on an early-September morning carrying a full complement of passengers, including Electa Plummer, and we waved and watched as Henry Plummer followed dutifully alongside the coach, taking Electa out of Bannack City and south, I never felt closer to Francis Thompson as when we stood in the middle of the street and I saw him wipe an erstwhile tear that had just escaped his eye.

BOOK III

HENRY TILDEN

CHAPTER 1

The argument had been in progress for only a few minutes when the guards from the train of freight wagons turned their rifles and shotguns upon the men of our small entourage. In this fashion, they continued what had been a debate but now was a foregone conclusion as they funneled their wagons past us, directing imperious and emotionless glares at Sidney Edgerton, who stood, unrelenting, arguing the injustice of their behavior.

Until finally their leader would suffer under it no more—under the oratory and harangue that seemed and was in fact endless, coming as it did from Sidney Edgerton's depthless and indomitable persistence—and the wagon master fired his shotgun into the air. And the sound of it, all at once exploding within and above the forest and then lingering somehow even after the quiet had returned, frightened our women severely. "That's all I intend to say about it," the man said angrily. "We arrived first, and we will cross first." And I thought it to be the final insult in a long series of effronteries that had befallen Sidney Edgerton since Lincoln's moderate Republicans had split the party and caused Sidney to lose his seat in Congress.

Sidney Edgerton had deserved far better treatment in every

respect. He had courted and fostered the powers of the great Ohio Radical Republicans, Ben Wade of the Senate and Governor Salmon Chase, being the same Chase who had almost become president and should have at that moment been president were it not for the absurdities of the nominating convention—and the same Chase who had so intimidated Lincoln that Lincoln had given him the Treasury post, from which, in reality, the country and the war were even at that moment being financed and directed. Uncle Sidney had lent great assistance to both men, keeping the name of Ohio prominent among the other Northern states, even going so far as to insist to his nephew, and my uncle, Wilbur Sanders (Sidney, in truth, being my great-uncle but, with only thirteen years between him and Wilbur, not very much liking the patriarchal title) that in the name of duty, and if not duty then at least in the name of honor, Wilbur should abandon his law practice in Akron to recruit Ohio volunteers that Wilbur would then lead against the rebels with a brevet officer's rank. This Uncle Wilbur had done with organizational success; but Wilbur had received very little recognition for his contribution of troops and political support. Then, following his transfer to a different regiment under an Ohio colonel, he did not even know, Wilbur had succumbed to a fever bred out of the miasma of the river swamps of the Mississippi. The fever brought with it the added indignity that Wilbur was wholly tent ridden at Pittsburg Landing, confined to a field hospital along the banks of the river where other men lay dying from the wounds of battle.

Wilbur thus could only admit that while he had been there at that place where so many men died in the fierce charges and countercharges through the orchards and thickets of trees, there at the place where Grant proved his leadership and his resolve and which the rebels called Shiloh or Shiloh Church with an almost reverent tone, that he had seen none of it: none of the valiant fighting, nothing of how the brave men he had known and marched with had stood and done battle and died. Instead, the fever had persisted and he, ultimately, had been sent back home to Akron and had been invalided out of the army just in time to learn that Sidney and James Ashley, another Ohio congressman and the chair of the House Committee on Territories had, with the help of Chase and Wade, succeeded in persuading Lincoln to appoint Sidney to a judicial position out West.

These coarse, indifferent men at the river ferry in the middle of the remote Idaho Territory knew nothing of any of that, nor of the fact that Sidney Edgerton finally had been appointed by Lincoln to be the chief justice of the territory, only to suffer more humiliation delivered by telegram from William Wallace, the territorial governor, advising Sidney that he was being assigned to the isolated eastern district, east of the great barrier of the divide, where Wallace could be assured Sidney would not interfere with the real government, which was comprised of western men and centered in Lewiston, west of the Rocky Mountains. From which intelligence we learned also by inference that there was little government in that portion of the territory east of the great mountains, the lack of which was more than amply demonstrated by the way these freightmen lawlessly threatened us with their shotguns as they disconnected their tripled wagons and began the time-consuming process of slowly shuttling their wagons and mules and oxen across the Snake River aboard the sole toll ferry that had been stationed there by the Mormons as a means of extorting profit out of travelers who had no choice but to pay the unconscionable tolls.

"You have no idea to whom you are speaking," Sidney had angrily said to the wagon master.

And the wagon master had replied, "I don't give a damn who I'm talking to. You shut your mouth or you'll find yourself facedown in the current."

So we waited while they loaded the ponderous wagons, one at a time unhitching them from each other and then unyoking all but the last team so that each wagon could be loaded on the platform and poled across the river with only a heavy guide rope to keep the raft from careening down the waters. And I could see the frustration building in both Sidney and Wilbur after more than two hours had passed and only a quarter of the freight train had crossed while we sat with the women and children and our two wagons full of our possessions, waiting in the heat of the day.

On one of the return crossings, the ferry brought over a wagon that had been converted roughly and curiously into a stage, the sight of the passengers in transit far out in the mountains being somewhat startling, like the first notice of land after months at sea. And as the passengers disembarked to stretch their legs and beat the dust from off their clothes and hats, I watched as the lone horseman who accompanied them dismounted and, with a perfect etiquette, assisted a young woman down to the ground in such a way that the romantic connection was evident and overt. Hand in hand they walked up the road on which we had braked the wagons while the Mormon freighters made their passage.

When he and the young lady at his arm approached our wagons, he said, "Good afternoon," and he gracefully doffed his hat to the women in our company. And it was notable that he carried himself with a great measure of self-assurance, which I did not attribute to the pistol he wore at his side nor the shotgun he left on his saddle. Those things, I assumed, were standard in the territories: the guns and knives and scars merely testamentary to conditions and not the personalities that tolerated and enjoined them. So that I surmised that his walk would have been the same and his countenance equal anywhere, no matter whether he strolled a Manhattan avenue or rode an unmarked trail.

"It was a good morning when we arrived here," Sidney answered from where he sat in the wagon. "And it may well be a good evening before we are allowed to cross." Wilbur and I nodded our heads in acknowledgment of the man's salutation.

"Allow me to introduce you to my wife," the man said. "I am Henry Plummer, sheriff at Bannack City. And this is Mrs. Henry Plummer, Electa."

"Good afternoon, madam," my uncles each answered. And I said, "Ma'am," also.

Henry Plummer looked back at the Mormon freighters before any of us could introduce ourselves. "Do you mean to tell me that these freighters will not yield the right of way long enough to allow you to pass over the river?"

"Almost came to gunfire," said my Uncle Wilbur, who was prone to exaggeration.

And then Sidney added, "We're badly outnumbered, as you can see."

Henry Plummer showed genuine concern. He looked back at our wagons, over the sunburned and dirtied faces of the women and children. "I will see what I can do," he said. "It would help if I knew your names and your purpose."

"Sidney Edgerton, at your service, sir. I am recently appointed by the president, President Lincoln that is, as the chief justice of the Idaho Territory. I have been sent to Bannack City by the territorial governor, pending further instructions. This," he said, proudly introducing my uncle, "is Colonel Wilbur Sanders, recently of the Sixty-fourth Ohio Infantry, and an attorney of some fame in Ohio. And this is my ward and nephew, Henry Tilden. The rest of our company is our family: our wives and children and one niece who hopes to teach school in the new settlements. And Almaretta Greer, Colonel Sander's servant. We are, as you can plainly see, greatly inconvenienced by the discourtesies of these . . . these villains."

Henry Plummer received Uncle Sidney's remarks with great hospitality, taking off his hat and extending his hand in greeting. "Welcome, your honor. Welcome indeed. It is a pleasure, Judge Edgerton. And to you, also, Colonel Sanders. And to you, Henry Tilden. If you will wait here, I believe I can remedy your problem." And he turned, after commending to our women his attractive wife, who had coyly stood by with a demure and modest smile.

There followed a heated discussion between the sheriff and the wagon master, which we could not hear but only watch as the two men argued their separate points of view. The wagon master gestured his feelings with great emphasis, portraying the burden of his responsibility with a sweep of his arm, and the inconvenience of delay by the vehemence of his anger. And all the while Henry Plummer responded with a staid and almost silent authority, listening but not wavering from his position, which carried the weight of fairness and courtesy. From the corner of my eye, I could see that Sidney watched them also, and that he had been favorably impressed by this man Henry Plummer, having observed the sheriff's sense of politics and position. "There," Uncle Sidney said, referring to Plummer with a directional indication of his hand, "is the first man of manners we have encountered since we left the train in Omaha. I will wager you my ten dollars to your one he's a Union man, tried and true."

In but a few minutes, Henry Plummer returned. "They have agreed to your passage on the next two crossings. It would be best if you moved up now and assumed your position." He had reason to be pleased with his success and, if anything, I thought he acted reserved in delivering the news to us. And my uncles were too adroit to play it up by asking how he had accomplished expediting our crossing. Then Plummer looked over to where the women had been plying his wife with questions. "I should retrieve Mrs. Plummer; I am afraid we are holding up the others. She is," he said in a delicate and almost whispered explanation, "on her way East to receive some medical treatments. I shall be ahead of you, on the road back to Bannack. May I make any arrangements in advance of your arrival?"

Sidney had carried with him all the way from Akron duplicate letters signed by Lincoln setting forth his new credentials as chief justice. He now retrieved one of them from the strongbox that had been bolted beneath the seat of his wagon, and he handed it ceremoniously toward Plummer. "These are my credentials and letters of introduction, Sheriff. I would appreciate your delivering them to whoever is the territorial authority at Bannack City with the statement that we expect to arrive shortly. The advance notice shall help to ease my assimilation into the government. Thank you for offering."

Plummer smiled but did not take the letter. "I would be honored to act as your courier for such a purpose," he said. "Only there is no ter-ritorial authority in Bannack City. There's a miners' committee, and a miners' court. I serve as sheriff by the vote of the miners themselves. If you would like, I can deliver your letter to the committee. That would be the best I could do."

Uncle Sidney frowned and then withdrew his hand, which still held the sealed letter. "Perhaps it would be better for me to withhold this pending our arrival. Thank you just the same, Sheriff."

Plummer gave us advice for the remainder of our journey to Bannack, and then he said his farewells to his wife and rode back to the river and forded it still mounted on his horse. He moved up the road, into the trees, north, and was gone.

Begrudgingly, the Mormon wagon master yielded to us and per-mitted us to cross the ferry, which was necessary to keep the wagons out of the sharp current of the river and its rocky bottom. He could not, however, refrain from remarking to us as we prepared the wagons for crossing. "You're making a mistake by befriending that man Plummer. You're likely to end up wishing you hadn't."

"And why is that, if I may ask?" Wilbur replied. "The man is every bit the gentleman. And, as you surely know, he is the appointed sheriff in Bannack City. He has every appearance of being a man of the people."

"Being sheriff of a mining district don't mean much when it comes to deciding who you trust and who you don't. Plummer's got a history that goes way back before Bannack. I can tell you that. Used to board in San Quentin, before the governor pardoned him out. Like I say, he's got himself a history all right."

"As do we all, sir. As do we all."

"Not as murderers we don't. Your man Plummer's killed men for less reason than most would need to kick a mule. An' that lot he rides with isn't too respectable neither. He isn't what he seems; I can tell you that."

"We will take our chances, sir," Sidney intervened. "And we will form our own opinions. Now, good day, sir."

~~~

It wasn't the difference in their age that caused Uncle Wilbur to be so deferential to Sidney Edgerton; nor was it the fact that Sidney was his uncle and therefore, by normal familial applications, entitled to the courtesies that come with such relationships. Rather, it was what Sidney Edgerton had already done with his life, whom he knew, down which halls and through which doors he had passed as he tangled in the political throes of what in the beginning of his career had still been an evolving nation, and was now a nation at war with itself, and soon would prove to be the greatest and most noble of any government of peoples to ever exist on the face of the earth. Sidney Edgerton had stared straight into the eyes of such men as Seward and Chase and Buchanan and Lincoln, and no doubt had at times persuaded them of the validity and truth of his perspective. He had worked the floors at the Free Soil and Republican conventions, and in subtle ways had dictated that certain planks be included in the party platform. And perhaps of greater ultimate consequence, there were officers now in the field who were owing to him for his earlier recommendation for their admission to the service academy at West Point or their promotion to a higher military rank, just as there were young men who held positions in various governmental offices in Ohio and Washington City who recognized an indebtedness to return a favor to Sidney Edgerton when called upon to do it.

So there was that—Sidney Edgerton's demonstrated achievements and the political affiliations he had cultivated during a time when the political climate was particularly mercurial and yet unyielding. There was that, and then there was the implacable drive deep within Sidney Edgerton that would inevitably compel him onward to even greater accomplishments in the western wilderness into which he had moved and which he, alone, if that was what was required, would tame and organize politically in a manner to his liking.

Wilbur Sanders knew as much, as did all of us who were blessed to travel in Judge Edgerton's company; and Wilbur had known it for the better part of his still youthful life. He had been given the opportunity to study at Oberlin, where Mary Edgerton's sister, a wealthy founder of that institution of learning and study, still maintained an aristocratic and social connection. But he had rightly seen that an even greater future rested with an association with his uncle, because while a formal education of the quality offered at Oberlin clearly would create the potential for achievement in the future, Sidney Edgerton offered even more of prosperity, especially at the time when Wilbur committed to study the law under his tutelage, when Sidney was still aspiring to gain position and power in the federal government.

In a very different way, however, Wilbur was almost Sidney's equal. They both knew that it is more than just the man that makes the man. And they both possessed a keen and refined sense of how to build upon opportunity and circumstance to further their ambitions and good fortune. So Wilbur had studied the law under Sidney's watchful eye and had come to interact as a legal advisor to many of the businessmen and local politicians who sought out Sidney Edgerton for the advice and privileges attendant to his stature.

Even in that respect though, Wilbur had not the foresight that carried Sidney along. When Salmon Chase lost the Republican nomination to Lincoln, it was Wilbur who was the most devastated. At the family Christmas dinner that year, his despondency was pronounced, until Sidney, who always discussed political matters at least generally at the table as though they were grist for the entire family, proclaimed there clearly would be civil war, and that it would be the most profound of mistakes for Wilbur to not involve himself prominently in it. "It will be a tremendous opportunity for you, Wilbur," he had said. "You will form a company of Ohio volunteers and you will be elected to lead them. Soldiers, alone, are in the public eye during time of war. And it is the backwash of war that makes great politicians. Washington, Jackson, Taylor—all soldiers. You must not miss the opportunity." And Wilbur had acceded to the suggestion, raising not one company but two, one of infantry and one of artillery. Sidney had no connections in the War Department run by Cameron, whom Sidney called the worst kind of thief and bungling fool. And Wilbur was further disadvantaged by his lack of the formal military education and experience that had catapulted half-rate men into colonelcies and generalships with meteoric effect. Then the order of reassignment came, sending Wilbur to an Ohio regiment from a different part of the state, and Wilbur had written to Sidney just as the word had come that Chase and Wade had finally repaid Sidney Edgerton at least a portion of their debt—the appointment to the Idaho Territory had been made by Lincoln.

Perhaps it was destiny that Wilbur Sanders was stricken by the fever, and it may be that it was fate that caused it to persist long enough that he was rendered unfit for prolonged service in the Union army. But it was his own personal will and determination that eventually defeated it before we even knew he was ill; by the time he had returned to Akron, Wilbur appeared to us to have regained his strength in full. And it took no great insight to see that a great epic stood before my reunited uncles, and I gladly seized upon Sidney and Mary's benevolent suggestion to my mother that my consumptive condition might be relieved in the mountain and arid climate to which they were removing a substantial contingent of the family.

Wilbur, in contrast, worried vocally whether the far West might condemn us all to mediocrity. And it frustrated me to no end to hear it. Because Sidney Edgerton's vision was far too great to be questioned by Wilbur Sanders. Sidney could survey what was transpiring in the world or in any microcosm of society or industry or politics and project where it might lead under the careful direction of those with the wisdom and inclination to make it so. At the family gatherings in Ohio, one could catch glimpses of this faculty: at the head of the dining table where he spoke in superficial generalities the women could understand, or in greater detail and with more emphatic argument in the parlor where the men would gather afterward to smoke their cigars and drink their brandy and discuss how best the nation could be managed. But as a boy amongst men, I never gained a full exposure to his intellect and perspicacity until we departed for the West; the confinements of the trains to Chicago and St. Joseph and Omaha, and again in the wagon as we slowly proceeded along the toilsome immigrant road, brought me in almost perpetual proximity to him.

And Uncle Sidney's view that a new territory should be carved from the Idaho Territory, from those lands east of the mountains, and that it should be governed by Republicans who could administer it in a manner consistent with the needs of the Union, became well known to me before we reached the Eagle Rock crossing and were told by Henry Plummer that Bannack City lacked a territorial representative. So that for Sidney Edgerton it must have been like hearing a vulgar and offensive joke, reiterated yet again, when we came down off the freight road that led into Grasshopper Creek and rode into what there was of Bannack, with its featureless streets and alleys and crude buildings, and saw that there was not a single Union flag displayed anywhere, nor for that matter any form of banner or seal or insignia at all to demark the fact that this place was part and parcel of the United States of America and subservient to the laws and Constitution Sidney Edgerton had sworn to uphold, so help him God.

CHAPTER 2

My Uncle Sidney was at fault in the matter, though I knew he would never consider admitting to it. He had said, "We must make every effort to identify Union men amongst the local citizenry," and I had acted on what I thought to be a clear and immediate instruction. And the response had been substantial, too. I had placed a sign outside of Oliver's Bannack City Express Office, where Sidney Edgerton's new influence had secured for me employment, asking for Republican Party members to come inside and register their name and place of residence together with the names of any other citizens known to be affiliated with the party. And I also had made inquiries, discreetly I thought, and with a certain air of eastern sophistication, as to who amongst the Democrats in town might be anticopperhead and thus, presumably, prowar. And when I was asked who was collecting the information, I openly told them it was Sidney Edgerton, the recently arrived chief justice.

So that it was natural for me to conclude that I was providing Sidney with not one service but two, in that I perceived that the spreading of his influence was best accomplished by publicizing his presence and his official status in the government. But when I brought the lists to him, proudly presenting them with an expectation of a warm and pleased reception, he as much as exploded with red-faced anger. "You fool," he chastised me. "When I want you to do something, you will know it by explicit direction. Never," he said with a scowl, "never, do you understand me, presume how and when I want things done."

In the end, his own conduct demonstrated that I had achieved something that was useful to him. He took the lists, and from them he and Uncle Wilbur made their own inquiries concerning certain individuals and their political inclinations. Afterwards, Sidney as much as apologized for being so harsh. "You must understand," he said only a few days later with his arm around my shoulder, "that these are difficult times, and this is a hostile place. One must take great precautions under such circumstances. It is not easy to distinguish our enemies from our friends. I will be clearer next time, Henry; I will ensure that my intentions and desires are fully communicated to you. So that you need not guess at what needs to be done."

Among the identities I had brought back to Sidney were the names of N. P. Langford and Sam Hauser, who had both been at Bannack essentially from the beginning and had observed its growth with somewhat of a jaundiced eye. Langford owned an interest in a rather profitable sawmill up a feeder creek of the Beaverhead and had been wise enough in the early going to join up with the likes of Bill Bunton, the proprietor of the Rattlesnake Ranch, in staking and perfecting some choice claims along Grasshopper Creek. He was also a staunch Republican, and as such he headed the nonpartisan Union League, which at the time of our arrival sported over thirty members, only a few of whom were Democrats. And I heard Wilbur mention that Langford was also a Mason; but word of that was never again repeated in my presence, and so I only learned much later that it was true, that Langford had taken the secret oaths and learned the secret signs and immersed himself in their shadowy shroud of mystery.

Hauser came from much the same cut. He had emigrated the prior year by steamship run to Fort Benton and had such a reputation as a businessman and entrepreneur that he was known about the region as a preeminent capitalist; it was said as a weakly sort of pun that he could make a profit out of Lucifer himself. And he was known to celebrate every Union holiday and war victory exuberantly, sometimes firing off the mountain howitzer that Captain James Fisk had brought overland with the wagon train he had guided across the mountains. Hauser, however, did not qualify to place his name upon the first of my two lists in that he was a Democrat. In all respects, though, he thought and acted as would a devoted Radical Republican; he despised slavery and the South, mostly for economic reasons, and promoted the war and free soil in the West at every turn. And there was something to him that suggested that he, too, had taken the secret oaths and would invoke them in the name of the Masons' secret purposes if and when the time arose.

Uncle Sidney chose to consult first with these two men, saying that he had as much to learn from a Democrat like Hauser as from a run-of-the-mill backcountry Republican like Langford. And as soon as Mary Edgerton was satisfied with her arrangements in the new family residence—a sizable log building on Main Street that Sidney had purchased at an auction efficiently run by Henry Plummer—Sidney invited them for an afternoon of political discussion and an exchange of news.

Before the guests arrived, Mary Edgerton took the children up to Yankee Flat to the cabin the Sanders family had rented, and when she was gone, Sidney rearranged the chairs more to his liking, correcting a woman's eye for proportion with a man's need for proximity and dominance. And I was so very surprised that I had been invited to attend that I did not feel the least bit slighted by the fact that Sidney intentionally placed my designated chair against the wall, back from the tight circle in which the others would be sitting. "You will each take great care not to say anything to offend our guests," he said in his final instructions to us. "And certainly do not overplay their significance. This will be a fine lesson for you, Henry. You can learn much just by listening and watching. I do not imagine the occasion for you to speak will arise."

Why he had invited me was unclear. I had been admonished by Sidney for what he called ineptitude, and I had never before been included in a private session amongst politicians. And while I was a family member and had been treated as such, there always seemed to be subtle reminders that my relationship was distant compared to the intimacies of the remainder of the family. Sidney had made that clear when he insisted I take on employment and then proceeded to locate a place for me to room on the opposite side of town, and when he referred to me as his ward when I was in reality his nephew and by some standards his adopted son. But I was still expected at the Edgerton table for the evening meal and was made to understand that, at my age, I was still very much in need of the supervision of an adult. In this sense I was answerable, and required to be responsive, to Sidney Edgerton; I was at his beck and call.

Langford and Hauser arrived together with considerable pomp and a good deal of commotion, and Sidney escorted them into the cabin graciously. "Good afternoon, gentlemen," he said in his stentorian voice. "Judge Sidney Edgerton, at your service."

Langford and Hauser introduced themselves with airs of sophistication.

"I trust your ride into town was pleasurable?" Sidney asked rhetorically. And when they said it was, he said, "Allow me to introduce my companions. This is Wilbur Sanders, my nephew and a veteran of the war. Wounded at Pittsburg Landing. Colonel Sanders was gracious enough to sacrifice a rather lucrative law practice in Akron in order to serve as my assistant. I expect he will practice law here in Bannack as well. And this is Henry Tilden, my ward and secretary. You may assume that you may speak frankly and in confidence before them both, and that any word Henry brings from me or Wilbur in the future is accurate and definitive. Now, may I offer you a cigar?"

Langford was equally cordial and yet formally affected. "Why thank you, thank you, Judge," he answered. He reached out and accepted one of the cigars Sidney handed to the two men. He drew it slowly beneath his nose and then artfully tasted it. "Excellent leaf, Judge. Tennessee?"

"Why, yes. Yes, it is at that," Sidney lied. The cigars had been given to him, before the war had started, by a congressman from the Carolinas.

Langford carried himself with an almost absurd affectation of propriety; he hemmed before he spoke, and he sat stiffly, and he gave a slight and affirming nod of his head with almost every word he offered. "You cannot imagine how relieved we are that you have come," Langford said, his head jerking in rhythm with the words. "We were beginning to believe the governor would not act."

"He has yet to act, as far as I am concerned," Sidney said. Theatrically, he struck a long stove match and with it lighted the cigars given to Langford and Hauser, and then his own and Wilbur's. "He sent me here as a means of keeping me from Lewiston," he said. "I am confidant that he expects me to return East and resign my duties."

"You mean he doesn't expect you to hold court here?" Hauser said. "That's absurd. It doesn't take a genius to know that law and order's what we need most. Wallace is an idiot. They ought to have him shot and save us the trouble of having to put up with him."

Sidney smiled grimly at Hauser's comment. "As far as I am concerned, gentlemen, I am authorized and expected by the president to do all things required of the chief justice of the territory. Only I have not been funded by the governor. I have been offered no facilities, no prosecutor, no library, no briefing clerk; I have not even been provided with any form of written territorial laws. No casebooks. No rules of procedure nor process for appeal. These, gentlemen, are the tools of the judiciary. They have been intentionally withheld, and I do not intend to allow myself to be made a laughingstock by way of a blatant political attempt to undermine my reputation."

Langford and Hauser looked aghast, although I cannot say whether their countenances reflected their real feelings or were formed to appease Sidney Edgerton's expectations. Langford's expression, in particular, looked surreal and assumed. "May I confide in you, gentle-men?" Sidney asked. And when Langford and Hauser both affirmed that he could, Sidney said in a low voice, almost a whisper, "The war does not go well. It does not go well at all, despite what you might have heard of these victories in Pennsylvania and at Vicksburg. The nation is insolvent. Bankrupt, gentlemen. Chase has told me so himself. Under the strictest form of confidence, you understand. Our banknotes and war bonds have not been well received by the financial community and the public. Our gold and silver reserves are insufficient to back up the currency. Some are questioning whether the war effort can continue to be financed by promises alone. Chase is concerned there soon might be a financial panic."

And then he paused, examined Langford's and Hauser's faces to see what effect his statements had made. "I think we understand each other, gentlemen. The Grasshopper strike, together with that at Alder Gulch, have all the makings of the greatest placer finds in the world. The government in Washington City is in need of the gold that is being mined here. It must not fall into the hands of the traitorous rebel sym-pathizers. And the secesh must not be allowed to control the territory. Certainly, the absence of law and order here increases the risk that the gold will be moved south. The only choice, it would seem, is to separate the territory in half; form a new territory of the lands east of the moun-tains so that Wallace's scheme will fail, and law and order will be estab-lished. That is our duty, gentlemen. To the Union. We must work together toward this end."

Langford and Hauser then knew they were in the presence of a real political force. They seemed unable to speak; Sidney Edgerton rep-resented something far beyond their experience. Here was a man who could talk of Chase as an equal, and who had access to the congres-sional and presidential powers back East.

Finally, Langford said, "We are with you on this, Judge. You will have to tell us what we can do."

"Yes," Sidney said. "I knew I could count on the both of you."

Much was discussed that day between the four men in terms of what the principal concerns of the region were, and what their course of action should be, and how their objectives could best be accomplished. It was agreed, first and foremost, that Sidney Edgerton and Wilbur Sanders must acquire mining interests so that they would be privy to, and constituents of, the miners' committee and its deliberations. "With any luck at all," Langford said, "you'll even make a handsome profit on your claims." It was further understood that Sidney and Wilbur must tread lightly when it came to Henry Plummer, whom Langford and Hauser both characterized as being politically shrewd and as having a very substantial backing amongst not only the miners but also the merchants and express agents who ultimately held and transported the store of gold mined in Bannack and Alder Gulch. "Even if a new territory is created," Langford said, "we will have Henry Plummer to contend with. He is the people's choice. Not only here, but in Virginia City as well. Only two days ago Buz Caven resigned the Virginia City sheriff's post that he was elected to only recently, so that the miners could have their first choice, which was Plummer. That had not been possible until Mrs. Plummer went back East. So there you have it, Judge. Plummer now runs both Bannack and Virginia City. We will have to reckon with him."

"And so we will," Uncle Sidney said. "For now though, I think it would be well for Wilbur and me to become better acquainted with our good sheriff."

Langford and Hauser agreed. Langford then further suggested that it would be appropriate for the chief justice of the territory to observe a miners' trial in progress. "There is a hearing scheduled for tomorrow that you might find interesting, Judge. Something about an assault and destruction of property."

"Fine," Sidney answered. "That will be just fine."

The next day, we gathered for the Edgertons' traditional Sunday dinner, which Mary had been constrained to delay while all of us—the remainder of the Edgerton family and that of Wilbur Sanders together with Lucia and Almaretta—awaited Uncle Sidney's return from the miners' trial he had attended throughout the day. Mary Edgerton had spent the better part of her morning cooking and baking. She had done so on a day that had been surprisingly warm for the first week of October. There were three fresh golden loaves to sop up the gravy from the roast, and soda biscuits and corn bread besides. And then there were the mince pies for which she could have been famous, the necessity of using dried apples in no way detracting from her art, and the crusts perfect and only slightly yielding to the touch. And there were gingersnaps, much to the children's delight, and the luxury of fresh milk purchased for an incredible 25 cents a quart. All this prepared on the single sheet iron cookstove that had been hauled across the plains at considerable inconvenience, and with expectations just as great.

The time spent waiting for Sidney's return seemed interminable, placing, it seemed, the food at a very real risk of spoilage before he might return. When he finally did come back to the cabin, brushing the children aside almost as though he did not see them, he was in a foul state of mind approaching one of his dark and arbitrary moods, which could so quickly dishearten the women and children. But Mary said a word to him and pointed out the table, which was so crowded with foods and silverware that its surface was totally obscured, and he eased some. And then it was all right. The children's lighthearted play revived, and Mary reigned queen for the hour during which the meal was consumed.

With the dinner finished, the children were dispatched behind the house to play along the creek and on the log footbridge that crossed over to Yankee Flat, while Mattie, the eldest of the Edgerton children, watched over them like a brooding hen. The women attended to the table, and Sidney drew us outdoors to sit under the eaves.

Once outside, we could clearly see the street and hear the sounds of music and laughter coming from the saloons, which had absorbed the sudden overflow of miners from the trial. Sidney Edgerton shook his head when he heard the noise. "Gentlemen," he said in a resolute and profound whisper. "Earlier today I witnessed one of the greatest mockeries of our time. I hardly know what to think."

Wilbur had been looking over in the direction of the creek, where the voices of the children carried through the few remaining trees. "Are you referring to the miners' trial, Uncle? I was surprised it took so long."

"It took so long because the fools had to recess every half hour just so someone could purchase more bottles of whiskey to keep them refreshed. I'm talking about the judge, mind you. Drunk at the bench. And the prosecutor, too. The whole lot of them. The witnesses, the accused, the crowd. They were all drunk as Irishmen when they started and they were in the same state seven hours later when they concluded." The self-invoked anger I had seen before now welled up in my uncle. It flushed his visage, highlighting the hawkish, piercing gaze of his eyes, the aquiline nose, and the sunken high cheeks that defined his face.

Wilbur merely shook his head with tacit understanding. "You knew it would be bad, Sidney," he said. "We knew we could not expect much from this sort."

Sidney gave him a sharp glance. "I knew it would be bad. Yes. I thought it would be inept. I thought they would show their ignorance of the law. I thought it would be a failure because of their inability. But it was far worse than that. It was a blatant mockery, a travesty to our entire way of life." Sidney's breath had become labored, and it was frightening to see because one could not know at what point an elder man might not explode his heart under extraordinary stress.

"Would you believe," he said, calming some and shaking his head, "the whole thing evolved around a practical joke. A practical joke, mind you, that ended up with one man being shot and another's cabin severely damaged. And can you guess what they decided, and by 'they' keep in mind I mean every one of them; every damned one of them is entitled to place their vote on guilt or innocence. They decided that the man who did the shooting was guilty of no crime, and that the man who induced him into the shooting and thus started the events that led to the destruction of a third party's cabin was liable for no loss. And do you know why they came to that result, other than the fact that the one who won had the most friends there and therefore the most votes? They decided that way because the joke was a good one and he deserved it, and the wound was not bad and the cabin could be repaired, the owner being rather heavy with dust. That's what someone in the crowd was allowed to observe. That the owner of the cabin, who was seeking damages, 'was heavy with dust.'"

Sidney expected Wilbur to say something in agreement with his commentary, which Wilbur did by noting that Sidney was now armed with "persuasive anecdotal evidence" that the territory was in an utter state of chaos. "Washington," Wilbur said, "will be appalled by Wallace's failure to implement a judicial system. They will have no choice but to take strong measures to correct the situation."

I sat for a long while listening to the two men talk. The fact that liquor had played a central role in the behavior at the proceedings, alone, was enough to cause them to be indignant and affronted. Wilbur was totally abstinent, and Sidney, who knew better than to preclude political interaction through absolute restrictions on personal habit, drank only sparingly and then only when courtesy or personal advancement required. They were equally astonished by the fact that the deciding body at the trial—in this case anyone and everyone who was present—could be weighted and biased simply by the success of one party in persuading his friends to attend, or his enemies to stay clear. They discussed the constitutional implications of the lack of a real jury, and the political ramifications of a trial to the entirety of the populace.

It was all over my head, the lexicon of the law being as foreign to me as the language employed by the Bannocks and Shoshones when they came to the cabins to beg for scraps of food and clothing. Somehow, it all seemed to boil down to the same universal threat to the Union that Sidney Edgerton suspected behind every closed door, around every corner, beneath every unturned rock. I suppose it was boyish of me, but I wanted to know what the practical joke was that had precipitated the shooting and destruction of property. But I dared not ask Sidney, who was incapable of looking lightly upon a situation he would later seek to manipulate. And it was not until the next day and into the evening that I was able to slip away from the express office long enough to corner Joseph Swift at his and Francis Thompson's store across the street. Of late, I had sought him out when I felt the need for male companionship. And he had shown some inclination toward me, treating me much as an older brother might, with wavering degrees of interest, antipathy, and ambivalence.

Joseph had been at the trial, as I thought would be the case. Francis Thompson, who had taken instantly to patronizing both of my uncles, and Joseph owned mining claims and maintained an active interest in the miners' committee. When I asked Joseph about the trial, and more specifically about the practical joke, he described it to me with relish. "I'm not sure you know who Jacob Lilner is," he began. "Lives out by Marysville, just down the road a way, a mile or two. The man drinks like no one you've ever seen. He wakes up and starts drinking, and he keeps right on drinking all day long and into the night for as long as he can until he passes out. Then he sleeps for two days straight. And when he finally wakes up, he starts all over again, unless he needs to put in some representation work on his claims upstream. Always works sober, and he always works hard. I've heard 'em say when Jake Lilner's working, he can bring up more gold in less time than anyone in the district. That's where he gets his drinking money. Once he gets in his representation work, he goes straight back to the saloons.

"That's where it all got started. He'd been on a three-day binge just before they struck it at Alder Gulch, and he'd only been passed out for a few hours when Hack Wilson, who's a friend of his, came into town to let his pals know about the new strike. Only Hack couldn't wake 'im for nothing. So Jake missed out on it. Didn't get there until four days after the first rush out of Bannack, and he wasn't willing to stake a claim out away from his pals. After that, he made everyone he knew promise they'd wake him up, no matter what it took, next time a stampede came up.

"Well, Hack thought it was all pretty funny, how all these men had been made to promise they'd throw water in Jake Lilner's face and shoot guns in his ears and do whatever was required to wake him up enough so that he'd get in early on the next rush. So one night they waited until Jake got all drunk up and had crawled back into the cabin he was renting, and then Hack and some other friends of Jake's got some chains hooked on his cabin door and locked it up from the outside as tight as a safe. Then they started shooting their revolvers and banging on his cabin door—all this after midnight and Jake Lilner only three hours into a sleep that could have lasted for days—yelling for him to hurry up or he's gonna miss out on a new find that was going to make Alder Gulch look like slim pickings. Took 'em half an hour just to wake him, and then he couldn't open the door. They kept yelling at him to hurry it up or they were leaving without him, and Jake kept blabbering that he couldn't open the door and couldn't fit through the windows, and they said he was too drunk to open it and he just kept yelling and jerking on that door and not moving it an inch. So Hack and his friends said that was it, they'd woke him like they promised they would, and they weren't waiting on a drunk just so they could lose out on the best claims. And then they went across the street and sat down to watch.

"It took Jake Lilner and an ax all of ten minutes to break down that cabin door, and half the wall attached to it. And the first thing he saw when he made it out into the street were all these men sitting there drinking and laughing like there was no tomorrow. So he goes back into the cabin and gets his pistol and goes back outside and empties it at 'em. And it was a good thing he was still as drunk as he was. He got off five shots, but only made one hit when it was over and done with." Joseph Swift told it with a broad smile, and I did not even have to speculate to see how he had voted when the time came for deciding the civil and criminal issues jointly presented at the trial.

"Guess that showed 'em," I said in an effort to show that I understood it all.

"Showed who what?" Joseph said back. "First thing Lilner did after he emptied his pistol was to come into Skinner's and get himself another bottle. And the first person he offered a drink to was Hack. Funny thing about it was what he did to that door. It was a beauty: solid tamarack, real hinges, and a real lock all the way from Salt Lake City. By the time he made it through, the door was good for nothing but kindling. And the one that Jake and Hack replaced it with, well, it's hardly a door at all. You could pass a letter through the cracks without ever touching wood. What it shows," he said with a sort of self-entertaining look, "is that if you're going to rent out to others, you had better remove more than the family china before you let 'em in."

A crowd had begun to assemble in front of Peabody's while Joseph Swift and I were talking. They were waiting for the stage that was to have arrived from Virginia City two hours earlier and which, it was assumed, had been detained by a broken axle or wheel or some other contingency. Peabody's stage, together with a line owned by Mr. Oliver, made regular runs between Bannack City and Virginia City, stopping at the ranch stations along the way—the Rattlesnake and Cottonwood and Pete Daly's— to take on and disembark passengers and mail and, more importantly, to change into the fresh teams of horses that allowed the sturdy Concord coaches to usually make the 70-mile trip between dawn and dusk.

I had already made the journey once with Wilbur, whom Sidney had sent to Virginia City for the dual purposes of scouting out the mining camps and spreading the word that Wilbur and the chief justice had taken up residence in Bannack. It had been an exhilarating ride, up and down the gullies and foothills and across the smooth tablelands of the high plain with the coach, which was suspended by heavy leather straps, tossing like a fishing cork on a stormy sea. Such that when we had arrived in Alder Gulch, we were almost exhausted, only to find that the diggings were supported by the wildest sort of lifestyle, with thousands of men working the mines under onerous conditions and the nightlife in Virginia City dominated by back-alley saloons and houses of ill fame and hurdy gurdys where a man could buy a dance with a pretty girl for a dollar a turn. But what had struck me the most about the place was the total lack of sanitation. Horses for riding and draft work, cattle and hogs for butcher, were kept in corrals and pens along the Daylight Creek, right there in Virginia City, and their manure and urine mixed in the muddy streets and ran into the creek, down into the Gulch with swarms of flies following its course all along the way. It made for a horrendous smell, and drinking water was only to be got by going up above the towns and the mining sites. And there was no semblance of order anywhere, although the settlements were clearly prospering with industry and businesses of almost every sort imagined.

We had spent a good portion of that day with a friend of Sam Hauser's and a man named Culbertson who ran a freight office, and then we had stayed the night at a new hotel there on the main street in town. On the return stage, we had been joined by several men who, once they became acquainted with Wilbur, confided that they were carrying in hidden belts under their garments substantial quantities of gold dust and nuggets. "You cannot be too careful on these roads," one of them said as we watched the countryside of sage and scrub pine pass. "I know at least ten men in these parts who have lost their gold to road agents. There will have to be a shooting before they take what's mine." And he patted his coat, implying that a firearm lay beneath. Yet the ride had proved uneventful, with the only excitement provided by the herders at the stations who made a game out of seeing how quickly they could switch the teams in and out of the harnesses and send the stage on its way down the road.

The crowd in front of Peabody's kept growing, and Henry Plummer finally came out of the Goodrich Hotel, where he had taken up residence since Electa Plummer's departure. When Joseph Swift saw him, he yelled out "Henry" to catch his attention, and then he crossed over the street to talk to the sheriff, and I followed after him.

"Stage still out, is it?" Henry Plummer said. "Expect it will be here soon." And then he recognized me. "Hello, Henry Tilden," he said. "I hear they've got you working over at Oliver's. He's a good one to learn from. Knows all the ropes, and all the tricks of the trade, too. And how is Judge Edgerton . . . and Colonel Sanders?" he asked. "Word on the street is that they're buying up claims left and right. I sure hope they haven't caught the fever," he said lightly. "'Bout as contagious a disease as is known to man."

"They're fine, Sheriff," I said. "I will tell them you asked."

Then you could hear the faint rumble of the coach coming down off the freight road, and then see it too, with a cloud of dust rising up behind. And then finally you could actually feel the thundering of the harnessed horses at a gallop as they came down onto the flat and up the street and suddenly halted in front of Peabody's, where the crowd had drawn back to the boardwalk.

The man who was driving the coach was not one of Peabody's regular men, and Henry Plummer knew it. "Hello, Tom," Plummer said to the driver, and then he turned to a second man who was riding in the muleskinner's seat. "What are you doing up there, Bunton? Hitchin' a free ride, I'll wager."

"We been robbed, Henry," the driver said, almost wholly out of breath. "Up at Spring Gulch. Two of 'em."

The passengers began to empty out into the street. And we almost immediately learned that one of them was Bummer Dan McFadden, who held a notable reputation in the mining districts. He had acquired his nickname by bumming on his claims, doing little to no real work while his neighbors through sheer labor proved up theirs and consequently his. In the last month, Bummer Dan had been caught stealing a pie in Virginia City and had been fined by the miners' court. When it was determined he had no money to pay the levy, the miners made him work it off by forcing him to stake a claim at a very unpromising spot on a feeder to the Alder. And to their chagrin, it had proved to be a wonderful placer, yielding up a fine dust with almost no overburden. After taking out the easy dust and scads, Bummer Dan McFadden had sold it out and had been heading for the road to Salt Lake City when the stage was robbed.

"Well, hello there, Dan." Henry Plummer said with a grin as Dan McFadden's head emerged through the coach door. "Don't tell me." And when Bummer Dan nodded his head affirmatively, Plummer asked, "How much?"

"All of it, Henry," Bummer Dan said with a doleful look. "At least $2,000 worth of the brightest metal the Good Lord ever placed in the ground."

Several of the other passengers, including Bunton and a man named Percy, had lost money to the road agents also, albeit in much smaller amounts. Once it was made clear that no one had been harmed, the crowd asserted itself. "Who was it?" a number of them asked. "What'd they look like?" "Did you recognize their horses; what were they wearing?"

But the robbers had been covered up with blankets and hoods, and none of the victims could recall anything noteworthy about them. Bunton noted that they had Irish accents, which was not all that peculiar in a region filled with European emigrants of every nationality. "They may have sounded Irish to the likes of you," Bummer Dan said, "but they were as far from an honest Irish brogue as I'm standing this moment from the stone at Blarney. If they were Irishmen," he said, "then I'm a Bannock, shore as can be."

From the door of the express office, Mr. Oliver had seen me in the street, and by his look he made it known that I was remiss in my responsibilities. So it was only through the window that I could watch with envy as Joseph Swift stayed by Henry Plummer's side while the sheriff interviewed first the driver and Bunton and then the remaining passengers, one by one. And from all I ever knew or could ascertain from Joseph and Will Pearson and my other friends who kept their ear to the ground, no one was ever able to determine who robbed Peabody's stage in the evening shade of the bluffs that overshadowed Spring Gulch's deep ravine.

CHAPTER 3

T he moment I saw Mattie at the door of Oliver's Express office, standing at the threshold stupidly staring at me but saying nothing, I knew that she had been sent by Sidney. The verbal agreement between my Uncle Sidney and A. J. Oliver, arranged without any consultation with me, was that when I was not in the service of Sidney, I was to report to Mr. Oliver, for whom I was expected to work obligingly from eight in the morning until six o'clock each evening throughout the six-day work week habitually recognized by the miners. The responsibilities of a clerk at Oliver's were myriad, but mostly involved the receipt and further administration of shipments of all sorts of goods, ranging from mining and building equipment and tools, to foodstuffs and an endless variety of specially ordered items. And this, Sidney explained to me, would provide me with a good experience in the ways of the business world.

From my remittance from Mr. Oliver, I was to defray the cost of my rooming at Mrs. Gibson's boardinghouse, with my remaining living expenses being covered by the Edgertons, who treated me rather well. So well, in fact, that it prided me to satisfy Sidney's every expectation, which I believe I did from and after my initial lapse.

My service to Sidney Edgerton was as broad and diverse as Sidney chose to make it. At his behest I helped the laborers under his employ to work the several claims he had purchased at auction and, in no time, I learned the rudimentary skills of a placer miner, working the heavy sands and gravels out of the bars and ledges and shafts and sifting it into the sluices and rockers, carefully treating the dirt not like the mere and common soil of Ohio, but as a precious medium for the flecks of gold that you could almost always see but only infrequently recover in sufficient quantity to justify your time. I exercised the horses with vigor and genuine affection, copied documents for him in a lacy flowing calligraphic style he greatly admired, and performed any errand he might direct. So when I saw Mattie standing there at the door, looking at me but saying nothing with that same vacant look that was only half real and half assumed, I knew that I was being called upon again; and the truth was that I was glad to escape the drudgery of my regular clerkship duties at Oliver's Express.

"Hello, Mattie," I said, prompting her to break her silence. And when she still said nothing, I added, "Did Sidney send for me?"

"Yes. Father wants you, Henry. Right away," she said, and she flicked her braids and turned and dashed out of the office and was gone.

The express office was directly up the street from the Edgerton cabin, sitting in the center of that congested congregation of commerce that seemed always to focus on Chrisman's and the Goodrich, all of it so close in proximity that one could yell out and almost ensure that your words would be common news throughout the town within the hour, should you so desire. And as I walked the modest distance to the cabin, I felt as I always did in Bannack, familiar and integral and participant with the men that smoked and drank and talked inside the buildings and on the street and in hushed voices in the nameless alleys where they struck dishonest deals and told great lies.

No one answered when I knocked on the door of the Edgerton cabin; nor was anyone in the main room of the cabin when I walked in. Then, through the closed door that led to Sidney's private office, I heard the judge talking in an impassioned voice. He spoke in a tone that came from deep within, summoning up a fire that, once raised, was most difficult for him to quell. "It is no different," he asserted as if he were in a heated argument, "than what has befallen the entirety of the South. Whether manifested by the enslaving of an entire human race or the rampant pillaging of an entire territory. It is the same godless immorality. Feckless robbery, wanton murder, heartless thralldom. All bred of the same base injustice of uncivilized and ungoverned men who are no more than dishonorable traitors to their country. And it must be put to an end. Once and for all. Now and for all time the evil must be eradicated. And the only way to accomplish it is by the absolute rule of order." A book or a hand slammed down onto a solid surface with a heavy thump, and an object, dislocated from its resting position, fell and clattered onto the floor. And then I stood there much as Mattie would, dumb and speechless, unsure what I should do since if I knocked to announce myself, he would know that I had been there and had heard his conversation with Wilbur or Mary or whoever was there with him.

He must have paused to retrieve the fallen object, and in the immense silence that followed, I tapped gently on the door.

"Yes. What is it? Come. Come," he said in a flustered voice from behind the door. And when I opened it and walked into the room, which, by the thickness of the logs and the low ceiling, seemed even more diminutive than it really was, I found him standing there alone with a broken vase in his hand and his face flushed and his breathing somewhat erratic. A mixed look of puzzlement and rage came over his face when he saw me, until he calmed some and then said, "I've told your aunt Mary a dozen times to not place these things on the edge of my desk where they're likely to be knocked off. Now what is it, Henry? I'm more than busy."

"Mattie said you sent for me," I stammered out, overtaken by the fact that he was alone.

"Yes. I did at that, didn't I." His composure slowly returned, and with it he summoned back his gracious mannerism. He placed the pieces of the broken vase down on an almost empty bookshelf, and then he sat behind the new desk he had bought from Francis Thompson, in the new black leather chair that had been made by a local carpenter. "I need for you to deliver something to Mr. Langford. At his mill, up Godfrey's Canyon. You know where it is, do you not?"

I recalled for him the location of the turnoff. Off from the freight road.

"Good," he said. He reached into his desk and pulled out a sealed envelope. "It is of great importance that this be delivered today. If Langford is not there, you are to find out when he will return. Otherwise, you are to await his written response. No matter how long it takes for him to formulate his reply. And no one is to read what either he or I have written. Not even you." He handed me the letter. "You will need to go over to Pearson's to get Jonah," he said. "He was to be newly shod yesterday. Do you understand your instructions?"

"Yes, Uncle Sidney," I answered as I took the envelope from him. "Is that all?"

"It is. Be on your way." And then, as an afterthought, he added, "And be cautious. The roads have turned perilous for us all."

It was a warm and brilliant day for being the last in October, and the road was all but deserted. The commotion that had risen throughout the region following the robbery of Peabody's stage had quieted almost immediately, the community far too occupied with the frenzy of the rush and the ensuing boom to suddenly come to a standstill, but a certain reluctance to travel other than in large and well-armed parties still prevailed. One such group passed me not far out of Bannack, and the glowers and scowls on the faces, and the firm and readied grip on the shotguns as the men approached, were enough to deter the most aggressive of road agents, I was sure. And the number and evident security of the traveling company made me wish for companionship or other occupation as the miles passed.

Langford and Robert Knox and some other investors had built their small sawmill in Godfrey's Canyon for the sole purpose of furnishing lumber to Bannack and the Grasshopper placers and mines. They had located their operation on an ideal ledge of rock, over which the water conveniently fell for a full 10 feet and then pooled again in a rocky basin. Nearby, several stands of cottonwood and pine and fir had defeated time and adversity to grow to trees of incredible height and girth. There the trees had withstood all that could naturally be set against them, all that a chaos of wind and fire, lightning and drought, flood and disease and infestation could summon from out of order to sling furiously down and through and over the canyon. When Langford arrived, the trees had already been standing there for 200, 300 years.

Here, they had built the mill and the small cabin in which Langford and his partners could set up and sometimes sleep and conduct their business. And then they systematically had cut and sawed the timber, broadening the absolute desolation of their work in an ever-widening arc, sliding and skidding the logs with the aid of heavy logging chains and sturdy mules, always taking the closest tree, moving the stands back with each felling cut of the ax, echoing the sound of change.

By the time I arrived with Sidney's letter, they had been at it for almost a year, and the mill now stood on the edge of an extraordinary wasteland in which dismal stumps protruded where great trees once stood, and the once natural surface of the forest floor was now rutted deeply where the great logs had dragged eroding furrows and where rocks and stumps had been blasted to clear passageways for the hauls. A mountainous inventory of cut logs and drying lumber was piled to one side, and enormous heaps of sawdust and peeled bark and slash rose up out of the ground in all directions. So that where there once was forest, there was only but a remnant of forest left, with even the understory of brush and saplings scraped roughly away and into piles that would be burnt bit by bit in the consuming stoves. And the impressive storage of sawed and unsawed timber portended plainly that in the days and months and years to come, the arc would become ever wider, broadened inexorably by the insatiable appetite of the migrants who were coming in ever-increasing number.

I found Langford outside, directing how the labor of the day was to be performed. He read Sidney's missive and then reread it with a prudish frown while I stood by and tried my best to not hurry him in any way. He muttered something about Washington City and a great distance, and then he looked at me as he folded the letter and slipped it inside his pocket. "What do you say to some coffee, Henry?" he said. "It will take me a bit of time to compose an answer."

Langford led me inside the cabin and motioned that I sit in a rough chair hewn and shaped out of a short stump of pine. He searched amongst a pile of pans and tin dishes until he found a dented and charred coffeepot. "Judge Edgerton is quite a man," he said with his back turned while he measured out the grounds. "I would think he would make a fine governor if he were ever afforded the chance."

I agreed with his sentiment, and I told him so. "But the way things are back in Ohio, what with the Democrats looking strong and the moderates amongst the Republicans weakening the party, I don't think Sidney—I mean Judge Edgerton—would have a chance just now."

"I suppose he could be made governor here," Langford said casually as he filled the pot with water from a bucket. "If a new territory were created, I mean."

I didn't know how they decided things like that, relating to the territories and their administration. And I said so to Langford.

"Has he ever talked about it? It would be natural for him to consider himself a candidate." Langford placed the pot on the wood stove that was used both to heat the cabin and cook meals, and then he came and sat at the table. "I don't mean to pry," he said. "It just seems logical that he would be interested in such a position, if it were available."

And then I understood that Langford wanted to hear something specific, but was reluctant to openly ask. "I would think," I said, "that he would consider it an honor to act as governor of a new territory; if he were asked, that is. And that he could do it with the help of men like you and Mr. Hauser. He speaks of you two often. Just yesterday," I said, hoping that the lie were not obvious, "the judge was commenting on how a few good men, like he and my Uncle Wilbur and you and Mr. Hauser, could make that part of the territory east of the divide into a great state, what with all the resources we've got. What was it he said? 'All it takes is a railroad, and men like Langford and Hauser, and a little hard work, to bring the future into the present.' That's how he put it, too. 'The future into the present.'"

"Langford and Hauser," Langford said caustically as he poured the coffee. "Hauser and Langford. Hauser is a Democrat. A good man, granted. But a Democrat nonetheless. Now, a railroad, that makes sense."

He wrote out his reply to Sidney while I sipped at the steaming coffee; and there was nothing there to occupy me other than to watch him as his hand moved across the page with an angry flourish, curling the ends and the beginnings of the words aggressively, and so forcefully placing the punctuation that he must have put holes in the paper when he did it. With correct and exacting precision, he folded and then sealed the completed letter with wax from a candle. And then he held it out to me without any intent of relinquishing his grip. "Now you must understand, Henry," he said, still holding on to his half of the letter while I held on to mine, "that this transmittal is of great importance. It must reach Judge Edgerton. And it must be read by no one else. Do you understand this, Henry?"

"Yes, Mr. Langford," I said. "No one is to read it. Not even me."

"That's correct, Henry," Langford said. "You are a fine young man." From his vest he pulled out two dull silver dollars, which he jingled in a half-closed fist before he placed them in my palm and nodded his head in affirmation.

Some might say I imagined it, but I now believe more strongly than ever that I was followed home that evening. Noises emanated above and behind and off the trail, more and more audible and regular as the darkness fell and the stars emerged. And twice I was approached by riders who slowed as they neared and then lingered behind me when they could have easily passed. I worried as to what I might do if I were confronted, of the probabilities of my escape and of how I could successfully hide or destroy the letter, which I knew contained some kind of information bearing overwhelming significance. And I regretted that my Uncle Sidney had denied my request that I be permitted to bring a revolver, with which, he said, I was more likely to bring myself harm than good.

Sidney had me remain still and useless like an untried militia soldier at attention, too stiff and too proper, while he read Langford's reply. It was late and the children and Mary were asleep and the cabin was soundless; only the music from Skinner's and the Goodrich and some local conversation from Durant's Billiard Hall and the trot of several horses along the street invaded the silence. I could see Sidney's eyes under the glow of the kerosene lamp as they moved slowly across the words, to the bottom of the page where something Langford had written displeased him. An angry glare overcame him, and he looked up to the beginning of the letter and then back down to the offending passage. "Damn these puny miscreants," he muttered, and he threw the almost weightless letter across the floor. "I know a Democrat when I see one. And I know when and how far they can be trusted, and how they can be used to our own advantage." He looked up at me. "Fetch me Wilbur," he said. "And hurry."

Wilbur was at his one-room cabin on Yankee Flat, sitting on his porch where he was attempting to read from his Bible by the light of the moon. My Aunt Harriet was there also, standing by his side. As I approached I found that she was engaged in a form of unilateral debate that severely impaired Wilbur's ability to read. "I am convinced the savages have identified us," she was saying in almost a whisper and anxiously gesturing with her hands, "as a permanent source of charity. This morning there were no less than four of them with their faces in the window, staring at me while I baked the morning's bread." She rambled on, alluding to the Bannocks that had set up camp near Yankee Flat as "beggars" and "scavengers" and "incurable heathens," and denouncing the very existence of the pagan and impoverished Indians in a settlement of civilized men. Such that I could only make my presence known and then wait for an opening, when I might speak without the implication of being impolite.

"Hello, Henry," she finally said in a curt acknowledgment. And then she continued. "I'm sure Henry here would agree with me. Don't you, Henry? I was emphasizing to Mr. Sanders how dangerous and immutable these Indians are. Scrounging around for scraps of food and rags when they could be putting their time productively to use. Tell him, Henry. You tell Mr. Sanders how intolerable the situation is."

"Yes. It is a problem, Uncle Wilbur. I've seen them myself," I said. Then I turned to my aunt and chanced the interruption. "I beg your pardon, Aunt Harriet, but Judge Edgerton has asked me to bring word to Wilbur. Sidney needs to speak with him immediately." At which Wilbur automatically rose and excused himself and departed into the night, leaving me to suffer under my Aunt Harriet's diatribe for the next half hour and more.

~~~

More than anything, Sidney Edgerton had succeeded in instilling in my Uncle Wilbur a strong if not somewhat myopic sense of determination. For years now, Sidney had emphasized and finally ingrained into Wilbur's way of thinking the necessity of forcing himself into and upon every situation that provided opportunity for his own advancement. And experience had provided Wilbur no basis to disbelieve the wisdom in Sidney's advice; it was Sidney's indomitable persistence that had brought Wilbur to at least peer over the very brink of power. So Wilbur followed Sidney's every cue, allowing his failures and setbacks to serve merely as points of divergence from which to transition toward even more enticing potentialities. And by this method, Wilbur Sanders far exceeded his own aptitude and limitations.

It had been obvious for some time that Sidney was embarking on some grand design to firmly carve his and Wilbur's permanent place in the burgeoning settlements of the eastern district of the territory. I knew Sidney's skill at politics, and the many associations he maintained back East dictated that he would nurture the sentiment in Washington City for the creation of a new territory east of the divide. And it was as easily foreseeable that, by Sidney's presence and position in Bannack City, he would be viewed by the Republicans—both the radicals and the moderates back East—as the logical, if not the sole, choice to assume the role of territorial governor. None of that, though, would be enough in the eyes of Sidney Edgerton. His political philosophy was one of preemption. It required, above all, that any opposition be outright eliminated, if not rendered powerless.

There had been riots in the past two years in Maryland and New York, engendered by the Union army draft and issues relating to emancipation and labor and taxation, and Sidney was ever aware of the social and political force that such mobs could bring to bear. He called them and their leaders the greatest threat to a true democracy, and in Ohio and in the halls of Congress, he had called for the suspension of their most fundamental constitutional rights in order that the great democracy might yet survive. And he and others like him—Wade and Greely of the *New York Tribune* and Thaddeus Stevens—had prevailed upon Lincoln to issue his proclamations suspending what the Democrats angrily argued were their basic liberties. So that while I never knew what Sidney said to my Uncle Wilbur that night, I knew nonetheless that some great and conclusive change was coming, and that with Sidney Edgerton as its catalyst and Wilbur Sanders as his lieutenant, it would be swift and determinative in a way that only their confidants could foresee and comprehend.

Wilbur returned home just as I managed to persuade my aunt that I needed to retire for the evening. He came up to me and stopped me before I could slip away. "Hold up there, Henry," he said as he grabbed my arm. And then he lowered his voice when he realized that his words could easily carry through the house and awaken the sleeping children and maybe even some of the closest neighbors. "You and I are going to Virginia City tomorrow. We have some business to attend to. Get your things together tonight, for a two-night stay. And go over to Peabody's and reserve two seats on the stage. Sidney says to wake Peabody if you have to. Just make sure you get those seats. And Sidney says to be sure you advise Mr. Oliver that you'll be gone." He looked over to to his wife and smiled warmly. "I'm sorry, my dear," he said. "There is no help for it. And you, Henry, I will see you in the morning. Be there a half hour before the stage departs."

It came as no surprise that Henry Plummer was there at Peabody's when the morning came. Lately, it was as though he and his deputies were everywhere at once, walking the streets on what they called patrol, intervening in even the slightest of afternoon disputes, attending the opening of businesses in the morning and the closing of every trial. Moreover, in the last month, Plummer had made it a regular practice to visit both the Edgerton and Sanders households, paying court, it almost seemed, to Sidney Edgerton in particular. On occasion, he would bring with him members of the Vail family, who seemed to hold Sidney Edgerton, whom they knew of from their past life in Ohio, in some kind of awe, as though he were not even a man but something else, a species even more complex and incomprehensible.

It was different with Henry Plummer; he stood up to Sidney and Wilbur familiarly, as if they had been acquainted before, on some equivalent and relative level of competition. And in exchange, Sidney and Wilbur treated him cordially, if not somewhat at arm's length, engaging him in diverse conversations regarding the goings on in the mining camps, exchanging ideas regarding how best the camps and the entire region might be administered and governed. And Henry Plummer plied them for information as well, artfully and with careful inquiry wondering what was afoot with the territorial government in Lewiston, or back East where most everything ultimately was decided. But if you watched closely enough, you could see that they never came together on any issue, in any way. When Sidney Edgerton declined Henry Plummer's suggestion that

Sidney act as a judge for the miners' committee, it was no more surprising than when Plummer spoke out against Sidney's proposal that an
excise tax be imposed on each mining district for the purpose of supporting the war effort in the states. I heard many such conversations,
although I seldom participated in them, and I sometimes wondered at
how Sidney and Henry Plummer could persist in what seemed to be
such fruitless and broad-ranging banter.

When Henry Plummer saw me walking away from Peabody's, I
thus knew he would come up to me and at least exchange a pleasantry.
"Off on business, Henry Tilden?" he said when he saw my small traveling bag. "It's a fine day for it."

I smiled wanly and looked about for Wilbur and, when I did not
see him, answered, "Yes, I am, Sheriff. To Virginia City."

I knew that Henry Plummer had killed more than just one man.
But so had a good share of the soldiers you could see walking down any
avenue in any city or town in Ohio. It had more to do with how deliberate and cool Plummer was, how he never flinched or wavered under
any circumstance. He was undeniably a leader of men, just as was Sidney
Edgerton, and that meant that he was far more capable of affecting a
large number of lives, like a general in the field, than might a single
sharpshooter, however remarkable his aim, picking off a careless officer
here and there. So you had to respect him in that way, and to fear him
also, since the two sentiments were mostly one in the same.

"Then that's a fine stroke of good luck for me," he said. "I'm off
in the same direction. We might even be going to see the same people.
You're not planning to visit Doc Glick, are you?"

"No, I'm not," I answered; and then without thinking I began to
add, "We're meeting with Sam . . . ," when Wilbur came up and grabbed
my shoulder sharply.

"Good morning, Sheriff," Wilbur said without enthusiasm to
Henry Plummer, who tipped his hat. "Seeing the stage off this morning?"

Wilbur was none too pleased to learn that Henry Plummer would
be on the stage for the entire ride to Virginia City. After offering some

utterly meaningless conversation, he excused himself and me from the sheriff's presence and then turned to face me directly. "What did he say to you, Henry? What did he want?"

"Nothing, Uncle," I said. And I was glad Wilbur had arrived and cut me off. "He just said he was planning to see Doc Glick. I mean we were just talking general like."

"Be careful," Wilbur said. "Our business is ours alone, and of no concern to anyone else."

Once Wilbur and Henry Plummer got in the stage together, the one almost seemed to try to top the other with courtesy and conversation, easing from one topic to the next in order to maintain their dialogue. But underneath their talk there was a constant strain, a tension such as that which exists between two newly introduced fighting cocks, with their necks stiff and their eyes watching every movement and gesture of the other.

All the way to Bunton's Rattlesnake Ranch, the conversation between Henry Plummer and Wilbur Sanders was particularly general, almost stupid in its lack of consequence and merit. Each seemed to struggle to outdo the other in mentioning and then dwelling on the mundane. By noon we were far past the Rattlesnake, and then it seemed they could not agree on anything. They had worn thin of their conversation, but they did not argue. Wilbur offered an observation regarding the war or the miners' committee and Henry Plummer politely listened and then observed that he firmly and on both philosophic and practical grounds disagreed. And then Plummer commented on how the various forms of recreation available to the miners were necessary to provide an outlet for the men, and Wilbur rebutted the proposition by phlegmatically characterizing the halls and hurdy gurdys and saloons with biblical allusions and indignant epithet.

They went on for maybe two straight hours, neither man being willing to quit the game first and suggest capitulation. And all the while, the remaining passengers—a couple of miners and a merchant on his way to Virginia City from Salt Lake City and a middle-aged smallish lady dressed in a somber black outfit from head to toes—pretended not to listen and yet heard it all, word for word as the stage jolted over the rutted and potholed road and the scenery of foothill and distant mountain passed without notice by the two men who would not and could not remove their eye from its vigil of the other.

It was the lady who finally broke the impasse by interjecting herself into the conversation. She lifted the black lace veil from over her eyes and laid it back along her hat where it still could not hide the grey and wiry aspect of her hair. "Excuse me, gentlemen," she said; and when she spoke her disformed and yellow teeth showed for the first time, protruding outward, distending from her skull in a most grotesquely gothic manner. "Am I correct in presuming you are Henry Plummer. Sheriff Henry Plummer?"

And Plummer said, "Yes, ma'am, I am," smiling at her courteously, with the same warmth he was known to offer to every member of the fairer sex, regardless of age or looks or disposition.

"I have been looking forward to meeting you," she said with an odd inflection. "I am Winnefred O'Malley. Nurse O'Malley. Your miners' committee in Virginia City hired me to come all the way from Sacramento to attend at your new hospital. When I wrote back and told them I would not accept the job unless there was law in place, they informed me that you had been hired as sheriff. Of course, coming from California, I had heard mention of you from your time as sheriff in Nevada City. You seem to have recovered from your illness. I'm sure that Governor Weller will be glad to hear that your health has been returned unexpectedly in full."

You could have taken the meaning behind her comments in any of several ways. To my Uncle Wilbur, they implied that Henry Plummer was experienced and well connected. "I didn't know you were acquainted with John Weller, Sheriff," he said. "A Democrat, is he not?"

"I'm not aware of his current politics," Henry Plummer answered. And yet he did not pick up on her conversation and instead moved to redirect it. "I am confident, Nurse O'Malley, you will find the facilities respectable under the circumstances. I supervised the solicitations of the donations myself. There were some very admirable contributions."

For my part, I thought I had detected something cynical in her tone. Maybe just disrespect for mining camps, I thought, and I let it go.

"I hadn't realized the hospital was ready for patients," Wilbur said.

Henry Plummer looked over to Nurse O'Malley. "I only wish that it had been built sooner. I was just about to suggest to my companion here, Colonel Sanders, that he join me in a visit there tomorrow morning." He turned to Wilbur and said, "Will you consider it, Colonel? You might find it interesting. I put one patient in a cot myself last week. He got to thinking he might rob Kiskadden's and it cost him a ball in the arm."

Whatever our business in Virginia City was, it was urgent, and so I was surprised when Wilbur said, "Yes, of course. You name the time."

For the remainder of the ride, including a change of horses at Dempsey's Cottonwood, which was effected so quickly by Dempsey's men that there was time only to drink from the well and stretch out the body cramps before returning to the tight uncomfortable carriage seats, there seemed a great degree of tension between Henry Plummer and Nurse O'Malley, who seemed to stare intently. But I easily could have imagined all of it. The sway of the Concord coach was enough to make one sick, as might be expected in a seagoing vessel during a high seas storm; and as if that were not enough, the dust kicked up by the horses and the wheels drifted into the coach through every crack and then seemed to float inertly in the carriage in a sort of diminutive cloud. So that if you were not made nauseous or head sick by the ride, the moted air would surely get you in the end.

~~~

That night, in Sam Hauser's cabin, Wilbur kept turning Hauser's Bible over and over in his hands, rubbing his thumb again and again across and into a deep indentation in the leather where a Crow bullet had struck the book that summer, saving Sam Hauser's life. "The Lord may not be your shepherd, Mr. Hauser, but he certainly is your savior. He must have greater plans for you than to die at the hand of a savage."

"That may be, Colonel. May be. But there were other men with us that day on the Yellowstone that held up to the expectations of the Lord and yet never made it back. Henry Geery and Ephraim Bostick and good ole Cyrus Watkins, to name the best. And when you consider that that blackguard George Ives was with us, and that he came out of it with only a flesh wound on his leg, you almost have to wonder whether it isn't God's will that his flock take care of its own."

"Certainly," Wilbur broke in, "I will agree with you if what you are saying is that the Bible tells us to protect what is ours, and to turn back evil."

And Hauser, who sensed that his agreement on the point would be prudent, affirmed that Wilbur's interpretation was a fair one.

"I will presume then," Wilbur said, "that we are also in agreement as concerns our need to seize control of the situation here."

"If you mean this bipartisan proposition that I join Langford on this journey East to promote the new territory, yes, I'll go as the Democrat to the entourage. Particularly after what that nurse told you about Henry Plummer. I don't care how much local support he has; the man was convicted of murder. Pardon or not, he has no right to accept the position of a lawman after that. And certainly not to apply for a deputy marshal's appointment. You may tell the judge that I will go, gladly, and meet with Congressman Ashley. Although I must say I'm surprised that Langford is willing to make the trip alone, if need be, at such a time when there's so much money to be made here. That is not like him, I can tell you."

Wilbur placed the Bible back gently on the table. "I think you can safely assume that there will be a lucrative role for both you and Mr. Langford once a new government is constituted. Besides, we are all going to have to take some risks and suffer some inconveniences in the days ahead."

Hauser's cabin was located on the edge of Virginia City, which meant nothing in terms of quietude or isolation because the entirety of Virginia City and its environs were churning with a random, endless flux of activity that knew no temporal or physical bounds, as an army camp in bivouac might be were there no reveille and taps and protocol to contain it and give it time to rest. So we had not even surprised him by our late-evening arrival at his doorstep, the advent of an unannounced visitor at any hour being almost an expectation, a given; and he had welcomed us genuinely and insisted that we spend the night as his guests. The two men spoke with each other for a long time while I sat and listened, late into the night, to the sounds of the saloons and hurdy gurdys surging in and out of hearing like the roar of a flooding river above the noise of a pelting rain and blowing wind, until I finally fell asleep and they threw a heavy buffalo robe over me and continued their conversation in lowered and yet emphatic voices that pulled me in and out of my slumber. And they were already discussing their business again in the morning when I awoke to the smell of the lighted kerosene lamp and the overbrewed coffee and to the permeating heat of the wood stove.

Throughout their conversations, I could hear Wilbur repeatedly impress upon Hauser how necessary it was for government to be brought officially and in all its tripartite aspects to the mining settlements. But Hauser only seemed to honestly agree when Wilbur raised points concerning the integrity of commerce and financial opportunity and the necessity for security from the highwaymen. Then Hauser would chime in with a plethora of ideas of his own. When it came to civic questions of schools and hospitals and churches, of improvements for the miners in general or for the Indians who scoured all the mining camps for anything they might be able to sell or eat, Hauser became instantly oblivious and nonplused; and when Wilbur said he had an appointment to inspect the new hospital, Hauser reacted with indifference. "You'd be better served by having breakfast with me and Paris Pfouts over at the Arbor. Paris is a good man to know, as long as you can keep him away from the cards. A first rate Union man."

Wilbur reached for his coat and then signaled for me to follow. "I'd say I'm better served at the moment by keeping an eye on our friend Henry Plummer, which is exactly what I intend to do."

Hauser shrugged his shoulders. "If you say so, Colonel. I'll expect you back this evening."

"Thank you, Mr. Hauser," Wilbur said. "We shall be here. And give my apologies to your Mr. Pfouts. Perhaps we can meet this afternoon should I return early."

The fact that it was a Sunday, the only nonworkday out of the week, made all the difference in the world. It was daylight, only midway through a delightfully cool early-November morning, and as I walked along Wallace Street, the crowds—mostly of men but a few women and children there amongst them—surged around and past me, in wagons, on horses and mules, afoot, up and down every side street and alley and into and out of every doorway and tent flap, anxious and self-consumed even though it was yet morning and the whole day and the entire night remained before it would be Monday again and the work would resume in earnest. It made me thankful that Wilbur had dismissed me from any obligation to visit the hospital. Because I had been to enough of them back in Ohio, where it seemed every other adult male friend and acquaintance and relative you had ended up, lying listlessly on an army cot in the cold sweat of an unbreakable fever or bereft of an arm or leg or eye lost in some great battle or minor skirmish with the rebels, and all you could do was to look at them and maybe wipe their brow with a damp cloth and try not to stare at the blank flat space where there should have been an arm, a leg, an eye, and tell them you were sorry and that you were their friend and that they would get better, when you knew all the while that they and you would never, never again be the same. So I welcomed the opportunity to run the errands Sidney and Wilbur had laid out, rather than walk about the sickly and the injured and smell their sickness and the rot the orderlies could never fully wash away.

At Dance & Stuart's I delivered a sealed letter to James Stuart. He laughed about the Bible when I told him that Sam Hauser had showed it to us. "Far's I know," he said, "Hauser never once opened that book until it stopped that ball. Whenever someone asked him why he was carrying it, all he'd say is 'For luck.' Makes you wonder why he don't keep carrying it, now that he knows it works." And as I left, the clubfooted cobbler who had been allowed to set up a stand in the back of the store, and who seemed to be doing a fine business with dozens of shoes and boots laid out for repair, winked at me once in acknowledgment of James Stuart's good company and sense of humor.

And then, having sought out and delivered the sealed envelopes to Captain Fox and several other men, all that remained for me was to purchase for Mary Edgerton the baking yeast and other sundries that had run short at Chrisman's and at Thompson & Swift's, and for the children whatever odds and ends might suit their fancy. And then my time was my own, and I began to spend it well, bathing in my own freedom and independence as I walked down the streets and into the menagerie of stores and shops and even the makeshift storefronts and offices.

What went on at most of the business establishments in Virginia City was not really any different than what went on in any other town. People went into stores and browsed and bought what they wanted or could afford, and then left. Through the door of the barber's an unshaven or unkempt miner would enter, while another, clean shaven and neatly groomed, would exit. Hungry and thirsty men moved into the restaurants and saloons, and others left, having had their fill. Orders were placed and filled; shoes were shined; deals struck.

But when I came to the hurdy gurdy and stood on the boardwalk and looked inside each time the door swung open and then closed, there was none of that reliable consistency that characterized the other establishments. Each time the door opened and I looked in, the scene within the dark, smoky confines seemed altogether different from the last. On one viewing, I might see a pretty girl, in a lacy flowing gown, being twirled across the floor gracefully by an unseen hand; and on another, a dirty and drunken miner stumbling across the floor, and somehow not knocking someone over as he fell. The door would open, and I would hear the steely twang of the music, and then close as I heard a whoop and a call for a different dance. And then the door would open again, and through the narrow view I would see a neatly dressed merchant or businessman holding one of the dancing girls closely and hardly even dancing at all. Then the door would close, and the brightness of the day would envelope me as the sounds became muffled, until it opened again, and the dancers had changed once more in appearance and demeanor and in almost every other way.

I stood there for a long while, wanting to go in but knowing that I could not. And then, suddenly, there was my Uncle Wilbur, looming up in front of me, with Sam Hauser and another man I did not know. "Why, Henry," Wilbur said playfully, in a manner very much unlike himself, as if he were trying to impress the others with his cleverness. "It is a good thing we have chanced upon you. Here you stand within a pitchfork's throw of the devil's very den, and you don't even know it."

The other men with him laughed and exchanged looks connoting humored wisdom and infinite maturity. But Wilbur only looked at me with a paternal and benevolent smile. And he put his arm around my shoulder and drew me even closer as he and Hauser and Paris Pfouts moved off across the street.

CHAPTER 4

By mid-November the coyotes had come down out of the elevations to slink and ply about the foothills in search of the deer and elk that lingered for the rut. You could hear their cacophony sporadically through the night and early morning, wild and erratic and full of play, and see their sign up to the very edge of the houses and buildings that to the human settlers defined and described Bannack, but which to the coyotes implied only unnatural intrusion. Just as the Crows and the Sparrow Hawks and the Blackfeet must have seen it as they were pushed back, deep into the diminishing wild. Leaving their marks clandestinely, as if to give notice, to aver, "You can move us back, take from us what is heritable to us, but we will never wholly succumb, not until the grasses die and never green again and the clouds wither in the sky and you and what is yours fails first, so that the last of us might see your fall before we return into the womb that is the earth." So you could walk out of your cabin in the morning and step behind it to relieve yourself in the privy, and you would see the coyote scat there in the middle of a path where you could not miss it, or you would note their track, the small sure even footprints of their tireless vigil, and you would know that they had been there while you slept, defiant and searching and vital late into the night.

When their sound woke me again, for the third time since I had dropped my head upon the pillow and pulled Mrs. Gibson's moth-bitten blankets over me, I rose, too tired of it to even fight it anymore and not even waiting for Mrs. Gibson's knock to wake me, or for the yet undawned light to invade my sleep through the narrow window. Then there was nothing to do but go to the Goodrich or LeGrau's Bakery, where they almost never closed their doors. Go and have coffee, I thought; find warmth from this merciless cold.

Along the street a few horses and mules were tethered to posts and railing, their dark forms standing out like motionless and riderless statues. Otherwise, the town seemed empty; no wind nor breeze nor sound but for the scattered yipping that had faded far downcanyon, nothing but a settled cold under an oppressive and starless sky. Then I saw them moving down off the slope on the south side of the creek in a thin silent shadowy line, one by one like grey apparitions from out of an ancient vision, picking their way down the freight road and over the creek where the water passed not far from the Edgerton cabin. A half score of them at least, silent and bowed and yet somehow still proud, still noble, despite the half-white man and half-Indian dress that I knew they wore. And I alone of every other soul in Bannack City watched them as they crossed the road and hugged the northern edge of the diminutive valley, their horses somehow perfectly silent also, fading back into the shadow of the dark, passing in a long line behind Skinner's and the Goodrich, where the lights shone and the smoke of a rekindled fire billowed from the chimney. And I alone noted how silent and ghostlike and unreal they were as they struck the road again and rode up, past the cemetery, which to them was heathen, and over the ridge and out of sight.

The quiet sat eerily upon and over the town, over Skinner's and the Goodrich and the long row of bachelor's cabins and shops and bakery and assay office, so that the faint tread of my footsteps seemed almost like an invasion into an otherwise silent dream. I stopped, intrigued by the light in Chrisman's store, where I knew Henry Plummer sleeplessly stood guard over a shipment of gold that Sam Hauser and Langford planned to carry east as a service to Stuart and Dance and several other Virginia City merchants. The light glowed behind the muslin curtains, and there was a noise in the back of the building; and I remained motion-less, hesitant, unsure that I should call on him and let him know about the Indians, notify first the very man that Sidney Edgerton would call upon last. And all the while, the calm, predawn silence pervaded, absolute and dimensionless, resistant to the very cold. And then from out of nothingness, a whispered voice broke the peace with words of violent promise: "Move 1 inch," it said, "and you're dead." Convincingly, it said, "Empty your hands and put them over your head."

The words terrified me, such that it was only natural that my stomach would twist and my nerves excite and my throat thicken when I heard them and felt the hard narrow circle of steel in the middle of my back. "I'm Henry Tilden, Judge Edgerton's nephew," I pleaded. "Don't shoot. I'm unarmed."

Then I heard a different voice behind me, different and yet formed by the same mouth, same throat, tongue, lips, lungs, saying this time, not whispering because somehow it was no longer necessary, "You're going to get yourself hurt, Henry Tilden, sneaking around in the dark like a thief," and then a strong hand on my shoulder turned me firmly and evenly until I found myself face-to-face with Henry Plummer.

It was the only time I ever saw him unshaved and unkempt. The faint light emphasized a fatigue that had settled darkly around his eyes; and even his overcoat, a fine woolen red-flannel-lined greatcoat, hung on him heavily, as though his tired shoulders slumped beneath its weight. "You must have something important on your mind to be here at such an hour," he said. "Come around back and we'll get warmed up some."

The heavy nasal snore of a restless sleeper came from the barred window of the jail behind Chrisman's, tempered by the running gurgle of the creek—probably a drunken miner receiving a free night's stay at what my Uncle Wilbur called the Henry Plummer Inn. The lock to

Plummer's office snapped open and the door swung and the light glared out intensely over both of us. He was taller than I remembered, and more drawn and dour.

Inside, the light starkly illuminated everything, the neatly arranged office brightly defined in every spartan aspect, and everything outside, the brush and jail and hills, spectrally vague and shadowed. And as he closed and bolted the door behind us, I heard, even farther off than before, a last chorus of the wild and piercing screams of a lone member of the coyote pack.

He took me through the doorway that separated Chrisman's store from his narrow office, setting the bolt there also; and he directed me to a chair behind the counter, on top of which he had stacked sacks of flour and sugar and potatoes to protect him from an assault. Only then did he release the hammer of his double action army revolver, slowly lowering it down; and then he pulled the second revolver, a Navy Colt, from his waistband and set it down also. He removed two extra loaded cylinders from his coat pocket. And then a Green River knife, short and thick and shining from a recent whetting. So that, all told, it was a most impressive arsenal, with the double barrels of the sawed shotgun each filled with a handful of lead balls, and the two revolvers loaded and ready to be changed out and fired again, and the knife, more reliable than the pistols that might misfire and the shotgun that lost in its accuracy as much as it gained in its devastation. Each weapon handled by Henry Plummer with a deft familiarity that bordered on unconsciousness, as though the weapons represented an extension of his hand, his arm, and very thought.

He removed his coat, the bloodred flannel flashing for a moment as he folded it and draped it over a chair. "Now, what is it, Henry?" he asked, his back turned. "I trust there's no problem over at Mrs. Gibson's."

I could see that he had barricaded the front door with packing crates and a heavy chest, and that a chain had been looped through an iron ring attached to the door. "No, it's not that, Sheriff Plummer," I answered. "It's Indians . . . a whole lot of 'em . . . just five minutes ago. Passed right through town. I saw 'em myself." The words tripped over each other as I told it.

"Is that right?" He said with a false tone of surprise. "And how, may I ask, did you alone happen to hear and see these Indians when no one else in Bannack seems to even have been disturbed from their sleep?"

"The coyotes woke me. I came out to . . . to listen to them. That's when I saw them, coming down south off the road and across the street and up the other side."

"And you decided to come right here when you might have gone over to Judge Edgerton's?"

"The fact is, Sheriff, I wasn't sure what to do. I reckoned the Edgertons were still asleep, but I knew you were over here guarding that gold Mr. Hauser and Mr. Langford are taking back East; so I came over to tell you."

A slow, easy smile came over Henry Plummer's face. "Did you ever stop to think, Henry," he said, and then he paused as if to afford me one last opportunity to discover on my own what he was about to reveal, "given as how Mr. Hauser and Mr. Langford took it upon themselves to boast to the whole town how much gold they were taking with them out of the Gulch, that every road agent and thief for a hundred miles around has heard about it? And that I've been sitting here all night waiting for one or five or ten of their number to show up and make their claim on it? Have you thought of those things, Henry? Because if you had, you wouldn't go sneaking around where gold's being kept."

Henry Plummer had always been kind to me, almost to the point of patronizing. So I said, "I'm sorry, Sheriff. I didn't mean to bother you. I thought they were going to raid the town. I wasn't sure what to do."

He cut me off then, before I could ramble on some more. "You're not disturbing anyone," he said. "I didn't say that. It's my job to be disturbed. And it's my job to shoot when there's a need for it. I'm only telling you what's best for you. So you don't go getting in your own way.

So that your time comes naturally and not prematurely in the middle of the night by a bullet or a knife in the back."

He poured out some of the steaming coffee that had been simmering on the top of the stove. "Now tell me all of it: how many there were; what they were wearing; which way they went."

I told him, and he asked more questions that made me remember more, of how they had no extra mounts, and the way they rode in single file.

He walked over to the stove and replaced the pot. A thin self-assured look came over his face. And then he asked, seeking reaffirmation, "And which way did you say they were moving, Henry?" And when I said north, up the freight road, he said, "Good. Because if it had been up or down the creek, we'd have us a problem, what with the way every miner and settler along the Grasshopper has got a mind to shoot the first intruder he sees." Up close, I could see the pale white trace of a scar running along his hairline. And when he moved to drink his coffee, an awkward stiffness was evident in the movement of his wrist.

In the silence that followed he seemed lost, looking backwards into his mind, processing thoughts. So I struggled with it too, puzzled over what I had seen and been made to recall. But it made no sense to me, a pack of braves out in the night without the wherewithal to spend any meaningful time in the cold of the failing autumn. Because I knew that much. You couldn't help but know some. You couldn't load up a wagon out of St. Joseph and travel all that way and see the smoke, at times, in the distance, and their wide, dark, expressionless faces up close at the trading posts and forts, and note the lonely graves along the trail, and hear the stories and the talk of anxious men in quieted voices, and not learn some things about them. So I knew at least that the Indians I had seen were not merely moving their camp from one place to the next, or hunting without the pack animals they would need to bring the downed meat back to their families and homes. "They must be up to something," I finally said.

Through the veiled windows I could see lights beginning to shine across the street in other buildings as the day came on. Henry Plummer saw them also, and he walked over to the curtains and slowly drew them open. "I suppose you're right, Henry." He did not look at me but rather peered out the window, carefully, with untrusting precaution. "Thing to do would be to find out anyways. There's folks depending on us to keep things straight." He walked across the floor to the counter. And as he began to remove the sacks and place them on the shelves, he said, "I could use a favor right now, Henry. I should say a second favor since you've already done me the one today. Will you fetch me Ned Ray, from over at Madame Hall's? And Buck Stinson, too, from Yankee Flat, if you can find him without trouble? Can you do that for me, Henry? I'd go myself, but I don't think Nat Langford and Sam Hauser would much appreciate the breach of trust."

~~~

Sidney Edgerton was furious when he learned, not much later that morning, what had transpired. "You went to him first, when I and your uncle and Sam Hauser and Mr. Langford were sitting wide awake at the Goodrich the entire time! Sometimes I cannot believe your indiscretion, Henry. Of all people to turn to. Henry Plummer. Of all people. It is far beyond belief."

In his condemnation he allowed me no opportunity to explain, to defend myself and my innocence. There had been no lights showing at the Edgerton cabin. And no reason for me to check at the Goodrich first. I had done the only logical thing under the circumstances. As it was, though, there was no viable defense to Sidney Edgerton's anger, being arbitrary and repressive and not receptive to reason and understanding. And I consequently did not even try, accepting the rebuke as I always did.

The irony of it was that what Sidney Edgerton no doubt perceived as punishment was, to me, an opportunity for expiation and relief. He said, in a pronouncement of sentence, you will go to Horse

Prairie this morning and herd the oxen and return by nightfall; and I said "Yes, sir," but in my mind thought "Thank God, a reprieve from this insanity."

Mary knew it was unjust of him to treat me so. She went to great lengths to prepare me a fine breakfast, utilizing several of the precious eggs and giving me the freshest biscuits when they might have gone to little Wright and Pauline; and then she packed me a more than suitable lunch to take upon the road.

What I wanted most to take with me, though, was a pistol; and now I could not even ask. Which was not fair, not sensible. Because I could shoot one well enough. Sidney had insisted on that much before we even left Ohio. And I had practiced at it sufficiently to be able to raise the revolver up and fire it with reasonably accurate aim without ever having to hold it up high, and sight along the barrel, like my Uncle Wilbur. Over at the stables where Jonah was always kept, I considered asking Will Pearson if I could borrow one from him. Only, when I subtly raised the topic of revolvers, he said he did not have one, had no access to one. "What you want one for, anyway?" he asked as he led out Jonah.

"Just want one for the road today. I'm going up to Horse Prairie to round up the oxen, and . . . well, there's been some Indians about today you know. I just thought it would be a comfort to have a revolver close at hand. Just in case, I mean."

He looked at me and shook his head and paused as if he were thinking. "You like to fish?" he finally asked.

"Sure I do." I answered. "Who doesn't?"

"Well, you never know." He bridled Jonah and I followed him as he went into the tack room for the saddle. "I'm heading out that way, too. To Horse Prairie, I mean. Got two horses to fetch," he said through the doorway. "Thought I'd show you my secret hole; if you're interested, I mean."

I didn't know Will Pearson all that well, other than to converse with him when the occasion might arise, at which times he most often regaled me with one tale or another in a manner that reflected that he seemed to know a lot about girls, and women too. And thus, while he seemed nice enough in his own slow Missourian way, it was difficult to become familiar with him. And my wish that the likes of him and Joseph Swift would let me into their inner circle never matured any further than a mere and passing acquaintance.

"You don't have to if you don't want to," he said. "I mean I'm not dying to let other people know where the best trout this side of the mountains are."

"It's not that," I said. "It's just that I'm not sure I've got the time."

And Will Pearson said, "Suit yourself. I was only asking."

When I knew I could not prudently resist the opportunity any longer, I said, "I'd sure like to take a crack at that hole."

There was a commotion on the street as we came out from around back of the stable, men teeming about Thompson & Swift's and Skinner's and milling in the street with that same wild frenzy I had seen a half dozen times, each new placer or mine or prospect that showed good color catalyzing a wild scramble, the same frantic panic starting up again after its last affair with disappointment and scarcity, predictable in its urgency no matter the time of day or the inclemency of the weather. And you knew that no matter what it was all about, within minutes the facts would become entirely exaggerated and reality entirely confused, and half the men, out of contentment or prudence or wisdom or maybe just laziness would see it sooner than the others and would go back to their own business, and the other half would identify the man whom luck had graced and would follow him about until he revealed the location of his discovery.

Will Pearson could only indicate his disgust as we rode by. "You would think they'd have learned by now," he said. And I was ready to agree until I saw several of them talking quietly, almost secretly, with Henry Plummer, and I could not help but wonder whether there had been another silver find.

We followed the freight road at a casual pace and I did not mind at all that Will Pearson talked in his usual boastful fashion while I merely rode along listening, looking up at the great expanse of sky and mountain, and more than half believing that I was seeing the occasional tracks of unshod horses. So he rode ahead of me, talking aloud without turning his head, as though I were in front of him and not in back, and his conversation seemed to hang in the crisp breezy air. After a while we turned off the road, onto the rutted path that mostly was used for stock but which also traced, in two narrow parallel lines that jogged irregularly around and over the terrain, the worn path of the wagons that had been used by the hay cutters and by the butchers too, and by any number of rustlers who would wend their way out to the prairie and slaughter and steal the cattle that were grazed there. Only, long before we approached the prairie, Will Pearson suddenly veered off the trail, and then we were departed from and disassociated with anything that connoted the presence of white men and civilization, moving toward the dark forested mountains into which the likes of Lewis and Clark and Jedediah Smith and the fur traders had cut their paths in search of new routes and beaver ponds.

By the time Will Pearson led the way into the drainage where the water from a substantial clear-water creek pooled and collected in a gleaming basin, into a smallish canyon dappled with elders and birch, he had earned from me a newfound and not inconsiderable respect. Because there was no place like it I had ever seen, no place else on earth where you could look down into water so clear, to such unclouded depths, and see such perfectly formed fish idly fanning the imperceptible current of the water in such utter contentment and with such absolute disregard for that other alien world that lay just above the surface. With the rock walls obscuring, and the trees thickly trunked and leafless now and yet still alive and vigorous with their roots reaching well into the water, and the rock itself smoothed by the winds and rains and splitting freezes of time, and yet resistant to it. And the fish more than idle, almost inert, as though, having reached this state of total perfection, there was nothing left for them but to rest, motionless and content in their own existence beneath the shading canyon walls.

We sat for a long while on the boulders above, and said nothing, sat watching the glassy surface and the flitting movements of silver flecked with shimmering color, until I finally asked what he knew I must be thinking. "How is it you know about this place?" Asking because it seemed impossible that it was there and more so that he had found it.

"I just kept looking for it," he said, and when he looked up at me, he saw that I did not understand his meaning. "I don't mean I knew it was out there somewhere," he said. "Just that I knew I wanted it to be here, that everywhere else I went was not good enough, not enough to make me want to stay, to stop looking for a better place where I could get away from all the madness." And still I did not understand, and I said so. "In a way it's just like all these miners down in Bannack," he said. "They're all looking for something too. And most of 'em have been looking for a long time. Not just for gold and silver because that's not enough to keep 'em long. Moving from place to place and never seeming to be happy with what they find even though they know that the next place can't keep holding out more than the last. Like most of 'em really aren't looking for anything at all and really are just keeping themselves busy. Like Hermie Fraily and John Dutton, giving and throwing away every lick of gold they dig out before the creek water even dries off it. You see what I mean? We're all looking. Constantly. Only there's some who aren't really trying to find something or wouldn't know what it was if it kicked 'em in the face. Wouldn't know enough to move on and admit that whatever it is they need is not where they're presently standing."

And I said, "Okay. I understand." Because I wanted him to stop. And then I thought I saw the fallacy in his philosophy, so I asked, "Only what happens when you look and look and look and don't find it and have no reason to believe you ever will?"

"You either quit, like Hank Crawford did, or you keep looking anyway, like Henry Plummer." And then he threw a pebble into the water and the fish spread instantly, outracing in flashes of speed the single concentric wave of ripples that spread out and faded across the surface, only to instantly stop and resume their perfect immobilized stasis. "And I'll tell you this much," he added. "The more I watch what goes on in Bannack City, I mean with all of us, my father and the Masons and Chrisman and Bunton and Judge Edgerton and even Henry Plummer, all of 'em, the more I can't tell which ones know what they're looking for or looking at, and which ones have quit looking or are likely to keep on looking until it gets the better of 'em. And the one thing that's for certain is that they all can't have at the same time whatever it is that they want. Least not in Bannack City. Because where the one sees white, the other sees black. And it can't be both. Not now and not later. No matter how much they want it to be, and no matter how long they try."

We sat there on the edge of his sanctuary for a long while with the world seemingly frozen and immutable in and below and above the water. And Will Pearson never did make any pretense of having brought with him a line or cork or hook or bait with which he might try to capture one of the trout that were even larger than life itself and which almost seemed to watch and tolerate us without concern. And it finally became evident to me that he had none of those things with him, that he never would have even considered it.

It was long past noon when we finally left, rising up reluctantly and moving with slow even motions to not disturb the fish in our final moments beside the pool. And I would almost swear that Jonah sensed it too, that he moved down out of the elevations trancelike and effortlessly. And when we came to the beginnings of the smooth waving grasses of Horse Prairie, to the edge of Martin Barrett's expansive ranch where the stock were allowed to freely range, it was as if the two geldings that Will Pearson had been sent to retrieve knew that he was coming for them, and they were thus waiting for him.

For two hours he helped me search out and then drive Sidney Edgerton's oxen across the prairie and by then the clouds that had moved in from the west had blanketed the ground with several inches of light powdery snow. And I knew then that I had delayed too long, because one of the oxen was still not accounted for and I had had ample time and Sidney Edgerton would not yet have forgotten enough of the morning to not carry his anger over with the least provocation into the night. "I can't help you anymore," Will Pearson said while we moved the animals into the common corral that stood out near the trailhead. "These horses are promised for this evening."

So I thanked him, and he melted into what was still merely blowing snow but could quick become blizzard, with his geldings roped and following blithely behind him. For another hour I search with the snow aggregating and the day failing and then failed, and I never did find that last ox. Which was the best for me in the end since it made my delay more plausible, and it was concluded long afterwards that the poor animal had been taken by thieves or wolves or Indians, or by one of the scavenging grizzlies that roamed far out across the western grassland plain. I shut the remainder of the oxen inside the corral, turning my back on the black, stupid eyes, and then I cut Jonah onto the trail that was fast becoming obscured and moved him out at a steady trot to beat the darkening storm and falling cold back home to Bannack City.

It had been far too long of a day, and I had hoped that it was now finally over. But it was not, the day that had been so lengthened by its premature beginning now unwilling to end. So that while that should have been the end of it, the ride home merely conclusory, it was not to be, because I was already late and I hurried to mitigate my tardiness. And in so doing, at the gallop at which Jonah took me through the blowing snow that was not white but instead bluish and grey in the night, I, we, horse and rider, first became lost and disoriented with nothing visible by which to know anything of direction, and then finally finding it, the faint indented snow-covered outline of the road and guessing somehow, rightly, what was north and which south, only to run faster, to make up the time that had been bargained away and then lost after it had already been spent, and blindly colliding with two riders who instantly drew their revolvers. And, I believe, they would just as soon have shot first and then ascertained whether I had some intent of robbing them, had I not cried out and showed them I was unarmed. Which only made me afterwards ride even harder, risking not only another collision with unseen and unknown riders, but risking also all the rest, all there might be of savagery and evil and misfortune in one wild race through the sheaf of frozen ice. And not even ending it then, the day that had been prematurely lengthened and then unexpectedly suspended and lastly prolonged by failure and misdirection, but instead running Jonah, who knew only that it was fear alone that we were sharing, and that the only way to share it, to have some comfort together in it, was to run to beat even the wind and time itself, flying over the snow-covered ground and the hills and past the shrubs and the trees, wildly and yet with an evenness that did not suggest rhythm but rather agreement in fear, into the Bannack ditch, which had been drifted over by blowing snow. Which is the last that I remembered until they woke me, Mary and Sidney Edgerton, with looks of great and real caring—recalling lastly and only the sudden complete collapse of Jonah's forelegs, and the effortless sensation of floating as I sailed over his head, which at once was below and then behind me, remembering that, and the seemingly distant sound of my scream that pierced the Bannack City night.

CHAPTER 5

or all the misery in which the nation was ignobly mired, with the dreadful squalor of the Civil War subsuming it daily and the overwhelming philosophic and practical questions of the day dividing it in every manner possible—politically, geographically, ethnically—Lincoln still justified decreeing that on a certain day in November, the nation would pause to reflect upon, and would offer thanks for, that which had been proffered divinely to it. And with the Edgertons being so proudly and religiously in the fore of organized support for the Union, and Mary Edgerton taking such matriarchal pride in the quality and sumptuousness of her table, I knew it to be a sore trial for her to accept that the entirety of the adult faction of the Edgerton and Sanders families would make themselves guest to the holiday feast to be hosted by Henry Plummer.

"We have no choice in the matter, Mother," Judge Edgerton said in response to her objection, throwing his scarf down on the table to show at least that he also was not pleased by the predicament. "He has made the invitation to us, and I was not prepared at the moment to contrive an excuse. You may take heart in the fact that Francis Thompson will be there, as well as Wilbur and George Chrisman and the Balls and plenty of others. I am sorry, Mary," he said, shaking his head, "but under the circumstances I thought it best to play along with him. I understand he has gone to great lengths to ensure that it be a day not to be forgotten in Bannack. That makes our presence imperative; if we fail to attend, we will be seen as being even less a part of this place."

My Aunt Mary sighed and wiped her hands on her apron and as much as shoved me out of her way when I was there to help her prepare the table. She removed his scarf and began to set out the evening's meal with a cold mechanical precision. "All right then," she said in disgust. "And you may fairly expect that I will be courteous about it, too. But I shall not exaggerate as to the quality of the food, nor the company. I can assure you of that. These Vail people are as common a lot as I have ever seen. I will not overplay their significance, no matter whether they have relation with your Mr. Plummer."

It had been a hard two days for all of us. Uncle Wilbur still had not fully recovered from the humiliation he had suffered after being compelled by Sidney, on the very day Will Pearson took me to his special place, to pursue Henry Plummer and a group of well-mounted miners who had dashed northward into the wintry weather for reasons rumored to relate to a new quartz strike laden with rich veins of silver. In his anxious, almost blind desire to capitalize on new financial opportunities, Sidney had insisted that Wilbur join the foray even though Henry Plummer had assured Wilbur that his purpose was solely to avert an Indian conflict like the one that had resulted the previous spring in the killing of a number of Shoshone horse thieves by a Bannack City posse led by Buck Stinson.

Wilbur never did catch up with them, which was just as well since it turned out that all anyone was really worried about was a herd of horses owned by Frank Parish, Bill Bunton's partner in the Rattlesnake Ranch. Parish was thought to be dying from the fever, and it had been perceived to be a prudent measure to keep the horses, upon which the stage lines and the public in general depended, from the tribe of Parish's squaw should Parish pass on. Wilbur ended up alone in a heavy snow atop a lowly mule that sat him no less awkwardly than did a horse, and which caused him to arrive late into the night at the Rattlesnake Ranch.

At the Rattlesnake, Wilbur had been forced to share a bed with Bill Bunton and Red Yeager, who was Bunton's hand, and several others, and had had what he described the next day as a life-threatening encounter with Jack Gallagher, whom, of all Henry Plummer's deputies, I thought to be the most noble in appearance and remarkable in carriage and demeanor. So I concluded that Gallagher had probably been drinking before he arrived, and that Wilbur had become disturbed by Gallagher's behavior and then had said so and then had come to regret it when confronted man to man.

And it made matters worse for Wilbur that, out of necessity, I had been forced to exaggerate my circumstances after they finally brought me out of the stupor of having been thrown off of Jonah, telling Sidney and Mary that it had been road agents that had stopped and tried to rob me on the road and had caused my imprudent headlong flight home. Because the fact of it, of a robbery at gunpoint on the same night on which Wilbur had followed the stampede out of town was far too much for Mary, who induced George Brown to fetch Wilbur back from the treachery of the night. And no matter how Wilbur examined me after his return, employing the best of his lawyerly skills, I ensured his further aggravation by failing to recall any particulars of the robbers, who were essentially fictions of my mind. So that when he would not stop, could not admit that there was nothing for him to learn from me, I finally said, "It could have been anyone that did it, Uncle. It could have been anyone beneath those masks and under those blankets. Even you or Uncle Sidney or even Henry Plummer, if you see my meaning."

By that time, Wilbur was reaching the point of either losing his sense of reality, or recognizing that the reality all around him in which men proved themselves by both base and heroic means was one in which he could not much longer survive. He was not, after all, what one would call a man's man in that day and age where men willingly died for the sake of friendship or argument or challenge. He could barely ride a horse at more than a walk, and the firing of a revolver, let alone the complex regimen of deftly removing the cylinder and loading the powder and the wadding and the balls and caps and fitting and plunging them all safely into place, was totally beyond his agility and ken. Nor was he a physical man, labor being as foreign and antithetical to him as is flying to a slug or killing to a deer. And it took little time for him to be so perceived by most of the men of Bannack, who all, at one time or another, took their turn at a pick and their aim with a pistol or a shotgun.

Wilbur appeared unable to comprehend that no great offense ought to be taken when a subtle joke was directed at him, as when Jack Gallagher strode into Wilbur's office and blackened his boots atop Wilbur's desk and then strode back out without a word. He could not return the prod and thereby achieve parity with the likes of Gallagher; and he therefore reacted to it otherwise, with great and emphasized indignation and affront. And his strictly moralistic rejection of the working ladies and the need for recreation of any sort no doubt was viewed by many as effeminate and adolescent. I thus felt embarrassed for him, and somewhat ashamed for us all, when Wilbur responded to Henry Plummer's and his deputies' constant and admirable displays of horsemanship and civic duty, to the way they selflessly protected the merchants and contained the miners' inevitable transgressions, and to the infinite and unequivocal courtesies they granted to the womenfolk, by childishly referring to Plummer as self-appointed king and to the likes of Stinson and Ray as loyal minions to the throne.

Sidney Edgerton was far more discreet and composed, although none the less chagrined by Henry Plummer's ever-growing stature and Wilbur's inability to engender a meaningful following amongst the more prominent townsmen, who were at least listening to Sidney's articulated vision of a nation and territory ruled by the iron strength of law and order. More and more, Sidney directed Wilbur's activities and contemporaneously grew impatient with Wilbur's shortcomings and lack of initiative and foresight. So that when Wilbur protested over attending

Henry Plummer's Thanksgiving feast, Sidney rebuked him sharply. "He has bested you again, Wilbur. It was something you should have thought of yourself. If you are ever to be rid of him as your nemesis, you must seize upon every opportunity, and you must gain the upper hand. Can you understand that, or shall I write it out for you in ink?"

~~~

At the day and hour of Henry Plummer's Thanksgiving dinner, the three of us, Sidney and Mary and I, crossed the footbridge over to the Sanders's family cabin. And then, despite the fact that the cabin sat immediately next to the Vails', where Henry Plummer's dinner was to be held, and much to the agitation of the women, who had spent a great deal of time in preparing their hair and dresses for the occasion, Sidney had us sit and wait for nothing other than the passage of time. So that when we finally crossed the opening and Sidney Edgerton knocked on James Vail's door, I knew that Sidney Edgerton had every intention of converting Henry Plummer's dinner into something of a political rally for himself. Sidney thus made it a point to quickly and yet cordially introduce politics into every conversation he held that day with Henry Plummer's guests, including the likes of Colonel McLean and George Chrisman and Thomas Pitt. And above all, he made his position on the question of a new territory known without equivocation and with little effort reinforced the idea that Bannack logically would be the named territorial seat. This then excited conversation regarding real estate spec-ulation and other such matters, which served to mask the real reason why the subject had been raised.

Henry Plummer's intentions seemed altogether different. He appeared far more concerned with fulfilling his obligations as host of the affair, and in facilitating a casual and social interaction amongst his peers. As if to ensure that no one might accuse him of being penurious or frugal, he covered the table that day with fine French wines and raisins and nuts and dates, and a turkey delivered personally to Henry

Plummer all the way from Salt Lake that was said to have cost $40. And what with the way the sheriff saw to it that none went without enough to eat and drink and smoke, and by his gracious and condescending attention to the women who, as was expected of them, gathered off to a side to discuss domestic and familial issues, it would have been difficult to argue that Henry Plummer's motivations were ulterior to simply providing for the social occasion over which he presided.

And yet there were hints, at least, that it was so. For Henry Plummer allowed others to provide a political service to him. Francis Thompson first mentioned the topic of the federal deputy marshal's position, and when Sidney subsequently spoke of a new territory, Francis offered his opinion on the subject. "I should think that our host would then be the logical, if not the only, candidate for the office of territorial marshal. Don't you agree, Judge Edgerton?" he said and then regretted it when Sidney Edgerton replied that he could not say either way.

And that is when Henry Plummer let his own thoughts be known. "I am not, at least at this point in time, inclined to throw my personal support behind a territorial designation," he said. "Although I might be persuaded to back the proposition if it were demonstrated that it would be in the best interests of the local population."

"And why is that, Henry?" Smith Ball asked as he allowed his empty brandy snifter to be refilled.

"Because there's no guarantee of democracy inherent in the creation of a territory. We will have little opportunity to choose leaders from amongst our own. The federal government back East will do that in our stead; that is unless we assert ourselves now and let them know that we will support the proposition only if they allow us to select our own representatives. It's their way of maintaining control until they've structured the government to their liking, without regard to the needs and desires of those who live in remote lands such as these. I would much prefer immediate statehood, or some such similar mechanism in which the populace has something akin to state's rights. So that we can elect a governor and a judiciary of our own choosing."

"It is my opinion," Sidney interjected, "that such federal intervention is precisely what is required here. These people, these miners, have already shown that they have no ability to govern. Now understand me in this. I am not saying that they are not good people; a very industrious sort they are, beyond question. It is only that they are so consumed with this endless search for gold that they can't stop long enough to learn even the rudimentary principles of government. What would it prove to allow them a second opportunity to demonstrate their incompetence?"

"Of course you would see it that way," Colonel McLean said. "As would any member of the party in power. But surely you can understand our point of view," saying this in a way that somehow seemed to emphasize that Henry Plummer and a significant majority of the other guests that day were Democrats, "that we are far enough removed from the war, and this being free soil and all, that there ought to be some form of self-determination here in order to ensure that we are not made puppets to those in power back East."

"You seem to forget, sir," Sidney Edgerton said, "that this already is part of a territory of the United States. We are merely talking of divorcing ourselves from the land west of the divide. The same federal controls would need to apply."

And as this seemed a solid point, Wilbur added, "Yes. I also fail to see the logic of your argument, Colonel McLean."

"The reason why you fail to understand me, Colonel Sanders, is that you Republicans find it convenient to not be accountable for anything. Lincoln and Chase spend millions every day, money we do not even have in the treasury, and react to the loss of tens of thousands dead on the fields of battle merely by drafting more men, or boys should I say, and finding new generals who are willing to kill tens of thousands more without gaining an inch of ground. Of course you don't see my point. It is your idea that none of us should even have a vote. That there are ten or twenty of you, or maybe only three or four, that should be allowed to run the entire show under some distorted concept of martial law, without anyone else having any say. Well, I say none of that here, out West. I say we are distant enough from their troubles, and that we have earned our keep such that we deserve better. And I say we can do better with men such as Henry Plummer, if only we are allowed to have them lead us."

This embarrassed Henry Plummer to a considerable degree, and he held up his hands and said, "Gentlemen, gentlemen, please," as if to end the debate. But Sidney let it be known that he would not permit its conclusion except on his own terms.

"Be that as it may, Colonel McLean," he said. "You state your position well. Nevertheless, your libertarian political philosophy being whatever it is, it does not, in any way, change the facts. This entire region is . . . well, I will not say lawless because that would suggest that our good sheriff is not performing his duties . . . but if not lawless then shall we at least say in need of government. Badly in need. And we have but two choices, the one being to get the territorial governor in Lewiston to act and the other being to have Washington declare this to be our own territory where we at least might govern ourselves."

And the matter having come full circle, Henry Plummer wisely saw that it now should be ended for the time being. "We can all agree then," he said with a reassuring look in all directions, "that one way or the other we should be permitted to govern ourselves. And I propose for the remainder of this day of thanksgiving, in any event, we leave it at that. A toast," he said as he raised his glass both to the men and to the women, who turned in unison when it was made clear that they were being recognized as well. "To our womenfolk, for gracing our little valley with their beauty and dignity."

"Hear, hear," Francis Thompson said, and we all drank to their honor.

I afterward thought it a mistake for Henry Plummer to have hosted the Thanksgiving feast, if only because it was such a great success. Through the diversity and support of his guests, he showed Sidney Edgerton that he had far greater political strength than one might have supposed by merely watching him quietly perform his duties. And this was something that would not be missed by Judge Edgerton, whose powers of observation were acutely refined. So that whereas Henry Plummer might have superficially appeared to have established once and for all that he was predominant amongst his Bannack City peers, I knew it to be the case that Sidney, by learning what he did that late-November day, became significantly more advantaged and determined than he had been before he decided to attend. And this, I thought, was the sort of thing that Henry Plummer, being far more open and trusting than Sidney Edgerton, would never come to see—that as between himself and Sidney Edgerton, Sidney was far more manipulative and intent on achieving his objectives, the desires of the local population and democratic principles and established precedent all be damned.

BOOK IV

BILLY HARPER

CHAPTER 1

For some of the miners of Alder Gulch, it was simply a matter of brute strength and persistent endurance, or perhaps just a raw and wanton imperviousness to hardship and cold and toil that pulled them through, that carried them forward from the end of one day of deprivation and struggle into and through the next. With others, it was almost the opposite, as though the ability to survive and even prosper amid the coarse milieu of the placers and mines was as much a matter of intellectual exercise as it was of physical effort.

That was how life was in Alder Gulch for most of them, almost all of them, I guess, except, that is, for X Beidler, for whom something altogether different was involved, something of purely snide and remarkable determination and effrontery and presumptuousness that dictated and asserted at every passing moment that he not only would somehow maintain, but that he would predominate also, in his own way and at his own time of choosing. I first saw it before he ever proved to me and Pap what he really was, before he verified himself in ways that could not be ignored. And in no way were his tendencies toward falsely subscribed and arbitrary violence more evident than in his recounting of his encounter with the vagrant Navajo, which I believed and accepted as fact, maybe not the first time he told it to us before a cold fire at Dead Missourian Gulch in the Colorado, and maybe not even the second time when me and Pap had come to know him well enough through a shared claim and camp, but by the third time for certain. And not just because he told it the same way in each instance, which he did with varying degrees of reconcilable detail, but because it fit neatly with X Beidler's character in every way.

It was a brief anecdote, at least by his telling, and darkly humorous too, if you didn't mind the way he drew it from out of the air and laid it on you. But most importantly, it was always the same, arising from a similar stimulus and containing the same cursory facts and concluding with the same dull remark. Beginning always with something concerning Indians in general: if not a passing or worried comment, then at least a tribal relic or artifact of some sort, carried by him or some other miner or traveler in a coat pocket or saddlebag and then suddenly or inadvertently displayed to or by X. And then he would introduce his tale, opening up the narrative of the encounter with an observation that only barely related to the arrowhead or moccasin or scalp or whatever it was on that particular occasion that he or the other held in his hand or stooped to pick up from off the ground. "I had me an Indian friend once," he would say with a sardonic smile that was also somehow warm and introspective. And then you knew it was coming, whether you liked it or not.

"Met 'em for the first time up at Taylor River, my Indian friend that is, along the bank where me and my hireds had set up a camp for the pack train we were runnin'. 'Bout nightfall this Indian rides up on an old swayback of a mare and him lookin' worse for a meal than her. We fed him some, fed the mare too, and bedded 'em both down good. Come mornin', we loaded 'em both up with breakfast and sent 'em on their way. Pack train made 'bout 15 miles that day, and when we went into camp, that Indian showed back up, actin' like he hadn't eaten in a week when he'd had two meals straight. But we fed 'em again anyway, seein' how he was nice enough as Indians go. Probably a Navajo, I imagine;

peaceful type. And we gave 'em some breakfast in the mornin' and packed 'em up a lunch and sent 'em on the road. Made maybe 15 mile that day too; and sure as stink on skunk, he come back into camp that night. Then I got tired. My hired hands had some picks and shovels, and the three of us dug a grave and buried that Indian and mare in it and covered 'em up good so's his friends wouldn't know. He wasn't a bad sort, really. As Indians go, I mean."

When X decided to put an outfit together out of Denver and head north to the Grasshopper in the Idaho Territory, me and Pap joined up with him and Johnny Grannis and George Berkingham and made our way to Bannack City just in time to get swept up in the stampede that threw men into the Alder Gulch like leaves off an aspen grove on a windy autumn day. And X said let's take the high ground, which we did, hauling the wagons and mules and supplies up only after the claims had been staked and the Highland District declared. But after the first week Pap said we wouldn't stay with them no more, and when our claim got jumped by a big Dutchman with black eyes, we just moved down some and picked a spot along the creek north of the new Virginia City and it turned out just fine. And Pap never said why we'd left, but I guess I could figure it on my own, because X Beidler wasn't one to work overly hard and the ditch digging to set the course for the water was plenty laborious and still nothing compared to what came next. So when X quit working at it, and took to playing chief and bossing and directing and administering the camp, Pap said, "Enough," and we moved down the creek. Pap kept on good terms with X, though, and as it turned out, that meant that we would have a lot to do with X in the days to come.

It wasn't but a few weeks after the stampede that Dillingham was shot right there on the main street in Virginia City, where, only twenty days before, there not only had not been a street but no town either, no trampled ground even to mark the passage of man or beast of burden. And X somehow got himself involved in it even though he hadn't seen it happen and therefore couldn't know who shot Dillingham and why.

When Judge Bissell said they needed a scaffold to hang Haze Lyons and Buck Stinson on, X said, "I'll build it," and when the judge said they'd be needing graves, he said, "I'll dig 'em," both of which he did, apparently in furtherance of some moral principle he'd suddenly acquired after living in the mud like any other Pikes Peaker I'd ever seen. And that's what got him started—building that scaffold on which no man was ever hung and digging those graves that sat empty and ridiculed until they finally filled with snow and froze. Because when Jack Gallagher got the committee to recount the vote for the third time, they set Buck Stinson and Haze Lyons free, and thereafter X had himself more than several men in the region who were not particularly partial to him.

X was what we called a gadabout back in Kansas. It seemed that no matter where you went, X was there, especially once he learned he could make the easy money buying goods in Bannack when there was a shortage in Virginia and Nevada City, and visa versa. You could go to Dance & Stuart's and there'd be X, selling gum boots on the boardwalk and not bothering Stuart nor Dance none either, since they'd just as soon see their would-be customers happy and still shopping than gone and shoeless. And there were some that said that X could smell frying donuts better'n a bear dead meat; so X predictably was at Star's Cafe in Nevada City whenever fresh pastries were on the counter. And at every one of the open-front saloons and at the grand California Exchange, where there was room enough for twenty card games and a dance at once, X was not only known to have a favorite stool and table but was allowed at most of those establishments to pinch out his own dollar's worth of dust in payment for drinks or a dance even though his thumb and forefinger were smaller than the average. In other words, X was good enough at making friends, and some good ones too. By which I mean good men to have on your side when it came down to getting the drop on a road agent, or holding your own against any one of the mix of desperadoes that were drawn to Alder Gulch like flies to a three-day dead mule.

Me and Pap pretty much minded our own business, but you couldn't help in making acquaintances both along the creek and up in the towns that sprouted up every 3 miles or so. And by making friends it seemed you couldn't avoid making yourself some enemies too. Because there was so much divisiveness, with the Southern boys letting it be known that their hearts were with Bobby Lee's troops, even though they themselves might never have worn a butternut uniform nor maybe even seen one; and the Republicans and the Democrats snarling at each other at every turn like a polecat and a snake; and the rowdies always rubbing wrong the more civilized townsmen who tried to bring maybe just a little too much dignity where it had never been before. So you went and made some friends, since it wasn't the kind of place where you'd always want to be alone and there were things you just couldn't do by yourself— throwing shafts and working windlasses and setting ditches—and with those friends came something else: not guilt, because everyone there had only themselves to blame for coming to such a remote and brazen place, but at least adversity, and if not that then risk, by the association with someone whom you might not have chosen to be a friend but who might have sought you out.

Fact is, I was just a youngster at the time, so it all comes back in a headlong rush of memory, like time was trying to return itself into one scrunched-up wad in which all of occurrence and happenstance exist at once, in one narrow jumbled frame of recollection. Whereas in reality it all just sort of unfolded naturally, just as an ancient cottonwood traces back to a single forlorn seed, having its own beginning and, later on, its own end. Only you don't know it until afterwards, when you can look back and fit together the pieces of a puzzle that didn't make anything in particular when you held them apart; you didn't know at first, or even in the middle when it was happening, that it would amount to an event with an obvious start and a logical conclusion. And you might say that insofar as concerned the happenings in Alder Gulch, the seed, or one of them at least, from which it all germinated, from which grew something large and notable from something small and indistinct, was X Beidler himself, who had spread his story of the Navajo and the swayback mare along all 20 miles of the Gulch within one week's time.

Pap and me, we were there when X and George Ives first went at it on the street in Virginia City. It wasn't even a town then, not the random collection of cabins and stores and stables, of hotels and saloons and cafes and brothels it came to be within the next few months. But it was a city nonetheless, into and through which a population of miners and itinerants flowed and set their tents and brawled and drank and ate and slept, whored and gambled, just like in any other mining hamlet in the West. We had gone in to fetch any number of items of which we were in need, and which could be purchased at an outrageous price from gougers who laid down the tailgates of their lumber and freight wagons and sold goods at five times the normal price. And Pap was just sending me off to look for matches and some salt and some pick handles, when up from out of the crowd that seemed to be doing more milling than moving comes X Beidler, who says his howdys and then asks if we'd seen Black Bess on our way in.

"Ain't seen her since we moved down to the Nevada District," Pap says.

And X says, "She's been stole, sure as snake sheds skin."

There was one thing you could always count on with X, and that was that he could build up a head of steam like no other man. And it was something to see since he was shorter than normal, and sturdy enough, and it wouldn't take but a minute or two after he'd start going that he'd start to looking like either the top of his head would come off or every muscle in his body snap. So it was a good thing when Pap asked who done it, since it opened up a valve, or something close, that permitted X to vent out a five-minute diatribe on how there weren't nothing more heinous than stealing a man's animal when there was work just waiting to be done. He wandered off after that, probably for the sole and instinctive purpose of rejuvenating that steam he'd lost up into the atmosphere; but the truth was that X had reason for being unhappy and chagrined, seeing as how Black Bess was by both my and Pap's reckoning the absolute best packing and working and riding mule we'd ever seen.

I found me the salt and some cheap sulfur matches for which I paid dearly. The pick handles, though, were another matter, there being none to be had along the whole 20-mile city and the prospect of having to cut our own out of the heartwood of a pine or spruce being none too attractive of a splintering alternative.

We had struck some pretty colorful gravel at our claim during the first week of work, the gold almost lying there for us to shovel and placer off the surface of the creek bed; and seeing's how you couldn't leave your treasure in your camp unprotected, Pap was carrying with him that day a good-sized heft of dust in a silk-lined leather pouch. Which is how it was with everyone, the distrust evident in their faces, and the location of their happy burden sometimes revealed by a bulge under a shirt or a heavily draped pocket in a coat. So that every man pretty much always had his shotgun at the ready and his revolver loaded and primed with the caps set, no matter where he went and with whom he sat. And the weight of all that heavy metal had a most peculiar effect not only on Pap but seemingly on most every other man, because no matter how much or how little they had, whether an ounce or ten times a pound, there came upon them this immediate and insatiable need to rid themselves of at least some of it; as though they could persuade themselves that once there was only half or a quarter of it left in their pocket they would be content and sated by it.

Before the Dillingham affair, someone had already begun to build a couple of cabins up on Wallace Street, cutting and notching the green logs with a great deal of effort and knowing full well that once that timber got to drying and twisting, the walls might just bend with them and the roofs cave in. Within its first two weeks, Virginia City therefore had its first real bakery, and its first real saloon, too, since that's what had spurred on the men that had felled the trees and dovetailed the ends—the prospect of throwing up some walls and draping tent canvases over them and calling them buildings and inventorying some flour and yeast and gin and whiskey and brandy and then opening up their businesses to every and any white man who needed some sustenance or wanted to lift his spirits. And that's where Pap and me were headed, to Morier's saloon I mean, after we'd exhausted the possibilities on pick handles and he'd bought himself some fresh powder and us both some leather working gloves.

"Might as well get some refreshment," he said; and I agreed, thinking maybe this would be the time he'd let me join him, in town I mean, in public. Because I'd had my swig or two around a fire or late at night when Pap would allow it. Only never in town, in front of other men who did not know me or him. But Pap told me to sit there on that wagon and not move unless it were the only way to save our goods, the flour and potatoes and the hay that was stacked loosely in the back, and he went through the doorway on which no door had yet been hung and into the smoky jumble of noise that came out of the saloon like the distant confused murmur of a Sunday service.

That's when X Beidler returned. He was leading Black Bess behind him on a lariat, and she was all lathered up, bad, unlike I'd ever seen a mule sweated before. And it didn't take but one look at X to see that that head of steam had built back up again and hadn't reached its peak, and that it had better be vented soon or something extraordinary would happen right there on Wallace Street.

From what Pap says, X went into that saloon and plowed his way through the crowd and headed right for George Ives; and when he got up in front of him, being not much more than half George Ives's size, X tore into him for taking Black Bess without even asking. George Ives told X he'd better keep his animals on a ranch instead of roaming loose in the district if he didn't want them rode. And that's when they came out, or were sent out by Morier, who probably didn't care much about a couple of men shooting at each other but wasn't too interested in seeing himself and some of his friends caught in the middle once the lead let loose.

So then I could not only see them but almost smell them both, because X made a point of going up to Black Bess, which he had tied to Pap's wagon spokes, and showing Ives how the mule was worn flat out. And George Ives followed him in a fearless humor, striding along next to X with his long shanks taking one step to every two by X and George Ives's white hat and blond hair and mustache each as light and handsome as the next. "She's a hell of a mule, I'll give you that," George Ives told X in a deep, good-natured voice. "Good for 70 mile a day." And then he pushed it too hard and said, "I know."

And X said, "You try it again and I'll see to it."

For all I know, George Ives never touched X's stock again; but Jack Gallagher did just a few days later, and Gallagher and Ives were known to ride together. And I suppose maybe X hadn't had time to let off all that steam he'd stoked up with George Ives and was therefore that much ahead of himself when Gallagher was three hours late in returning the mule that X reluctantly said he could take for thirty minutes. X was pretty hard that day, labeling Gallagher with names and invective that weren't repeatable in mixed company, or even in good company either. X later claimed that Gallagher took off on his mule to arrange for the murder of Dillingham, which brought the matter full circle in explaining why it was that X had such an interest in building that scaffold on which someone finally hung a couple of elk carcasses, and in digging those graves in which Buck Stinson later urinated, he said, just to piss off X.

But that was in the summer, when things seemed fairly plain and simple, with it being hot and dry and the creek yielding dust at whatever point you stuck a shovel into the gravel, and it still being a rush in every sense, and there not being enough of any one faction for any other to worry much about. By late fall it was very much a different story. Pap says there must've been 5,000 souls in the Gulch by the time of Abe Lincoln's Thanksgiving remembrance, but I figured it was closer to 10,000, what with every district now having its own town and the towns by then taking on the character of real communities. Of which Virginia City was by far the most dominant both in size and political structure, being Henry Plummer's town, presided over by Henry Plummer's deputies, with a miners' court and committee composed of a decidedly Democratic constituency that was openly sympathetic to the South.

That's what bothered Pap the most. Because although we hailed from Kansas and were therefore almost border state in political origin and geographical proximity, Pap had been a Free-Soiler, just like X. In the last days before the war began, he had journeyed all the way across the plains of Iowa just to help build the fortifications on the Mississippi at which one of his brothers not much later lost his life and Pap his closest friend. And that was enough for Pap to maintain his belief in the Union, and for Pap that meant being loyal, and loyalty meant action when the time came and it was clear that the words of argument and faith and belief had not sufficed. Not that Pap was a fighting man, because he wasn't, not at least in the sense of resorting to violence first and reason only later. Instead, he was first and foremost a Lincoln man, a Union man from the western states—meaning Illinois and all else west of the Ohio and Mississippi—moderate and yet resolved; and he therefore supported only those things that Lincoln advocated and of which we read in the dated and torn and disintegrating papers that passed through the camps.

X liked to think that he stood for the same virtues of dignified honor and defense of country—of country, but not of God and country, because there, in the Gulch, there was no God present in any visible form, not a single church nor grotto nor even icon outside a miner's tent or cabin to suggest that God had come too, had attended at least as witness to the greed and want that drove men to the Gulch and then into the ground like worms or insects frantically avoiding the sun or rain.

So for X it was just love of country and, as X liked to put it, what's right. But I can't help but believe that X was none too capable of differentiating what exactly fell within the right, and otherwise within the wrong. And being unable to distinguish between the two, he chose to deal with the question, when it came up, in a summary and arbitrary and decisive manner, like he had with that Navajo Indian who at first had been acceptable or at least tolerable, and then, for some reason apparent only to X, had become worthy of disdain such that X could rationalize dispatching him into a grave once and for all and with good riddance. Which meant, when it came to X, that if a man associated with George Ives, that man was every bit as undeserving as Ives, and that the associates and friends and maybe even the acquaintances of those men were equally tainted by the relationship, despite their distance and removal from George Ives, whom they might never have even met.

The same held true for Stinson and Lyons and Gallagher and any of two score others, as far as X Beidler was concerned. Which at first made some sense to me since I had seen enough of things in my time spent in the mining camps in the Colorado and then in the Gulch to know that men survived only by holding together against those who sought to take from them what was theirs. So I could see and understand and even admire X's resistance to Ives and Gallagher and the others, until X carried it too far afield and swept into his growing dung heap of approbation and mistrust Henry Plummer, of whom I had reasons for forming a different and more reserved opinion than did X Beidler and the like.

Henry Plummer didn't make his first appearance in the Gulch until a full month after the strike and the stampede that followed as naturally as would thunder lightning. But he was nonetheless there from the beginning, his spirit and will carried and enforced and exemplified not only by his deputies, but also by a majority of Bill Fairweather's rowdy friends and by the stampeders themselves, who, after all, at first mostly descended from Bannack City and its environs and therefore had already voted en masse to hire and recognize Henry Plummer as their enforcer of the law. He was also, to my way of thinking, generally the voice of reason. Which is what set Henry Plummer apart from all the rest, from the X Beidlers and the Jack Gallaghers and all their counterparts and corollaries—the fact that Henry Plummer called a spade a spade and a fact a fact, and thereby gave credence and consideration to the realties that virtually everyone else in Alder Gulch, out of greed and bias, chose frequently to argue against and blatantly ignore.

And X Beidler hated Henry Plummer for it. Whenever X had something radical and rousing and somewhat arbitrary to say, Henry

Plummer always seemed to be near enough to calm things down before they took a leap. So when the Union League got word out in Nevada City that a self-confessed cannibal and known rebel sympathizer named Boone Helm had staked a claim at the edge of the Fairweather District, X was amongst the first to move to throw him out. And Henry Plummer as quickly stopped it. "This man Helm has committed no crime against us," Henry Plummer said. The truth and significance of which angered X Beidler to no end because it was known for a fact that Boone Helm, as X Beidler put it, "had et a man," and, in his past, had also been formally accused of several murders for which he never had been tried due only to the failure of the witnesses to appear. "Probably et them, too," X had noted out loud to the committee. "May be," Henry Plummer had answered with a laugh. "But let us not convict a man based only on the speculation of his diet."

So X Beidler would show up at every miners' meeting in the Fairweather District, and in some of the others too, and on his own volition would even call a few meetings to convene, and each time it would be Henry Plummer, or one of his designees standing in his stead, that would divert the attention of the membership toward a less radical solution than that proffered by X Beidler and those that followed in his lead. X wanted George Ives arrested for the robbery of Anton Holter, whose freight and lumber yard serviced the growing ambitions of the entire Gulch; but there was no evidence to support the issuance of a warrant. Then, X Beidler, and Charley the Brewer with him, led a movement to restrict the sales price of flour and salt to something within reason; but Ned Ray, all dandied up in his neatly fringed buckskin and his knee-high boots, brought it to an end by pointing out that such market regulation might warrant a reduction in the price of gold, which, to date, had held its value despite its proliferation. And when X protested aloud that Aleck Carter and Talmadge Jersey and other friends of Stinson and Lyons had threatened him on the streets, all Henry Plummer had to say was, "I'll calm them down for you, X," and X Beidler knew, to his escalating chagrin, that it would be done just at Henry Plummer promised.

Of course, I didn't catch on to all of it firsthand; a body seldom does. But Pap and others brought it clearly to me nonetheless, retelling, out of irritation or humor, how Henry Plummer, with the lash of his smooth and articulate tongue, was able to outdo X Beidler and his cohorts at almost every confrontation between them. And the balance of their perspectives and attitudes toward Henry Plummer were sufficiently diverse and antagonistic to allow me to synthesize it and form my own opinion of Henry Plummer's worth.

From the very beginnings of Alder Gulch, Pap and me thus had reason and cause for forming an opinion of Henry Plummer. On this question we differed from the start and avoided the expression of our thoughts as much as was possible in light of the bond we shared. And maybe it would have ended there, with Pap and me differing some, but not enough for either of us to do other than what Pap would've been inclined to do if it had been up to him alone, and me stuck in a no-man's-land between adolescence and manhood where an individual feels all the yearnings of life and knows not one iota of its pleasures. It might have remained that way forever, or if not forever then at least long enough that it would not have mattered since events would have passed us by and left us bobbing in their wake like most of the other flotsam of the Gulch, had it not been for Jotham McKenzie, whom I had never met except to see him draped over Henry Plummer's horse.

When I first saw him, I thought the man who was Jotham McKenzie was dead, gunned down by Henry Plummer in the line of duty, until Plummer and his companion rode by, sitting two to the one horse and leading the other, across which the apparently lifeless person had been slung and tied, and I saw through Henry Plummer's open coat that he was shirtless, his silken blouse having been wrapped as a bandage around the broken leg of the unconscious man, the blood now dried and clotted on the splintered limb that bounced only lightly at each jog the horse took along the road. Pap would have said no, had I asked; so I never even considered following them to Doc Cox's office in Virginia City, where it was said they were heading in the hopes of saving his leg.

By the time they passed by our claim, which wasn't but a bit off the road, I knew that the trim postured figure who sat first atop the mounted horse and who constantly turned his head to check the man in tow, was none other than Henry Plummer, of whom I had heard told so much. It didn't make much sense to me at the time since there were mining camps all along the way, at any one of which Henry Plummer might have exerted his authority and officially borrowed a wagon with which to cart the man with a much higher degree of comfort. But I didn't ask, contenting myself to hear that this was Henry Plummer and knowing that on the next occasion I would recognize him without having to inquire.

Next day, Pap sent me into Virginia to purchase some short logs to be used to timber up the small shaft we had dropped in the center of our claim. As I drove the wagon into town, I came upon a small crowd that had formed in front of Doc Cox's office, and there in the middle, atop a hogshead, stood Henry Plummer's companion of the prior day. He seemed to be well known by a number of the crowd. And when I asked someone near me who the speaker was, he said, "That there's Joseph Swift, Thompson & Swift's in Bannack. He's a deputy of Plummer's, or some such." And as I stood near the rear, I watched as the crowd pressed him for information.

"What you say his name was, Joseph?" a voice yelled out.

"Is," I heard Joseph Swift say back with some pride and even more impatience. "Is, not was, because Doc Cox says Henry Plummer saved his life, and most probably his leg too, by getting him up here quick as he did and letting that leg go free so that that crushed bone didn't go banging all over a wagon for 15 miles."

"What's his name," a second miner says.

And the answer comes back, "Jotham McKenzie."

This brought a murmur of interest from the gathering, because it was a name that was well known throughout the placers. John Lott claimed that Jotham McKenzie had made more money than anyone in the whole eastern portion of the territory by buying and selling mining

claims, and had done less work than even the bummers who were growing in number with each passing day. Most recently, it had been rumored
that McKenzie had sold out the claims along the Grasshopper that he
had bought for a pittance just weeks after the rush vacated Bannack.
Word was that he was heading east to Benton to take his gold down the
river in a mackinaw, being the fastest way out of the territories.

"What happened to him?" a suspicious and angry voice demanded. "Robbed I suppose. Is that it? You and Plummer found him,
but only after he'd been relieved of his gold. Is that what we're supposed
to believe this time?"

I figured there'd be a fight then; you could see that sort of thing
evolve by the way hands moved toward the revolvers and knives that
everyone stuck into their belts, and in the manner in which men tightened up to prepare themselves for violence.

"That's Henry Plummer you're talking about. I'd be more careful
if I were you," someone retorted. And I could hear more than one hammer click into place.

Pap said to stay clear of trouble when I was alone in town, and so
I began to move backwards to extricate myself from the middle of the
circle. And in so doing I bumped into someone behind me by whose
stature I would have figured to be a boy had the person not seemed so
immovable and solid as to be made of stone. I turned to meet X Beidler
face-to-face.

"Move back, Billy," X says and pushes me toward the rear. "Might
be trouble comin'."

Just then Joseph Swift stepped up onto a window ledge so that he
was higher now even than those who had come up to his altitude by
standing on a chair or a wagon seat. "Hold up, boys," he says, and then
adds, "You're drawing some wrong conclusions. Jotham McKenzie had
20,000 in gold when he left, and he had 20,000 when Henry Plummer
found him unconscious with his leg twisted in that broken wagon wheel.
And I can tell you that 20,000 was still there when I rode up an hour
later and found Henry working on that leg; and it's still there now, right

there in the Doc's office under Jotham's bed." And when the crowd quieted some, Joseph Swift said, "All you got to do is go on in and ask Jotham yourself. He's sitting up with two shotguns at his side, and he says he ain't lettin' anyone but Doc Cox and Henry Plummer within 10 feet of that bedside."

And so it ended almost instantly, with half the crowd being justified in their faith and reliance in Henry Plummer, and the other half disgruntled by the fact that the evil they abhorred had not occurred.

After X Beidler had withdrawn, I made my way up to Joseph Swift and waited a turn to speak with him. "Billy Harper," I said. "Pleased to make your acquaintance." And when Joseph Swift just looked down at me, I added, "Me and Pap got a lot of friends who claim Henry Plummer's the best man for most any job. Now I see why."

And Joseph Swift said back: "Henry Plummer's a born leader. I'd place my bet on Henry Plummer, anywhere, anytime." Then someone else attracted him away, and the crowd filtered off to leave me standing there, leaning against a post and wishing that I could see Henry Plummer and shake his hand.

No one was really totally right or absolutely wrong in Alder Gulch when it came to suspicion and paranoia and affiliation. I now knew Henry Plummer to be an admirable man, but the plain fact was that by his equanimity and calm reason, he necessarily accommodated the bad along with what was good. And while there were plenty of good honest hard-working souls in the Gulch, among whom I proudly counted Pap, putting in a full day's work measured from dawn to dusk, there was also an almost endless spree of violence and thievery such that the highest topic for conversation, aside from the placer mines themselves, was who had been shot or knifed or robbed where and when and by whom, and of what they had lost, and what they or we or someone else might do about it.

They played cards and tendice nightly in twenty different saloons in Virginia City and Nevada City; and on most nights some fool of a miner would come dangerously close to getting shot up with lead either for cheating or winning or losing or drinking far too much. And while one might have thought that the arrival by the wagonload of sporting ladies with their silky low-cut dresses and willowy hats would have softened this aggression amongst the miners, the fact was that it only made things worse. The new supply of amorous offerings only increased the demand, such that there were far too few women of easy virtue to satisfy their increasing clientele, who, more often than not, found the ladies' services easy enough to desire and all but impossible to afford. So that if they couldn't have these women whenever they might please, the miners fought about it or over them or maybe just to gain the release in another manly way. Pap claimed that most Gulch miners would just as soon fight it out at the drop of a hat; to which I replied that most miners wouldn't go so far as dropping their hat since it either hid some dust or paper money or was the only one they'd be likely to afford for the next year or more. Pap and me, we stayed clear of the conflicts as much as was possible for someone living in the mining camps. And things went along well enough that Pap said in but a year or so we'd have us enough in dust to head back East, or out West to Californy, and buy ourselves one big farm and settle down.

~~~

Late one night in early October, X Beidler showed up in our camp. He'd been drinking some; I could hear it in his voice and see it in the way the campfire flashed dully in his eyes. "There's someone in the district claims to know you way back from Kansas," says X to Pap.

"And who might that be," Pap says back, in a way that showed just a little distrust.

"Name's Williams," says X. "James Williams. Know him?"

Pap walked away from the fire then, so that you could not see the expression on his face. "I know of him. He's a good man. A hard man, too. Proved himself along the Kansas border wars years ago. Why you askin'?"

"I ain't askin'," says X. "I'm confirmin'. How about Jack Slade?"

"Don't know him."

"I'm told he come up partways from Denver with Williams," X says. "Turned off toward Salt Lake to get him a load of freight. He's here now, too. If it matters to you."

Pap threw some sticks atop the fire, and they caught instantly to flash a light into Pap's solemn face. "Then I'd figure he's a good man too," he says into the flames.

"Even if he carries a dead man's ears in his pockets?"

"We're all carrying a lot of baggage with us these days," says Pap. "You and me, and Billy there. And it's gettin' to be a heavier load all the time."

And then X rode off.

Afterward, Pap pulled out the good bottle and took himself a drink. And then he passed it over to me. "You better have one too," he says. And that's when I knew that things wouldn't stay quiet forever in Alder Gulch.

CHAPTER 2

Things mostly went along fine for me and Pap until the last few days in November when Abe Lincoln as much as ordered the nation to drop the tools with which it worked and the arms with which it fought and to join hands and give thanks to the Lord above. And Pap, being stoutly in favor of this man whom they claimed split the very planks on which he walked to Washington City, held out as to how we'd best spend the day amongst men of common thought and ties. Which brought us, along with hundreds of others, to the main street of Nevada City where the largest part of the crowd congregated at the door of Doc Byam's house, on the second floor of which the Union League had opened a paltry office as if to counterpoise the Southerners who regaled themselves 3 miles up the road in Virginia City, which was ten times the place Nevada ever was and ever had a chance to be.

There, under the very banner of the Union League on Lincoln's Thanksgiving Day, plenty of speakers had gathered out on the roadway with more than their share to say, and drunks with an excess of drink, and none too few of any element you might describe, except for copperheads and Johnny Rebs of which there were none, these latter avoiding, for this day only, the open doors of Nevada City's hurdy gurdy, which was just a few buildings down from Doc Byam's place, atop of which on a lodge pole someone had hoisted and unfurled the Union's flag and a facsimile of the regimental colors of the Irish Brigade, which, at times alone of all the Army of the Potomac, had more than held its own against Lee's and Jackson's troops until Burnside sent it into oblivion before the stone wall at Marye's Heights.

At first, the crowd seemed immobilized by the hard news that had been delivered the day before that Lloyd Magruder and the Chalmers brothers and one or two others apparently had been murdered somewhere up above the Bitterroot Valley and their bodies left to the wolves. So it was understandable that the crowd gathered outside Doc Byam's was initially somewhat subdued. It didn't have that much effect on Pap and me and the Colorado boys though, maybe because the killings seemed to have all the earmarks of a localized west Idaho Territory affair.

Magruder, who was from Lewiston, had been on his way home to his wife after making a trading fortune in Alder Gulch. And his probable murderers—Doc Howard and Jim Romaine and Chris Lowry—actually had hired on at Cottonwood to guide Magruder into Grasshopper Creek and thereafter worked for Magruder, hauling his freight for him, and handling his line of mules for him, and then finally hiring on with him again as guards and traveling companions on the return trip to Lewiston three months later. And maybe it didn't seem that big to us because they hadn't even found the bodies, the conclusion of murder and treachery having been deduced by a lone friend of Magruder's named Hill Beachey, who had begun to piece together the clues and evidence when Magruder's train became a week and then two weeks late.

So that we could only be somewhat shocked by the idea that you could not be safe even amongst your own professed and time-proved friends, a fact that made the prospect of the endless struggle against the creek even that less enticing, seeing as how you could do every bit of it right, the prospecting and the selecting of a claim, the water work and the drifting and the placering, and still lose it all to a thief or a murderer in the night. And it caused me to see Lincoln's great wisdom in offering up to the common people this hiatus in the midst of their toil and effort. If the labors and worries in the Gulch were in any way representative of the war energies recently expended in the remainder of the nation, the Union was in great and dire need of refreshment and regrouping.

Somewhere along the line Pap and me got separated, which was just as well; he seemed intent on achieving some degree of inebriation, and I could see that I was at best an unwelcome deterrent to his ambition. At the first opportunity I thus wandered off, leaving Pap and Bill Clark and John Lott and X Beidler, who had carried with him for the last hour a bottle of whiskey in the one hand and a flask of brandy in the other. I wandered about the town, which at the time was comprised of no more than twenty real buildings made of logs and ten times that many shacks and wickiups and structures in progress, up and down its narrow alleys, through the clotted wagons and unattended stock and the knots of drunken men, twice passing the Finney house, where someone inside was playing nationalistic songs on a poorly tuned and weakly strung piano. "John Brown's Body" and the like could be heard plainly and sourly through the open window and door.

Next to the Finney house was a small cabin owned by a miner whose surname was Richards. He was a Pikes Peaker too, and I knew he wouldn't mind that I climbed his roof for the better view. There was a large cottonwood next door, its thick trunks branching up and off in all directions. And through its leafless limbs, from atop the roof, I not only could see down into the Gulch where a few die-hard asocial miners worked even at that moment, but also across the panorama of Nevada City at the great aggregation of men who, despite Lincoln's overture and good intentions, were really kin only to themselves and their own venturesome kind.

It was from my lofty perch on Richards's roof that I saw Joseph Swift as he rode into Nevada City, sitting tall on his horse with a string of mules lolling lazily behind, and his fancy Indian buckskin jacket and fine hat as obvious as a churchgoing maiden on a workday week. He was about to pass when I called out to him and he stopped but made no movement to dismount. I shouted, "Working on Lincoln's holiday?" and then he saw me up on Richards's roof.

"If you call this working, then I guess so," he said as he rode up to the side of the cabin. "Billy Harper," he said. "That's it, right? Observing the day off, I suppose."

"More like observing those that's observing. What about you? You're for the Union, aren't you?"

"As much as any other man," Joseph Swift said assertively. "Democrat, and proud of it."

And then he was next to me, and only slightly lower, with the edge of Richards's roof being typically low slung in the standard trapper's style. "Me too," I told him. "A Union man, I mean. And maybe a Democrat, too, if I was old enough to be voting."

"You don't have to be old enough to vote to be a Democrat," Joseph Swift answered from his saddle. "I'm not old enough by almost two years. But I'm still a Democrat. If I'm old enough for them to draft me and send me into the lines, then I'm old enough to decide for myself which man it is that gets to send me."

"Then I'm a Democrat, too," I said, even though I didn't really know what that might mean.

"Well then, by God," Joseph Swift said as he reached into a bag slung across his horse and pulled out a bottle, "we'll vote to it ourselves."

We drank to some unnamed principle of faith and belief, with Joseph Swift sitting atop the same horse on which Jotham McKenzie had been hauled—Henry Plummer's horse, that is—and me slightly above him on the roof. Then we drank to the war's end, though I proposed the toast in terms of victory to the great armies of the Union and Joseph Swift restated it in terms of peace. And then it was his turn again, for which I was glad since the hot liquor had twice burned my throat and lungs and gut. "To Henry Plummer," he said, and he raised the bottle up in the air. "His health and prosperity." And then he drank deeply and proudly and then passed the bottle up to me.

"To Henry Plummer," I said none too loudly, and I drank for the third time.

Things had gotten pretty animated in Nevada City by then; a large group of men were engaging in a variety of knife throwing and shooting contests behind Doc Byam's, and every twenty minutes or so a heat of horses lit out on a race that took them halfway to Virginia City and back. Along the roadside someone had built a temporary hearth of granite boulders and they were roasting deer and elk quarters over it and selling the cooked meat at a dollar's worth of dust to the pound. And while it all came to me somewhat in a reeling blur, I judged by the state of drunkenness into which Joseph Swift had fallen that he had either been taking far greater draughts than me or had felt their effect in even more telling proportion. He dismounted and staggered to tie Henry Plummer's horse and the mules to a rail and climbed up to join me on Richards's roof.

Over the hour and more that we sat and talked and watched the raucous behavior of the Gulch miners, I heard Joseph Swift say many things that later would help bring it all together for me, providing me in piecemeal fashion with bits of that puzzle that made no sense until time itself put a frame around it all and said, "Here, all this scrambled up confusion of fiction and fact fits neatly to form a single picture, piece for piece." So that when Joseph Swift said as to how Henry Plummer was not only hosting a big Thanksgiving feast in Bannack City but had recognized the civic and political prudence of inviting Judge Edgerton, I had no reason to know who this Judge Edgerton was and every reason to surmise out loud that he must be a newly appointed jurist on the Grasshopper miners' court.

"You mean to say you ain't got word here 'bout Judge Edgerton," Joseph said, slurring the words as he spoke. "You people here in the Gulch are behind the times. This here judge, Sidney Edgerton's his name, is a real judge, sent out personally by Abe Lincoln to straighten out the territory. Only thing is, he's a Republican, from way back."

"Well, what's he waiting for then," I said.

And Joseph answered in a whisper, "There's to be a new territory if things go right. Our own territory. Henry Plummer says so himself. Says we Democrats need to stay on our feet or the Republicans, the radicals like Edgerton in particular, will beat us to it and cut us out." And after a long and pregnant pause, during which I tried in silence to comprehend the meaning of what he had said, he added, "Don't take long after you're made a territory that you're made a state."

It may be that Joseph Swift would have added more to further clarify his point, except that just at that time X Beidler supplanted the last of a long series of impromptu speakers who had regaled the throng with drunken diatribes and dissertations on a spectrum of topics ranging from alluvial theory to Indian management and everything in between. He mounted up atop a freight wagon seat and, by the mere gesture of waving above his head a shotgun, drew a boisterous cheer from the crowd that flowed around him as fluidly as a school of minnows in water or a flock of juncos in flight.

"Storm's comin'," X Beidler yelled out. And the crowd yelled back even though it was safe to bet they had no idea what X Beidler meant by it. "Changes are in the wind," X shouted, and the crowd hooted and hollered in waves of chorus.

"Come on X," someone said loudly. "We can see the weather as good as you. Out with it, whatever it is."

And X Beidler, in a voice far exceeding his stature, said, "You all ought to know by now that Lloyd Magruder's been murdered up the Bitterroot. Magruder and the Chalmer boys and Charley Allen. Left a wife of ten years behind him, Magruder did. Enough dust stolen to make any twenty of us rich. And I'm bettin' there ain't but a handful here that knows that old Jeb Tayback was robbed last night. And shot up bad, too. We're takin' contributions from you that's a little flush. Means you, Web Blainey. And you, Arnie. And the rest of you tightfisted slugs."

And this was X Beidler as I knew him in a different mood. He was happy in his own angry sort of way. He was glad to be who and where he was, in front of other men, and seemingly taller than the rest of them. "Last week it was Anton Holter," he continued. "Week before that, Wayne Coffee. Don't know who it'll be next week. But it'll be one of us for sure. We know that much boys. We sure as sin do. And the week after that, same thing.

"Now you boys know the deal. There's plenty here who've seen these cards before. We do somethin' 'bout it now, or nothin' gets done. Boys," he said amid the catcalls and affirmations, "what we need's some law and order around here. Now there's some that say we already got law. Well, you can say that if you want, but you can't say we got order. All we got for certain is a band of highwaymen robbin' us blind. And for the present, we're as good as on our own. To me, that means no law, least for now. But boys, that don't mean we can't have order. We don't need no lawmakers for that. We don't need no sheriffs and deputies wearin' badges. We don't need no judges or courts of appeal. All we need is resolve. And resolve is somethin' we know we miners already got plenty of. And I for one," X Beidler yelled at a higher pitch, that shotgun as high over his head as his short arms could hold it, and the crowd by now with him entirely, holding back only long enough for him to finish, "am planning on seein' that's exactly what we get." After which, the pistol shots and shotgun blasts and the noisy cheers of the crowd made any further conversation between Joseph Swift and me nigh on impossible.

~~~~

Two weeks later, being then almost the ides of December and the snow line in the mountains moving down rapidly, Pap's and my drifting work was stopped cold by the single constrained and involuntary cry of a man under the lash. There'd be the perfect air-splitting crack of oiled leather, and then the cry of pain that it made no sense to even try to contain. Again, and again. So that I could hardly bear it, standing like Pap leaning on the shovel, and me wincing at each repetition of the tandem sounds. Until finally, when it seemed that the sound had somehow pierced and immobilized my heart and breath, it stopped, the sudden silence itself unsure and anticipatory with pain and regret. And I, at least of all the others who heard and yet did not see it, was sure the man was dead.

But when we got up to Hal Meacham's mining camp on the bench above the Gulch, to where we knew the sounds had come from, Pap having suggested that we see what had transpired only after the sound had halted as suddenly as it had begun, we found that the victim was not only alive, but was still conscious as well. He seemed almost contented and relieved to know that the only pain he now had to bear was the aftermath of that punishment that had already been inflicted upon him, that the dead tanned flesh of the one animal would not again be laid with intolerant force upon the living, coursing flesh that was his own. And it was an even greater marvel to see them untie him and watch him first crawl and then pull himself to his feet abreast his mule, onto which they shoved him. And then they drove the two of them off down the Gulch, the indifferent mule and the rider who had been reduced to something less than man, toward the camps that lined the road heading to Laurin, on the way to Fort Benton and beyond.

A large and varied congregation of miners stood around the post where the man had been tied and whipped. When James Williams arrived, the crowd parted some. Pap had introduced me to Williams on the holiday, and he was a man you could not miss; his small beady eyes and wild shock of black hair and thick sloping shoulders and heavy legs all were unmistakable. Then X Beidler arrived, and Elk Morse. The three of them gathered to the side with a small group of men who seemed both occupied with the morning's events and determined to exclude the remainder of the crowd from their deliberations. And I thought, here again is another instance by which Pap's good stead and reputation served him well: they welcomed us, almost drew us in as gold dust seems naturally adhered to mercury, within the exclusivity of the inner circle where it appeared James Williams and Elk Morse had taken assertive and predominant control. Several of them acknowledged Pap by name; but Pap said nothing, chose instead to nod or touch an arm and integrate without statement or inquiry.

James Williams was midcourse into what would have been an interrogation had not Meacham been a proven friend. "Who else did he name?" Williams as much as demanded.

Meacham, no less tall than Williams but still smaller, less imposing physically and in confidence as well, said, "Aleck Carter. And Marshland."

There was a rumbling of voices around the circle; it carried a somber and disgruntled implication that something negative and unacceptable had been unexpectedly revealed. Then Williams grabbed Meacham by the collar and drew him up close so that their faces almost touched. "Did he say Jack Slade's name?" And when the other said no, Williams said, without releasing him, "Who else then? Who else did he name?"

And the other said, "That's all. They're the only ones."

Only then, when he otherwise would have been circumstantially excluded, did Pap pose the simplistic questions that would endlessly into the future assure that we, meaning Pap and me, would be forever entwined with the confused and confusing history of what was to come. "What? What is it, James?" Pap asked with a familiarity and association that I at once heard but did not understand. "What's it about?"

And James Williams answered, "Road agents, the whole damned lot of 'em."

Fate would have it that the man who was whipped would not die that day from the lashing, but instead from a pistol shot to the head as he slowly rode on past Laurin's ranch down the Stinkingwater Valley near Wisconsin Creek. Some said George Ives perpetrated the deed after learning that the man had saved his own neck from a lynching by identifying others who had joined him in the commission of his crimes; others claimed that it was a lieutenant of Williams's who performed the act. But no one really seemed to know, even though the body was found on the open road at a busy section where the crime should have been viewed from Daly's and the Cold Spring Ranch. And since no one claimed to have seen it, and no one cared much for the man who nearly died once and then did die on the same day—either for the crime he admitted to committing or for the breach of trust to others—the question faded almost as soon as it was raised. "Let 'em kill each other off," X Beidler said when he heard about it. "Saves us the trouble."

But the trouble was not to be so easily resolved. Down deep they all knew that much, and some even might have hoped that it could be that way, because in every difficulty is born opportunity alike, and in all such cases there are those prepared to seize upon the day and make it theirs. A week at the most went by although it seemed a month. Word came of a shooting at a dance hall in Virginia City, and of a second up at Johnnie Grant's ranch at Deer Lodge. And no one did a thing other than to learn the victims' names and the place they called their home. Those that declared them dead took their guns and buried the dead men in the cold ground. And these events, too, failed to bring the matter to a head, even though Johnnie Grant was a big man with a big name; for as angry as they all—we all—were about the killings, there was no identified antagonist against whom the mighty powers of frustration and retribution could be directed.

~~~~

I had met Nick Tibolt any number of times when he was living, but I only really knew him as an orphaned Dutchboy turned man early and by savage circumstance, whom Burtchey and Clark had as much as adopted when they were back in the Colorado and whom they took with them, almost as the surrogate for a son, when they came north to establish their freight line in Alder Gulch. And having never really known him in life, there was thus no way for me to picture how he looked in death as he lay a good half day in that wagon on the main street in Nevada City while the curious and the morbid filed by to glance upon his last remains and pronounce that no, they did not know or recognize him either. And to my chagrin, no matter how hard I tried I could not picture X Beidler's gruesome and lifeless description of how Tibolt had been pecked and bit at about the face and eyes by ravens and magpies and the Lord knows what other critters, could only guess at how death could change and degrade and atrophy the very face of time.

"Was Bill Palmer that found him," X explained as I watched Pap throw a saddle blanket over the mare and then straighten it in his normal, meticulous manner. "And Tom here who figured who it was." And here was X Beidler again, as though he were the angel of mercy, or at least its cousin, come to see that justice be done in a form to his particular liking.

Pap threw the saddle up and cinched it, again with care and slow precision. "Was a pocket knife that turned the trick," X Beidler said into the silence, and I noted how the words billowed out, separate and distinct in the form of frosty steam and slow expression. "Ole Tom'd lent it to him months back. Nicky still had it in his coat when Bill Palmer found him laying in the brush."

Bill Clark said nothing while X told it, and I could see that it had been hard on him. He just stood there, mostly looking down at the ground and kicking at the dirt with the tip of his boot while George Burtchey and Tom Baume held their horses, their faces as grim and awesome and silent as that of Clark's.

Pap led the mare around once in a circle to be sure of the tack and then went into the tent and came back out with one of the pistols and the shotgun. "Is this all?" he finally said to X. "Just the five of us?"

"We'll have James Williams and Jack Wilson and Palmer shortly," X answered. "Elk and Al Hamilton are over at Story's now. We'll pick up Chas and Franky at Junction. That's thirteen by my count. My lucky number." He turned and chawed at something in his mouth. "That's plenty for this business," he said.

Not one of them told Pap exactly where they were headed, and Pap never asked. They just rode off to join Williams and Wilson when they appeared over the rise in the twilight, with Pap saying nothing other than to tell me to stay put until he got back. And X Beidler looked like a child amongst the rest of them, sitting straight in the saddle of his mule like a dwarf in the shadowy land of the giants.

~~~

The way X Beidler told it later, George Ives almost escaped on his American stallion by persuading his captors to engage in a horse race or two along the road back to Nevada City. But most who heard it knew better; because while Pap and the others might have been overtolerant of things in general, they were not to be made fools of by the likes of George Ives. The truth, I am sure, was that George Ives was more than aware that no man would risk the ire of Ives's friends by shooting Ives in the back. So Ives made the run for it and they caught up with him at last and made him ride the remainder of the way with his hands tied up front. Which made for a motley sort of parade: Ives with his hands tied but he no less secure in his character and carriage, leading the way into town in the failing light, and George Hilderman's face showing what looked to be an incredible grin but what really was only an extraordinarily wide-shaped mouth, and Long John Frank as quiet and solemn as an undertaker in front of Pap and the others who talked amongst themselves earnestly and in careful whispers.

They came through our camp on their way into Nevada and they were a troop now, their number at some point having swelled to twenty at least. And at first I thought that Johnny Gibbons was one of their prisoners, too; the whipped man had implied that some of the ranches and stations along the stage route, including the Cottonwood, of which Johnny Gibbons was one of the owners, harbored road agents and served as clearinghouses for rustled cattle and stock. But then I saw that he and George Burtchey, who did plenty of business together, were sharing a bottle and that Gibbons still wore a pistol and a knife at his side.

They waited only long enough for Pap to grab a slab of salted pork and his brass padlock and the good bottle of brandy and then they moved on up the slope toward the town where the lamps were coming on and from which the sounds of a banjo and a fiddle emanated from Palmer's dance hall. And I followed, just as Pap told me to do, as quickly as I could saddle one of the team and secure the camp.

The sheer noise that a hundred and more men make is an unmistakable marker. So I knew where they were before I even crossed over the road that separated Nevada City from the Gulch itself. And in my hurry I failed to check for traffic, and I was almost run over by Clubfoot George Lane on a beautiful steed flying north up the road like a proverbial bat straight out of hell.

At the row of cabins behind Doc Byam's, James Williams had taken control of the martial aspect of the situation and had encircled Palmer's small storage cabins with a cordon of men armed with shotguns. There were twenty of them, at least, elbow to elbow and as grim as they could be. Several of them were familiar to me—John Daddow and Nelson Story and others—and I had seen a good number of the remainder at times about the Gulch. They made for a curious sight, at once both deadly serious and still boyishly timid, conversing with the gathered crowd and all the while holding their line and their deadly shotguns firmly and with resolve. All, that is, except for James Williams, whom I heard several refer to as captain; he marshaled and kept order amongst the appointed watchmen with a consistent and unmitigating air of authority, in a manner that seemed utterly alien to a mining camp.

Out front, near the door of the cabin, Pap and Burtchey and Clark and X Beidler and most of the rest of the posse stood debating. When Pap motioned me to move alongside him, I did so obediently. "Then we're agreed," Burtchey was saying. "They stay here in Nevada." There were general nods of consensus amongst the rest. Then Burtchey said, "Best we find us a prosecutor tonight."

"If we can find one that'll do it," Pap said.

The mob around the cabin soon numbered several hundred and took on an air of partisanship and violence. Voices from out of the crowd angrily demanded that the prisoners be set free for the lack of a warrant or the miners' committee's involvement, and just as many shouted for the instant execution of all three of the men, who had been bound in light logging chains and had been kept out of sight. An equally heated argument featured the question where the proceedings should be held, with Ives's supporters advocating Virginia City and his captors favoring Nevada as the closest practicable situs to the crime, aside from Junction, which bore only the seeds of a townsite. And it was not until Doc Byam arrived that things calmed some being as how, as the elected judge of the Nevada District, he represented the highest authority there was.

"All right now, boys, let's tame it down," Doc Byam said after making his way to the front of the crowd. And when that failed, James Williams fired first one, and then the other, of the barrels of his shotgun; and it got reasonable close to being quiet.

Someone filled Doc Byam in on what happened, and every so often he would nod his head to show he understood or shake it to reflect his general empathy with the condition into which the Gulch and perhaps all of mankind had fallen. And then he finally stared out at the crowd. "It's far too late to be worrying over this tonight, boys," he announced from where he stood on the step of the cabin. "There'll be a miners' meeting called at eight sharp in the morning. That's when the question of whether these boys are to be tried, and, if so, by what process, will be decided. Meanwhile, you all best go back home and take care of your own business. Go on now," he said. "And don't any one of you think about knocking on these windows in the middle of the night."

There was some grumbling and some disappointment, but mostly they slipped off without much complaint. "They'll never hang 'em now, if they ain't done it yet," I heard one miner say. "That Ives's got more lives than a cat."

Doc Byam had a way to keep you calm that must have come from his days doctoring back East. It had been that manner that got him the job of judge in the first place; anyone who'd lived in a mining camp knew that presiding over a miners' committee took a lot of patience, and

Doc Byam was known to have more of that commodity allotted to him than most any man alive. And more than that, he could pass his equanimity on to others in a way that not only reassured but also tempered their anxieties, if only for the while. So when Doc Byam said, "Go on now, go back home," that's pretty much what the miners did, and you could see Pap and William Clark ease some when it happened. And then, but a few minutes later, the captors of George Ives, including Pap with me behind him, rode straight off for Virginia City leaving Williams and his men to stand at guard.

What with a dozen or more saloons and three dance halls and the houses of ill fame and the reckless assortment of cabins and houses, businesses and cafes that Virginia had become, it seemed unlikely that we would find any of the lawyers whose names had been suggested as candidates for the job. But that wasn't going to stop them. George Burtchey dispatched the entire group one by one, leaving me to act as herald, bringing news to certain residents who lived in houses along Cover Street and up against the hillside in Virginia City. Only a few of them were home, and to these I gave the information that there would be a murder trial in Nevada City on the morrow. When I told it to them, their reaction was mostly disinterest, and then I would mention that it was George Ives who was to be tried, and they would raise their eyebrows or let out a hoot or word of doubt. And as I walked from one place to the next, I noticed the peculiar, almost unearthly odor of Virginia City, and I thought how very like a young bull elk it smelled and looked, just after the rut, rank with its own overambition, disoriented and restive, just a bit too satisfied with what it had accomplished, oblivious to its own weakly condition.

I later came to realize that George Burtchey and the rest of them pretty much knew where to find the men for whom they were looking; it was apparently a fact that the lawyering complement of the Gulch populace spent all of their waking and nonworking hours in public places, as visibly as possible, so that, I suppose, it would be widely known both who they were and what they were about. George Burtchey came up just a few minutes after Al Hamilton and I had returned to the appointed place, being James Williams's livery there along Wallace Street. "They were there all right," he said to Hamilton. "The two of them sitting at that same damned table in the Exchange like they owned it. And Gibbons is sitting there with 'em, as snug as can be, sharing a new-bought bottle and all smiles."

"You saying Gibbons hired Richie and Smith to defend George Ives?" Al Hamilton said incredulously. And when George Burtchey reaffirmed the fact, Al Hamilton said, "That bastard is going to hire every lawyer in town. He's just the one to do it, George. You just watch."

Elk Morse walked up next; he had been down to Star's Billiard Hall on Wallace, and then over to the Gem Saloon. "Davis is over at the Gem," he said. "Just like I thought. Setting there more than halfway drunk and only a quarter on his way to wherever he's heading."

George Burtchey had quickly grown impatient for the return of the other men. "What did he say to it?" he asked.

"Never had a chance to ask him, George. Was a whole passel of miners around him when I got there, and him in the middle tellin' 'em how he'll get those boys free by the first motion he makes."

Which made three, and actually four, because it was assumed, and easily confirmed by J. M. Fox, who nonetheless brought back the news with great disappointment, that James Thurmond would represent his solid friends and clients, George Ives and Long John Frank, once asked.

Pap came up next, and I looked at him with anticipation since things never went wrong when Pap was around. But he said, "Wayman Randle's left the Gulch for the winter. Two days back."

And that was five.

The last of the number they had identified and counted was Y. W. Pemberton, a lawyer of some great reputation both for his tenacity and political perspicacity. And when Harry King finally returned, George Burtchey could not even wait to hear it. "Let me guess, Harry," he said. "Gibbons has been to see him already."

"Gibbons has been there all right," King said, and Al Hamilton shook his head knowingly. "But that didn't make no difference."

"You saying he'll do it; Y. W. will prosecute the case?"

And Harry King said, "I ain't saying no such thing. Gibbons got there first, and Y. W. said no. And I got there second, and he said no to me too. And in case you're thinking about it, he also said he'll shoot the next man that even asks him because he don't want nothing to do with it either way. And he means it, plain as day."

"Then that's it," George Burtchey said. "Six lawyers and not one of them willing or able to serve justice."

They stood there stunned, the whole lot of them not knowing what to next do other than propose that someone in their camp attempt to prosecute the case against the four experienced practitioners who had each gained some modicum of fame for prevailing in at least one notably tight situation. So I finally spoke. "There's one more. One more lawyer I mean." And I saw Pap turn sharply and glare at me with admonishment. "His name's Wilbur Sanders. Some of you've heard of him," I said. "He's from Bannack."

"I know about him," J. M. Fox said. "But we don't have time to be looking in Bannack for lawyers." And Pap gave me more of that same look that said be quiet, be still.

"He's here though. In Virginia," I said, now looking directly at Pap. "Mr. Culbertson told me so. I wouldn't say it otherwise. He says Wilbur Sanders is here talking privately about our getting our own territory."

"Well, it's true that he was here," J. M. Fox said. "But I thought he'd left days ago."

One of the men asked Fox what kind of a lawyer Sanders was, and another stated as to how the last thing they needed was an attorney turned politician from Bannack to prosecute a case against George Ives in Alder Gulch.

So I spoke up again, directing the words at Pap. "He's a court-room lawyer mostly. From back East. Studied law under Judge Sidney Edgerton; you know, the new territorial judge over in Bannack."

"I've heard some about Judge Edgerton," George Burtchey said, and now Pap was just staring at me with something other than anger, something more like wonderment or maybe just a little pride.

And then J. M. Fox said, "I've received some correspondence from Edgerton myself. He's the new territorial chief justice."

"Appointed by Lincoln himself," I affirmed. "Only he's not holding court until they bring in some government."

"Then let's get him to do it," Harry King said. "This Judge Edgerton, I mean."

"There ain't no time for that," Burtchey said. "The rest of you boys best get back to your camps and round up some support for the morning."

~~~

As I made the short ride down Cover Street along Discovery Creek, I thought, so that's what it means to be a lawyer; they pay you more than you're worth to defend something you're training tells you is a wrong; and if you're lucky, the pot's big enough to pay all of your colleagues just so you don't have to be fighting with your friends. And if you're even luckier, they're satisfied just to pay you for not taking the other side; so all you have to do is tell the one you'll take it and the other you won't and then do nothing at all since the one that's without knows it isn't even worth the time it would take to try. And I pictured an exodus of the legal profession flowing into Nevada City and taking their reverse toll of gold dust at its nonexistent gate, like the Mormons at the ferries, only different.

Some of the Cal Gulch boys had split apart from us as we left Virginia, going up the Gulch instead to the Highland District where they and X Beidler ran their claims and enjoyed their greatest influence. James Williams was well known there also, up among the meadows at the headwaters of the Gulch, since he and his brother had established their ranch just the other side of Summit, along a creek they named for themselves. There, they grazed and corralled horses and stock that had been over- or underused, bringing them back up to the norm or keeping them fit for the next long ride to anywhere. Most of the miners that James Williams had led up out of Colorado, to what they thought would be the established placers at Bannack but what turned out to be the strike at Alder Gulch, had also staked claims in the high elevations of the Gulch. That stretch of the 20-mile find was more to their liking in that it reminded them more of Colorado. And they mostly kept their animals at the Williams ranch and had their friends did the same; all of which made for a pretty good business for the Williams brothers. And together with his livery in Virginia City and his early cabin building efforts and later freighting endeavors, it suggested that James Williams would have his way financially wherever he might go.

Some of the others kept riding when we hit Nevada, with the intent of going to Junction and as far as Laurin, which was a job I would not have wanted for the world; the prisoners' stronghold was north of Junction along the stage road, past Bivens Gulch and up to Wisconsin Creek where Ives kept his tent-camp ranch, and where Long John Frank also kept his. Which left Pap and me and only three or four others to quietly raise the word in Nevada. We went first to Palmer's storehouse where the prisoners were kept, and when we came up, James Williams stopped us with his shotgun pointed low until he was satisfied with what he saw.

"Any trouble here?" Pap asked.

And James Williams said, "None. Not expectin' any either. Aleck Carter and Bill Graves showed up demandin' to know what we intended to do with Ives and the others. They complained some when they heard, but there's far too many guns here for their likes. Rode off 'bout an hour ago. Expect we'll see them and their entire crowd of yahoos in the mornin'." And then he looked across all of our faces, his pinpoint eyes emotionless and deathlike. "Didn't find yourselves a lawyer, did you?" he said. "Should have hung 'em when we had the chance. I told you that before."

Night had fallen over the Gulch with an expectant quiet. And yet most everyone in every camp was wide awake, sitting about a fire with their partners and friends arguing the case before most even knew much of what it was about. And it took only an hour or so for Pap and me to see that the word had spread through the Gulch like a grass fire in autumn. "Let's go get some sleep," Pap said. And I could tell by that voice that I knew so well, that voice that had guided and been with me throughout my life, that Pap was dead worn out from his exertions, and that what lay ahead would require even more fortitude and conviction than simply riding out and seizing a man so that justice could be done.

We set out our bedrolls in the tent, and I watched him as he checked the shotgun and laid it by his side. "Pap. You think they'll hang George Ives?"

"Wouldn't bet either way."

"If I were betting, I'd put my money on X Beidler," I said.

"You'd have lost that bet last summer," Pap said, and now he was into his bedroll and instantly motionless. "Stinson and Lyons won out then. Why won't Ives win out now? Besides, X ain't runnin' this show. He'll get to play his part I imagine, but it ain't his party. And without a prosecutor on our side, a real lawyer I mean and not just some easterner who thinks he wants to be a real lawyer or knows how to play one, we ain't got a chance in hell. If it were me, I wouldn't go bettin' on anything around here right now. Unless I bet on the opposite of what seems right and logical. Seems to me this place is about as upside down and inside out as it can get. Wouldn't surprise me tomorrow if the whole damned rebel army rides in here and claims this place as their new capital, and if the next day Satan himself drives them out and claims it as his. No, sir," Pap said, and now he was on his side facing the tent wall. "I wouldn't trust nothin' to no one around here if I were a bettin' man."

CHAPTER 3

Clubfoot George Lane's clubfoot was an item of much curiosity in Alder Gulch, although I couldn't say whether anyone had ever seen it in all its glory, bare to the skin. It was mentioned and joked about with some frequency in the barbershops and cafes and around the camps, openly by metaphor or simile or exaggerated comparison; and there were some who, in moments of either reckless indifference or warm reflection, referred to George Lane by any of a dozen other sobriquets, including the mighty King of Clubs. And the irony of it was that Clubfoot George himself made sure that it was so. When you rode up to Wallace Street in Virginia City, he was usually the first man you saw. When the weather tolerated, he'd set up his bootblack stand in front of Dance & Stuart's and then sit there in a chair with that clubfoot up on the rail while the wagons and other traffic rattled by all day long, as if to draw attention to his business by the obvious and severe deformity of his foot. As if to proclaim: Clubfoot George is my name and there it is to prove it.

It couldn't help but make you feel sorry for him, seeing that crippling defect and knowing that he couldn't, nor ever had been able to, do what you could do. And since the miners in the Gulch generally were a charitable sort, Clubfoot George did a more than reasonable business tending to the footwear of others, including a host of notables that frequented Virginia City, Henry Plummer and his deputies included, who sought out a shine even when they were not in need. And some of the most reckless and frivolous class, George Ives and Jack Slade and their attendants, also were known to pay more than a pinch of dust for a particularly good job of cleaning the mudcake from a road-weary boot. So, when George Lane dashed off down the Gulch in clear haste and obvious intensity, it made sense to conclude that his mission was to seek aid for his patron George Ives; and that George Lane's destination was Bannack City, where Henry Plummer would be advised of the doings in Nevada City and would come to impede or insure justice, depending on one's point of view.

That was the first talk Pap and me heard the next morning as we walked up the slope toward Nevada. "Hey, Yank," a miner shouted to Pap from a camp along the trail. "If ya'll er thankin' a lynchin' Ives, ya'll best be doin' it fore Henry Plummer makes it in." And then a second time from William Clark, whom we ran into as we crossed the stage road and came up to Doc Byam's place. "Word has it Plummer's been sent for," Clark said in a disappointed voice.

We didn't have a chance to learn more though, because at that moment John Lott and George Burtchey came striding into the crowd with a slick and somewhat pale and fragile-looking man between them. The newcomer was dandied up in a crisply starched shirt and a fine looking greatcoat and boots the like of which were rarely seen in the Gulch. And yet for all his appearance of being a wealthy and accomplished merchant, he bore a mixed look of nervous anticipation and hesitancy. He struggled to keep his mouth tight-lipped and without expression, and in so doing his hands took over unconsciously, stroking his thin black mustache and his cropped beard.

"Boys," John Lott said as he broke into the circle. "I've brought you our man. Step up here, Colonel." And Wilbur Sanders eased awkwardly into the middle of the crowd with his back up like a rooster in a barnyard. "Gentlemen, I am pleased to introduce Colonel Wilbur Sanders of Ohio. Of the firm of Edgerton and Sanders. That's Judge Sidney Edgerton of Bannack, for those of you who don't know, sent out here to the territory by Mr. Lincoln himself. Colonel Sanders is an Oberlin man. A trial lawyer from back East. And he's our man now, so let's give him our best support and finish with our task."

There were doubts of course, and I wouldn't exactly say you could hear an audible and collective sigh of relief at the announcement. This Colonel Sanders was essentially an unknown, and that fact would work as a negative before a group of miners judging one of their own. And there was something to him that didn't look right; he was too neat, almost too feminine by the way his face looked like it never saw the sun or his hands the handle of a pick. And he seemed too young to be a colonel, or if not that then at least not manly and determined enough to lead a regiment of men in a charge across an open field against a rebel line. And as though that were not enough to raise concern amongst the friends of William Clark and George Burtchey, Sanders kept stroking at that beard and mustache and plunging one hand, and then the other, deep into the pockets of his greatcoat and fidgeting with some unseen object in them.

Across the way, in Star's Cafe, the lawyers Richie and Smith and Thurmond and Davis were meeting with Johnny Gibbons and Harvey Meade and Bill Hunter and a few others who were the most prominent or wealthy of Ives's supporters. Occasionally, we would see one of them emerge and then return awhile later with what was generally surmised to be a potential witness, who each time evinced great seriousness as he moved through the rapidly growing numbers of men who were funneling in from the surrounding districts to observe the spectacle that had been promised. The skies were clear, and but a little ice showed in the shadows; and the snows in the elevations deflected the brightness of the day with an almost religious light. It was the morning of the nineteenth day of December in 1863. And at eight o'clock sharp someone started ringing the cowbell that had come to represent the signal that a miners' meeting was being called to order in the Nevada District.

It had been assumed that the meeting would be held at the normal location, in a small bowl-shaped depression just across the road that accommodated the average attendance and provided a good view of the center of the proceedings, so that any member of the district might participate simply by speaking out loudly on the subject of a particular line of questioning or argument. Someone had hauled a table over for Doc Byam to sit at, and Doc Byam was there now with Y. W. Pemberton and Bob Hereford standing at his side talking. And a great crowd of men, and a few women too, had already assembled, with others streaming in by a steady flow from up and down the Gulch, as though every creek and canyon and defile were being cleansed at last of the mass of human detritus that had accrued over the last six frantic months.

It took a good hour for the lawyers and their employers to make their way down into the meeting area, the prisoners conspicuously being absent and presumably still under guard. And by the time they all congregated in front of Doc Byam's table, it looked more like a prayer meeting than a trial. Pap always said to not be bashful about taking what was free, so I claimed a spot up close, where I would be afforded a clear viewing of the entire process, but after a while I thought better of it and moved up the slope some so that I might be able to observe what was happening in the crowd as much as what was transpiring down below. And all the while, Doc Byam pretty much sat there, with Pemberton and Hereford at his side, and the three of them smoking cigars like animated chimneys enjoying some well-seasoned cordwood on a cool winter's night. And every so often, Doc Byam would call out to one of the lawyers and ask whether everyone was ready to proceed.

But the lawyers couldn't seem to agree even on that, or apparently on anything else. George Ives's four lawyers set upon Wilbur Sanders with every pretrial argument they could conceive regarding such matters as where the trial should be held and by whom and to what deciding body when and through how many witnesses over how much time and toward what end. And each time one of the former made their point,

Wilbur Sanders would rebuff them by suggesting an alternative and usually opposite solution.

It went on so for an hour, maybe more, and at last Doc Byam lost his patience. He rapped on the table with the butt of a pistol and caught the attention of Ives's four lawyers, who virtually encircled Sanders as they presented their endless series of proposals. "You boys come over to the bench here," he said. And when the five of them did, he asked loud enough for the entire crowd to hear, "Now what's the problem?"

And James Thurmond immediately stepped forward. "We have some preliminary matters to attend to, Judge. Their disposition seems plain to me, but we can't seem to get Mr. Sanders here to agree. If you will allow me to explain, I am confident I can persuade you that certain jurisdictional questions exist here that preclude this district from exercising its authority over the men that are being held prisoner."

At which, and I believe to the great surprise of Pap and George Burtchey and their group, Sanders loosed a reckless and caustic laugh that everyone in the natural amphitheater heard quite clearly. "Jurisdictional questions indeed," he scoffed. "Must we continue with these delays?" And then he strutted in front of the audience, only to turn all of a sudden and slam his fist down upon the table, thereby startling Doc Byam, who had not been watching him closely enough. "The jurisdiction of the court is established by the district's nearest proximity to the crime committed. The court's power over the subject matter is concurrent with that over the persons accused. Let us not," Sanders said, "be deluded by the farcical arguments of the defense, despite their numerosity." There were murmurs both of agreement and opposition amongst the ever-growing crowd, and George Burtchey and John Lott drew Sanders back and spoke to him at length in hushed voices.

Sanders, of course, was wrong on all points, both factually and legally, since, while apparently unbeknownst to him, the Junction District recently had been formed south of Nevada and it thus, being the closest district to the locale of the crime, was the logical place for what the miners called the venue for the trial. During their lengthy conference, Burtchey and Lott must have persuaded Sanders that such was the case, for when Sanders finally turned back to Judge Byam, his position on the question was altogether altered. "We propose, your honor," he said with a great theatrical flourish of compromise and condescension, "to avoid these preliminary squabbles by employing a procedure we are confident will be acceptable to the public at large."

"And what might that be?" Judge Byam asked with more than a hint of sarcasm.

"That the accused be tried before an advisory jury comprised of twenty-four men good and true, with twelve being allotted from the Junction District and twelve from Nevada. That you and Judge Wilson, whom I am advised presides over the Junction court, try the case jointly. And that the question of guilt be submitted to the public in its entirety once it has considered the jury's advisory verdict."

From there, things deteriorated rapidly. Someone in the crowd questioned the need for a jury of any sort, and then a second suggested that the only thing that had been proved so far was that the lawyers were more of an obstruction than a catalyst to the process and should thus be barred from participating in the case. "We don't need these here slickers tellin' us what questions we need to have answered to know who done what," the objecting party said. "I say let the miners themselves submit the questions. These lawyers here ain't gonna do anythin' other than to drag this out." But in the end the lawyers, each and every one of them I mean, established beyond doubt that if the parties desired lawyers, they were more than entitled to them.

Then, Buz Caven, who with the missus had just given Virginia City its firstborn child, interjected by waving before Judge Byam and Judge Wilson, who had unilaterally assumed a seat next to the Doc, a sheet of paper on which something had been written. "I have in my hand a list of twelve prominent citizens from Virginia City," Caven shouted out less to the two men who sat as judges than to the throng that now numbered at least 600 or 700, "whom I move be added to the twenty-four jurors from Nevada and Junction." And then he read them off loudly, giving their proper Christian names in full and with great clarity and emphasis, as though by so doing he demonstrated the high quality of their character.

I thought the motion was a fair one, both because Nevada had expressed no inclination to administer and adjudicate the case on its own, and since Virginia's interest in the proceedings was as dominant as Virginia was to the Gulch as a whole. And I suspect the assembly would have approved the motion en masse with little consideration had not Wilbur Sanders stepped forward and loudly objected. "The prosecution objects," he stated definitively. And then there was a long pause during which no one said anything while the crowd waited for Sanders to explain the basis for his opposition to Caven's idea. Then he finally spoke. "The motion has no foundation or basis in law. What reason is there for involving the Fairweather District in this proceeding? If Virginia, then why not Summit and Highland? And if them, why not also Bannack and Spanish Fork? The motion is plainly ill founded."

"Do you object to one or more of these gentlemen I have named?" Caven demanded, and it was clear that he had calculated that Sanders either knew none of them or would not dare defame them in the presence of so many locals.

But Sanders surprised Buz Caven and the whole gathering a second time. "I believe Mr. Dearborn is a professional gambler, Mr. Caven. Is he not? Shall we have those that are advising on a verdict bet on it at the same time? In which case it will be most difficult to speculate whether the probabilities of the verdict determined the wager, or the amount of the wager the verdict. And since I do not know the reputations of the rest of these gentlemen, and since I obviously cannot trust to their reliability based solely on your motion, and since I am not a gambling man, Mr. Caven, I object to the remainder of them also. I object to all of them, Mr. Caven. In the singular and in the plural."

This was a little hard for the miners to interpret since, by the sheer fact of being there in Alder Gulch during its speculative beginnings, they were all more or less predisposed to gamble in their own right. And at least half of them compounded that vice by then gambling at the tables, or at any other opportunity, with the golden fruits of their original good fortune. So that close to half of those present were unsure whether they should be offended by Wilbur Sanders's castigation of what they considered to be the natural habits of the working class. And there thus were angry shouts and rejoinders mixed in almost equally with the vocalized support for Wilbur Sanders's argument against the inclusion of Buz Caven's dozen with the other twenty-four.

It became necessary to call a vote on the question and, since the issue was perceived to be of some consequence, a recess of fifteen minutes was called in order that those who had wandered off to buy a haircut or a meal or to do some other business might be notified and recalled. And sure enough, at the expiration of that period, the attendance was considerably larger than it had been fifteen minutes earlier.

On the first call for the vote, the yeas were distinctly louder than the nays. But it was evident that the former had gauged the volume of the latter who expressed their disapproval of the motion first; this brought the somewhat unusual complaint that those against somehow had been cheated by not realizing the vehemence of those that were for. As if to prove their point, on the second vote, and even more so on the third, which was demanded by those in favor, those opposed to the expansion of the jury did succeed in shouting down the motion. The court declared the motion denied amid some rather serious upheaval in the crowd. And it was clear by the nature and substance of their invective that the anger of those who had been denied was directed solely at Wilbur Sanders, who fidgeted nervously in the face of a barrage of criticisms and threats.

Thurmond saw this to be opportune, and he thus argued that although the court had determined the composition of the jury, it had not necessarily determined where the trial should be held. He swept his hand across the panorama of the overflowing amphitheater, taking in everyone with one munificent gesture. "We cannot accommodate such a crowd here in Nevada," he said with a voice of civic concern. "In the name solely of convenience, let us transfer the proceedings to a locale more suited to the trial's magnitude." At which, and before the entire question that had just been resolved could be reignited by an uprising from the congregation of miners, Judge Byam held up his hand and then stood up. "It is near the dinner hour," he said. "We shall continue, and it shall be here, in Nevada City, up on the road where we can accommodate Mr. Thurmond's concern, before an advisory jury of twenty-four. Judge Wilson and I shall have their names for you when we reconvene. And gentlemen," he said, and now it was clear that Judge Byam would at last assume control over the trial, "be prepared to begin in earnest when you return."

~~~

You wouldn't think that one and a half hours could mean much to men who parceled out time and effort in measures of full half days and longer; but that holiday of Abe Lincoln's must have set them thinking different than they had before. As soon as Judge Byam said the words, there was a mad scramble every which way and at every which speed. And within five minutes' time every barber chair and gaming seat and dance spot and restaurant table and bar stool was occupied by someone who five minutes earlier had been in the outdoor amphitheater prepared to cast a vote on any question posited to them. And I would have done the same, gone off I mean, to do something that Pap's strict tutelage forbade or at least inhibited, were it not for X Beidler, who as much as seized me by the neck and stopped me cold. "Be needin' some help here, Billy," says X. "Judge Byam says to move the trial up across the road and to get some arrangements on it, too. Be best if you came with me."

We went across the road to the dance hall and X Beidler made me wait outside while he went in. I could smell the fresh whiskey on his mustache when he came back out. "They've got plenty of chairs and benches along the wall," he said. "Bring 'em out and set 'em under that tree, over there. Two rows for twelve men each. In an arc. And don't run off."

Without more, he turned and walked away with a jaunty air of authority and a smart bounce in his gait, carrying that long shotgun that seemed
at least as tall as him and maybe taller. And then he turned back and said,
"If anybody gives you any trouble, just tell 'em Judge Byam's order."

The dance hall was unlike I had imagined it would be; but each
time I walked back in and grabbed a couple more chairs from someone
and said my apologies and stated my authority, it made a little more
sense. Because the first time I went in, it was too unreal for me to even
fathom. The dark, poorly dressed and drab figures of the miners holding and dancing as close as they could get to the brightly dressed, silky
radiance of the women. And the women, despite all their charms and
womanhood, unable to overwhelm the harsh smells and manners the
miners brought in with them. That, and the music, did it. So that the
first time it stopped me square in my tracks until the dance ended and
the abrupt conclusion of the music almost knocked me over. On the
second pass it was only moderately easier, merely quickening my breath
and speeding up my heart. But by the time there were only a few chairs
left, it all seemed perfectly natural, if not somewhat necessary, and I
thought to stay there, and only by the lack of choice did I discount the
notion.

Next to the dance hall, under the cottonwood that stood between
the hall and Richards's house, X Beidler had pulled up two large freight
wagons. He placed several chairs in each, and then, with no regard to
questions of ownership, he directed me to move from Finney's house a
full stack of cordwood that Finney had laid up against the wall. I asked
about it, but X said, "Don't be worryin' none about that. We'll be
needin' a fire." Then he made every man owning a wagon or a horse or
a mule to clear out of an area of 200 feet in radius. "This land is
claimed temporarily by the miners' court," he proclaimed out loud. He
mounted one of the two freight wagons and made me get up, too; and
then he sat there, with his shotgun stretched out across his lap, and kept
the area clear of obstructions.

The miners started coming back a good half hour before the

appointed time, and they seemed more intent, more interested in where might be the most advantageous spot from which to both observe and participate in the trial. And they clearly had been refreshed by the break. Many of them carried with them food and bottles and glasses, and they mostly seemed in better moods than in the morning. There were plenty among them that knew X Beidler, and it seemed an accepted practice for them to come up to X and try to harass him somehow. And somehow they never got the better of him, including one young miner who seemed overenthused by the concept. He kept making caustic remarks about how little X Beidler looked sitting high up in that wagon. And when he finally said, "You look like a little old man up there, Beidler," X called him on it and said, "Bet I've seen fewer birthdays than you." The young miner looked at him and said, "Not a prayer," and X Beidler says, "Five dollars," and they agreed and gave it to me to hold. And then X Beidler says, without waiting, "February 29, 1836, what's yours."

At first the other didn't get it and he blurted out his birthday, which barely made him twenty, and stuck out his hand for me to pay him. And then he did get it, and he got mad and called X Beidler a cheat and a liar. That shotgun came up from X's lap as fast as wind and stuck straight in the other's face, but a foot away. "That's the second mistake you've made since you showed up here, boy," says X. "Best say your apologies and move off." And when the other just stood there with an intense look in his eyes, X said, "Move on, boy. Now." And the other backed away slowly and then angrily turned into the crowd. I gave X his $5.00 and then X let me go, saying, "Stay clear of trouble," and I was glad to climb down off that wagon and get away since it seemed he had trouble written all over everything he did.

There was interesting talk going on all around during the break, but you could only hear snatches of it; so you couldn't come close to guessing what would happen and who really meant what. Meanwhile, the crowd grew more and more restless, while the lawyers and prisoners and potential witnesses were sequestered in barren, ill-lit rooms. Rumors began to circulate exonerating Ives and Long John Frank via

irrefutable alibis; and in a different segment of the crowd, men with desperate and violent looks about them were vehemently asserting that Bill
Clark and John Lott would die long before George Ives came anywheres
close to getting hung. A wild air of secrecy and connivance and appre-
hension prevailed, with many a word exchanged in veiled whisper, and
messengers and seeming spies delivering information furtively back and
forth between the assembly and the teams of combatants who savored
every last minute of preparation available to them. And all the while
more and more people funneled in from up and down the creek until it
was all but impossible for a wagon to make it from one side of Nevada
City to the other.

Someone must have drawn the conclusion that Wilbur Sanders
was just a bit too metropolitan or eastern to stand it alone, and Charles
Bagg, a relative newcomer to the Gulch, had therefore been enlisted to
render him aid. Judge Wilson made the announcement as soon as he and
Judge Byam had taken their seats in one of the wagon beds and behind
the table that had been set in it at X Beidler's direction. "On its own
motion," Judge Wilson proclaimed once he had quieted the crowd, which
came to order most reluctantly and not without its share of humor and
sarcasm, "the court recognizes Charles S. Bagg, Esquire, as additional
counsel for the prosecution. For those of you who are unacquainted
with Mr. Bagg, you should know that Mr. Bagg is an attorney of some
reputation from Indiana and the owner of a newly recorded claim in the
Junction District."

This brought a chorus of hurrahs and disparaging remarks, none
of which affected Charles Bagg in the least. A squat, red-cheeked man
in dilapidated clothes, he strode out in front of the wagon and bowed
once, looking very little like a lawyer and rather like a clown. The names
of the appointed jurors were read aloud, first from the Nevada District
by Judge Byam and then those from Junction by Judge Wilson, and the
named men made their way up to the two rows of chairs and benches.
And almost concurrently, from out of the crowd a substantial number
of armed men came forward, including Embly Sutherland and Charles

Weatherbee and Tom Whitly, and with a predetermined precision they formed a solid ring around the jurors and showed clearly by their shotguns that they were there to guard the jury until the end.

X Beidler must have figured I had the best viewing spot of all up there on Richards's roof, and being as how X was not one to stand in a crowd, he handed me his shotgun and climbed up to join me, pushing a miner next to me over more than just a bit. "Good place to see what happens," he said once he got situated. "If shootin' starts," he said as he scanned the crowd, "be best for you to slip up over the roof there and come off the other side."

And X was right; you could see virtually everything from that one position—the jurors, of which only twenty were present, thus requiring the judges to select four alternatives, and Pemberton, who had assumed the neutral role of court's secretary and was sitting next to the fire that had been kindled with Finney's wood, and the crowd that had settled some and yet seemed to teem with its own unique form of static activity. The prisoners, though, were not to be seen, and Pap, also, had not yet returned. Nor had Sanders nor any of the other lawyers reappeared, except for Thurmond, who no doubt was there now to prepare the assembly and to ensure that nothing happened without his side knowing it. As he made his rounds between the judges and members of the jury and crowd and even amongst some of the guards, who held firm and yet were congenial to him, Thurmond seemed to be on familiar terms with everyone, offering a cordial word or a ribald comment wherever he might do so to his advantage, taking a social drink from a bottle extended to him through the wall of arms. And then Bagg showed up, and from thereafter, wherever Thurmond turned next, Bagg followed him closely, much in appearance to a lowly squire at the heels of his knightly lord.

Finally, Judge Byam summoned Thurmond and Bagg over to the bench; they exchanged some conversation, and then the two lawyers went off—Thurmond into Star's Cafe and Bagg to the row of buildings behind Doc Byam's office—and it was clear that things were about to begin.

When they marched out George Ives, it was under a guard commanded by James Williams. Pap was there among them, and George Berkingham and Phil McGowen and Elk Morse, too, and a half dozen others I knew well. It seemed like half of the old Cal Gulch District had come all the way to the Alder diggings not so much to find gold as to see George Ives hanged. And as soon as Ives came into view, an upwelling of support was expressed in as many different forms as vocalization and gesture allowed. "Don't go worryin' none, George," one miner in front of me and X Beidler yelled. "We'll have you free by sundown." And true to form, Ives cut a figure of confidence and alacrity as he followed Williams's lead up to the tribunal.

"That George Ives sure is a cool one," I remarked to X Beidler.

And X almost sneered at Ives before he answered. "We'll see," he said. "Things ain't even warmed up yet."

I thought that Williams would go back then and get Long John Frank and George Hilderman, but he never did. Instead, he picked for himself the most prominent place he could find, midway between the jury and Ives, and then grimly assumed his own post, holding his sawed-off double-barreled shotgun like most would hold a pistol. That was when I, and anyone else who was paying any attention, knew the scuttlebutt that John Frank had agreed to testify against George Ives was the truth. Because this one trial was going to take plenty long enough that there wasn't going to be a second one after it, not with the creek still running and the daytime temperatures moderating slightly above the freezing mark. And if they simply had decided they weren't going to try John Frank and George Hilderman, they would have freed them. So they were holding them for something else, be it to protect them from Ives's friends or to ensure the coercion of their statements. And George Ives's friends saw this also, and bitter complaints were voiced by Bill Hunter and Johnny Gibbons, and thereafter by their lawyers, but to no avail.

"You boys are no more entitled than they are to know what the other side's got up their sleeve," Judge Byam said in denying Smith's motion that John Frank be produced to the court. "Let's move this along."

At the time, I didn't know much about trials and how they were conducted, or I might have thought this one just a bit peculiar. They started out by letting Bagg on the one side, and Davis and Smith on the other, argue what they called "the facts" but what in reality were plainly distorted and largely unverifiable contrivances to sway the crowd toward their way of thinking. And Bagg very much surprised the audience in his ability to advocate and, more importantly, persuade; he stood up on that wagon, utterly impervious to the chastisements of Ives's friends, with his clothes hanging on him like rags off an overweight scarecrow, and the first thing he said in a well-projected voice was, "I don't know." Which I thought was an auspicious start; and I was about to say so to X when Bagg did it again. "I don't know," he said, "who to thank more—that grouse for being slow enough for a bad shot like Bill Palmer to hit it full in flight, or the Almighty for dropping it from the sky right there on Nick Tibolt's body where Bill Palmer could find them both." And having got the crowd's attention, Bagg said, "Don't let there be any doubt about that much, gentlemen; it was divine providence that brings us here and accords to us this opportunity to rid ourselves of the evil that has settled over this community. And let us not be mistaken about why we are here either; we've been brought here so that it can be shown that George Ives murdered Nick Tibolt, so that we can decide what we're going to do about it." And Charles Bagg was off and running.

When Bagg first started, I could see that Wilbur Sanders was somewhat appalled, embarrassed no doubt by his association with the colloquial Bagg and concerned, too, that Bagg would undermine his case and his good name with it. But Bagg did a good enough job of maneuvering his way through his opening statement, laying the foundation for justice by reminding the miners and merchants and teamsters how hard they had worked and what the Lord above expected of them, and then by detailing the litany of robberies and murders in what seemed an infinite itemization—the names of Magruder, Southmeade, MacFarland,

Carrhart, Dillingham, and plenty of others whom I had never heard of, and some who might not have even existed, running on top of each other like horses herded into an undersized corral.

And when Bagg spoke of the cruelty of Ives, who John Frank would testify shot Tibolt while he knelt to pray, and who Palmer would state kept friends that would not even lend the ten minutes it would have taken to help him load the body into a wagon, it became clear to everyone that George Ives had just entered a struggle for his life. And Bagg did not stop then, either. He went on somehow to involve Ives in every crime that had been committed in the entire region over the prior four months, explaining how Oliver's and Peabody's drivers had offered statements implicating Ives in virtually every robbery on the roads between Salt Lake City and Fort Benton, and in several killings, including that of the man that had been whipped into submission up at Hal Meacham's camp. And you could not help but tend to be persuaded by Bagg's implicit argument that it was these roughs out of Lewiston—Ives in particular, and Zachary and Romaine and Howard and Skinner and Marshland and all the rest—who bore the responsibility for the lawless decline that had befallen the Gulch.

From the way Davis and Smith conversely told it, the world was virtually the opposite of that described by Charles Bagg. They offered a little bit of George Ives that everyone could relate to, whether it was his respected association with the officers' corps of the U.S. Army up in the Washington Territory, or his good sense of humor, or his affiliation with James Stuart's ill-fated Yellowstone expedition that had, after all, given birth at least indirectly to Alder Gulch itself. And, well, Nick Tibolt was dead and the Gulch was a hard place and times were at least bound to get colder if not harder here in the coming months. And of course it wasn't George Ives that was doing all that robbing since everyone knew George Ives when they saw him and no one rode a horse the way George Ives rode one, so that there would have been no way for George Ives to hide his identity if he had been guilty of all those robberies Bagg had itemized in neat chronology.

"So," H. P. Smith said as he caught his breath. "Let us not get carried away with all this speculation of who did what, where, when, and why. Honest Whiskey Joe and George Brown will tell you that George Ives was with them over at Dempsey's Cottonwood on the day Tibolt died. If George Ives was with those gentlemen, then he could not have committed this crime they think he might be guilty of, but which not one person observed. We need to stick together here, boys. Let's not get carried away. I ask you," Smith said directly to the jury. "George Ives and James Thurmond and my colleagues ask you to go forward carefully in this endeavor. If it is George Ives today, it may well be you tomorrow." And then Smith stepped back.

There was some grumbling after that, and some catcalls in favor and against both sides. But Judge Byam held things in fairly good order and, when he had quieted the crowd sufficiently, he called for the prosecution's first witness.

They made Bill Palmer swear under the fear of God that the testimony he would offer would entail only the truth. And Wilbur Sanders made a great point of the fact that he coincidentally had a Bible available that would serve that very purpose, there in the inside pocket of his coat where, we were made to believe, it was always kept. So Palmer swore to it solemnly and then Sanders placed the Bible back into his coat and then patted it once, as if by so doing he ensured that it would settle back into its own permanent place of repose.

I had already heard Palmer's story several times; and with each subsequent telling it had not varied much from the way X Beidler and Pap had told it to me. And sitting there on that wagon with his long greasy hair hanging loosely over his shoulders, Palmer told it again as I had heard it, in a confident and assertive tone: of how he had gone down to the Stinkingwater hunting grouse and after a long fruitless day finally had shot a hen only to have it land straight on top of the disfigured body that proved to be that of Nicholas Tibolt, and then had gone looking for help at the nearest place he could find for someone who would assist him in prying the body off of the frozen ground and loading it into a wagon in a decent manner. And then he told of his conversations with John Frank and George Hilderman. "Fact is," Palmer said, nodding his head over at George Ives, who sat alone in the other wagon, "George Ives's friends all seemed to be plain knowledgeable of the fact that there was a body layin' over there and just as plain against helpin' anybody to move it."

"And why is it that you say that, Mr. Palmer?" Wilbur Sanders asked.

"Because when I told Hilderman and John Frank there was a body layin' in the sagebrush just a mile back, all they said was, 'There's men dyin' on this road 'bout every day.' And when I asked them for some help in gettin' that body loaded up into my wagon, all they said was they didn't have time to be wastin' on dead men." Then Palmer recounted how he worked the frozen body off of the ground all by himself and struggled to get it into his wagon and then got enough people out on the street in Nevada until someone figured how it was Nick Tibolt.

"That's when they got up the posse," Palmer said. "Bill Clark and George Burtchey did. And of course they wanted me along since I was the only one that knew where I found him and knew where Hilderman's wickiup was at." And when Wilbur Sanders served up to Palmer an open-ended question that asked him to tell what happened with the posse, Palmer explained in detail how they came up on Hilderman's wickiup in the early morning and caught the whole bunch of them—John Frank and Ives and Carter and Zachary and Shears and Johnny Cooper and Whiskey Bill Graves—some of the same ones that Ben Bailey, who'd been caught stealing, had named as his cohorts and was spared with only a whipping for telling it. "And as soon as we took John Frank outside and told him we were takin' him to Nevada for murderin' Nick Tibolt, he said, 'I didn't do it; it was George Ives that killed the Dutchman.'"

"Did John Frank explain how he knew Ives murdered Nicholas Tibolt?" Sanders inquired of Palmer.

And Palmer said, "Frank said that Ives followed Tibolt after he retrieved those two mules, and when Ives came back he had 'em both, plus the one Tibolt was riding, being X Beidler's Black Bess he's so proud of, all in tow."

"And is that all John Frank told the posse out there at George Hilderman's wickiup?"

"Well, no," Palmer said. "I guess there was more. He said how when Ives came back he asked Ives what happened to Tibolt and Ives said he had made Tibolt pray and then shot him in the head while he was down on his knees."

Sanders asked a few more questions, and Palmer told about how they found at least fifteen revolvers and rifles and shotguns in the wickiup, which seemed to me about the right number for that many men in those times in the Idaho Territory, and then he told about the ride back and how they captured Hilderman out on the road and how Ives almost got away.

That was about all Palmer had to say; but Wilbur Sanders dragged it out a lot longer anyway. He made Palmer describe twice what the body looked like when he found it, and when Palmer detailed how the face had been pecked at unmercifully by birds, Sanders shook his head. "Where did you say that bullet hole was?" he asked.

"Right here," Bill Palmer answered, pointing above his left eye. "That's where Ives shot him, right about here."

"Mr. Ives wasn't concerned much about Nick Tibolt getting a proper Christian burial, was he, Mr. Palmer?" Sanders asked.

And Palmer said, "Not one bit," before Thurmond and Richie and Colonel Wood, a vocal supporter of Ives with a Georgian Baptist lineage, could shout out their objections.

I thought that the first portion of Palmer's statement was pretty much a nonevent. The truth was that having a ranch like George Ives did, and a brush wickiup like George Hilderman did, along the wagon road that followed the creek, could amount to a major inconvenience to the owner. The road was heavily used, and travelers were always breaking down, or getting stuck in the mud, or getting hurt or sick, or needing help for some other reason, or just plain looking for a place to get out of the rain. Twice, earlier in the year, men had been run over by wagons, and one of them had died not far from Wisconsin Creek. So it wasn't as though it was fair to be expecting those that lived along the road to carry society's burden for it. Not that that meant George Ives didn't do it either; it just seemed that Palmer's testimony about them not wanting to bother with a body that was already dead didn't shed any light on the question at all.

X Beidler reacted to it altogether differently. When Palmer said how Tibolt's face had been eaten at, X said out loud, "Poor Nicky." And when Palmer stated how Hilderman and Frank wouldn't lift a hand to help him, X said, "Those sons of bitches." And plenty others in the crowd reacted similarly, especially when it came to the part about the Christian burials. Because there were certain things that George Ives wasn't, and one of them was the sort of man that thinks in terms of chapters and verse. Which was probably why H. P. Smith spent a long hour going over with Palmer what he had said and a lot more besides. The result of which was that before Palmer was through, we had to consider not only that he had found Tibolt's body in bad shape with a bullet hole in the head and rope burns on his neck and that Ives's friend wouldn't help him, but also that Palmer ran a dance hall and made a profit off his sporting ladies and hadn't owned his own Bible since he'd come out West, and that, by William Palmer's own admission, it was just possible that Long John Frank had said all those things to protect his own neck at the expense of George Ives.

I was glad that I had heard most of it before, since it made me feel comfortable in ignoring a lot of it and instead watching what was going on in the crowd. It looked like maybe neither side had had enough time to fully prepare. Even as the trial progressed, if you looked hard enough, you could see their emissaries working through the collection of men, searching for witnesses and information and support, which they gathered with great subtlety and connivance. At the same time, I watched Smith and Bill Hunter or Bagg and Clark and Burtchey occasionally meet behind the wagons, between themselves or with someone else, and every five minutes or so a rider would head up or down the Gulch, no doubt in an attempt to retrieve more witnesses or informants or at least more men to vote their side when the time came for deciding.

They finally let Palmer step down off the wagon and they as quickly ushered in Long John Frank, with James Williams providing a full guard until Frank was sitting up there in the witness chair next to Judges Byam and Wilson. And you could see that John Frank was a might nervous as Williams led him through the crowd, with Long John Frank a head taller than the crowd in general, and Frank turning his head this way and that, all the while looking down at those all around him and never once, not even when and after he climbed into the wagon, looking at George Ives, who still maintained an appearance of calm good-natured confidence.

Then John Frank retold it exactly as Bill Palmer had, and from that point on the expression on George Ives's face was changed. Where before that moment he had wore a light carefree countenance that I imagine hundreds of those present had known or seen as Ives cavorted on the roads and through the towns and shops and saloons astride his American stallion, which he took any and everywhere, now all of a sudden he seemed pallid and ashen and wan. And when Long John Frank concluded his testimony by reiterating, "Ives told me he shot the Dutchman and gained $200 and two mules by doing it," George Ives said, almost inaudibly, "That's a lie."

There wasn't anything H. P. Smith and Davis could do about it, no matter how hard they tried. Because it all made enough sense that it not only was believable, but was easy enough to believe that no one had to work too hard at coming to grips with it. The mules that Clark and Burtchey had sent Tibolt to retrieve were being kept at Dempsey's Cottonwood, and since Ives was Dempsey's hostler and herder, it was Ives that Tibolt would have to see first to get them back. And Tibolt would have to make payment for the grazing and herding fee and Ives was the one to pay, which meant not only that Ives knew Tibolt had got the mules but that Tibolt had money with him also. And here was Long

John Frank, known to be a friend of Ives and having his own ranch but a few miles from Dempsey's telling in logical fashion how it all happened. Which was the only thing that a good portion of the assembly had a hard time believing; not that what John Frank was telling was the truth, and not that George Ives had murdered Tibolt, but that John Frank would stoop so low as to skunk on George Ives, in miners' terms that is, when John Frank had nothing to gain by it, seeing as how he hadn't done anything himself. So that now cries came out of the audience to hang John Frank, there on the spot with no more waiting; and James Williams tightened up his guard some, and the animosities quieted just a little.

Finally, Davis asked John Frank outright, "What'd they promise you for giving this testimony, Mr. Frank?"

And Wilbur Sanders objected loudly and, through a long-winded explication of particular aspects of the code of criminal evidence, succeeded in having the objection sustained such that, much to John Frank's evident relief, Frank was instructed by Judge Byam to not respond.

George Ives's lawyers had no more questions then for Long John Frank, and Frank half rose his lanky body on the supposition that he was finished when Bagg stepped up to the wagon and said, "Just a minute, John. Just so there's no question about it, tell us again. This testimony is given of your own free will under your solemn oath, is it not?"

And before Thurmond could catch him by his own objection, John Frank said, "Yes, sir, on the Bible."

John Frank stepped down off the wagon then, and the entire assembly burst into hundreds of contemporaneous and excited conversations, as though the gift of speech had descended on them all at once. And it was so loud as to be collectively and individually incomprehensible. James Williams formed a guard around John Frank and then they led him through the crowd, back again behind Byam's where he presumably was kept secure. And still the vocal pandemonium prevailed, until Judge Byam rose and finally quieted the crowd.

Darkness by then had fallen, and the scene took on an eerily shadowed aspect, localized by the light of dozens of kerosene lamps and candles and torches and by the fire that by now had consumed close to a quarter of Finney's wood. Judge Wilson called the trial back into session and James Thurmond immediately walked up to the wagon in which the two judges sat, and then Thurmond moved that John Frank be joined as a defendant in the proceeding.

"And what is the basis for your motion, Mr. Thurmond?" Judge Byam asked.

And James Thurmond answered, "We now have reason to believe that it was Long John Frank that murdered Nicholas Tibolt."

"Well, I don't see why that would require us to try the two of them together. If Ives is found innocent, the committee here can still try Mr. Frank."

"You don't understand, Judge," Thurmond said as he moved over in front of Judge Wilson. "The statement would have to come from George Ives himself. And, I am sure you can perceive, we are reluctant to have him testify solely on his own behalf with everyone believing he's the only one accused when he could be testifying in a proceeding in which the real guilty party is being tried. It makes no sense to handle it otherwise. We could just as well be trying John Frank here first with George Ives's trial set for the second, and then it would be John Frank sitting up there in chains listening to George Ives tell how Frank murdered the Dutchman. This has evolved into a gross inequity that must be rectified."

With that, James Thurmond seemed to have sufficiently confused the two judges, and even Wilbur Sanders saw as much and objected to the proposition under diverse theories of procedural delay and substantive waiver, which, it seemed to me, only muddied the waters further. And I think the judges looked at it in the same way, or at least did not want to be saddled with such a momentous decision and thus, after the two judges conferred between themselves, Judge Byam announced that the question raised matters beyond the jurisdiction granted to them by the committee and that they therefore were not entitled to adjudicate the question on their own.

They called for the miners to vote on the matter, resulting in a ten-minute recess in order to allow for the absent participants in the trial to again be retrieved from the saloons and dance halls and cafes and shops so that they could voice their opinions as well. And when that had been done, the crowd was at its greatest strength for the day, numbering a thousand and maybe more, and every one of them willing and anxious to have their say on what transpired next.

The judges made Thurmond restate his argument, and he did it with great eloquence and yet with such sincerity that it was difficult to disagree with his logic and conclusion. "If we are going to do this thing," he said in closing. "If we are to sit here and act in judgment of our fellow man, let us do it in fairness and with regard for what is equitable and unimpeachable and right. Lest we condemn ourselves to less than mediocrity, to something lower than our own potential."

Had they voted at that moment, I believe Thurmond would have prevailed, and the setting would have changed significantly. But the process allowed for rebuttal, which Charles Bagg offered in a single sentence. "I don't know about you boys," he said, "but I'm planning on finishing the Lord's work here on this one trial against George Ives and then getting back to Claim No. 157 down at Junction while the weather holds, George Ives be damned." And the crowd erupted in a wild cheer. So they took the vote then, and Thurmond's motion was denounced thoroughly, and Judge Byam recessed the trial until nine o'clock on the morrow.

I hadn't said anything to X Beidler for a long while, the both of us being captivated by the proceedings and he eagerly watching out for interlopers and me proudly keeping one eye toward Pap. And when he moved to slide off the roof, I recalled what had been on my mind and then had been forgotten, and I said to him, "I didn't know Nick Tibolt had Black Bess with him when he was murdered."

X looked up at me with a hard, self-confident look about him and said, "I told Ives I'd fix him if he ever touched her again." And then he added, as his short legs slipped to the ground, "Now it's almost done."

By the time I could wedge my way through the tightly milling crowd to where the wagons were, Pap and the other guards and their prisoners and the judges and lawyers were all gone. I had had enough of it anyway—the posturing and untruths and biases far more than enough for one day's observation; and I made my way back through the dispersing miners to Pap's and my camp with the thought that the traditional Nevada City Saturday-evening debauch would now pick up in the night to carry forward the near insanity that had ended with the day.

The sudden quiet of the camp was almost overwhelming, especially in the darkness; and I worked quickly to kindle a fire to return light and warmth back unto myself. Pap returned about an hour later. He was exhausted by the strain of the last two days; I could see that much without him even having to say it. But he needed to talk about it some and so I drew him out while I heated up a meal. Mostly, he talked about nothing in particular, saying how hard it was to stand motionless for that long and how the smoke from Finney's wood had kept stinging his eyes, and other things like that. But in between times he also said some things that told me he was just a bit uneasy with the role he was having to play. "That Williams is a hard one," he said after talking about how Williams refused to allow Ives to be given anything to eat until after his lawyer had paid for the food. And when I told him how I had sat with X Beidler the entire afternoon, he just shook his head and didn't say a word.

We ate the corn bread and fried beef in silence and then Pap told me to get the bottle. He took a few solid drinks and then handed it back to me without stating his intent. So I waited, looking over at him until he said, "Go on. Have some if you want. If you can spend all day watchin' 'em try to hang a man, you might as well have a drink over it too."

There were a lot of things I wanted to know from Pap, like whether he believed Long John Frank, and what George Ives was like, and what they had done with all those jurors for the night; but no sooner had he finished eating than he slumped over and fell into a deep slumber, and I decided I had better let him be. Which left me with nothing to do but cover him with the blankets and then sit there myself and pull at that bottle every once in a while and ruminate over it all while the sounds of a fiddle and a tambourine and the muffled shouts in Nevada City floated down from the dance hall and saloons. Mostly, my thoughts were of George Ives and his lawyers and of what the latter might be doing at that very moment to prepare for the second day.

It was my guess that for the rest of the night, there would be men out searching everywhere, at the direction of Johnny Gibbons and Bill Hunter and George Ives's lawyers, scouring the entire northern half of the Gulch and the Madison Valley for Aleck Carter and Bob Zachary and Johnny Cooper and the rest of them that were identified as being in George Hilderman's wickiup when the posse rode up. And by the way I figured it, they wouldn't find a one of them since things looked like they had the potential to turn any which way, which meant that anyone testifying for George Ives might find himself being accused next. And besides, there were other possibilities that might alter the situation altogether, the most significant of which remained that Henry Plummer might come, and that he might bring with him his favorite deputies—Stinson and Ray—the three of whom alone were capable of carrying enough of persuasion and influence to change most any situation.

Except that there really was not time for that, given that it would take Clubfoot George Lane at least one full day to make the 70 mile ride to Bannack City, and a second day for Plummer to ride the same route back, which made it seem logical that Henry Plummer would conclude that any trial would be over long before he got there. And then I remembered Joseph Swift, who seemed more than willing to believe that Henry Plummer was capable of anything. And that brought me full circle to Wilbur Sanders, whom I had first heard of on the afternoon of Lincoln's holiday and who seemed to have been thrust into the center of an uncontrollable vortex.

So far, Sanders's performance had been less than impressive, except that his timing had been either perfectly accurate or remarkably fortuitous. He appeared to have the uncanny ability or good fortune to say and do things that, standing alone, would seem foolhardy or naive and yet which in the course of the trial somehow advantaged him and the prosecution repeatedly. Such that when George Ives blurted out a denial of an alleged and unproved fact that Sanders asserted in leading John Frank, all Sanders said was, "Please, Mr. Ives, you'll get your chance." And, at first blush, one might have thought that Sanders's remark was a natural and meaningless enough way to countermand Ives until one considered that, by saying it, Sanders might have been challenging Ives to dare to testify on his own behalf or, alternatively or concurrently, might have been reminding the crowd there was a reason why Ives's lawyers wouldn't let him testify even though Ives wanted, and maybe even was able, to rebut certain aspects of the prosecution's case. And in thinking about it, of how illogically it all was unfolding, with the crowd partisan and the motives suspect and the process more than imperfect, I began to see how my friend Joseph Swift might be just a bit too sure of some things, and more than a little unaware of others.

~~~~

The morning brought with it more of the same unseasonably pleasant weather, with the temperature above the freezing point even as the sun rose. Pap was already gone when I awoke, or reawoke really, because he had brought me just far enough out of sleep hours earlier for me to understand that he had been called upon to serve in the guard again for the second day and that he was going over to get Harley and eat a bite with him before they reported to James Williams. So I made and drank the coffee by myself and cooked the johnnycakes and ate them alone, too, while I watched the miners from the camps begin their short trudge back up to Nevada City. They seemed almost like pilgrims, drawn by some unseen and irresistible lure toward a salvation or resolution they could neither predict nor understand. And when I finished my meal and checked the camp, I followed them in their slog up the slopes of gravel and rock.

I had thought to walk around for a while that morning and thereby gain a better sampling of the mood of the miners as they milled about. But the concentration of people around the site of the trial was already so great that I worried I might not find a place from which to view the second day. Which was wrong, and not even coming close enough to giving X Beidler the full credit he was due, because I should have known by then that once X determined that there was a means by which he might gain any form of advantage, he would seize it if he could. So I should have known that he would be up there, elevated so to speak, back up on Richards's roof where he could mitigate against his shortness and, at the same time, watch the backs of those he did not trust with his long-barreled shotgun charged and ready in his hands. "Been waitin' for ya," X said when I came up. "Had to fight off a half dozen yahoos to save you a place." And I believed it to be true, more because it was in X Beidler's nature to welcome and invite confrontation than due to a misconception as to X Beidler's charity toward me.

So we sat through it together for the entirety of the second day too, X Beidler and me like two vultures on a cliff watching a herd of buffalo below us and wondering which ones we should be turning our attention toward. And the first thing I noted about him that morning was that he'd had his hair cut, which meant for X Beidler that the trial had become something special.

Judge Byam started it up again by asking the lawyers whether they were ready to proceed, and what immediately became apparent was that if you gave a bunch of lawyers a whole night in the middle of a trial to stew over matters, they'd come up with enough argument and theory to stop the trial altogether if the trying judge would let it happen. But Judge Byam was not that sort. He promptly overruled Thurmond's motion that the trial be continued until witnesses could be found and acknowledged several procedural points advanced by Sanders and then ordered the prosecution to pick up where it had left off. Wilbur Sanders called Hal Meacham to the witness stand; Meacham stepped up to the wagon and Judge Byam swore him the same oath as before, after borrowing that same Bible from Sanders and then returning it so that Sanders could slip it back into that same pocket where it apparently always rested.

I had seen plenty of Hal Meacham around the Nevada District over the last half year and even had some conversation with him on the few occasions after they'd agreed that I could do enough of a man's work to represent Pap's claim by working on the water ditch with the other miners. And I had come to look at him as being one of the more respectable of the Nevada miners, being as how he was book read and even had some reading materials, which he was good enough to lend to me on more than one occasion. When I saw him holding the lash in his hand on the day he whipped Ben Bailey, I was thus taken somewhat aback, maybe a little because the blood had not even dried on the leather or even stopped flowing out of Bailey's skin, but probably more so because all sign of caring and sympathy had been removed from Hal Meacham's face. And it never returned thereafter. So that when he climbed up on that wagon and took the chair they had set in it for the witnesses, he wore the same emotionless mask of determination that I had seen when we had walked up that day of the whipping and then watched as James Williams asked his curt, exacting questions and demanded the answers, as if they were his alone to own.

It became clear immediately that the whole purpose of Hal Meacham's testimony was to recount the confession that Ben Bailey had given in exchange for being whipped rather than hanged. And James Thurmond and Colonel Wood both objected to it as being hearsay. "This testimony is not Hal Meacham's testimony that the learned gentleman from Oberlin is attempting to introduce here, your honors," Thurmond said. "It's the testimony of a dead man, and it is rank hearsay. Your honors, please. I do not mean to instruct you on what is and is not hearsay. But the supposed confession of Bailey is plainly an out-of-court statement. It is being offered here to prove the truth of matters asserted in the so-called confession. That causes it to be hearsay under the English Rule, which, as I am sure you know, is followed by the

American courts. As hearsay, the testimony ought not be admitted. It is prejudicial and unreliable. I cannot cross-examine a dead man, your honors. To allow Mr. Meacham to testify as to what this dead man would say if he were here today and alive is intolerable."

Judge Byam responded by saying that, yes, he'd prefer to hear it direct from Bailey, but, as Mr. Thurmond had noted, Mr. Bailey was deceased; and, well, Mr. Thurmond at least could cross-examine Mr. Meacham, which was better than nothing. Then Wilbur Sanders intervened. "I believe an exception to the rule applies here in any case," he said. And when Judge Byam looked at him in absolute quiet, Sanders continued, "Under the exception providing for the statement of a dying man, your honors."

"That's absurd, your honors," Thurmond rejoined. "Bailey wasn't dying when he made this supposed confession. He made the statement to avoid dying. It's highly prejudicial."

"He confessed the truth to avoid the penalty that came with being guilty of horse theft," Sanders asserted. "It is no different than a dying man offering up the truth to clear his soul. Ben Bailey confessed the truth to save his life. It is the same bargain, either way, and the exception should apply equally in both situations."

Which apparently was enough for Judge Byam. He held up his hand with his palm out, as if to say stop, that's all I need, and then he thought better of it and leaned over to confer with Judge Wilson. Judge Wilson seemed less sure of the matter, and between whispers he gestured out across the assembly. So the two judges called for a vote from the miners on the question. And the response was so great in favor of admitting the testimony, which virtually everyone was interested in hearing, that with the first voice vote the issue was decided. "The court will hear the testimony," Judge Byam said, "and give it the weight it deserves."

Sanders strutted over to the wagon in which Hal Meachan sat, brusquely ignoring Thurmond as he passed him, the word "absurd" no doubt still ringing in his ears. "All right then, Mr. Meacham. Now that we've determined that your testimony is indeed relevant, contrary to Mr. Thurmond's protestations made on behalf of the accused murderer Mr. Ives, please recount for us, in as much detail as is possible, the exact confession Ben Bailey made to you and the others who were with you."

And that's what set Hal Meacham up to redeem himself. Because for the past week, ever since he'd extracted the confession from Ben Bailey and then let him ride off after a whipping that some said wasn't enough for a horse thief and road agent, there had been many in Nevada and up along the creek who said that Hal Meacham had had no right to be taking district business into his own hands. Some, like James Williams and John Lott, had spoken daily of how they would have gotten more information from Bailey and might well have brought his accomplices to justice all at one time had they been there before the deal was struck. While others claimed that the parceling out of punishments was reserved unto the committee alone. And still others complained only that they had not got the chance to see the whipping or take a hand at the lash.

So when Judge Byam announced that the court would allow Hal Meacham's testimony, Meacham finally gained the opportunity to show that he had done the best thing in the interests of both justice and the community at large. "I guess it's important," he began, "for me to start out by saying that there wasn't ever any question about whether Ben Bailey stole Welton's mare. We caught him with her in tow in the middle of the night coming out of our camp. And the same thing's true about the saddle he had on his riding horse, since George Mitchell only'd been missing it for two days and his initials were burned under the stirrup if you knew where to look. So we're really not talking about a confession as much as we're talking here about a man that knows he's got to give up something to save his skin. And what Ben Bailey gave up is exactly what we asked for, which was all he knew about the string of robberies that had been occurring along and down the Stinkingwater over the past couple months.

"At first you can bet he denied knowing anything about it. But that hound didn't hunt for long, not with ole George Mitchell standing next to him with a nice length of cord and working on tying up a noose. So Bailey came clean and we got what we wanted to know.

"First thing he said was that some of the ranches down on the Gulch was where his friends were operating out of. Said a lot of 'em worked or took their drink at the Cottonwood, and some others over at Daly's place, though he never did say that Dempsey himself, or Pete Daly, were involved. And he mentioned George Ives here more than once, saying that Ives and Aleck Carter and Zachary robbed the stage whenever they got the chance and had been rustling stock and keeping it hid in the foothills until they could slaughter and butcher out the cattle and sell the mules and horses.

"Fact is, I couldn't remember all of it after he told it because there was just too much. But once I started hearing Bill Palmer tell his story, the rest come back clear as a bell. All these boys that Palmer named as being in Hilderman's wickiup were part of the gang. They'd rob a stage or a wagon coming up the freight road and then they'd split up and meet back at the wickiup and divide up what they'd got. Bailey wouldn't say if they'd done any of the killing that's been going 'round, but it was pretty plain by the way he described their activities that they weren't the kind to let shooting a man stop them from getting what they wanted."

"All right now," Wilbur Sanders said after seeing that Meacham was beginning to wander just a might too much. "You say that Ben Bailey specifically identified George Ives as being part of the gang?"

"Yes, sir," Meacham said. "It was Ives and Carter that robbed and shot at Anton Holter. And it was Ives that robbed that coach that Bummer Dan was on up by the Rattlesnake Ranch."

"And that Ives maybe was even one of the leaders?"

"That's what Bailey was saying. Ives and Cy Skinner and a couple of others from Bannack way—Bill Bunton I think it was—are all wanted in California or Washington or Salt Lake for one murder or another; and Ives is one of them that's been organizing them since they come to Bannack over a year ago."

"And you're saying that Shears and Zachary and Graves and Carter were all implicated by Bailey's confession, too?"

"Every single one of 'em. And more besides. Doc Howard's part of their bunch. And Steve Marshland. That whole gang that came out of the Oro Fino mines near Lewiston. That's where Bailey was from."

"And those are some of the same men, are they not, who were all hiding in George Hilderman's wickiup when they were found by the posse that came looking for Nick Tibolt's murderer? Isn't that true, Mr. Meacham?"

To which James Thurmond objected before Judge Wilson allowed Hal Meacham to answer yes.

I thought the irony of Hal Meacham's statement was evident. Much was being made of the confession of Ben Bailey, as though it were gilded in truth. And yet the confession itself had come into existence, had been extracted from Bailey, because Bailey had been intolerantly dishonest. So we were supposed to believe that this dishonest man's self-serving confession was the honest truth when the man who had given it not only was not credible, but was not even alive to verify what they were now saying he had said.

Sanders got Meacham to say a lot more, too, about any crime Meacham could recall hearing about over the past four months. And it was a fairly long itemization, ranging from stolen tools and hardware and sluice dust to robberies at gunpoint and murders and brawls. And occasionally Sanders would interrupt him and ask if these were the sorts of things that Bailey confessed that he and the others were doing, and each time Meacham would state yes and then go on to offer more.

By the time Meacham had finished, the assembly was made to understand that George Ives somehow was guilty of, or if not that then at least responsible for, virtually every transgression that had occurred in the Gulch since Bill Fairweather had made the discovery that last summer. It was even suggested, since Ives sometimes rode with Lyons and Stinson and Forbes, that Ives played a role in Dillingham's death. And it seemed somewhat odd to me that the law provided for this guilt by association, and that Sanders would make so much of it, since it was known that Ives also was closely acquainted with Henry Plummer, whose integrity neither Sanders nor anyone else apparently was willing to risk assailing and whose name was never mentioned by Meacham either.

Thurmond and Richie had the same difficulty with Meacham as they had had with Palmer and John Frank. About all the two lawyers could do was to suggest to Meacham that he didn't personally know whether all these things were the truth, going over the alleged facts one by one and each time having to listen in silence as Meacham said that's what he'd heard, and that he believed every word of it. Out of frustration, Thurmond finally said, "And I suppose you know for a fact that George Ives killed Ben Bailey too?"

And Meacham answered, "I believe he did, Mr. Thurmond. Who else would have done it?"

"I suppose anyone could have done it, Mr. Meacham. Bailey was obviously running short on friends at the time."

"If you mean by anyone, Aleck Carter or Shears or Graves and that lot, then I'd agree with you," Meacham answered back. "But that's just the same as if George Ives done it himself, isn't it, Mr. Thurmond? I mean the whole lot of 'em wanted to get rid of Bailey at that point. Does it really matter which one of 'em put the ball in his head?"

"It matters to George Ives, Mr. Meacham. I can assure you of that."

Somewhere early along the line I noticed that Pap wasn't standing guard in front of the jury where he had been posted the day before, and no matter where I looked in the crowd I couldn't see him. "Seen Pap this morning?" I finally asked X Beidler.

"He's working with Burtchey and Lott on witnesses," X Beidler said. "Been a lot of boys coming forward that wants to give testimony against Ives."

If that were so, you wouldn't have known it by the remainder of the prosecution's case. The four or five remaining witnesses were presented in quick succession. They identified a couple of guns found in Hilderman's wickiup as being taken from them in recent stage robberies, and two of them told how they were sure it was Ives that had robbed them at the point of a revolver. One of these subsequently admitted, on cross-examination by Thurmond, that Ives had returned the money but a week later. "Well then you can't really say he robbed you, Mr. Steele," Thurmond said. "Seems to me he only borrowed it for a while."

This brought the crowd's humor back to life some, revived it from a perfectly serious state in which each sworn word was now heard and considered as being potentially determinative of some important point. Not that the miners had suddenly become behaved and full of decorum. If anything, there was more drinking going on than before. And there certainly was more animosity and anger from both sides of the fence. So much so, in fact, that there no longer was any of the play and jesting that had marked the prior day. So that when Thurmond suggested that George Ives had shown more of an intent to borrow than to steal when he would ride his horse into a shop and demand money with his revolver drawn and then pay it back a few days later, there was some laughter and catcalls and other levity, but only for a moment, and then the air of dread and resolve returned itself in earnest.

All through the morning, X Beidler had been sipping at a flask; and he was not alone amongst the formal members of the court and guard in this respect. I saw Judge Byam more than once hit on a bottle and watched as he shared it with Pemberton, who continued to act as the court's secretary. And even some of the lawyers, Thurmond and Richie and Bagg in particular, fortified themselves from time to time. And it was thus a good thing that the court took an early recess for the dinner hour, being as how it seemed that if some of them didn't get a meal into themselves soon, they'd all be fast asleep within another couple hours. And to my misfortune, X said that it would be best for me to stay put and hold our places, which I obligingly did while he eased off into the crowd.

CHAPTER 4

Now I'm not saying that Doc Byam and Sam Wilson weren't qualified to be serving as judges in the trial of George Ives, but it did seem that the two judges should not have been doing a lot of talking to the one side in the absence of the other. Yet that is exactly the way it went. As soon as the dinner break was called, George Burtchey and John Lott went over to the freight wagon in which the judges sat and offered up to them healthy platefuls of food that must have come steaming hot out of Star's Cafe. And then Burtchey and Lott graciously refreshed the two judges by handing up to them a full bottle of brandy. And maybe it didn't matter one iota since, even if they hadn't done it, the relationship would still have been there—the ineradicable fact still being that Byam and Lott and Burtchey and Clark and Paris Pfouts and Elk Morse and the whole lot were not only Masons, but mostly Republicans as well. So that the mere gesture of offering a meal, and perhaps commenting in muted voices as to the progress of the trial, was probably of no consequence at all in that Byam and Wilson in all likelihood already knew by then that Wilbur Sanders also was a member of the Order, and that his uncle, Sidney Edgerton, not only had some influence with the

Masons but had a real voice in party matters relating to the Radical Republicans back East.

And, besides, it was not as though George Ives's supporters were totally without their own means of influencing what came next. The good Colonel Wood, alone, made sure of that. And as one of those who remained pat still over the dinner hour, I witnessed the colonel's oration as he maneuvered the remaining and not inconsiderable crowd through a mixture of sermon and argument showing not only that George Ives was innocent, and not only that the Almighty had made room for the likes of Ives in His all-knowing plan, but that the evidence, too, established as much, both by the fact that Ives could not have killed the Dutchman due to lack of opportunity and selfless motive, as well as by Ives's good reputation amongst all the many kinds that had made their way into the Gulch.

"Friends," Colonel Wood boomed out. "Fellow Christians and fellow miners. Hear me. Hear the word of God and the wisdom of our Lord the Savior as it relates to this trial of men. Come on up here, Jason Barnes, and you Hiram Bean, and you Tom Bentson. And the rest of you as well. Hear what it is that Jesus Christ himself says of this question of how we treat George Ives on this precursor of the Christmas day." And the crowd moved toward him, perhaps as it may have done to accommodate any speaker, but with a certain interested resolve nonetheless, zombielike, baying back at the colonel with colloquialisms and formalities as from multifarious pews to the generic pulpit. Until, at the colonel's insistence and repeated urging, full half of those who had remained at the meeting site had encircled him to look up where he stood on the cottonwood stump.

"Friends," the colonel preached, "we are at this very moment at the summit of the mount. Brought into the Lord's very wilderness to be tempted of the devil. Given the riches of pharaohs and brought to the pinnacle of the temple. Taken to the highest mountain and shown the glory of independence and all the luxury of freedom. Satan has brought temptation to us as he did to our Savior. Be not deceived friends. This is our great and lasting test, and it is the same that was levied upon Jesus our Lord. And we must remember and be guided by his and his father's words.

"These things the Lord says to us as we proceed with this trial of George Ives, our brother. Blessed are the merciful, for they shall obtain mercy. Blessed are the peacemakers, for they will be called the children of God. Blessed are they which are prosecuted for righteousness sake, for theirs is the kingdom of heaven. Blessed are ye, George Ives—nay friends, his name is not written; but it might as well be—blessed are ye, George Ives, when men shall revile you, and persecute you, and say all manner of evil against you falsely."

In between each sentence, at which Colonel Wood paused just long enough to invoke and encourage response, some in the crowd would say back their "amens" or "praise bes" as if to verify not only that the words were true, but that they themselves, God's lowly children, were imbued with a quality of sacramental holiness.

"Friends," Colonel Wood spoke out in his great projecting voice, "these are not my words but the words of our Lord." And as he spoke, he gestured with the closed tattered Bible held tightly in his hand, waving it at them with emphasis and direction, as if it were the final, unassailable proof that more than verified and sanctified what he said into graven unimpeachable word. "Think not that I am come to destroy the law. This is the word of our Almighty; this is His response to those that would deny the quality of His mercy. I am not come to destroy, but to fulfill. Because I say unto you, that whosoever is angry with his brother, without cause, shall be in danger of the judgment. That means you, Jason Barnes, and you, Emmett Peterson, and me and all of us. The Lord says unto you thusly: Love your enemies; bless them that curse you; do good to them that hate you; and pray for them which spitefully use you."

And on he went in this manner for a solid hour, interweaving great subtleties regarding the innocence of George Ives and the virtues of restraint, such that I could only marvel at his ability to retain so much of the written word and recall it at a moment's notice. And all the while,

he tuned the audience to the emotional chords of his words and inflections, drawing out at least some of the guilt-ridden humility and doubt
and empathy they all harbored subconsciously in some obscure and neglected corner of their minds.

I didn't buy any of it myself, maybe because my own slate was still
clean. And yet the words that Colonel Wood spoke nonetheless had an
effect upon me, if only in the way they showed, in one way or another,
how easily men got caught up in the tidal thrust of emotions, the
"amens" and the "praise bes" being not much different from the phleg-
matic curses to "hang 'em" and be done with it once and for all.

The crowd began to swell again as the participants returned from
the dinner break, and they collected again in their partisan groupings
with the secesh boys feeling their oats and being some of the loudest in
favor of George Ives, their adopted brother. Pap returned too, X Beidler
leading him right up to the edge of Richards's roof where I sat; and Pap
bore that same look of involuntary resignation that he had brought back
with him to the camp the night before. "You had something to eat?" he
asked dully, almost as if he were in a sleepless daze. And when I said no,
he handed me up a roll of wax paper, inside of which I found a cold cut
of boiled tongue and some scrawny carrots.

"There's talk there might be some shooting here before this is
done," Pap said. "You'll make a target setting up there on that roof."

And he was about to say more when X Beidler intervened. "Hell,"
he said. "If there's shootin', they'll be too busy takin' aim at me to be
bangin' at Billy." And then X climbed back up on the roof and Pap
moved off to the back side of the trial, where he joined up with William
Clark.

They brought George Ives back out, and it looked that he might
have caught cold that morning because now he was bundled up in a
heavy Union greatcoat and wearing that cream-colored cavalry hat he
always seemed to wear. He looked chilled, too; a bluish tinge seemed to
haunt the bony structure of his face, and his shoulders were hunched
tight to ward off the cold.

I leaned over and whispered to X Beidler, "Looks like death warmed over." And X expressed some satisfaction of the fact with a carnivorous grin.

When Judge Byam called the proceeding back in session, it was with a particularly solemn air, almost as if he were saying that the trial was as good as done but that George Ives's lawyers still ought to have their chance to try to show that things were different than they seemed. So Judge Byam turned and looked down at James Thurmond, who, with Wilbur Sanders, was standing before the judges' wagon, and he said, "Does the defense have any evidence it wishes to present?"

"Of course we have evidence, Judge," James Thurmond answered in a somewhat flustered voice. He turned to the crowd and muttered a profanity. "Ample evidence exists," he asserted loudly to the assembly, "to show that George Ives did not kill the Dutchman and that he was nowhere near the Dutchman when he died. We call Honest Whiskey Joe Basak to the stand."

The assembly had become big enough at that point that any aspect of common familiarity had been totally lost; there were far too many faces thrown together at random for any of them to know, or even know of, anything approaching a majority of those present. And when James Thurmond called out for Honest Whiskey Joe, most in the crowd thus thought that Thurmond had slipped in a subtle commentary on the credibility of the witness. There were hoots and laughter and general amusement when the name was pronounced and its owner summoned.

When the crowd quieted and the witness made his way up to the wagons and took his seat next to the judges' bench and was sworn in, now with Colonel Wood's ragged Bible rather than the neat tome that was owned by Wilbur Sanders, the first thing James Thurmond did was to ask the witness his name.

"Honest Whiskey Joe Basak," he answered. And for some reason the crowd hushed.

"And how do you come by such a name?" Thurmond asked.

"My folks give me the Joe Basak part," he answered.

"And what about the rest?"

"The Whiskey part I guess I got cause I'm partial to the spirits. And the Honest part I got out in Californy for returnin' to a miner a cache of gold he'd lost along a trail and I found afterwards. Five thousand dollars worth was in that pouch. I figure that's what it cost me to get called Honest. Five thousand dollars and ten years since of work."

"I see," James Thurmond said. "And is it your character to always be honest, Mr. Basak?"

"Yes, sir, that's a fact. They don't call me Honest Whiskey Joe for nothin'."

"Well, fine. That is precisely what we need here to clarify this question regarding whether George Ives had anything to do with the death of Nicholas Tibolt."

Honest Whiskey Joe then explained in easy talk how he and George Brown saw Nick Tibolt retrieve Clark and Burtchey's mules from George Ives, and that they, together with Ives, watched Tibolt ride off up the freight road along the Gulch.

"How long did the three of you watch Tibolt?" Thurmond asked.

"Not long really. Because we'd all been busy workin' on that new roof for Dempsey's stable when the Dutchman rode up; and we had plenty of work left before we were through."

"Are you saying George Ives was with you and George Brown the whole day?"

"I'm sayin' more'n that. Ives was with us the whole day puttin' up rafters, and then he supped with us afterward over some fresh steaks George Brown grilled in Dempsey's kitchen, and then he helped me all night long with a bottle I'd been wantin' to get rid of. That's why I can't figure what you all are even doin' out here in the cold. George Ives couldn't have killed the Dutchman. You boys have got the wrong man on trial here."

That was about all that Honest Whiskey Joe Basak had to say. And I think that was a problem for James Thurmond, in that Wilbur

Sanders and Charles Bagg had taken a full day putting on their witnesses and it didn't look right for Thurmond's witnesses to not consume an equal portion of time rebutting the prosecution's case. Or maybe it was just that Thurmond enjoyed the limelight enough that he was not inclined to abandon opportunity too easily. Whatever the reason, he led Honest Whiskey Joe through a meandering series of questions relating to whether George Ives had participated in any of the long itemization of crimes that Hal Meacham and the others had ascribed to George Ives. And Honest Whiskey Joe either knew a lot about George Ives or had been prepared well for his testimony. Through direct observation, or by way of circumstantial knowledge, he provided diverse reasons why it could not have been George Ives who robbed Bummer Dan and Anton Holter and who shot Ben Bailey up near Wisconsin Creek. And when James Thurmond announced that he had finished with the witness, Honest Whiskey Joe added gratuitously, "It's like I said. Seems to me you boys are after the wrong man."

To that point, Wilbur Sanders had shown no particular talent in examining the witnesses; but then the witnesses so far had been his own, which meant that all he had to do was lead them along and protect them from Thurmond's own examination. To be sure, he had had his moments of aggression when it came to arguing a point. But that was not the same as demanding helpful answers from an uncooperative witness. Now, as he walked up to the wagon in which Honest Whiskey Joe sat, he bore a look of indignant anger, and I thought that maybe he was bitter over the fact that this one single witness had in forty minutes undermined and negated a day's worth of condemning evidence.

Sanders stood in front of Honest Whiskey Joe and stared for what was only a minute, maybe two, but what seemed like eons. And when he finally spoke, that look that was part disdain and part anger became even more exaggerated and evident. "Are you telling this court, sir," he said most acidly, "that you have never told a lie or committed a wrong of any sort? That you have never misrepresented a fact even when you thought it might be best to do so? Never told just one white lie, thinking it was better for everyone involved? Never lied once to your mother when you were a boy?"

And this confused the witness some. "I ain't never said that. No one asked me that."

"Well, what is this testimony, sworn on our Lord's Bible, that it is your character to always be honest? Always, mind you." And when Honest Whiskey Joe failed to answer that question, Sanders said, "You've lied somewhere down the road, Mr. Basak; we can safely assume that, can't we? And it would be safe to say you'll lie again; now wouldn't it, Mr. Basak?"

"I imagine I have," Basak answered. "But I can't say what I'll be doin' in the future."

"But you have lied; you admit that much."

And that's when Joe Basak lost his tempter. "Don't go giving me your lawyer's bullshit, friend," he said in an angry outburst. "Ain't nobody said I was some kind of saint."

"That's what I thought," Wilbur Sanders said with a smirk. And he paused briefly. "Now that we've established that you're no more honest than any other man, let me ask you some questions. You're acquainted with George Ives here, aren't you, Mr. Basak?"

"Known him for years."

"And he's a friend of yours now, isn't he, Mr. Basak?"

"You could say that."

"In fact, he's a good enough friend of yours for you to share a good bottle of whiskey with, isn't he, Mr. Basak?"

"I already told that."

"And you don't much like the idea of Mr. Ives being hanged, do you, Mr. Basak?" Sanders fired off the questions in rapid succession, and the answers came back fast too, Joe Basak saying, "I don't like the idea of any innocent man bein' hung," with spontaneity and growing impatience. And it apparently troubled James Thurmond some, and he moved up close to Sanders, to intimidate him perhaps.

"And it would be fair to say, wouldn't it, Mr. Basak, theoretically speaking I mean, you could lie to help George Ives and, as a practical matter, you would not have done it for your own good?"

"I object to this line of questioning, your honors," Thurmond finally interjected. "The question calls for speculation. No foundation has been laid. The answer would be irrelevant and immaterial. Mr. Sanders is harassing the witness and it must be stopped."

"Overruled," Judge Byam instantly responded. "The witness will answer the question.

"I didn't get the question," Honest Whiskey Joe said.

"Then let me ask it another way," Wilbur Sanders said. "You've testified that you've told white lies before to help others than yourself. And you've testified that George Ives is your longtime friend. Now I ask you, it would not be out of character for you to tell a white lie here for your friend George Ives, would it, Mr. Basak? For instance, if you believed in your heart that George Ives didn't murder Nick Tibolt, you might lie a little to help him even though you couldn't really know for sure whether Ives murdered him or not."

And the witness answered in a subdued voice, "I ain't lyin'."

To which Sanders responded, "And that could be another of your white lies, now couldn't it, Mr. Basak?" And when Honest Whiskey Joe didn't answer that, Wilbur Sanders said, "It seems to me that you've got no more right to be calling yourself by the name 'Honest' than any other man. In fact, Mr. Basak, the only thing that is clear here is that you are friends with George Ives and that you've known him for years and that the two of you are close enough to spend long nights drinking together. I don't care what anyone else thinks, Mr. Basak. I think you're a liar and you're lying here. And I don't mind telling it to your face."

"Is that a question?" Thurmond interjected just in time to keep Joe Basak in his chair.

And Wilbur Sanders said, "No, sir, it is not. I am not disposed to ask this witness any more questions given that we already know of his proclivity to tell what he calls white lies to help his friends." And he stepped back in a huff and strutted over to where Burtchey and Lott and the others stood, shaking his head the whole while and scanning the crowd, as if they and Wilbur Sanders all knew that the witness could not be trusted or believed.

That set the crowd all astir, and X Beidler liked it in particular. He slammed his hand down on the roof and let out a couple of whoops, and the assembly as a whole got set all in motion by Wilbur Sanders's handling of the witness. And this caused Thurmond and Davis to huddle together with Richie and H. P. Smith, undoubtedly to revisit their strategy and alter their approach.

Richie came forward and advanced a long-winded series of arguments concerning why Sanders's cross-examination should be stricken from the record: it was prejudicial, he argued, with the support of a dozen obscure and only half-reported cases; it was designed to inflame the jury; it undermined the judicial process and, on balance, failed to substantiate any fact.

Sanders responded by reciting every rule and principle he could recall or construct relating to the impeachment of witnesses and evidence regarding character and credibility. And then the assembly voted on the issue, overwhelmingly in favor of the prosecution.

Richie seemed somewhat drunk by that time, and I believed that to be the case; but he was every bit the equal of Thurmond in elocution and he far surpassed him in eloquence. And, if nothing else, he bore a dignified aspect of respectability unlike any other man who participated in the proceeding. "I call George Brown as a direct witness to the defense of George Ives," he said with what might have been a slight slur, or only the effect of the December cold. George Brown came up and took the witness seat. He nervously looked out over the crowd, no doubt saw many that he knew from the time he had spent in Bannack and at the Rattlesnake and lastly as Dempsey's bartender and cook. And then, in response to Richie's inquiry, he told the same story as Honest Whiskey Joe, relating with great specificity how the three of them had spent the day and night together working and eating and drinking. And that made it different since one man could tell it and it would be a lie, but for two men to tell it and for it to be a lie, it also had to be a conspiracy, and that had to be at least a little harder to accept and believe.

Up to that point, the crowd had only participated sparingly in the questioning. Someone would shout out a question and, at a time when it would not too greatly interfere with a line of inquiry then in progress, one of the judges or the lawyers would propound it to the witness. Generally, I thought the questions from the crowd to be fairly mundane and unhelpful in resolving the main issue, although, on occasion, a particularly good point was made by a query. And until the moment when Richie concluded his examination of George Brown, it was obvious that none of the lawyers were in the least interested in, or appreciative of, the crowd's involvement.

Now it was different. Even after a long conference between Wilbur Sanders and Charles Bagg and their employers, it began to appear that the prosecution had little to ask George Brown. Not that they left the proceedings hanging in some form of pregnant silence; but the questions they asked seemed not to hit on anything of consequence, drawing out only useless information about Brown's former life in Minnesota and of his wagon trip out West only a year or so earlier. It obviously frustrated Wilbur Sanders, who would have liked to have built on the success he enjoyed with Joe Basak and yet who knew that he could not repeat his performance simply by attacking the next witness in the way he did the last. It finally became evident that they were in need of assistance, and scattered voices began to call out proposed inquiries.

"Ask him if he knew Ives back East," someone yelled, and the question was asked and a negative answer was given.

"Ask him if Ives owes him money," someone else called out, and another negative answer was returned.

Then Granville Stuart, who together with his brother James had been present throughout the trial, spoke out. "Ask him if the steaks they cooked that day were fresh butchered," he shouted out. And this drew laughter both because Dempsey was known to advertise the freshest steaks between Virginia City and Bannack and because many in the crowd knew Granville Stuart from his days as a butcher in Bannack City. And when Sanders asked the question playfully, George Brown smiled, to be politic if nothing else, and said, "You can bet on it Granville; still pulsing blood, as always."

Then Granville Stuart said, "And who did the cutting, George?"

And Brown said, "I did, Granville. You know I do my own butchering."

"I ain't never believed it, George," Stuart said; and the crowd laughed, thinking this was at least fun. "Come on now, George," he said. "Who helped you?"

"I did it all myself, like always, Granville. And just as good as you'd do, if I don't say so myself."

"With no one even there to tell you where the sirloin is?" Granville Stuart said with a laugh.

And George Brown said, "You know better, Granville. You know I don't let no one in my kitchen and no one in my butcher shop. Them's my rules."

"Isn't Dempsey's slaughterhouse up by the ranch house, George?" Granville Stuart asked. And now it all seemed a bit silly, because the lawyers weren't stopping it, and the judges were enjoying the release of tension, and it almost was as though George Brown and Granville Stuart were having a fine old talk between themselves in the middle of the street with no one else even around.

"Yep," George Brown confirmed. "Around back the kitchen."

"And isn't that new stables George Ives was working on at the other side of that big stand of aspen in front of the ranch house?" To which George Brown did not answer. So Granville Stuart said, "With all that butchering and cooking you were doing, George, seems to me that you were busy enough and far away enough that old George Ives could have done anything and you'd never have known it."

I suppose Wilbur Sanders knew better than to open up the door wide so that George Brown could resurrect himself. Instead, Sanders walked over to the witness and then paced back and forth before the judges, usurping time and causing Granville Stuart's point to ferment throughout the crowd. And all the while George Brown twisted in his seat and avoided meeting eyes with George Ives, who sat rigidly and stared, disbelieving, at the strutting Wilbur Sanders.

Sanders finally dismissed the witness, saying, "I have nothing more, your honors," and Richie took the witness back and tried to undo what had been done. And in no time he had George Brown correcting himself by saying how the steer had been slaughtered and butchered that morning before the Dutchman had even arrived, and how in between the times he flipped and seasoned and tenderized the steaks, he was tending the bar at which George Ives and Honest Whiskey Joe both sat. And while Richie did a fine job of it, leading Brown through an organized series of corrected recollections, you couldn't help but still be left with a bad taste in your mouth when he was finished.

Thurmond next had Doc Glick to testify as to his experience in rendering medical services at the stations between Bannack and Virginia City; and it was more than a little difficult to see the connection. Then Thurmond asked, "And have you ever seen any sign that any of these boys named by Hal Meacham were conducting the road agency business out of the ranches?"

And Doc Glick said, "The only thing I've seen out of those boys is a good horse race now and then."

So Wilbur Sanders did not even bother with him other than to ask if the good doctor had any knowledge, either way, concerning whether Ives had killed Nick Tibolt. And when Doc Glick said, "No, I sure don't," Sanders dismissed him aloofly.

Apparently, Richie and Thurmond had been planning on calling a couple of other witnesses in defense of George Ives. Now that the time had come, those witnesses were nowhere to be found; and an argument broke out amongst Thurmond and Johnny Gibbons and H. P. Smith regarding who had been responsible for keeping an eye on those who were to testify. A recess was called while Ives's four lawyers sent out parties to search Nevada City for the men, one of whom was identified as Tex Crowley, a sometimes drifter and gambler who had made none too good of a name for himself in the Nevada District. And when the time allotted for the recess had elapsed without the witnesses being located, Thurmond requested that the proceedings be continued until the morrow.

Sanders was opposed to it, and he said so in vehement terms. But it was a Sunday, and what little of it was left still had a certain value to the miners who had lost most of the only day of the week they felt entitled to squander. A vote was taken and a large majority favored Thurmond's suggestion, and with no more ado the judges adjourned the trial and the crowd began to dissolve in streams of men heading toward the saloons and dance hall and up the road to Virginia City.

Pap came home even later that night, and he explained the lateness of his return only by saying that there had been a meeting and that he had already eaten.

Sometime late into the night, shots rang out from up in Nevada City. And shortly thereafter, there was a commotion of horses galloping north along the freight road, out of the Gulch. This, I figured, was the much anticipated breakout of George Ives, and the last we'd ever see of him in Alder Gulch. Pap heard the noise only as a subconscious disturbance to a dream, and he let out a grunt and rolled to his other side and resumed his slumber. The sound of the horses faded almost at once, and I too fell back into sleep imagining the cold emotionless face of James Williams leering out into the night in search of the man he had held at gunpoint and by chains for three days going.

When the morning came, it brought with it nothing of the rumor or report of the escape of George Ives, and so I knew that it had never happened, that the gunfire and horseplay involved something more commonplace and of less significance. And once again, with the dawn, the camps began to empty in long mesmerized files up toward Nevada City, where the trial would come on now for its third and final day. Pap was gone when I awoke, and this time he had not even called me out of my sleep to say that he was leaving and that the camp was my responsibility. And in like manner, I did not even bother to boil coffee or break my fast before I, too, trod up the path that intersected the freight road and came up just to the left of Finney's house.

It was almost a full hour before the trial was scheduled to restart, and yet there were already more people congregated than at the peak on the yesterday. And the crowd was different in gender as well; whereas before there had been but a few women, now it was as if every lady in Nevada and Virginia City had turned out for the final day. Even Mrs. Sheehan and Mrs. Grannis and Mrs. Harley were there, standing in close proximity to some of the sporting and hurdy gurdy ladies and not seeming to be bothered by it one bit. And X Beidler was already there too, up on Richards's roof with his shotgun across his knee and space enough for me to sit there too. And the Judges Byam and Wilson were mingling with the crowd, and most of the jury were already seated, and Pap and two dozen others already were cordoning off secure areas for the jurymen and the accused. The air of a political event prevailed in every sense, with conversations lively and heated and women dressed up in their Sunday best and men smoking and debating every point that came to mind.

"Today's the day," X Beidler said when I came up.

"What day is that?" I asked as I pulled up onto the roof.

And X Beidler said back, "The day George Ives gets hung."

I doubted it, but I didn't say so to X, didn't tell him of the shots in the night and of my subsequent dream in which George Ives was a free man and happy for it. Because three days of trial was a lot different than one or two, in that it afforded time for a rescue of George Ives to be mounted from almost any place, whether it be Bannack from which Henry Plummer and his deputies might come to restore order and process or Cottonwood or even Hell Gate, where some of George Ives's friends had retreated when the posse first set out. Instead, I only said, "It'll be a good day for it then," as I looked up to the morning's

cloudless skies, which held great promise for a moderating winter afternoon.

All of Finney's wood by now had been consumed, and the judges
had let it be known at the end of the prior day that each participant in
the trial was expected to bring with him in the morning at least one log
to contribute toward a fire. Those that forgot scrounged around for a
twig or branch and offered that, but mostly the people had complied;
and as they came up to the site of the trial and laid their cordwood in
the rapidly growing pile, it was with a compliant solemnity that made
them look like they were tithing to some greater power.

They finally brought out George Ives, and James Williams himself
ushered Ives over to the wagon and gestured for him to climb up and
take his seat. And when Ives did this, Judge Byam called the trial back
to order.

After Thurmond again sought and was denied a continuance for
the purpose of locating witnesses, the lawyers announced that they were
through presenting their cases and were now ready to argue the law and
the facts. That did not sit well at all with certain members of the crowd
who had contrived their own theories of the case and who therefore
desired now to ask additional questions to some of the witnesses who
had already testified. And not being inclined to lose their good stead in
the districts they each represented, the Judges Byam and Wilson permitted this at the cost of two unproductive hours in which Hal
Meacham and John Frank and George Hilderman offered absolutely
nothing new. Throughout these revisitations, X Beidler grew more and
more anxious and impatient. "Let's get on with it," he shouted once in
the middle of some nonsensical inquiries from a well-meaning miner.
"That's been asked and answered two days back."

Once the crowd had been placated and their questions exhausted,
the two judges apparently presumed that the court would then entertain
closing arguments and that the matter would then be submitted to the
advisory jury. But Wilbur Sanders had other ideas, and he expressed
them in no uncertain terms as soon as the judges declared the evidence

closed. "The prosecution moves," he announced in a loud and staged voice as he moved in front of the judges' wagon, "that the entirety of the testimony of Joe Basak and George Brown be stricken from the record on the grounds that it is suborned for the purposes of perjury and therefore is irrelevant and prejudicial." A louder reaction than what followed could hardly be imagined. X Beidler let out a wild huzzah, and it was joined instantly by scores and then hundreds of others through-out the crowd. To a lesser degree there were deriding and vocal objec-tions to the proposition. Several miners in the back of the crowd could not even agree to disagree on the point, and their argument evolved into a minor scuffle that was only finally contained when some of James Williams's men took the bloodied offenders into a rough form of cus-tody, hauling them off by their hair. And then the crowd quieted enough that Judge Byam could be heard.

"What evidence is there to support this motion, Colonel Sanders?" he asked.

"You've heard the evidence, your honor. The two witnesses are sworn friends of the accused. They couldn't even keep their stories straight as between themselves. They have been brought to this trial for a single purpose: to provide false testimony on behalf of George Ives. The question is at issue, and it should be put to the assembly at large."

At which point Wilbur Sanders's tactic became obvious; the motion provided a free shot at ensuring Ives's guilt through preliminary argu-ments, since if the testimony were stricken, it would leave Ives's lawyers with nothing other than to argue against the prosecution's witnesses and, if it were not, the prosecution would be no worse off for having tried. It also could serve to greatly relieve the pressure that had been mount-ing on the advisory jury, which more than once had been the target of vocal threats from the crowd. It would be hard on the jurors to have to vote that Brown and Basak were both liars, and much easier to say that the lack of evidence left them little choice other than to find Ives guilty as accused.

And Richie said as much. "This motion advanced by the gentle-man from Ohio is ludicrous," he remarked contentiously. "There is no evidence of perjury here, and I take exception to the suggestion that perjury has been suborned. The credibility of every witness is at issue in any trial. I could as easily accuse Mr. Sanders here of suborning perjury. What then? Must we vote on that question also? Please, your honors. This motion makes absolutely no sense."

You could tell by Judge Byam's reaction that the motion made him uneasy. And when he turned to Judge Wilson and whispered something to him, the way in which Judge Wilson shrugged his shoulders suggested that he, too, was unsure of what to do. Charles Bagg must have seen this, and he came forward now to reinforce Wilbur Sanders's concept. "The motion is not that unusual, your honors," he said. "I saw the same thing done in Cincinnati once. Before Judge Peter T. Craighead. Ole Judge Craighead struck down every word the witness in question offered, and since that was the only witness offered by the defendant, he held the defendant liable without ever letting the jury return a verdict."

"We will not do that here, Mr. Bagg," Judge Wilson said. "We, I mean Judge Byam and I, are not the final arbiters here. We are only here to ensure that this trial proceeds in an orderly and logical fashion. It will be for the entirety of the assembly to decide on the question of guilt after having been advised by the jury."

"Yes, Judge," Bagg responded. "But it is not for the advisory jury to decide on questions of admissibility. That should be for the entire assembly on so important a matter." And on this the crowd in general shouted out its approval from all directions, leaving the general impression that virtually everyone present wanted a voice in the issue and trusted neither the judges nor the jury to decide it for them.

When it came time for voting on the motion, it was plain that there was nothing to stop me from adding my voice to that of the others, and every reason to do it with X sitting there next to me and watching over me, and me visible not only to Pap but to dozens of his friends; so I had no choice other than to join with the assembly in voting down the testimony of George Brown and Honest Whiskey Joe, but not before Smith and Davis and Wilbur Sanders were allowed over an hour's time to argue the matter thoroughly. And Davis must have known when he tried the same tactic with respect to the testimony of Long John Frank and George Hilderman and Hal Meacham and the others, that it was fruitless since it no longer was a trial. It was something far less dignified and more in keeping with what James Williams had had in mind from the beginning.

A certain restless and anxious attitude crept across the crowd. More and more, you could see miners and lookouts turning this way and that, checking their backs and peering down the road, expecting anything at any moment to change the momentum; and with an escalating urgency voices from the crowd hurried the process along. By consensus it was agreed that the lawyers would conclude by three o'clock. And the shotguns that a majority of the crowd carried seemed more poised, more tightly held for action, if the need arose.

Charles Bagg opened the final arguments in the same manner he had opened the trial. He referred openly and constantly to divine providence and of how the Almighty had descended on the Gulch to afford this one opportunity, this one and only chance for those with a conviction for clean living and pious thought, to instill order and morality in their community. He related a realistic day in the life of a placer miner: of the fingers smashed from working the drift; of forever aching backs; of feet that could not bear to stand the icy waters any longer. And he juxtaposed the miners' lives, in demeaning ways, to the life of George Ives and his road agent friends who in a minute's time plundered what it took days and weeks and months to extract from the great overburden of Alder Creek.

"At what cost?" he asked as he worked the crowd. And now, somehow, his awkward and stublike stature no longer mattered; every word he spoke was heard and given serious consideration. "Ask yourself not only what the cost has been for what you have gained through your labors; ask yourself also what you will spend and expend here in the future, in the next week and month and year. Are you willing to lose that also; are you willing to sacrifice even your own dignity and purpose for fear of doing what the Good Lord has already ordained? It is not just for retribution that George Ives must be cast down; his fate must stand as an example to others who repudiate the word of God." And so on, with an underlayment of righteous prophecy and compassion that showed that Charles Bagg was a miners' lawyer from the beginning to the end.

He concluded with one last definitive reference to God's will, not only deferring to it but defining it also with specificity and certitude, and then he, in his own opinion, pronounced George Ives guilty of the murder of Nicholas Tibolt and equally responsible for all the other misdeeds that had occurred since the strike at Alder Gulch. And to Charles Bagg's statement, as prolonged and emotional as it was, the crowd responded with a heightened fervency that seemed at least to ice the air if not darken the very skies.

Richie came forward and, for the better part of an hour, castigated an unjust and biased process by which one of our own was to be judged. He spoke of the trial as being amongst a dozen of the greatest outrages of the millennium, comparing it in scorching terms to the Inquisition and the Salem trials, reviled any one of the assembly who dared to so usurp the most fundamental rights of the Constitution by the grotesque assertion that the will of the majority always will prevail. And he would have gone on longer, I am sure, had not the crowd turned angrily and violently against him, by the score and even the hundreds at a time, shouting him down with catcalls and blasphemies and vile threats. So Thurmond pulled him back and sent him off to compose himself in one of the saloons that had to be all but empty, and Thurmond picked up with a different tack that called in more gentle and commonplace terms for reason and dispassionate behavior. And by the power of his voice and character and will he calmed the crowd some, brought it back at least from the brink.

From my perch on Richards's roof I had noticed that, for over the last hour, a steady stream of men had been coming down the Gulch from the higher districts. Without exception, their purpose was to participate in the final stages of the trial; they would park their wagon or secure their mounts wherever convenience allowed and then hurry over to the assembly and join its ranks. And many of those who were of more prominent positions in Virginia City in particular would first approach George Burtchey or Paris Pfouts or John Lott and exchange a veiled and hurried conversation.

If James Thurmond did not believe in his client's cause, you never would have known it. And whether the profanity that crept into his argument was a manifestation of his frustration or style or personality could not be told from his bearing, which was both powerful and controlled. And while in another setting he might have been mistaken for a gambler, with his broadcloth suit and black pants and silken tie against his perfectly white silken shirt, tall in his polished boots and his hair and mustache black and thick and long, he showed himself as being first and foremost an advocate of great capability and demeanor.

"Two great responsibilities lie before us today," he asserted in an instructive and insistent manner. "To fail in either is to fail in both. We first and foremost must guard the life and rights of George Ives as if they were our own; we must protect them as we would protect what is most precious to us, with our last ounce of determination and hope. And we must secondly protect the future for ourselves and those who are yet to come; we must ensure that the freedom and privileges and assurances of democracy do not fail here where they are yet to be tested and established by precedent and history's graven word. Do wrong to George Ives and you will do a wrong that will last into the next century, and perhaps even beyond. Because from the wellspring of events such as these is spawned the watershed of the future. My friends," he said as he moved along the fringe of the inner crowd in long even strides with his strong hands placed on his hips and his coat tails fluttering in the cold breeze, "think thusly of the future: that it is as fragile as a human's life; as easily altered as one unplayed hand is to the next; as dependent as a newborn babe. Think not that what is done today can be forgotten at will tomorrow. Because tomorrow will be what today ordains." And then at length he reviewed the criminal law regarding murder and other capital crimes in a manner totally contradictory to that asserted by Charles Bagg, and then unequivocally declared George Ives innocent both in fact and by reason of a lack of countervailing evidence.

Making a speech like that could draw a man down some. I knew that right off, and I consequently was not much surprised that after Thurmond had finished, it was as though he at once lost all further power to stand, let alone influence the crowd. But the crowd, being an aggregation of emotions and minds and personalities, was not so easily dissipated, and it therefore lost little momentum by James Thurmond's statement. If nothing else, it seemed probable that the endlessly growing number of participants only gave further weight to its resolve. Thurmond's argument was received with nothing more than moderation by the vast majority of the miners, and with random and enthusiastic applause by the remainder.

Wilbur Sanders already knew that the trial was won when he came to the fore to make the final statement. But he knew also, as did everyone who had attended the proceedings and become a part of them, that winning the trial and having their way with the prisoner were two altogether different matters. Stinson and Lyons had been convicted for Dillingham's murder and they not only lived but remained prominently in the community. The same was true of Moore and Reeves back in Bannack. Blaze Fulton was found guilty of the murder of Art Wilkerson in Cal Gulch but two years back, and me and Pap and plenty of others had been caught by surprise when Fulton's boys swept in and freed him moments before he was to swing from a tree. And while there were plenty of armed men in the crowd under the command of James Williams, the plain fact was that not one of them bore the reputation of a lot of other men when it came to quickness with a gun and versatility on a horse. And besides, the crowd itself was filled with faces that had no names but which spoke volumes in terms of hatred and anger toward Wilbur Sanders and George Burtchey and the boys from Pikes Peak in general.

This reality, understandably, made Wilbur Sanders nervous. Now more than ever he seemed to be toying with that unseen object in his pocket as he paced back and forth in front of the wagon in which George Ives sat, pacing to and fro and summoning either the courage or the words he required to close the record and submit the matter to a final disposition.

When the shot rang out, it was more like an explosion, maybe because the crowd had quieted into an awkward silence, and maybe because the commencement of gunfire had been expected all along. So that when it finally came, that first shot seemed immeasurable, of impossible proportion, like the first round fired in what would be a long and drawn out war. There was the explosion that clearly was gunfire and yet which sounded like something far greater and more insidious, and then the noise of the crowd as it shifted uneasily. And then something akin to inert pandemonium broke out, particularly toward the back of the crowd where the view was most obstructed.

Those in front, or who had clear views like those of us atop Richards's roof, saw immediately what had transpired, since the roar of the firearm was followed instantly by a blossoming of orange and red at Wilbur Sanders's right side where his pocket and a good portion of his coat had caught fire upon his inadvertent discharge of one of the Police Colts he had kept hidden in his pockets throughout the trial. Sanders, above all others, was startled out of his wits by the noise and sudden concussion, and I believe that had not James Williams rushed to his side and stripped Sanders's coat from off his back, Wilbur Sanders would have stood there immobilized and would have burned on the spot, like the great effigies of Lincoln that repeatedly had been torched in Atlanta and Richmond and a dozen other Southern cities over the past few years.

I thought it rather humorous, but X Beidler saw it differently. "Goddamn it," he said. "Just our luck." And when I asked him what he meant, he said, "Things were movin' along pretty smartly. Last thing we need's a distraction."

It took awhile to calm things down and exhaust the inevitable remarks in jest and play that kept emanating from out of the crowd, but Judge Byam finally did it by threatening to call a recess until the morrow. And then Wilbur Sanders came forward wearing someone else's coat, which was too large for him, and he embarked on a long and somewhat unnecessary summarization of everything that had been said and done the last three days.

I expected Sanders to pull out the one last trick that would ensure George Ives's conviction through an artful maneuver. But he never did. To X Beidler's disbelief, Sanders opted for a long-winded Unionist explication of the origins of the country and the sovereignty of the power from which the territorial law was derived and of how no one man can be allowed to circumvent the purpose and sanctions of the laws of the United States. This brought the Southern boys out angrily, as X knew it would, and Sanders was forced to alter his direction by reverting to more simplistic arguments, explaining what the code of criminal law said about prior bad acts and witnesses against the character of the accused, and then articulating the finely honed principles regarding the crime of murder by premeditation. And when he finally concluded, a dead silence filled the air.

With no other instructions than to vote their conscience in light of the facts as they saw them and the law as they understood it, Judge Byam directed that the jury be sequestered in Star's Cafe, where it should deliberate the case and then return with its advisory verdict. And with great solemnity and an even greater degree of martial righteousness, James Williams and his guard marched the jurymen to the cafe, carefully crossing the ice and slush, and passing through its door. And as I watched them funnel in, one by one, I was more than glad that Pap was not amongst their number.

~~~~

Harney Blake stood before the entire assembly and fulfilled his civic duty. "We, the undersigned twenty-three jurors find George Ives guilty of the murder of Nicholas Tibolt." He read the words off the paper with no more emotion than that expected from a man reading the label on a can of peas. Blake handed the paper to Pemberton, who handed it to Judge Byam, who had risen off his seat. And then Blake sat back down and shifted in his seat and looked anxiously about the crowd.

There were some angry rumblings and expressions of relief and congratulations, but even these were constrained by an ominous foreboding. "Did you say twenty-three?" Judge Byam asked as he scanned the writing.

And Harney Blake answered, "Sure did, Doc. Henry Spivey here says he can't vote neither way."

Someone shouted the words "hung jury," and in but another second Wilbur Sanders lunged out into the center of the opening.

"Move that the committee adopt the advisory jury's recommendation as its verdict," he said loudly and assertively; and his motion was seconded by scores of hurrahs from the crowd. So Judge Byam, being politic in all such matters and apparently not hearing or not heeding the objection that James Thurmond tried to make, put the question to a vote; and by a clear and almost overwhelming majority, the motion was approved.

Then Wilbur Sanders instantly again edged in front of the judges' wagon and, as loudly as he could, shouted out, "Move that George Ives, having been convicted of the wanton murder of Nicholas Tibolt, be forthwith hanged by the neck until dead."

There was nothing James Thurmond could do then, but he tried nonetheless. He argued for leniency; he questioned the authority of the committee to levy such a sentence; he moved alternatively for banishment from the Gulch. But when Judge Byam put Wilbur Sanders's motion to a vote, an even greater majority than before supported Sanders.

Things got blurry after that. It was as if with that one final determination, the whole crowd sprung loose and then coalesced in a different form. James Williams's guard gathered tightly around George Ives and the two judges and the jurymen, and friends and acquaintances of Ives came up to the front and began to say their farewells and to express their outrage. From different angles in the crowd, the occasional high and piercing voice of a woman cried out for mercy and pardon. And then, into a great and awesome silence, George Ives stood up and descended the wagon and was allowed to walk over to Wilbur Sanders. He took Sanders's hand, and then said loudly, "I have a request."

"And what might that be?" Sanders asked indifferently.

"I would like to have the time to write my mother and arrange my business affairs. If you will allow me until the morning I will give you my word that I will make no effort to escape."

To which X Beidler, who frowned and snorted even as Ives made his plea, shouted down from where we sat, "Sanders! Ask him how long he gave the Dutchman."

Someone found Ives some paper and a pencil, and they sat him down beneath the cottonwood and allowed him to make his final arrangements in that way. And I couldn't but wonder what traversed a man's mind at such a moment, and I watched as he wrote some and then dropped the pencil to his side and sat with his head bowed while Williams and Sanders and Judge Byam barked out diverse orders.

Hereford and Davis returned to the inner circle minutes later and reported that they had not found a suitable place for the execution. And that drew X Beidler down off the roof. "Hell," he said loudly. "Any place'll do for a hangin'. All we need's a decent rope." And he began to move about with his eyes up, searching for a makeshift gallows and looking rather like he had been knocked insensible in the head.

He found what he sought in an unfinished log building just to the rear of the trial site, and somehow when I next saw him, he was already atop the unroofed structure, straddling a rafter that protruded beyond the walls and waiting for the rope that someone finally brought and tied and threw up to him.

They walked George Ives over to the building, and I could see that he now wore moccasins instead of his tall saddle boots, and I watched as someone placed a dry goods crate long end up beneath the rope. There were shouts from every direction now, some crying out for George Ives's release and others for his neck; and everywhere in front and behind and around the rope, which swung lightly in the cold, were James Williams's guards with their shotguns up and ready.

Robert Hereford led Ives up to the box and stood him on it while Adriel Davis loosened the noose and set it around Ives's neck. And still, George Ives maintained his composure and with an expressionless look surveyed those all around and below him. And for a second, he seemed to glance hopefully over and past the entire assembly, down toward the freight road and into the darkness.

"Do you have anything you would like to say before your sentence is carried out?" Judge Byam asked.

And George Ives said in an unrelenting voice, "I am innocent of this crime. Aleck Carter killed the Dutchman. Go on," he said as he teetered on the crate. "Bring John Frank back out here. He'll tell you as much himself, now that I've said it."

There were cries from the back of the crowd for Long John Frank, and several men rushed toward the hanging site only to run directly into the guard. Simultaneously Judge Byam nodded at Robert Hereford, who shouted out, "Men, do your duty," and two of James Williams's men kicked the crate out from beneath George Ives's feet.

In the next instant it was as though time and dimension and circumstance had all devolved into a dreamlike state, with the shadows of the bonfire dancing in the flickering light, and the crowd utterly immobile, and the body, alone, making noise, swinging in the icy mist, perfectly weighted, and the rope by which it was suspended rubbing out a rhythmic squeak as it worked against the rafter. And, perhaps only for me, another sound that would not die, an echo far in the back of my mind, the reverberation of the clear and definitive snap of George Ives's neck; and it too lingered into the silence, perpetuating and demanding, reminding of the fact of what had just transpired, until it faded into whatever follows next, into memory, into the past.

And excited talk began in a hundred circles. Yet no one broke from their position, nor made any movement toward removing or even touching the body that now no longer swung but only twirled slowly, first one way and then the other, with George Ives's eyes staring out widely and without focus, almost bulging in the specter of his death, blankly surveying the entire gathering beneath him, passing direct in front of me once, twice, a third time until someone slowed the motion. And it would have been none the less startling if Henry Plummer or Buck Stinson or Steve Marshland or any combination of the swiftest riders in the territory had at that moment descended from off the hills in a wild gallop to cut the rope and carry off the injured but in no way lifeless body of George Ives, as when the spell was finally forever broken by one of the guards who said, asked loudly, in a childish insecure manner, "He's dead . . . ain't he, Doc?" and it was over.

CHAPTER 5

That should have been the end of it. But not then, not there in Alder Gulch, with James Williams and Tom Baume and Elk Morse and William Clark and Charley Beeher and plenty of others more discontented by what they had heard over the past three days than sated by what they had done. So when Pap didn't come back to the camp until late the night they hanged George Ives, and even later on the next night after the business of acquitting John Frank and banishing George Hilderman had been completed, I knew that there would be more to it still. Pap wouldn't talk about it though, even when I asked.

X Beidler stopped by the claim on the morning of the twenty-second. He seemed somewhat agitated, which to my way of thinking was his normal state and condition. We exchanged some pleasantries regarding the weather, and then he asked, "Pap around?" He had Black Bess behind him, and she was packed up and spoiling for a ride.

"Pap's been out all day, X," I said as I stroked Bessie's smooth muscled flank.

X was always fussing over Black Bess, checking her ears and mouth and confirming her tack. "Where's he at then," he said from under her belly where he was reaching to feel the tightness of the cinch. "I've got some business for him."

I went back to working the rocker while we talked, since Pap said he expected an ounce a day from the claim while he was off, and I was having a hard time getting that much color out of the drift that we had piled high along the bank. I shoveled in more of the coarse gravel and sand we had removed from the shaft we had bored straight down toward the creek bed. "Don't know, X," I said. "He's been mighty busy though. Probably with Mr. Burtchey and Mr. Williams, I imagine."

"Ain't with them," said X. "And I can't find Tom and Elk neither."

"Can't help you, X," I said back while I shoveled another scoop of the gravel into the tub.

"You tell him Kiskadden's train is havin' trouble in the high country. An' I been hired to find it an' pull it out. You tell him I could use some help, an' that it pays better'n he's gonna get out of that claim."

The rocker shifted the gravels back and forth and washed the lighter sediments out unevenly. "I'll tell him, X," I said.

"You're rockin' it too slow," he said. "Speed her up some."

The weather held for that day too, and it seemed that the Gulch was in mighty fine spirits. A month and more back, the representation requirement for working claims had been suspended until the spring, and the volume of work being done had receded instantly. The beginnings of cabins had begun to show everywhere along the creek, first sill logs and then whole walls and finally roofs covered with poles and thatch and in some instances even shingles. And all Pap and I lacked was the poles and rafters to make a roof, and then we'd be living in a cabin too, instead of lying on that cold hard ground that seemed to sprout up rocks like an unattended field does weeds.

The logs came from any of a variety of places where the timber grew more thickly in stands of pine and fir, some as straight and true as a rail line across a flat. There were men in the Gulch who were good enough with an ax or who had the right kind of workhorses and chains to make a business out of it. They felled and trimmed and sometimes even peeled the trees and cut them to length so that all you had to do was to pull up and pay them for it and dovetail them on your own. But that wasn't Pap's way either, and we had done all the work ourselves, including the hauling, which was no easy matter, even though we kept the logs down to 12 foot spans and only moved a few at a time. And when we went up into the trees and saw the axmen working all day long out there in the pine fresh air, I more than once wished that me and Pap were in that business, instead of having to work in that cold water with all that rock that always seemed to be right where you didn't want it.

With no work obligation, and winter threatening to intensify, men had gone out in twos and threes on hunting forays and often had returned with huge black-tailed bucks and an occasional elk or bear, which they would dress out and hang up in their camps, the skinned bear carcasses looking so very much like the musculature of a man that sometimes you had to look twice to make sure it wasn't a human body you saw hanging upside down with no skin on it. And even the gaiety from the saloons and dance halls had seemed more pronounced, and the traffic in and through Nevada City less hurried and more leisurely, and the days easier, albeit shorter and with longer nights, now that the miners' committee was no longer insisting that each claim be worked with timed regularity at the risk of enforceable forfeiture.

~~~

When I awoke the next morning after X's departure, Pap was already up and cooking a breakfast of bacon and hotcakes. I took the scalding coffee that was sitting on a rock, and I wrapped a cloth around the tin cup, and then sipped at it repeatedly to ward off the freeze. A grey mass of clouds had moved in during the night, and it had settled midway down the ridgeline so that the hill standing above and in front of Virginia City—the hill on which the cemetery had been located, and murderer and victim alike buried—was topped with an impenetrable and formless mist. Somewhere up in the cloud I knew that Nick Tibolt and George

Ives both lay, with the newly turned dirt softly mounded over them and the paint that noted their span of years hardly dried upon the markers.

Pap leaned over the fire, cooking with his back to me; and as I watched him through the whorls of steam that lifted off the coffee, he seemed undefined and without identity, the two coats that he wore obscuring the contour of his body and his hat and scarf masking his neck and head so that he could have been shapeless and disembodied without me knowing it. In a slow, almost mindless motion, he turned the fat strips of bacon with his knife, and then he pressed them down and held them so that they sizzled and popped in the iron skillet. Then, at the risk of being burned by the spattering grease, he methodically spooned out some of the boiling lard and put it in with the hotcakes so that they bubbled and burned on an instant all along their edges. Then he turned them over and pressed them down into the pan so that they spat and sizzled more.

When the hotcakes were cooked, he pulled them out of the pan, and then he handed them all to me on a tin plate. Then he made a second batch for himself, still without having said a single word, mixing the batter hurriedly before it could freeze, and then heaping the grease on that second batch too and burning their edges with the same slow hypnotic intent. And then he split the bacon between us and commenced to eat his meal without pause. When our plates were cleared, he pulled out an end from a sourdough loaf and we sopped it in the congealing grease and relished that also, and then we wiped what was left from the skillets with our fingers and licked them clean.

And still he did not speak, which made me both uneasy for myself and worried some for him. So I finally said, "Got an ounce and a half yesterday, Pap."

He put his coffee down on a rock and wiped clean the knife and stuck it back in its sheath. And then he smiled, not a real smile with some form of happiness or gladness, but a smile filled with compassion for me and with irony for all of life and living. "Knew you would," he finally said. "Be even more near the bedrock, I expect." Indifferently. As though it didn't matter whether we ever found another ounce of gold or had money to buy another thing.

"X stopped by," I said, wanting it, the conversation that alleviated the almost unbearable silence, to continue. "Said to tell you Kiskadden's train's lost up in the mountains. Said the driver went on a drunk and let the oxen get buried in the snow. I think maybe X needs your help."

"X don't need my help," Pap said with matter-of-fact certitude. And then he said, almost apologetically, "We banished Hilderman, Billy. Gave him ten days to vacate the territory on pain of death."

And I said, "I heard it already. From Con. He was down here · looking for you and Charley the Brewer."

"Well, he found us. Did he tell you we let John Frank off?"

"Yea, he did Pap. Only I figured that deal was already made. Con said they did something with Ives's money, too."

Pap kind of nodded and then smiled with a sort of nervous look I'd never seen on him before, being some of resignation and some also of regret. "That was Sanders's idea. Said there was law supportin' the idea that a man convicted of a crime had to pay the costs of the trial. Meanin' for the guards and lawyers and their food, and even the lodgin' for the prisoners. And the same thing for the jury too. That's what he said, anyway; even that Ives's estate had to pay for the coffin and burial, and for Nick Tibolt's too."

"Sounds like a pretty sum of money," I said.

"That's what I thought. I even said it. I told Sanders and Williams that it was a fine thing to lay down a rule like that, but it was a different thing gettin' a dead man to pay for debts he never knew he had, especially if that dead man didn't have the money to be takin' on those kind of debts in the first place. Turns out I was wrong about that, though; Ives and Hilderman had a stash out there at their ranches, including the stock and harness and coin and dust. Williams sent some boys to get their property and they come back with a load. And then they did the same thing with John Frank, too."

That was all he said. He stared into the fire and moved a stick around in the ashes and coals and didn't look up. So I asked him what took so long getting back.

"There was another meetin' I had to go to," he answered with his head still bent and that stick still drawing meaningless lines. And when I asked him what it was about, he said, "I can't say, Billy. I swore an oath." And then he did look up, straight at me so that I could see the sleepless red that defeated the whites of his eyes, and he said, "I'm gonna have to leave for a few days, Billy. You need to look after things while I'm gone." He stood up and dug into his pocket and pulled out some real gold coin—$40 worth of U.S. mint. "Here," he said. "That's my share for workin' the trial. You spend it as you like."

It was a lot of money, and it made me uneasy. "You keep it, Pap," I said. "You earned it." And I meant it, because Pap was never one to spend anything on himself, always thinking in terms of the two of us, what our needs were, which almost always meant what my needs were because Pap didn't seem to have any needs beyond an occasional bottle of whiskey and a game or two of cards.

His hand was still stretched out with the coins collected in his fingers. "I didn't earn nothin'. I said, take it. You understand. I don't want it. Get yourself a good meal or two, and go up to Virginia and buy yourself something. Whatever you fancy. I mean it, Billy. And Burtchey says you're to have Christmas dinner with him and Bill. You'll need to find out what time. And don't be worryin' about that rocker until I get back."

He placed the coins in my hand and I liked the way they felt heavy and perfectly balanced in my palm. "Well, where are you going, Pap? You can tell me that, can't you?"

"I can't tell you anything, Billy. Not now. We agreed to swear and sign an oath. It's bein' written up right this minute."

And when I asked who was going with him, he told me he couldn't say that either. But it was not as though I couldn't guess at most of it myself. Because anybody who sat through George Ives's trial knew that George Ives wasn't the only one who might be blamed for killing Nick Tibolt. When George Ives finally stated that Aleck Carter killed the

Dutchman, just before Nelson Story and Ben Ezekial kicked that box out from beneath Ives's feet and gravity took over, anybody in their right mind had to know that it was fact. And that was just the part of it. The complicity of Shears and Cooper and Graves and the rest of the band from Oro Fino in any number of killings and robberies had now become open and public knowledge. And that being the case, it was also plain that certain of the participants in the trial, like Williams and Beehrer, who had a penchant toward the imposition of rule and order on terms of their own choosing, and Elk Morse and Tom Baume and William Clark, who held Nick Tibolt as more than just a friend, were not likely to call things even until they were made even in a way more in line with their specific way of thought, which meant that anyone from the other side of the mountains, meaning particularly the gang from Oro Fino, had better believe that the Colorado boys would stick together when it came to taking care of their own. So I said, "I under-stand," and meant it in more than just a general way.

It began to snow before Pap got ready to leave, and the flurries came in small icy flakes indicating it would be getting colder quick. "You'd better take an extra blanket, Pap," I said. And I packed him twice the food he asked for and made sure that the powder and wadding for his revolver and shotgun were high and dry and safe.

~~~

You could pretty much figure where the posse would be headed by process of elimination since by that time the snows in the mountains had all but closed off the passes to Lewiston and Salt Lake. Not that it was impossible to traverse them; there were those who, for a hefty price and with no concern for risk of freezing to death, would still bring mail and news of import, or who had some more private reason for having to get from one place to the next. But any man who might try it had to be prepared to lose his stock or risk starvation on a barren windswept mountain ledge. That's what had happened to Boone Helm in 1859, and he had survived the ordeal only by eating one of the legs of his dead companion and by carrying the other leg out with him as he struggled on foot through the snow for weeks on end.

That made Deer Lodge or Hell Gate the probable destination since the road agents weren't likely to flee to Bannack, into the hands of Henry Plummer. Nor did it make sense that they would hole up at Dempsey's, who surely would not want them and whose ranch was still in the Passamari Valley, an easy ride out of Virginia City. Besides, Cottonwood had its own way of doing things, as did Hell Gate, which mostly meant they had no rules at all, being only way stations and not places where anyone but the ranchers and the saloon and dance hall proprietors and freight merchants would stay at long enough to call it home. So I figured I knew which way Pap would be heading; and, yet, I took little comfort in the knowledge. And Pap probably knew that it would be that way, that I would worry for him, about whether I would even ever seen him again. Which was why he gave me that $40 when he'd never given me more that a tenth as much before.

Now $40, being seven or eight days worth of mining labor wages, might seem like a lot for one young man to have loose in his pocket just for spending. But I can tell you that it only goes as far as you can stretch it. To be sure, you could get plenty of any one thing in Virginia City with that kind of money, be it a pistol or a few days of eating and drinking on the town or an hour at a friendly faro table at the Shades or the Cal Exchange. But you couldn't have them all. And that was the problem, because even if you had five times that amount, it would only enable you that much incremental pleasure. Which was never enough. And since one man or group of men could not placer and drift and windlass enough gold out of any claim to ensure that kind of behavior for more than a day or a week or at most a month before they would have to go back down into the creek and under it at risk of life and limb, it almost seemed like it was worth it to spend everything you had at once and make the most of it in that maximizing and debaucherous way.

Which is not to say that I spent it all on that very day on which I received from Pap those two bright and only somewhat worn $20 pieces, although I might have had I had the chance. The problem was that I couldn't be sure that Pap was really gone when he rode out of our camp long before noon with the snow flying. And, as the new blast of icy winter rolled in not long after the fall of dark, and I tried to fall asleep inside the tent that suddenly seemed too large and too empty, I could only speculate that the steady and ordered tramp of horses that I heard were those of the friends and avengers of Nicholas Tibolt as they rode from out of the past and into retribution.

When I awoke I found that I was fortunate to have slept away from the tent wall; it had snowed heavily throughout the night, and the snow had drifted against the tent. Outside, much of the camp was buried and invisible. And it was brutally cold as well, the water in the pans and jugs not merely sheet frozen across the top but solidly trans-formed to ice, and the wind piercing and relentless enough to have warded every miner off the creek and into their wickiups and cabins or the towns for shelter. Which left no choice as to the disposition of a portion of my windfall.

I had no interest in sitting amongst Pap's friends, and that left, as my only alternative, one or another of the commercial establish-ments in one of the towns, where they expected some form of com-pensation or purchase in exchange for the comforts of a closed room and wood-burning stove and the space and time it cost to provide them. So I walked through the blowing snow that had accumulated to 6 or 7 inches, for the whole 3 miles to Virginia City, not wanting to spend the time in Nevada where the aftershocks of the trial were still most immediate and dominating. And my mood was lightened by the way the new blanket of snow brought the Gulch back to a pristine state, seemingly untrammeled and unscarred by the heaps of tailings and the random broken rusting implements and shattered long toms and wheels and various refuse that normally were visible all along the road.

Virginia City itself had changed considerably since I had last seen it in the daylight, over a month prior. Someone had whitewashed the facade of the Virginia Hotel, and it looked like a real building now, the stark bright clapboard front dominating the featureless log walls to the rear. Up on Wallace Street, J. E. McClurg had expanded his store. His clerk was out front as I walked by, moving barrels and kegs as quick as he could so he could get back out of the cold. And he nodded to me smartly, with a measured expression of confidence and in an almost conspiratorial acknowledgment of our commonality in youth. A billiard parlor now stood on Van Buren, and its success could easily be confirmed by a chalkboard sign outside that gave notice both as to how long the estimated wait for a table would be, and of the names of challengers who sought to wager a bet on a friendly game of tens. There were new restaurants and bakeries and stores of every kind, some not even fully stocked and yet still open, and others not even completed in construction and yet still advertising their pending opening by a sign or with a stall in which a sampling of their wares and goods would have been displayed were it not for the sudden adversity of the weather.

The wind whipped and curled through Virginia City; it hurried the traffic along the streets and boardwalks and caused even the hardiest to draw their hats down low and their collars and mufflers high across their face. At Holter's lumberyard and over at the freight office a few wagons were being loaded, the drivers stomping their feet in the snow and flapping their arms for warmth. But no one unnecessarily lingered out of doors; instead, they clustered inside whatever refuge they happened upon, so that you could see them through the windows, crowding around the stoves or warming themselves to a hot drink or pretending they were doing as much through the deceptively burning swallow of a Tom & Jerry or forty-rod. And as I looked into the buildings and at the miners, they seemed to be distorted somehow, their conversations loud and yet still muffled and lost by the barrier of wall and window, their images blurred and confused by the dirty and cheaply opaque panes of glass.

Once I had gone up Cover Street and back down Wallace, I got to thinking it was more than just pretty cold and I was wanting to be less that way. And when I saw that the thermometer outside Dance & Stuart's was reading at fifteen below, I knew that was the case. And the warm air that struck me as I entered the store was almost like a furnace blast from the opened door of a boiler burning at full pitch.

James Stuart was there, sitting near the stove and smoking at a pipe together with his brother Granville. They were talking about how Mrs. Grannis had finally obtained her divorce through the territorial government and how hard Johnny Grannis was taking it and how maybe Mrs. Grannis should be waiting just a little longer before letting it be known that she was planning on marrying another man. And every once and a while one of them would make a statement and then turn to Clubfoot George Lane, who was over in the corner diligently working on some shoes, and say, "Don't you think so, George?" and George Lane would answer back saying, "Shore do, Mr. Stuart; shore do." I was tempted to ask George Lane what had happened to Henry Plummer and his deputies, of whether he had made the ride to Bannack City before the trial and why no one had come. But I refrained, not as much because I didn't know George Lane as because I didn't want to offend James Stuart, who was about as middle of the road as anyone in the Gulch.

There were plenty of store items there in Dance & Stuart's that anyone would have wanted to own, ranging from tools and pulleys and boots and hats to iron cookware and leather tack and all kind of canned fruits and vegetables at a pretty price. But what really caught my eye was a new kind of rifle I had never seen before and which they had set up on display with a lock looped through its sling pivot so you could see it and get an idea that it might be worth something but still not be able to take it down without first getting permission. There were things about it that were intriguing—its short thin barrel and that long levered handle that had to have some kind of purpose not readily apparent. When my curiosity finally got the better of me, I asked James Stuart what kind of firing piece it was. "That there's a Henry repeater," he said like I was supposed to know what a repeater was. "Shoots fifteen cartridges before you have to reload."

I let out a low long whistle, and then the thought struck me that maybe that was the sort of thing Pap was in need of now—now that he'd taken it upon himself to be getting in situations where firepower might mean the difference between living and dying. "How much is it, Mr. Stuart?" I asked. "I might just buy it from you."

And James Stuart answered, "One hundred dollars gold."

That seemed a might high for a rifle, and I said so. And James Stuart said back, "Not when it's about the only one in the territory. Walt picked 'er up last week from a Union cavalry pensioner who was down on his luck. Probably not another one in town."

And that was the standard mining camp rule of economics: charge what you thought you could get, and not what a thing was worth. "John Nye's got a used breach loader in the window right now for $50," I said.

"And that's $10 high for that rifle," James Stuart answered. "The way I see it, this here repeater's more like fifteen rifles, seein' how you can shoot it fifteen times as fast. That makes it a bargain at $100." And I wanted to say that when every rifle could shoot that way, the argument wouldn't hold water any longer, but I held my tongue.

And George Lane, who was about the nosiest cripple who ever limped a boardwalk, asked, "Why're you worryin' over it? You an' your daddy strike the vein down there finally?"

So I could only smile a bit and say, "Hardly," and then take my leave to walk back out into that biting wind that cut through clothes like a hot knife through soft wax.

~~~

I got myself a juicy cut of steak at the Arbor, with a side plate of potatoes and some fine flat bread that was still warm out of the oven. The whole while I ate, two Georgians at a table behind me agreeably discussed the myriad reasons why the rebel capital should be moved to

Atlanta and how Bobby Lee should just move up and take Washington and be done with it once and for all, and of how if Jeb Stuart and his cavalry had been at Gettysburg, the war would have been over before harvest time.

Back on the boardwalk the snow blew in sliding windswept sheets, and every piece of stock along the rows of buildings was turned tail to the wind, every horse and mule in sight facing east like there was something there to closely watch and as much to the west to carefully ignore. At each window or door along the way, I stopped and looked in and considered whether there was something on the shelves and racks that I might want to own. And each time my mind drifted back to that repeater that fired fifteen shots without needing to reload and which I knew Pap badly needed even though he'd never seen one and probably didn't even know that one existed.

That's when I got to thinking that $38.50 in gold could be turned to a lot more with a little risk and a little luck and that the risk was worth it and the luck would just have to follow. I thought to stop first at Skinner's, but when I got there, I learned that Skinner had packed up again, just as he did with his saloon in Bannack, and that he now was up at Hell Gate on the Mullan Road with yet another saloon, so I went to the Shades, where Henry Plummer and his deputies often stopped to catch up on news and have a drink.

It was a dark place, merely by the fact of its too few windows and too many confinements. And at the moment it seemed filled with a particularly hard lot of miners. The talk was mostly bitter and angry, centering as it did on the injustice that had been done to George Ives and George Hilderman. And I heard it said that Aleck Carter and Bill Graves had boasted how they were good for any thirty of the strangling bastards that hanged George Ives. And so I stayed long enough to not make it look like I was uneasy in the place, although no one ever mentioned Pap's name and it was doubtful any of them even knew it. And then I left, despite the fact that I badly wanted to play and had watched the games for long enough to confirm that I understood the rules and could reasonably assess the odds. I pulled out and walked further up the street, shuffling through the snow with my back to the wind, just like those mules and horses that stood motionless as statues, and I landed at the Cal Exchange, which was doing a business like nowhere else in town.

Beyond the door and into the smoky atmosphere of the Cal Exchange, into the noise of the fiddle and the bright oil lamps, it was evident that something big was happening. At first, it seemed it might be a fight by the way the men were crowded in a big circle with those on the fringe standing tiptoe or atop chairs so that they might better see what was going on. But up closer, I could see that a single man was at the center, and before him on the bar were a half dozen bottles of whiskey and gin, and from them he was filling tumblers and passing them out to the crowd, who quickly drank them down and handed the glasses back for more. All the while the crowd kept hollering out toasts: "Here's to the luckiest son in Alder Gulch," and "To Lucky Hansen," and half score other variations.

"What's it about?" I asked a miner close to me after he'd drunk down his free glass and wiped his beard.

"Hansen just won himself $2,000 in a faro game. The boys wouldn't let him out 'til he agreed to buyin' three rounds. This here's the third round," he said with a wink, letting it be known that he'd had more than that and how it was a good joke to be getting away with it.

The man in the middle of the circle kept pouring out the whiskey and gin while the crowd bumped him and toasted him and put them down like they were water. And occasionally the man they were calling Lucky Hansen would drink down some of the whiskey himself, each time becoming just a bit more drunk and a bit more free with the pile of dust that sat in a pouch in front of him and from which the bartender drew a measured number of pinches each time a new bottle was opened. And the whole pouch, and more besides, probably would have been spent by Hansen had not some of his friends finally seen what it was leading to and then pulled him out of the crowd clutching that pouch and two more just like it, and then moved him out of the Cal

Exchange, where Hansen would only have to risk something less ominous, like the mercury at fifteen degrees below.

The Cal Exchange was big enough that you couldn't see everything that was happening in it at once; and maybe it was for that reason that it took me another ten minutes of watching faro and monte games and looking for my lucky table before I noticed a man off in the corner slouched down over a table with an empty bottle toppled over in front of him. At first I thought he was drunk and had passed out from inebriation, which was an all too common sight in the Gulch, where on a good day there seemed to be a man lying in every corner of Nevada and Virginia City, paying homage to the ground. But when I came up closer, moving from table to table to watch the play, seeking the right game at which to win at least enough to buy that Henry repeater and maybe more, I saw that it was Meise Garner, who but a week ago had sold out his claim for what Pap called a tidy sum. "Howdy, Meise," I said to him as I came up.

He looked at me in a funny way, as if I was supposed to ask him something, and when I didn't, he said, "I lost it. Lost it all." So then I knew that it was Meise Garner that had lost all that money to Hansen, and that I was on the verge of playing the fool by thinking that I could turn $38.50 into something significantly more. Because Meise Garner was known as one of the best faro players in the Gulch and was generally presumed to be incapable of losing. "How'd it happen, Meise?" I asked.

And he said, "How do I know? How's anything happen? All I know is that it did." And then I think he realized it was me. "What're you doin' in here, anyway?" he said. "Where's Pap?"

"He's out helping X," I lied.

"Well, what're you doin' in here then?"

"I was thinking of playing me a little cards," I said. "I got me a little recreation money."

From the way Meise Garner's chair shot back, I thought maybe he'd gone into some kind of apoplexy, and I stepped back just as he grabbed the butt of his pistol, which was stuck into his pants, and said, "Get the hell out of here." And I turned and hightailed it out onto the street like nothing you'd ever seen.

I probably would never have noticed Wilbur Sanders had I not run straight into him as I hurried away from the Cal Exchange. He seemed even paler than from a distance, and more frail, too, by the way he knocked over when we collided. Two of the men who were with him stooped to help him up, but not one of them, not Paris Pfouts nor John Lott nor J. E. McClurg, lifted a hand to help me out of the tangle of barrels into which I had dropped.

"Watch where you're going, boy," Pfouts said up in my face so that I could smell the liquor on his breath. "That's Colonel Sanders you've knocked over by your carelessness."

And before I could apologize or introduce myself, they rushed off, into J. E. McClurg's store, where the clerk I had seen earlier closed the door behind them.

～～～

Pap didn't return by Christmas, just as he had projected. And not for another week after that. With each passing day I got to worrying more and more, thinking of more and more diverse reasons why I would never see him again, of how his horse could have fallen in the frozen river or how he and the rest of them might have been bushwhacked by Aleck Carter and Bob Zachary and their friends who claimed that, man for man, any one of them were good for thirty of the men who'd hanged George Ives.

By the time the New Year 's Day came and went, I knew I'd never see Pap again. My mind sort of went south then, and I don't mind saying now that I got to crying and couldn't make it stop for quite a while. And in the span of the next day and a half, I concocted a hundred ways to avenge his death by every means available to man, and some that had never been thought of then or since.

"There's no cause for worryin' about it," George Burtchey said at the Christmas table when it had been only two days. "He's with some of the best men I've ever known. Probably dinin' on fresh venison this very moment." And then a week had passed and Burtchey and William Clark stopped by the camp where I insisted on staying, and Burtchey said, "They'll be back in a day or two, you can be sure of that."

But that day and then two more passed also, and I heard and saw nothing of them. Then it was twelve days, which was too long, the distance between the Gulch and even as far as Hell Gate too short, and the vivid detail of their deaths that my mind contrived—the horrible vision of Pap's lifeless body lying in the icy snow with only the wolves and coyotes and wolverines there to scavenge his remains—was almost too much to bear.

I slept late on the morning of January 5th, there being nothing left for me to do with the drift all placered and the shaft more than one man alone could handle and the weather still cold enough to persuade me to stay in my bedroll as long as possible. And so I never saw Pap when he rode up alone and got off his horse and came into the tent to stand above me and watch while I slept. And I don't know how long he stood there either—only that he was there when I awoke, standing motionless and looking down at me with tears in his eyes where I had never seen tears before, not even when my mother had died and there was no one there but me and Pap to bury her and say the words over her grave.

"Pap," I said, and then I started crying too, and he crouched down and took me in his arms as I sat up.

It wasn't that day or even the next that he told me where he had been and what he had done. He just took to working at the claim like we had never worked it before, denying the darkness with a lamp or a torch and forbearing the cold that was somehow different than the cold in Colorado, somehow more native and thereby less antagonistic. And for those two days and into the third, no one came by the claim, not William Clark nor X Beidler nor any of the dozens of others with whom Pap had spent so much of his time and effort and emotion over the last three weeks. Until it seemed like too much just to be coincidence, and so I finally said how it was strange that none of them had come around when they were always stopping by before.

"You won't be seein' them no more, Billy," Pap said. And when I asked why not, he just said, "Because that's the way it's gotta be."

Pap and me had this rule against secrets that went way back. He had first made me promise not to hold them, and then several years later I had extracted the same concession out of him. And he had held true to it too, at least until that morning on the twenty-third when he said he couldn't tell me why he was going and with whom and where. So I said to him, "You're holding secrets, Pap. That ain't playing by our rules."

He kept seeming to want to cry; it would well up from out of nowhere and bring just enough water to his eyes for me to see that he was hurting bad. And that water came up again when I told him he was breaking his promise. "I'd tell you if I could, Billy," he said. "But I swore an oath."

"You swore an oath with me, Pap. Or you made a promise, anyway. It's the same thing, ain't it. And you promised with me first. Seems to me if you got to go breaking one of them now, the second one's the one it makes the most sense to break. I mean, since that's the one you really couldn't have made anyway, being contrary to our own."

He smiled then, the first real smile I'd seen out of him since before they brought in George Ives and said they were going to try him for murder. And while it wasn't much of a smile, being more out of relief than anything else, it was a smile nonetheless. "All right then," he said. "I'll tell you. But you've got to keep it to yourself. Because I could die if the word gets out; you understand, Billy? They'd as soon kill me as blink an eye if they knew I told."

"I understand, Pap," I said. "I ain't never broke a promise to you yet."

"All right then. But I don't expect you to accept what I'm about to tell you. I don't even know if I understand how they got me to go along in the first place. All I can tell you is what happened. That's all I can do.

"It started up with George Hilderman's trial. It didn't go the way some of them wanted—Williams and Charley Beehrer and Bill Clark and the rest of the Colorado boys. They wanted him hung too, just like they did Ives. And maybe that's what should've been done since Hilderman was a part of it. Only there were too many voices against it. Some said he was too old, and others said the hangin' had to stop with Ives. There's plenty of boys in the Gulch that ain't no friend to law and order; and there's plenty who think that anyone who's for the Union or from the Pikes Peak rush or a Mason—and you can never repeat that I ever even said that—has got a way of thinkin' that don't fit out here in the West. So when they let Hilderman go, Williams and Tom Baume and some of the others said we couldn't stop there or we'd be right back where we were in but a few months.

"Williams called a meetin' and said we had to band together and swear an oath and bring in the others that were responsible for Nick Tibolt's killin'. He got John Lott to draw it up, and I wouldn't have signed it but Tom and Elk and Bill Palmer made it plain that I owed it to Nick Tibolt and George and Bill, so I signed it with the rest of 'em. And then we rode out to get Aleck Carter. I imagine you figured that much on your own. We guessed we'd probably get one or two of the others, too. The idea was to bring 'em back and try 'em ourselves for the murder of Nick Tibolt and for all these other robberies and murders they'd been doin' up and down the Gulch. That's the way it started out anyway. That's what we all agreed we were goin' to do. We'd catch 'em ourselves, and we'd try 'em ourselves, because that trial of George Ives took far too long and lettin' all those lawyers play their game didn't serve no purpose other than to risk justice bein' done.

"You know how cold it was the day I left. The snow was driftin' pretty bad so we didn't make it any further than Dempsey's on the first night; and then we had to go around McCarty's Mountain just to be sure we didn't get stuck up there in the pass. That meant we had to follow the Big Hole and cross it at the places where it ran up against the rock. It was hard weather, Billy. I kept thinkin' how I shouldn't have left you alone here at such a time as that.

"Must've been the third day we went over the mountains and came down on Deer Lodge Creek. That's where we ran into this fella named Yeager who was headin' in the opposite direction. Short man with bright red hair. Baume and Palmer and Williams were up front and so they were the ones who talked with him the most. Yeager told them that Carter and Graves and a few of the others were up at Cottonwood, just like we figured, havin' the party of their lives. So we moved up slow after that and spent the night along the creek, without any kind of fire because Williams said it would give us away.

"We'd brought Long John Frank with us. That was Beehrer's idea. He said we'd be needin' someone to point out who some of these boys were who we'd heard of but didn't know from Abe Lincoln. We took him with us into Cottonwood and there were some folks there who acted like they'd seen a ghost when they saw John Frank's face.

"I don't mean to say we just marched in. Williams is too smart for that. He had us split up so that we would come in from all angles at once. And that's the way we came into Cottonwood, in twos and threes so that we'd just look like we were travelers passin' through on our way to Hell Gate or the Passamari. Cottonwood's a small place. Maybe a hundred folks, mostly Frenchies and a few greasers set up on a corner of John Grant's ranch.

"We went into the livery and saloon and hotel that way, in twos and threes, askin' for Carter and his boys and makin' like we were friends from Oro Fino. But it was a waste of time. They'd been there all right, drinkin' and whorin' for two days straight. But they'd been warned we were comin'. One of Grant's hands knew all about it, and Grant made him tell it to Williams. He said that Red Yeager had come up all in a hurry just two days back and had sought out Carter, and that within an hour Carter and a dozen others had lit out for who knows where. It's the only time I've seen Williams get mad, and even then he didn't yell about it or lose his temper and take it out on the other men. He just got more determined. He got Charley Beehrer to put up some of that money he's been makin' brewin' beer, and he paid for bunks and meals for all two dozen of us, and Grant put up the horses and mules in his stables. And I mean to tell you it ended up bein' quite a bash once the boys got to drinkin' and playin' cards. That was Williams's way of keepin' us goin'. I didn't see it then, but I do now.

"We stayed in Cottonwood for two nights. Some of the boys had got sick sleepin' out in the snow and soakin' in the creeks and then freezin' up after, and all that drinkin' didn't help their condition much. So Williams decided they'd better recover some before we moved out. Then we headed back toward Dempsey's.

"Beehrer had bought some buffalo robes and plenty of meat there in Cottonwood, and we were pretty loaded up and some of us weren't feelin' too good for one reason or the other; and I thought we weren't in that much of a hurry anymore. So it seemed a bit odd that Williams moved us along like we were still on the hunt for Carter and his boys.

"We made it back to Dempsey's in two days. And the first thing Williams does is to take Dempsey into a back room and have a long talk; and then he comes back out and says Red Yeager headed west toward the Rattlesnake and that we're goin' after him. Some of the boys were still sick or weak from the long rides and sleepin' in the snow and cold, and awhile back a couple of the others had been pretty loud in favor of hangin' Buck Stinson after Dillingham was murdered; and they didn't much like the idea of goin' into Bannack, or anywheres near, and causin' trouble. 'We ain't goin' to Bannack,' Williams says back. 'Dempsey says this here Red Yeager is Bunton's cook at the Rattlesnake and that he come over from Oro Fino with Doc Howard and the rest of 'em.' And when that met with silence, Williams said, 'Listen, boys; this Yeager fella warned Carter. That much is plain. That means he's the reason we didn't get Carter. And it means they might have a way of keepin' up on us, too. That makes him a source of information that could save us a lot of time and effort now and in the future.' And Charley Beehrer, and the other Dutchman, Charley

Brown, agreed to that and said they'd go along, and pretty soon Williams had Con Khors and Elk and Tom and Bill Palmer sayin' they'd be willin' to go, too, and that they were sure I'd be willin' to join 'em.

"The eight of us made it as far as Stone's ranch that night, and Williams let us sleep for maybe four hours and then we headed back out. Right after daylight a lone rider approached us from the opposite direction. He was all bundled up and you could see he was short like Yeager and was ridin' a mule like Yeager, so when we got close enough Tom and Williams lifts their shotguns and Tom calls out for the rider to throw up his hands.

"Ends up it was X. And by the way his eyes got big, you'd have thought he figured he had just enough time left to praise the Lord and be done with it. After X calmed down some, he told us he'd just come from the Rattlesnake and that Red Yeager was there. 'What you want him for?' he asked when Williams said we were after Yeager. 'He's just Bunton's cook.' So Williams told him how it looked like Yeager had warned Carter and the rest of 'em that we were comin'. When he heard that, X said, 'You boys best be quick about it then. Those sons of bitches Stinson and Ray are at the Rattlesnake, too, claimin' George Ives never would've been hung by the committee if they'd known about it and had their way.' And then X says, 'And from the talk in Bannack,' which is where he had just been, 'I understand Henry Plummer says there ain't to be no more hangin's. Least not unless there's a full-blown jury trial with rights of appeal to the territorial court.' And when Williams asked if Plummer was up at the Rattlesnake too, Beidler said no, that Henry Plummer'd been ridin' escort for a gold shipment to Fort Benton and had just got back to Bannack City after bein' gone for two weeks straight. Williams suggested that X go with us, but X said no, he and Stinson were like oil and water ever since X helped build those gallows last summer and dig those graves, and that he and Ned Ray weren't gettin' along any better, especially since X says he's been lettin' it be known that the word from the Salt Lake freightmen was that Ray had escaped less than a year ago from the penitentiary down there and was a wanted man. So X kept on toward Dempsey's by himself.

"Stinson and Ray were still there at the Rattlesnake when we came up. And they didn't like it much when Williams told Beehrer and Elk to take Yeager into custody for horse thievin'; and they liked it even less when Williams told 'em we were takin' Yeager back to be tried in Virginia City. Stinson said, 'You boys don't have jurisdiction here or in Virginia. Those are Henry Plummer's towns. There's deputies there if they're needed.' And then Ray said somethin' about Plummer havin' promised the marshal from Lewiston last fall that there'd be no more hangin's unless it was accordin' to territorial law. When Williams didn't answer to that and instead just kept barkin' orders for takin' Yeager and headin' back out, Ray added, 'You boys are makin' a big mistake goin' up against Henry Plummer. He ain't gonna let you keep hangin' people just 'cause they don't see things the way you do.'

"There wasn't a thing they could do about it though, not with the eight of us havin' our shotguns out and ready and there bein' only the two of them. And all the while, Yeager kept protestin' how he hadn't stole a horse ever in his life and demandin' that Williams show some proof that justified makin' Yeager go all the way to Virginia City when he had just come from that way. And Williams didn't answer that neither. He just moved us out of there with Red in tow and Charley Beehrer and Tom guardin' our rear, just in case Stinson and Ray got an idea.

"About halfway to Dempsey's, Williams pulls us over under some rocks where there ain't much snow and he puts Yeager out in the middle of us all and asks him why he warned Carter we were comin' to Cottonwood. And Yeager says, 'What're you talkin' about? I didn't even see you 'til after I left Cottonwood.' And Williams says back to him that we had it on good word that as soon as Red talked to Carter, Carter and his boys moved out of Cottonwood like the whole town was on fire. And Yeager says back, 'You got it all wrong. The only thing I did was to deliver a letter to Carter from George Brown. There ain't no crime in that. I don't even know what it said. All I know is that after they hung

George Ives, Brown asked me if I'd deliver a letter to Aleck Carter and I said shore, for a price that made the trip worth while, and when he said $30 gold, I said I'd do it.'

"That threw Williams a little, especially after Elk said it looked like we got us the wrong man. 'This here ain't the wrong man,' Williams said back. 'Don't tell me he didn't know what was in that letter and why he was deliverin' it. If he knew about Ives's trial, then he knew Carter was as guilty as Ives.'

"And that made the rest of that night and the next day's ride back fairly unpleasant since we'd already been gone from the Gulch for longer than we had planned and here it looked like we still might end up comin' in empty-handed or at least lookin' a little foolish. You could see that Williams was still workin' on it; his eyes kept fixin' on nothin', like he might be daydreamin'. Only that wasn't his way; seems like once he latches onto somethin', he don't let go 'til he's through.

"We got to Dempsey's and the boys were mighty glad to see that we had Yeager with us. X was there, too, waitin' on us. And the only thing he says when he sees Red Yeager is, 'Hidy, Red. Where's your pals Stinson and Ray? They ain't talkin' loud now, are they?'

"Before Williams even took off his coat or had a meal, he got Dempsey to bring out George Brown and then he told Brown we had read his letter to Carter and that his game was played out. That shook up Brown plenty. Then finally Brown said, 'So what. Ain't no crime to write a letter.' And all Williams said back was we were takin' him to Virginia City for trial. Williams tried to get more out of Yeager and Brown, but neither of them had much to say, and I think Brown finally figured out that we hadn't seen that letter after all. They claimed they didn't know anythin' about any gang, and that they were just passin' acquaintances with Carter and Zachary and the rest. The boys were pretty hard on Brown in partic-ular. They kept askin' him why he'd lied on behalf of George Ives durin' the trial and he kept sayin' all he'd done was tell the truth.

"We spent the night at Dempsey's and there was plenty of talk amongst our group about whether what Brown and Yeager had done was enough to be called a crime. Most of us thought it was bad enough to at least have a trial over it and decide whether they ought to be banished from the Gulch since it wasn't any different from what George Hilderman had done. Williams didn't talk about it much. He just sat and listened to us, like he was judgin' us instead of helpin' us decide what to do next.

"When we left the next mornin', John Frank stayed behind. And he was plenty glad to see us ride off without him. The trail'd been packed past Dempsey's and we could have made it back that night, only Williams insisted we stop at Laurin's, where we could get us a decent meal instead of comin' in late and goin' to bed hungry. So that's what we did. And there were too many of us for that little roadhouse Laurin's got down there, so we had to eat in shifts.

"Later on, Williams and Beehrer and X had a long talk off in a corner, and a little after that they took George Brown and then Yeager separately into a room and had a talk with each of 'em. And when they'd finished with Brown and Yeager and had sent 'em off to a room upstairs to remain under guard, the three of 'em went back off in that corner and went at it again, like three old gossipy hens whisperin' and arguin' and noddin' their heads in agreement.

"The rest of us were goin' at it too, talkin' about Ives and Hilderman and all those boys from over the mountains, and each of us was statin' our own opinion just a little louder and more insistent with each drink. So the fact that X and Charley Beehrer and Williams were doin' the same thing didn't seem to merit much attention. That is until they broke away from each other and Williams sent Laurin's bartender off by payin' him and then said to the rest of us, 'Boys, we need to talk some.' And then Williams gave us a long speech about how Brown had lied at George Ives's trial, and how Brown and Yeager had just confessed to bein' part of Ives's old gang and that, just as had been suspected, Carter and Graves and Cooper and Zachary and Shears and the other boys who had murdered Magruder and his men, bein' Doc Howard and Jim Romaine and Billy Page and Chris Lowry, were all part of it.

"I could tell he was lyin' by the way X's eyes kept dartin' back and forth, lookin' at the rest of us to see how we'd react. And I don't think it bothered Williams much to know that at least some of us knew that Brown and Yeager hadn't given any information at all. Williams went on talkin' about how the Oro Fino gang used the ranches along the road from Virginia to Bannack as their shebangs, and how Brown would obtain information about gold shipments and travelers from the likes of George Lane and Billy Twerlinger and then pass it on to Red at the Rattlesnake so he could get it on to the gang.

"By then I knew what was comin', but I didn't know how to handle it. Williams started talkin' about how Carter's gang had plenty of friends in Virginia and how the town was still a little fidgety from Ives bein' hanged and that if we brought Yeager and Brown in, the chances were high that they'd be free within a day. Then he walked into the middle of us all to remind us he's twice as thick as any man there, and he says, 'We'd better hang 'em here and now. We've done an awful bit of hard work to be lettin' others waste it.'

"That's when I finally said somethin', because it had never been my intention to go out on a lynchin'. 'I ain't bein' no part of no lynchin',' I told 'em. And I told 'em if they were goin' to go hangin' those boys, they'd be doin' it without me, and I turned and grabbed my coat and moved for the door. The next thing I know there's three shotguns on me and no one sayin' a word, so I got the message and sat back down. Williams looked at all of us and said, 'We're doin' this together. That's already been sworn to.'

"That's all there was to it. I tried to do somethin' about it, Billy. But there weren't no way. I tried. I really did."

Then Pap became totally silent; and when he wouldn't look up at me, I knew that he was fighting back tears again. And I struggled with it, or maybe against it, because he wouldn't give me the ending and I didn't want to conclude it myself. And when I had waited long enough to know he wasn't going to say any more, I said, "Are you saying they hung 'em, Pap?"

"I'm saying we hung 'em, Billy. Right there at Laurin's. Do you hear me? We. Not they. We hung the two of them on a cottonwood along the road and we put signs on 'em saying, RED! ROAD AGENT AND MESSENGER and BROWN! CORRESPONDING SECRETARY. And as far as I know they're still hangin' there now, in plain sight for anyone comin' up or down the road to see."

BOOK V
ALTON QUADE

CHAPTER 1

They say history has a way of repeating itself, as if there were something mystical and determinative to the events surrounding human civilization. It's the sort of thing you hear everywhere, whether in a tavern in conversation amongst working men, or in a parlor room between gentlemen in after-dinner discussion. The occurrence of a recent fact is noted, one of an earlier date is recalled, and then the seemingly profound mention is made of the remarkable similarities between the two. And then the axiom is stated and the talk centers around its truth. But don't go believing it. The redundancy is in human nature itself; the more we think we've changed, the more we stay the same.

What had occurred and was occurring in Alder Gulch was nothing new; I had seen it before, despite my youth and narrow range of experience. The drama was a repeat, a replay if you will, of a theater of the absurd produced and staged in San Francisco only a few years prior when twice in the span of a half decade, William Coleman formed vigilance committees that needfully took the law into their own hands and exacted justice consistent with their own collective judgments. And within the first month of my arrival in Virginia City, I recognized the beginnings of its reappearance, the same manifestation of criminal greed and unlawful violence followed by fear and retribution, culminating in the hanging of one George Ives, a man of superior intellect if not eclectic humor and poor discretion.

I mentioned it to my employer, J. E. McClurg, the day after the hanging. "This sort of thing happened a few years back in San Francisco," I told him. And when he asked, "What sort of thing?" I explained how in 1851 and 1856, the citizens of San Francisco rose up against the corrupt ineptitude of the local authorities. "It started out with just one man being hung down on the Plaza, just like with this George Ives. And by the time they were through the second time around, in 1856 when I actually saw some of the executions, they had formed a vigilance committee of almost 10,000 men." And I went on to explain in detail that my father was prominently among the vigilantes, and how it all had come to pass.

But Mr. McClurg was a stoic. He did not see the connection between the California episode and what had transpired in Nevada City. "The two situations bear no similarities that I can see. You say these men that were hung in San Francisco were given no trials, whereas George Ives was allowed three days to prove his innocence. And you talk of secret meetings and deals when what was done here was done openly and fully in public. I'm sorry, Alton," he said, "but I cannot agree with your sentiments, nor their implications. I know the men who prosecuted George Ives. They are gentlemen and deserve a place of honor in our community."

"Oh, I couldn't agree with you more, Mr. McClurg," I replied as I continued stocking the shelves. "I was just pointing out that in my opinion, the situation has yet to run its course. It was only after the first hanging that the citizens in California realized that a vigilance committee was needed to ensure the peace. Its function was really one of deterrence." Mr. McClurg seemed disturbed by the fact that I had mentioned it at all, and I thus left it at that, not wanting to risk the loss of my clerking position and the accompanying privilege of sleeping accommodations. But I knew better than to believe that the issue had been put to rest, and I had more than enough reason to suppose that throughout the Gulch that evening, the testimony given at George Ives's trial would be the favorite, if not irrepressible, topic of conversation.

Mr. McClurg's shop was well situated in terms of location; it stood next to Kinna & Nye's, where many of the Unionists liked to meet to discuss the issues of the day, and across the street from several of the most prominent saloons and dance halls, which seemed always to be bustling with noise and entertainments. The result was a steady flow of foot and horse and mule traffic past the store, and a consequent patronage that only a good location could achieve. This fact, in turn, allowed Mr. McClurg to enjoy a certain reputation, particularly amongst his fellow Masons, whom he often called in from off the street to join him in the enjoyment of an imported cigar or bowl of flavored pipe tobacco. And from these easy and fairly inexpensive gestures and associations, Mr. McClurg found himself included in the counsels of men like Paris Pfouts and Nicholas Wall and Nathaniel Langford, all who were strongly inclined to engage in the sport of politics whenever opportunity allowed.

Just one day after my conversation with Mr. McClurg, John Lott and John Nye came into the store in an obvious hurry. In his boisterous voice, John Nye bid me a good morning and asked whether Mr. McClurg was about. "He's in the back room attending to the books," I told them both.

And John Lott said, "You had better call him for us, Alton."

There was a remarkable blizzard passing through at the time, and it had almost froze John Lott stiff as he rode up the Gulch from Nevada City. The ice was crusted into his beard and eyebrows, and his cheeks, which were always somewhat rosy, had been turned a decidedly glowing and bloody shade of red. "Messieurs Lott and Nye to see you, Mr. McClurg," I whispered as I poked my head through the back door and came instantly to within a foot of where he sat, cramped into the narrow back-room quarters and peering at the ledgers as if they were written in a foreign and unintelligible script. "And it appears that Mr. Lott has made a special trip in through the storm."

Mr. McClurg rose and came up front instantly with his writing quill still in hand. "Gentlemen," he said. "Out on such a day as this?"

"We have news, Jason," John Lott said as he moved toward the stove to thaw his hands. "We need to find Paris. Williams and his boys went after Aleck Carter." And when Mr. McClurg said nothing to that, John Lott added, "They formed a posse and swore an oath in writing."

"An oath. What kind of oath?" Mr. McClurg said. "That will not do at all."

"John has it with him here," John Nye said. "He promised Williams he'd hold on to it until they return. That's how John here found out about it. It really doesn't say much, except they each promise to tell no secrets. That's the bothersome part. 'Reveal no secrets,' it says. Some of those boys are lodge members from Colorado. They know better than that. Reveal no secrets, my ass."

Mr. McClurg readily agreed to go with them. And as the three of them tramped out into the cold and snow, I assured Mr. McClurg I would closely watch the store.

John Lott and John Nye were Masons, just like Mr. McClurg. And in his time, my father had been a Mason also. Through him, I came to understand the political expediency attendant with joining the Mason's ranks, and to appreciate the clandestine means by which they sought to accomplish their agenda. And I found, after his death in one of the many arson fires that swept San Francisco, that it was productive for me to ascribe to their beliefs and adopt their point of view. As soon as I had done so by informal means, at the time still being but a youth and thus not qualified for official membership, I was accorded such condescending treatment, as an orphaned son of an Ancient Free and Accepted Mason, that it almost seemed I was heir and beneficiary to some great trust established for that very purpose. They guaranteed that I was fed and housed and employed, all in a manner exceeding the norm; and when, after several years, I expressed the desire to return to the East by the transcontinental route, it was the worshipful master in San Francisco who granted me a sufficient stipend to secure my passage at least to Illinois where I had relatives who were awaiting to receive me.

I thus traveled by deck passage on steamboat to Eureka and Celilo and Umatilla and finally, by wagon, in to Walla Walla. Amongst my California acquaintances, some thought such a routing ill conceived. "Why not go via the Isthmus?" they had asked. And others had argued in favor of the wagon route east from Salt Lake City. To which I needed only reply that the Isthmus route took too long and ran the unnecessary risk of encounter with Confederate corsairs along the Texas coast, and that the wagon trails took too much out of a man in jolts alone, even if one maintained no interest in keeping one's scalp attached. "Where I come from," I had told them, "a river is nothing but a highway for the upper class. Why fight the countryside with hoof and wheel when you can observe it from the rail of an upper deck?"

From Walla Walla I had made the land portion of my sojourn with relative ease, as a civilian accompaniment to a small army survey team, the late-summer season having sufficiently hardened the roads, and the inland Northwest weather so pacific as to be almost tropical. So that when we arrived at the gates of Fort Benton, I felt as though I had essentially completed my trip, all that remained being the easy 1,500-mile steamboat ride downriver to St. Louis, and then downriver to Cairo, Illinois. That is until a leathery and rancorous man at the lead of a freight train approached us and then stopped directly in our path as we came up to the fort.

"Where's the dregs of the U.S. Army off to this time?" he had asked our major rudely. And before the major could answer, he added, "Not out makin' treaties with the local savages, I hope."

Major Preston stood up to the abuse well and merely smiled as he noted to his antagonist that he had not had the pleasure of making his acquaintance.

"Jack Slade," the man had said back roughly. "Captain Jack Slade.

Formerly of the Overland Express. Where'd you boys say you were headin'?"

"I did not say, sir. But if you must know, we are returning East by steamboat. She was to have arrived but yesterday and is scheduled to depart Monday next."

"That so. Well then you'll have a year's wait if that's your plan. I've just come from past Cow Island. That's as far as the *Cap Walters* made it before she ran out of water and had to drop her freight. She's long gone, Major. Long gone."

That being the case, I had had no option but to part company with Major Preston and to join with Captain Slade, who agreed to take me with him to Virginia City. "Yeah, I'll take you along," he had said. "As long as you can pull your own weight in drivin' a team and shootin' a Crow." And when I assured him that I could, he rudely laughed and said, "Then get your ass up on the rig next to Hatchet there and make sure the sonofa keeps that load movin'."

It was thusly by the Masons of San Francisco that my transport to Virginia City was funded, and by the good graces of Jack Slade that I arrived there at all, after a ten-day wagon ride during which Jack Slade cuffed more than one of his men roughly on the ears, and over the course of which every profane expression and ribald joke had been graven into my mind by endless repetition. And upon my arrival, and in more than small part in an effort to avoid further association with Slade's class of men, I quickly had made as much as I could of my association with the Masonic fraternity.

By discreet inquiries, I found out the names of many of the members of the newly forming lodge—Pfouts, Hereford, Langford, Holter, Hughes, Fox, and a dozen others. From these men I then sought employment and assistance and quickly found as much and more from Mr. McClurg, who also was courting the favor of the more prominent and established citizens of Virginia City and who had, upon the suggestion of Paris Pfouts, therefore immediately hired me on at a respectable wage. What's more, Mr. McClurg needed me badly. I knew ledgers and accounts, and he did not. I also had an eye for bargains and economies of scale. And in respect to customer relations, particularly with the ladies who sought out the powders and perfumes, the cosmetics and combs and brushes that I persuaded Mr. McClurg to keep apart for them on a separate counter, I proved myself most adroit and indispensable. But most important for both Mr. McClurg and me were my insights and accuracy in analyzing issues of local politics, and my willingness to share my perceptions with Mr. McClurg liberally and without invitation.

Benefited by my many observations, Mr. McClurg succeeded in ingratiating himself into the innermost circle of the elites. And I do not believe he would have allowed me any credit for his social elevation had it not been apparent to both him and me that it would do him more harm than good to ignore me. So that, after a time, he began openly to characterize me as his "right-hand man," and I permitted the reference, only because it suited me as well.

~~~~

So secretive were Paris Pfouts and Wilbur Sanders and the other men with whom Mr. McClurg joined in discussing the formation of a vigilance committee that I did not know of their efforts until Mr. McClurg invited me to attend what was to be their third meeting in as many nights. I had been in the process of closing up the shop for only a few minutes, during which time the early winter darkness had declared itself in full, when Mr. McClurg began to talk, almost to himself it seemed, about the same subject that now seemed to be festering everywhere and all day long. "Something must be done. That much is clear," he muttered as he counted the notes and coins and weighed the dust as he did every evening at the close of hours. "Henry Plummer hasn't even been to Virginia in a month now. There's no jail, no court to speak of, nothing even resembling authority to govern a city of thousands. Absurd. That's what it is. A paradigm for anarchy." And then he said, "Something must be done; don't you think so, Alton?"

That was what I had been telling him all along, and I said so.

"You think there should be a vigilance committee, then. Is that what you're saying?"

And I said it didn't really matter what I thought. "There will be one whether I desire it or not. It is merely coincidental that I happen to believe that it is the only way to bring sanity to this place. If it is done correctly, that is."

"Yes. Of course. Then you must assist us," Mr. McClurg said excitedly, the word "us" hanging ambiguously and undefined. "We have formed such a committee. Come with me tonight, Alton. I am confident you will not be disappointed." At the time, I was more than pleased by the fact that I had received the invitation. In their early going, the vigilantes of San Francisco had proved themselves to be not only formidable, but also highly respectable in their manner of operation and purpose.

That evening was Christmas Eve, being the same day that John Lott and John Nye had dropped by with the information that Williams and his men had embarked on their secret mission; and the cold that had descended a day earlier kept on with a conviction that was most remarkable. The subzero temperatures hurried one along, the snow crunching and squeaking all that more loudly underfoot and the wind cutting at the skin as with a sharpened razor. So that Mr. McClurg and I moved quickly along the boardwalk, up to Kinna & Nye's where the windows had been shuttered closed, allowing only the interior light to show weakly through the slats.

Mr. McClurg knocked on the door and it opened only enough for a single eye to peer out, and then the face of John Nye showed and the door opened just wide enough for us to pass before he quickly shut it again and set the latch. "A Merry Christmas to you, Jason. Merry Christmas, Alton my boy," he shook Mr. McClurg's hand and patted my back. "And a white Christmas at that."

"Yes," said John Lott, who had come up out of the crowd to greet us. "And a cold day in hell for George Ives, I'll warrant."

There were perhaps a total of thirty men in the store, every one of whom I recognized as not only being proponents, to one degree or another, of the recent hanging, but also mostly as men who had been Masons before they ever even heard of Alder Gulch and Grasshopper Creek. And as I moved through the crowd so that I might mix company and demonstrate my social upbringing, I brushed shoulders with some of the most outstanding citizens of Virginia City—J. M. Fox and Nick Wall and men of that caliber—only to find myself standing next to Colonel Wilbur Sanders, who was sitting in a cane chair, in a world all unto himself, examining a single sheet of paper.

They all seemed to be in a uniformly grim state of mind and, in connection with each new member, John Nye offered a brief comment about the man that somehow enhanced his dignity and qualifications. But when it came to me, all that John Nye said was, "I believe most of you are acquainted with Jason's clerk, Alton Quade." Wilbur Sanders, who had been in Mr. McClurg's store earlier that day, looked up at me over his glasses and nodded his head in a form of acknowledgment. And then John Nye said directly to me, "Your employer, Mr. McClurg, believes you can be of unique assistance to us, Alton."

"One minute, please," Wilbur Sanders interrupted. "Let us take care of a few formalities first." He rose and paced across the front of the counter with his head down as though he were in deep thought, and then he turned abruptly to face me. "How old are you, Mr. Quade?" he asked. And when I answered, he said, "Rather youthful for such matters as this, I would say." He drew a deep breath and held it for an unduly long period and then exhaled in a sigh of resignation. Then he said, "We are here on very important business, Mr. Quade. Our lives and the welfare of our loved ones may depend on it. I hope you can appreciate that confidentiality is of the utmost importance to us."

I had stood perfectly still as he nervously walked the floor. And now I answered with a measure of calm that was meant to impress. "I understand that perfectly, Colonel. I should advise you that my father was the recording secretary of the San Francisco vigilantes. I know better than anyone of the need to keep information privileged."

"Then you already know why we have called for you?" Colonel Sanders asked. "Mr. McClurg has revealed our purpose?"

"No, he didn't, Colonel. The inevitability of what would follow from the hanging of George Ives was apparent to me instantly. And I told Mr. McClurg as much. The presence of so many reputable citizens of Virginia merely confirmed for me that a committee was now being formed."

"That is a fact," Mr. McClurg blurted out. "Young Quade here said to me just the other day how it all reminded him of the events in San Francisco. Truth is I didn't listen to him. I should have known better. Alton's father was a lodge master in his time, you know."

"And have you been degreed, Mr. Quade?" Colonel Sanders asked.

To which I answered no, I was too young when I left San Francisco just months back and had yet to have been invited to join the Masons here in the Idaho Territory. And when a substantial silence afterwards ensued, I added, "But I would be honored by the invitation and am satisfied that I would quickly prove my worth."

There were some murmurs of approval and no further questions. Then Colonel Sanders said, "You have come direct to Alder Gulch from California then?"

And I said, "Yes, sir. I have."

By then I knew what they wanted—the knowledge of prior precedent, behind which men hide to justify what they are about to do, being therefore nothing that had not been done before and which, presumably, would be done again. "I have the vigilante oath, if that is what you gentlemen are seeking, and the regulations and the bylaws of the San Francisco Vigilance Committee, as well. I am more than willing to share them with you."

Over the next four days we worked into the night, secretly debating and revising the regulations and bylaws, mostly to suit Wilbur Sanders's archaic taste for legalese and the usage of the English language.

And each evening our number grew, the new arrivals all being men of great dignity and high reputation in the Gulch: names like Al Brockie and Harry King, all of whom had transported respectability and education to the wild frontier. In the first instance, they were nonetheless made to take the vigilante oath, which they repeated, word for word, just as had been written in the pages of my father's diary.

The debates over those four days showed that what the members maintained in desire they lacked in backbone. Mostly, they seemed to be afraid—afraid of everything and everybody ranging from Aleck Carter and Bill Graves to James Williams and Charley Beehrer and Charley Brown and even X Beidler, who seemed to me a little man in the body of a boy. They seemed equally concerned over gaining too much notoriety by their self-appointments as vigilantes, so much so, in fact, that when the time came for electing officers to the executive committee required under the bylaws, no one stepped forth to volunteer to take the committee chair.

"I nominate John Lott," John Nye proposed as the discussion focused first on the selection of a president.

And John Lott as quickly said, "Decline the nomination."

Then Robert Hereford was proposed, and he too declined on an instant.

It went on that way until someone finally proposed that Paris Pfouts, who was in Nevada City attending to personal business and therefore not present, be given the role of president. The motion was seconded and approved without dissent. "That'll show Paris," John Nye whispered to Mr. McClurg. "I told him he'd better not be missing these meetings."

The question of who should be selected as the executive officer was an altogether different matter.

There seemed to be a consensus that for any of a variety of reasons, the position should be offered to James Williams, who had yet to return from his secret mission. "We need a man like Williams," Ad Davis stated, "to ferret out these hellhounds and bring them to us for trial."

"And how shall we induce these men to take on such a dangerous task when the need arises?" Harry King asked.

And Wilbur Sanders answered, half in jest, "With a ferreting fund. How else?"

I did not much appreciate Colonel Sanders. He was an opportunist, and nothing more. He seemed to have little appreciation for the logic that underlies the law; and had it not been for his talents with the English language, he would have been a failure of a man from first to last. I found myself subtly contradicting him, more often than was prudent. "The fact is," I said, "that is exactly the function of the property seizure provisions of the regulations: to provide capital for the committee's operations. Without our being too specific, it should be made known to the captains who take a company out to make arrests, that it is assumed that their efforts will be rewarded, and that the source of the monies in that regard will be, first and foremost, the estates of the criminals they apprehend. Call it a ferreting fund, or by whatever label you prefer. But a fund there must be. It will be the engine that drives the committee's operations and the greater its purchasing power the more that will be accomplished. I'll venture that much with odds."

"I am not a gambling man, Mr. Quade," Colonel Sanders responded.

"Nor am I, Colonel Sanders," I said. "Nor am I. That is why the fund must operate as I have described. Consider it to be insurance. James Williams and X Beidler might volunteer to make a few arrests before they lose their enthusiasm, and Charley Beehrer and Charley Brown might make a few more just for the thrill they will derive from it. But it is the promise, or guarantee if you will, of reward, whether by payment in gold or in new horses for Williams's ranch, that will remove speculation regarding whether they will persist until the job is completed. That is what I have been trying to impress upon you all over these past few days. The California vigilantes operated on three premises. First, that with the lure of money, a sufficient number of men can be found who will gladly patrol the streets and make the necessary arrests no matter the hour or place. And second, that a select group—the executive committee—must be designated to try the accused and sentence them if necessary. And third, that once the power of the executive committee and its captains and lieutenants is known and witnessed, the vast majority of the population will follow their lead like willing and docile sheep."

When Wilbur Sanders said nothing at all in response, I knew that I had offended him; and it was a mistake I could only mitigate. And so, after the nomination and approval of James Williams as executive officer, I argued that the bylaws should be changed to admit the designation of an official prosecutor, whom I then proposed be Wilbur Sanders, who had, through his legal talents, brought George Ives to justice. A motion was made and seconded, and the position formally established and appointed. From thereafter, Wilbur Sanders no longer perceived me as a threat. And to be sure that it remained just so, I made it a point prospectively to be condescending to him.

They named John Lott treasurer, and this time he could not avoid the nomination; and when a secretary was appointed after it was noted that the rules of secrecy and expediency ensured that little would need be done by that officer, the slate was filled. Then there was nothing to do but to wait for what we would do if the posse succeeded in capturing Aleck Carter, and perhaps others of his band, and returning them for trial before the committee.

New Year's Day came and went with all the revelry and emotion, well-wishing and resolving, that one might expect in view of the ongoing war and the success of the trial and the richness of the Alder strike; and still we had no news of James Williams and his men. By then, it had become common knowledge that the posse had set out, and rumors were circulated daily concerning the fact that they had slaughtered Carter's gang or had been ambushed themselves or had froze along the banks of the Stinkingwater after having been trapped in a blizzard of freakish proportion. There were some who said good riddance for whatever misfortune had befallen them, and others who bemoaned the apparent failure

of the posse, with the newly formed vigilance committee members uniformly among this latter group since, without James Williams and his
men, the committee would be bereft of its operative heart and soul.

"I fear the worst for them," Mr. McClurg said on the afternoon of
the third after it began to snow yet again and the mercury dropped back
toward the zero mark. "They have been gone far too long. Can it be that
the hanging of George Ives unleashed an even greater evil?"

Then, on the afternoon of the fifth, word spread through Virginia
that Charley Beehrer and Charley Brown and X Beidler were at the
California Exchange. That was all. There was no report of James
Williams nor prisoners nor anything else, only that the three men were
at the Exchange and that Charley Beehrer had brought in a couple of
kegs of his best beer and opened them up to whoever might imbibe. And
that information, alone, set off what looked like a gold rush stampede,
up and down the snow-encrusted streets and alleys of Virginia City.

Mr. McClurg was a man of great decorum, and it was thus predictable that he would think it below himself to join in the scramble to
get the news. "We'll find out soon enough," he said. And that proved to
be true, because when an old haggard miner whom we knew as Weasel
stuck his head in the shop fifteen minutes later and asked if we had
heard, and then said, "Hung two," when we said no, it was as if the
world came to an abrupt and perfectly unnatural stop.

"What do you mean, 'hung two'?" Mr. McClurg shouted at the
figure who had already closed the door to hurry along the boardwalk to
Kinna & Nye's. And when the footsteps did not stop, Mr. McClurg
went out into the wintry cold in pursuit of the old man who by then
might already have thrown open the door at Kinna & Nye's and said,
"Hung two," and then closed that door too so that he might repeat his
information again to another set of anxious and waiting ears in the next
place of business down the street.

They called a meeting that night at J. M. Fox's Blue House, and
by then we had learned that it was not Aleck Carter nor any of his
henchmen that had been hanged, but merely the lowly George Brown,

who had cowered and shook when he gave his testimony at the trial, and a man named Red Yeager, whom Granville Stuart knew as a boy back in Iowa and who was known only as the cook and bartender at Bill Bunton's ranch on the Rattlesnake Creek, a goodly distance from the Gulch. John Nye and Ad Davis stopped by to deliver the information, and they were obviously displeased and affronted by it. "What are we going to tell people?" Nye said. "What do we do when we're asked what their crimes were and we can only say, 'We don't really know; we hanged 'em before we had a chance to ask.'" And when Mr. McClurg asked John Nye what James Williams had had to say about it, John Nye answered, "We don't know that either. Williams won't say a word about it. That's what we're hoping to find out tonight."

~~~~

"Trial!" X Beidler exploded. "What do you mean, why didn't we give 'em a trial? You ain't heard a word we've said. This ole boy Red Yeager confessed to it all at Laurin's. What would've been the sense in bringin' 'em back here and spendin' a week gettin' 'em hung? They deserved hangin', and we gave 'em what they had comin'."

Wilbur Sanders had left for Bannack to begin the preliminary groundwork toward establishing a vigilance committee there and in his absence Paris Pfouts apparently thought it was incumbent on himself to play the role of chief interrogator. "You say they had it coming, but I'm not even sure what they did," he said to X Beidler. "Surely you hung them for something more than writing and delivering a letter."

Through it all, during the whole time the vigilance committee posed their questions, James Williams said nothing beyond the brief explanation that they had caught Red Yeager and George Brown warning Aleck Carter, and that they had been hung. Someone would ask a question and Williams would simply stare back at them and not answer, with X Beidler each time jumping in to make an emotional statement justifying the executions.

Finally, Williams stood up and began to walk toward the door. "I've had my share of this," he said in a hard voice with his jaw clenched. "If you all don't like what we did, find someone else to do the rough work next time. I'm goin' back up to my ranch to get me and my horses some rest. If you want me," he said as he swung open the door, "you know where I'm at."

That left X Beidler alone to explain what had happened at Laurin's, because not another member of the posse was there despite the invitations they had received. Which meant there almost was nothing left to meet about since, if X departed also, it would be over entirely. So Pfouts backed off some. "Let's go over it again, X," he said. "From the beginning. What is it Yeager told you that made you decide to hang them then and there and be through with it?"

"Get me somethin' to write with," Beidler said in a frustrated voice. "And some paper." And when J. M. Fox brought him the writing materials, X Beidler commenced writing without saying a word.

"What're you up to, X?" Al Brockie asked.

"Keep your pants on; I'll be finished in a second." When he was through, X Beidler put down the pencil and lifted up the paper and turned it toward the group of men and said, "There. These are the men we're after. These are the men Red Yeager told us were members of the road agent gang. And that's why we hung those two yahoos then and there. Because we ain't got the time to be patsyfootin' around with this many of those bandits when they're busy figurin' how to rob us blind and cut our throats."

The paper was passed from hand to hand, with each successive reader blurting out a name or an expletive, until John Lott got hold of it and read the names out loud. "Red Yeager—messenger, George Brown—corresponding secretary, George Ives—captain, Aleck Carter—captain, Sam Bunton, Bill Bunton, Cy Skinner, Steve Marshland, Weldon Hall, Dutch John Wagner, Whiskey Bill Graves, Twofingers Carson, Johnny Cooper, Bob Zachary, Doc Howard, Mexican Frank, Billy Page, Harry Peterson, Tex Crowley, Gad Moore, Buck Stinson, Haze Lyons, Frank

Parish, Jim Romaine, Chris Lowry, Billy Twerlinger, Pete Saxon." When he had finished reading, the paper came down to his knee, and then John Nye grabbed it and read it and passed it on to the others. A long silence followed during which Paris Pfouts looked at X Beidler and X Beidler returned the stare with an intense and unwavering squint, as if he might be capable of looking straight into the sun. "You're saying Yeager identified each of these men as being part of an organized gang of road agents?" Paris Pfouts finally asked.

"That's exactly what I'm sayin'." Beidler answered. "Every damned one of 'em. And there's plenty more besides. You can count on that. The whole damned gang is working out of the road stations and ranches. They've got lookouts and spies and the whole shebang. They've been runnin' out of Bunton's Rattlesnake and Ives's ranch along the Wisconsin. They've even been usin' Dempsey's ranch when Dempsey don't know about it. That's how they know when someone's travelin' with gold on 'em. And the one thing that ain't written there that you boys had better come to face is that Henry Plummer and his deputies are lettin' it happen right beneath their noses. You ask Jim Williams, when he cools down some, what Buck Stinson and Ned Ray told 'em at the Rattlesnake when Jim and his boys arrested Red Yeager. They said there ain't goin' to be no more hangin's if Henry Plummer has his way."

"What's Henry Plummer got to do with this?" someone in the back asked. "You're not saying he's part of this gang, are you?" And someone else asked what Beidler was saying about Ray and Stinson.

"He might as well be," Beidler answered the one question. "This ain't the kinda deal where you can sit on the fence and not take sides. Either you're for cleanin' up this country or you ain't. Either you're for findin' Nicky Tibolt's killers or you're against."

The paper was in Nick Wall's hands now. "There's twenty-five names on this list. Are you saying we need to arrest all these men?"

"Three of 'em's already dead," X Beidler answered. "And Doc Howard and his boys are already arrested and gettin' ready to be hung in Lewiston. So it ain't twenty-five. Fact is, there's plenty of others who ain't on that list that oughta be. We got our work cut out for us, if that's what you're sayin'. That's a fact. And we better get to it before they get more organized and we end up with a war on our hands."

"What do you mean by that?" Harry King asked.

And X Beidler said, "If you boys can go organizin' committees and makin' plans, what makes you think they can't do the same thing? Especially with all these secesh boys hangin' around here lookin' for ways to get even for what we did to 'em at Gettysburg and Vicksburg. We're settin' on a powder keg here boys. Be best if we did somethin' about it."

"You suggesting we go straight back out there and try to catch Carter again? We're going to have trouble getting men to go when you boys couldn't get him the first time."

"We'll get Carter," X Beidler said. "Don't go worryin' yourself over that. He ain't goin' nowhere we can't get to now that the snow's closed off the passes. Seems to me that Bannack's our problem at the moment. We need to get over there and see that Colonel Sanders does somethin' to make sure Henry Plummer and his boys ain't gettin' in our way. Besides. Someone needs to let 'em know about Yeager and Brown. And they need to be on the lookout for Carter's boys tryin' to make it out of here by goin' south."

"And how do you propose we get control of Plummer and that bunch?" Paris Pfouts asked.

"How the hell am I supposed to know," Beidler answered. "I'm not one for makin' decisions before I have to. Maybe Sanders and that Judge Edgerton can answer that for us."

This last observation by X Beidler reminded me of something from the past, and so I spoke out. "That's what the San Francisco vigilantes did right up front," I said. "They got some of the local judiciary to go along with what they were doing. It made it a lot harder for people to complain."

"That makes some sense," Paris Pfouts said. And a number of the others agreed.

"All I know," X Beidler said, "is that it's got to be played out somehow. I'm willin' to go to Bannack so long as I'm not alone." He stepped up onto the counter and looked out over the group of men. "I've been out in that weather for two weeks straight. I'm bettin' some of you boys got enough hide on you to make the two-day trip to Bannack without turnin' into snowmen. Now who's willin' to go to Bannack and get the judge's blessin'?" He surveyed the faces that looked up at him vacantly. And when no one said anything back, he added, "It'll be kinda like goin' to see the Pope."

CHAPTER 2

From over the crest of the freight road we looked down at Bannack City in the waning light. And the little hamlet looked so diminutive and peaceful in its isolation, so bucolic and idle and contained at the bottom of the vale in which it sat, with the new-fallen snow to smooth the rocky terrain and the creek frozen half solid from the bitter cold and the streams of smoke so thin and the glow of lights so faint, that it seemed almost a shame to invade its tranquility with words of desperate need. "Looks almost like a painting," I whispered to John Lott as he came up on his horse next to mine.

"Don't let it fool you none," X Beidler answered. "There's a den of thieves down there, thick as snakes."

We came down the road in a single file, John Lott and X Beidler and Harry King and me, at a slow, steady, almost indifferent plod. And with each step, Bannack City loomed more real and extant, negating my imagined portrait of the place and instilling in its stead the actual fact of its composition and personality—the conceived and the real merging finally into one.

At a point on the road but several hundred feet above the town, which by then emitted audible sounds and showed movement on its streets, we came upon a cemetery alongside of which were the smoldering and anomalous remains of a campfire. And from thereon we rode in silence until we came up to Pearson's stables, where Pearson himself greeted us, and John Lott especially, and then introduced us rather coldly to his son, whom he instructed to groom and feed our mounts. And I felt that the younger Pearson looked at us with suspicious and distrustful eyes as we gave over the reins and followed his father into the stables.

"I've been expecting you, John," Pearson quietly told John Lott. "Colonel Sanders said to look out for you within the week. What news from Alder Gulch?" Then he seemed to think better of talking openly, even in the confines of his own stable, and he said more loudly, "Why don't you gentlemen come into my cabin. My wife is out at the moment, but I know she would insist on your having some coffee and pie." He turned to his son, who was taking X Beidler's saddle off Black Bess. "Be sure to clean the floor, too. And put a bit of soap on those saddles."

Inside the cabin, Pearson regained the sense of immediate interest he seemed to have lost a moment ago. "How are things in the Gulch, John?" he asked almost anxiously.

"There's been more hangings," John Lott replied quietly. "Yeager and Brown both confessed to being road agents. We've come to meet with Colonel Sanders."

"I understand," Walt Pearson said. And then he added, "Do you mean Red Yeager and George Brown? They're both cooks, aren't they?" And when no one responded he said more loudly, "Perhaps you gentlemen should make room arrangements while I inform the Colonel. There's trouble about. It's not a good idea for you to be seen making for Yankee Flat. It would be best if you looked to be in Bannack on ordinary business."

"What kind of trouble?" X Beidler demanded. And he moved up close to Pearson.

"A couple of boys brought Dutch John Wagner in for robbing Moody's pack train. Henry Plummer and Ned Ray tried to take him from them but they refused. Plummer says there has to be a jury trial based on the territorial code, or that they've got to set him free. Plummer claims he made a promise to the federal marshal that there'd be no more hangings after Peter Horen."

"Who's they?" Beidler said. "Who's got Wagner?"

"Neil Howie and a freighter named Featherstun. They've got him over in an empty cabin on the flat. They say they won't give him up to Plummer. And they mean business. Come morning there'll be trouble for sure. There's a bunch over at Durant's Billiard Hall who says Wagner's to be hung, and there's another bunch over at Jimmie's Bar, including Buck Stinson, that are making some pretty loud noises about letting him go."

X Beidler was about to say something more when John Lott cut him off. "I had better see the colonel myself," Lott said. "I'll head over to Judge Edgerton's; that way someone can bring the colonel over and I won't have to cross the creek. X, you see what you can find out over at Durant's if you want. You've been around Bannack enough that your presence won't seem unusual. Harry and Alton, you get us a couple of rooms at the Goodrich and then check with Bill Roe. And be careful who you boys go telling about Yeager and Brown." Then he turned back to Pearson. "We'll be needing a place to meet where we won't be noticed. What do you suggest?"

Pearson shook his head. "You can't go unnoticed in this town. The best you can be is unsuspected. I'll get out the word for a lodge members' meeting this evening at Peabody's; Ben's down in Salt Lake. I'm taking care of the place while he's away. You've got news regarding a charter for a lodge in Virginia City. That way we'll at least be assured of privacy and confidences."

John Lott slightly lifted the curtain from the window next to the stove and peered out onto the street. "Fine," he said. "At eight o'clock."

When we met in the back of Peabody's at the appointed hour, I expected there to be a fair gathering of men since Wilbur Sanders had assured the Alder Gulch committee that a substantial portion of the

Bannack population was under his sway and would join in the vigilante movement. But it was not so. Other than the four of us and Wilbur Sanders and Walt Pearson and Bill Roe, there were only five other men, and not one of them had yet been persuaded of the need or wisdom of forming a branch committee in Bannack.

Among them was Smith Ball, who held a high reputation not only as a Mason but also as a loyal Unionist and a man of education. Ball, not so incidentally, was also one of the diverse men who had been deputized by Henry Plummer. "I understand what Mr. Quade here has told us concerning the effectiveness of the vigilantes in San Francisco; and I do not intend in any way to demean what was accomplished there by his father and others. But what you gentlemen don't seem to appreciate," Ball said midway into the first hour of the meeting, "is that the general consensus in Bannack City proper is that the town is in good hands. Even George Chrisman and Tom Pitt believe that Plummer is as fine a law officer as we could hope for under the circumstances. You're going to have a difficult time persuading them, and some of our wives I might add, that Plummer's responsibilities should be taken from him and reposed in a committee whose only charter is to execute those it finds guilty. There must be some other way to break this road agent gang that Yeager identified, without having to wrest control away from Henry Plummer. Perhaps Henry will join us in the effort."

"Join us!" X Beidler exclaimed. "You ain't listenin' to what we're sayin' here, Smittie. Plummer's a part of it; he's lettin' these boys get away with all this killin' and robbin'. Do you understand what I'm sayin'? These road agents are Henry Plummer's friends; he knew half of 'em on the other side before he ever came to Bannack. He's part of it, and he deserves to be hung just like the rest of 'em."

"You're saying you want to hang Henry Plummer?" Smith Ball said, stunned by the proposition.

"You're damned right that's what I'm sayin'," Beidler answered, and as he said it, I saw John Lott roll his eyes.

"Now wait a minute, X," Lott said.

But Beidler would have none of it. "You boys had better listen to what I learned over at Durant's. The word is that Plummer and Stinson and Ray have given Howie and Featherstun twenty-four hours to cool down and hand over Wagner. Then they're gonna take Wagner from 'em whether they like it or not." He pulled back out the paper on which he had written the names he had said Yeager identified, and he said, "There's one name Red Yeager gave me an' Jim Williams that ain't been written down yet; and the only reason it ain't been done yet is that I've been waitin' to see how many of you out there are willin' to do what's got to be done. The plain fact is there ain't no more time to be waitin' on it, so I'm gonna have to tell you who that name is and be done with it myself." And when he had seen that he had captured the attention of all of us who stood there, he said, "That name is Henry Plummer; and he's the chief of the road agent gang."

No one said anything for a long while, each of us individually suspended in our own disbelief or awe of the moment. Finally, Wilbur Sanders walked up to Beidler and handed him a pencil and said, "Then write it down. Put it down on that paper too so that it will be written at least." And then he said, "Given what we now know, it is obvious that we must recruit more men, and then we must take Plummer and Stinson and Ray into custody and try them according to the bylaws of the committee."

Smith Ball shook his head. "You're saying hang them, too, then. Aren't you? You're saying seize them and hang them on the same gallows Henry built to hang Peter Horen." Throughout the debate he had held a pair of gloves in his hand, and now he slapped them down in frustration. "Ever since Plummer killed Jack Cleveland I've believed he ought not to wear a badge. And I've known for a long time that some of the boys he's friendly with have been doing some of the robbing and maybe even some of the killing that's been going on around here. And I know you feel the same way, George," he said to George Copely, who had been nodding affirmatively to everything that X Beidler and Wilbur Sanders said. "But there is no way in hell you're going to get many of the men in this town to agree with what you're proposing unless you come up with some good evidence to show that it's the necessary thing to do. Henry Plummer's got more friends than you can shake a stick at, some of the best citizens included; and most of 'em are wondering whether you boys from Alder Gulch have lost your minds and are coming after them next just because they don't agree with your viewpoint on the war or the weather or which leg is the best to start off on when you're racing a horse. You better have something better than a list with Henry Plummer's name on it, especially when the last one is Henry Plummer and it's obvious that it was written long after the others had been placed down on that paper."

Again, there was silence, and it was unclear whether the debate had ended in a stalemate. Then X Beidler said, "All right then. If it's evidence you want, it's evidence you'll get. But once it's laid out in black and white, there'd better not be any more of this shit here or the next debate is goin' to be in Virginia City and the topic is goin' to be why folks in Bannack are so protective of the road agents. I vote we get Dutch John Wagner in here and let him tell us whether Plummer and Stinson and Ray have been helpin' these boys with their thievin'. We already know Wagner's a member of the gang. Yeager said so," he said, waving the paper that was becoming more and more battered and torn each time he folded it and placed it in his pocket. "He come over from Oro Fino and Lewiston with Yeager and Doc Howard and Carter and his boys. And he knew Plummer from those days just like Yeager did. Let's see what a man who's preparin' to meet his maker has got to say about clearin' his conscience and givin' up the truth." And when he had obtained the general agreement of us all that this was a reasonable manner in which to proceed, he added, "I'll fetch him over here while you boys round up some more of the brave citizens of Bannack. If we're gonna put on a show, there ought to be an audience."

It would have been more than imprudent for all of us to suddenly appear out on the streets trying to round up men, so only four of the men from Bannack—George Dart and Smith Ball and George Copely and John Innes—went back out into the cold. And as the remainder of us began to discuss the new direction we had suddenly taken, Wilbur Sanders became more and more agitated until he finally rose and put on his greatcoat and said, "I am going to consult with Judge Edgerton on our course of action, gentlemen. I will not be long."

It was a long wait before anyone returned; and among the last was Wilbur Sanders, who appeared much more excited and enthused. "How says the judge?" John Lott asked.

And Wilbur Sanders pompously answered, "It is his decided opinion that we have no option, in the face of the lawless alternatives, other than to proceed." With that, Sanders took off his coat and sat off in a corner as if to think.

The others had enjoyed similar degrees of success, and there were almost thirty men assembled when X Beidler and Neil Howie and John Featherstun entered through the back door of Peabody's warehouse room with their prisoner. "We had some time of it," X Beidler said as he kicked the snow off his boots. "But I think we made it in on the sly."

The man they called Dutch John Wagner was in a particularly sorry state. His hands had been severely frostbitten during his failed attempt to flee over the mountains to Salt Lake City, and his fingers, which had turned a deadly black, appeared to be utterly useless to him. And X Beidler, all on his own, seemed to have placed the Dutchman in a pitiful frame of terror as to what Beidler might intend to do. Every few moments, Wagner's head would turn to look down pathetically at X, who stood just inches from his side; and on each such instance Wagner's eyes would meet the double barrels of X's shotgun, which, by the way the weapon was cradled in Beidler's arms, almost casually pointed up at, and directly into, John Wagner's face. It made for a most peculiar juxtaposition, for Dutch John seemed fully twice X Beidler's size and three times or more his match in strength; yet by X Beidler's visage, one might have thought X capable of any vicious act, whereas John Wagner's countenance was almost pitiful and gentle and contrite.

It all proved to be a waste of time. Two good hours worth to be exact. Because John Wagner had concluded from the start that the purpose of the inquiry was to prove he should be hung, and X Beidler did everything he could to reinforce Dutch John's impression. When X asked if Dutch John had robbed Moody's train, Dutch John denied it. And when X suggested to the prisoner that he was a member of the road agent gang, Dutch John disclaimed any knowledge of the gang's existence and did his best to disassociate himself from Aleck Carter and Doc Howard and the remainder of the roster that Beidler read off, one by one. "Why do you ask me these questions?" Dutch John finally asked. "This Red Yeager you name is no friend of mine. He owes me money; that's all. He gives my name so that he won't have to pay me back."

"Your friend Red Yeager is a dead man," X Beidler answered. "Last time I saw him he was wearin' a rope necktie and decoratin' a tree."

By the time Wilbur Sanders could inject himself into the process without alienating himself from some of the newly arrived Bannack men like George Chrisman and Francis Thompson, there was no opportunity for him to even ask if Henry Plummer was also a member of the gang. And when Dutch John Wagner requested that he be placed in Henry Plummer's custody in order that he might prove his innocence to the Bannack miners' committee, the matter abruptly ended and Howie and Featherstun returned with their charge to Yankee Flat.

By then, a certain and fairly smallish number of the Bannack citizens had come to believe that the time indeed had come when at least Buck Stinson and Ned Ray must be brought to justice. In a detailed accusation orchestrated by X Beidler, George Copely and Smith Ball and Wiles outlined how Stinson had murdered the ancient Flathead named Old Snag and then scalped him ignominiously in front of his people, and then had murdered Dillingham in league with Plummer's other deputies, and now was suspected of a half dozen robberies and other crimes, including the shooting of his own dog in the middle of the street. And then Harry King, who had spent a considerable amount of time in Salt Lake City, told how Ray had been jailed for horse thieving only to escape from the territorial prison under cover of night. And as each man added more and more fact and rumor to support their contentions, the enthusiasm amongst the crowd grew. Until George Copely, who fancied himself a lawyer of sorts, advocated that the two deputies be seized and tried according to the vigilante bylaws; and Smith Ball and Wiles joined him in the motion, prompting X Beidler to call for an immediate vote.

"What about Plummer?" Sanders instantly asked. "He's the one who has permitted all this mayhem to persist. Why should he escape punishment when he's no less guilty than the others? We know he murdered a man in California, and that he escaped from San Quentin. And it's said he killed another man in California afterwards, and another over at Oro Fino. I say Plummer is the first and foremost on the list of those to be executed."

A great deal of dissension and confusion followed during which George Chrisman observed that Plummer had not escaped but had been pardoned by the governor of California only after a mistrial and continuing questions regarding the validity of Plummer's conviction. "I've seen the pardon myself," he said. "Henry's got it in his office. I, for one," he said angrily while looking directly at X Beidler, "am opposed to such radical action as is being proposed here unless it can be shown that Henry Plummer has knowingly supported the road agent gang's activities. I am not ashamed to admit that Henry is a friend of mine. I have never known him to be anything but a gentleman."

When Francis Thompson—who roomed and boarded at the house of Henry Plummer's sister-in-law and who was closely acquainted with Wilbur Sanders and Judge Edgerton—was asked how he felt on the question of the guilt or innocence of Plummer, he answered that he had heard only rumors of transgressions being committed by Henry Plummer in his past, and that he was inclined to defer to Judge Edgerton as to what the law provided regarding crimes committed in other jurisdictions. "I would certainly prefer to see some proof of the charges," he said, "before we hang the man."

The hour had become late, and it was agreed that the meeting would be continued on the morrow after everyone concerned had the opportunity to sleep on what they had heard. And then, one by one, and only after swearing their solemn oath of secrecy as Masons or members of the Union League did the men of Bannack slip off into the night, leaving alone only the four of us from Alder Gulch together with Wilbur Sanders.

"I'll hang the three sons of bitches myself if I have to," X Beidler said as the door closed for the final time.

And Wilbur Sanders, who seemed at least to never stop thinking, said, "Don't give up on our obtaining some assistance, X. There may still be some evidence against Plummer that has not yet been considered. Let's give it until morning."

"You got somethin' specific in mind?" Beidler asked.

Sanders smiled back weakly. "I might have," he said. "Let's give it until morning."

~~~~

As soon as Wilbur Sanders announced the reason why he had brought his nephew, Henry Tilden, to the meeting the next morning, I knew it was a sham. And so did most of the others. Wilbur Sanders had said, "My ward, Henry Tilden, was robbed by Henry Plummer and two other highwaymen out on the road to Horse Prairie this November," and the first thing I had thought was, "I don't believe it." But no one said anything, and Wilbur Sanders proceeded to lead Henry Tilden through a concise series of inquiries beginning with a request that he generally describe the incident on the road from Horse Prairie, which Henry Tilden did by explaining in a shaking voice how he had been approached after nightfall by three masked horsemen who demanded money and then hurried him on his way after relieving him of the sole $10 banknote in his possession.

"And was one of those men Henry Plummer?" Wilbur Sanders asked immediately.

"I believe so," Henry Tilden answered as he looked down to the floor.

"Well, you know so, don't you? Was one of those men wearing a coat lined with red flannel?"

"Yes, sir."

"Just like Henry Plummer wears?"

"Yes," Henry Tilden said. "It was like the coat Henry Plummer wears."

"And was one of them holding a cavalry pistol like the one Henry Plummer owns?"

"Yes. I remember that."

"And didn't you tell Judge Edgerton and me that very night that one of the men who robbed you was Henry Plummer?"

"I guess I did," Henry Tilden answered timidly.

"What do you mean, you guess you did? You did in fact, did you not?"

"Yes. I guess so."

"Well, Henry," Wilbur Sanders said, easing off considerably and giving the boy a chance to catch his breath. "Why don't you tell these men in your own words whether Henry Plummer was one of the men that robbed you that night? And speak carefully. This is very important to all of us, myself and Judge Edgerton included."

And after he took a deep breath and raised up his head to look across the faces that were watching him, Henry Tilden said, "It was Henry Plummer. I'm sure of it."

Wilbur Sanders patted Henry Tilden benevolently on the back and then pulled away from him to face the gathering that totaled only twelve, George Chrisman and Francis Thompson and a few others having sent their apologies. "There you have it, gentlemen," Sanders said. "Judge Edgerton and I have refrained from mentioning this until now in order to protect the boy and our families. The judge has given me permission to verify to you that he specifically recalls that Henry Tilden identified Henry Plummer as being one of the road agents that robbed him. As do I. I trust," he stated smartly, "that we are now in agreement regarding the disposition of our good sheriff, Henry Plummer."

But there was no agreement, and that fact was made clear by Tom Pitt and Doc Leavitt, who both expressed their belief that Henry Plummer was not involved with the road agent gang. "Perhaps the boy thought he saw Plummer," Pitt said. "But he easily could have been confused, what with the darkness and the masks and the excitement of the moment. Why, old Frenchie Robert's got a red-lined coat. Surely we aren't going to go suspecting him of the crime too." So Wilbur Sanders escorted Henry Tilden back to Judge Edgerton's home and then returned only to find that Smith Ball also now was equivocating on arresting the sheriff.

Ultimately, it was agreed that at least the two deputies, Stinson and Ray, should be dealt with expeditiously. And with the hour past noon, the group disbanded in order to recruit further members under the express understanding that nothing would be done about Henry Plummer absent a clear consensus on the point. The dinner hour was appointed as the time at which we would reassemble.

It was a Sunday. And the cold was insufferable and unrelenting; as soon as you went out one door, the weather forced you into another. I went to Durant's, of which I had heard so much from X Beidler, and I listened for a while as a freighter told how all along the freight road south between Bannack and Ricker's Ferry, on the route to Salt Lake City, pack trains were strung out and foundering in the heavy snows and the brutal cold. Neil Howie had told much the same thing, of how there were at least sixty men holed up at Dry Creek Ranch losing their stock by the score. And everywhere else along the road, from Barret and Shineberger's ranch on Horse Prairie to the open meadows at Red Rock, trains of wagons laden with flour and groceries and winter staples were broken down and thwarted by the snow and ice.

From Durant's I went over to Chrisman's, where I thought I might purchase some sugared candy for the long ride home. Only when I came up to the window, I observed George Copely and John Innes inside talking with Chrisman and several others. I turned away, and as I stepped off the boardwalk, I could see around the corner of Chrisman's building, to the back where Henry Plummer would have been in his office at that moment were it not for the fact that he was ill with the fever. And as I took a few more steps, the jails themselves came into view, their heavy log walls all but impregnable and their windows narrowly barred and perfectly secure.

That left only Thompson & Swift's as a place at which I might find the candy and the calamine and laudanum that were in such short supply in Virginia, and when I walked into the place, the first thing I thought was how neat and businesslike it was. Francis Thompson was there talking to a well-dressed, middle-aged man with extraordinarily harsh features—an emotionless face, hawkish nose, icy piercing eyes. Thompson introduced him to me; "The Honorable Sidney Edgerton, chief justice of the Idaho Territory," he called him. And then he said, "Judge, this is Alton Quade, the gentleman from San Francisco whom I mentioned earlier."

The Honorable Sidney Edgerton rose partway out of the chair in which he had been sitting. "A pleasure," he said blandly. And then he sat back down without otherwise meeting my eyes or acknowledging my presence and instead continued with some conversation in which the two men had been engaged.

"The privilege is mine, I'm sure," I nonetheless said. And then I chose to ignore them both and examine the inventoried goods that were as diverse as in any store in Alder Gulch.

"So you see," the Honorable Sidney Edgerton proceeded to explain to Francis Thompson, "every single witness for the claimant perjured himself blatantly before the court. And the court could not help but realize that it was happening, and yet it elected to do not one thing about it."

"You mean to say the claimant prevailed by such a tactic?" Francis Thompson asked.

And the Honorable Sidney Edgerton answered, "Yes. That is exactly correct. Judge Blaney ultimately ruled in favor of the claimant because he knew full well, even though it could not be proved in a legal sense, that the claimant had meant all along to exercise that option and had simply forgot to do it when the time came up. There is an old adage that says, 'For those grievances for which the law does not provide a remedy, the hand of justice still might rule.' You might remember that in the days to come, Francis. It is a principle tried and true."

Just at that moment the door opened and a handsome, clean-shaven man stuck his body partway through the door and peered in, this way and that. "Everything all right, Francis?" he inquired.

"Fine, Buck," Francis Thompson answered. "Just fine. The judge and I are just enjoying a cigar."

"Hello, Judge," the man said. And after the Honorable Sidney Edgerton nodded back, the man eased out of the store.

I saw Francis Thompson and Sidney Edgerton exchange sober and knowing looks and then Thompson turned to me. "Buck Stinson," he said, and then he turned back to the judge.

~~~

There were but slightly more than eight hours of daylight at that time of the year, and when darkness began to fall that evening, it almost seemed that the day was over before it had begun. Back at Peabody's, I found only Harry King and Bill Roe, together with X Beidler and John Lott and Wilbur Sanders. They were in an intense conversation as I walked in, and to my discomfort they discontinued it abruptly upon my arrival, which made me think that our mission had failed altogether, because the objective from the beginning was to ensure the organization of a vigilance committee there in Bannack and it now had begun to look as though no one would join.

Then the rest of them arrived one at a time or by twos—Innes, Dart, Copely, Pearson, Porter, Wiles, Roe, Ball, and eight other men—each obediently carrying the shotgun they had been told was the vigilante's weapon of choice. And after an hour's wait, it became clear that was all there would be.

John Lott was now clearly in command, and I thought it strange how at this one moment in X Beidler's life, he seemed perfectly content to say nothing at all and to acquiesce in another's plan. "Every man is to have his shotgun loaded and ready for firing," John Lott instructed. And as he spoke, it was evident there would be no further talk of a hearing of any sort regarding the guilt or innocence of the accused. "One group led by Harry King will arrest Ray and a second led by Bill Roe will arrest Stinson. Their hands are to be bound behind their backs and they are to be taken immediately to the scaffold behind the jail. X and Colonel Sanders and I, and Alton here also, will go to Colonel Sanders's cabin where Judge Edgerton is waiting now. We will escort him to the hanging site and he will preside over the executions. There is to be no noise, no gunfire unless absolutely necessary. When we get to the gallows, we do our work quickly. We allow the prisoners time to speak; we give them a good drop; and we leave them there to be seen in the morning. Are we agreed on this, gentlemen?" he asked. And after he received only murmurs of approval, he said, "Then let us be on our way, and with God's speed."

It was fully dark as we came out of the warehouse and split up according to John Lott's directions. And had it not been for the fact that we were instantly seen by several faces peering out of cabin and store windows, we nonetheless would have been heard, for the sound of the crusted snow crunching beneath our boots was loud and obvious. Harry King took his men and headed straight for the saloon run by Madame Hall, the courtesan and concubine of Ned Ray. It was known that Ray both slept and gambled regularly at the place; and it was logical that he would be there now, late into a Sunday night. So we watched as Harry King's troop moved down along the second row of buildings to the south of the street, and as Bill Roe took his men and moved toward Yankee Flat, where Buck Stinson and his wife were living in Bill Toland's cabin. And after Roe had distanced himself from us by only several hundred feet, John Lott said, "Let's move. And keep your guns cocked and ready."

I did not know what there was to Yankee Flat other than to look at it and see that it lacked storefronts and thus was essentially residential. There was no way for me to know which of the two dozen or so cabins was owned by Bill Toland or Wilbur Sanders or whoever else resided there on the edge of the town, across the creek. So when we came over the bridge and moved into the thicket of rough buildings I could only look from one to the next and wonder in which cabin the Honorable Sidney Edgerton sat at that moment, waiting for us to hoist him up like some great personage and bring him to the ceremony. And there was no way for me to even have known, as we came up to the cabin door and Wilbur Sanders knocked on it and the door came open and a woman's face showed, smiling and almost welcoming, that this was not the Mrs. Sanders nor any other member of that household, but Mrs. James Vail instead. There was no way at all for me to have known it, nor what was to follow next, until Wilbur Sanders said, in a neat calm friendly voice, "Martha. Will you bring Henry to the door? We need a word with him." And then I knew that things were not as they had appeared to be.

"Henry's not feeling well, Colonel Sanders," Martha Vail said. "Is there a message I might bring to him?"

"We need to speak with him directly, Martha," Sanders said. "Please. It is rather urgent. Tell him it relates to John Wagner."

And then Henry Plummer himself appeared at the door and X Beidler and John Lott raised their shotguns and Lott said, "You'll be needing your coat."

I looked upon Henry Plummer for the first time in my life, and I saw a man of proud and graceful appearance. And his eyes showed a high level of comprehension, reflecting a capacity for patience and introspection. "It's all right, Martha," he said back to Mrs. Vail. "They want to talk to me about Dutch John Wagner. Bring me my coat and pistol, won't you?"

"He won't be needing a firearm, Martha," Sanders interjected. "Just his coat will do."

And as I looked through the door to see Martha Vail scurry to lift Henry Plummer's coat from off a chair, I saw three other men—one whom I took to be Martha Vail's husband, and another, a tall youthful fellow who stared protectively at Henry Plummer's back, and Francis Thompson, who looked at us and said not a word.

We turned away from the cabin quickly, John Lott and X Beidler each closely at one side of Henry Plummer with Wilbur Sanders and me following behind, and before Martha Vail had even closed the cabin door, the shrill high-pitched scream of a woman came from another cabin nearby on Yankee Flat.

"Let's pick it up," X Beidler said when he heard the sound; and as if on signal, Lott and Beidler grabbed Henry Plummer at the elbows.

From thereafter, we virtually ran the entire way to the gallows, where Harry King and his men were already gathered with their prisoner bound and angrily stamping in the snow.

"What the hell is this, Henry?" Ned Ray demanded. "These bastards think they're gonna hang me."

"More than think," X Beidler said. Some of the others held Plummer, whose protests were ignored, while John Lott and Harry King cut lengths from several long ropes.

Then Bill Roe and his troop came up, and they had their prisoner as well. And within almost seconds, it seemed the townspeople began to descend from out of their cabins and down the streets and alleys to see for themselves what the noise was all about.

"You men form a circle around here," John Lott directed. "Somebody tie up Plummer. And bring your shotguns to bear on anyone who interferes." Lott and Harry King worked frantically now to tie the three nooses, and having done so they threw them over the crossbeam while Harry King and Bill Roe and X Beidler kept their shotguns level on the three lawmen who had begun to complain loudly together with members of the crowd and even some of the vigilantes who insisted that there had been no agreement to hang Henry Plummer.

"You can't do this," Henry Plummer asserted firmly. "We've done nothing. You can't do this sort of thing without giving a man a trial." And Buck Stinson and Ned Ray swore every oath and curse and blasphemy they could think of at the men who stared back at them wordlessly.

Through it all I stood there as in a daze, holding my shotgun up and at no one in particular only because there was no real choice. As the crowd formed, I vaguely saw faces that moved in and out of a memory of the last twenty-four hours: George Chrisman and Tom Pitt, who sadly watched the proceedings without saying a word; Doc Leavitt pleading with Wilbur Sanders in the name of decency and what is right; and the faces of the three youths—the Pearson boy and Henry Tilden and the tall fair boy named Joseph Swift, who had been sitting at the table in Martha Vail's cabin when John Lott said to Henry Plummer, "You'll be needing your coat"—all three of them aghast and Joseph Swift crying and yelling out Henry Plummer's name and Will Pearson swearing at his father and Henry Tilden staring at the ropes swaying between the posts and beneath the crossbeam as if they were the talismans of a hypnotist; and then, lastly, up on a knoll above the gallows, the lone and darkly shrouded, top-hatted and ominous figure of the Honorable Sidney Edgerton staring down at the proceedings like some unearthly being, observing the realization of evil, incarnate and reaffirmed.

"Bring up Ned Ray," X Beidler said, and the crowd quieted by the fact that it was going to happen. Beidler put the noose around Ray's neck, with Ray now struggling to somehow escape from the iron grip of Bill Roe and George Copely. And then, without a word of command, Roe and Copely and X Beidler pulled back on the rope with great effort, and Ned Ray was hoisted into the air with his feet kicking and his face and eyes instantly and violently contorted, his body jerking in wild disjointed and involuntary spasms until the last few twitches ended; and then they tied the rope down on the post and Beidler said, "You're next, Bucky, my friend. It's been a long time comin'."

Buck Stinson begged for mercy, pled for banishment or dismemberment or anything short of death. But there was no mercy to be had. All the while Henry Plummer argued at and cajoled anyone whose attention he might gain, all to no effect because John Lott and Wilbur Sanders and Roe and King had encircled him and would acknowledge no one's presence other than to hold at bay with their menacing weapons anyone who might think to intervene. And the crowd could only apologize and make similar pleas and then watch in awe and astonishment while the body of Ned Ray swung on the rope and Copely and X Beidler fought to keep Buck Stinson standing as the noose was fastened round his neck.

They hanged Buck Stinson in the same way they did Ned Ray, pulling the rope back with great effort and Buck Stinson fighting at it uselessly until he rose off the ground, as if by magic, and the rope tightened around his neck to enjoin and deny first air and then the blood and finally life itself from the body that kicked and struggled but which could not even scream or cry out or choke for the utter lack of breath. And when John Lott said, "You're next, Henry; is there anything you want to say?" an absolute silence fell within the crowd that now numbered well over a hundred.

"You can't do this to me, John," Henry Plummer said, standing and facing his executioner with his hands tied behind his back. "I have a wife. I am an innocent man. I have committed no crime that warrants hanging. Give me a trial at least."

And John Lott answered, "I'm sorry, Henry. It's over."

Harry King and Bill Roe seized the sheriff by his arms and pulled him beneath the two limp bodies. And Henry Plummer resisted, not in a manner by which he sought to escape but only by dragging his boots enough that he might live another minute, a few more precious seconds. When John Lott placed the rope around Henry Plummer's neck, the crowd came to life. There were shouts and screams, and in a wild reckless rush the youth Joseph Swift broke through the guards who themselves did not know what to think, and he fell to his knees at Henry

Plummer's feet and through his tears repeated "Henry, Henry," again and again until George Copely and Smith Ball pulled him back.

"It will be all right, Joseph," Henry Plummer said in a cracking voice. And then he turned and looked at John Lott and said, "All I ask is that you give me a good drop." And John Lott nodded his head and motioned to Harry King and Bill Roe with his finger pointed to the sky, and those two men lifted Henry Plummer at the thighs as high as they could and John Lott and Walt Pearson and X Beidler tied back the rope, and they dropped Henry Plummer and there was a muffled pop and Henry Plummer was dead.

CHAPTER 3

For the entirety of the two-day ride back to Alder Gulch, I could not help but dwell on, and be confused by, what had transpired in Bannack City, not as much because it was impossible to comprehend the hanging of Henry Plummer and his two deputies as because of what happened afterwards, after daylight broke and the Bannack Committee reconvened and, over the objections of some of the men who wanted the hangings of the three lawmen to mark the conclusion of it, the talk began anew. And I had not even wanted to be there, and I had told Harry King of my disinclination when he woke me. But John Lott said, "No, we need you with us," and I only later came to see that what he really meant was, "We do not trust you enough to leave you on your own."

Mostly, at first, the debates were exculpatory in nature, many of those present not wanting to be associated with the dead men and thus professing both their belief that the lawmen had been road agents and at the same time expressing their previous lack of suspicion that such had been the case. Others, like Francis Thompson, and George French, in whose carpentry shop we were standing at the time and in which we had deposited the frozen and contorted bodies of Plummer and Stinson after having gone back to the gallows only to find that someone had already cut down Ray and removed his body from the execution site, were more concerned with giving the dead a proper burial. And still others, and most particularly Wilbur Sanders, could do nothing beyond exult in Henry Plummer's demise.

But X Beidler was interested in none of it, and by his own assertive nature, he quickly took control of the assembly by asking if Jack Gallagher recently had been in town; and when he was told no, he proceeded down a memorized list of names that somehow seemed considerably longer than the one he had written down on paper, each time receiving the same advice that, no, that individual had not been seen in Bannack for some time now, until he said, "What about Mexican Frank?"

"What's he look like, X?" someone asked.

"Like any greaser," X answered. "Greasy hair, greasy skin, greasy liar. 'Bout John's height and build."

And what was most remarkable about it was that other than X Beidler, not one of them knew anything about the man Beidler alluded to as Mexican Frank and, yet, they were all suddenly anxious to accept as fact whatever X Beidler had to say about him. And all that Beidler could purport to know was that Mexican Frank was a saloon-hall brawler and a member of the road agent gang and that he had last been seen living in a vacant cabin down at the small settlement at Marysville, just a few miles downcreek from Bannack. Then someone else said, "We got ourselves a greaser right here in Bannack that fits that description; claims he rode with Joaquin in California." And within ten minutes they were there, as an angry crowd in front of the greaser's cabin, making plenty of noise and George Copely and Smith Ball banging on the door with the butt of a shotgun and demanding that the greaser come out and answer some questions to the Bannack Vigilance Committee.

Their call went unanswered. Then, I had watched as Copely and Ball, in a peculiar blend of wild enthusiasm and misperceived invulnerability, kicked in the door and entered the small ill-lit confines of the cabin only to be met by a hail of pistol shots that struck Copely square in the gut and dropped him instantly to the ground and which only modestly wounded Smith Ball in the hip such that he was able to drag back Copely who was in excruciating agony, before Ball worried to stop the bleeding from his own body.

And as if abject stupidity were not in and of itself enough, they then turned to wild abandon, with every one of them, the Honorable Sidney Edgerton and Wilbur Sanders included, opening up on the cabin with every firing piece available until Francis Thompson called for a halt after several vigilantes were almost injured by ricocheting shots. Which meant only common absurdity had been left untested; and that came next. With Edgerton's permission they wheeled out the polished brass mountain howitzer that Captain Fisk had left with the judge just months back; and Wilbur Sanders, who really had seen one fired and who on an instant assumed all the aura and composure of command, directed that it be loaded and the fuse cut variously and fired four separate times with the fourth round actually detonating inside the structure so that when it took effect, the cabin was in a shambles with one wall down almost completely and the rock fireplace collapsed and the roof half caved into the cabin's single room.

And what came next, after Doc Leavitt proclaimed that George Copely was dead, is what would not escape my memory—of Walt Pearson and John Innes pulling out the riddled and yet still living body of the greaser, and of X Beidler saying, "Hell, that ain't Mexican Frank," just before Smith Ball and the whole of them commenced firing their weapons into the dying man anyway; and of the way Sidney Edgerton came up and looked at the body and then at X Beidler and said, "Throw him in the cabin and burn it," which the crowd did with great industry and enthusiasm. And the smoke that it made funneled up into the cold breezeless sky like some great nebulous monument until it caught an upper wind and dissipated eastward, toward Alder Creek.

No one said a word about it while we rode, Beidler and Lott and Harry King all lost in their own wanderings and I in no way interested in invoking conversation with them. And I believe if we had talked, it would have been Dutch Wagner of whom I would have spoke; of how the big Dutchman looked and acted almost like a child as he begged for leniency and of the way he dictated the letter to his mother in his own language while his countryman sadly wrote it out; and of how, from the barrel on which he stood, he peered down almost curiously at the distance from his feet to the floor; and of how he seemed wholly innocent, or if not that then at least repentant, before the barrel was pulled out from beneath him and he violently strangled by his own weight against the taut rope, with the frozen bodies of Henry Plummer and Buck Stinson grotesquely lying on the bench and on the floor below him.

~~~~

John Lott would only allow us a five-hour sleep when we arrived at Stone's ranch, and long before dawn we were back on the road and more than thankful that the weather had moderated to such a degree that it seemed almost mild compared to the relentless cold of the last three brutal weeks. And it thus would have been a pleasant ride, with the skies clear and the sun warming and the snowy vista of the Beaverhead and Mount Baldy and the Rams Horn mountains breathtakingly soothing, had X Beidler not engaged in a rambling indictment of a dozen or so men, against each of whom he held a particular grudge of one sort or another.

　　With all my ability, I did my best to ignore him, straining my imagination to invoke awestruck sensations of the first explorers, listening to the faint sounds of birds, of the trees popping as their thawing wood split. But I could escape him no more than the fact of the executions and my own involvement in them. And just as I could not have done a thing to avoid the reality that I had carried the shotgun that John Lott had handed to me, and that I had held back the Bannack citizens as the deed was being done, and that at Harry King's direction I had tied the rope around the empty barrel so that it might be jerked out from under John Wagner upon command, I could not escape from X Beidler's harangue, which went on and on with Beidler being both the speaker and the audience, perfectly happy to both articulate and hear his case.

Foremost amongst those he castigated were the others who he claimed conspired in the killing of Dillingham—Lyons and Forbes and especially Gallagher, who X claimed had commited another murder in Denver before coming to the Grasshopper in a wagon train along with Paris Pfouts and the Waddam family. "You all know how that murderin' son of a bitch shot Jack Temple in the back last month just because Temple tole Gallagher to quit kickin' on a dog," X said. And then, after noting how Wilbur Sanders and others had also been aggrieved by Gallagher, he moved down the list that seemed graven in his consciousness, complaining that Clubfoot George Lane had almost saved Ives's neck and that Carter and his boys had yet to answer for Nick Tibolt and of the fact that Steve Marshland was still on the loose even though he bore as much blame for the attempted robbery of Moody's train as did Dutch John.

John Lott and Harry King said very little and instead only let it be known that they were listening as they peered about in silence and into the greater quietude and tranquility of the looming snowcapped mountain ranges and the blue skies that seemed to extend almost forever. Occasionally, Lott would ask X a question regarding a road agent that X had been discussing, such as where he was last seen or with whom he last rode or of what his history had been before he arrived in Alder Gulch. And on each such occasion X would have an answer spontaneously available to him. So that it almost seemed that X had been conducting an investigation on the gang ever since he arrived in the Gulch, cataloging and sorting the bits and pieces of rumor and innuendo and isolated fact, as the scientists of France were then doing with the fossilized fragments of bones and teeth they uncovered from the earth and which they then described in detail to the world as creatures from another era.

Lott pushed our mounts hard, and Black Bess set an example for our horses that forced them on, wearily through the snow and into the lower end of the valley of the Passamari and then past the tree where X Beidler had said they hanged Yeager and Brown, and then into and through Nevada City, where John Lott parted from us to rejoin his brother Mortimer. And as we rode the last 3 miles up to Virginia City, a small but growing crowd of men fell in behind, anxious for news from Grasshopper Creek.

~~~

I had no way to know how long I had slept except to see by the light coming in beneath the door that it was already daytime. And I would have slept even longer, perhaps as much as the whole day so that darkness would have returned and I could have hid in it again to avoid confronting the self-effacing doubt that came with light and waking, were it not for the noises emanating from the streets and up on the heights, the curt commands and acknowledgments and the ordered tramping of feet that made it sound as if the army had come to Alder Gulch.

Mr. McClurg had not opened the store even though it was almost ten o'clock. But the shutters were pulled back, indicating that he had already come and gone, and revealing a confusing and anomalous sight. There were men with shotguns and rifles posted in front of every store, at the intersection of every street and alley, and a ring of men was also visible along the hillside that looked down on Virginia City from the south. And all the way down the length of Wallace Street, mules and horses were tethered in front of every store and shop.

Outside, and just beyond the door, I encountered a man with a shotgun. He turned and looked at me, almost examined me I should say, and then he inquisitively stared at me until I said, "Good morning, sir." And then I asked him what was happening.

The man relaxed his shotgun and looked over to me with a smile that suggested he was glad to be relieved of the tension of standing so erect and grim. "You're Quade, aren't you?" he asked.

"I'm Alton Quade. Where's Mr. McClurg?"

"He's with Beehrer's company," the man said. "Down on Van Buren, I think."

"What do you mean, Beehrer's company?" I said, because none of it was making any sense. "You mean the brewery?"

"Guess you don't know, do you? They said to let you sleep; that you'd done your share already."

"Done my share of what? If I may ask. All I've done is sleep away half the morning."

"Your share in this road agency business," he said. "I didn't mean no offense." And when I stood there silently staring at him, he added, "It's a roundup. They put out a call late last night, or maybe it was morning by then, saying the vigilance committee expected every able man to be in Virginia City at first light with a shotgun and a primed revolver." And when I still said nothing, he continued, "We're rounding up road agents. The town's closed. They're letting in anyone who wants, but there's no way out."

The skies were partially overcast, the sun moving in and out from behind the clouds every few minutes and the temperature rising and falling in tandem so that one moment, with the sun on your face, it was almost warm enough to feel springlike, and on the next the chill was enough to make you draw your collar and bury your hands in your pockets. Yet the temperature had moderated enough to start a melt. And the streets that for over a week had been packed solid by snow and ice were now roiling with slush and mud that was tracked everywhere that horse and mule and dog might venture.

It was Mr. McClurg's practice to have ready for me in the morning some coffee and bread and perhaps some cold boiled beef or bacon in order that I might go straight to work when he arrived to open the store. There had been none that morning and as I very much desired a meal, I walked down to the Arbor and took a table at which some other men were already eating and I ordered a breakfast of biscuits and gravy and ham. I vaguely knew one of the men sitting at the table, a gentleman named Christiansen who bore a good and kindly reputation; and he knew of me through my clerkship with Mr. McClurg. I found him scrutinizing me critically. "Hello, Alton," he said stiffly, and then he turned to his two companions and they exchanged knowing glances. "I understand you were with Beidler and Lott when they hung Plummer," Christiansen said. And when I affirmed the fact, he said, "Did he confess to anything?"

"Not that I know of," I said. "He claimed he was innocent until the end."

"That's what I've been telling you," one of the other men said to Christiansen and the third man. "Beidler claims that's their password, saying 'I'm innocent.' Beidler says that's what they call themselves—The Innocents—but that's just turning around what most any man would say when someone was trying to hang him."

"What about that, Quade? Were those men innocent?" Christiansen asked. And now he could no longer contain the indignation that had not been immediately evident. "For what crimes were they hanged?"

There were others in the Arbor who by then had picked up on the conversation, and some of them had turned toward our table. "To be frank with you, Mr. Christiansen," I answered, "I do not know the answer to your question. X Beidler and Colonel Sanders and a few others are possessed of the relevant facts. You would need to ask them for that advice. I only happened to be there at the time." I ate at some of the plate of steaming biscuits and gravy while the three men finished their meals and gave each other more of the same silent seemingly knowing looks. And then I said, "For what it is worth to you, I am against this whole business. It has gone far beyond what was called for. As far as I knew we were going to Bannack merely to facilitate the formation of a branch committee. I had no way of knowing what they had planned."

My father liked to say that the marvelous thing about pain was that if you gave it enough time, it would always pass. It was a perverse sort of axiom, and I am sure he knew it, since sometimes the only way for pain to end is by death. I had not thought much about the saying when John Lott had stated at one of the vigilante meetings that the vigilante process would be somewhat painful; but I thought about it now. And the perversity of my father's axiom came fully to the fore since the vigilantism that was now running rampant, being lawless itself, inherently threatened to perpetuate its own painful and malignant effect upon a society of men and women. I thought how the social pain that ultimately arose from the hangings might not lapse for a year or a decade or a century. Or that it might evolve into something even more nightmarish if the civilization it ultimately spawned never acknowledged the wrong it had entailed, and of how a state, or even a nation, could rise up and accept vigilante rule as a heritage of which to be proud. And I concluded that the pain then, however subtle, would never end. And that my father, and John Lott, would then have been wrong on all accounts.

By twelve o'clock they had already taken Frank Parish and Clubfoot George Lane into custody, and the word had come out of Kiskadden's Mercantile, where the hearings were being held, with Paris Pfouts presiding, that the two men had been found guilty of being road agents and had been sentenced to be hanged. There, in front of Kiskadden's store, a large restless crowd had formed. And I joined in with them, drawn to it by an overwhelming curiosity that was no different than that suffered by the populace as a whole. "Parish admitted to cattle rustling," someone said from within the crowd. "And that he's been providing a base for the road agents at his ranch."

And someone else said, "I'll bet Bill Bunton's glad he ain't in town," before the myriad conversations within the throng moved on to the names of other men who might be hauled before the executive committee.

Every ten minutes or so, one or several vigilantes would come up to the store and be admitted, and more often than not James Williams would emerge with them and go off for a while and then return and go back inside. And in every way, Williams acted the role of a command-ing officer, receiving his direction from the executive committee inside of Kiskadden's and then implementing action without ever going too far afield, no doubt distrusting the committee to act without him if left too long alone; and when his men addressed him or made reference to him within hearing of the crowd, he was "captain" or "the captain" or "Captain Williams."

As Williams and the others engaged in side conversations with those who stood by and watched, news of the trials passed through the gathering. Soon it was heard that George Lane, too, had confessed in detail and had acknowledged how he utilized his post at Dance & Stuart's as a place to gather information of gold shipments and the comings and goings of pack trains laden with gold and greenbacks.

But not everyone believed it. "I've known George Lane for years," I heard one muffled voice say. "He's as innocent as the day is long." And I thought of X Beidler and of how he had derided Lane for having gone to Bannack to deliver word of the pending trial of George Ives.

Perhaps an hour went by with the crowd growing in size and com-position, and then a phalanx of men suddenly broke through, and X Beidler and Jack Slade were at the lead, pushing men aside with their shotguns and shouting, "Move back. Make way," as they led the com-pany of armed men up toward the mercantile. They had Jack Gallagher in their midst and he struggled against them at every step, making their task all that much more difficult and their treatment of him that much less gentle by a roughly equivalent degree. "You goddamn bastards," Gallagher swore. "You'll pay in hell for this."

"I been to hell already, Gallagher," Jack Slade answered as he pushed Gallagher along. "They sent me back. I can tell you everything you'll need to know. Now move up or I'll take out your knees."

When they got up on the boardwalk in front of Kiskadden's, you could see how big and strong Gallagher was next to Beidler and how lit-tle love there was between Gallagher and Slade. And yet it was Beidler who dominated the scene, throwing open Kiskadden's door and pulling

Gallagher by the pinioned arm and then pushing him through by placing the butt of his shotgun in Gallagher's back and shoving him with little regard as to how the stock of the gun might affect Gallagher's spine
and disposition. And I heard Gallagher say, "You little son of a bitch"
once more before one of the vigilantes shut the door and closed us out.

The next two men that were hauled in were unfamiliar to me. But
all you had to do was wait. "That's Arden Hawly," old Gabe Westfall
noted from out of the crowd. "I always wondered if he was out there
thievin' with that bunch of no goods he follows around." And when
someone said, "They got Boone Helm," I turned and saw Mr. McClurg
coming through the crowd, red faced and huffing at the exertion and all
the while following the directions of Bill Palmer, who was pushing
through the crush of observers with one arm and hauling Boone Helm
with the other as Helm complained at Palmer's indifference to the arm
that Helm had wrapped heavily in a sling. "They got the cannibal,"
someone else yelled. And a second voice shouted out, "Look out there,
Bill; he might take a bite outta ya."

And then the word came back that Gallagher and Helm had confessed, too. Which made little difference with respect to Boone Helm
since, for months now, he had had a reputation as having murdered men
in Missouri and up by the Fraser River and over near Walla Walla. But
it mattered as to Gallagher since he was a staunch Union man and was
known to have a brother in the Army of the Potomac who wrote often,
lastly delivering word to Gallagher of the three-day fight at Gettysburg.
And Gallagher had a reputation of another sort as well—as being good
with the children in the camps. More than once I had seen him atop his
magnificent stallion with a child at his front and another behind him,
parading up and down Wallace at a courtly trot with those happy youthful faces as enlivened and entertained as any caring soul might hope to
see. And what made it most unsettling was that Gallagher had not even
been in the camps that much, instead having opted to join in the second
expedition to Colter's Hell, which took him away from the Gulch for
the better part of the late summer and early fall, so that he was not even

present when many of the stage robberies had occurred. And there were few in the crowd who could have seriously believed that he was a member of the gang, if a gang there even was.

Just before Elk Morse's company brought in Haze Lyons, they let Arden Hawly go. The door of Kiskadden's opened and the crowd hushed and Hawly came out and walked down the steps with his face an ashen and ghastly shade. "What happened, Ard?" a voice shouted. "They change their mind 'bout ya?" But he did not answer, and instead walked hurriedly off on shaky legs toward the Virginia Hotel.

Haze Lyons looked a desperate man when Elk Morse and his men dragged him up Kiskadden's steps. He pled and begged that they release him, and he used those same words that X Beidler claimed showed he was a member of the band. "I'm innocent," he said. "I ain't done nothing. You've got to believe that." And every man in the crowd who watched it knew not only that Lyons had already escaped the hangman once, but that the same hangman, in the form of X Beidler, was there inside Kiskadden's waiting for him now.

There were others they were looking for, and they let it be known that anyone hiding them would suffer at the hands of the vigilantes. But these were exactly the men who had to have known better than to come anywhere near Virginia City or even Alder Gulch once word of the hangings of Ives and Yeager and Brown had reached them. So no one could even say that they had seen Carter or Marshland or Graves or Cooper or the others in town for weeks now. And once it had been determined that Bill Hunter, who ran a saloon in Nevada and who had lived along Discovery Creek, had somehow managed to escape from the network of guards that surrounded Virginia City, it became evident that their roundup had been completed and the streets fully cleansed of what X Beidler called the lowest scum of the earth, and several layers of hell.

Gradually, the companies all returned to Kiskadden's, as did a substantial number of the vigilante guard, which had grown by forced enlistment throughout the day until they surpassed in number the general crowd that had wasted away the afternoon in front of the store. And then the vigilantes, too, had to wait, while we all anticipated the executive committee's pronouncement as to what came next.

When the door of the mercantile finally opened again, James Williams emerged, and the expectations of the crowd and the vigilantes instantly refocused. But Williams merely took X Beidler and Robert Hereford aside, and then Beidler and Hereford departed in a hurry and Wallace and Williams went back indoors. More time passed; the sun threatened to set below the highline to the west. Complaints began to sound from the crowd, implying and asserting a public right to an expedient disposition of the issues, and when, at last, James Williams came out yet again, he was met by an impatience he could not wholly ignore.

"What about it, Williams?" a member of the crowd demanded. And someone else shouted, "What the hell they doin' in there, rewritin' the Constitution?"

And just as Williams asked out loud whether Beidler had returned, Beidler and Hereford came trotting down the street and up to Kiskadden's. "We're ready for ya," Beidler said, short of breath. "Bring 'em on."

"Where?" Williams asked.

And Beidler answered, "Wallace and Van Buren."

Williams had the company leaders reform their squads, and then he placed the six groups of men in a formation that made it appear they were readying for an infantry maneuver. Charley Beehrer's men were placed directly in front of the mercantile and two ranks of companies were positioned to each side with the sixth company stationed at the door and split in half so that you could have walked right out of Kiskadden's and into the secure heart of Williams's army. Which was exactly what Williams had in mind. He returned inside the mercantile one final time, and when the door opened, this time he led them out, the five bound prisoners each held tightly by two of Williams's men and three of them—Parish and Lane and Helm—crippled in one fashion or another with Parish limping from frostbite and Lane on his clubfoot and Helm with his knife-throwing arm in a makeshift sling, and all five of them dumbfounded by the size and impregnability of the guard and by the ignominious fact of their conviction before the citizens of Alder Gulch.

And then, by a gesture of James Williams, who stood with X Beidler at the front of the brigade, the army of men began to move.

My mind began to race wildly, because the fact that it not only was happening, but happening again, was at once both incredible and somehow vaguely irresistible. I thought of what Beidler had said—Wallace and Van Buren—yet I could picture nothing at that intersection that would provide for a gallows. And then I remembered what I had heard Beidler say once before, that all you needed for a hanging was a good rope. And I knew that Beidler could make a gallows out of anything once the need arose.

At the Virginia Hotel the parade abruptly stopped and I moved along the edge of the men and toward their front to gain both the better view and the advantage when the time came to seek a position from which to witness the final act. And this brought me face-to-face with Mr. McClurg. He was very much animated and at the same time quite taken by the fact that I was suddenly there before him.

"Alton, my boy," he said awkwardly, as if I had caught him in a dishonesty. And the tone of his voice, and his discomfort in seeing me, only confirmed what I had already suspected: there had been a discussion of me that morning, with Mr. McClurg and others involved; there had been talk of my reliability, and I had been intentionally left behind. I saw how peculiar he looked holding the shotgun and standing in his row, and I could not help but despise him for his weakness and his faults. Behind him, in the inner circle where the prisoners were held, Walter Dance had fallen to his knees at the request of Haze Lyons, to deliver a prayer for the redemption of the latter's soul. "I had hoped you would not have to see this," Mr. McClurg said to me in an unsure voice. "You seemed quite shaken last night over what happened in Bannack."

The words of the prayer ascended over the crowd like some great voice of doom: "Oh Lord, we beseech you to have mercy upon the spirit of Haze Lyons, and to deliver him from evil in the hour of your judgment."

But before Dance could finish, Boone Helm shouted out, "Let's get on with it, goddamn it," and Dance abruptly ended his prayer with an "Amen." The army began to move again, surging forward slowly and massively such that the sudden renewed momentum of the crowd separated me from Mr. McClurg. And then I recalled the open beams across the half-constructed building owned by Griffith and Thompson, and I realized how conveniently the ropes might hang across its span.

Then I began to run, as did plenty of others from the crowd who knew, or thought they knew, which way the vigilantes were headed. I outran them all and gained a crow's nest perch atop the building next to Griffith and Thompson's partially completed store where I looked down at the procession and clearly saw the five doomed men in the midst of the guard. Every one of them—with the exception of Helm—resisted their destiny mentally or physically, by word or action or sullen disposition, with only Helm walking upright and silent and apparently unmoved. Others caught up with me, the five ropes that had been draped over the beam being plainly visible through the unroofed rafters and the windows and the doors. And men swarmed like ants up onto the roofs of the surrounding buildings or found other ways to scale walls and achieve a greater altitude so that they might also be able to look down inside the skeleton of the half-constructed store.

Then the vigilantes were directly beneath me; and had I jumped at that moment I could have come down hard on top of Jack Slade's troop. Slade himself was drunk, and everyone else in his company was in the highest range of spirits; and as he passed below me, I saw how Slade had Gallagher by the arm in an icy grip with a revolver to Gallagher's head. Williams shouted, "Halt," and Beidler ostentatiously reiterated the command and the entire mass of men stopped in unison, like some kind of gigantic centipede all abristle with deadly barbs and stingers and its innumerable legs wholly anomalous and yet somehow coordinate and facilitating.

Beidler took Williams inside the building, and from where I sat, I could see only half of Williams's head and none of Beidler's until Williams stepped up on something directly under one of the ropes, and then his entire torso was visible to me. He must have concluded that Beidler's arrangement would suffice, for he came back out and said loudly to Elk Morse, "Bring 'em in," and Morse shouted some commands and the five prisoners and a score and a half of vigilantes funneled into the building through one of the two doors at its facade. The doors closed and then someone must have realized that that made no sense and they were reopened so that some of the guard that had been left outside could see in; and with that, the ranks of the remaining vigilantes and of the crowd broke and there was a mad rush to gain access to the windows and the top logs of the walls until every place from which one might view the executions was taken.

It became necessary to stand on the apex of the roof where I had hoped simply to sit and watch; and only then was I able to see over the row of men that sat on the log wall of the structure. Which altered my line of sight in several ways, in the end giving me an even better view of the five condemned men, who now had all been made to stand on something to bring their heads sufficiently close to the ropes looped and knotted across the beam. And it was my misfortune that Williams and Beidler chose to stand the men so that they faced toward the east, whereas I faced the building from the west; I thus could only see the backs of their heads as X Beidler stepped up on each of the boxes on which the prisoners had been placed in an evenly spaced row—Lane, Helm, Gallagher, Parish, and lastly Lyons—and each time, Beidler rose up on his toes to fit the noose around each man's neck and then tighten it through its slip.

There was some talk between Williams and one or two of the other vigilantes and the condemned men, but you could not hear it through the noise of the crowd, which now mostly seemed to be enjoying the spectacle. All I could see was Williams suddenly angered and one of the other vigilantes arguing with him and then Williams waving the man off toward the door, which the man exited in a great hurry. He

dashed across the street to a saloon and then returned at a run, breaking through the crowd and carrying a bottle of what appeared to be
whiskey together with several glass tumblers.

Paris Pfouts had made his way into the building by then, as had
John Lott and his brother Mortimer and J. M. Fox and the rest of the
executive committee. Pfouts also seemed to argue against the liquor, and
he fought it still as the vigilante poured the glasses and Helm and
Gallagher were untied and the two men drank down the drinks in long
insistent swallows with the nooses still around their necks, tilting their
heads back as if to sneak a look at the rafter and the rope above them.
Their hands were then retied and then more talk followed; and it seemed
that they would never do it, that there was something to time that had
mercifully enjoined the final act by causing the vigilantes to debate every
point regarding last words and wishes and who in what order and at
whose command, when suddenly George Lane jumped from whatever it
was he stood on and hung himself in that expedient way.

The four other prisoners looked in horror at George Lane as he
jerked and bounced and his face turned an opaque blue below them. And
then Boone Helm yelled out, quite audibly, "Hurrah for Jeff Davis!
Every man for himself!" and then he jumped also, followed closely by
Jack Gallagher, who swore at his executioners even as he fell. And that left
only Parish, who looked dazed with his head turned and staring at the
bodies that swayed and jerked, and Lyons who appeared to be sobbing by
the way his bowed head would slightly lift up every second or two.

By the time something was located to place over Parish's head, presumably at his own request, the three hanged men appeared to be unconscious, not motionless, because they still hung by the ropes, which
twisted and swayed in a way that eventually ensured you would see every
possible profile of the horrid faces and bulging eyes, and not lifeless
either, since every few moments a shock would course through one of
the bodies and it would all of a sudden jerk in a way that connoted life
and living. And then, while I could not see it, someone must have kicked
out the box or barrel on which Parish stood. Because Parish suddenly

and unexpectedly dropped, bounced once on the rope, and then fought against his death with extraordinary violence for the few minutes it took him to fall into darkness from the lack of air and blood. Leaving only Lyons, who now looked frantic, turning this way and that in search of a friend to help him, or perhaps for his paramour, Catherine, whom he had asked for only to be rebuffed by Beidler. His eyes met only denial and judgment until he, too, dropped seemingly into a chasm and died in much the same way as had the four other men who hung to Lyon's right, twisting and twirling at the end of their ropes while a great cheer rose up inside and then beyond and above the macabre scene.

CHAPTER 4

B ill Fairweather was among the least likely of miners to have discovered a great placer find such as was Alder Creek. He was far
too inclined to drink and as much prone to procrastination, and
even more than half crazy with tricks and humor, to have been indus-
trious and aggressive and prudent enough to not only be in the right
place first but to have been the first to have tried it properly, with an eye
toward geology and mineralogy and placer mining itself. But it nonetheless was he that panned the first color out of the Gulch. And the name
Fairweather thus gained fame immemorial.

It was equally true that Bill Fairweather's good fortune determined much regarding the demography of Virginia City. Because when
Barney Hughes returned to Bannack to obtain supplies so that the discovery party could prolong the search and stake the very best of
claims, it was Hughes's and Fairweather's friends who first realized
that a new strike had been made; and it was they who thus instantly
followed Hughes back to the Gulch and, too, staked claims along
Discovery Creek. So that after they sold into partnership and staked
more claims and split those also, it was as much as predetermined that
Virginia City would play residence to the rowdiest, liveliest, and most

boisterous segment of those that formerly called Bannack City their home.

And a few hangings were not about to stop them.

On the day after the five men were executed in Virginia City, James Williams and a contingent of twenty-five, being many of the most prominent of the hangmen—Beehrer and Brown and Beidler included—rode out in a solemn double file. And within an hour after the posse was beyond sight, Fairweather and Dan Harding and Jack Slade—the latter who, having come to the Gulch late, seemed intent on making up for lost time—went on a spree, buying drinks for every man they could find who was willing to join them in shooting out a window or breaking up a chair. And the irony was that despite the hangings, there were still enough men willing to do it, and that it was only by Kiskadden's intervention that Slade and Fairweather did not spend every ounce they had.

That was on the first day of my unemployment, having only that morning announced to Mr. McClurg that I was terminating my clerking position immediately, and having refused to listen to his protest to the effect that I was violating my responsibilities to him.

"Be that as it may, Mr. McClurg," I told him. "I cannot work here any longer."

"And how is that?" he asked in a wounded voice. "I've done nothing different than you."

And I said, "It's not worth talking about, Mr. McClurg. It's just time for me to move on, that's all." And then, when I was almost out the door with my scant belongings slung in a duffel across my back, I turned and said, "I'm sure you understand, Mr. McClurg, that things here went way beyond what was done in San Francisco." So that he had to then understand that what I wanted to say outright, but couldn't, was that the hangings were wrong; and that he should have known that fact by all accounts.

Outside, the day was in full progress with the sun already over the eastern hills and the sky cloudless and the night frost melting in pattering drips from off the roofs and eaves. And yet the streets were strangely empty, almost cleared of traffic it seemed by an unseen force or an unpublished decree. And over at Dance & Stuart's, from where you could look down into the Gulch, the entire valley looked frozen except for the smoke rising lazily out of the chimneys.

For a long while I sat in the cold in George Lane's chair on James Stuart's porch, considering what I might do. Thinking where in all this desolation and madness I might retreat: to Hell Gate, along the Mullan Road, where at the first opportunity I might join company with someone heading somewhere away from the Gulch, or Fort Benton, which seemed such a dreary and isolated place, with everything contained behind those four featureless walls and the towers peering over everything within and everything without like some watchful untrusting god. And that was all, since the snows had been extraordinary and the pass to Salt Lake too much for a single traveler.

The day came on painfully and slowly, the citizens only cautiously and in numbers easing out into the streets. Until, finally, necessity perhaps, and if not that then curiosity, brought them out en masse, still cautious at first like the early skaters of the year, testing the apparent frailty of the ice, and then with greater excitement and conviction once the boldest had determined it was safe.

They went first to Griffith and Thompson's half-completed store, where the five men had been hanged, and now the curious could no longer simply peer through the windows to see the lifeless bodies, because the victims had been cut down, removed at least from line of sight after little Mollie Sheehan had come home from school and had peered wondrously into the building only to see the throttled Gallagher, who had befriended her and her family on the road from Denver the prior summer, little Mollie seeing the man who had complimented her reading and who was hanging with the rest of them like so many butchered cattle, their heads all twisted and their faces showing nothing of the human countenances they had known in life. So they had cut them down and laid them on the ground inside the half-built structure, which meant only that those who wanted to gaze and wonder at them now had to make enough effort of it that their morbid curiosity was even more apparent. And that is exactly what they did, every other one of the citizens who chanced onto the streets at the first hour of the workday, funneling almost mindlessly toward the open windows and forcing their way inside so that they could get up close and examine the face of a cannibal and the shoeless and deformed stub of a foot of a cripple and join with their friends and neighbors and enemies in knowing and ensuring that in the future they could note, "I was there; I saw them hung," and maybe even claim to have played a part, regardless of whether it was true.

Williams and his contingent of men came down off the high placers that morning riding and leading fifty or so horses and mules that were mostly not even theirs, coming down the road past Virginia City like the town was not even there except to the two or three men who broke away only long enough to retrieve other riders who had been waiting for them all along. And somehow, they all seemed impervious to the cold and icy background as they moved down the road with Williams at the lead and X Beidler lingering behind as if to guard the rear.

All that day I moved from one establishment to the next, to the City Bakery, where I breakfasted, and the Gem Saloon, where I wasted an hour at a small-time game of tendice, and over to Kiskadden's, where I looked on the wall for posted news and potential opportunities. Nowhere I went could I find a sense of comfort, a place where I did not feel the cold glare of eyes that now might be disfavorable to me for a variety of opposing reasons. Twice I encountered and then narrowly avoided Fairweather and Slade in the throes of their funereal celebration only to meet them again at a third location, this time out on the street with Slade completely in a drunk and Fairweather not far behind. And I never even considered directly intervening when Slade stood out in front of John Roe's store and methodically and with his usual accuracy shot out every pane of glass and then two lamps above the door, one after another without missing once.

Then it was a week that had passed since Williams and his men rode out, and nothing had been heard of them other than that Steve Marshland had been found strung up on the east edge of Clark's ranch near the Big Hole. Which came as no surprise in that it had been made clear by Moody and Howie and others that they were able to identify Steve Marshland as Dutch John Wagner's partner in the failed robbery of Moody's train. And from the way Marshland's frostbitten and gangrenous hands and feet were described by those that cut him down and buried him, some argued that the vigilantes did him no small favor in saving him from the amputations that probably only would have painfully and briefly prolonged his life.

But that didn't make it any easier to hear about. Marshland's hanging set off debates in every corner of Virginia, where I at last had concluded I must stay until the late-spring breakup. And there were those who began to suspect that just maybe the time had come when it was Williams and his men who needed to feel the weight of law and order.

As if that were not enough, the news arrived that an entourage of Bannack businessmen, led by Sidney Edgerton, had decided to brave the south road and head for Salt Lake to make the journey back to Washington City, where they intended to make their case for a new territory carved out of the lands east of the Bitterroots. Both the Democrats and Southern men deemed the information as discomforting, since the steady and contradictory rumors of the details regarding the hanging of Henry Plummer and his deputies suggested plainly that there had been a conspiracy to assume Henry Plummer's mining claims and relieve him of his power. There was even rumor that some of the most prominent citizens of Bannack had claimed the power of attorney over all of Henry Plummer's possessions and holdings, and that the entire estate had fallen into the hands of those who had hanged him. And this type of information, needless to say, caused even more talk of violence and retribution. So maybe it was a good thing when the word started flying up and down Virginia City's streets that a new bonanza

had been struck up the Gallatin Valley by Barney Hughes and his partners, and that there was five and ten and even twenty dollars showing to
the pan. Because, if nothing else, it provided the diversion so very badly
needed in the Gulch.

~~~

"It's Alder Gulch all over again, boys. Word is, Barney Hughes pulled
out 200 on the first day alone. An' Charley Edwards claims he saw a
nugget the size of a goose egg." The man told it not with relish and exu-
berance but rather in great haste, giving the information only because it
was the only way to get free of the erstwhile friends who had seized him
and literally held him back when they saw him buying new prospecting
supplies on a cold winter's day.

"How thick're the bars?" someone shouted.

And someone else asked how long it had been since the word got
out.

"I just heard it an hour back," the man answered. "And I wouldn't
be tellin' ya 'bout it now if it weren't for Jeff and Art here havin' spotted me buyin' up my outfit. Be my guess there ain't that many that know.
An' we'd be doin' ourselves a favor if we kept it that way."

But he was wrong. Everyone knew; and most everyone was thinking seriously about joining in the stampede to the new placers that were
rumored to yield dust in such great quantity that one could merely
shovel it direct from the creek beds and the banks.

"I've done tole ya all I know," the man with the information said
when the crowd pressed him for more. "I shouldn't have even tole ya
that much. Next man that stands in my way is gonna find himself with
one of Kiskadden's new picks stuck in his ribs. Now let me through."
They stood back then enough for him to leave, and then the rest of
them scattered in every possible direction, never stopping to thank the
man for his time and courtesy, nor to slow enough to not run into and
over whoever might be in their way.

From inside Kiskadden's you could hear the noise on the streets, the jostle of laden mules and the activity along the boardwalks, which all of a sudden had quadrupled in volume and then quadrupled again in intensity. And you could see the instant workings of their madness as they ran up and down the town seeking out their friends and scurrying to secure supplies and whatever additional information might be had.

"They're crazy," I said to Kiskadden as we jointly watched it through the window.

"We're all a little crazy," Kiskadden said back. "Just a matter of degrees that separates each of us from the next."

Over the next few days, I tried my best to ignore the insanity that seemed to have emptied the entire Gulch. And yet with each passing day the rumors of the new find were more and more spectacular, with descriptions of water that flowed a golden color and of some miners who had already sold out to others at extraordinary gains. And as I walked over to Kiskadden's and the Virginia Hotel on the next two mornings and then up to Washburn's in search of employment to help stem the continuing loss of my savings, the prospect that I might join in the rush and make a fortune in just a matter of weeks became more and more enticing.

Then it was ten days since the hangings, and then it was two weeks; and the executions almost seemed forgotten until a young man rode into town on a badly overworked horse and then sat there, stupefied, in the middle of the street with the sweat on his mare slowly freezing. Kiskadden saw him first, and he went out to the rider. Then Kiskadden called on me from where I stood inside the store, again looking for posted situations, and I went out also.

"Come off that horse, son," Kiskadden said to the boy who looked very much afraid. "You look like you could use some warming up."

The boy said nothing, looking down at us with obvious fear, until he said, almost in a whisper, "You vigilantes?"

"We're just townspeople," Kiskadden said. "You needn't be afraid of us. Come on now; get down off that horse and give her a rest at least."

As the boy came off the saddle slowly, with great caution, Kiskadden said, "Why're you asking us about that, son? If we're vigilantes, I mean?"

"They've been to Cottonwood," the boy said in a hushed voice. "They hung Bill Bunton."

By then others had come up just to see what news this rider might have brought from the stampede. "Bunton?" one of them said. "You mean the rancher over at the Rattlesnake? What'd they hang him fer?"

"They said he'd been involved in the stage holdups, and that he'd killed some men."

"Which men?" someone else asked. "What were their names?"

And the boy answered, "They never said names. They just pulled him out back and gave him his choice of being dropped or jumping, and he jumped." Then the boy broke into tears and Kiskadden led him into the store with a considerable number of men following.

The boy calmed some after Kiskadden's whiskey and stove warmed him up a bit, and then the boy finally gave his name, which was David Meiklejohn. Everyone wanted to know more about it, but the boy was distraught and Kiskadden stood over him protectively. So we only learned that Williams and his men had headed off toward Hell Gate after asking for the whereabouts of Aleck Carter and Bill Hunter and Bill Graves and two dozen others, and that they had left behind X Beidler and Tom Baume, who had seized everything Bunton owned, including a line of pack horses and a third interest in a Cottonwood saloon he had won only two days back in a card game. "They sold it all in an hour at auction prices," the boy said. "And then they put the dust in their saddlebags and rode off to catch up with Williams. And that isn't all," Meiklejohn said with an outpouring of emotion. "There's a man down by Rock Creek that's been hung outside his cabin. No one even knows who he is. A hermit some say. And no one's willing to get close enough to cut him down."

"The hanging sons of bitches," someone in the crowd said.

And Meiklejohn said, "Bill Bunton hadn't done nothing. I've been working his horses for two years now, back before he even came to the

Grasshopper. He's never done nothing that would deserve him being hung." And then he started crying again.

A silence followed until someone said, "That makes sixteen. They've done hung sixteen men we know of in three weeks. And there ain't no tellin' how many more are out there they've already strangled or are about to."

"I'm moving on," someone else in the crowd said. "For all we know, they'll be coming back this way soon, and I'd rather be on the trail to the Gallatin than sitting here waiting to see if I'm gonna get lynched just cause I don't use a fork the way they do."

The one thing that had become more and more clear was that, sooner or later, the vigilantes were going to have to start worrying about who might bring them trouble in the future, as opposed to those who had brought them trouble in the past. There were plenty who now thought that it was nothing short of murder to be executing men on a daily basis for reasons that were never revealed and perhaps did not even exist. And that was something I began to consider seriously, in that I had been with them in the beginning and now had left them behind and therefore, arguably, I was no longer to be counted on to keep confidential the information that had already been trusted to me. So I began to think that I also might try the Gallatin's new placers, if only because I needed to not be there when Williams and his men returned.

I asked Kiskadden about it, about whether there would at least be a labor job for me at the new placers. And he said, "We don't know for certain that there are new placers, Alton. I haven't seen anyone bringing in canteens full of dust yet. Have you?"

And I admitted that I had not, but then questioned how such a prolonged and extensive rumor could be so untrue. "That doesn't make much sense to me, Mr. Kiskadden," I said. "Meaning no disrespect, of course. I just don't see how that many people could all be wrong."

Kiskadden smiled then and said, "Well, we can't all be wrong and all be right. So your guess is just as good as mine. I'll tell you what I'll do. I'll stake you for 20 percent. You can take a couple of my mules.

They're spoiling right now anyway. Do 'em good. Mind you, I'm not being charitable about it. Twenty percent doesn't sound like much until a man sees it paid out of a pocket he's already put it into."

I told him I didn't know anything about it, about prospecting and placering and mining. "That's the beauty of a stampede," he said. "All you got to do is follow along and do what everyone else is doing. Ends up pretty much being a matter of luck who turns up the best claims. Bummer Dan could tell you that much. Then, in a week or two, or a month, you can sell out if you want and make a good dollar without working it much at all. Truth is, I'd go myself," he said as he looked out the window and into the streets. "But with the way things've been around here, I wouldn't feel good about leaving the store in someone else's hands." And as I thought maybe this was my chance, maybe it could happen to me, Kiskadden touched me on the shoulder and said, "Go get your belongings. I'll set you up."

~~~

"I've made arrangements for you to travel in company," Kiskadden told me several hours later as we began to load the pack mule. "There's no single road to the Gallatin, and with all the snow and all these yahoos heading off in every direction, I thought it would be best if you went with someone who knew the way."

And this was illustrative of why I had come to appreciate Kiskadden. He seemed more honest and caring than most of the other merchants in town and had kept in the background during the hangings despite the fact that he was a Mason and had allowed his store to be used as the site for their inquisitions. "Fine, Mr. Kiskadden," I said. "Who is it? Who am I going with?"

"Jack Slade. He and Bill Fairweather said for you to meet them in front of the Exchange in a half hour."

When I got there, they were waiting for me just as Kiskadden had said. And they were both drunk. They had with them three other stampeders who apparently had paid Slade to take them direct to the mouth of the Gallatin.

Slade saw me as I came up with Kiskadden's mules, and he staggered over with a bottle in one hand and the other resting on his holstered revolver. "We've been waitin' on you, boy," he said in an accusing tone. "I've drawn and quartered men for keepin' me waitin' this long." And when I told him Kiskadden had said this was the hour of our departure, he said back, "That's Kiskadden's time. You're on Slade time now, and that's whenever I say it is." Then he tipped his bottle and drew down on it hard. "Jack Slade's the capt'n. Now let's get."

It was a high price to pay, having to put up with Slade's intoxication and profanity for two or three days, but I calculated it would be worth the time and aggravation to be saved from not risking a wrong turn that could lead into a defile or into the tangle of unnamed mountain drainages. So I sat Kiskadden's mule quietly, in the rear of our little train, as Slade and Fairweather led us out of Virginia City before we turned north and east, heading for Meadow Creek.

I more than once had seen the winding trail on which we now rode, but had not thought much about it since the mountains that surrounded the Gulch and the Passamari, and which formed the west flank of the Madison Valley, had become infested with miners who sought out every creek and wash and draw in search of gold and silver and game animals and logs by which they might make their own lasting fortune or at least survive while they tried to do so. Which meant that there were roads and trails and pathways everywhere that a man could ride or drive or walk. And this one on which we traveled, up over the top of the last rise so that the world to the east loomed up suddenly and freshly before us, was really little different from any other, were it not for the fact that it led directly to Jack Slade's house.

I didn't know it at the time as we rode along and listened to the quiet that was interrupted randomly by a drunken song by Slade or a whoop by Fairweather. But when I saw Virginia Slade come out from the front door of a small but sturdy rock house we approached near sundown,

I knew that this had to have been our first day's destination all along. And it really did not matter because the day had been long and the snow increasing in depth, and the idea of sleeping in the cold with only a gum blanket was hardly an attractive thought. And, in point of fact, Virginia Slade was a sight at any time of the night or day, and it was almost a joy to think that she would be present to take the edge off of what suddenly seemed a long and weary ride.

The moment she appeared at the door, all of the contradiction and anomaly that was Jack Slade came to life and was illustrated in one perfect form. Because Slade was some of everything in the Gulch—some of miner and some of merchant, a man with whom any man might drink and yet who was loyal to the Union beyond cavil, rowdy and lawless and yet indignant and righteous to the point of having joined the vigilantes and even having agreed to serve as a captain once it was accepted that he and his boys would only be responsible for capturing the road agents of their own choice.

But it was not merely what he did once he arrived in the Gulch that made his reputation. Because by the time of Barney Hughes's stampede, Slade's reputation had preceded him and then caught up with him and then grown by that much again. He called himself Jack Slade of the Overland or Captain Jack or just plain Cap, but to most others he was known as the man who had been gunned down and left for dead only to have not merely recovered but to have removed the ears from the man who had shot him first. And he claimed to have shot and killed at least a dozen others that he could still remember. And that was how he was known to those who did not know him or knew him only to drink with: a reckless, loud, and drunken villain who challenged Jack Gallagher on Wallace Street and who, by God, would have shot him down had not someone intervened.

Those who had done business with him, Mr. McClurg and Kiskadden included, knew him otherwise. He was something of a maniac, to be sure, but not a hardened criminal. And he was considered not only to be perfectly reliable but as having a unique ability to move freight from one difficult place to the next, this attribute having been proved by his work for the Overland company and having been reestablished when Slade had rescued the steamboat freight offloaded at the Milk River and which I had helped him to move from Fort Benton all the way to Alder Gulch.

And still to others, he was seen as a man who commanded a great deal of authority, if only because of his own arbitrary penchant for violence and his imperious way of influencing his cadre of ruffians to follow him in whatever action he might engage. Some thus said that Jack Slade was possessed of great courage and even greater judgment or powers of exaggeration or intelligence or brashness or bravado, but the fact was they were all seeing the same quality through different eyes. Because the only trait that Jack Slade really had, other than an arbitrary mixture of gentleness and volatility that was no better and no worse than a dog that will only take so much, was that he had the willpower to do and have exactly what he pleased.

There was that, and then there was Virginia Slade, who could only be described as perfect in every way. In short, she was worshipped, and not from afar, in that she alone of every lady and courtesan and prostitute in the Gulch could turn every head at the Virginia Theater by her looks and bearing and then the next night take $500 off a newly arrived monte sharp at the Cal Exchange. And she was, above all, and without equivocation, Jack Slade's woman, as true and devoted to him as a woman can be to a man.

It was hard to say exactly what made Slade a man of reckoning, but for my money I would say it was a combination of circumstances, of Virginia Slade and his own determination and the mythology of his reputation, that brought him to the fore in Alder Gulch. Because any one of those characteristics was not enough to distinguish him much from the remainder of the brave citizens of that place, and any two of them only would have put him in the company of men like Beidler and Williams and Plummer and a dozen others. The truth was that Jack Slade was above all of them, if only by the implausibility of his being such a person and yet remaining in reasonably good graces with every element in the gold camps from the Highland District all the way to Hell Gate. And it took little observation to realize that it was Virginia Slade that softened him up at least enough to make him human.

We rode up to the corral, in front of which she stood waiting, and the first thing she said was, "You're late, Mr. Slade." And when he suggested that he'd been unforeseeably delayed, she added, "Don't give me any of your guff."

"All right, boys," Slade said with a grin as he moved to dismount. "The welcome mat's out. Might as well come on in and get some abuse."

Virginia Slade had us to come in. And for all of us, the almost formal aura of the place, with its neatly crafted rock walls and fireplace and the rock floor covered by bearskins and Indian rugs, and the soft scent of lavender, reminded us of another world in which everything was not composed of logs and roughly cut lumber and invaded by the acrid smell of sweating men. She brought out bottles filled with gin and brandy and whiskey and freely poured us glasses to drink and then offered us some of his cigars when he went outside to bring in some cordwood. "I'll have steaks and potatoes up in thirty minutes," she said. "You boys make yourselves at home."

There was a banging at the door while we were eating, and it caused Slade to immediately reach for his shotgun. "Who the hell is it?" he shouted out gruffly. And when a voice announced that it was Ad Davis, Slade shouted, "Well, come in then goddammit. No need to break in the damned door."

Slade's stone house, which a moment before seemed comfortable and cozy, with Virginia Slade's presence almost sanctifying the stone walls and hearth, now was crowded with the six of us and Mrs. Slade and Ad Davis and his two companions. And they had not eaten on the long ride from Virginia City through the deepening snow. Which meant that the quality of our dining was disturbed also, with Virginia Slade no longer ours alone to admire and engage in idle conversations regarding the weather or the stampede or the food, which had been both plentiful and excellently cooked.

Davis seemed displeased by the fact that he had not found Slade at home alone. And he and the other two men, neither of whom I knew by name but both of whom I had seen in the streets in Davis's company on the morning and afternoon of January 14th, avoided all but the smallest of talk. When Davis evaded answering Slade's query regarding what they were doing on a road that led mostly to nowhere unless you were heading out prospecting, Slade said, "Keepin' secrets, are we now? You know what that did for ole Bill Fairweather here." And when Slade looked out the window at their mounts and said, "Well I'll be a horse's ass. Not a goddamned pick or shovel between the three of ya," Davis grabbed him by the arm.

"Let's go outside for a minute, Jack," Davis said. "I've got some freight business for you."

The four of them went outdoors while the rest of us remained in a sort of uncomfortable stasis. So we waited, and Virginia Slade entertained us by the absolute power of her looks and personality, her raven hair and dark blue eyes and womanly form almost too much for any one man to bear.

When they came back in, they kept the nature of their business to themselves, Slade saying only that Davis and his men would be joining us to the stampede. And, as if to explain the fact that they had no prospecting tools, Davis added, "We're hopin' to start up a freight-line business in the Gallatin if the strike proves up."

The new arrivals joined us in our meal, and then, more out of need to show my complicity than to sate a desire, I participated for a while in the drinking from Slade's inventory of bourbon. And then the eight of them gambled all night long, Fairweather, Slade, and Davis and the rest of them drinking and swearing and falling into a lowly drunk while Virginia Slade served them and played along with them, taking from them ultimately a sum that she counted as over $400 in winnings.

All the while, they reminisced over the days in Colorado and the recent hangings and of what came next. "I'll tell you what ole Jack Slade's thinkin'," Slade said as he threw down a weak hand on which he had thinly and unsuccessfully stretched a bluff. "I'm thinkin' that by the time this whole thing's over, Jimbo Williams is gonna be runnin' the entire Gulch like it's his town."

Ad Davis shook his head with his eyes widely opened and yet unfocused, in frustrated and yet condescending disbelief as Virginia Slade pulled in the coins and banknotes she had just won, adding them neatly to the already substantial stacks she kept arrayed before her. "I don't know about that, Jack," he said as he clumsily dealt out a new hand. "There's plenty of politicking going on for Jim Williams to have him some pretty good competition. There's some that's even taking bets on who'll be the new marshal once we're a territory. The odds are running in favor of Hereford and Beidler at the moment."

"I ain't talkin' 'bout titles," Slade snapped back. "Even if there is a new territory, which is more than a little doubtful if the Lewiston boys have anything to say about it. I'm talkin' 'bout fact. Between Beidler and Williams, it's Williams that's takin' the most credit for the hangin's. Beidler is usually there all right, and that little son of a bitch does more than his share of talkin' 'bout it. But we all know Williams is the one givin' the final order each time, and that means he'll make hay by it when the time comes. Hell, he didn't bring in one of the five that were hung in Virginia. Me an' my boys got Gallagher, an' Williams never as much as said thanks for it." Slade took two quick drinks from a bottle and frowned injudiciously at his cards and then threw them down. "I know that bastard Williams well enough. He an' me led a train up from Colorado, you know. And he let it be known right off that he had to be the chief. Got to whinnin' and pissin' 'bout it so bad that I had to let him have it. He's in it for himself; that's as goddamned sure a thing to bet on as there is. This is pure business to big Jimbo Williams. He didn't get himself where he's at now by being a high and moral type that's got religion."

"Makes you wonder why Williams wasn't at the Plummer hangin's," one of Davis's companions said. "You'd think he'd have wanted to be there for the big fish."

"What about that, Quade?" Ad Davis asked, turning over to where I sat, in a corner near the fire. "You were there, weren't you? How is it that Jim Williams didn't go along to Bannack? Him and X flip for the privilege, did they?"

"You'd have to ask John Lott," I answered carefully. "He set up the trip."

Slade had been resorting his cards while he chewed on the end of a cigar, as though he somehow might be able to change the hand that had been dealt to him merely by changing their order. And now he stopped and poured more whiskey into his tumbler before he passed the bottle to Fairweather, who had reduced himself to the extent that he was recklessly losing his money. "I heard you did all those hangings by yourself," Slade said sarcastically. "Captured 'em and tied 'em up and set the nooses and jerked up every one of those sons of bitches while every dumb ass one of that Bannack City crowd stood there and watched. That right, Quade? That the way it went, is it?"

And I said, "Just about," and then smiled in a way I thought would look to be wryly conspiratorial.

I probably should not have said it, at least not in a way that was boastful and convivial. But sometimes you have to do what your company expects or requires. So I said, "Just about," implying a proud and substantial role in the hangings of Plummer and Stinson and Ray and Wagner, and maybe even in the extermination of the Mexican whose real name I still had not learned. And that was enough to reinforce whatever it was that adhered one man to the next.

We rode out in the morning with Slade and Fairweather and the other men in a stupor, and it was a credit more to Slade's horse than to Jack Slade himself that we picked our way down the trail into the Madison Valley at a sure and even pace.

It took all that day and some of the second for us to reach the

waters of the Gallatin. And when we arrived, we received the first confirmation of what we had heard from stragglers we'd encountered at the
fords of the Madison River and atop the next ridge that separated the
rivers' valleys. "There ain't no strike," one haggard frostbit miner said to
Slade when we stopped at a desolate camp along the high waters of the
Gallatin. "Ain't seen as much as a scad." But when Slade asked how far
down river the group had been and where Hughes was at, all the miner
said was that he didn't know where Hughes was but that he'd seen and
heard enough to know it was a bust.

So we moved on for the remainder of the second day, downhill
and crossing one creek and then the next where they emptied into the
mainstream, and looking up at a great and almost endless expanse of
forest that had been burned so recently that the undergrowth had not
even recovered enough to begin to hide the blackened char of the standing denuded timber. And at each turn in the river where the banks
sanded up and beached, and up each feeder creek and drainage, we
would see men, or their sure and determined signs, and yet neither hear
nor note anything implying that the Gallatin would offer anything of
the 20 mile find that was Alder Gulch. All the while, at each camp and
prospect at which we stopped, Ad Davis made discreet and cautious
inquiries that the rest of us could not much hear, until finally I overheard one of the brief and unilateral conversations in which Davis asked
a miner where he might find Wes Emery's cabin; and when the miner
said he had no idea, that he had never as much as heard of Wes Emery,
Davis dropped the subject on an instant.

As we rode on, you could not help but notice that Jack Slade
always seemed to know just where we were. "'Bout 40 miles from the
Missouri," he would say, and you would know that he was right even if
he had never before been to the place at which we were standing when
he said it. So that when he noted we were only perhaps 20 miles from
the mouth of the Gallatin, we all knew that we were nearing Barney
Hughes's strike, which Fairweather claimed was 15 miles up from the
muddy waters of the Missouri. It was at that point that Davis finally

found someone who knew Wes Emery. "Right down the river a ways," the man said. "Up the first crick on the left; 'bout a mile." And as we moved on, it was more than apparent that Davis and his men had come up to the front of our procession to ride alongside Jack Slade.

Emery's cabin sat alone above the creek, and the sign of Emery's trap work was everywhere: a scattered pile of discarded bones sat behind the cabin, skulls of predators and prey sat along the roof line like a long row of gargoyles, wolf and wolverine and badger and beaver pelts of various shapes and shades were pegged up against the walls. And a row of broken and rusting traps sat near an anvil that Emery had mounted on a stump, at which he conformed and repaired the steel legholds and water traps to suit his purpose.

Emery came out to see who we were, and Slade made some introductions before he and Davis drew Emery off to talk in private. And the whole while, Emery did little more than nod his head and look back and forth at Davis and then Slade and then Davis again, nervously agreeing with what they said and seeming not to want to lose eye contact with either of them.

After a while, Slade finally came back over to us and then walked up to Fairweather while Davis remained next to Emery. "Billy," he said. "Why don't you take these boys down to Barney's so they can get in on some prospectin'? Emery here says it's just 4 mile down. They're callin' it Hughesville."

"What's he say about it?" Fairweather asked. "Is it big?"

"He ain't sayin' neither way. Don't seem to be one for talkin' much. Probably not too happy 'bout all you Gulch boys invadin' his trappin' grounds. You'll need to see it for yourselves. I'll be down to find you in the mornin'." And Fairweather said all right, and he led the four of us— me and the three men who had paid Jack Slade to lead them to the stampede—back down that creek and down along the river and not once turning our heads to look at or for the men we had left in front of Wes Emery's trapping cabin.

~~~

They had named it Hughesville, and they even had gone so far as to paint that name on a board that they placed at the trailhead in and out of the area of Barney Hughes's find. But it didn't really deserve that name at all, because it was a bust, just like the man had said up in the highlands 20 miles back. To be sure, Barney Hughes had hit what looked like a fine claim on a bar that ran along a sweeping bend in a feeder to the river. And, in fact, it had yielded a respectable amount of gold for the two days he worked it before the word leaked out. And the prospects indicated that there would be even more of it in the immediate vicinity of Barney Hughes's claim, that a few claims, at least, would indeed be worth working after the spring waters ran. But that was all there was, that one long bar along that one sweeping and longish curve, every other prospect up and down that creek and out into the river and up and down the next three creeks on both sides being as dry as the desert sand.

At first Bill Fairweather did not believe it. He had insisted on searching out Barney Hughes when we came up to the camp and had finally found him and had demanded by their friendship that Hughes reveal the next best prospect that had not been staked. And Hughes had said, "They've all been staked, Billy. It's just this one bar."

And Fairweather had cajoled him and pushed him for the information anyway, until he decided he'd have to go and find it himself. And I followed, only because there was nothing else for me to do. For the rest of that day and into the dark and then early into the next morning we panned everywhere that Fairweather suggested might be a gold-bearing sand, working to the point our fingers were frozen and numbed, and yet never once turning up enough color to pinch between two fingers.

When Slade came up the next day, he found us sitting around a fire that was large enough to mark the fact that we had been idle for over an hour. "It's a bust, ain't it?" he said. "Just like that ole coot warned. Coulda tole you as much myself before you even left. You know how you know it's a bonanza, Billy?" he said. And when Fairweather bit and asked how, Slade said, "When the whores show up. An' you know why? 'Cause they can smell gold like most men can smell them.

"I'm headin' back," Slade said. "Got me a case of brandy at home that needs some company." And when he asked if we were coming with, Fairweather said, "Yep; I could use some of that company myself."

We rode up the trail past the broken camps of disappointed prospectors, Fairweather side by side with Slade, and the two of them passing a bottle back and forth just as fast as the one could take a drink and the other could reach out so as to not lose time when it came to his turn. So that in the fifteen minutes it took us to come back up to Barney Hughes's sandbar, Slade had fallen back into the same belligerent stupor into which he descended every time he drank more than a glass of beer or two shots of whiskey. Twenty feet before he reached the board on which someone had painted "HUGHESVILLE" he drew his revolver and blasted the sign with five rapid shots, and then he whooped and hollered and rode up to it and yanked it out of the ground and sent it flying into the first tent he saw. And then we rode through the camp, with Fairweather making every bit as much and maybe even more noise than Slade, with Fairweather this time drawing on that second sign and shooting it full of holes before he, too, rooted it out of the ground and sent it spinning over the heads of several miners who were walking wearily along the trail. Then we rode on, around the bend of that curve and into and past a line of alders and then around another curve and out of sight of the camp.

Slade and Fairweather drank some more while I rode behind, and I kept my distance if only for my own protection. At some point, intermixed with all the rest of their nonsensical conversation, Fairweather asked the one question that had been on my mind but which I had feared to ask. "What'd you an' ole Ad Davis an' his boys do with that Emery fella?" he asked in a slur.

And when Slade muttered that Davis had headed back already, Fairweather said, "What'd they want with 'im though? The ole boy seems harmless enough."

Slade answered that they really didn't want anything with Emery, and Fairweather persisted. "Well, what the hell were they doin' talkin' to 'im then?"

And Slade answered, "Hunter. They were looking for Bill Hunter."

My heart raced when I heard it, because I had seen Hunter actively pursuing Ives's defense at the trial at Nevada City and then had heard of the confrontation between Hunter and Charley Beehrer and some others the day after Ives was hung, and how Hunter somehow had escaped the dragnet in Virginia City the day the other five were hung. And I had wondered where he and so many of the others had escaped to in the middle of winter with the snow deep and the cold unforgiving.

"They find him?" Fairweather asked. "Emery know something about it?"

"They found him all right," Slade said with a curious look of satisfaction. "Now quit asking so many goddamned questions and let go of that bottle."

We came around another bend in the river. And even from a distance you could see that something did not look right with the tall cottonwood that stood out over the bluff. It was like glancing at a woods or up on a hillside and instantly noticing an object that was not part of the immutable landscape, like a deer or an antelope or an old broken wagon. Only with the cottonwood the anomaly seemed vaguely insidious and incongruous, whereas spotting an elk from afar was more a compliment to one's hunting and survival instincts than anything else. And as we slowly approached the bluff, and then followed the trail up the rise where it led away from the cutbank in the river, I could not take my eyes off the dark linear spot that seemed detached from the tree and heaven and earth.

Slade was not the least surprised when we rode up the trail and came up even with the body that hung there at the end of the rope. He merely sat on his horse and watched as Fairweather and I got up even closer and then saw the numbers "3-7-77" scrawled on the paper that had been pinned against the dead man's clothes.

"Well, I'll be damned," Fairweather said. "It's Bill Hunter. You help those boys do this, Jack? I never considered Hunter as a bad one, even if he had a friendship going with Ives. Hell, you an' me had drinks with 'em at the Arbor just last month."

"You know how that goes, Billy boy. When a man's time comes, it comes. Wouldn't have mattered one bit whether I helped those boys with that rope or not. Not one bit, one way or the other."

"Well, what's these numbers all about?" Fairweather asked. "They numbers they've given themselves when they signed up to be vigilantes?" And when Slade said only that there hadn't been any numbers pinned on the body when he parted ways with Davis and his men, Fairweather said, "Suppose it might be Ad's idea of the measurements for a grave. That Ad Davis ain't none too bright."

And the more I stared at the paper and then up at the frozen tortured face, the more I knew what the writing meant. It had gotten to the point that all they had to do was scribble some numbers on a body or a door frame, and without even understanding what the writing stood for, you would know that they had either summarily done what they wanted or would do so in the immediate future unless you instantly left them and all you owned far and permanently behind.

CHAPTER 5

It was after noon when we rode down into Virginia City by the back way, and the weather was warm and even pleasant. Yet there was an unlikely quiet on the mud-ridden street, as if the town had been removed of people and had been left with only their smells and works. Into this vacant eeriness Jack Slade now invaded by his booming drunken voice and reckless riding and the very way in which he held his head unreasonably high. When we reached the Cal Exchange, Slade looked, searched out the boardwalk and the length of the street just long enough to see that there was no one outside at that point either; then he pulled out his revolver and fired off shots in all directions.

They came out then—the merchants and storekeepers and denizens of Virginia City—to see what it was about this time. But they showed no enthusiasm for it, nothing of humor or camaraderie or even disgust or irritation, staring up blankly at Jack Slade like he represented something that instantly wore and tired them immensely, almost ignoring him, when he whooped once or twice to stir them. And when Slade rode up on several of them and fired off his revolver, still no one said a word, so that Slade, in the end, had to break the silence himself. "Whose gonna buy a drink for the man that hung Bill Hunter?" he

417

shouted out, his horse spinning in a circle beneath him. And when no one said anything yet, he shouted even louder. "Do you lazy bastards hear me? I hung Hunter for you. Captain Jack Slade slew the beast that Jimbo Williams couldn't even catch."

And that's when Kiskadden emerged from the mercantile and hurriedly came up to us and grabbed the halter of Slade's horse and pulled the horse's head and muzzle down so that Kiskadden looked straight up into Slade's face. "Quiet down, Jack," Kiskadden said in a contained and anxious voice. "The word's already been brought. The town already knows about Hunter."

Slade leaned over his horse so that he looked like he might slide off and come down, head first, onto Kiskadden. "What of it?" he said. "So the sons of bitches already know I got him. I'm gonna let 'em know some more; all day maybe. Maybe all night."

"Ad Davis is telling it different than you, Jack," Kiskadden answered.

"What do you mean?" Slade sneered back. "What's that lyin' bastard sayin'?" And then he pulled back up and moved his hand to his pistol and scoured the town in search of Davis as if he would have shot him down at that moment had he seen him.

Kiskadden jerked at the halter and regained Slade's attention. "He's saying he and his boys hung Hunter after you led 'em over the mountains, Jack. That's all. Let it be. Let it alone."

"I don't let nothing be, goddammit. Where is he now?"

But Kiskadden held firm. "There's more, Jack. Why don't you come in the store and I'll tell you about it."

Slade pulled back at his reins, but Kiskadden continued his hold. "Tell it here goddammit. What else did that son of a bitch say? Davis'll wish he'd never heard the name Jack Slade when I'm through with 'im."

"It's not about Davis," Kiskadden said, no longer even purporting to try to maintain a whisper against Slade's invective. "It's about Williams." And when Slade suddenly quieted his horse and became still, Kiskadden added in a lower voice. "They hung six others before you boys even left for the stampede. The Gulch has had enough of it. Signs were posted before Hunter was even hung threatening the vigilance committee with five hung vigilantes for any one man the committee hung thereafter. You're not doing yourself a favor boasting about hanging Bill Hunter. He's got more friends in Virginia than you've got in the entire Gulch."

And that's when Slade went totally slack. It was as if in one fraction of a moment in time he calmed completely, went sodden and drunk to sober and deliberate so that even his breathing came almost to a standstill. "Who was it?" he said to Kiskadden in a voice without emotion or inflection. "Tell me their names."

"It was Carter and his boys, Jack. They were bound to catch 'em, or most of 'em anyway. Shears in Frenchtown, Graves and Zachary at Fort Owen, and the rest of 'em—Carter, Cooper, Skinner—at Hell Gate. That's all there is, Jack. It's over. It's got to be. You need to let it lie."

By then Slade was off his horse, moving toward the Cal Exchange and yet not removing his stare from off Kiskadden. "Skinner don't ride with those boys," he finally said. "You know that."

And when Kiskadden repeated, "Let it lie, Jack," Slade spat on the boardwalk and answered, "Whose gonna tell that to Jim Williams? You gonna tell him? That woman Pfouts gonna tell him? Look at these yellow gutless wonders," he said, indicating at the townspeople who had stood the whole time and watched the exchange without word or movement. "Which one of them is gonna tell Jim Williams and Beidler and Beehrer and the rest of their lynch mob that they're through? Don't go tellin' me what to do when you haven't got the stomach to be tellin' them." And then he strode into the saloon with Fairweather behind him and the door swinging wildly from the violence of their entrance.

It was as if the numbers rolled through my mind as I walked with Kiskadden back to the store: nineteen, twenty, twenty-one, twenty-two, twenty-three. And I said the final number to Kiskadden. "That's twenty-three then. By my count, I mean."

And Kiskadden answered, "Yes. I suppose that's as good as any other number." Then he told how Williams and his men had come back the day after we had left and how it wasn't until after Williams and Beidler and some of the rest had met with the executive committee that the information was released. "That's when it started," Kiskadden said. "There was a lot of complaining and threats being made in all directions. So the committee said it would hold off if the Gulch could show the committee wasn't needed. And Williams hasn't been in town since."

Over the next few days an unnatural and uneasy calm prevailed in Virginia City, punctuated by a renewal of the cold wind and blowing snow. You could see it in the icy street without ever having to go outdoors, the furtive conversations between erstwhile vigilantes or Southerners or a dozen other classes of men, all ending abruptly and the men scattering in all directions at the first sign that someone else had taken notice of, and exception to, them. As if the mere congregation of more than two men in any one place was enough to violate the unwritten truce.

Then, on the fourth day, a saloon at Junction was robbed at gunpoint in open daylight, and when the vigilantes declined to form a company to pursue the perpetrator, the trail and description of the man quickly became confused so that the ramshackle posse of angry Junction miners succeeded in doing nothing more than exercising their mounts. And then, not two days later, James Dorsett brought in the bodies of his brother, Rudolph, and of John White—the latter being the discoverer of Grasshopper Creek—and James Williams refused to raise a single man to take up the two-week old trail of the murderer whose name and looks were well known to Dorsett and dozens of other men. "We've been told we're not needed and not wanted," Williams responded blithely when asked for vigilante intervention. And so at last Henry Thompson rode out by himself in a fruitless search for the murderer who led him across the snowy mountains and on to Oregon and California before Thompson lost him in the teeming crowds of San Francisco.

These events, and others of lesser offense, revived the call for law and order, so that the reluctant silence of the varying factions now broke into scores of lively debates in the saloons and in the camps and on every street corner in the 20-mile city. There were those, like Beidler and Beehrer, who demanded a recognition of the effectiveness of vigilantism. And others, in particular the Democrats and Southerners, who argued strenuously for the reinstatement of the miners' committee and who openly rued the absence of Henry Plummer, who, they asserted, would have put matters to rest.

A majority, including Kiskadden, now advocated vehemently in favor of the creation of a real tribunal in which, as Kiskadden put it, "a man's right to a jury will be ensured and the public's right to law and order still guaranteed." And this newfound voice of reason, which seemed to gain momentum with every reiteration, prevailed within a matter of days such that when a drifter was arrested on a Sunday night in mid-February for the shooting of a fellow monte player in the Cal Exchange, the man was given two days worth of a fair and public hearing before he was hung off a rafter on Wallace Street.

The orderly trial and execution of the man pleased Kiskadden greatly, and as much chagrined X Beidler who recently had adopted Kiskadden's store as a comfortable spot at which to warm himself and gather and disseminate a gossipy form of information, and who let it be known that the two-day trial wasted, by his calculation, a year's worth of man hours that could have been put to infinitely greater productive use.

For my part, I was happy to let them argue it out, for I had no desire to impair my newly established employment with Kiskadden. And Kiskadden took this for a form of quiet acquiescence, so that when he debated the issue with Beidler, he utilized me as a perfect foil for the making of his points. "This vigilante movement was just an understandable reaction to the moment," he said to Beidler as he recorded the inventory that I read off. "Don't you think so, Alton? The vigilance committee is played out now that the people's court is up and functioning. This way there can be no doubts, no room for outsiders to question our ability to govern ourselves. The last thing we need is the federal government coming in here and asking questions."

"Think so?" Beidler answered while he smoked at a pipe and sat on a barrel with his legs dangling like those of a little boy. "I wouldn't be so quick to make that pronouncement myself. That gambler they hung yesterday was guilty, plain as day. Alex Davis has had an easy time of it so far, playing the judge like a one-tune piano. I'll wait 'til he's got a tough one to deal with before I believe it works. Wait 'til they try somebody who's sharin' a camp or who rides with some shooters."

And we did not have to wait too long on X Beidler's or Alex Davis's account. Jack Slade made sure of that. Just one day after the hanging of the drifter, J. M. Fox, who had bravely assumed the role of sheriff, arrested Slade after he rode his gelding into the billiard hall just across from Kiskadden's and shot up the tables and the mirror before he rode back out with a bottle in one hand and his reloaded Colt firing off in the other. They tried him and fined him and he immediately paid in full, all of which was taken by some as a demonstration of the efficiency of the people's court.

"What did I tell you, X?" Kiskadden said to Beidler the next day. "I doubt the vigilance committee itself could have handled it as well."

"Hardly see that as a test," Beidler answered.

Within the span of ten days, the people's court considered more than a dozen matters. And in each instance, and only after a hearing in which the accused was allowed to present his evidence in public, the perpetrator was fined a considerable sum that more than compensated for the injury to the peace that had been inflicted. And this, too, gave Kiskadden reason to contend, before not only X Beidler but others as well, that the people's court was now the legitimate successor to the vigilance committee. "I think the time has come," Kiskadden said, "for the entire Gulch to give its thanks to the vigilance committee, and to reward those who served it so nobly, and then to disband it once and for all so that the people's court can have an air of permanence about it."

"And how is that?" Beidler asked when the rest of the men in the store carefully held back their opinion.

"Well, look what has been accomplished," Kiskadden answered. "Every wrongful act that has occurred over the last ten days has been accounted for and remedied. If that is not the efficient administration of justice, I would be pleased to be instructed on what is."

And that's when Paris Pfouts, who had just staggered into the store, spoke out. "It may be that, and it might not," he said in a slurring voice that showed he was about his regular habit. And when Beidler offered him a bottle, he took it and drank heavily from it. "What it is not, however, is a means by which to stop these disruptions to law and order in the first place. Why, Jack Slade, alone, has appeared before the court on four separate occasions."

"And he has paid every fine levied against him, has he not?" Kiskadden said. And I could not help but to wish that Kiskadden would rebut Pfouts by noting that Pfouts no doubt wanted a greater retribution against Slade for publicly deriding Pfouts for his well-known addiction to the amorous and not inexpensive attentions of one of the more prominent sporting ladies of Virginia City.

Pfouts swore as soon as he could swallow. "And with the payment of every fine, that son of a bitch has made his way back into the street with a loaded and primed revolver pointed at the head or property of another man. The way any reasonable citizen would see it," Pfouts said as he paused to draw down again on Beidler's bottle, "is that all your people's court has succeeded in doing is setting a fee schedule that allows the likes of Slade to know in advance how much it is going to cost him to shoot out a lamp or break up a chair. And from the looks of things, Slade and his boys are more than happy to pay the price for the enjoyment they get in doing it." Kiskadden had no answer to that and, as it was well known that he was more than a little friendly with Jack and Virginia Slade, it came as no surprise when he looked at Paris Pfouts with a modicum of distrust and dislike. And Paris Pfouts, alone of everyone else who had gathered in the store, was too drunk to see it.

"All I want to know from you boys," Pfouts said to the entire group with a snide and arrogant tone, "is what's going to happen when Slade's gang gets big enough, or maybe just bold enough, to not pay the next fine that's levied against him. That, and what the fine for murder's gonna be. Because when those boys do get bold enough, someone's gonna get shot or stuck with a knife. I'll give anyone here five to one against my twenty right now. And when it happens, you can bet they're not gonna sit back and watch their boss get hung."

~~~

After that, I knew it was just a matter of time before something happened. Not only because Jack Slade could never let the insults and aggravations die down on their own, and not simply for the reason that Paris Pfouts and his confidants would never be content until every last irritating contingent of the community had been subverted and thoroughly contained, but because there was even more to it than that, all woven into a complicated formula in which everyone competed and jousted for position like so many wolves in a leaderless pack, waiting for that one vital opening, that one passing moment of lapse into weakness or forgetfulness when they could instinctively strike and gain the final advantage that would ensure their dominance.

I tried my best to stay clear of it, saying nothing, going nowhere I did not have to go, hiding from the cluttered interaction of the cramped town where nearly all the traffic moved up and down the three or four most central streets. And even that was not enough to provide total insulation, since at least the word of what was occurring could not be stopped from siphoning into Kiskadden's like a faintly telltale and poisonous gas.

The first week of March came and went and the wintry cold would not relent for more than a day or two at a spell. And during that time, within the span of seven short days in which Jack Slade and plenty of others became more and more openly resistant to restrictions on their reckless behavior, the faces of the most prominent vigilantes—

Beehrer and Williams and Brown and many others—became visible on the streets once more.

Still, Slade and his followers continued in their vandalism, the latest transgression being Slade's disruption of Kate Harper's performance the previous night at the Virginia Theater, where Slade had burst in and demanded that Miss Harper remove her costume comprised of nothing more than a ballet dress and hosiery. X Beidler brought that information into Kiskadden's as the next morning's news, and Kiskadden had shrugged it off as he instructed me on several deliveries I was to make about the town. "If you see Slade," Kiskadden said as an afterthought, "tell him I'd like to talk with him."

And as I walked out, Beidler added, "If you find him, give me a five-minute warning. Five minutes is as close to that sonofa as I want to be."

I never did find Jack Slade; he was on a particularly circuitous and arbitrary route that morning that would involve him lastly in a drunken brawl with Dan Harding and Charley Edwards, being two of Slade's closest associates, out front of the Shades. But I would nonetheless encounter his trail, in the form of a small stream of cow's milk that had spilled from a dairy wagon that Slade and Harding had sent driverless down a side street, at the bottom of which the wagon had crashed and splintered into a hundred pieces. There on the street, dogs and miners alike fought over the pooled and muddy fluid, smearing it involuntarily on their clothes and faces in a desperate combat for its final remnants.

By the time I made my last delivery to a small camp just the other side of Discovery Creek and then had returned to Kiskadden's, Slade and his companions had been arrested and hauled before the people's court. When the word was brought to Kiskadden, he shrugged his shoulders, even making a bit of a joke about it; and it did, indeed, seem a bit fun that Slade could play so many pranks in so short a span of time. Then Slade himself, together with Fairweather and Harding and Edwards, came into the mercantile laughing and hollering as if they had just won the war or struck a vein.

"What was the fine this time?" Kiskadden asked at they came up to the counter.

It was Fairweather that answered. "Weren't no fine at all. Did ourselves a little lawyering that made sure there wouldn't be no fine."

"You saying you boys won one?" Kiskadden said with a laugh.

And Slade, who had just plucked a pickled egg out of a tall jar on the counter, said, "We're sayin' we didn't give that bastard Davis a chance this time. I tore up their chickenshit warrant before they could read it aloud. And Billy boy here let Davis know there'd be gunplay if they tried to do something about it." And then he shoved the egg into his mouth and ate it whole.

I could see Kiskadden was dumbfounded. Then Beidler came in with his shotgun in his hand. He walked straight up to Slade and looked up into Slade's eyes with that squinting and otherwise expressionless look that was unique to X Beidler. "You best be hightailin' it outta here," he said. And when a look of anger spread over Slade's face, Beidler added, "Davis turned your case over to the vigilance committee."

The rest of it confuses me some because Jack Slade instantly saw the wisdom in heading for his stone house down on Meadow Creek, and when he went back out into the muddy street and mounted his horse and Bill Fairweather joined him, it seemed that this time he would succeed in not even having to pay a fine. And as they rode off and Slade sang out the words of a well-known limerick of rather bawdy meaning, replacing Paris Pfout's and the courtesan Lily Winshaw's names for those normally associated with the poem, it almost was as if the comic relief of the moment was welcome and very badly needed.

Williams and his men must have encountered Slade before he ever made it out of the Gulch. In less than a half hour after Slade had left us, we saw Jack Slade again, this time in the center of Williams's cavalry and this time, alone of all the times I ever saw Jack Slade, groveling vocally and begging Williams to spare at least his life.

They gave Slade the same abbreviated hearing that the others received in Bannack and in Virginia City and at Laurin's and in Hell Gate and the other places that will never be known, and then they hung him behind Pfouts and Russel's stone building on the gateposts of a corral. And then they cut him down for fear of the wrath of Virginia Slade, who was sent for by Kiskadden at the moment he saw what was about to come to pass. And when Virginia Slade rode into town with her beautiful jet-black hair blowing behind her and her mare sweated and she screaming at a pitch so high and pure and perfect that it might have been a sound from out of the heavens, Jack Slade was already growing cold.

~~~

Only one more man was hung in the three months of March and April and May, and we, the whole town I mean, went out to see it since the man was an outright murderer having knifed a citizen in the back and taken his gold when he thought he would not be seen. But the vigilantes were not at rest. The executive committee convened regularly, and the townspeople knew about it and could do nothing to stop it; and James Williams and his men were kept occupied for most every day, with Williams and his company arresting men in every district, up every creek and draw, and the executive committee trying them for complicity with the road agent gang and then exiling them on one day's notice.

By the beginning of June, the count of those whom had been formally, or in practical reality, banished by the committee was over thirty, including the likes of Harvey Meade and James Thurmond and Colonel Wood, who had defended Ives to the last. On each occasion the possessions and property of the banished man were seized or auctioned off quietly by the vigilantes, who were said to be buying claims and stock and equipment at a tenth and less their actual worth. And it seemed that it might go on forever until the Gulch was made up solely of members of the vigilance committee.

There were complaints to the committee, by good men like Kiskadden and others who took a great chance in speaking out. And when no change in policy ensued, there were secret meetings and posted threats and a not inconsiderable attrition from the vigilantes' ranks. But even that would not stop them, not even the threats against their lives could hold back Williams and Beidler and Beehrer and those that acted at their command. And when, in the middle of June 1864, they hung James Brady for the murder of a man who shortly thereafter, and some said miraculously, recovered, it was apparent that only some greater power of intervention could bring about an end to vigilante rule.

And it thus was with great enthusiasm that the people of Virginia City streamed into the streets on a late day in that very month to hear more about the wild news that a new territory had been formed of all the lands east of the Bitterroots. And I was with them, as was Kiskadden and so many others, bumping and crowding into each other in desperate search of someone who was fully informed, anxious for the relief that at long last had to come from the federal government thousands of miles away in Washington City, from Abe Lincoln himself, who had to take the time away from his troubles over the war and the political infighting in his cabinet and the treacheries of his own party to resurrect the Northwest gold field from the anarchy of its own ways. So that the wait was almost intolerable, painfully unbearable as the express rider from Fort Benton drank down a glass of beer and then another, tantalizing the crowd it seemed as he tried to catch his breath and slake his thirst enough to speak. Until the crowd would not stand for it any longer and some-one hoisted him up on a wagon and the news was demanded from him.

"We're a territory," the man said. "That's all there is to it. Everything east of the Bitterroots for 400 miles. From Colter's Hell north to the border."

And when someone asked what we were to be called, the man spewed out the rest of it, matter-of-factly, as if all of change came by the territorial designation itself, with nothing else determining what it might ever come to be, as if the institution of the processes of govern-ment alone would heal the wounds, and eradicate the evils, and forever ensure that all in the future would be right and just. "It's called Montana. And Sidney Edgerton, Judge Edgerton from Bannack, is gov-ernor of the whole damned place."

AFTERWORD

Enough time passed for the mountain grasses to grow back over the graves of the hanged men, and for someone to have broken the ground again enough to remove the skeletal remains of the clubfoot of George Lane and the skull of Henry Plummer and the shotgun ball that had been lodged in his elbow, and to place all of those objects on public display. Still, many of the willing and unwilling participants in the above-recounted events continued to live, and in many cases to prosper, in what was to become the state of Montana. Their stories are too complex and lengthy to be set forth in detail here and, instead, can only be mentioned in the briefest of fashions.

The elevation into public life Wilbur Sanders enjoyed as a result of the trial of George Ives carried him forward for the remainder of his career. When the time came for the new territory of Montana to select its nonvoting delegate to the U.S. Congress, he was twice a nominee—first as the Union party candidate in 1865, and then again as the Republican candidate in 1867. In both instances he lost. From 1873 to 1879 he served in the Territorial House of Representatives and from 1890 to 1893 as one of the first two United States senators from the state of Montana.

He also was active as a trial lawyer and in a number of prominent private institutions that exist in the state to this day. For a period of twenty-five years, from 1865 to 1890, he presided over the Montana Historical Society, and in 1885 he founded and served as the president of the Montana Bar Association. When the Grand Lodge of the Masons of Montana was formed in 1866, Wilbur Sanders was named its first grand secretary.

Territorial Governor Sidney Edgerton, in contrast, remained in Montana only briefly. The advent of formal territorial elections resulted in the consolidation of the power of the Democrats in the Montana Territory. Democrat Samuel McLean defeated Wilbur Sanders in the 1865 race to be the territorial delegate to the U.S. Congress and the ascendancy of Andrew Johnson to the presidency of the United States threw the Radical Republicans into an angry frenzy that culminated in the impeachment of the president. All the while, Sidney Edgerton resisted the influence of the Democrats and so antagonized Democratic representatives to the territorial legislature that one prominent representative resigned after his loyalty to the Union was formally challenged by the governor.

Contemporaneously, investigations into the vigilante hangings both in Washington and Utah brought pressure to bear on Sidney Edgerton and others, forcing Wilbur Sanders to travel to Salt Lake City in the spring of 1865 to defend the vigilantes' actions before the Utah courts. Faced with mounting animosities with the Democrats and President Johnson, and contending that the only way he could recover the monies he had personally extended on behalf of the government was to plead his case in Washington, Sidney Edgerton left the territory in 1865 and never returned.

The vast mineral resources of Montana allowed for the accumulation of great fortunes such that at one time the new capital city of Helena boasted to have more millionaires per capita than anywhere else in the world. Among them William Clark became one of the richest and certainly one of the most powerful. His interests spanned the industrial spectrum, ranging from copper and silver mining in general, to real estate, banking, electricity, railroads, sugar, and newspapers. While his investments gained him influence and wealth throughout the West and Northeast, he remained, for the time, most prominently in the Butte area where his silver and copper mining and smelting operations were world class in scope and production.

In 1877 Clark was elected as the twelfth grand master of the Masonic Grand Lodge of Montana. In the same year, he received the brevet commission of major and led what was known as the Butte battalion against the Nez Perces and Chief Joseph. He presided over the Third Montana Constitutional Convention, which resulted in the ratification of the constitution of the state of Montana in 1889, and then, in the infamous dual senatorial elections of 1890, was elected as one of two Democrats to serve as the first Montana senators to the U.S. Senate. Simultaneously, Republicans Wilbur Sanders and T. C. Power were elected in a separate proceeding to the same positions. The U.S. Congress ultimately recognized the Republicans, and Clark was not permitted to take the senatorial seat. He subsequently was again elected and then was later appointed as senator only to either never be sworn in or to fail to be recognized. Finally, in 1901, he was again elected as a senator from the state of Montana, at which time he officially became a member of Congress. He never ran for public office again and instead occupied himself by overseeing his businesses from the vantage point of the greatest cities in the western world, and by enjoying the luxuries of his 121-room New York mansion that was said to contain four art galleries that were in no way sufficient to display his extraordinary collection of art.

The other great capitalist of the vigilante era, Samuel T. Hauser made his friend N. P. Langford a partner when, in 1865, he formed the first bank in Virginia City. A banker, mining magnate, and railroad man, and a Democrat throughout his life, Hauser was appointed as governor of the Montana Territory in 1885 by President Grover Cleveland.

When the three existing Masonic lodges in the territory were merged in 1866 into the Grand Lodge of Montana, Langford was cho-sen as the first grand historian of the Masons; three years later, in 1869, he became the fourth grand master. Langford's writings of the vigilante days, together with those of Masons Lew Callaway, Wilbur Sanders, X Beidler, and "Professor" Thomas J. Dimsdale, as well as works written more recently by Masonic authors, form the core of the written history of the Montana vigilantes.

In 1872 Langford was appointed as the first superintendent of Yellowstone National Park, and as the bank examiner for all U.S. terri-tories and the Pacific states.

Little is known as to how Electa Plummer lived the remainder of her life after her departure from Montana. Francis Thompson claimed, some forty plus years after the hangings, to have sent to Electa funds representing the remainder of Henry Plummer's estate less the costs of burial, but no evidence exists to support that contention, and some exists to refute it. Electa is known to have joined the Vails in the Dakota territories after the Vails left Bannack and is said to have vigorously insisted on Henry Plummer's innocence. In 1874 she married James Maxwell, and together they raised Maxwell's two children plus two of their own. Some sources indicate that prior to his death Henry Plummer was already making preparations for a reunion with Electa to occur in the spring of 1864.

The first session of the territorial legislature of the Montana Territory was convened in December of 1864, and Francis Thompson participated as the delegate of Beaverhead County, where Bannack is located. It was at that time that he designed the territorial seal, which became, and remains, the Great Seal of Montana. After spending a number of adventurous years in the West, he returned to his native Massachusetts, where he ultimately became a member of the judiciary.

John S. Lott was appointed by Governor Edgerton as the first auditor of the Montana Territory. He and Paris Pfouts acted in leader-ship roles when, in December of 1864, the Grand Lodge of Kansas authorized them, and other applicants, to form a lodge in Virginia City.

James Kiskadden was appointed the first junior deacon of that same lodge upon its formation. Kiskadden married Virginia Slade in March of the following year. The hiatus between Jack Slade's death and Virginia's remarriage allowed her time to transport Slade's body, which supposedly had been stored in a tin coffin filled with alcohol, to Salt Lake City, where Jack Slade was buried. The marriage between Kiskadden and Virginia ended only three years later.

Granville Stuart became one of the founders of the Montana cattle industry. In 1882, together with Con Kohrs, he purchased 12,000 head of cattle for $400,000. He later served as the president of the Montana Stockgrowers Association and participated in many of the vigilante hangings of cattle rustlers that occurred in Montana in the 1870s and 1880s. In 1891, he was appointed as state land agent, and in that capacity he selected over 600,000 acres of land ultimately given to the state by the federal government for school purposes. In the later years of his life, he acted as envoy extraordinary and minister plenipotentiary to the republics of Uruguay and Paraguay.

James Williams also ranched in Montana, although his efforts ultimately resulted in financial ruin and may have contributed to his losing battle with drinking. Facing potential legal prosecution for his role in the vigilante hangings, and having lost in his bid as the Republican candidate for county sheriff of Madison County, in which Virginia City is located, Williams died in 1887, alone and outdoors on a cold winter day from an overdose of laudanum. The question whether his death was an accident or a suicide will never be resolved. He was survived by a wife and seven children.

John X. Beidler was appointed as deputy United States marshal in 1865, serving under Marshal George S. Pinney. He was often seen atop his mule with shotgun in hand, patrolling the streets of the new mining town of Helena, the downtown of which was located in the center of the gold find at Last Chance Gulch. In 1870 he received a letter, signed by 200 men, threatening to accord to him no more time to prepare for death than he had given those whom he helped hang. He was to live for another twenty years. Upon his death in 1890, Senator Wilbur Sanders delivered the funeral oration at a ceremony sponsored by the Montana Pioneer Society.

Dave Meiklejohn, Bill Bunton's stable boy, also became a deputy U.S. marshal in Montana. Throughout his life he continued to assert that Bill Bunton, as well as those who associated with Bunton, never committed any crime.

Joseph Swift and Henry Tilden made no further contributions to the history of Montana, although their proximity to the life and death of Henry Plummer shall cause their names to never be forgotten.

Throughout their reign, the Montana vigilantes utilized the designation "3-7-77" as their symbol of terror and authority. While the true meaning of the symbol has never been definitively established, it is likely that the designation originally represented three specific numbers assigned to three members of the vigilante organization. It is well known that both the San Francisco and Montana vigilantes used numbers, rather than names, in order to ensure secrecy and thwart retribution.

The numbers 3-7-77 are inscribed above the epitaph on X Beidler's gravestone. Those same three numbers appear today on the shoulder patch insignia of Montana's State Highway Patrol.

ABOUT THE AUTHOR

James Gaitis is a trial lawyer, arbitrator, editor, and academic. Born in Chicago, he has received degrees from the University of Notre Dame and the University of Iowa. For more than ten years, he lived in Montana's remote North Fork of the Flathead. He now resides in Scotland.

Chasing the Powhatan Arrow

A Travelogue in Economic Geography

Michael Abraham

Pocahontas Press
Blacksburg, Virginia

Chasing the Powhatan Arrow

A Travelogue in
Economic Geography

Copyright © 2017 by Michael Abraham
Printed in the United States of America
Signature Book Printing, www.sbpbooks.com

Book design by Michael Abraham
Cover design by Jill Darlington Smith
Maps by Robert Pearsall

Photographs by the author unless otherwise noted.

ISBN 13: 978-0-9967744-2-0
ISBN 10: 0-9967744-2-4

First printing: 2017
Second printing: 2018
Third printing: 2019

Pocahontas Press:
http://www.pocahontaspress.com/

Also by Michael Abraham

The Spine of the Virginias
Journeys along the border of Virginia and West Virginia

Union, WV
A novel of loss, healing, and redemption in contemporary Appalachia

Harmonic Highways
Exploring Virginia's Crooked Road

Providence, VA
A novel triumph over adversity

WAR, WV
A novel of a fight for justice in the Appalachian coalfields

Orange, VA
A novel of political intrigue

Keepers of the Tradition
Portraits of contemporary Appalachians
With artist Leslie Roberts Gregg

The author can be reached by e-mail at:
<michael@mabrahamauthor.com>

For updates and ordering information on the author's books, excerpts, and sample chapters, please visit his website at:
http://mabrahamauthor.com/

Acknowledgements

I AM DEEPLY INDEBTED to many people who supported my effort. The people I met in Norfolk, Cincinnati, and everywhere in between were unfailingly gracious, generous, and accommodating, making my job much easier and more rewarding. I appreciate the honesty, openness, intelligence, and candor I was shown.

Additionally, my editors worked countless hours (at recompense so meager that I'm embarrassed to admit it) to help me make my book readable, relevant, and grammatically correct.

Jane Abraham, Blacksburg, Virginia
J. Preston Claytor, Village of Golf, Florida
Mary Ann Johnson, Blacksburg, Virginia
Phil Ross, Blacksburg, Virginia
Sally Shupe, Newport, Virginia

I thank these lovely folks for their hospitality, encouragement, information, and support:

Paulette and Larry Bailey, Lynchburg, Virginia
John Burchnall, Cincinnati, Ohio
Howard Gregory, Appomattox, Virginia
James Hughes, Reading, California
Mark Kinne, Cincinnati, Ohio
Christina and Kaleb Matson, Lynchburg, Virginia
Dave Mullins, Blacksburg, Virginia
Phil Ross, Blacksburg, Virginia
John Singleton, Roanoke, Virginia
Katie Walser, Petersburg, Virginia
Jane and Sam Webster, Norfolk, Virginia

I give special thanks Jennifer McDaid, archivist at Norfolk Southern Corporation, who met or exceeded every request I made and to the entire company for supporting my work and keeping the dream of railroading alive in America.

I also thank Bob Pearsall for the wonderful maps and Beverly Fitzpatrick Jr. and his staff at the Virginia Museum of Transportation in Roanoke for their cooperation and support.

Timetable

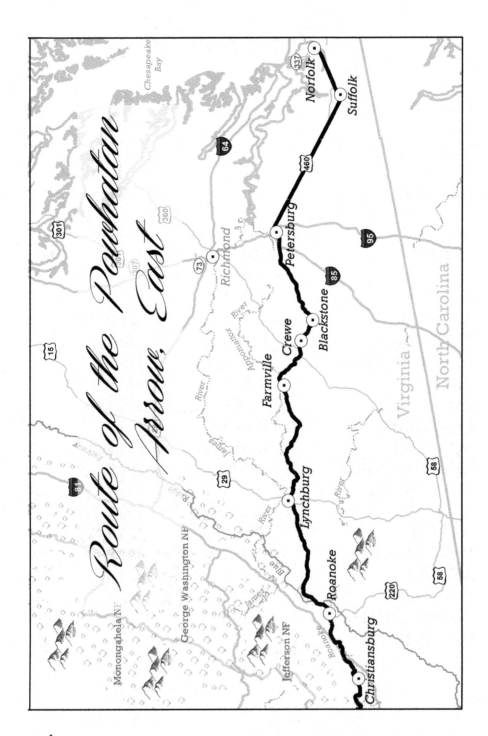

Route of the Powhatan Arrow, East

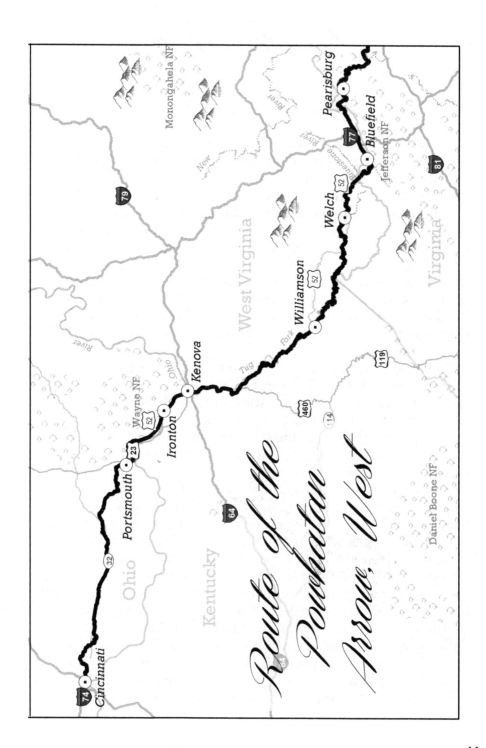

Route of the
Powhatan
Arrow, West

Dedication

THIS BOOK IS DEDICATED to **J B. Jones**, PhD, retired professor of Mechanical Engineering at Virginia Tech. J. B. was the head of the M. E. Department when I earned my degree. He was one of my Thermodynamics professors and he literally wrote the book we used in our classes. He was supportive of my writing career and lived to read and enjoy this book. He died in May, 2017.

Thermodynamics is the study of heat and its relationship to work and energy. Thermo was a painfully difficult course for me – and as it turned out for most of my classmates as well – but Dr. Jones' brilliance made it relevant and relatable to everyday life, including cars, motorcycles, and locomotives. I entered Tech with an interest in machinery but under his guidance left more interested in energy, the ability to do work, and how it enables economies and provides for the earth's climates and ecosystems.

THIS BOOK IS ALSO POSTHUMOUSLY DEDICATED to a man I never met: **Robert Claytor**. Bob was born in February, 1922, and died in April, 1993, and is widely credited for adding N&W locomotives to the Norfolk Southern's steam excursion program and thus extending life to the famous Class J 611 locomotive.

He was the son of the late Graham Claytor, Sr. who while vice president of Appalachian Power Company, supervised the construction of a dam and resulting lake in Pulaski County, Virginia, that now bears his name. He was the brother of the late W. Graham Claytor, Jr., who was president of Southern Railway and later CEO of Amtrak. He was the father of Jane Claytor Webster and Preston Claytor who helped me enormously with this book.

Bob Claytor was president of Norfolk & Western Railway and oversaw the merger with Southern Railway, and then became the first CEO of Norfolk Southern. Bob died of cancer long before this book took shape in my head, but his name is spoken reverentially by legions of railfans who have never forgotten and always appreciated his contributions to the legacy of railroads in the mid-Atlantic. I never heard anything negative said about him and it is one of the great regrets of my life that we never met.

Preface

The Greek philosopher Heraclitus long ago said, "No man ever steps in the same river twice, for it is not the same river and indeed he is not the same man." Thus is the nature of change, I think to myself, as cool, clear New River waters sweep past my naked feet, swirling away the summer heat that has just prior been enveloping me, wrapped in my motorcycling helmet and suit. The river itself seems entirely timeless, flowing northward, downstream to the Kanawha, then the Ohio, Mississippi and to the Gulf of Mexico in this same corridor for eons. And yet the movement is constant, the molecules of the earth's most abundant liquid following gravity's command, downstream.

I lift my feet and place them into the cooling waters again, as if to test the theory. A yellow-legged little green heron spikes a 2 inch fish on a sandbar 75 feet away, deftly swings it face-first to its beak and swallows it whole. Sunshine glimmers off its dark, wrapped wings and ruddy chest. The water now swaddling my feet is not the same as it was moments ago. It is a different river.

A flowing river represents one of the most easily illustrated images of the juxtaposition of change and stability. For all intents and purposes, at least from our temporal lives, the river is always there. Yet the water that comprises the river is in constant change.

More subtly, I'm in constant change as well. The river has swept away thousands of dead cells from the surface of my feet as my body undergoes the life-long process of jettisoning old and adding new. The blood reaching my feet moments ago has been re-circulated already, and like the flowing water, the flowing blood is not the same as before. We all have an expiration date, and I've aged closer to mine, however minutely. That moment is gone and will never be back.

Everything about us is constantly changing, perceptibly or not. Nothing stays the same. On the level of atoms, there is eternal motion in all objects, whether solid, liquid or gaseous. On the level of planets, it's the same story, ever-changing, even in seeming stability.

Our bodies replace almost every cell every eleven months, except brain cells which live for years. Yet miraculously, every cell has a perfect blueprint of our entire body within it. A child is the same child, even as she grows.

Change is part of the basic nature of everything. Yearning for stasis, for eternal stability, is futile and angst-producing. Resisting change is like asking the child not to grow. Or old men not to pass away. Or a river not to flow.

The New River at McCoy in Montgomery County, Virginia, has an abiding beauty, and as we in our temporal beings understand the concept of "always," it always has. Wildlife abounds. The river teems with fish. Wading birds like the little green heron are all around me. Swarms of insects play above the rippling water. Blazing red cardinal plants grow along the shore, bursting forth in an ephemeral profusion of color that will last mere days.

This river is in the area of my birth and my current residency. It is the area I know better than any other. And yet every time I see, touch, smell, and experience it, it is new.

Long ridgelines clad in a carpet of green stretch into the distance from the opposite shore, mostly covering occasional rock outcroppings. A jet airplane flies overhead, trailing a long white pencil-line on a blue background, its sound too faint to hear over the natural sounds of the river, the bird songs, the rippling water, and the leaves flowing in the gentle breeze. Three kayakers, dappled in neon yellows and greens, play in the rapids. I pick up pebbles and toss them into deeper waters, hearing their plop as they penetrate the surface tension of the water and emit concentric waves that are quickly swept away.

A pulsing sound grows above the others, a deep, guttural sound, throaty, masculine and mechanical, reverberating across the valley, ricocheting off the mountains. Visually, nothing changes. The chuffing sound increases in intensity and the other sounds of river, birds, and insects seem to quiet, as if in reverence. I turn to see a plume of white smoky-steam arise from upriver. I stand and look towards it, and from below the smoke emerges a massive, black machine, a locomotive, streaming towards me. It has a hemispherical front like a woman's breast, with a single yellow headlamp at the nipple. Below, between the hemisphere and the track, is a plow-like prow. Framing the hemisphere are two shiny tubes, pipes that form hand-railings, which sweep upwards on the front and then traverse the massive horizontal tubular skin back to the cab.

The massive leviathan locomotive approaches, moving with power, forcefulness, and intensity, and my adrenaline level increases. The side comes into view, where a 2 foot wide horizontal band painted in Tuscan red framed in yellow pin-striping, sweeps from front to back, the numbers "611" painted in yellow, mid-engine. Above is a grand horizontal cylinder, gloss-black, emerging from the front hemisphere and running the length of the machine to the rear cab. A tiny American flag flaps madly above it, near the exhaust where smoke and steam throb upwards into a plume above.

Below the Tuscan stripe are four colossal black metal wheels, six feet in diameter, the drivers, linked by enormous silver dog-bone shaped linkages, all pulsating and reciprocating in an intricate, frenzied, kinematic dance.

The track is twenty feet vertically above me and fifty feet back from the river. Because it is at a higher elevation, I can't see the track itself. But I see the slope of track ballast, the tan-white embankment of rock which supports the rails. The ground below me seems to vibrate under the onslaught of the massive machine, and I feel the air move with a more humid hint of steam. The smell of burning coal wafts through the air, pungent but not bitter or unpleasant. I'm showered by a light dusting of coal cinder particles.

The locomotive's cab passes me and inside I see the hefty, smudged-faced fireman with white striped cap. Then the tender car passes, it, too, resplendent in its Tuscan red stripe, with the words, "NORFOLK & WESTERN," emblazoned on it.

Then a parade of passenger cars follows. The Tuscan stripe has now widened to encompass nearly the entirety of each car's sides. My eyes are drawn overhead as the grey-black plume of smoke trails high above, spouting vertically from the locomotive, then trailing off horizontally as if a banner over the cars.

Refocusing on the cars, I watch a procession of square windows, inside which are passengers barely discernible in dimly lit cars. A child waves at me and I return her wave.

I see a man's face framed in the window. He is bald, bespectacled, and his forehead is familiar and resembles my own. He has a knowing but melancholy face. Our eyes meet for an instant, or at least I envision they do, and the corner of his mouth widens in a smile, as I sense my own is doing. My thoughts sweep back a quarter-century to my mind's eye image of my grandfather, the last time I saw him alive. And like the beat of the hummingbird's wing, like the molecules in the river, the visage of the man behind the window is gone.

The locomotive sound fades into the distance, supplanted by the screeching sound of the cars' wheels, the flanges on the outside, uphill wheels fighting to keep the wheels centered on the rails.

Just that fast, the final car, rounded at the back, sweeps by and the train has gone, moving westward, following that great ribbon of steel, to Eggleston, Pearisburg, Narrows, Glen Lyn, Bluefield, Bramwell, Welch, and beyond, to the banks of the great Ohio River, and onward to the bustling city of Cincinnati.

I turn back to the river for a moment, and then my eyes are drawn back towards the tracks. I see an endless convoy still flowing by, not of passenger cars but of empty coal cars headed back to the coalfields. I realize that I've been duped. My earlier vision was a ghost; my fantasy has been shattered. My imagination tricked me into seeing a passenger train, pulled by a hulking steam locomotive. In reality, I saw a prosaic gloss black diesel locomotive and a train of dirty aluminum coal cars, each printed with the NS logo and the words "TOP GON."

There are no passenger rail trains on this corridor any more. The last one pulled through, delighting those aboard with the fantastic river scene I've been enjoying, nearly fifty years earlier. The stegosaurus. The dodo bird. The teletype machine. The rotary-dial phone. My grandfather. The molecules of water that just prior had cooled my feet. They've all gone, long ago swept away in the tidal vicissitudes of time.

We can dam a river, but we cannot stop it. We can look back on days gone by with longing and even romanticism. But we cannot stop time from flowing.

I SIT AGAIN ON THE ROCK beside the river, the New River,

paradoxically named because it is one of the world's oldest, and the scene returns to quiet. I'm intimately familiar with this river, having grown up in Christiansburg, a town 20 miles away, in southwest Virginia. Much of the area has changed dramatically since my childhood, but this spot has a refreshing stability. I came here as a child, watching my dad fish. Once, I went canoeing with a group of Boy Scouts over the nearby rapids and most of us swamped. We spent a long cold night in wet sleeping bags.

Christiansburg was a modest town, arching past 5,000 people during my upbringing in the 1960s. It's quadrupled in size now, with over 21,000 people and a maddening number of traffic lights and exasperating traffic. The commercial center of my youth was centered in the three-block-long downtown, but now it's on the edge of town at the shopping malls. My parents live in the house in which I was raised. Mom bemoans that she can't buy stockings in downtown any more. Other than the county courthouse and town offices, there is painfully little activity. There is a poor bus system, scarcely any bicycling and walking amenities, and a car is necessary for every trip into and around downtown Christiansburg.

There were several factories around town, including a towel and sheet factory, a garment factory, and a furniture factory. My father owned a commercial printing factory where I worked in the summer to make spending money and which I would later be gifted and run for 17 years. Almost all of the factories are gone now including ours, although some of the buildings are still in service. The old printing company building is now a vacant office. The garment factory was repurposed as the county's government center.

In Cambria, a separate town then, now annexed by Christiansburg, was an N&W passenger train station. Mom tells me that as a child, I'd want to spend every moment there, watching the trains go by. There was a long pergola-like canopy covering the passenger platform. Several distinctive wooden carts that with a single pair of wheels could be balanced either front or back were parked haphazardly here and there. Inside the building were long, wooden couches, whose surfaces had been polished to a slippery sheen by the posteriors of countless thousands of travelers. On the walls

were framed black-and-white aerial photos of steam trains chugging through the picturesque nearby valleys.

I picture myself as being gregarious and uninhibited, even as
a child, approaching people at the station and asking where they
were going. And why. And for how long. These things fueled my
wanderlust. Special indeed were the times I got to ride the trains
myself. My maternal grandparents lived in Richmond, and sometimes I'd get to take the Pocahontas or the Powhatan Arrow to
Petersburg where a family member – neither grandparent could
drive – would pick us up. But my memories are scant, illusory.

In hindsight, it was a simpler time. A man – or a woman, but
mostly men, as more women stayed home – could make enough
of a living to provide for his family, buy a car every few years, and
take an occasional vacation on a workingman's salary. We Americans had the world's largest middle class, and I think everybody
thought we always would. If you wanted a job and were willing
to work, you could get one. You could open a restaurant or start a
business and local customers would support you. People belonged
to Kiwanis Clubs and Lions Clubs, Cotillion Clubs, and Women's
Club. Boys like me were in the Boy Scouts. People golfed and
bowled. Downtown was filled with locally owned stores – furniture stores, shoe stores, phonographic record stores, and drug
stores. Diners. Movie theaters.

People cruised the streets in cars that got 15 mpg burning
gasoline that cost $0.28/gallon. Folks went to Myrtle Beach in
South Carolina or Virginia Beach for a week every summer.

Life was good. Stable. Or at least it seemed that way to me. In
my youthful naivety, I assumed other places were much the same.

Slap me upside the head about now, as it is undeniable that as
a child, I lived in a stratified society. Schools weren't integrated
until I was ten or twelve, and the blacks in town clearly didn't
fare as well or have the same opportunities as we whites did. But
Geneva, the black woman who babysat for my parents when they
wanted a night on the town, was as peaceful as anyone I've ever
met, imbued with sangfroid. There was blissfully little racial tension. Or so it seemed to me. There was order in things.

But like the water flowing past my feet, like the coal-car train
still rumbling on the tracks behind me, things changed. Presi-

dent Eisenhower's Interstate Highway got built and I-81 wrapped around town, drawing commerce to the exits. The movie theater closed and a parking lot was built on the site. The two department stores moved to the mall three miles to the north on the way to Blacksburg. The drugstore closed when the new syndicated store opened. My old high school building closed and a new one, a soul-less, windowless edifice, an architect's worst nightmare, emerged on a hillside a mile away. The tallest building in town, the five-story Mensh Building, had a minor fire but was demolished anyway. Another parking lot replaced it.

I was aware that the passage of time had impacted other communities in the area in vastly different ways. Nearby Blacksburg, home of Virginia Tech, was like Christiansburg, a bustling place. Roanoke, the region's only real metropolitan area, had suffered with the loss of the headquarters of the Norfolk & Western Railway to Norfolk after its merger with Southern Railway to form Norfolk Southern. But Roanoke had transitioned to a new economy of primarily health care. Lynchburg, farther to the east, had also transitioned its economy from manufacturing to education and was doing well. But the coal mining regions to the northwest had fared miserably and were among the poorest and most destitute in the country.

The cacophony behind me finally ended as the last rail car – there are no longer any cabooses on trains – rumbled by. And I got to thinking… what about that time of my childhood, long ago? What about the Norfolk & Western Railway, now the Norfolk Southern Corporation (NS), and its ribbon of steel, that indelible metallic strip across the landscape from Norfolk, Virginia, to Cincinnati, Ohio, and the communities along the way, like this spot in McCoy? How have they fared?

I should go have a look, I thought to myself! And so a plan was hatched. I'd venture to Norfolk, to Milepost 0, the place where the famous Powhatan Arrow began its journey westward every morning, and trace as closely as possible the route it took to Cincinnati. I would follow the path of that defunct train and see how change had played on the communities along the route. I would metaphorically and metaphysically chase the Powhatan Arrow.

Foreword

Railroads incite passion and infatuation in people in ways other transportation media cannot match. Icons of our nation's industrial history, railroads fostered our nation's growth and expansion and became and still remain emblematic of the best our country ever produced.

One of the storied railroad companies, the Norfolk & Western Railway, emerged in the latter part of the 19th Century and quickly gained a reputation as one of the best managed, most profitable, and most innovative railroads in the country. Their main line from Norfolk, Virginia, to Cincinnati, Ohio, traversed an incredibly varied, scenic swath of the mid-Atlantic. Through a wholly owned subsidiary in Roanoke, Virginia, they built most of their own locomotives and rolling stock. Few lives in southern and southwestern Virginia, southern West Virginia, and southern Ohio, were not touched by the company.

From its earliest days, the Norfolk and Western (also "Norfolk & Western" and simply "N&W") Railway concentrated most of its effort and made most of its profits from carrying coal from the Appalachian coalfields either east to Norfolk for export or west to the Rust Belt cities of Cincinnati, Columbus, Cleveland, Pittsburgh, Youngstown, Detroit, and beyond. But like many of its competitors, it offered passenger service as well. Corporate pride ensured that the N&W's service would be a cut above the others.

Locomotives with colorful names like the Cavalier and the Pocahontas plied the main line from Norfolk to Cincinnati, but the premier train, the exemplar of corporate excellence, was the daytime streamliner, the Powhatan Arrow. Leaving Norfolk at 7:00 a.m. and arriving in Cincinnati at 10:45 p.m., with a parallel train moving in the other direction simultaneously, it was in its era the model of speed, efficiency, and elegance.

Beginning in 1946, the Powhatan Arrow was pulled by the magnificent Class J steam locomotives. Engineered and constructed in N&W's shop in Roanoke, the Class Js were widely considered the finest steam locomotives ever built. The Class Js were fast, efficient, reliable, and stunningly beautiful. Their legacy was crystallized in their fate, in that they superseded the end of the era of steam. By the late 1950s, steam locomotives bowed to the inevitable, the inexorable advancing technologies of modern diesel locomotives, and began vanishing from the nation's rails. N&W, as a coal-hauling railroad, was the last major company in the country to make the shift. But when the shift came, it was swift and irreversible. Of the 14 Class J locomotives built, a single specimen, the 611, avoided the terrible fate of the cutting torch and remains alive today.

After its last revenue run, the 611 was mothballed three times, interspersed with brief duty as a conveyance for excursion rides, the most recent run beginning in 2015. These runs were extremely popular with riders and watchers who lined the tracks in the thousands.

The corridor of the Powhatan Arrow is one of immense geological, economic, and cultural diversity. From the flat Tidewater to the rolling Piedmont to the mountainous Ridge and Valley regions in Virginia, the Allegheny Plateau of West Virginia, and the Ohio River Valley of West Virginia and Ohio, each region has its own racial and ethnic history and economic make-up, legacies of the wealth of the landscape and decisions of the people who settled in it.

This volume is mostly travelogue, but also part history, part living history, and part prognostications of the future. By the conveyances of car, motorcycle, bicycle, canoe, and even a smidgen of passenger railroad, the author followed the route of the ghost train, the Powhatan Arrow.

Chasing the Powhatan Arrow

A Travelogue in Economic Geography

7:00 a.m.

Norfolk

Mile 0

City on the world's greatest natural harbor – the Port of Hampton Roads. Gateway to the ocean playground that is Virginia Beach. Naval Base, Langley field, and many other military installations. Near Cape Henry, Jamestown, Williamsburg, Yorktown, other Colonial and Revolutionary landmarks. Extensive N. & W. coal and merchandise freight piers, including new $6,000,000 Pier "N," largest single-deck pier on the Atlantic Seaboard. Seafood prepared in the genuine Norfolk manner. *(From N&W Powhatan Arrow description of cities and points of interest.)*

Ostensibly, every travelogue is based around the notion of going from a proverbial "Point A" to another proverbial "Point B." So it was vexing to my soul that I couldn't physically locate "Point A," Milepost 0, the Norfolk Terminal Station. This was in spite of my best efforts, assisted by the lovely Jane Claytor Webster, on a beautiful day of exploration together as she tour-guided me around the sights and scenes of Norfolk, the city where she and her husband, Sam, had lived for four decades.

Jane is a trim, auburn-haired woman with contemporary stylish tastes who graciously offered her services in helping me launch my trip as I attempted to chase the long-extinct Powhatan Arrow from Norfolk to Cincinnati. She has an incredible pedigree, part of arguably Virginia's First Family of railroading. Her grandfather was W. Graham Claytor, Sr., a vice-president of Appalachian Power Company for whom Claytor Lake in Pulaski County is named. Her uncle was W. Graham Claytor, Jr., who was CEO of Southern Railway and Amtrak. Her father was Robert B. "Bob" Claytor who was CEO of the Norfolk & Western Railway and the first Chairman and CEO of the new Norfolk Southern which he oversaw the creation of effective June 1, 1982, in the merger of those two companies. Not only was she an eager, proactive participant in my explorations, she also served as my house-host, providing me a comfortable, attractive room in her spacious home, surrounded by blooming azaleas, rhododendron, and tall pines.

She drove as we traveled together in her late-model Volvo station wagon (Her personalized license plates read "RR FAM."). Her recollection, corroborated by others, was that the old station was east of town near the Elizabeth River, just east of where Interstate 264 crossed over from Chesapeake and Portsmouth, near the new Harbor Park baseball field.

We motored directly through downtown to the east side of the Berkley Bridge landing and along Waterside Drive, she doing the hard work of tolerating city traffic while I arched my neck looking at skyscrapers and construction cranes. We passed underneath the Interstate where Harbor Field, home of the Norfolk Tides, the Triple-A farm team of the Baltimore Orioles, loomed ahead of us. A "Tide" light rail train glided silently before us. There was construction all around, some that appeared to be part of the Tide and other relating to buildings or parking lots.

The Norfolk Terminal Station was a shared facility between the Norfolk & Western and Virginian Railways. From photos of it, it was more a skyscraper than a traditional terminal, with a full eight stories of shared office spaces. It was built in bright red brick after an October 13, 1909 fire destroyed the original wooden station. It opened for business in 1912 with offices in the upper floors and passenger services at the ground floor. By 1959, the N&W had absorbed the Virginian. But with the decline in passenger service, the station was demolished in 1963. Still, I had hopes of finding a few of its skeleton bones lying about on the ground.

Nothing we found looked like a train station site, a footer, or anything recognizable. It bothered me that on the 676.6-mile course I planned to follow, finding "Mile 0" was not to be possible.

So we did what we thought might be the next best thing – drove around the baseball field to the new, modern Amtrak station on the other side. It was staffed by a young African American man who said he was transferred there from someplace else and knew nothing about the history of Norfolk & Western's passenger program. It probably ended before he was born. In complete contrast to the constant frenzy of the international airports of cities the size and importance of Norfolk, the Amtrak station was so silent you could hear a grasshopper fart, as deathly quiet as a small-town morgue. There were only two arrivals and departures each day, all headed to Petersburg and Richmond with options to other destinations from there. I had to rap on the glass to even roust him from the inner sanctum to the customer service window.

The complex of waterways that comprise Hampton Roads cannot be quickly grasped. (More accurately, it should be "Hampton Roadstead" as a "roadstead" is a sheltered body of water outside a harbor where ships can stage awaiting their turn to port.) Deemed by many the finest deep-water port in the world, the roads is comprised of principally the James River, but to a lesser degree the Elizabeth River and its three branches, the Nansemond River, the Lafayette River, and several others, as they converge on the Chesapeake Bay. So the current Amtrak route as far as Petersburg follows the route of the Powhatan Arrow, leaving the eastern terminus metropolis headed not west or north but actually southward over twin draw-bridges over the East Branch of the Elizabeth for several miles before turning right, westward, towards Suffolk. But my tracing of that route would have to wait while I explored Norfolk.

Jane Claytor Webster

Human activity at the Amtrak station was bare, but the outside landing where we explored was heavy with the noises of traffic and industrialization. Jane and I took ceremonial photos of each other, admired the bizarre sculptures, and then drove northward along the eastern perimeter of her city to the northern edge, the shoreline of the lower Chesapeake Bay and through the community of Ocean View, with its seashore-themed murals and condos. We drove to the extreme northwestern edge of the city on Willoughby Spit and back around to Willoughby Bay where she pointed out the many naval ships moored at the U. S. Naval Base, the largest naval facility in the world.

We continued over the Lafayette River Bridge, past the campus of Old Dominion University, and towards an area of great interest for me – the Lambert's Point coal staging facility. I had seen aerial photos in books and magazines and the sheer size of it was staggering. This is the destination of all the hundreds of thousands to millions of coal cars headed eastward through my home region of Southwest Virginia for nearly 130 years.

Lambert's Point was named for Thomas Lambert, who acquired the land by virtue of being the first person who wanted it. English settlers arrived in three little ships in 1607 and established a colony twenty miles away, upstream on a small island they named Jamestown. Almost 30 years later, young Thomas patented 100 acres and cleverly named the protrusion into the east side of the Elizabeth River after himself.

We can assume that not much of anything happened there for around 250 years while it waited for William Mahone, a man I'll tell you more about soon, to supervise the construction of a railroad from Norfolk to Petersburg which he imaginatively named the Norfolk and Petersburg Railroad. Mahone completed by 1858 a trio of engineering marvels of the day bridging both the Eastern and Southern Branches of the Elizabeth River and negotiating across the Great Dismal Swamp along with several other swamps we need to assume were less great and less dismal on the way to Petersburg, devising an ingenious method of swamping thousands of cypress tree trunks to form a corduroy surface upon which to lay the tracks. It is difficult for me to fathom enormous destruction of tens of thousands of cypress trees and the immense work in laying them trunk-to-trunk over tens of miles of fetid swampland. But their work was invaluable, as this stretch of rail is still in use today.

Once to Petersburg, connections could be made northward to Richmond, southward to the Carolinas, and notably for me, westward to Lynchburg on the South Side Rail Road (not "Southside Railroad," I'm told) and on the Virginia and Tennessee Railroad to Bristol.

The Norfolk and Petersburg Railroad, like most others of the era, carried a variety of cargo materials along with passengers and played an instrumental role in the Civil War. But don't forget, it terminated near downtown Norfolk, not a few miles north at Lambert's Point.

Immediately the new railroad brought new prosperity to what was becoming Virginia's primary port in Norfolk, until the unpleasantness of the Civil War which put a damper on things for a few years. Promptly after the war Mahone managed to gain control of all three railroads, renaming the new corporation the Atlantic, Mississippi, and Ohio (AM&O) Railroad, indicating his vision that the sky was the limit, so to speak, with Norfolk representing the easternmost terminus and likely recipient of the commerce and wealth the railroad would direct its way.

It cannot be overstated how crippling the damage was to the infrastructure of the Confederate states inflicted by the war. On a more positive note, significantly greater knowledge became available as to the vast coal resources in far southwest Virginia and southern West Virginia. The Financial Panic of 1873 ripped away control of the AM&O from Mahone and for several years it operated under receivership. By 1881, it was placed at auction where Mahone was outbid. The new owners, Philadelphia financiers E. W. Clark & Co., renamed the line the Norfolk & Western and placed Frederick Kimball in charge. Kimball immediately pushed through a new line from the point where the AM&O had reached the New River just east of Radford northward along the river to reach the coal resource areas. Norfolk welcomed the first carload of coal in 1883 at their Eastern Branch Terminal. Finally, by 1886, coal operations moved to Lambert's Point where the first of many facilities for loading coal onto awaiting ships were constructed.

Jane and I drove a semi-circle around the facility at Lambert's Point, cordoned off with a chain-link fence and ominous warning signs. Not wanting to risk any good relations I hoped to establish with the folks at the headquarters of Norfolk Southern, we stayed where we belonged.

As IRONIES GO, Norfolk's is a whopper.

Norfolk is sinking. Seas are rising. The world is getting warmer, and it's mostly due to anthropogenic activities, principally burning fossil fuels, especially coal. Norfolk hosts the largest coal port in the world. Hmmm.

Norfolk has dealt with issues before; this is just one more issue for one of Virginia's largest and most important cities. The city's motto is "Crescas," Latin for "Thou shalt grow." What's a bit of flooding compared with what Norfolk's been through in the past? Turns out, a lot.

For example, in 1776, seventy years after the city's incorporation, the English navy under the command of Lord Dunmore, shelled the defenseless community of 1,200 buildings for more than eight hours, destroying 800 of them. Dunmore had only three ships, but you apparently can do one helluva lot of damage if you've got all day to do it and with nobody firing back. What Dunmore didn't destroy, the patriots took down themselves, torching the others two months later, apparently to keep what was left out of enemy hands. I don't imagine that went over well with the homeowners who survived the first onslaught. Or the realtors who found there was no longer any inventory.

After the war, plucky Norfolkers (Today's word is demonym, the name used for people who live in a particular place. Here it's either Norfolkers or Norfolkians. Don't let your mom hear you practice pronouncing "Norfolkers". Incidentally, many Norfolkers scarcely pronounce the "r" calling their city a subdued "NAW-fawk". Local joke: "We don't smoke, we don't drink, Norfolk, Norfolk!) spent the next couple of decades rebuilding the city only to see much of it burn to the ground again in 1804. Three hundred buildings were lost in that fire. It was worth rebuilding, apparently, as it is located on one of the world's finest natural harbors. The city rebounded.

Somehow the city managed to weather the War of 1812 unscathed, but the 1820s brought a widespread recession across the nation, particularly the South. Almost from the beginning of English settlement in the new world just upstream at Jamestown in 1607, tobacco had been the most significant cash crop in the region, and by the 1800s, the soils were largely depleted of nutrients. So hundreds of citizens of the city, at that time with a population of around 9,000, left for perceived better opportunities.

Again the city rebounded.

The 1850 census counted over 14,000 residents, most of whom found work on the bustling port. But on June 7, 1855, a ship arriving from the West Indies brought the yellow fever virus. A month later, a machinist died of the disease, and soon thereafter dozens were dying every day. An estimated 5,000 citizens of Norfolk and nearby Portsmouth caught the disease and 3,200 eventually died from it. Thousands more fled to escape it, some permanently.

Again the city rebounded.

Like many places in the South, Norfolk has had a complicated history with slavery. Norfolk was a busy slave port and by the outbreak of the Civil War, more than 7,500 slaves toiled away in Norfolk city and the surrounding county. Yet native son Joseph Jenkins Roberts helped establish the new colony of Liberia on the coast of Africa to "repatriate" free blacks, ostensibly improving their lives by sending them back to their homeland. Roberts became the fledgling nation's first president. While many blacks did move back to Africa, most did not, preferring to stay in their new country in spite of its oppression.

Like most Southern people in slave-owning states, in 1861 Norfolk's citizens voted for Virginia's secession. As an important coastal city, Norfolk was destined for conflict, and it arrived on March 8 and 9, 1862, with a fusillade of shells barely a year after the war began. That's when the Battle of Hampton Roads ensued, which history would prove not to be the war's deadliest battle but one of the most important, literally changing the course of naval history forever.

HERE'S A SHORT VERSION of that story of naval history.

A mere week after Confederates fired on Fort Sumter in Charleston, South Carolina, President Abraham Lincoln declared that the United States Navy would blockade the entirety of the Confederacy. At the time, the Navy faced a daunting task indeed! It had 42 ships and needed to patrol 3,500 miles of coastline along the Atlantic and Gulf of Mexico, with 12 major ports, including Norfolk.

The enormous industrial capability of the North came into play and dozens of ships began emerging from its shipbuilders. They were of similar designs of multiple masts, sails, and cannons, to what naval shipbuilders had produced for decades, with a curious, special exception.

Prior to the war, just as the Union held Fort Sumter in South Carolina, it also held the Gosport Navy Yard in Portsmouth, across the Elizabeth River from Norfolk. As Virginia seceded from the Union, naval commanders in Washington sent orders to evacuate all federal military bases, including Gosport (pre-cursor to the Norfolk Naval Shipyard). Anchored at the base was the Merrimack, a modern ship of 275 foot length, equipped with both sails and a steam boiler, commissioned in 1855, and named for the Merrimack River near where she was built at the Boston Navy Yard in Massachusetts. The night before Union commanders were to sail her northward to prepare for wartime duty, the secessionists had sunk small boats in the channel between Sewell Point (a few miles north of Lambert's Point) and Craney Island, blocking her evacuation. So the U. S. Navy burned her to the waterline and then sank her to avoid having her fall into the new enemy's hands.

Not a year later in February, 1862, Confederates raised and rebuilt her, this time with a covering of iron plates. The Merrimack, now renamed the "Virginia" by the Confederate navy, steamed into the harbor to attack blockading ships. On March 8, 1862, she was able to sink the USS Congress and the USS Cumberland and was on her way to destroy the USS Minnesota when darkness intervened. The Virginia's fatal blow to the Cumberland was delivered by ramming her, an action that might have taken the Virginia to the bottom of the bay herself, had her ram not broken off as the Union ship sank.

The next day, with eerie simultaneity, the Virginia found a new enemy in her way, one scarcely recognizable as a warship, but clearly the most potent weapon ever developed. Awaiting her was the peculiar, devilishly deadly USS Monitor.

Swedish inventor John Ericsson had immigrated to America and was almost 60 years of age when the U.S. Navy commissioned him to build an ironclad ship. Overseeing the construction of the Monitor in New York, which went from plans to sea trials in a mere 100 days, Ericsson established himself as one of the most influential mechanical engineers in history. The Monitor was completely unlike every other ship ever invented. At 179 feet, it was smaller and lighter than the Virginia, and it sat low in the water, almost flat, propelled by a single steam-boiler driven propeller and notably no sails. Amidship above the hull was a large, rotating cylindrical gun turret, with a pair of cannons inside. The turret was an easy target, but it was heavily fortified. There was nothing else to shoot except the tiny pilot house.

The two revolutionary warships fought for three hours with neither doing significant damage to the other. Nevertheless, the battle was fierce! Witnesses described the ships' proximity as "close range," but how close is close? It's like asking how tall a tall building is. Regardless, sailors on the lumbering ironclad ships must have been terrified by the concussion of large shells being blasted from their guns and enemy shells smashing into the iron plates of their own. Picture yourself inside the Virginia, furiously loading the cannons with gunpowder and cannonballs, with an enemy shell striking the Virginia's iron cladding a few feet away. Firing back, your own cannon's terrible explosive sound ricocheted through your vessel. I can't imagine that a single eardrum survived intact.

The battle ended when the Monitor's pilot house was hit, wounding its captain, blowing shrapnel into his face and eyes, and temporarily blinding him.

The North actually had more casualties in the Battle of Hampton Roads, with 261 lost compared with 78 Confederate deaths, but both sides claimed victory. Ironically, neither ironclad ever fought again. The Confederates destroyed the Virginia deliberately two months later lest she re-enter Union hands. The Monitor, a brilliant warship in calm waters, was no match for the tempestuous Atlantic Ocean. She had nearly sank two days before the battle on her way from New York and then on Christmas Eve, 1862, before her first birthday, she sank in a storm during transport farther south off the coast of North Carolina's Cape Hatteras. Her remains were not found until 1973.

The Monitor's impact upon the world's navies was significant and instantaneous. From that point on, neither England, Spain, nor France ever again built wooden warships, and everything that came from their shipbuilders for decades employed the shallow draft, heavy armament, swivel cannon design that the original Monitor inspired.

In May, 1862, Norfolk's mayor surrendered the city to the overwhelming Union army which placed it under martial law for the rest of the war. Thousands of slaves used that opportunity to escape captivity, some staying as free people in Norfolk and some fleeing northward. In short order, a separate, black society emerged in Norfolk with businesses, churches, and schools. Fortunately, Norfolk escaped the terrible fate of Petersburg and Richmond, which by April, 1865, mostly lay in steaming, smoking piles of rubble.

FORTY YEARS LATER, Americans were ready to party again and planning got underway for the tricentennial of the 1607 founding of Jamestown. Because the real location of Jamestown was remote and mostly abandoned, Norfolk was named the site of the 1907 Jamestown Exposition. It opened on April 26, 1907 exactly 300 years after Admiral Christopher Newport landed at Jamestown.

The Exposition was a grand failure in most tangible ways. It never drew the audiences the promoters had projected, and it lost millions of dollars. However, it put Norfolk "on the map," so to speak, and drew naval planners' attention back to its fabulous harbor. As world war appeared on the horizon, the U.S. Navy began pouring millions of dollars into Sewell Point to develop the Naval Station Norfolk. Meanwhile, the new Virginian Railway – we'll talk more about that later – built expansive coal piers nearby, competing with the Norfolk & Western's port at Lambert Point. The Naval Station Norfolk would soon become the largest naval complex in the world.

Nothing particularly noteworthy happened in Norfolk for the next fifty years or so, other than the two World Wars and the Great Depression, which of course impacted everyone. But commerce was good and Norfolk's population grew from 67,000 in 1900 to its zenith of more than 300,000 in 1960.

Two things helped de-centralize the city and the region beginning in the 1950s and continuing through the 1970s. First, the Supreme Court ruled that segregated public schools were unconstitutional, thus mandating integration. In 1959, seventeen black children began attending six formerly all-white schools. Second, superhighways, primarily in the Eisenhower Interstate Highway System, dramatically improved mobility throughout the Hampton Roads region. Norfolk, Portsmouth, Newport News, Hampton, and Virginia Beach blended into a single metropolis. "White flight" ensued, as many Caucasians fled the inner cities and established suburban communities. By 2000, the population within Norfolk's city limits had dropped to 234,000 residents.

Norfolk's city leaders fought to keep the economy viable, working to re-establish and gentrify the waterfront and downtown. Historic retail corridor, Granby Street, was revitalized, as were many of the decaying piers and port warehouses, some turned into upscale shopping areas. The Norfolk Scope convention and sports complex opened in 1971 which at the time was the second-largest public complex in the state (Note: Number 1 was the Pentagon.). The Harbor Park baseball stadium opened in 1993, and Nauticus, the National Maritime Center, opened in 1994.

Norfolk Scope

Today the U. S. Department of Defense is the city's top employer, followed by Sentara Healthcare, the public school system, and Old Dominion University. Smithfield Foods, Dollar Tree, and the Norfolk Southern Corporation are headquartered in Norfolk. The latter resulted from the merger of the Norfolk & Western Railway and the Southern Railway in 1982. NS built its headquarters skyscraper in downtown, after consolidating operations from the former's headquarters in Roanoke and the latter's headquarters in Washington, D.C. in 1986, much to the consternation of both cities, especially Roanoke. But that's a story for a later chapter.

But what I want to tell you about is the encroaching Atlantic Ocean.

We all know that the planet is getting warmer and has been for centuries, due largely to the massive amounts of greenhouse gasses produced into the atmosphere since the dawn of the Industrial Age. Rising global temperatures turn more Arctic and Antarctic ice into seawater, thus raising sea level overall. The colder the climate of the world, the more water is trapped in ice and the lower the sea level; the warmer it is, the higher sea level. Estimates by this century's end are anywhere from one foot to three feet higher sea level. One foot may not seem like much, but there's another problem.

In the mid-Atlantic coastal areas, and in particular the ports dotting the Chesapeake Bay, the ground itself is subsiding. That's right, good old terra firma turns out not to be that firma. This is caused primarily by two factors, one caused by humans and the other purely natural. First, much sinking along the Atlantic coast is caused by water withdrawals, mined groundwater from underground aquifers. When you pump out the water, the ground sinks. This is most acute in Florida and Louisiana and could be mitigated with reductions of that activity. The second factor is strictly natural, millennia old, and has no cure.

Glaciers carved New York's Finger Lakes, as well as many of the hundreds of other lakes across the state and into New England. Mid-state Pennsylvania was the southernmost extension of the glaciers. Virginia has only one natural lake and West Virginia has two, neither of which were formed by glaciers. Other "lakes" are actually reservoirs, watercourses that have been dammed.

As the glaciers retreated, the weight was released, and the mantle began to settle and return to its previous thickness. Ergo, the land south of the glacier's terminus, surrounding the bay, began to subside. This phenomenon may continue for hundreds, perhaps even thousands more years. This may account for another six inches or so before the current century's end.

Rising seas and sinking land, when combined with high tides and storms, produces massive flooding that has already occurred and will only get worse.

What's already happening in Norfolk is the loss of several piers and during high-water events the swamping of streets and neighborhoods and the inundation of lots of basements. Insurance companies are studying the risk, and homeowners insurance is increasingly expensive and difficult to purchase.

Norfolkers have seen a couple of wars up close and personal, several recessions, racial strife, pestilence, and white flight. From all, the great city has overcome. Rising seas might become Norfolk's Achilles' heel, the one from which it may not ever fully recover. Water is the lifeblood of the area, but if a Katrina-intensity storm arrives with a high tide, subsiding land, and rising seas, the damage might be unrecoverable. And you can at least partially blame all that coal shipped out of there.

Jane and I headed to her beautiful white house hidden amongst tall pines on the Lafayette River inlet just south of Sewell Point.

THE NEXT DAY, another beautiful day I might add, I sought out some folks that I thought might know some answers about Norfolk's vulnerability: Greg Steele and Susan Conner at the Norfolk office of the Army Corps of Engineers.

Greg is the Chief of the Water Resources Division at the Army Corps of Engineers in Norfolk. His office is on the third floor of a building on the edge of the water, alongside the historic Fort Norfolk. Because of the work going on there, the building has a lot of security. I had to show my driver's license to an outside guard at the parking lot and a second guard at the front desk in order to simply be admitted into the building. Even at that, I had to be escorted from the lobby to his office. He was waiting for me with Susan, a coworker who was a biologist.

Greg was kind enough to begin our conversation with an overview of his organization. He said, "We are the nation's public engineering firm. We provide engineering support and combat engineering support. We have a military program requirement to support the troops, and we have a civil works component as well, supporting states, localities, and non-governmental organizations. Susan and I work in our civil works world.

"We are civilians, working for the Department of Defense. My boss is a colonel in the army. He has two deputies, one military and one civilian. The Corps sustains a workforce of about 25,000 or 30,000 people worldwide. Of that, perhaps 1,000 are in the military. A lot of people don't realize when they interact with us, particularly on the civil side, is that we are actually structured like an architectural and engineering firm. We are a project-funded organization. We need projects that are funded by Congress as well as local sponsors. We do not have a sales department; in fact sales is a bit frowned upon. We are not looking for a profit. But we need a certain workload so that we don't have to lay off people.

"We are not a well-loved organization. People who want to do something on the coastline, for example, have to get approval from us.

"Here's an example of something we have done recently. We got an authorization to study the Lynnhaven River and do environmental restoration and provide aquatic vegetation and wetlands restoration. It ended up being about a $35 million to $38 million project. Congress got our report and then authorized us to actually construct that project. So we do both the analysis and fulfillment. I head up a division that has planning, operations, and regulatory functions. It is all water resources. Whatever touches water or deals with water will come through my office."

Greg and Susan dealt with the Chesapeake Bay and the rivers that feed into it, the York River, the Rappahannock River, the James River, the lower Bay, and the Blackwater, Nottoway area.

We began to speak about my interests in being there: community success, resiliency, and sustainability. Greg said, "Honestly, I think fundamentally what adds resiliency here in Hampton Roads and everywhere is a general understanding of the interrelated dependencies of communities, people, businesses, and resources. When groups or communities are myopic they tend not to have that resiliency. They need to understand how they fit into the bigger network, the living fabric of this community. That is what's happening here, particularly with the threat of sea level rise."

Now that we were getting to the crux of the matter, I asked. "How bad is it? How bad is it going to get, and when?"

He said, "People always ask for a number. As is always the case, there is some uncertainty. When you look at hurricane tracks you see a cone that tries to encompass all of the potential directions it might go. We have a cone of sea level rise. We know that we will see impacts within a certain range. Here in Hampton Roads proper, within this area, we have two problems. First, we have sea level rise impacts. We also have subsidence. This is like salt on the wound. They are happening at almost equivalent rates. It is almost 50-50.

"The relative land elevations are subsiding. Everything is relatively lowering from that subsidence impact. The biggest reason is groundwater withdrawal."

I said, "I thought the biggest factor was the ongoing subsidence after the retreat of the glaciers from the last Ice Age."

He said, "If anything, you might think that there was a certain lift component, depending upon the soil properties. Everything that we have looked at recently shows that the lack of sufficient groundwater recharge is the biggest driver in the regional impact of subsidence. This is based on primarily industrial ground water usage. Many companies simply sink a well and draw out thousands upon thousands of gallons of water. The rate at which it is replenishing naturally is insufficient."

I said, "Can't you simply go to these guys and say, 'We need you to stop doing that?'"

He said, "They may be an economic driver in that community. That is the whole point. We help them look for other technologies and other ways of accomplishing what they need to accomplish. That may involve reuse."

I said, "This seems analogous to me about the extraction of coal in the coalfields. The resource has always been there, so we might as well extract and use it. Groundwater is useful and so we might as well use it. It seems to me that that thinking has been pervasive. As a species we really do not fully understand the proper ways to evaluate the greater ramifications of doing something like that. When you blow off the top of the mountain to get a few years of coal and the mountain is destroyed forever, the people who do that are not really thinking about the long-term ramifications to stormwater, streams, floods, biological resources, aquatic life, and even the people who live in those areas."

"That's right," he said.

"I see construction cranes all over Norfolk. I get the impression that people are ambivalent about this crisis," I continued.

Susan said, "I think the people here and the local governments have turned around to a great degree in the last three to five years and are taking this more seriously. The public will always be a bit behind. People think of this as a 50 year to 100 year threat rather than something that is imminent. I think it is incumbent upon the government to take this seriously, and I think that it is. It is a long-term issue, and we have time to deal with it. It doesn't mean that construction stops. It means that we start looking at the long-term trends that we need to implement in order to get to where we need to go."

Greg agreed, "The great thing is that we have time to plan for it. The horrible thing is that we have time to plan for it. Long-term solutions for land-use and things of that nature are not politically expedient. So it takes concerted leadership to make decisions that will posture ourselves for 50, 60, or 70 years from now when it is an issue. We don't want to wait for 40 or 50 years before we start doing things."

Susan said, "I think Norfolk is more progressive than other coastal cities and other areas. The city in fact has a chief resiliency officer. You don't see that in every city. Storms cause an imminent threat and gather a lot of attention and potentially a lot of money to the issue."

He said, "We have many problems. Storms. Sea level rise. Loss of ecosystems. We have lost some of the high functionality that we once saw in the bay. This once was the most productive oyster system in the world."

I had done some reading about the oyster depletion problem. I learned that when the settlers arrived, the Chesapeake Bay hosted an abundance that was difficult to fathom. The oysters were huge, too, often three to four times larger than those in England. The habitat was ideal. The depth was mostly shallow and the forests alongside the bay retarded erosion that could damage their gills. Each oyster acts as a tiny pollution treatment plant, filtering organisms and keeping the waters pristine and clear. It was said that a boater could see the bottom of the bay in twenty feet of water. The European settlers began eating the oysters voraciously. They waded into the water or used rakes from boats. They were mostly eaten in the winter months, supplementing scarcer foods.

By the mid 1880s, over 20 million bushels of oysters were taken annually. The delicate flavor made them a worldwide delicacy, but the shells were in demand as well for mortar and plaster for buildings and roads, for agricultural lime for fertilizer, and grit in chicken feed. People made fortunes trading oysters and shells. The take rapidly exceeded the ability of the resource to regenerate. Worse, because the shells were not being returned, new oysters found a less suitable environment. By the late 1900s, the annual catch had fallen to 2 percent of its peak.

Because the filtering capability of the oysters was gone and because of increasing population around the bay, the bay became more polluted. Where the bay was once dominated by bottom dwelling species like oysters, today it is dominated by microscopic life suspended in the water.

Greg continued, interrupting my reverie, "Norfolk really has no more developable land. Almost anything that gets built now is on redeveloped land. So density is an issue. We are a coastal city and so storms will always be a risk. We have been lucky. Hurricane Sandy did some damage, but it did much worse damage north of here. Our last really bad storm here was in the 1950s. It is not a matter of 'if' but 'when.'

"The nor'easters are really our biggest issue as far as storms are concerned. They stay and stay, and cause hours of flooding. They actually shut down entire localities for hours. Floods here are slow moving and pervasive. There is significant standing water all over the place, over the roadways and in basements."

Susan said, "In the last one, there was water all the way up to the door of this building. It is 10 feet above the bay. No water got inside, but it did get inside other buildings. Sometimes it will stay inside for as long as a complete tidal cycle. It can be 12 to 24 hours. Even 2 feet of water is impassable. That can happen to some streets around here in simple rainfall events."

He said, "What makes the nor'easter so bad is that we get a combination of sea level rise, land subsistence, high winds, lots of rain, and tides."

I said, "What is the worst case you can envision? Will you need to abandon some neighborhoods? Will build sea walls need to be built?"

She said, "We have a Norfolk flood risk study that we just kicked off. It looks at the entire city. There was a study along the entire East Coast that was funded with money that came forth after Hurricane Sandy. Norfolk is one of nine study areas. We are trying to look comprehensively at what all those solutions might be. The team is definitely focusing less on sea walls and levees and more on natural and nature-based features.

"There is a lot of hardened shoreline here, unlike New Orleans which is more than 100 miles from the Gulf of Mexico. We do not have a delta here. We are looking at more progressive alternatives. We may be thinking about moving things to fingers of higher ground and letting the lower ground trend back towards what it was. We are looking at restoring original floodplain areas.

"That might mean abandoning some structures. If I were to guess, I don't think we will see full-scale migrations out of communities and neighborhoods, but we are looking at a whole suite of opportunities to do things differently."

Greg said, "The answer to your question then is 'yes.' We do see some people abandoning property. We see some levee building. People will be adapting. All of those things are part of the answer. We know that some areas will get inundated more.

"The clarion call at least for local governments and the communities is not looking at this so much as a problem but as an opportunity. We live with water. That is part of our biology here. We ask ourselves how we can effectively live so close to the water. We are not about fighting the water. It is living with the water. We are looking at what makes sense for the communities."

I asked him if there were any naysayers, people who just didn't believe any of it.

He said, "Yes. The benefit is that we don't talk about the 'why.' We don't blame Norfolk Southern or the coal industry. The fact of the matter is that the sea level is rising. It doesn't do us any good to blame anybody."

She said, "In the scientific, academic, and political and agency communities, there are no naysayers. Sometimes we like to call it 'recurring flooding' rather than sea level rise. It is the same thing. The fact is that it is flooding in Norfolk, it is flooding more often, and it is flooding with more duration. That is what we need to acknowledge. Our job isn't to try to save it from certain amounts of greenhouse gas omissions. The climate scientists deal with that. We have a boundary we think the sea is going to (remain in) during our planning horizon. We look at things that we can recommend and do to address that and achieve resilience.

"We hear from the city's sustainability official that it doesn't help us to keep the city dry if nobody lives in it. We need to keep Norfolk a good place to live."

I thanked my hosts for their time and descended to the lobby. I realized an inconvenient truth: barring the implementation of a radical program to geo-engineer the earth's climate, the die has already been cast, and it is a virtual lock that sea levels are going to rise and keep rising for decades and will likely stay high – who knows?, 5 feet, 20 feet, or even 50 feet higher than today – for hundreds if not thousands of years, inundating significant portions of Norfolk and all our coastal cities. The impact will be inestimable.

I emerged outside to another gorgeous day and wandered around the whitewashed buildings of the old Fort Norfolk, built under congressional authorization by President George Washington in 1795 to protect the vital harbor.

WITH HER FAMILIAL CONNECTIONS, Jane had graciously offered to set up an appointment for me to meet with a former CEO of Norfolk Southern, David Goode, at the corporation's exquisite office tower in downtown. Goode was CEO from 1992 until 2005 and holds the dubious distinction of being the guy who shut down Norfolk Southern's steam excursion program that ran at that time. So I drove back into the city center and found a place to park for our meeting.

Today's Norfolk Southern is an amalgamation of between 300 and 400 once separate, predecessor railroads. The earliest history of worldwide railroading began in England when in 1825, George Stephenson perfected his "locomotion" steam powered engines to pull trains that were at the time on rails but drawn by horses. The idea spread almost immediately to the United States when in 1827, the Baltimore and Ohio Railroad was chartered. It took 26 years for that train to reach Wheeling, Virginia (but in West Virginia now, after that state formed in 1863).

Meanwhile, a locomotive named the Best Friend of Charleston, built in New York for the South Carolina Canal and Rail Road Company, took its inaugural run on Christmas Day, 1830. This is the starting point of the Southern Railway and thus the modern Norfolk Southern Corporation. The Best Friend of Charleston was able to achieve two historic milestones. First, it took its passengers on the ride of their lives, at an astounding 15 to 25 miles per hour. Second, it was the first locomotive to explode and fatally wound its crew. Accounts of the day say the fireman, tired of listening to the persistent, annoying wail of the pressure relief valve, affixed it shut and the pressure soon overwhelmed the boiler. He'd never do that again!

True to my quest, I focused most of my attention not on the Southern Railway but the Norfolk & Western, since the companies hadn't merged by the era of the Powhatan Arrow.

In the years after 1830, it was thought that the railroads would supplement the various roads and canals around the nation rather than supplant them. Here in Virginia, city leaders in Lynchburg planned a new railroad westward, naming it the L&NR, to stretch from Lynchburg to the New River. Note that this was before the Norfolk and Petersburg Railroad and the South Side Rail Road. The thinking in Lynchburg was that materials could transport between Lynchburg and the coast via the James River and Kanawha Canal, but to go farther they needed a railroad. I'll tell you more about the canal when we reach Lynchburg.

By the 1830s, financing and construction techniques for canals and roads were common. There were thousands of miles of roads and 1,500 miles of canals. Public funding was necessary for the railroads, along with rights of way, which most communities eagerly supplied, understanding the economic benefits.

The economic and political realities of the day prevented the L&NR from ever being constructed, but by 1835, another attempt was made to go westward, and the Lynchburg and Tennessee (L&T) was proposed. Not a single spike was laid until 1849, at which time the General Assembly renamed it the Virginia and Tennessee Railroad (V&T). It took six years to complete it, but by the late 1850s, the line had stretched through Salem, Christiansburg, Wytheville, and Abingdon and had reached Bristol, spreading prosperity along the way. Neither Roanoke nor Radford existed at that time; they were products of the train era.

Meanwhile, by 1854 the South Side Rail Road reached from Petersburg to Lynchburg, and by 1858 the Norfolk and Petersburg Railroad connected those two cities. So by the outbreak of the Civil War, railroad tracks stretched all the way from Norfolk to Bristol, providing carriage that would greatly benefit the Confederate war effort and would represent a constant target for the Union.

After the war ended William Mahone located the corporate offices of his AM&O to Lynchburg, along with principal operations. Assisted by his spirited wife Otelia, Mahone oversaw an ambitious program of renewal and improvement to the line, along with the plotting of several new towns and rebuilding of many stations destroyed during the war.

After Mahone lost control of the railroad and it emerged as the Norfolk & Western Railway, Frederick Kimball decided that a tiny village named Big Lick in the Roanoke River Valley seven miles east of Salem would be the best place for their operations. So they renamed the place Roanoke and moved their headquarters, maintenance facilities, and manufacturing operations there. Their reasons were many, principally that the Shenandoah Valley Railroad, extending southward from Hagerstown, MD, would join the N&W there, and that Roanoke boasted considerable suitable flat land for railroad operations.

Kimball, a partner in E. W. Clark & Co., became First Vice President of the new N&W and eventually President. He was a civil engineer by education and had a keen interest in geology. Aware of the massive coal reserves in the Pocahontas coalfields of western Virginia and southern West Virginia and through a combination of new tracks and acquisitions of existing lines, in 1882 he spearheaded a route along the western side of the New River from near Radford through Pulaski and Giles counties in Virginia and Mercer County in West Virginia reaching a village called Higginbotham's Summit, then renamed Blue-

David Goode

field. Rails rapidly reached a multitude of the Pocahontas Coal Field's remote hollows and a black gold rush was on. Coal camps, tipples, coke ovens, stores, and churches burst forth with a rapidity of a spring flowering and coal almost instantaneously became the nascent N&W's largest commodity. By the turn of the 20th Century, Norfolk was the nation's leading exporting coal port.

Under Kimball's leadership, the N&W quickly gained a reputation for being a top-notch, efficient, and well-managed operation, with the finest rolling stock and most meticulous maintenance standards in the world. Notably, they made much of their own equipment at their own Roanoke Shops, which between 1884 and 1953 produced 447 steam locomotives. The N&W continued to operate profitably though two world wars and the Great Depression, hauling principally coal, but also general commodities and passengers. By the late 1930s, the N&W with its focus on quality and corporate image, planned the stunning Class J locomotives, designed specifically to power passenger trains along its primary route from Norfolk to Cincinnati. From 1941 until 1950, fourteen were built, numbered from 600 to 613, of which a single one, the 611, is still in existence. The 611 will play an essential role in my journey. These trains were numbered but also named. The Pocahontas. The Cavalier. And of course the Powhatan Arrow.

A route map of the N&W dating from 1948 shows a main artery

from Norfolk to Cincinnati. There were important spurs from Lynch-burg south to Durham, Roanoke south to Winston-Salem and north to Hagerstown, Radford west to Bristol, and Portsmouth, OH, north to Columbus, with dozens of smaller capillaries spreading throughout the coalfields.

In 1980, the N&W joined into a marriage of equals with Southern Railway, and after consideration of literally hundreds of new names selected Norfolk Southern (NS). In 1999, it absorbed much of Conrail, increasing its size by half.

Throughout its history, the Norfolk & Western had a dramatic and I think mostly positive impact on the communities through which it passed. It had its hand in almost every aspect of commerce, and it made many communities and broke others. I suspect that if you handed a piece of paper to 50 people throughout central and western Virginia in the 1960s and asked them to name a corporation they were familiar with, the N&W would be on virtually every list.

NS built its headquarters in Norfolk in the building where I was headed. I entered the lobby and went through security in preparation for my elevation to one of the upper floors of their magnificent 21 story skyscraper. I was escorted by one of David Goode's assistants to his palatial office with a commanding view of the harbor. It was filled with books, memorabilia, and artifacts of railroading.

DAVID GOODE GREETED ME wearing a black sport shirt, a tan sport jacket, and wire rimmed glasses. He was 75 years old and grew up in the Roanoke suburb of Vinton. He was educated at Duke University and Harvard Law School where he earned his JD in 1965. For most of our conversation, we were joined by Jane and NS's historical archivist Jennifer McDaid.

As we got acquainted, David told me about the recent succession of leadership since the merger of N&W with the Southern Railway in 1982, largely engineered from the N&W side by Jane's father Bob Clay-tor. David told me, "Jane's dad was succeeded by Arnold McKinnon (in 1987), then me, and then Wick Moorman (in 2006). Wick recently retired and now Jim Squires is in charge. Since 1982, there were only four chairmen, now five.

"We had this building built for us. In 1982 when the companies merged, we moved into another building here (in Norfolk) until this one was built."

I asked about current business at the railroad company he used to run.

He said, "We are in a period of huge transition. Everybody knew there would be an end to coal someday. My perception is that it occurred much more suddenly than (our corporate leadership) anticipated. And that has forced the company into a major transition.

"The company, on the Southern Railway side, traces its roots back to the Best Friend of Charleston railroad back in the 1830s. So we are more than 175 years old.

"With that many years of history, we should not look for its demise simply because of the decline of the coal industry. Companies like this always have to transition. Everything Amazon sells has to be transported somehow. These days, there are typically three or four different ways. Virtually everything that is sold on the Internet this week will at some point need to move by rail."

I asked him about his own upbringing and experience.

He said, "My father was born in the coal country of West Virginia, in (the coal camp of) Tams in Wyoming County. He moved to Vinton as a young man and was in the retail business. I grew up there. I could hear the Virginian Railway railroad trains growing up. Our house was near the Roanoke River. Everybody in the Roanoke Valley grew up with trains around.

"I had no intention of going into the railroad business until Jane's father (Bob) hired me out of Harvard Law School. He was a Harvard Law graduate himself. I interviewed with the railroad in Roanoke and got the job. I worked my entire career with the N&W and then the Norfolk Southern. That was from 1966 through forever," he laughed.

I asked him if he was involved with the decision to terminate the passenger trains such as the Powhatan Arrow in the 1960s.

He said, "No. That decision was made while I was working there but I was not involved. As a young whippersnapper tax lawyer, I just watched it happen. I was nowhere near the decision-making process. I do remember riding it. It was a good decision to terminate it. It was a huge loser."

I attempted to make a joke and said, "We are just talking about money here, David." I immediately regretted it, reminding myself that I was talking to a no-nonsense former CEO of a fortune 500 company.

He said matter-of-factly, "This is a 175 year-old-plus company. We didn't get that far by making bad business decisions. We have to pay attention to the bottom line. We employ over 30,000 people. We all love the hardware but let's face it: we have got to make a profit.

"I don't know if the passenger service ever made money. But I certainly never saw it make any money in my career. The industry saw the ability to get out of the passenger business almost as a key to the survival of the rail system as a private enterprise system. If you go back into the late 1960s and early 1970s it was a low period for much of the railroad business. Norfolk & Western did better than anybody primarily because it had the coal business and it had very limited passenger business. My recollection is that the N&W was anxious to see Amtrak come into existence and let them get out of the passenger business because it was a losing operation.

"One of the last holdouts was the Southern Railway. Jane's uncle, Graham, just loved passenger service so much but I can't imagine that it was profitable for Southern either." (Graham Claytor, the uncle David referred to, was CEO of Southern Railway, serving from 1967 until 1977. I made a mental note to ask Jane about him later.)

David continued, "I don't think that there is any railway in the world that is making a profit running a passenger rail business. They all require subsidies. In Europe and in Japan, the rail passenger networks are socialized."

I said, "Our interstate highway system is subsidized. Airports are subsidized..."

He asked, rhetorically, "Should we as a society be supporting high-speed rail? The answer to me is clearly, yes we should. Rail as a transportation system makes every sense in moving people in certain places. The decision that every state had to have its railroad was fatal to the passenger transportation business in the United States. Every senator got his piece of the pie. If you give me the Northeast corner and let me run it as a real business I could make some money. As far as a transcontinental network for passengers, give me an airline."

I said, "The great distances in this country, particularly across the sparsely populated areas, simply do not support passenger rail transportation. Cities are much closer together in Europe."

He agreed, adding, "I love the idea of expansion of Amtrak service, for example, from Charlottesville to Washington. It runs on our rails. We get paid a little bit for doing it. But we are not operating it."

We talked about the resurgence of the excursion program. He told me that he had ridden behind the 611 as it returned from Spencer, NC, where it had undergone refurbishment back up to Roanoke. He said, "It was extraordinary! People were hanging from the trees and off of bridges. It was a remarkable outpouring of both interest and love. Now, the question is will that sentiment translate to people who will actually pay the fare and get on regular service trains in Roanoke or Blacksburg and ride to Washington and beyond as opposed to hopping in their car and driving on the Interstate? The answer to that is harder. But I would be optimistic if the service was right.

"There is service now from Norfolk to Washington and New York. It is small but growing. If I was looking at this from the helm of Norfolk Southern, as a businessman, I would do whatever we could make profitable. I suspect there is some combination of scheduling and pricing that would make passenger rail more attractive throughout the region. I would be surprised if it can ever be done without it being subsidized, significantly. It is a political issue. It is a societal interest in having the alternative transportation mode available in there to operate. You have to make the political decision that it is what society wants and then put the money into it.

"At one point we decided to build an interstate highway system. When you fly to JFK Airport in New York, you will find that the most difficult part of your journey is getting from the gate to the taxi line and then from the taxi line to downtown New York. You would say that one of the simplest things in the world would be to build a high-speed rail line from JFK Airport to downtown New York just as the Chinese have done in many of their major cities. Why have we not done that?"

I ventured, cynically, "Because we don't invest in this country anymore."

He said, "Because the political decisions have not been made to do it. I don't question the utility or the love or the interest in passenger rail and whether that can be translated into a modern high-speed line."

We talked about the Powhatan Arrow and the fact that with the Class J locomotives, the Norfolk & Western spared no expense. They ran on a corridor that had few people on it. Roanoke was the only city served that had more than 50,000 people in it. And yet Norfolk & Western decided that it would do a better job than anybody else in the country. It had the finest locomotives, the finest cars, and the finest accommodations of any railroad in the country. They went all-out. What kind of company would do that?

He said, "The last time I actually rode the train, there were a few people on it. I had a pass because of my employment with the company. I think everybody on the train worked for the company. It was a really pretty ride and I got to know everybody on the train.

"I don't really have much of a personal recollection of passenger rail travel as a luxury travel or something that my family ever did when I was a kid. I didn't come to the railroad because of fond childhood memories of riding it. I remember going to the station in Vinton and watching the trains come by and talking to the workers."

I said, "A company like Proctor & Gamble makes Crest toothpaste. I'm sure the people there are proud of it, but I can't imagine it has true fans. You ran a railroad. There are thousands of people who are really passionate about trains. I don't think people get really excited about toothpaste. People love locomotives and airplanes. Did you have a different feeling about it then as CEO of this company?"

He said, "There is a strong culture in the company. You are talking about two separate but strongly related things. There's great pride in what the company does and love of the company and it is palpable as you go around and talk to people on the road. You see and feel that. In the overall populace, the people that don't work for the railroad, I would notice that when I would go to Washington almost every congressman had an uncle or grandfather who worked for the railroad. They had warm feelings and if we could bottle those and turn them into support it would be great.

"But you're right. I have been on the board of Delta and I see it in the airline business. There is something about working with the machinery and the equipment. There is a culture that develops. It is very powerful. I used to tell people, I still do, that being a CEO is a great thing but being CEO of a company like Norfolk Southern is far greater. It is because of the culture, the things that people feel about it, and the passion."

I asked about the formation of NS and the move to Norfolk in the early 1980s. As I did, I looked at the awesome view outside the window. In front of the window was a three-foot tall carved wooden sculpture of a stallion, the company's graphic image mascot.

He said, "I was not involved with that. There was a merger of two relatively equal companies with headquarters in separate cities. I'm sure that there was an impulse to have the combined corporation located in a third city. Jane's father was involved with that."

Jane said, "They looked at Richmond. They looked at Tysons Corner. Southern was located in Washington already. For a company named Norfolk Southern and whose base started in Norfolk and went west, it was a natural to come here."

David said, "The new headquarters was not going where either of the two companies was before, no matter how disappointed Roanoke might have been."

Jane told me she was in Norfolk already and knew Norfolk Southern might come if the city embraced them. "Norfolk moved heaven and earth to get them here." The company employs around 1,000 people in Norfolk.

Although regular passenger service had long been terminated, NS was still providing excursion runs when he was CEO. He said slyly, "Jane's father put them in and I killed them. It is true that a lot has been written about that but the actual story has never been done. It will be in my memoirs.

"It was well thought out, and I think it was the right decision at the time. I was not prepared for the depth of feeling. I fully knew what we were doing, and I think we did it for the right reasons. The reaction was greater than I had anticipated. There were some very strong personal, angry reactions. There are still some hard feelings and it was 25 years ago. But it was still the right decision."

On a more positive note, David gave himself credit for gathering archival materials stored within the company, at the Virginia Tech library, and at Southern's facilities in Atlanta all into one place in their main corporate building. "I made the decision that we had history here and that we needed to preserve it, sort it out, and get it organized. There is strong history and cultural tradition. So we decided to pull it all together. There is a question as to whether the company itself is the best place to do this. We are not a library, but we have over 200,000 archival negatives and we keep them in cooled, climate-controlled units. I don't know if every company does this; I know a lot of companies do. But we deem it important to maintain and cherish the history of the company. The general public has many questions about their family history and the railroad. Many people working on dissertations or theses are interested. We are filling a need by facing outward."

David escorted us downstairs to the room that kept the archives. There was a series of portraits of the corporation's CEOs through the years hanging on the walls. About the merger of Norfolk & Western and Southern Railroad, I asked David, "Was this a good wedding?"

"Oh yes," he said. "It created the structure of the modern railroad industry. It dictated the form of the CSX system and the absorption of Conrail after the Penn Central system broke up.

"People love the company and trains. In many towns our company served, the train was how you got in and out. There are not a lot of 175 year-old companies around. When you have one that does exist, it has adapted consistently to change. It started as the South Carolina Canal Company. It started to move cotton to the port. The people of Charleston financed the Best Friend of Charleston because they didn't have a good river port. So they got the canal company to build this new thing so they could compete with Savannah that had a better river port. Then they discovered kaolin deposits in the hill country for making

Wedgewood china. They needed this clear white clay. The Georgia Railroad followed which became the Southern Railroad and on and on. Coalfields developed. The Clark brothers, who had coal resources, needed a way to get the coal to market. Billy Mahone had built this east-west railroad and they acquired that.

"Now we see the decline of the coal business. NS has now been able to accommodate intermodal cars (that carry shipping containers) to replace that. If you have an intermodal facility, you have more business. There are intermodal terminals that bridge the road/highway/rail link.

"You've got to be fast afoot. You've got to be developing. I have no doubt there are people thinking right now, 'What can I move? What can I sell? What's the next market?' That's how we've got this history."

JANE AND I RETURNED to her home to rest and wash up before the evening's activities, dinner downtown with several of her friends and then a Norfolk Forum lecture. The Norfolk Forum is a four-times-per-year lecture series begun in 1933, the oldest of its type in the country. Not surprisingly, it receives corporate sponsorship from charitable Norfolk Southern. Lectures are held at the Chrysler Hall across the pavilion from the Scope, Norfolk's large domed arena. The planned speaker, famed Duke University Coach Mike Krzyzewski, called in sick as he was recovering from knee surgery, and he sent former players Shane Battier, Jason Williams, and Jay Bilas in his stead.

Jane and I were joined by her husband, Sam, and we proceeded to a nearby restaurant where we met their friends at a long table inside, across the street from the Chrysler Hall. The restaurant was so severely understaffed that we were told by the waitress as she scurried by that we were unlikely to be served for at least 45 minutes. I was frightfully hungry and tempted to pick from the scraps of food left behind by other customers and still sitting on unbussed tables. I decided this was uncouth and would garner me no respect. But when Sam suggested that we look elsewhere for food, I readily agreed.

We arrived at the Chrysler in time to join their friends on the front row of the theater, where Battier, Williams, and Bilas spoke about their careers and their tutelage under Coach Krzyzewski. Williams' story was perhaps the most compelling, in that he played only one year of NBA ball before suffering a severe motorcycle crash from which he never re-covered well enough to play again. All three were accomplished speakers, with Battier being the most engaging and Bilas the funniest and most self-deprecating. By the time they were done, looking upwards to the stage at three tall speakers left my neck in a knot.

THE NEXT MORNING I parked my car in a paid parking lot (only $1 for three hours!) and walked back to the NS tower for my follow-up conversation with NS historical archivist Jennifer McDaid.

Norfolk had all the pleasant and fun accouterments of a prosperous mid-sized city, including fountains, street art, and those decorative flags so many cities fly. My favorite was a cast metal disk, probably 15 feet in diameter, imbedded into the sidewalk, with a raised-relief map of the old downtown with historic sites and etchings. Ubiquitous were gaily and individually painted mermaid statues of fiberglass and metal.

As I got closer to the NS building and the other skyscrapers in that neighborhood, I saw that the people on the sidewalks were better dressed, many women with pumps and men in suits and ties. These were the professional class, people with Ivy League MBAs and Porsches and six-figure incomes, people who shower when they wake rather than when they go to bed and who wouldn't be caught in public without perfume, even the men. Both white and black races were represented, along with many of indeterminate race. It was all very pleasant, and I felt out of place, alien, scruffy, and inferior.

JENNIFER WORKED FOR MANY YEARS at the Library of Virginia as an archivist. She had been at Norfolk Southern for six years. I asked if she was looking for them or if they were looking for her. Her answer seemed to indicate that it was a combination of the two.

"I have a Masters degree in history from William and Mary," she told me. "NS was looking for a historical archivist. I had been at the Library of Virginia for quite some time. I wanted something different, I think. One of the good things about that job is that they have a very rich business records collection at the State Library. I think I was well prepared for this job here.

"It is great! It is challenging to go from a state library where there are lots of archivists to being here and being the only one. Archivists call being in a place like this being a 'lone arranger.'"

I said, "NS has over 30,000 people. It has made a corporate decision to fund archival work. Do I understand that you are the only employee who actually does that?"

She said, "Yes, that's true, but I have never felt alone." She described a close relationship particularly with the graphic arts people to help her with this place in the museum and publications. Her office was on the 18th floor, a few floors up from David Goode's executive suite on the 13th. "Managing the archives has always been a job that involves lots of outreach. I am not the kind of archivist that would be satisfied with putting items into folders and putting folders into boxes. The company has always completely supported my work."

I said, "I assume people show a lot of interest in this company."

"Yes. It is a mix of people within the company who have reference needs and people from the outside. People need things for presentations. The graphics people need things for whatever they're working on: pamphlets, magazines, or displays. People work on genealogies. People work on histories of train stations. People work on exhibits or books like yours. People work on theses and dissertations."

I asked what she had learned in her years with Norfolk Southern.

She said, "The collection (constantly) yields surprises. When I was little, I always wanted to be Nancy Drew. I feel like I solve a mystery every day. Sometimes it is not the mystery I thought I would solve. Sometimes I find something one day and end up using it a week later.

"Here's an example. A month ago I found photos of Robert Kennedy campaigning from the back of a railcar. A while later, I found Dwight Eisenhower campaigning from a railcar. With the presidential election coming up, one of my coworkers said we need to talk about presidents and campaigning from railcars.

"I had good articles from the Norfolk & Western magazine on both of them. There they were and I filed them away. On Facebook, I post something from the archives every Thursday. The Social Media Team puts things like historic photographs and historic maps. I often post things that people haven't seen before."

I said, "It seems to me that the Powhatan Arrow and all other passenger trains were public relations efforts. Sure, it was a transportation thing as well, and you could ride it from Norfolk to Cincinnati and all spaces in between. But in every regard in terms of the graphic design, in terms of the stylishness of the locomotive, the upfitting of the cars, and the beauty of the stations, it was important for Norfolk & Western to proudly show their corporate prowess. Comfort. Showmanship. It was a statement. The Norfolk & Western said to their passengers, 'We are the finest and best run railroad in America. You can see that when you get on this train and ride with us.' It seemed important to them then." I asked her if she got that feeling as well.

She said, "Yes. They wanted to make a statement about what type of corporation they were running. I think they wanted to say that they were the best in transportation. It was definitely a PR push for them. You can see that in the advertising that we have in our archives. They were focused on photographing things along the line as well."

I said, "I remember going into the train station in Christiansburg where I grew up and on the wall they had beautiful black-and-white photographs of their trains motoring through the farms, forests, and valleys of our area. It wouldn't surprise me if they were still there. It is a particularly scenic area. They could have put anything on the wall or nothing."

She said, "We have lots of pictures of Virginia Beach or Luray Caverns and other things that were considered attractions. Trains carried students back-and-forth to college and so we get requests for pictures of area colleges.

"We have an online photographic collection that is now available for anybody to see. Sometimes we cannot identify people in the photographs. We had an elderly woman who e-mailed me from Florida. She got a link to the website and patiently went through the photos. She found a picture of two men together who turned out to be her father and her uncle. We did not know who these men were, but she did. It was a goosebumps moment for me. It was amazing that she took the time to find it. She got her picture, and she was very happy with it."

I said, "I don't think there has been a single corporation that has ever had a greater impact on my part of the world than yours. It was visible. Everybody loved the Norfolk & Western."

She said, "The pictures here they tell the story of an engine or a machine or a building and that is important too. But it is people that make a railroad. Archives tell the stories of people. For me it has always been about the stories behind the documents and the people behind the events. The archives are a small part of Norfolk Southern, but it always impressed me that the corporation committed to maintaining an archives.

"I took my daughter on the inaugural run of the 611. It was like a parade. I knew it was a big deal but I don't think I expected people to literally stop traffic. It was incredible; it really was. People have very strong feelings about trains."

She concluded, "I try to take it one day at a time, but taking care of the archives is an awesome responsibility."

LET ME NOW TELL YOU more about 19th Century Virginia's most illustrious power couple, William "Little Billy" Mahone and his wife Otelia Butler Mahone.

William Mahone was born in 1826 near Courtland in Southampton County, Virginia. At age five, he and his family escaped death at the hands of Nat Turner's rebellious slaves who massacred 55 to 65 whites in that area. The boisterous, freckle-faced Irish-American Mahone pursued an engineering degree from Virginia Military Institute in Lexington, graduating in 1847, four years before Thomas J. "Stonewall" Jackson accepted a position as professor of Natural and Experimental Philosophy and Instructor of Artillery.

After graduation, Billy carried the mail and taught school before his entry into his field of education, getting hired in 1848 to build the Orange and Alexandria Railroad. By 1853, he had gotten the job as chief engineer on the new Norfolk and Petersburg Railroad, the corridor between those two cities later used by the Powhatan Arrow and miraculously still in use today after its eventual incorporation into the Norfolk & Western and now the Norfolk Southern. He pioneered the use of wooden logs laid at right angles below the surface of the swamp to form a foundation for the track across the Great Dismal Swamp. It is difficult to imagine the tonnage the Mahone track has carried over 160 years! The stretch from Suffolk to Petersburg is, at 52 miles, the longest completely straight stretch of railroad track along the Powhatan Arrow's corridor and the entire N&W line.

On February 8, 1855, Mahone married the intelligent, cultured, and feisty Otelia Butler of Smithfield, daughter of one of Virginia's state treasurers. Skirting death once again, Mahone evaded the yellow fever epidemic of that same summer by spending time away in Clarksville, Virginia. The epidemic killed almost a third of the populations of Portsmouth and Norfolk, and put the completion of the railroad linking those two cities on hold. When the rail line was finally completed in 1858, Billy became the company president.

His tenure, as with so many other men of his era, was interrupted by the drum-beats and cannon fire of the Civil War. At the outbreak of the war, where he supported Virginia secession, he was still a civilian. Given his obvious intelligence and leadership ability, he soon rose through the ranks and by November 1861 he was a brigadier general. A photo of him shows his hand under his grey woolen, pleated jacket – Napoleon style – and a white, wide-brimmed hat, atop a deeply-bearded, intense face.

Little Billy, all 5 feet 5 inches and 100 pounds of him, was a skilled tactician and fierce fighter. He was involved in many of the war's most famous and critical battles, including Seven Pines, Malvern Hill, Second Manassas, Fredericksburg, Chancellorsville, Gettysburg, the Wilderness, and Spotsylvania Court House. Meanwhile, Otelia served her renegade nation as a nurse in Richmond.

Mahone's military career is best known for his actions at the Battle of the Crater near Petersburg on July 30, 1864, which I'll tell you about in more detail when we get there.

After the war, Mahone returned to railroading, which at that time desperately needed him, as much of the mileage of track in the former Confederacy had been decimated. He oversaw the merger of three of Virginia's primary lines, his own Norfolk and Petersburg, the South Side Rail Road, linking westward 132 miles to Lynchburg, and the Virginia and Tennessee from Lynchburg to Salem and on to Bristol at the Tennessee border, a distance of 204 miles. At that point, a single line reached from Norfolk to Bristol. The section of rail from Norfolk to Walton Junction, the wye, which is railroad-speak for a triangular junction, at the New River between Christiansburg and Radford, would be the path of the Powhatan Arrow 75 years later. He also oversaw the rebuilding of many of the railroad stations that had been destroyed during the war years earlier.

As I mentioned, Mahone lost control of his railroad, but his career and contributions to the people of Virginia were far from over. In the midst of the war while he was actively engaged, he was elected to the Virginia House of Delegates from Norfolk in 1863. And he served as mayor of Petersburg. He ran an unsuccessful bid for the governorship. After his loss, he became leader of a coalition of Republicans, Democrats, and prominent African Americans that termed themselves the Readjuster Party. They sought to readjust Virginia's prewar debt and allocated an equitable portion to the new state of West Virginia. When "his" railroad sold, he fought for an allocation of some of the state's windfall to be invested in a school for blacks that ultimately became Virginia State University in Petersburg.

Billy died from a stroke in the fall of 1895, and Otelia lived in Petersburg until her passing in 1911. After his death, Virginia and West Virginia continued to dispute the debt with the final issue settled in 1915 and not fully paid off until 1939.

I MENTIONED EARLIER that my hostess, Jane Claytor Webster, came from one of the most illustrious of Virginia railroading families. After spending two nights at her house, I finally had a chance to speak with her in detail. She and her husband Sam fixed us a wonderful meal of crab cakes – a delicacy I don't see much of where I live in the mountains – green beans, and rice. Afterwards we sat down in their living room to talk about their life histories.

Sam was a lawyer, originally from Columbus, Ohio. He and Jane met at Dartmouth College in New Hampshire. He was attending there and she came as a transfer student. He graduated from Washington and Lee Law School in Lexington, Virginia. From there, they moved to Norfolk in 1977 and had been there ever since.

Jane was born in New York City and moved with her family to Roanoke when she was two years old. Her brother Preston was 11 years younger, and I would learn that he was one of the primary architects of the new excursion program using the 611 locomotive.

She said, "Sam and I got married in 1973. We have two children. Both are adults now and live in Colorado. So we were living in Norfolk before the merger of Norfolk & Western and Southern Railway and their ultimate move to Norfolk."

Sam joked, "Jane's father got accused of moving the company to Norfolk to be closer to his grandchildren. The real reason was to be near to his sailboat."

Jane laughed, "Neither story is true! My father was hired by (then N&W chairman) Stuart Saunders in 1952. Saunders had talked to my uncle Graham, my father's older brother, and told him that he needed some lawyers in his law department at Norfolk & Western. Uncle Graham told him that his kid brother was a lawyer, fresh out of Harvard Law School. So Saunders interviewed my father and the next thing I knew, we were moving to Roanoke."

Her grandfather, William Graham Claytor, worked for Appalachian Power Company. "He grew up in Bedford and he came to Roanoke as a trolley operator. He eventually went to VPI (later Virginia Tech) and got a degree in electrical engineering."

Sam said, "In those days, railroads, trolley companies, and electric companies frequently were all the same company."

Jane said, "(Grandfather) was tapped to manage a hydroelectric dam project on the New River that built the lake that ultimately was named after him. My father became a railroad lawyer. He made continuing progress up the management chain."

Sam said, "Corporations have lots of lawyers to manage all sorts of things. They also employ outside contract lawyers. Bob didn't want to be a tax lawyer or an employment lawyer. He wanted to be the lawyer for the operating department. He was bright, and he understood transactions, taxation, and finances. He would not have gotten where he was without that. But he wanted to be the operations department lawyer. So he learned how to operate trains."

Jane concurred, "He wanted to be connected. He wanted to understand, physically, in the cab, how to operate a locomotive. He was a boots-on-the-ground guy."

Sam said, "He was as happy at the throttle of a diesel engine as anybody ever could be."

She said, "Whenever he went out on the system he always made a point of meeting everyone he could. He wanted to know the employees. Lots of CEOs in those days were lawyers. But he didn't see himself as just in the law department. He wanted to be a part of everything, and he loved the operating end. He loved trains!"

Sam said, "There was a strike in 1978. Managers were forced into doing operations work. He literally ran merchandise trains from Roanoke to Norfolk and back again the next day and then still got his own work done. This went on for three or four months."

I said, "It pains me that I never got to meet this man. I already like him a lot."

She said, "You would've liked him. Yep. He was Princeton and Harvard educated. But he was a man of the people, a down-to-earth person."

Sam said, "We became close friends and he was very much a father figure for me."

I asked, "If you had been up on stage at the Norfolk Forum last night talking about lessons learned not from Coach K but from Bob Claytor, what would you tell the audience?"

Sam paused thoughtfully and then said, "His lesson was in the way of life: a love for the arts, a love for the church, and a level of generosity."

Bob Claytor's daughter said, "He was also about his sense of humor. He never thought too highly of himself. I think those are my lessons from him. He was a very loyal person. He was ambitious but not overly ambitious."

Sam said, "Bob was assertive, but not aggressive. He could have easily had an engineering degree as well as his law degree. He understood how locomotives worked. He understood how the coal pier worked.

"Bob Claytor was instrumental in the merger with Southern Railway in 1982 and was the first chairman and CEO of the new Norfolk Southern company. He is fondly remembered by many for reactivating Norfolk & Western's steam locomotive excursion program."

Jane said, "He was smart, but personable and approachable. He was the right guy in the right job at the right time. It is tough to merge two companies. Everyone says this was a good merger. He and his compatriot at Southern Railroad worked hard and gave a lot of thought how to balance each company. It was not loaded with one side or the other."

Sam said, "Bob was adamant about the fact that it was now one company. There were several managers and executives who were dismissed from the new company because they did not buy into that ethic. They actually lost their jobs because they did not understand the teamwork aspect of the new company."

She said, "Everybody wanted this to work from day one. It was not going to be one side or the other dominant."

I offered for approval, "This was a merger of willing and motivated equals."

Sam said, "Yes, they really got hold of the synergy of the combination almost before it fully happened. It is textbook. It is one of the finest mergers in American history."

She said, "And I think my dad was a major architect of that."

I said, "Do you think your father's lack of pretension and superiority contributed to that?"

She said, "Yes. Potentially a more self-proud manager could not have pulled that off. It is safe to say that it would not have happened if he hadn't wanted it to happen."

Sam said charitably, "It wouldn't have happened if the Southern people did not want it to happen, either."

I asked them both if they could recall a single proudest moment.

Sam said, "I am always proud to be able to say that Norfolk Southern is now

Jane Webster's license plate

my client. I have had my share of success for them. I am proud of my relationships I've developed with their senior management. When Bob retired, there was a lot of ceremony surrounding that. It made us both feel really good.

"My proudest moment was riding in the seat behind a fireman on the 611 with my children (when they were younger) riding on the jumpseat on the tender behind me and their grandfather was running and their great uncle firing. It was really cool.

"Please don't leave Bob's wife, Frances out of the story. She was supportive of him in his career. In their marriage they were a great example for us in our marriage."

I said, "Sam, it appears to me that you married up."

He said, "I would go home to Columbus, and my best friend would say to me, 'Webster, do you know how lucky you are?' I went to my reunion at Dartmouth and people there said, 'Webster, do you know how lucky you are?' I went to law school and people there said, 'Webster, do you know how lucky you are?' I definitely improved."

Jane and I spoke earlier in the day about a tragic accident that occurred while her father was at the helm of the 611 during one of the excursion runs. I asked her to comment on it.

She said, "Well, the facts are facts. It was a very hot day in May, 1986. One hundred twenty eight people were injured. There were one thousand workers and their families on board. Sam and I were on board as well. We were going westward towards Petersburg through the Great Dismal Swamp. Dad was at the controls but he wasn't speeding. The man who normally ran the train was, I'm certain, standing right next to dad. Amazingly, the locomotive did not derail but the third fourth and fifth cars fell off the track. They always send a track inspector right in front of any excursion. There was no issue with the track. Investigations that followed were inconclusive.

"One car was lying on its side. One car was still upright but off the tracks. I think a third car was partially derailed and the last three cars were not."

Sam described the scene. "In all the cars, people were slammed around. So people were hurt even in the cars that did not derail. The cars were properly equipped for braking. But you have to understand that trains do not come to an immediate stop even when the brakes are actuated. We were in the last car that did not derail. We came through and the car behind us separated from us. That sets the emergency brake for every car."

"There was the chaos that follows any accident," Jane said. "People were running from the front to the back trying to figure out what happened. We were all doing anything we could think of to help. Emergency helicopters began arriving. We were in the Great Dismal Swamp so nobody could drive there."

Sam said, "The railroad sent a train with several cabooses from Suffolk and backed it in to carry injured people to hospitals in Norfolk. The most seriously injured people were airlifted."

Jane said, "My father was devastated. He never talked much about it. But he absolutely felt responsible. And yet, no fault was ever proven. But it was still his company and the victims were his employees and friends. It was his beloved engine. The only thing you could say about this was that it was an accident. To this day, nobody knows why it happened."

I noted that at that point, the accident still did not cause the discontinuation of the excursion program, which actually continued on for several more years.

Sam said, "Yes, but they did put new speed restrictions on it. I don't know why David Goode ultimately shut it down. My speculation is that he took a hard look and realized that there was potentially a lot of liability out there for the railroad that they didn't want to accept."

I said, "All of those situations that entered into his decision still exist today, and yet we now have another new excursion program. Wick Moorman, who was chairman of Norfolk Southern when the new program got underway, apparently faced that same set of circumstances and yet he made a different decision. Do you have any idea why?"

Sam admitted that he didn't. "You will need to ask him."

"Is that a fair question?"

"Yes, absolutely," Sam said. "Make no mistake, though; David is also a real fan.

"Norfolk Southern is a great corporate citizen. Wherever the employees are they are generous to the communities they live in. We are beneficiaries of that, especially because they are headquartered here. Their people are on (philanthropic) boards all over the area."

I SPENT MY FINAL night in Norfolk with the Websters and departed early the next morning, headed southward on St. Paul's Boulevard, US460-alternate, towards downtown. I crossed the Eastern Branch of the Elizabeth River over an impressive bridge, noting that on the other side, inbound traffic was backed up for miles. I knew the track of the Norfolk Southern, the original route of the Powhatan Arrow, was to my left, parallel, with both of us headed towards Suffolk, but I couldn't see it.

My route became I-264 and I continued towards the southwest. I then took US-58/US-460 on a straight-arrow six-lane divided road, the Military Highway, across the Great Dismal Swamp towards Suffolk. There was a nice divided highway bypass around that city, but I dutifully drove the old business highway that followed the tracks into the city center.

7:23 a.m.

Suffolk

Mile 21.9

Where King Peanut rules. More peanuts are processed and marketed here than anywhere in the world. This is Virginia ham country, too. Fishing and hunting are excellent in the Dismal Swamp and its lakes to the south. At Kilby, three miles west, there begins a stretch of over 52 miles of N. &. W. double-track without a curve.

The Powhatan Arrow was launched with great fanfare on April 28, 1946, as the sleek streamliner, with its signature Tuscan red and gold striping and fantastic new Class J locomotives, chugged westbound from Norfolk and simultaneously eastbound from Cincinnati. Multitudes of rail fans lined the tracks and overwhelmed overpasses along the route as people sought the view of this fantastic new conveyance provided by the venerable Norfolk & Western Railway Company.

Jennifer McDaid, the archivist, had given me a photocopied version of an original typewritten document, the

PRESS BOOK

of the

NORFOLK & WESTERN'S
"NEW POWHATAN ARROW"

It said, "The Norfolk & Western's new Powhatan Arrow traverses a land of varied and unusual scenic beauty – sparkling beaches, majestic mountains, broad, lush valleys, and winding rivers – a land of rich natural resources – a land steeped in the history of the Republic."

Although the Powhatan Arrow had much of the same equipment as some of the other named trains like the Pocahontas and the Cavalier (which, incidentally, traversed much the same route, although at different times of day), it was still considered special. The coaches had been engineered and manufactured just a few months prior to the Second World War. There were typically six coaches and one dining car in each train.

When new cars were put into operation in late 1949, it truly represented the finest of everything one of America's highest-quality railroads could offer.

The Class J locomotive was engineered prior to the Second World War. Norfolk & Western made a series of technological advancements during the Great Depression. As the Depression began to wane, locomotive designers began investing in advanced designs. They built the Class A first. Shortly after that they built the Y-6s which were compound engines that were an improvement over the older designs of the 1920s, and then class J locomotives. Needing increasingly more power and speed from their locomotives, they began looking to a wheel configuration of 4-8-4. The Norfolk & Western was watching the strife in Europe and anticipating World War II perhaps without being fully conscious of the perniciousness of it. In particular, between 1936 and 1941, they were building exceptional new designs in locomotives.

The Southern Railway put in a new train called the Tennessean that ran from Washington, DC to Memphis, Tennessee. It had streamlined equipment and it was powered by diesel. Norfolk & Western wanted to show that they were not behind the times, so they built the streamlined Class J.

The first Class J was built in late 1941. The first unit was designated the 600. With the bombing of Pearl Harbor, the schedule of the 603 was rushed and it was released from the shop on Christmas Eve, 1941. The employees hung a wreath on it the day it was released. The 604 followed soon thereafter. They built five Class Js during the war that were in the same specifications as the regular Class Js except they were not streamlined. They were built, theoretically, as freight locomotives because the railroads were not allowed to build passenger locomotives during the war. After the war, all of the Class J locomotives were again streamlined and re-designated primarily for passenger service.

Although the Norfolk & Western did not serve major metropolitan markets and passenger service was always a sideline, they took pride in it. Even though the N&W was a mid-sized, mostly coal-hauling railroad, it was clear that they intended for their post-war passenger service to make a strong, visible presence, providing the most modern locomotives, equipment, and facilities anywhere in the country. Passenger service was a window into the corporation. People would form their impressions about the corporation overall by their passenger experience.

As the decades wore on, ridership dropped as did revenue. Incurring these losses became less palatable. Eventually N&W discontinued all passenger service. During the early days of laying tracks into the coalfields, passenger rail was really the only way to get people in and out of those areas. For example, it was the only efficient way to get from Bluefield to Welch. There were several short run passenger trains on this route every day. People were surprisingly mobile but everywhere they went, they went by train. If the train was two or three hours late, there would be an article about it in the Bluefield newspaper the next day. Even though service fell off during the Great Depression, N&W still felt like faster service was an obligation to the public on through World War II. Afterwards, the nation embarked on a significant improvement in the highway network and people began to do more travel by car. Air travel became preferable for longer routes.

Railroads, like any other businesses, exist to make money. But at the same time, the N&W had some corporate conscience and wanted to keep a good relationship with the public. In bygone decades, the railroad was the center of much economic activity. Eventually, N&W began to decommission and in some cases demolish the depots, roundhouses, tracks, and repair facilities in many communities along the corridor.

Because the region between Norfolk and Cincinnati was sparsely populated, the Powhatan Arrow, the Pocahontas, and the Cavalier never met their ridership expectations. The N&W actually ran three trains every day along this general corridor and there was not enough passenger traffic to support it.

In its 676-mile run, the Powhatan Arrow refilled its tender of water every 75 miles or so. There was no checked baggage or mail service, so most stops were only long enough for loading and unloading of passengers. They changed engine crews about every 100 miles, which was a long-standing tradition from the earliest days of railroading. Another reason for changing crews so often was because particularly in the mountainous areas, there were many changes in elevation and significant stretches of tightly curved tracks. It was important for the crew to be intimately familiar with the route.

The specifications for the Class J locomotives are impressive. The weight overall is 494,000 pounds, with a 378,600 pound tender (when loaded). The overall length is almost 110 feet long. The driving wheels are 70 inches in diameter, meaning each revolution takes the train 18.3 feet down the track. The boiler generates 300 psi of working pressure, which is piped to two 27 inch diameter by 32 inch stroke cylinders, one on each side of the locomotive. The boiler has 290 tubes and is 19 feet long. The tender has a capacity of 35 tons of coal and 20,000 gallons of water, which is a good thing, because fuel economy sucks (pardon the pun); the firebox consumes a ton of coal every 10 miles and the boiler heats and then spews into the atmosphere 250 gallons of water per mile.

These monsters generated an unfathomable 80,000 lbs. of tractive effort! Wow! To be honest with you, 50,000 lbs. or 250,000 lbs. would have sounded equally impressive. I have no idea how much tractive effort it takes to pull 12 passenger cars up a mountain, or for that matter even what "tractive effort" is, and I'm too lazy to research it.

The original route of the N&W, and thus the route of the Powhatan Arrow, went from the eastern terminus in Norfolk south to Suffolk, then generally westward for the entire length, with major stops in Petersburg, Blackstone, Crewe, Farmville, Lynchburg, Roanoke, Christiansburg, Pearisburg, Bluefield, Welch, Williamson, Kenova, Ironton, Portsmouth, and Cincinnati. Trains like to avoid elevation changes, so every effort was made to keep the grade as smooth and gradual as possible. The elevation gain was consistent and gradual from Norfolk to Blue Ridge between Bedford and Roanoke (with a minor dip on the old routing through downtown Lynchburg), topping out at 1296 feet before descending into Roanoke at 905. From there, it climbed again to 2,052 feet just shy of the Christiansburg station before descending again to the New River and downstream to Glen Lyn on the border with West Virginia, elevation 1520. It then climbed 1,000 feet to its highest point in Bluefield before descending all the way to the Ohio River at Kenova and then Portsmouth, Ohio at 534 feet. It climbed back to 1,077 on the circuitous "Peavine" route into Cincinnati and the terminal elevation of 505 feet.

One engine crew would take the train from Norfolk to Crewe and another engine crew would take the train to Roanoke. At Roanoke they would change locomotives and get a new crew that would drive the train to Bluefield. The next new crew would drive the train to Williamson and the next to Portsmouth, Ohio. The final crew would drive it on its last leg into Cincinnati. Meanwhile, another train was making exactly the same route in reverse. The crews working on the cars would run from Norfolk to Roanoke, Roanoke to Williamson, and Williamson to Cincinnati. So there would be six engine crews and three train crews.

The route's 676.6 miles had 17 stops, about 40 miles apart on average, not including conditional stops. Trips were accomplished in an amazing 15 hours and 45 minutes. After each stop, train was powerful enough to rapidly accelerate back to cruising speed. Top speed on the route was limited to 78 miles an hour in the 53 mile straightaway from Suffolk to Petersburg, but Class J locomotives were capable of much greater speeds. Climbing the mountain from Roanoke to Christiansburg, the train was limited to 40 mph. The limitation was based on the tight curvature of the track rather than on the capability of the locomotive.

There was a dining car with kitchen on each train. Cooks prepared and served terrific food. They cooked fried eggs and ham and fried apples. They baked pies and dinner rolls. In those days, dinner cost $1.75 and that was considered extravagant. The dining cars were serviced by a commissary near the Roanoke passenger station. They had refrigeration in the dining car and electricity in each car. Each car had its own electrical generator that was powered through the axles and a pack of batteries so the lights could stay on even when the train was not moving. If there was an extended stop at the station, they could plug into grid power.

The three trains plying the same route – the Pocahontas, the Cavalier, and the Powhatan Arrow – were spaced in intervals of several hours apart. On overnight routes, sleeper cars were provided. There were collaborative arrangements with adjoining railroad companies to provide continuous service to points beyond the Norfolk & Western's service area. Some routes had more intermediate stops than others. Their on-time performance was good.

The company named the train the Powhatan Arrow, the winning entry in a contest they held amongst their employees. Winner Leonard A. Scott, a retired section foreman from Belspring (near Radford), received a prize of $500 and a free ride on the maiden run. Powhatan was the Native American chief who ruled the tribes of coastal Virginia at the time of the arrival of English settlers in 1607. His daughter Pocahontas was the first Native American to marry an Englishman and the first to travel to England. She too was honored by the N&W in having a train named after her.

Through the 1950s and into the 1960s, passenger service continued to wane, making it increasingly less profitable. The Powhatan Arrow made its final run in the spring of 1969. When the Pocahontas stopped in 1971, N&W passenger service ended permanently.

IT WAS STILL EARLY MORNING when I arrived in Suffolk, so almost no commercial establishments were open. Its historic train station was now a meeting facility monitored by the city's Department of Parks and Recreation.

Illustrative of the fluid nature of American railroad companies and NS in particular, Suffolk had at one point been host to a whole series of railroads, including the Seaboard Air Line Railroad (later the Seaboard Coast Line Railroad), The Atlantic Coast Line Railroad, the Southern Railroad, the Virginian Railroad, CSX Transportation, the Atlantic & Danville Railway Company, and the Commonwealth Railway, in addition to NS.

As far as I could tell, Suffolk's major claim was that it is the home of Planters Peanuts and the birthplace of its cartoon mascot, "Mr. Peanut." I wondered if the person who named it got anywhere near the $500 Mr. Scott got for naming the Powhatan Arrow.

In 1974, Suffolk absorbed the county that surrounded it, Nansemond, and instantly became the largest city by land area in the state and jumped in population from around 10,000 to 45,000. It is a prosperous place, with an influx of high-tech and government-related jobs in the area nearest Norfolk.

With all due apologies to the wonderful people of Suffolk who hadn't bothered to come to work by the time I got there, I motored on.

I STAYED ON US-460, pointed towards the Powhatan Arrow's next stop in Petersburg. US-460 is one of Virginia's longest roads, closely paralleling the route of the Powhatan Arrow all the way to the state line with West Virginia and into Bluefield. In this area, N&W's tracks and passing trains were often in view on my left.

As I mentioned, the track is ruler-straight. The roadway is nearly so, but the highway designers threw in a couple of curves, so to speak, around the tiny towns of Windsor, Zuni, Wakefield, and Waverly, shooting straight through Disputanta. My guess was that in engineering these mild curves, traffic could be slowed in the modest commercial areas.

An interesting side-note to Virginia lore of the Mahones is that they were responsible for naming the towns along this stretch. Otelia began naming stations, and thus towns, for the places she was reading about in Sir Walter Scott's novel *Ivanhoe*, places like Wakefield, Waverly, Windsor, and the town of Ivor, named after the Scottish clan "McIvor." After a while, they must have been wearing on each others nerves, as by the time they were ten miles from Petersburg, they couldn't agree on a new name for the next place. Their spat gave way to a dispute, and the village became Disputanta. This stuff you can't make up.

The highway itself is a relic, a four-lane undivided road, with oncoming traffic separated only by a double-yellow line. In this era, it's unusual and disconcerting to be flowing past semi-trucks with a combined speed differential of over 110 mph.

The towns themselves offered a smattering of convenience stores, tanning salons, volunteer fire and rescue squad buildings, fitness centers, and Dollar General stores. Waverly was one of the larger towns, with its Main Street across the tracks, southeast of the highway. It had several nice buildings in town dating back to the early 1900s, with most of the storefronts empty.

THIS IS PEANUT GROWING COUNTRY, and who doesn't like peanuts? So with morning hunger pangs growing, I was drawn off the highway by a 7 foot tall sign image of an unshelled peanut at the business location of the Wakefield Peanut Company.

peanut sign in Wakefield

Before walking into the store, I decided to walk into another door that had the word "Office" posted outside. Inside I met Steve Laine, sitting at a desk by the door working on his computer. He was a young man with a big dark bushy beard. I introduced myself, told him about my project, and asked about the business.

He said, "My grandfather, Henry Ellis, started the company in 1965. My father, Jimmie Laine started working here in the early 70s and he built up the peanut shelling business to a larger operation. Local farmers grow the peanuts and contract with the company. The company selects the varieties it wishes to market and the local growers buy the seed from it. Currently, we have about six to eight main varieties.

"Peanuts grow underground. There are machines that are pulled behind tractors that actually plant the seeds. The seeds are pushed about two inches into the ground. The seed itself is just a peanut, shelled, that has been treated with a fungicide. It is just like a peanut that you would eat. When we get the peanuts, before we process them, the state will grade them. We dump them into a pit. They will go through a cleaning machine that takes out excess dirt, roots and sticks, and other materials. Then they will go into a sheller. These are just a series of screens. Based on their size they will fall into different slots.

"A spinning machine will knock the husks off and then a vacuum will suck out the shells. They will be sold for (animal) bedding or whatever. The peanuts then will go to a second cleaning process. Then an employee looks them over to make sure that they are all in good condition. Then they will be sized. The largest ones we cook and package for sale. The second largest group will be set aside for seeds. The rest of it goes into peanut butter and other foods.

"We also sell to other peanut retailers. A relatively small percentage of our production is actually sold in our store."

"How is business?" I asked.

"We don't have good and bad years, but we have better and worse seasons. Most years in recent memory have been pretty decent. After Christmas, things drop off. Then when the beach traffic begins things pick back up again. It is not really a seasonal product; we have about the same product year 'round. The harvest is in October. We are super busy in production then. Some of our growers can grow 6000 pounds per acre from 100 pounds of seeds.

"We want them to make money. We pay a bit more than the big companies. There are tight margins. I guess they wouldn't do it if they couldn't make some money. They also grow corn, wheat, soybeans and other crops.

"Peanut production is a huge part of our economy in this area. Peanuts like a sandy soil. The ground here is complementary to raising peanuts. The growers rotate their crops. You don't want to grow peanuts two years in a row (on the same acreage). Sometimes they will let the soil rest and just grow a cover crop. I am a third generation in this business. The pressure on me is to keep it up, at least to maintain it. With new regulations and such, there are always new challenges. We have about 15 or 16 employees when we are busy and eight or nine when we are not."

Wakefield Peanut Company

"Do you like peanuts?" I asked innocently.

He said, "Yes very much. I love them. I eat them every day, and I never get sick of them. All of the peanuts we sell are grown and cooked right here. The Virginia type peanut is larger, more oblong. Virginia type peanuts can be grown other places like Mississippi, Georgia, Florida, and Alabama. There is another variety called a Georgia Runner and they are rounded. Valencia peanuts are red. They have different colors of skin. The colloquial term is 'Redskin Peanuts.' That just means a peanut with the skin still on it.

"When any growing area gets a lot of rain or hurricanes at harvest season, it can be devastating. When the tractors can't get into the fields, they lose their crop. In farming, the weather is always a challenge. We deal almost exclusively in extra-super large peanuts. Our peanuts are bigger. I think they taste better."

Agriculture is Virginia's largest private industry, and peanuts are one of Virginia's main agricultural commodities, annually bringing in around $10,000,000 in farm cash receipts.

He took me on a walk through the warehouses and processing areas. The whole place had a wonderful pea-nuttiest smell. There were enormous nylon-weave and canvas sacks containing peanuts. Several workers moved around on foot and on fork-lift trucks. Then we went into the store. He gave me a can of peanuts for the road. It's amazing what people will give you when you're writing a book.

JUST PAST WAVERLY, a train appeared beside me, going my way, west. It was pulled by three of NS's jet-black diesel locomotives, with their distinctive logo of the silhouette of a thoroughbred and the letters NS and five thick horizontal lines in white on the black background. It carried a deep rumble that I could hear from the highway and carried a sense of power and invulnerability. Behind was a long row of empty coal cars, headed back to Roanoke, Bluefield, and then wherever else throughout the coalfields where they were pulled for refilling.

It is impossible to overstate the importance of the railroad to the development of our nation. As the new United States of America progressed from its founding years to the great industrial and economic superpower it is today, railroads have always provided an essential element.

The Industrial Revolution, beginning around 1760 in Great Britain and a few decades later in the United States, saw the introduction of scores of manufacturing processes in machinery, chemistry, metallurgy, and energy. Particularly important was the shift from wood to coal as a fuel and the use of steam to generate motive power.

Prior to this, neither the plantation owner, the mountaineer, the city dweller, nor the slave had access to anything more than rudimentary metal devices. The first steam engines, designed in England in the early 1700s, were used to pump water from underground coal mines. Work by Thomas Savery, Thomas Newcomen, and James Watt proved that steam could provide power substantially greater than animals, the most prevalent prior source.

When early 19th Century mechanical engineers figured out how to harness that expansion and turn it into motive power, the locomotive era was launched. The movement of people and goods at what was for then breathtaking speeds in excess of 12 mph became the very definition of progress.

Early viewers were awed to reverence by the seemingly lifelike qualities of animated masses of steel and iron, as the steam locomotive took on god-like qualities to be exalted. We can scarcely imagine today the rurally based homesteader's or mountaineer's first sighting of a self-mobile, metallic machine, when his prior experience had only allowed him access to metallurgy in the form of a door hinge, a hoe, a plow, or a nail. His eyes beheld a metal boiler on rails, a wondrous assemblage of pistons, linkages, wheels, bolts, and pulleys, enshrouded in smoke and steam, self-propelling down a laid pair of steel rails. How dumbstruck these viewers would have been!

In the early years, welding technology was still far into the future. So riveted boilers were the order of the day. They were frightfully dangerous, with frequent explosions and concomitant injuries and deaths. But the ability of a locomotive to move large numbers of people and heavy commodities couldn't be denied.

The opening of the Erie Canal, proposed in 1808 and completed in 1825, and the proposed construction of the Chesapeake and Ohio westward from Washington, DC, threatened the viability of the port of Baltimore, Maryland. Water travel was the preferred commercial option of the era, and Baltimore's industrial titans feared that the then thriving port in their city would be rendered irrelevant. Without access to a major river like Washington's Potomac or New York's Hudson, Baltimore was desperate for a new solution.

They found it on metal rails.

August 28, 1830, can legitimately be called the birthday of American railroading. Baltimore industrialists incorporated the Baltimore and Ohio Railroad with the intent of linking their harbor with the Ohio River. A mere thirteen miles of flat track was laid from the harbor to Ellicott's Mill (Now Ellicott City), and a locomotive engineered by New Yorker Peter Cooper pulled a single car at an incredible speed of 18 miles per hour, with the inventor at the throttle. The "Tom Thumb" as it became nicknamed, was joined en route by a horse-drawn cart and a race ensued. The Tom Thumb was the clear leader until a belt slipped off the pulley that drove a blower feeding air to the fire, and with the resultant loss in heat and power, the locomotive slowed and the horse passed and won. Nevertheless, the die was cast and the iron horse would rapidly improve and ensure its long-term superiority.

Sadly, like many of our nation's most prized antiquities, the Tom Thumb was relegated to the scrap bin. A replica, built in 1892, is on display now at the Baltimore and Ohio Railroad Museum in Baltimore.

In any event, the race was on to develop more powerful locomotives and to build more miles of track. By 1840, over 2,800 miles of track had been laid and by the outbreak of the Civil War, barely 30 years after the famous run of the Tom Thumb, the nation had over 30,000 miles of track! The newfound ability to move significant tonnage and great numbers of people previously unheard of distances forever changed the face of the nation. By 1850, every state east of the Mississippi River except Florida had some miles of track and regular railroad service. And by 1860, travel from New York to Chicago was routinely accomplished in as little as two days.

The speed of industrialization in the United States during that time was unparalleled in the world, and likely only matched historically by the recent industrialization of China. From time immemorial, energy was applied to the processes of civilization from two sources, almost exclusively: human and animal muscle. Progress to more powerful sources such as wind, falling water, tides, and wood came at measured rates. But the emergence of ground-based fossil fuels, peat, gas, oil, and predominantly coal, brought about unprecedented changes in the ways people fed, clothed, housed, and transported themselves.

Particularly important was the symbiotic, codependent relationship between coal, steel, and trains. You see, you couldn't make steel without the energy supplied by coal. You couldn't transport coal without railroads. You couldn't build the locomotives or rails without steel. And you couldn't power locomotives or trains without coal. Their development and use progressed hand in hand.

In addition, coal-fired steam boilers powered steamships, furniture factories, grist mills, looms, sewing machines, and the electrical dynamos that seemingly powered everything else. Streetcars replaced horses. Electric lights replaced oil-burning lamps. Factories sprung up across the land and rural dwellers flocked to the cities for paying jobs.

Railroad companies in those days were frequently short-run, often with a single line of rails, with only one or two locomotives, and often limited rolling stock. These railroads were often built for a specific purpose and specific cargo. For example, one of the nation's earliest commercial coalfields was the Richmond Basin Coalfield, some 13 miles to the west of downtown Richmond. In 1831, The Chesterfield & Manchester Railroad (later the Brighthope) was constructed to carry coal into the capital city. Similarly the Clover Hill Railroad was chartered in 1841, linking several Chesterfield County mines to the Richmond & Petersburg Railroad at Chester.

Still, many of the lines were disconnected. Most were concentrated in the Northeast, with fewer lines in the Southeast and Midwest. This would become a particular problem for the South as war broke out, as only a third of the national miles of trackage was theirs. And most of that was of shoddy workmanship and built to light-duty standards and often varying track gauges.

Of course, there were no safety or engineering standards, no governmental oversight, and little or no coordination from one railroad company to another. Thus accidents like that which destroyed the Best Friend of Charleston were frequent.

A map of the railroads of America prior to the Civil War reveals two interesting aspects for me. First is that there seemed to be clusters of rail lines. One was throughout the New England states. Another was around the port cities of New York, Trenton, Philadelphia, Baltimore, and Washington. Still another was in the Midwest, stretching from St. Louis to Chicago to Columbus to Pittsburgh. Second, there were almost no rail lines whatsoever in the Appalachian Mountains. In fact, from the east-west stretch of the B&O Railroad across the northern tier of what was then Virginia and now is West Virginia to the Chattanooga, Tennessee area, there were no trains that crossed the mountains into western Virginia, central Kentucky, and central Tennessee at all.

Trains would make their first forays into the mountains in the decades after the war ended, specifically to exploit the coal resources. Even today, there are only two rail lines that cross the barrier of mountains that run initially at the north along the Virginia/West Virginia state line northwest of Winchester all the way to Bristol. One is the Chesapeake and Ohio line, now CSX, burrowing under the Allegheny Mountain west of Covington alongside Interstate 64. The other follows the New River northwards from Radford and was the route of the Powhatan Arrow. As modest as the central Appalachian Mountains are compared with the lofty heights of the Rockies, the Andes, and the Himalayas, they always presented considerable challenges to rail engineers.

The coalfields west of Richmond are little known to modern

travelers as no commercial coal is still being mined there. The great Appalachian Mountain coalfields, stretching from Alabama to New York, but principally in eastern Kentucky, western Virginia and especially West Virginia, were experiencing an influx of workers and industrialization that would flourish for 70 or more years before reaching a zenith in about 1950. A relentless decline has been at play ever since.

But in the 1870s, no end seemed to be in sight for railroad development. An astounding 6,000 miles of track were laid annually between 1871 and 1873, ending abruptly by the Panic of 1873. This first worldwide depression, termed the Great Depression until upstaged by the events of the late 1920s and early 1930s, had several causes. German monetary policy depressed the US market for silver. Post-Civil War inflation was ongoing. The railroad construction boom exceeded demand, with overbuilding of not only rails but all ancillary facilities. The hostilities of Native Americans on the Great Plains drained railroad and government resources. Regardless of the relative influence of the component causes, the panic caused the first of many hiccups in the frantic path to industrialization.

In 1880, thirty of the nation's prominent machine builders and technical innovators met in the office of the magazine American Machinist in New York to discuss the tools, machines, and work practices going into boilers. This group formed the American Society of Mechanical Engineers, an organization that is still headquartered in New York. The ASME pooled the expertise and engineering savvy of the nation's engineers to specifically prevent boiler explosions. By that time, in spite of the considerable risks, there were no legal codes in any state.

Still, it wasn't until the early 1900s, following the disaster at the Grover Shoe Factory in Brockton, Massachusetts, on March 10, 1905, that boiler construction, inspection, and operations standards were legally mandated. In that accident, a four-story wooden structure, almost a city block square, was flattened, killing 58 and injuring another 150 when its boiler exploded. A newer boiler was out of service for maintenance, so an older boiler was put back into service. That Monday morning, as the boiler was being stoked to provide heat for the workers, it exploded, rocketing upwards through three stories and through the roof. Many workers who survived were trapped by pancaking floors, glass shards from broken windows (estimated at over 300), and heavy machinery, and the worst was yet to come. Burning coals from the boiler's fire box ignited broken timbers which set the place ablaze. More fires ignited when gas from severed lines exploded. The resulting inferno left wreckage like one of those photos of Hiroshima after the bomb.

On a more positive note, the 1880s saw continuing rapid expansions and improvements in the rail network and in the locomotive technologies. The standard gauge of 4 feet 8-1/2 inches (That's 1435 mm for you metric fans.), which is still used today was adopted, specifying universally, or at least nationally, the width separating the two rails on the track. Automatic knuckle-couplers were invented and were quickly deployed, as were air-brakes. Bridges were completed over many of the nation's largest rivers, such as the Mississippi, Ohio, and Missouri. By 1883, the Atchison, Topeka & Santa Fe reached New Mexico. That same year, the Northern Pacific had crested the Rockies, tunneled under the Cascades, and linked St. Paul, Minnesota and Seattle, Washington. Meanwhile, the Southern Pacific was arching across Texas, the southern deserts, and into Los Angeles.

By 1890, there were over 163,000 miles of track and by the turn of the 20th Century, over 193,000! The zenith was reached in 1916 at an incredible 254,037 miles, and we were indeed a nation of railroads, with the largest track mileage in the world. As a frame of reference, that is more than seven times the approximately 33,000 miles of Interstate highways that crisscross the nation now. Afterwards, track mileage began an inexorable decline that continues today.

Partially causal of the downturn was an increasingly emboldened federal government, which worked to rein in the greedy and monopolistic practices of the railroad magnates, along with similar practices in energy, finance, and other industries. Heavy restrictions, read "overbearing" depending upon your political makeup, were implemented, many of which remained in place until the deregulatory environment of the Reagan administration. Also, in the aftermath of World War I, other modes of transportation ate into the railroad stranglehold, increasingly including tractor-trailer trucks and private automobiles. Airplanes were becoming more reliable as aircraft such as the famed Ford Trimotor, introduced in 1925, gave travelers the opportunity to move from city to city with the reasonable expectation of being alive at the end of the flight.

Furthermore, most of the intercity trollies, the "interurbans," were discontinued, as travelers found modern automobiles more reliable, new expanded highways more convenient, and personal travel more desirable. In 1916, interurban lines across the country had over 15,000 miles of rail, but by the beginning of World War II, the number had fallen to under 3,000 miles.

The Great Depression cut deeply into the revenue streams of most American railway companies, and many fell by the wayside or were absorbed into stronger corporations. Somehow, the Norfolk & Western hung on.

Rail aficionados of the era did have one upbeat sign: the introduction of new technologies in locomotives and rolling stock that assumed the name "streamliner." Steam locomotives, as well as nascent diesel locomotives, emerged with aerodynamic looks and lighter-weight cars. One of my favorites is the 1933 model German DRG Class SVT 877, commonly known as the Flying Hamburger which could reach a top speed of 99 miles per hour!

Into this environment from the Norfolk & Western Railway East End Shops in Roanoke came the first batch of Class J locomotives. History would be unkind to the emerging Js, which were already facing the oncoming headlights of World War II and the dominance of diesel.

THE LAST LITTLE TOWN nearing the outskirts of Petersburg was Disputanta. As I mentioned, by legend it was named by the esteemed Mahones, Little Billy and Otelia, for their inability on what was presumably a shared bad hair day to come up with a mutually agreeable name.

I can only imagine what it must be like to live as a married couple in a town so named today.

Husband, "Let's have hamburgers for dinner, honey!"

Wife, "Let's have hot dogs!"

"Hamburgers."

"Hot dogs."

"HAMBURGERS!!!"

"HOT DOGS!!!"

"Oh, whatever."

"Fine!"

"FINE!"

I didn't stop the car in Disputanta.

8:20 a.m.

Petersburg

Mile 80.9

Colonial settlement built on an Indian village site. City is now a diversified manufacturing and distribution center with accent on tobacco. Much to interest students of Revolutionary and Civil Wars. (Battle of the Crater fought here.) National Military Park, City Point Rail Road, first N. & W. predecessor, built from James River nine miles to Petersburg in 1838. Connecting point for Richmond and Washington travelers. Camp Lee is nearby.

I got panhandled in Petersburg. In a most unusual way.

I am not a prejudiced person. I figure we're all the same inside, regardless of skin color. I have black friends who are kind and generous people, educated and involved in my community. But I live in a town that has about four percent blacks. Petersburg is around 80 percent black, the highest percentage of any city in the Commonwealth. And I have to admit that a street gang of black teens would worry me a bit if I was walking towards them. I really didn't know what to expect, but I was comfortable that walking on a city street in broad daylight wouldn't present any issues. I was wrong.

My quest in this travelogue was to seek out interesting places and people passionate about trains, their community, and history. This typically takes me to old downtowns, to the places that have seen the least change. I didn't know where downtown was in Petersburg, so I pointed the car towards what on the map looked like the greatest concentration of streets, and I went there.

I parallel parked on Sycamore Street, one of the main drags, and wandered about, carrying my satchel containing my iPad, my wallet, keys, and voice recorder. I'm sure I looked confused to two people sitting on a park bench. So I stopped, told them what I was doing there and had a chat with them. Her name was Cynthia Myers and his was Ronnie Howard. She was originally from Richmond but had been in Petersburg for 15 years. He was from Petersburg. After asking about the layout of the city and some places that I should visit, I asked him how the city had changed over the years.

He said, "Petersburg at one point was a beautiful place. Everybody would come downtown to shop on Saturdays. On Friday everybody got paid, and on Saturday the whole street here would be filled with people walking back-and-forth. There were all kinds of stores. There was a Red Cardinal drugstore. There was an A&N shoe store. There was a jewelry store. They are all gone now.

"I am 54 years old. Thirty years ago, when I was growing up, people were doing plant (industrial) work. They were working at Brown and Williamson in tobacco. Petersburg had lots of woodworking companies. Furniture factories. We had lumber stuff. Also, we had a Pepsi-Cola plant."

Cynthia said, "My family came down here for church services. You could go anywhere on the buses. People used to be all over the sidewalks, walking here and there. It was a really busy place, Petersburg was."

Ronnie said, "It was a town that nobody knew about. Now the only way we are in the news is if somebody gets killed. Petersburg was quiet and a very likable town, and people would want to come and stay here."

I joked, "It doesn't look dangerous to me." I looked up and down the sidewalk and only saw a smattering of people. There wasn't much traffic on Sycamore Street and most of the parking spaces were vacant.

He said, "It is not dangerous at all. It is very historical. There used to be a market down by the train tracks and the station. There were antique stores. That is how Petersburg was. It was very exciting."

I asked, "Is it depressing now?"

"Yes, oh yes. It is like a ghost town now," she said.

Ronnie agreed. "We need somebody to come in now, remodel everything, and fix it up. But it would still be a good historic place for anybody to come and see."

I said, "Are there drugs or gangs or violence?"

They both agreed there were no gangs. He said, "There is very little violence. It is a nice place for anybody to live; I can tell you that right now."

She said, "You are going to love it. Go on down to the old town."

I thanked them for their good cheer and turned to walk away towards old town, thinking about how different, how less affluent and less upscale, this downtown was from Norfolk's. A black man in his forties approached me. He was carrying a couple of plastic grocery bags. He said, "Can you help me, brother?" He asked if I could give him some money. "I have been diagnosed with prostate cancer," he told me, "and I lost my job. I was a fork-lift driver."

I kept walking. He walked with me. He was friendly, not threatening. He whipped out a company ID card that showed me his name: Junior. "Can you help me so I can buy some bread?" Junior pleaded with me. "I have two children, and I don't have my job no more." He wore a dark grey t-shirt and jeans. He had a broad smile. Good teeth.

I kept walking. It was a beautiful day with a perfect, comfortable temperature. He continued to walk with me. I didn't want to feed a drug habit if he had one, but I didn't want to create a scene, either.

I kept walking. "Junior," I said. "Tell you what. I'm headed down towards the old town and the railroad tracks. If we can find a grocery store, I'll buy you a loaf of bread." I was thinking that I'd just been the beneficiary of two night's free lodging, many kind gifts, and a couple of meals. It wouldn't hurt me to share some generosity.

I kept walking. Junior kept walking with me.

Junior the panhandler

As Ronnie and Cynthia alluded, Petersburg is dripping with history. It is the site of one of America's most important wartime battles, the Civil War siege of Petersburg in 1864-65. The "Cockade City," was founded as a trading post upstream of the confluence of the Appomattox River and the James River. By the outbreak of the Civil War, Petersburg was Virginia's second largest city and the seventh largest in the Confederacy, 23 miles south of Richmond, the largest.

In 1861, the city had about 18,000 people and would grow to a high-water mark of around 41,000 by 1980, but no further. The population has been on the decline since.

For most of the 1800s, Petersburg was more prosperous and even cosmopolitan than Richmond. By the outbreak of the war, it had a network of granite-paved streets, gas-powered streetlights, and a large reservoir that fed water through a municipal pipe system to town residents. It had two daily newspapers, several banks, 159 grocers, and various employers including textile and flour mills, a customs house for assessing import and export duties, slave auction houses, and of course the infrastructure to support the Virginia and Tennessee Railroad, later the Norfolk & Western.

At that time, about half of Petersburg was comprised of African Americans. Here's the part that's still mystifying to my 21st Century perspective: 3,000 of those were free and the other 6,000 or so were enslaved. How would they have countenanced this obvious dichotomy, with in some cases free and enslaved blacks working alongside one another? Fictional conversation: First black guy, "I just got a raise! I make 38 cents an hour. How about you?" Second black guy, "Oh, I'm a slave. I don't make anything."

Just north of downtown on a peninsula in the Appomattox River was a settlement called Pocahontas Island which housed one of the oldest and largest communities of free blacks in the country. Even in those days, many, both free and slave, were employed by the railroad, with the slaves' wages paid to their owners. Others worked as laborers or in owners' homes. The percentage of blacks increased steadily.

Petersburg has always been a major transportation center. The Virginia and Tennessee Railroad came through the city in the 1850s, linking east and west on our corridor of interest. The CSX came through the city as well, linking north and south, the modern incarnation of the Chessie System and the Seaboard System Railroad, formerly the Seaboard Air Line Railroad. The CSX and NS now have a duopoly over all rail traffic east of the Mississippi River, excluding Amtrak whose trains run on the rails of one or the other. The city's metro area is also served by Interstate Highways 95, 85, and 295.

Petersburg was founded in the 1630s by English colonists moving westward out of the Tidewater from the initial colony at Jamestown. Their arrival at Pocahontas Island and to the core of present day downtown Petersburg occurred in 1635. Ten years later, Fort Henry was built at the falls of the Appomattox River. Shortly thereafter, explorer Abraham Woods began a series of expeditions to the west, one of which took him all the way to the New River; he was reputedly the first European to ever see it, and in effect charted what would later become our corridor of interest. I'm still not sure why the New River isn't the Woods River, or better yet (for me at least, for obvious reasons) Abraham's River. I still lament that.

Around 1675, Wood's son-in-law, Peter Jones, established a trading post near the fort which he commanded at the time. The store became "Peter's Point" and eventually Petersburgh and now Petersburg. The fledgling city was incorporated in 1748.

The city remained mostly quiet during the Revolutionary War, but in the War of 1812, a group of men assembled into a fighting unit they called the Petersburg Volunteers. President James Madison named Petersburg the "Cockade of the Union" or the "Cockade City" after the cockades which festooned the Volunteers' hats. If like me you didn't know, a cockade is a rosette or knot of ribbons. I mistakenly thought it was a feathered thing. Learn something new every day. Petersburg is the knotted city, so to speak.

The city continued to grow, attracting many free blacks due to the availability of jobs there. Two of the oldest black churches in the country were established. The large population of free blacks made Petersburg an important way-station on the Underground Railroad.

Petersburg avoided much of the bloodshed that occurred throughout the South and especially Virginia in the early years of the war. Its luck ran out in a major way as Federal troops under the command of Ulysses S. Grant gained proximity to the city in 1864. Then all hell broke loose and fighting continued for 292 days, the Siege of Petersburg, almost ten months of ongoing assault and bombardment.

So let's go back to that summer of 1864. Through three long years of war, President Abraham Lincoln was determined that an all-out effort be made to crush the Confederacy, with the Confederate capital at Richmond being the ultimate prize. He thought he found a man for the job in the relentless Grant. A cigar-chomping man with a reputation for unflinchingly moving forward towards his strategic objectives in spite of horrific casualties, Grant proved himself determined to achieve victory irrespective of staggering losses. When winter gave way to another killing season in early 1865, he would be undeterred in pursuing Lee's Army of Northern Virginia, whatever it took.

When the war began, Richmond had already been Virginia's capital and most important city for a hundred years. When the Confederates moved their government there in May 1861, Richmond became a military headquarters, prison, transportation center, hospital, and munitions manufacturing and staging arsenal. In doing so, it fell squarely in the bulls-eye of Union commanders.

Grant's army had arrived in the Petersburg-Richmond area by early June, 1864, and conducted multiple raids and fought many battles aiming to cut supply lines between the two cities and eventually force the withdrawal of rebel troops from both. In a series of battles north of Richmond collectively known as the Overland Campaign, Grant's Army of the Potomac and Lee's Army of Northern Virginia engaged in some of the bloodiest contests the world had ever known. The names of those hallowed battlegrounds live on in horrific memories: The Wilderness. Spotsylvania Court House. North Anna. Old Church. And finally the bloodbath at Cold Harbor. In each of these engagements, Lee's dwindling army of battle-hardened but hungry, tattered, outnumbered, and outgunned men repelled a well-equipped, continually re-enforced enemy. But with each battle, Lee's grey-uniformed men became more exhausted.

In a month of fighting, the Grant's Army of the Potomac suffered almost 40,000 casualties, almost as many as his distinguished foe's entire army, yet the unremitting general kept moving forward, undeterred. The butchery to which Grant submitted his men was the subject of newspaper columns throughout the northern cities, but Lincoln continued to send him reinforcements, new troops and armaments the Confederates couldn't match. Grant would entertain no outcome other than the complete, unconditional surrender of his Confederate foe.

As most of this carnage occurred north of Richmond, Petersburg was spared, yet virtually completely vulnerable, as most able-bodied men had long before been sent to Lee's command. Few remaining men in Petersburg possessed any fighting skills or even working weapons.

At the conclusion of the battle at Cold Harbor, named for a tavern that did not serve hot meals, Richmond was still held by the Confederates. Stinging from utter defeat in one of the war's most lopsided battles, Grant abruptly changed course and sent his entire army in a clockwise direction east and south of Richmond. Under Grant's command, 450 engineers, mostly New Yorkers, constructed a 2,100 foot long, 11 foot wide pontoon bridge over the James River in a single day, over which he transported his entire army of 100,000 and all manner of cannons, baggage wagons, ambulances, and hearses, literally before Lee even knew he was gone.

Grant's new headquarters was established at City Point, the confluence of the Appomattox and James rivers, ten miles northeast of Petersburg. Thus on June 9, 1864, the siege began, and it would last until March 25 of the following year, subjecting combatants on both sides to seemingly endless, abject misery.

Because of the gathering of rail lines in Petersburg, Grant recognized its importance in supplying Lee's army and the city of Richmond. So Grant's priority was to sever those lines, an action that predicated the construction of more than 30 miles of trenches from the eastern outskirts of Richmond to the east and south of Petersburg with frequent assaults and raids.

The trench warfare was a precursor to the same style of war that would occur 50 years later in the forests of France in the Great War, the war we'd later rename World War I.

It was clear at this point that Grant had the upper hand. Grant's plan shifted from a campaign of direct confrontation during the Overland Campaign to a more patient, measured war of attrition where he could pin Lee down and starve his armies of the food, weaponry, ammunition, and other supplies they needed to maintain the fight. Lee, believing Richmond to be Grant's main target, allowed only meager defenses of Petersburg, much to the suffering of the Cockade City's citizens, who were victims of continuous bombardment and increasing scarcities of everyday necessities.

There were lots of back and forth assaults, victories and losses, which finally culminated in Lee's retreat westward toward his ultimate fate in Appomattox. Our new best friend, then Brigadier General William Mahone, distinguished himself in several skirmishes, notably the Jerusalem Plank Road on June 21 through 23, 1864, and the Battle of the Crater on July 30 of the same year.

On June 21, Mahone observed that the Union army in the area of the Jerusalem Plank Road about four miles south of Petersburg had split itself, allowing a gap between two corps. Knowing the area well from his railroad surveying work prior to the war, he knew about a ravine where he could hide his troops and attack the enemy under the command of Brig. Gen. Francis C. Barlow from the rear. Mahone commanded only 8,000 troops versus 27,000 Federals, but Lee approved Mahone's plan and by 3:00 p.m., Mahone's men attacked. The surprise routed Barlow's corps which quickly collapsed, and the rout continued until darkness ended the fighting. Playing the numbers game, with Mahone losing 572 casualties to Barlow's 2962, it was a firm Confederate victory, but by no means enough to turn the tide. The dapper Little Billy Mahone, with a cavalryman's hat and a jet-black long pointed beard, lived to fight again.

While our view at this distance in time indicates that Grant was more than willing to wage a protracted siege, in fact, he may have been a bit more impatient than we realize. His experience from his siege at Vicksburg a year earlier convinced him that this type of warfare was debilitating and costly. So when Lt. Col. Henry Pleasants, commander of an infantry unit from Pennsylvania, approached him with a bizarre scheme to shorten the war, he was apparently ready to listen. Pleasants had been a mining engineer prior to the war, and he proposed digging a tunnel over 500 feet long and 20 feet below ground under the Confederate trench works, filling it with 8,000 pounds of gunpowder, and blowing it to smithereens. And so he did.

It was an impressive feat of engineering, with a clever ventilation system using a constantly burning fire at a secondary entrance to create a draft and an upslope towards the end to preclude moisture accumulation. The roof was supported by timbers from an old bridge and an abandoned wood mill. Construction took just over two weeks and was undetected by the Confederates, less than the length of two football fields away, the entrance hidden down an embankment.

Lo and behold, in the pre-dawn of July 30, a deafening explosion rocked the Confederates from their slumber. The immediate blast killed 278 soldiers and left a crater 170 feet long, 60 feet wide, and 30 feet deep and showered the area around it with dirt, guns, blood, and broken men.

The Federals' plan was to commence an attack on the rebel soldiers in proximity, taking advantage of their surprise and shock. Somehow, in what today we would describe as a clusterf*ck, the Federals failed to take advantage of the chaos they had created. There was much discussion beforehand as to which troops would be used for the initial foray. Finally, Brig. Gen. James H. Ledlie's division was chosen, in spite of his known propensity for taking to the bottle before critical battles. As the clash ensued, Ledlie was reputably well behind the battle line, drunk. His staggering ineptitude later caused his dismissal. So his men, rather than encircling the hissing, blood-spattered crater, entered into it, with nobody alive to shoot and no easy escape from the crater walls.

Many of the Federal soldiers Ledlie sent into battle were pinned in. The commanding general, Ambrose Burnside, ordered the United States Colored Troops to follow Ledlie's men into battle. But rebel reinforcements under Mahone's command arrived and counterattacked. He roused as many of his Confederates as he could and began shooting at the Federals who had entrapped themselves, an action he later called a "turkey shoot." When all was said and done, the Union suffered 3,798 casualties and the Confederates 1,491. Grant wrote to Chief of Staff Henry W. Halleck, "It was the saddest affair I have witnessed in this war."

For many historians, Mahone is better known for what happened during and immediately following that battle than anything he did before or after. Rebels were particularly incensed by being killed by Negroes and reacted with unparalleled brutality. Those blacks that weren't killed in battle but were captured were paraded in front of enraged Confederates. An estimated 200 blacks were killed in captivity after the fighting had ceased. At some level, Mahone was culpable, with the moral responsibility affixed on Confederate leadership. Yet after the war, as we'll see in a moment, Mahone is associated with post-war policies to improve the lot of blacks. Thus Mahone's legacy is complicated.

In spite of the carnage, heavier again on the Union side, the stalemate continued as the strategic situation remained as before. The siege continued.

On March 25, 1865, the Union finally broke through and ransacked Petersburg. Richmond fell on April 4, and Confederate President Jefferson Davis skedaddled, along with his Cabinet and fractured government, to a new capital in Danville in the home of tobacco mogul, William T. Sutherlin, where it remained for only a week before Lee surrendered to Grant at Appomattox on April 9, ending the war. Davis, not one to ever give up needlessly, evacuated again, this time to Greensboro, North Carolina. He eventually gave up the cause and was arrested on May 10, 1865, and charged with treason.

After the war, life resumed in Petersburg, with a steadily improving economy and growth. Many freedmen came to the city to benefit from the society of freed blacks from before the war. In 1869, at Howard's Grove Hospital, the General Assembly incorporated the Central Lunatic Asylum, which from its opening until 1915, treated psychosis and its supposed causes, including emancipation, marriage, desertion, abortion, masturbation, and typhoid fever. We all know that masturbation causes psychosis, eh? And of course marriage.

And in 1882, the state opened Virginia State University to educate Negroes. It was the nation's first fully state-supported four year college for blacks. Our old friend Billy Mahone was a founding member of the Virginia Readjuster Party, a biracial political organization formed to "break the power of wealth and established privileged" among his planter peers. In apparent contrast to his Confederate service, Mahone was a major proponent of the education and socioeconomic advancement of the former slaves of the south, a noble cause that engendered widespread scorn from many of his contemporaries for the rest of his life.

As we reach into Petersburg's 20th Century history, we find a city increasingly dominated by Richmond and suffering terribly from "white flight", as wealthier whites left the city for the suburbs.

Beyond our Mahone, who at one point was mayor of Petersburg, famous natives are civil rights leader Vernon Johns and the late basketball player Moses Malone. I kept thinking, due to similar surname spelling, Malone may have been Billy Mahone's great-great-great-grandson. But probably not, given that Mahone was 5 feet 5 inches tall and white and Malone was 6 feet 11 inches tall and black.

So my new friend Junior the panhandler and I continued to walk downhill on Sycamore Street. The commercial buildings were mainly two- and three-stories tall and about half were occupied.

On our right was Petersburg's beautiful 1838 Courthouse. It was set back from the road up a small hill. It had six white two-story columns framing a yellow painted exterior and topped with a two-tiered octagonal cupola with a dial clock above, and above that a statue of some famous Greek mythological hero. Or somebody. Its grand entrance was above a long sidewalk, some stairs, and a brick street. It was fetchingly charming and impressive.

We ambled farther downhill and around the unique octagonal city market building, which was locked. We wandered over to the Petersburg Union Station that was also locked. Behind it to the north were train tracks and beyond that the Appomattox River. The station looked as if it had been restored and refurbished. All the streets were paved with granite bricks, and there was scant traffic.

There were a number of interpretive signs that told of the city's history. One of them told me that I was at Corling's Corner, the center of historic Petersburg's industrial past. Here, wealthier farmers, manu-facturers, railroad companies, and building contractors inspected and rented enslaved people to work for them. Petersburg's tobacco factories were probably the largest users of this rented labor. Renting slaves was a common form of commerce prior to emancipation.

Junior and I went inside the Old Towne Petersburg Visitors Center on Bollingbrook Street (which if you ask me, is a great name for a street). It was housed in a former Farmers' Bank building, built in 1817 and operated as a bank until 1866. I asked the two nice ladies inside, one white and one

Petersburg Train Station

black, about their city. They mentioned their most adept local histo-rian, a man named Delaney Ward, would be by later, and could I stick around? I told them I'd do some exploring and then return in an hour.

In asking us if we would sign their guest book, they also asked if were together, me and my new friend, Junior. I assumed they were skeptical, as we shared no resemblance. I just shrugged with one of those polite shrugs that hopefully indicated I wasn't sure the best answer to the seemingly simple question. And then Junior and I departed.

By this time, I had no idea whether Junior was for real or not, and whether he indeed had cancer and starving children and other related deprivations. I had no idea whether he liked me by now, whether he still held hope that his hour of peaceful, directed panhandling had any hope of being fruitful, or whether he was looking for an opportunity to mug me and make his get-away. But I was tiring of having him as my shadow. So while he wasn't looking, I checked in my wallet to see if I had a couple of dollars to give him. Finding only $5 bills, I handed him one and said, "Here you go," and wished him well. What was I going to do, ask him to make change?

"Thank you brother!" he shouted, and pranced merrily away.

I walked back downhill to the railroad tracks, under the high overpass of US-1. I thought to explore Pocahontas Island, the old community that once housed free blacks before the Civil War. I realized I had become frightened and wondered if it was a good idea to walk alone in a totally black neighborhood. Half-way there, I turned and walked back to the city market area.

I spoke with some guys doing construction on an older building's brick façade. Workers had made and bolted to it a wooden frame. They were stapling to the frame a vinyl covering that merely looked like the same brick; it was a forgery.

I spoke with one of the guys, a bandanna wrapped around his head, who looked to be a foreman. He said they were building a set for a made-for-TV movie, *Mercy Street*, set during the Civil War. He said the show had been filmed for several years, and each year they came back and rebuilt the set and then tore it down when they were done.

"As long as they want to use this building," he told me, "we will be putting (the set) up and taking it down. That is what we do. We are building both interior and exterior sets. This building is the exterior of the hospital. In a building over yonder," he pointed, "we have a tunnel entrance where a guy can look like he came out of the ground. We are building stuff all around here."

Behind us, somebody was shooting an air stapler. An air compressor churned.

I asked if it required much carpentry skills to set up something and then tear down a week later.

He said, "The goal is to make it look like it is the greatest carpentry in the world. We are always looking for fast, quick, and easy ways to put it up. I think some of the top carpenters in the country are in this industry. We make doors and frames from scratch. We like putting it up and taking it down!" He told me that they traveled all over the country building movie sets. But, "I live here, and so I happen to be at home for this job where I can spend every night with my family."

I WALKED BACK TO THE MUSEUM where Delaney Ward awaited me. He had a mop of white hair and wild eyebrows flowing enough to ski on. He bore a passing resemblance to an older Bob Denver, the actor from Gilligan's Island.

Delaney told me that the building we were in was built in 1817. "There was a huge fire in this area that burned about 800 buildings in 1815. Immediately afterwards, 300 new buildings were constructed. Many of them were not as fancy as this one. So many of the buildings that you see here in downtown Petersburg date back to that event."

I told him about my route following the Powhatan Arrow and asked him if Petersburg was the most important city historically on it.

He said, "This and Norfolk, probably. In 1860, Petersburg was the second largest city in Virginia and the seventh largest in the entire Confederacy. It was larger at that time than Atlanta.

"Tobacco made it important initially. It was also the sphere of influence for a vast hinterland to the west and south. In North Carolina, the next real port is all the way down at Wilmington. The Appomattox River was navigable by oceangoing vessels as far as Petersburg.

"Tobacco was transferred to cities like Petersburg either by cart on the roads or by bateaux on the rivers. (I'll tell you more about bateaux shortly.) Here it was stored and prepared for shipment overseas. As early as the 1830s, the railroads replaced that. They were fully replaced by the end of the 19th Century.

Delaney Ward

"The first railroad in Virginia, and the fifth railroad in the entire country, was created by the Petersburg City Council. It was simply called the Petersburg Railroad. It ran to Weldon, North Carolina, south from here. That was part of the hinterland, in the Petersburg sphere of economic influence. The railroad made it a lot easier to move the tobacco here. It was opened in 1832. This was vitally important and dramatic because it was the first interstate railroad in the United States.

"Within a decade, there was another railroad to Richmond and still another one to City Point, which is now Hopewell. The Appomattox River was difficult to keep open, because it constantly silted up. It was really not a good river to support commercial traffic.

"The next railroad to reach here was in the 1850s. This was the South Side Rail Road. It went to Lynchburg and is the route that you are now following. In Lynchburg, it connected with the Virginia and Tennessee Railroad all the way to Bristol. It was also largely subsidized by the city of Petersburg.

"Until the 1850s, Petersburg was among the most prosperous cities in the east. The Civil War hit the city massively. Billy Mahone bought some property in 1858 to build the station here and he settled here. After he consolidated the South Side Rail Road, the Norfolk to Petersburg Railroad, and the Virginia and Tennessee Railroad, he built his headquarters here in Petersburg. But understand Petersburg was a center for actual roads because prior to that it was a prominent settlement for the Native Americans before the English settlers arrived. This was the southwestern corner of the Powhatan world."

He said that the city became the principal entry point for African slaves in the Chesapeake region. "There really weren't a lot of Africans here until the 17th Century. We now know that there were a handful of Africans here before 1620.

"In 1620 the first legislative assembly occurred and the first African-Americans were brought here as slaves. There were many English indentured servants as well. The standard in England at that time was that almost all kids were apprenticed out at some time. They were not raised in their own families, even rich kids. If you were an orphan, meaning that your father was dead, you were always going to be apprenticed out. That shifted into slavery. And it was race-based. It was excused in everybody's mind by the basis of race.

"When the apprentice supply dried up, slavery became even more prevalent. In the early part of the 18th Century, the British got hold of a license from the Pope to run slavery trade in the Western Hemisphere. By 1620, Petersburg had more people than Jamestown, the first settlement."

Jamestown was always a rotten place to settle. The soil wasn't good. It was swampy. There was no good drinking water.

Delaney continued, "In the years between 1740 and the Revolutionary War, most of the slaves came in through City Point. That means it was the largest importation place in Virginia. At the outset of the Civil War, there were 3,500 free blacks in Petersburg. There were 18,000 people overall and approximately 9,000 were black. So a little more than a third of the blacks were free."

I said, "How could that work? How can a third of the population of black people be free and the other two-thirds enslaved?"

He said, "It was a complex social situation. Thomas Jefferson had written in the *Declaration of Independence* that all people are equal. Everybody knew slavery was untenable.

"The slave trade here was much more than in Richmond. It was much like Lynchburg's in size and scale. Railroads were used for the trade. In 1776, there were not many slaves in Virginia. Between 1830 and 1860, those three decades, 350,000 Virginia slaves were sold down the river, meaning to the Deep South. This is a phenomenal number. And yet Virginia's number of slaves had not decreased. In Maryland, the number of slaves during the same time decreased 80 percent. Virginia was growing slaves, having babies that would later be sold.

"During the siege of Petersburg, hundreds of buildings downtown were struck by shells, including this one. The shells varied in size and in destructive power. Many of the buildings that were hit were not destroyed. Some of the shells had explosives in them and some didn't. Probably more damage was done by the force of the shells than by the explosions. One shell was recorded as literally having gone through 14 walls.

"As they did in Richmond, the retreating Confederates set fire to the tobacco warehouses and to the munitions stores as they abandoned the city. Union troops were closer here, and they quickly put out those fires. We didn't have large arms manufacturing here like they did in Richmond. But the Confederates set almost everything on fire. In this case, the Union soldiers were the good guys.

"The station that has been refurbished is the Union Station. It housed both the Norfolk & Western and the Atlantic Coastline railroads. The oldest railroad in any southern state is the South Side Rail Road. It is the only one that survived the Civil War. After the war, once Billy Mahone linked all the railroads here, the city became less important. Norfolk was a more natural port, and it took less time and money to get the goods down there on the rail. So taking the goods to Norfolk became more sensible. Mahone did that back in the late 1860s and early 1870s. When the depression hit in 1873, Mahone began to lose control of the railroad that he had pieced together. It was completely out of his hands by 1877.

"Petersburg was still a vigorous community. Jubal Early was a conservative political rival to Mahone. One of the issues was the share of pre-war debt. On honor, Early and his faction wanted to pay it entirely. That included any debt that may have been owed by what became West Virginia. Mahone asserted that there needed to be a readjustment of this. He felt that (Virginia) should not be paying West Virginia's portion of it. And if we did pay the whole thing, we would have to close the public school system. The public schools system that educated all whites and blacks regardless of income was one of the good things that happened during reconstruction."

I asked, "Why do you think a conservative wanted to do this?"

He said, "To be honest with you, I think they felt that only rich people should be educated.

"Petersburg hit its zenith in importance in the 1850s. But it was still vigorous and had a lot going on for several more decades. Mahone was the last Virginian to (personally) own a railroad within the state. That is a sign of importance in a community. There were a lot of really nice houses built during that period. There was still a strong tobacco industry here.

"For decades, Brown and Williamson was the largest employer in the city. They're completely gone now. Today we have a lot of empty storefronts downtown and a lot of poverty. In 1850, the population was probably 55 percent black. Now it is probably 75 percent black. It is only about 15 percent white. The rest is Hispanic folks."

I took a quick look at my watch and realized that I was probably overdue on my two-hour streetside free parking. The lady at the museum said that I shouldn't worry about it. She said the meter maids almost never ticketed anybody. I said, "One of the good things about a city that is struggling is that there is typically no problem in finding a place to park."

Delaney said retail companies were not coming into downtown Petersburg or really anywhere else. He said most new development was by young people, entrepreneurs, who were finding these older buildings were good places to start things. There was a new restaurant with 160 seats next-door with $1 million in new investment.

Delaney then took me on a walking tour of the city. We went past the 1909 Union Station again that I'd seen before with Junior. "It is owned by the city now. The city renovated it to look like it did before. They use it for council meetings."

We toured the old city market that also had been refurbished. We looked at an old warehouse along the track that was half in ruin, torn apart by a tornado in 1993. "It is the Southside Depot. It was a passenger station, built in 1854. It was 450 feet long. It was struck by shells during the war. The shells were not intended to be damaging to the buildings as much as to create terror among the residents, hoping they could be driven out."

We walked on granite brick streets. He said they were likely laid in the late 1800s. "It was cut granite. Petersburg has a significant seam of granite that runs along the Fall Line all the way from Richmond to Georgia. The Fall Line was a hard, physical line. Both the James and the Appomattox cross the line and turn and run alongside it, the James to the south and the Appomattox to the north.

"There was manufacturing here for machines like peanut shellers and harvesters and things."

We walked past the tracks. He said they were largely unused now, as coming into downtown required a descent to the river and then a climb back out. Also, the newer route south of the city was straighter and thus shorter. We headed over towards Pocahontas Island, the original settlement of many freed blacks. He noted that we were only ten feet or so above sea level, but that rising seas weren't as much an issue for Petersburg as for Norfolk.

"There have been two tornadoes here since I arrived. The first took off twenty roofs in 1984. In August, 1993, a massive tornado swept right through town. It destroyed a Walmart and killed five people there. It damaged half the buildings in old-town. It was like a run-away truck running through dough. I don't think there is a record of tornadoes in the past. But in those two years, tornados hit this place.

"We have had some floods; all river cites have had them. And we've had fires. And one or two earthquakes. But no large ones."

I asked if the city had bottomed out, economically.

He said, "I think so. This area has been coming back for 30 years. It's gaining some steam now."

I enjoyed that railroad imagery and decided that was a wrap! I thanked Delaney, returned to my car (which, incidentally, had no parking ticket), and set a course for the apartment of Katie Walser.

ONE OF THE TRAVEL TECHNIQUES I planned to use to make this trip was an Internet-based hosting service called Couchsurfers. Anyone interested looks at its website and finds information on people willing to host travelers who want to come to their location. Back home, my wife and I had hosted dozens of people at our place. Here in Petersburg,

I had made arrangements to be a houseguest this night with a young woman named Katie Walser.

Katie was a high school history teacher. I found her apartment on the second floor of a new apartment complex. It had two bedrooms, a kitchen, a living room, and two bathrooms. It was absolutely immaculate. I was surprised that a young single woman would take in strangers, but she was open and friendly. She drove me to a BBQ restaurant for dinner together. Thanking her for taking me in, I said, "I hate motels. If I was staying in a motel tonight I'd be eating alone and reading a book in my room."

Katie smiled. She told me that she was from the Chicago suburbs, a town called Downers Grove. She was a high school teacher, but frankly didn't look much older than a high school student to me. Maybe I'm getting old.

She told me she started off teaching at Petersburg High School. "It was one of the most challenging experiences that I have ever had. I had great co-workers and often very good-hearted students. But the day-to-day behavioral and academic challenges were like nothing I had ever experienced before. I went to school every day not sure what I was going to find. Every day was an emotional roller coaster, and I would come home exhausted with more work to do, it seemed.

"It was really hard. I was pushed closer to my breaking point than I have ever come. The school was overwhelmingly African-American. Of the 70 or so students that I taught at Petersburg High School, maybe four were not African-American. I think overall, perhaps 95 percent of the student body was black."

Thinking about my own experience earlier that day with Junior I wondered if she had ever been threatened. She was diminutive, a waif. I asked her about being a small, female, young white teacher in an overwhelmingly black school.

"I was never threatened. One time after school I was meeting with a student who was not my own, but he came into my classroom and said things to me and I felt extremely uncomfortable. I have never walked away and locked my door so quickly as I did in that instance. But I was never threatened beyond that."

I asked how she felt about the city.

She said, "Honestly, my experiences are limited. It is a really beautiful place. There are lots of good things about Petersburg. There are lots of challenges as well because of corruption or drugs. There is still a lot for me to discover. I am fairly new, a transplant. Petersburg has done many good things for me. It has provided me with a job out of college. It has provided a really good learning experience. It has definitely changed my life.

"The schools in Petersburg have an opportunity to be better. They have the chance to offer the students a better education and therefore to live a better life. The fact is the students are being robbed of that, because of the administration at the school level or at the district level, or it may be a combination of both.

"The time I worked in Petersburg High School was challenging, but now I have gone on and have a really good opportunity to work at another school, the Appomattox Regional Governors School, and that has been wonderful.

"I plan to stay here for a few more years and then go to graduate school. You never know what is going to happen in life. I am not dating anybody right now. I would eventually like to meet somebody on the way. We'll see when that happens. I am not going to push anything that is not going to happen on its own eventually."

"Are you happy here?"

"Yes. I am. I am really happy here. By the time your book comes out, my situation may have changed. But hopefully I will still be happy. That is the plan."

After dinner, she drove me around town, first through some of the poorer sections to the east and then into the National Battlefield Park. It was dusk and a blaze-orange sun stretched towards the western horizon. Deer grazed lazily on the former killing grounds. Massive mortars still sat in place from 150 years earlier.

We went to the Crater area and saw the entrance to the tunnel, now blocked with a door. We walked around the crater itself. It looked like a low, oblong impression in the ground. It was a scene of incredible peace and serenity, at a former scene of unspeakable horror and bloodshed.

Were Katie and I not ineligible for a romantic moment, this would have been one, a crepuscular stroll with a lovely young woman.

DELANEY HAD TOUCHED on the history of tobacco in early Virginia and the incredible impact it had on the emerging colony's economy. Tobacco's history is almost as old as the country itself.

When European explorers came to the Americas and claimed various regions for their supporting countries, it wasn't just for the joy and satisfaction of exploration, to boldly go where no man had gone before; it was largely for economic exploitation.

Within days of reaching land, Columbus observed Native Americans carrying and using the plant. By the time of Christ, Native Americans were thought to be using tobacco, by smoking, by hallucinogenic enemas (Let's think about that one for a moment... or perhaps let's not.), and mostly by chewing. Tobacco was widespread throughout the Americas. A pottery vessel dating back to the 11th Century depicts smoking tobacco. Among the natives Columbus encountered, these dried leaves were traded like spears, precious metals, and fruits. Some of Columbus' men, uninitiated to the pleasures of a nicotine high, threw away the gift leaves.

Columbus seemed to have been focused on precious minerals, sending home gold and silver and launching a rush into Central and South America. Apparently, a crewman named Rodrigo de Jerez took an interest in the smoking habits of the natives and thus ignominiously became the first European in history addicted to tobacco. Upon return to Spain on the Niña, he brought tobacco with him to his hometown of Ayamonte. His nasty habit caught the attention of the local constable who imprisoned him for seven years, reasoning that only the Devil could give man the power to exhale smoke from his mouth.

Petersburg granite brick street

Let us take a moment to envision this conversation between Jerez and a fellow inmate. "What are you in for?" Jerez asks. "Rape and murder," his cellmate replies. "You?" he asks. Jerez moans sardonically, "Smoking. From my mouth." By the time his imprisonment was over, smoking was widespread, and hapless Jerez gained nothing from it.

By the 1520s, many Spaniard users were already addicted, and tobacco arrived in France in 1556 and Portugal in 1558.

Around about that time, Englishman Francis Drake emerged as a fierce rival to the established Spaniards, making his first transatlantic trip at the age of 23 in 1563, earning their enmity, as they considered him a pirate. He's also the second person to circumnavigate the world, an extraordinary feat for which he never received any accolades. (Nobody ever remembers the second person to do anything! Do you know the second person to fly solo across the Atlantic? Do you know the second person to run a sub-four minute mile? Of course you don't.)

Drake returned from the Americas and introduced pipe smoking to Britain. Later knighted in 1581, presumably for addicting an entire nation to nicotine, Drake also carried from the New World the potato. Both were met with some suspicion in England, but in a stunning twist of irony, the potato was thought to be poisonous while tobacco was rapidly broadly accepted. And both, in their own way, changed the world.

From an historic perspective, we never seem to be able to utter the word "potato" without the word "famine" behind it. Sadly and somewhat undeservedly, the potato was vilified as being the cause of death to a million Irishmen from 1845 until 1852. The blame was not entirely justified. In the decades prior to this "Great Hunger," the Irish had cultivated, disproportionately, a single species of the potato, the Irish Lumper, and its high nutritional value and hardiness made it a staple food, dramatically increasing the overall population of the island. When the blight developed, essentially the entire crop was devastated, leaving millions of people malnourished. At that time in Ireland, there were no equivalent stores of other varieties, as there were in the Americas, to take over the nutritional workload for burgeoning populations. So, the lack of genetic variability in Ireland produced a dire situation that wasn't replicated elsewhere in Europe or in the Americas. Why am I telling you this seemingly unrelated story in the midst of this travelogue? Because it presents a valuable lesson applicable even today, as monocultures, while momentarily and monetarily efficient, lack ecological resiliency.

England and all of Europe seemed to have developed an instant infatuation with tobacco. By 1580, the pestilence was complete and tobacco could be found throughout Europe. In 1585, Drake introduced smoking to Sir Walter Raleigh, who fifteen years later convinced Queen Elizabeth to take up the habit as well. To this day, for his transgressions, Sir Walter is still imprisoned in a can.

Three years later, in 1603, just after he took the throne, King James I was besieged by physicians demanding consumer protections. Astonishingly, tobacco was envisioned to cure over three dozen diseases. Many smokers complained that physicians were keeping tobacco's medicinal benefits a secret fearing they would no longer be needed. Physicians complained that if everyday citizens could buy tobacco without a prescription from them, their livelihood would be threatened.

In response, King James, with insight we hope all monarchs might exhibit, said that smoking is a "custom loathsome to the eye, hateful to the nose, harmful to the brain, dangerous to the lungs, and in the black and stinking fume thereof, nearest resembling the horrible stygian smoke of the pit that is bottomless." I suspect those physicians didn't ask for his help again after that.

And thus, in an inexplicable twist of fate, tobacco began its dance with the medical profession that seems to have lasted until about a generation ago regarding its health aspects and medicinal qualities. There would forever be an increasing workload for physicians due to nicotine!

By the 1600s, a vast trading network became established across the Atlantic, many taking advantage of the predominant winds and currents, in what became called "triangular trade." Commonly a merchant vessel would depart England laden with alcoholic spirits and manufactured textiles and other goods, headed south for sub-Saharan Africa. There, it would off-load this cargo and re-stock with human cargo, slaves destined for the Americas. Slaves would be deposited in Savannah, Norfolk, Baltimore, or Philadelphia while sugar, cotton, and tobacco were loaded for the trip back to England.

Always seeking a competitive advantage, Spain in 1614 proclaimed Seville the tobacco capital of the world. Interestingly, Seville, like Petersburg, is a port city 50 miles inland. Spain's law mandated that any incoming tobacco from the new world be off-loaded in Seville, quickly establishing it as the world's leading center for cigar production. England and France passed similar laws dictating the movement of tobacco through their countries. King James I of England established taxation on tobacco, while in France, Louis XIV made tobacco distribution and sale a governmental cartel.

Coincidentally and ironically, while governments and citizens were benefiting monetarily from the tobacco trade, it was increasingly obvious that tobacco was in fact not providing health benefits; rather it was prematurely killing people. Physicians of the day were unhesitant in performing autopsies, and the filthy, oleaginous black goo that permeated deceased smokers' lungs was obvious to even untrained eyes. And nicotine's addictive property rapidly asserted itself.

Seemingly responsible governments began imposing increasingly dire punishments for tobacco use, including fines, torture, or imprisonment, which seemed to have had all the efficacy of reducing consumption as today's prohibition on marijuana. The Catholic Church got in on the act by stating that tobacco use was sinful, but since there were no biblical references – remember, tobacco as a New World product would not have appeared in the Holy Land – nobody took much mind.

The bad news is that tobacco has a really good chance of killing its user. The good news is that Virginia, and Southside Virginia in particular, was a great place to grow it. From the first years of permanent English settlement in what was to become the United States of America, tobacco was colonial Virginia's most successful crop, and for a time essentially the only cultivated plant of any export value back in the Mother Country.

John Rolfe, one of the early settlement's most prominent and now famous individuals, obtained the seeds of Nicotiana tabacum from Spaniard sailors in 1612, and found it to be smoother and less bitter to the English taste than the Virginia Indians' Nicotiana rustica. Tabacum originated in the Orinoco River valley of South America, mostly in modern Venezuela and Colombia. But when planted in the loamy, flat soil of the James River it produced a milder leaf that was readily accepted by English, and then European, consumers.

The Spaniards who preceded Rolfe had already brought tobacco from the Americas back to Europe and had established a market in England. Rolfe's earliest attempts at growing hadn't produced the fine quality and taste the market demanded. But inventive Virginia farmers have always worked to improve their crops, and Rolfe's later efforts with tabacum were so successful that by 1617, over 20,000 pounds were shipped home. Growth in exports doubled, and then doubled again in only a few years, as Rolfe learned appropriate cultivation, harvesting, and curing techniques.

By 1619, the budding Virginia House of Burgesses, later the General Assembly, established laws for the growth and inspection of tobacco and warehouse and port cities, including Norfolk, Petersburg, Richmond, and Alexandria, for storage and export. The following year, a trade agreement was reached between King James and the Virginia Company to ban growing in England for commercial sale, thus ensuring a market for the Virginia product.

Within short order, tobacco became currency itself, used to pay for slaves, taxes, and manufactured goods imported from England. Anything that could be bought or sold, from liquor to wines, land to seeds, could be bought with tobacco. No other cultivated crop could match the value and transportability of tobacco. Then as now, tobacco is extremely profitable to grow, as the per-acre yield in generated cash may be several times that of corn, soybeans, or other agricultural crops.

Rolfe's success engendered other efforts, and by 1622, over 100 miles of settlements along the James River were producing exportable crops.

Virginia and North Carolina planters found tobacco to be the perfect crop, for several reasons. First was the seemingly insatiable demand, as millions of people rapidly became consumers. Second was the abundance of cheap (read: free) labor, in the form of indentured servants (read: slaves). The soil was perfectly suited to the crop, as was the hot summer, mild winter climate. A governmental system of regulation kept the quality high. And lastly, an expansive system of east-flowing rivers allowed for inexpensive transport to waiting ocean-going ships.

During the 1680's the farms surrounding Jamestown were producing over 25,000,000 pounds of tobacco per year for sale in Europe. Within the next 75 years, 80,000 to 100,000 Africans, destined for eternal servitude, reached Virginia. Tobacco and free labor made many Virginians astonishingly wealthy.

Tobacco is notoriously hard on the land, rapidly exhausting minerals and nutrients from the soil. Generally, restoration of the fertility of soil, if to be restored naturally, takes ten or even twenty years. There were no artificial fertilizers and natural fertilization with animal manure was impractical as most livestock were allowed to free-range. So when the soil depleted, farmers simply moved on. The wealthiest farmers obtained massive land holdings, allowing them access to fresh soils. However, those fresh soils were typically underneath ancient forests. The process from verdant forest to depleted field began by destroying the trees, either by girding them or burning them or both. Then planting ensued, often between the stumps. Then the crop was hand harvested. Then the land was allowed to fallow.

By the 1620s, farmers were already seeing reduced yields and Virginia's government sought to regulate planting. Ever opportunistic, farmers moved farther northward into the lands between Virginia's many Chesapeake Bay rivers, the York, Rappahannock, and Potomac. Then farmers moved inland, eventually crossing the Fall Line into the Piedmont, where soils proved to be equally verdant and suitable. Most of the counties of Tidewater Virginia were sustained economically by tobacco, soon to be joined by the Piedmont counties of Buckingham, Culpeper, Albemarle, Nelson, Cumberland, and several others.

By the mid-1750s, as Swedish taxonomist Carolus Linneaus assigned the plant's genus as nicotiana and two species as nicotiana rustic and nicotania tabacum, the York, Rappahannock and James River basins were the centers of production. The primary transportation option in the Piedmont down to the Fall Line ports was the bateau, a long, canoe-like vessel, packed with hogsheads, barrels specifically designed for conveyance of packed, dried tobacco leaves, paddled down the aforementioned rivers.

The standard length for a bateau was 58 feet with a width of 6 feet. Like canoes, they were pointed at each end and had no keel or rudder. Each could carry ten hogsheads, 4 feet tall and 30 inches in diameter at the foot and head. Each hogshead contained 1,000 pounds of tobacco, so a bateau could carry 10,000 pounds of cargo alone, plus its crew and various other supplies! Eventually bateaux were used to carry other cargo and passengers.

Before the James and Kanawha River Canal extended to Lynchburg, some 500 bateaux and triple that number of bateaumen plied the James River alone, with more on the neighboring rivers. Bateaux were typically crewed by 6 people. One man stood at the stern and another at the aft doing the steering with rudders. Two more men on each side walked from front to back on the walk-boards in rotation carrying long, sturdy poles used for polling the boat.

Each summer, as the plants grew, slaves built bateaux and hogsheads for the wintertime trip. The tobacco was harvested and cured, then packed in the hogsheads and the bateaux were paddled downstream during the freshet to ports of Richmond, West Point, City Point (Hopewell), Norfolk, and Alexandria to be packed for the transatlantic voyage. At that point, the bateaux were demolished and the bateaumen, almost all of them black, walked home, likely without lodging.

Tobacco is picky about the soil, moisture, and climate where it will grow profitably. Each type of tobacco has its own distinctive flavor, texture, mildness, and tar and nicotine content. Even from the same particular plant, the position on the stalk will yield a different set of characteristics. Weather conditions during growing and curing, and the curing method and duration can also impact the crop. In southern regions, tobacco matured earlier in the season, while farther north the season ended later. Typically flue-cured tobacco in Virginia was planted throughout May and harvested from early August until the end of September, ending in early October.

Each farmer's crop was brought to a centralized warehouse where it was auctioned to one of the many major production companies. Buyers walked among the rows of stacked product doing their examination, and then an auctioneer would begin the pricing wars amongst the prospective buyers. These were anxious, exciting times for growers, for those brief moments dictated whether they were to make a profit for a year's work. These events brought crowds and all manner of economic activity. Virtually every town had such a warehouse, with the largest in Richmond, Petersburg, and Lynchburg.

Throughout mid-century, business was good for Virginia planters, in spite of the discoveries by John Hill, a London physician, that snuff users were vulnerable to cancers of the nose. Of course, with all commodity markets, there is a never-ending dance between supply and demand. By the 1760s, fluctuations in the economy in Britain and tightening credit put the squeeze on Virginia's wealthiest plantation owners. By the time British banks collapsed in the credit crisis of 1772, these owners, already angry, began beating the drums of independence. British efforts to tax and control the colonies led to the revolt in Boston Harbor we now call the Boston Tea Party on December 16, 1773, an act that remains arguably the most renowned political protest in our nation's history.

With the loss of access to the British markets, and with many growers switching to food crops to support the troops, domestic production levels in tobacco plummeted from 55 million to 14.5 million pounds annually during the Revolutionary War. By 1775, Norfolk was Virginia's largest city and busiest port.

Business returned to somewhat normal for the next few decades, punctuated by the additional unpleasantness of the War of 1812, when shipments to England were again interrupted. But when there is money to be made, nobody stands in the way for long.

By the 1830s, more serious efforts got underway to rid the nation of tobacco's nasty and dangerous effects, with the first organized anti-tobacco movement forming as part of the temperance movement, bolstered by the New England Almanac's editor Samuel Green, who wrote that tobacco was "an insecticide, a poison, and can kill a man." Money is a strong motivator, and tobacco remained the Southside Virginia farmer's best cash crop.

The next big boost to consumption was the invention of the cigarette in 1832 by Egyptian soldiers. The word cigarette, incidentally, is French for the diminutive form of cigar, le cigare. Tobacco in colonial years was mainly produced for chewing, snuff, and pipe smoking. Cigars came into popularity in the early 1800s. The cigarette was smaller, cheaper, and more portable than the cigar, thus more compatible with workers in an Industrial Revolution.

The 1850s were great years for tobacco. Matches were invented and British soldiers discovered from their Turkish allies how convenient cigarettes were and brought their new habit back home. Robert Gloag, a veteran of that war, opened England's first cigarette factory in England in 1856. Phillip Morris had begun selling hand-rolled Turkish cigarettes in a London store in 1847, and his business benefitted from these returning soldiers.

Although cigarettes were gaining in popularity, dipping snuff was all the rage, particularly in the South. Across all income and status levels, fine pulverized leaves of tobacco were insufflated into the nasal cavities of mostly women. Men were primarily smoking cigars or chewing.

Still, while cigarettes were becoming more popular in the cities of Europe, they were rare in America prior to the Civil War. Most smokers preferred cigars, including Federal General Ulysses S. Grant (who would later die of throat cancer), who was often photographed with his stogie. Federal soldiers, as they infiltrated the Confederacy, got their first taste of southern tobacco. Sherman's army, during his march of destruction to the sea through Georgia in late 1864 and Grant's march through Virginia enabled soldiers to salvage and hastily consume tobacco before ransacking the warehouses.

The Bull Durham brand was prized and soldiers rolled their own smokes. Factories such as Allen and Ginter in Richmond and F. S. Kinney & Sons in New York sold hand-rolled cigarettes, often made by young Eastern European immigrant women who brought the technique from their home countries.

Tobacco mogul James Buchanan "Buck" Duke of the family that would later give its name to Duke Energy and Duke University, obtained a license for a cigarette making machine developed by James Albert Bonsack, in 1885, and almost instantly cigarettes gained a predominant position in tobacco consumption in America.

By the turn of the 20th Century, cigarettes and cigars were a major international economic powerhouse, with 3.5 billion cigarettes and 6 billion cigars sold annually. In 1902, Phillip Morris set up a subsidiary in New York to market its brand in America, including the world's most popular cigarette, the Marlboro. That's right: the Marlboro Man is from England. The Lucky Strike brand had been introduced by the American Tobacco Company in 1871, and by 1930 was the top-selling brand, engendering a fanatical following. Then in 1913, R. J. Reynolds introduced Camel, which within ten years amounted to 45 percent of the domestic market. Thousands of soldiers in World War I were introduced to smoking, and cigarette use expanded dramatically. American Tobacco introduced Pall Mall in 1939, named for a street in the city of Westminster, London. Soon, American Tobacco became the largest tobacco company in the country.

Mid-millennium public opinion was that tobacco use provided a variety of health benefits. However, logic and statistics started to rear their ugly head, as facts are, well, facts. Scientists and medical researchers began irrefutable studies linking tobacco use to a whole host of maladies which we're familiar with today, including respiratory illnesses, heart problems, and notably cancer. German researchers in Cologne in 1930 statistically correlated smoking with cancer. In 1938, Johns Hopkins University physician Raymond Pearl published his studies that smokers die earlier than non-smokers.

It is often said that war is good for business, and the tobacco companies knew an opportunity when they saw one. They donated billions of cigarettes to the War Department during World War II, which were included in a soldier's C-rations. By the war's end, there were hundreds of thousands of new, already addicted customers. Cigarette sales in America reached their zenith.

Throughout the 1950s, the terrible health problems associated with tobacco became irrefutably apparent and the foes of tobacco use became increasingly vocal and strident. The industry responded predictably by undermining or refuting every dire claim. Nevertheless, because the public was becoming more informed, the industry produced several "innovations," that at least on the surface appeared to minimize or mitigate the damage. One of the most ill-fated and ill-conceived was P. Lorillard's new Kent brand whose "micronite" filter contained asbestos. As if nicotine wasn't bad enough!

Other brands began sporting various types of filters, ostensibly to make cigarettes less toxic. But in January 1964, in a landmark event, the United States Surgeon General Luther Leonidas Terry, issued a scathing report called "Smoking and Health: Report of the Advisory Committee to the Surgeon General of the United States," which became the basis for a new wave of governmental efforts to regulate the sales and advertisement of cigarettes. The Terry Report concluded that smoking was causally related to chronic bronchitis, cardiovascular disease, emphysema, and many cancers. Later that year, the Federal Trade Commission instructed the manufacturers to display strongly worded warnings on their packages. Interestingly the report failed to define nicotine as an addictive substance.

The industry reeled! They began to distance themselves, at least publicly, from tobacco. R.J. Reynolds Tobacco Company became R.J. Reynolds Industries. The American Tobacco Company became American Brands, Inc.

Phillip Morris, looking to broaden demand, introduced Virginia Slims, a spin-off to their Benson and Hedges brand, expressly marketed to young professional women, glorifying them by claiming, "You've come a long way, baby!" Longer and narrower than traditional cigarettes, they were an instant hit, spawning several copy-cat brands from competitors and dooming millions of new female smokers to cancer and heart disease. By 1985, lung cancer was the leading cause of death among American women, overcoming breast cancer.

As I was making my way through high school in the early 1970s, tobacco ads on televisions were finally banned. By the late 1970s, the first Great American Smokeout was organized, imploring every smoker to go a day without a drag. Congress began banning smoking on airline flights.

You'd think all this negative publicity would doom the tobacco companies and banish consumption forever worldwide. You'd be wrong. The industry intensified its marketing outside the United States, especially in the developing world.

The peak year for Virginia tobacco production was 1981, reaching almost 160,000,000 pounds. Today production numbers are typically twenty-five percent of that, hovering around 40,000,000 pounds. In 1998, after decades of lawsuits, the Attorneys General of 46 states reached what was termed the Master Settlement Agreement that required tobacco companies to pay the states over $200 billion dollars over the next 25 years to compensate for losses in health care costs associated with tobacco. Virginia's legislature agreed to join the lawsuit, resulting in an award of over $4 billion.

In the intervening years, this windfall has become a political football, as various agencies have constantly fought over access to it. One of the results is that consumers were faced with huge price increases, and smoking or chewing became much more expensive, reducing demand. Meanwhile, the state commission established to manage the money has allocated it to education, roads, tourism, broadband infrastructure, economic development initiatives such as industrial parks, and direct compensation to affected farmers.

By 2010, Marlboro was the leading brand in the world, with 42 percent market share. The next ten brands together amounted to 38.7 percent. Marlboro is produced by Phillip Morris USA, and the largest manufacturing plant in the world is in Richmond. Production has grown from 200 million to 600 million cigarettes per day, with individual machines that can make 350 cigarettes per second! Phillip Morris officials are well aware that cigarettes cause 400,000 premature deaths per year nationally and 5 million worldwide, and that many of their customers wish they could quit.

Meanwhile, many of Southside Virginia's old tobacco warehouses have been converted into upscale housing and retail buildings.

Smoking is the most preventable cause of premature death in the world and as I mentioned, nicotine is one of the most addictive substances there is. A series of new products have been introduced, such as chewable polymer disks containing nicotine and e-cigarettes which turn nicotine-based liquids into vapor, designed to reduce the health damage.

People continue to find a way to ingest nicotine. Despite the known health risks, tobacco products are readily, legally available at convenience stores and supermarkets throughout the country for as little as a quarter per cigarette.

Similarly, alcohol is responsible for a variety of health and safety problems, including cirrhosis, pancreatitis, gastritis, ulcers, liver cancer, and accidental deaths. We tried banning it once, during Prohibition. That didn't work very well. There's still a prohibition against marijuana, which today is rapidly being re-evaluated. Along the road from Suffolk to Petersburg, farmers grew lots of tobacco. I suspect there were marijuana patches hidden far from sight.

While at one time or another, almost every county in Virginia has seen some tobacco production, today's traveler on the Powhatan Arrow corridor will find farms in Southside Virginia, but then not again until the Ohio Valley approaching the western terminus in Cincinnati.

WE DEPARTED SIMULTANEOUSLY the next morning, my host Katie and me, as she drove to her teaching job and I continued my journey, chasing the Powhatan Arrow. I was driving my wife's new car, a Ford C-Max hybrid. We'd only had it a few months, and I was still in *Future Shock*.

I pulled a toggle under the steering wheel and an expressionless, accentless female voice, emanating from the dashboard, said, "Please say a command."

I said, "Please fix me a nice cup of hot tea."

She said with what I perceive to be repressed exasperation, "I do not understand that command. Please say for example, 'climate,' or 'navigation.'"

I retorted with an attempt at self-amusement, "Climate! Please solve global warming and save Norfolk."

She repeated back, "I do not understand that command," with that same monotonically pleasant voice.

And on it went. Meanwhile, I was distracted enough to have crossed the center line a couple of times and nearly sideswiped an oncoming car, and I hadn't even left Petersburg's city limits.

I bought my first car, a Volkswagen Rabbit, in 1976 after I'd started my first job. I drove that little guy for twelve hard years before selling it in 1988. Then I bought a Colt Vista wagon that I kept for the next twenty. I sold that in 2007 for a Subaru Forester that my wife drove and I got her hand-me-down Honda Accord. We traded her Accord for the C-Max and I got the Subaru. I'm always getting her hand-me-downs.

So there you have it: 45 years and only three cars, now four. Buying cars so infrequently helped me see the enormous technological innovation overtaking our transportation devices. The Rabbit's innovation was its transverse (across the car, left to right) in-line engine, powering the front wheels, during a time most cars were still rear-wheel driven. The Colt upstaged the Rabbit by having all-wheel drive, as does the Subaru. But otherwise, the cars were much the same. Ignitions had progressed from the primitive points-and-condenser systems to electronics, and fuel injection replaced carburetors, but most of the controls were still analog. From the standpoint of the car/driver interface, not much changed between the 1976 Rabbit and the 2007 Subaru.

Not the miraculous C-Max! This magnificent marvel of modern engineering has an owner's manual that must rival the international space station's. The car starts not with a conventional turn of a metal key, but with the push of a dashboard button, activated by the mere proximity of the key fob. Once "started," it remains eerily silent; there is no motor noise whatsoever. When in reverse, it has a camera in the rear that shows a picture on the dashboard of the rear view. The car instantaneously calculates fuel economy and mileage until empty and shows this information on the dash. There's a clever display showing the transfer of energy from the batteries to the motor, or vice versa, and then to the front driving wheels. It has regenerative braking, meaning when the brakes are activated, energy returns to the batteries. It has heated seats (which are awesome in the winter, let me tell you!), heated outside rear-view windows, and interior automatic temperature management.

That this extraordinary technological advancement would appear to the motoring public in a mere blink of a proverbial eye between our 2007 and 2013 models makes one wonder what's next. Maybe my next car will fix me a nice cup of tea.

Meanwhile, I set the C-Max's navigation system to point me home, not because I didn't know the route, but to give me a sense of the estimated distance. The route was simple: take US-460 all the way. However, as soon as I got to the outskirts of town, the nice lady in the dashboard started berating me.

"Make a legal U-turn and continue on this road," she said.

I had no interest in a U-turn and wondered why she'd suggested it. I knew I was going the right way. What got up in her craw this morning?

Don't get me wrong, I'm sure GPSs are great, especially for directionally-challenged people who just want someone or something to tell them where to go. I'm sure they allow a new level of comfort and security in knowing that you can push a few buttons and be directed to an unknown place without the necessity of mindfulness. Or knowledge of how to read a map. How did people ever get anywhere before they were invented? How did people ever get to the buggy whip store in Pearisburg or to the place they repair typewriters in Cincinnati? Somehow we muddled through.

Sure, you'll argue, but if he'd had a GPS, Columbus would have known he was in the East Indies instead of India and the course of world history would have been forever altered. He did the best he could, and in spite of his monumental bigotry and brutality, he got a holiday named after him. And a city in Ohio.

And it's not that the woman's voice isn't pleasant enough. "In 100 yards, turn left onto Franklin Road." Frankly, there's probably an app that somebody's invented that plugs in a much snider, more sarcastically wretched mother-in-law style voice, just for spite, for people driven to self-flagellation. "WHAT! Did I not tell you to make a U-turn as soon as possible? What part of 'make a U-turn' do you not understand? Will you EVER listen to me?!? I go OUT of my WAY to give you CLEAR and *CONCISE* directions, and LOOK at you; you insist on making it up! Sometimes I don't know why I even **BOTHER**!"

And it's not that they aren't accurate, because typically they are.

And it's not even that so many people blindly obey them, although they do. Admit it; you've followed yours before even when it countered your best judgment and intuition.

And it's not even that it won't let me get lost. This doesn't seem like much of a problem to many folks, but in my life, more good things than bad have happened because I got lost. I've never been permanently lost, as evidenced by the fact that I'm in a position right now to faithfully report to you. But I've always maintained that you can only *BE* lost if you care where you are. Cool things tend to happen when I stop my motorcycle and spread out a map over the entirety of the gas tank, handlebar and dashboard assemblies. By their nature, motorcycles are conversation starters, but lost motorcyclists are magnets to helpful people. Sometimes I'll stop, take off my helmet, and throw open my map, just to see how long it takes for somebody to stop.

With GPSs, it's more of a subtle thing really, which I will attempt to articulate. The problem that I have with the GPS is that everything that used to exist between the proverbial Points A and B now effectively vanishes. There are no longer any discernible landmarks to be mentally studied, appreciated, and catalogued. Before the GPS, Point B was spatially related to the things on the way there. There was the entrance to the National Historic Park. There was the antique store with the giant carved gorilla sitting on a bench on the porch. There was the bridge over the James River. Now everywhere is nowhere, evidenced only by commands produced by that woman's voice, "Well, you're FINALLY here!" rather than a connection with anywhere else. GPSs have turned us into somnambulant zombies, wrapped in our comfortable cocoons, insulated from what's beyond the windshield, away from the realities of time, place, and situation.

All of this relates, of course, to that profound adage that it's not about the destination but instead about the trip. It's surely a metaphor for life itself, that the journey is more important than the terminus. "Be here now," spiritual teacher Ram Dass implores. Good plan.

I have maps in my head. My mind's eye envisions maps when I see landscapes and vice versa. One of the reasons I'm attracted to the mountains is that there is always a discernible horizon. Each distant rise, ridge, or peak has its own signature shape, and as they're imprinted on my memory, I relate to their spaces. Unless it's totally overcast, the sun is a reliable compass, rising in the east and setting in the west. At midday, my shadow is north. Everything else is just a matter of precision. In Virginia, there's only so far east you can go before things get pretty wet (Note: either the Chesapeake Bay or the Atlantic Ocean). Otherwise, it's just a matter of time until something recognizable comes along. These days there are Interstates everywhere. I doubt there are many places anywhere in Virginia, West Virginia, or Ohio that you can go more than a couple of hours before bumping into one. This happens well before you encounter an international border crossing where somebody is asking how long you'll be staying in the country and what your business is. So even when I'm in the C-Max and I have a GPS, I don't use it much, at least until I'm nearing specific addresses I've never been to.

And give my long-suffering wife some credit here; although she doesn't know which way to turn a screwdriver, she's adequately spatially literate. Often when we drive someplace new, I'll do the driving and she'll have the map in her lap the entire time. I vowed not to send my daughter to college before she could do two essential tasks of adulthood: juggle three balls and read a map. For the record, now a half-dozen years later, she's better at the latter than the former, but can still do both.

What maps can do that the GPS can't, especially when the map is 40 inches wide by 18 inches tall, like the official Virginia state map, and the GPS is barely 4 inches wide, is give you a sense of scale. When one map inch equals 12 miles, for example, you can gauge how long it takes to ride your bicycle or your motorcycle or drive that car that one inch, and see if you've got three inches to go, about how long it will take. And for that reason, it has you more attuned to what's out there, and how it relates to that blue or red line on the piece of paper.

Fortunately for this trip, our federal highway system's US-460 does a pretty good job of following the Powhatan Arrow from Norfolk to Roanoke to Bluefield, then US-52 to Kenova, and then SR-73 and SR-32 into Cincinnati. How lost could anybody get?

Cartography is one of the great sciences and arts of all time. Early map-makers drew maps by hand and embellished them with fanciful figures and vast gaps indicating terra incognito, tantalizing explorers. While perhaps not as useful as modern editions, they certainly lent an urgency of exploration; who wouldn't want to go where the map stopped, just to see what was there?

In our modern world, somebody has been just about everywhere before. Nevertheless, there's a sense of awe and satisfaction that comes with getting yourself where you want to go by using a map instead of the insistences of a synthetic female voice.

WHILE WE'RE ON THE SUBJECT of geography, the corridor traversed by the Powhatan Arrow, the Norfolk & Western's main line, from Norfolk to Cincinnati, is wonderfully, almost artistically complex and appealing to the modern eye, although with significant challenges to those who originally plotted it. It is simple to say that it emerges from the coastal lowlands of Virginia, gains altitude, crosses the great Appalachian Mountain chain and ends on the banks of the Ohio River. Topographically, it is much more multifaceted.

Virginia itself has three major topographic regions, or perhaps five, depending upon who you ask. The eastern region is the Tidewater, characterized by flat landscapes of loamy soil and bisected by brackish rivers, steeped in colonial history: the James, York, Rappahannock, and Potomac. The uppermost reaches of tidal water, principally on the James and Potomac, produced the great cities of Richmond, Georgetown, and Alexandria. To the west laid the vast Piedmont, a region of rolling, gentle hills of red clay soil. This is the transition at Petersburg that Delaney described.

The westernmost area is singularly called the Mountain and Valley region or in triplicate the Blue Ridge region, the Valley of Virginia region, and the Allegheny plateau region. The great Valley of Virginia stretches from Winchester to Bristol, northeast to southwest. It is unique in that most valleys are of a particular river whereas this Great Valley is bisected by several: the Shenandoah, the James, the Roanoke, the New, and the Clinch, radiating outward. Thus the Shenandoah (via the Potomac) and James flow eastward to the Chesapeake Bay, the New flows north to the Kanawha and into the Ohio and the Clinch flows southwestward to the Tennessee and ultimately the Mississippi.

In our area of study, the rail line is initially in the coastal swamp around Norfolk and Suffolk, drained mostly by branches of the Elizabeth River. From there, the track is in one of the tributaries of the Chowan River, mostly the Blackwater River, which flows into North Carolina's Albemarle Sound. Then it's into the Appomattox River watershed, a tributary of the James River and then near Lynchburg, the James River itself. Then in passing over the low rise in the Blue Ridge Mountains at Blue Ridge east of Roanoke, it enters the Roanoke River watershed, which also drains into the Albemarle Sound. It crests the Eastern Continental Divide near Christiansburg and enters the New River drainage. It follows the New until Bluefield, where for a short time it follows the Bluestone, a tributary of the New. Crossing under Coaldale Mountain between Mercer and McDowell Counties, it follows the Elkhorn Creek until it reaches Welch, where the creek and the rail line join the Tug Fork of the Big Sandy River Valley which the rail line follows to the Ohio in Kenova. It remains in the Ohio River drainage the rest of the way into Cincinnati.

Ohio topography is generally rolling hills to the south, our study area, with flatter areas to the north, sloping to Lake Erie.

Aerial views of the landscape between Roanoke and the Ohio River at Kenova show a mosaic of intense diversity, a diversity that has played into the social, economic, and geographic condition of the region since time began.

Into this varied environment, Norfolk & Western Railway and its predecessor companies plotted a great ribbon of steel.

9:01 a.m.

Blackstone

Mile 118.2

Station for Camp Pickett, training point for myriad World War II soldiers. Tobacco and livestock auction markets.

It's about 40 miles from Petersburg to Blackstone. A relatively new community, Blackstone's population has for over six decades hovered around 3,500 people. Blackstone was incorporated in 1888. Its original name was "Blacks and Whites," after two families that built taverns there. Likely the Whites are still angry about being dropped. Being in the eastern Piedmont where loamy soils predominate, there are few stones of any size at all and none I could find were black.

Like many towns in the region, it began as a location of tobacco sales. Warehousing and shipping of tobacco were through its Norfolk & Western Railway station.

When I pulled into town in mid-morning, the Schwartz Tavern museum, the oldest building in town, was closed. Formerly an inn and tavern, its original section was built in 1799, with its current three sections of 99 feet in length. It is a handsome wooden structure on a stone foundation. After use as a public meeting space, it served as the private residence for seven families. Please go see it. Take my advice and pick a day it's open.

I WANDERED ONTO MAIN STREET where many of the buildings had decorative, interpretive brass plaques beside the doors to tell of their histories.

Inside an antique store I found the office of Jane Barnes, the Executive Director of the Chamber of Commerce of Blackstone. She told me that Blackstone was doing well. "I am from here and I went to school here. We now have a bypass around town. Before that, all the traffic including the logging trucks came through town. Downtown used to have everything – grocery stores, hardware stores. Then things started expanding out. Downtown got sparse looking.

"Then in 2005 we had a fire in two big buildings, which were totally destroyed. It could have spread through town. We formed Downtown Blackstone, and were able to get grant money because we had blight. We now have a two-block historic area where businesses were able to get re-development loans. We got focused on service companies like lawyers.

"We're trying to get better Internet service. We still have some dial-up. It's a small community, a wonderful place to live.

"We are attached to Fort Pickett. That's a good thing, economically. They're bringing in the Foreign Affairs Security Training Center which will bring thousands of people here. We want to keep them here. They can commute from Richmond, but we want them to live here. The students will only stay short times, but the teachers will be here for a while. We only have one motel and one B&B. We want to build a hotel. We want them to eat in our restaurants, to shop, and to become part of our community."

I asked if they were trying to attract passenger rail service.

She said, "No, but I think that would be so cool. My father was from Louisville, Kentucky, and he grew up riding the train to and from UVA (University of Virginia). He told me stories. They were romantic. We would love to see passenger service here."

PERHAPS THE MOST REGIONALLY FAMOUS company in Blackstone is Bevell's Hardware Inc., owned by Bobby Daniels, an energetic septuagenarian who has built and annually manages at the holiday season a fantastic electric train exhibit inside the store. The store was housed in a modern, steel and glass building where paints, animal feed, lawn and garden equipment, household chemicals, hunting and fishing gear, and building materials were sold. But if truth be told, it was really the means Bobby employed for feeding his model train habit.

Collecting and running scale model trains has been a hobby for Bobby since his childhood. To say he is an avid toy train collector shortchanges the concept. In addition to the display which is 18 feet by 56 feet in size and consumes what would otherwise be productive retail display space, he had literally hundreds if not thousands of other locomotives, cars, and rural and urban settings. The top of every retail shelf nearby had more closed boxes of similar toys. It had been a 30 year effort. In 2010 the display was featured in Classic Toy Trains magazine and thousands of people line up each season to have a look.

Bobby said, "My father was a ticket agent at the station here in Blackstone. From 1960 until 1977 I was in the food business. I ran a little Tastee Freez restaurant. I always wanted to own a hardware store. A friend of mine started the store in the late 1940s or early 50s. I bought it almost 40 years ago.

"We have done a (train) layout every year since then except one year. I don't have any rhyme or reason for what I'm doing. I collect things from all sorts of places and have model railroads in several different gauges. I have so much stuff!" We went into his main office. Every wall was lined with racks of trains. He said, "At home I have even more rooms of packed away stuff. But for years I was buying stuff

Bevell's Hardware

wherever I could find it. I've got to the point now where I have slowed down. There is no point buying just to pack stuff away. I don't have time to run the display year 'round. When I first bought the store, we had a toy department and a housewares department. That was in the days before the big box stores and Walmart came to town.

"I only run the display during the Christmas season. It helps to bring a lot of traffic to the store. I don't know how many feet of track it has, but I can run four different trains at a time.

"Every year I change as many things as I can. I have hundreds of individual buildings. One part of the layout has a complete amusement park, with a roller coaster, a Ferris wheel, and various rides. I set up a drive-in theater and several wind turbines twirling on a hillside. There are hot air balloons that rise and fall over the entire display. It is a cross-section of various things I have collected over the years.

"I just got back from a meeting in Pennsylvania of the Train Collectors Association. They draw 10,000 or 12,000 people. Every building is filled with train collecting items. If you are not a member, you cannot go in. Everybody is buying and selling and trading. All of the manufacturers are there."

He gets help from his friends to control the trains in the display by remote control handheld devices. He said, "I have inventoried all that I have before. I am probably four or five years behind now. It is hard to say what it is worth. A lot of the stuff cannot really be valued. I keep books on that all the time. I have some individual cars that are worth nothing and I have some that are worth $400 or $500 apiece.

"We only have about 15,000 people in the county. There is no interstate here. The population has not changed but perhaps 400 or 500 people in my lifetime. At one time, they had 2,500 buildings at Fort Pickett. They had movie theaters and bowling alleys. They still have a lot going on out there. The State Police have a driving school where they teach troopers how to do high-speed chases. They have an indoor firing range for law-enforcement.

"When I first (bought Bevell's) there were three hardware stores in town. There is a shopping center with a Walmart. What you see downtown is what is left over. The downtown looks pretty good for a small town. The shopping center has 15 or more businesses out there. They have been there for about 25 years. We have lost lots of merchants over the years. But I am still here.

"We sell lots of lumber. But we change our business based on whatever we can sell. It is a nice store. We try to keep it clean and up-to-date. I still wonder where we are headed. I am 77 years old and am drawing Social Security. I could retire, but I still need to work in order to support this," he pointed at his train layout.

Bobby Daniels

IT'S A SHORT, 10 MILE DRIVE from Blackstone to Crewe, the Powhatan Arrow's next stop. On our way, I thought I'd tell you a bit more about the nuts-and-bolts of growing tobacco, both in historic and current times.

In the early days of Virginia settlement, poor people did subsistence farming to feed themselves. Tobacco was extra money. Almost everything else they grew was consumed by the family. For many people, going to the grocery store was not an option. They had to live on what grew in the fields and the pastures and the garden, things that could be preserved to eat during winter.

Tobacco has always required extraordinary amounts of labor to produce, thus its success where labor was cheap.

Planting was done in early winter, tended in the beds until spring, and then relocated into the fields. Historically, re-planting was done by hand. A hole was poked into the ground with a tobacco peg, either a curved wooden tool or deer antler. When the frost threat passed, the slips were replanted, in mid- to late-April. As spring gave way to summer, the task became increasingly hot, humid, and miserable.

The growing plants needed constant attention. They were frequently topped off to encourage the spreading of the leaves. Weeding between the plants was ongoing. Without pesticides, tobacco worms and other insects were removed by hand. Prior to emancipation, an adult slave may have planted and tended two acres of land with as many as 10,000 plants, requiring him to bend over tens of thousands of times each season. This toil was duplicated year after year. Tobacco leaves are notoriously painful to touch, and rashes developed on the hands and arms of the slave workers. Child labor was part of life, so a baby born into slavery faced a lifetime of toil and agony with no hope of respite.

There are different types of tobacco, more acclimated to their area. The "bright-leaf" is the area's predominant variety. It produces a golden leaf that is 3 feet long by 1 foot wide, with 16-24 harvestable leaves per plant. A mature plant is 5 to 6 feet tall. The leaves are at shoulder-level on a grown man.

Several tobacco leaves branch from the stalk at the same height in an arrangement of leaves that botanists call a whorl. In harvesting, the lowest leaves are snapped off first. They are dirtiest and most likely to have bugs and weather damage. The higher up the plant, the larger the leaves. Those are the money leaves. The lower leaves are for chewing tobacco.

When it is growing in the field, tobacco produces a resin. Workers holding a leaf or two might not notice, but when working with it for hours, hands and other exposed skin and clothing becomes coated with this sticky resin.

Tobacco resin is insidious, nasty brown/black stuff, and is notoriously difficult to remove. The only solvents that will take it off are Ajax cleanser and diesel fuel; neither was available to pre-modern farmers and slaves. Slaves working the fields prior to the Civil War were always covered with this resin from the time the harvest started until weeks after its conclusion in the fall. Only sand from the creek or something else equally abrasive would take it off.

The Piedmont of Virginia is ideally suited for tobacco growing. It has a gawd-awful hot climate. In mid-summer in Southside Virginia, generally the area bounded by North Carolina to the south, the James River to the north, and the Blue Ridge Mountains to the west, by 9:00 am, it's already 85F and nearing 100F by midday with oppressive humidity on many summer days.

NOWADAYS, MOST OF THE TOBACCO grown in Southside Virginia is exported. The government paid people not to grow it or to grow a lot less of it. This gave farmers the chance and incentive to diversify to growing broccoli or decorative flowers or even wine grapes. Farmers have always been entrepreneurial by necessity. There's more diversity now, at least in this part of the country. Farmers are getting into agricultural tourism, bringing people to the farm to see what's done and to assist with things like picking.

Back in the 60s and 70s, nearly everybody who lived and worked in the tobacco areas smoked. There were ash trays at restaurants. At stores. In offices and factories. In movies. The stigma that has been attached to smoking within the last 25 years or so has made it such that smokers are largely banished to the out-of-doors. Many smokers feel a degree of shame and humiliation.

A pack of cigarettes costs around $5 per pack, up to $12 per pack in more heavily taxed states like New York. Virginia legislators have been timid in raising taxes. Even in the low cigarette tax Virginia, someone smoking two packs per day is spending $3500 annually on feeding a habit that has a good chance of killing him. There are gums and patches to help people quit. When a smoker decides to quit, cessation aids are not paid for by insurance. Medical insurance will pay the astronomical costs for treatment of cancer or heart disease, but not the products that will help a smoker quit.

For decades, the tobacco industry and many manufacturing companies throughout Southside actively fought against other companies moving in that would draw from their labor force. If an incoming company paid $1 more per hour, it would drive up costs for the existing company as they would be forced to pay their workers more. And they fought any efforts at unionization.

High labor operations in manufacturing have always been opportunistic. They move to where labor is cheap. For example, the furniture industry moved from New England to the upper Midwest to the South (principally Southside Virginia and North Carolina) and in recent decades to Southeast Asia. Especially those hand-work manufacturing jobs that are difficult to automate have gone where people are still moving from subsistence existences to factories and are willing to work for almost nothing. Farming has reacted by mechanization and increasingly on employing migrant workers, principally Latinos.

IN TERMS OF RACE RELATIONS, many Southside counties had 50 percent African American populations. It's only increased since, with many whites seeking better opportunities elsewhere. There were almost no other ethnic or racial minorities. Folks now in their 60s and 70s went to either segregated schools or newly integrated schools. Many white kids were sent to private schools, many of them military academies or church-related schools. Many schools were founded before the civil rights movement and integration. There were many military schools in the South due to the tradition of military service. Most of the generals in the South during the Civil War were classically trained in the military. Meanwhile, many in the North were merely influential, rich, or powerful politically; their deficiencies in military operations and tactics were exploited by their opponents to the South's advantage early on.

The old-timers in Southside have their own distinct accent and dialect, minimizing their "r"s, sounding like "fawty" for forty and "Fawd" for Ford. "I bakked uppa da Fawd up in'a bawn, buta I couldn'a git tha daw open. The daw wouldna open a'caz it wazza too narra. I hadda clim outta da winna."

9:20 a.m.

Crewe

Mile 128.8

N. & W. mid-division point named for the English railroad center. Repair shops and engine terminal. (Appomattox River)

The railroad giveth and the railroad taketh away.
     The Norfolk & Western originally had five divisions: Norfolk, Shenandoah, Radford, Pocahontas, and Scioto. Even in its heyday, although Crewe, Virginia was a diminutive town, it was actually the headquarters for the Norfolk division. Crewe was founded in 1888 and named after a railroad town in England. It owed its existence to the Norfolk & Western, which chose Crewe as a staging yard as it was roughly equidistant from Norfolk and Roanoke.
     As the N&W's business grew through the early part of the 20th Century, Crewe became increasingly more important and vibrant. With the conversion to diesel and improvements in operation and maintenance, Crewe's significance evaporated and its population stabilized. According to the census records, it reached 2,100 people in 1920, and now, almost 100 years later, there are only 2,300.

CREWE IS A LINEAR PLACE. The highway I was on is sandwiched between the parallel railroad operations on the left and the parallel Main Street and commercial district on the right. I drove over to Main Street and saw several storefronts, including Crittendon's Drug Store. Booker's Supply. Crewe-Burkeville Journal Newspaper. Crewe Florist. Other buildings were vacant, some boarded up. Nothing interested me enough to entice me to stop.
     Back on US-460, I drove another block and pulled into the Crewe Railroad Museum. There was a building that resembled a train station,

although newly constructed, with several period piece locomotives and cars outside.

INSIDE, I MET VOLUNTEERS Karen Blankenship and Chris Klocke who were sitting together at a table in the center of the room. There were various displays on the perimeter of the room celebrating the town's history, including a scale model of the former roundhouse (a building used for servicing and storing locomotives, often semicircular in shape).

Chris told me there used to be a roundhouse near the current museum. Several hundred people worked there. "It was 100 feet from here, to the southeast. There were maintenance operations going on 365 days each year."

He said the town was incorporated in 1888. It thrived until about 1960 when the N&W made the transition from steam locomotives to diesel. "They used to have a large number of office personnel here as well. That is almost all gone now.

"There were facilities to load coal and water. There were more than a dozen parallel tracks. The company used to keep a lot of stuff in the yard. Obviously, the town was badly impacted by the change. We had a good 60 year run."

Karen said, "I moved here from Newport News with my husband in 1960. The railroad was still a big part of the town. He was from this area and wanted to move back."

"The merchant class was supported by the railroad here as well," Chris added. "My grandfather came here from Pittsburgh in 1904. He had a large farm and became president of the bank and he had an auto dealership. My family has been here ever since. I was in the laundry and dry cleaning business for years. Then I worked for the town of Crewe and the town of Blackstone, and I still run a little tax business. We have been merchants since 1904."

Chris said the building in which we were sitting was constructed specifically as a museum about 20 years earlier, modeled after an old railroad station. "The people that put this thing together really did a great job for such a small community. People can enter the box cars, the locomotives, and the passenger cars. And we have a nice model train exhibit. I think Mr. Daniels in Blackstone helped put that together."

Karen added, "Attendance really has picked up. We see lots of schoolchildren. Boy Scouts. Things like that. We are on the path between the mountains and the beach. Lots of people stop and visit on the way."

"We are still surviving," he said. "We haven't disappeared from the face of the earth. We've been able to diversify our economic base to some degree. We have an electrical cooperative headquartered here. We had smaller factories, but they're gone too. We lost a garment company. It is difficult for our young people to find jobs. The internationalization of trade has cost our smaller communities lots of jobs in small factories, particularly where working class women could help their families to make ends meet.

"Lots of kids are not college bound. There is nothing to absorb (a college educated) workforce. They end up moving wherever they can find a job. Richmond has always been a big draw. Most farmers are part-time. It's hard to make a living farming. When I was a kid, you found tobacco grown everywhere. Everybody has quit raising tobacco. Much of our land is still forested.

"The people who did stay here worked for the railroad. The population has stayed stable for 60 years. We have a prison and a rehabilitation facility and some people have moved here to service those. In downtown, all that's left is a bank to sell you money, a liquor store to sell you liquor, and a drug store to sell you drugs. That's indicative of the age of the population." He found this extremely funny, laughing heartily.

Karen said, "Neither of my kids gave any thought to staying here. They went to Raleigh and Alexandria. Kids always move away. It's been really depressing to me, watching it decline. It was a beautiful little town. Everybody is affected."

In the outdoor museum collection, there were several locomotives, both steam and diesel, and a nicely preserved Powhatan Arrow passenger car. Inside, it had a dozen rows, four across seating, of upholstered chairs in Tuscan red cloth with headrest covers in white with the "N&W Railway" logo embroidered on them. Elegant! A small dining area at the back had a table covered with a white cloth tablecloth, also with the N&W logo printed on it, and four place-settings of fine china and silverware. There was even a basket of artificial flowers on the table's edge for a splash of color. The napkins were white cloth, again also featuring the embroidered N&W logo. It was a lovely museum for such a tiny town.

It's FIVE MILES from Crewe to Burkeville, a place that time forgot (I love that expression!). Burkeville is where US-460, on its way across the state from Norfolk to Bluefield, and US-360, from Tappahannock through Richmond to Danville, cross. From our standpoint,

Burkeville's history, like so many other places, was borne of the railroads, which incidentally followed much the same paths.

US-460 followed the South Side Rail Road, the precursor to the Norfolk & Western, while US-360 followed the Richmond and Danville Railroad. The Virginian Railway came through town as well for a couple of miles nearly paralleling the Norfolk & Western.

Burkeville's population today stands just under 500, and the official town flower is the dandelion that grows in the cracks of the decaying parking areas. Just kidding. But with some seriousness.

Arriving on US-460 from the east, drivers are automatically directed away from downtown, as the highway merges with US-360 and the two of them share a bypass on a crescent over the north side of town. I took the left turn and proceeded along 2nd Street, the main drag, right through town. There was a large, vacant complex of buildings on the left, a former veneer factory owned by Bassett Furniture, another relic of a bygone industrial age. The downtown had only a smattering of public buildings, with the police department sharing a nice gray stone building with the town library, and a few modest homes.

SOME THINGS ARE MEANT to be in pairs. Salt and pepper. Sylvester and Tweety. Batman and Robin. Lewis and Clark. Trains and train stations. So it's a bit unnerving when you drive into Burkeville on the main drag, 2nd Street, and there's a train station on your right and the tracks on the left. They're literally across the road from one another, physically disconnected.

The station had that unmistakable architectural style; with large ubiquitous overhanging eaves, wrapping all the way around, it couldn't

Author at Burkeville train station

be anything else. It was placed in the middle of a grassy lawn. Stopping to have a look at the various interpretive signs, I learned that it had been moved there from across the road! Even the pigeon droppings on the roof supports had been moved. The station had been built in 1924 at a cost of $67,000 and moved in 2013 at a cost of $1,430,000. Actually, those data are completely and utterly false; I just made them up. Really, I have no idea what it cost to build or to move. But still, I imagine it cost more to move it than to construct it in the first place.

Peering in the windows, I could see that interior reconstruction was still underway, although to what end I couldn't discern. The only people I could find to ask about it were two volunteer firemen draining filthy brown water from a hydrant beside the road. Strangely, they were from nearby Rice and not Burkeville at all, and even after hearing their explanation I couldn't properly understand why they were there. Something about Rice not having hydrants.

So that was about it for Burkeville. Not much going on.

SPEAKING OF TRACKS, while locomotives are big and flashy and sexy, there is more to those two parallel lines of steel than you may think. The interaction between the high-flanged wheels of railroad trains and the rails themselves seems simple enough, but is astonishingly complex. Let me see if I can make this potentially mundane subject interesting for you.

If you look at your basic rail, it has three segments, the head, the web, and the foot. The head is the top, upon which the wheels ride. The foot is at the bottom, the portion that bolts to the wooden ties through a plate. And the web is the vertical section holding the head above the foot.

The first measurement is the gauge, the distance between the innermost points of parallel rails. The standard gauge is 4 feet, 8-1/2 inches. Wider gauge is "broad gauge" and narrower is "narrow gauge." Federal safety standards allow for variations in tolerance from 4 feet 8 inches to 4 feet 9-1/2 inches for operation up to 60 mph, but the N&W wouldn't tolerate anything that broad.

When building track, designers were continually aware of elevation. So they first "shoot the grade," figuring how to modify the topography with cuts and fills, and to a lesser extent tunnels and bridges, to ideally maintain a grade of 2 percent or less. Upon the natural ground or subsoil was a foundation of coarsely graded gravel. Above that was placed "ballast," which is a finer grade of rocks about the size of golf balls. Upon that was laid the ties (or "sleepers"), wooden beams perpendicular to the direction of train travel. Then the rail was placed on baseplates which together were then nailed with spikes to the ties.

Maintenance is primarily comprised of two functions: keeping the ballast clean and properly situated and keeping the rail itself in good condition.

The ballast supports the ties which support the rails, and is important because it is permeable, allowing rapid dissipation of water. Water wreaks havoc on the ballast, especially in winter when freezing, thawing, and re-freezing occurs. It is vital to channel the water away as quickly as possible. Norfolk & Western, as a primary coal carrier, always had problems with coal dust falling on the ballast. That, and any mud, clogs the "pores" in the ballast, inhibiting water runoff.

As trains ride over the rails, the enormous weight induces some flex in the rail vertically, thus causing the rail to "pump" up and down. Any water sloshing around underneath the ties further degrades the ballast. This forms weak spots and the train loses efficiency in pulling over it. Clean ballast maintains the track integrity. Thus ballast is routinely cleaned, replaced, and added to. Large machines that ride the rails can remove ballast from underneath a short section of rail replacing it with cleaner rock, without removing the rail.

Ballast is typically 12 inches above the sub-grade for new construction, but with each addition of new rock, it raises the track a few inches. If new ballast is put in place every two to three years, in a few decades the track can be a foot or two higher. The frequency is based upon overall tonnage that has gone over the rail.

Coal trains carry a double-whammy in that they throw off lots of dust that clogs the ballast and they are very heavy. So tracks that carry coal trains need to be maintained more often.

Modern locomotives are equipped with accelerometers that monitor the vertical or horizontal movement of the rail. If a weak spot is detected, information can instantly be relayed to maintenance people, giving them an exact location of the problem.

Track maintenance is typically done on live rails. So work crews work between the arrivals of the next trains so they can get out of the way. Sophisticated computerized tracking systems, using GPS and crossing signal actuation allows for continuous assessment of the location of every train so that workers aren't taken by surprise.

The wheels on trains are always paired on solid axles. When a train is moving in a straight line, this is no problem. But when trains go around curves, the wheel on the inner radius travels a shorter distance than the outer wheel. Therefore there must be some slippage. Additionally, each wheel has an inner flange of a greater diameter than the surface of the wheel that grips the inside of the track and keeps the wheel positioned directly above the rail. So each rail counteracts two forces: the vertical force supplied by the weight of the car and the lateral force against the inner side of the head of the rail, supplied by the flange. The high rail on a curve sees more wear than the low rail, peeling off steel from it over time. In areas that have lots of curves, maintenance engineers place reservoirs of grease alongside the track that inject grease onto the inside of the flange to lessen the friction, to achieve greater rolling efficiency and reduce wear on the rail.

Locomotives carry sand with them in containers called (What else?) sandboxes, to drop sand on the rail in front of the driving wheels in wet or slippery conditions or on steep grades to improve traction. There is an ongoing balance struck between too much friction and too little.

The head of the rail has a rounded surface that interacts with the rolling surface of the wheel in such a way that only about ¾", the diameter of a dime, is in contact. The enormous pressure on that point from a locomotive the weight of the J-class, which was almost 500,000 pounds, is difficult to envision, even as that weight is distributed over 16 wheels.

Rails are made in many countries and have different metallurgy. America. Britain. China. Canada. As with many things, there are different grades of rail. In this case it's like gasoline: regular, plus, and premium.

The pumping of the rail under the weight of the train fatigues the rail. Additionally, when metal gets warm, it expands. In the winter the track is in contraction and in the summer it grows. With the temperature fluctuations we have around here, every mile of rail will vary as much as two feet. The expansion and contraction needs to be controlled, typically through expansion joints. If not properly built and maintained, the thermal stresses and fatiguing will break the steel. Or the expanding rail can deform itself and come out of alignment. If severe enough, the train will derail.

To assess the condition of the rail, engineers developed mobile X-ray machines that drive over the rail and take X-ray photos of it. When they find a crack in the rail, they locate it, mark it, detail the type of fracture, and report that to the maintenance department. If bad enough, they can put in a new segment of rail on the spot.

Another machine that travels over the rail is a grinder machine. It re-grinds the profile to provide the optimum contact between the wheel and the rail. As the rail wears down, it becomes flatter, which is inefficient and cuts fuel economy. The grinder returns the profile to the original contour so that the wheel can ride directly over the centerline of the rail, putting its weight directly over the web where it can be distributed evenly into the foot. After a rail is ground multiple times and there isn't enough metal left, the entire rail must be removed and replaced. As you can imagine, grinding steel causes sparks, and brush fires have started from this operation.

Historically, rails were joined end-to-end by bolting on side-pieces. Now rails are welded together in place, a process that began in the 1940s but achieved widespread acceptance in the 1970s and 1980s. When a track is worn, it is typical to replace the rails not individually but to bring in panels of track, typically 39 feet long, already spiked to the ties. These are lowered by cranes into place, end-to-end. Then the ends of the rails from one panel to the next are welded together. The heat for welding is provided in one of two ways, either through electrical resistance (arc-welding) or through chemical burning using thermite, a pyrotechnic composition of metal oxide and gunpowder. A team of technicians can place sixty to seventy welds per day.

Regulatory agencies "class" each segment of track, giving allowable speeds, from one to five. The higher the class, the higher the allowable speed. Class one has a 10 mph speed limit while class five jumps up to 100 mph or so. The higher the class, the tighter the tolerances on the smoothness of the track.

In a curve, the outside rail is higher than the inside rail. This is called elevation. In extreme cases of higher speed and tighter curves, the N&W built 4- to 5-inch elevation. This is needed to counter the centrifugal force of the weight swinging around a curve.

Both rails are tilted slightly to the inside, meaning towards each other, about 2-degrees. This is camber and is set by the design of the baseplate.

Traditionally, the standard rail was 39 feet long. Having some fun with a calculator, the length of the route of the Powhatan Arrow from Norfolk to Cincinnati was 676.6 miles, or 3,572,448 feet, meaning 91,601 individual rails were needed – actually double that for the other side, or 183,202 total. Railroad ties are commonly set 21 inches, center to center. So roughly 6,251,784 ties were required. All were continually subject to maintenance and replacement.

When most people think of railroad workers, they think of the engineers and conductors. But there are vast numbers of workers who keep the trains and the public safe by maintaining and building track. Boredom is a problem for engineers, and more than a few have fallen asleep on the job, causing accidents. In many ways, track engineering and maintenance are more interesting than driving the train!

Onward!

9:46 a.m.

Farmville

Mile 150.1

At Appomattox, near here, Lee surrendered to Grant on April 9, 1865. Longwood State College for Women is here and Hampden-Sidney College, founded in 1776 is nearby. Farming center and tobacco Market. (James River)

You can't tell the story of Virginia, West Virginia, and Ohio, or of anywhere in America – let's be honest here – without discussing race. Few places have experienced racial strife in a more direct, destructive way than Prince Edward County, Virginia, and its county seat, Farmville.

Before I dive in on *that* story, I want to briefly recap the history of race in America.

The region of the world, specifically the North American continent that is now defined as the great nation of the United States of America, is a racially diverse place and it always has been. The beginning of human habitation, let's set at the receding of the Ice Age glaciers around 10,000 years ago. At that point, much of the world's water was tied up in ice, allowing for a lower sea level and a waterless land bridge over what is now the Bearing Strait linking current Alaska with Russia. The humanoids that originated in Africa and spread from there, crossed that bridge, and began the population of the Americas. By the time Vikings visited parts of modern day Canada and Columbus stumbled upon the islands of the Caribbean, the Americas were already home to millions of people we now call Native Americans, Columbus called Indians, and they themselves called variations on "the people".

I envision that given that people are sexual animals, it took approximately one microsecond before the gene pool in that region changed forever upon the arrival of the Spaniards. Okay, not that fast, but you get my gist.

Anyway, the great European powers of the day rapidly began colonization, and ultimately domination, of much of the rest of the world. Principally as far as the Americas were concerned, first the Spanish and then the Portuguese, French, and English made rapid inroads. At the same time, these powers were dominating and subjugating the African continent. Their military superiority, along with their cultural sense of prominence and supremacy, led them to believe that they should and indeed must deem others as genetically inferior and appropriate for conquest, enslavement, suppression, and mistreatment.

Well before Columbus landed on what he thought was India, the Portuguese were plying Atlantic waters south of the homeland, reaching the coast of sub-Saharan Africa. Portuguese and Spanish traders were already raiding Africa for human contraband before the English arrived in Jamestown in 1607. So it wasn't long thereafter when the English got into the act and the first Africans arrived in the embryonic settlement, forced into the manual labor the English were loathe to do. Originally, the Africans were termed "indentured servants," but in no time the terminology and rigid caste system of slavery was crystallized. How else could anyone term someone who was forcibly held in hard labor for life without ever the possibility of freedom? And as well, the people born to these slaves were slaves themselves for life, and on into perpetuity, with human beings considered property, bought, traded, and sold like any other product or service.

As we might imagine, many Africans forced into hard labor and separated from their families and culture reacted with rebellion or violence, and were met with brutality and often death. Those who survived developed their own culture, music, and religious interpretation of the Christianity forced on them.

Slavery was primarily, but not exclusively, a feature of the southern colonies and later states of the new nation. By the late 1700s, two percent of the Northern population were slaves, mostly personal servants, but more than 25 percent of Southerners overall were slaves, working the hard life of farming, brick making, carpentry, and other manual labor. In some Southern counties, well over 50 percent of the population was enslaved.

It is my view that Virginian Thomas Jefferson's immortal words in the Declaration of Independence, "When in the course of human events..." became a manifesto of hypocrisy, decrying the need for personal freedom and human rights of English descendants now on American soil but not the blacks those descendants enslaved! Most Southern signatories, including Jefferson, were slave owners themselves. Ignoring this duplicity, Founders turned their backs on freed blacks' petitions to terminate slavery. Nevertheless, about 5,000 blacks took arms against the English army alongside their white neighbors when the Revolutionary War broke out. Recognizing this, the British offered freedom to any slave willing to fight with them against the Revolutionaries. Slaves, caught in the middle by the thousands, used the chaos of war as an opportunity to escape from bondage, mostly northward to Canada.

After the new nation of the United States of America had been officially born, cotton joined tobacco as a lucrative cash crop for southern growers. Both were labor-intensive, and thus relied heavily on the free labor provided by slaves to be profitable for the landowner. As I mentioned earlier, many plantation owners became exceedingly affluent on the backs of their increasing numbers of slaves.

Meanwhile, resistance to the "peculiar institution" was forming in both the black and white communities. Sympathetic white abolitionists such as John Greenleaf Whittier, Gideon Welles, Harriet Beecher Stowe, William Lloyd Garrison, John Brown, and in a sense Abraham Lincoln, joined influential blacks such as Solomon Northup, Sojourner Truth, Harriet Tubman, and Frederick Douglass to call for ultimate emancipation of all slaves. Congress passed a series of laws in an attempt to placate a restless nation, divided on the moral, ethical, and economic quandary of human bondage.

A federal proclamation in 1808 made new importation of slaves illegal, but did nothing to cease existing slavery. By 1857, the U. S. Supreme Court issued a landmark decision in the case of *Dred Scott v. Sandford*, which held that no African American could be a citizen and thus had no legal rights anywhere in the nation. *Dred Scott* is widely regarded as the worst decision the Supreme Court ever made, inflicting aspersions on itself from which that revered institution might still suffer. *Dred Scott* also indirectly provided a catalyst for the Civil War. Thus, by the 1850s, slavery became primarily, but not exclusively, the cause of the Great War Between the States.

Abraham Lincoln, interestingly enough, in freeing the slaves in his Emancipation Proclamation of January 1, 1863, changed the legal status of enslaved people from "slave" to "free," but only in the South. In other words, he only freed slaves in states that had already seceded from the Union, and thus felt themselves not bound to anything their erstwhile government, or President Lincoln whom they so loathed, decreed. Thus it applied to the 3 million or so slaves in the new nation of the Confederate States of America but not the additional million or so in states that hadn't seceded. I imagine the reaction of that news to the slaves in the North was not the same as those in the Southern states!

Anyway, the outcome of the Civil War and the passage of the 13th, 14th, and 15th Amendments to the Constitution abolished slavery and granted civil rights and the right to vote to black men. America then instantly became one big, racially diverse but economically and socially equal, blissful family, to live happily ever after.

(Hopefully you're issuing a deep, sardonic laugh right now at that absurd notion. If you haven't yet, please do; physiologists tell us that a hearty belly-laugh is good exercise and promotes long life. I'll stand by.)

There has existed in this nation since the beginning a notion that continues today among scores of European-Americans that they are genetically and socially superior to blacks. This racism, as the decades passed after the war, gave rise to supremacist groups like the Ku Klux Klan, the Aryan Brotherhood, the White Aryan Resistance, and many others.

The Civil War ended in 1865, but the entirety of the former Confederacy was occupied until 1877, when federal troops were withdrawn. Freed from that restrictive force, quickly all hell broke loose. Pernicious acts spread like wildfire across the land, as some of the vanquished former Confederates instantly set about making life miserable for the newly freed blacks. Widespread campaigns of intimidation, terror, and even murder ensued. Black men hanging from nooses became a tragic but frequent sight throughout the South, and to be fair many northern states as well. Estimates of the number of lynched blacks, many of whom committed nothing to be construed as a crime, vary into the thousands.

Racists instituted a variety of literacy tests, poll taxes, and other means to deny black men the right to vote which had been granted by the 15th Amendment to the Constitution. They ordered that all facilities, public and private, be segregated by race. And they kept blacks impoverished by denying them opportunities for land ownership. Imagine the plight of the Negro family on the Southside Virginia farm finding that while no longer enslaved and no longer legally considered the personal property of the land-owner upon whose land they resided, they had no money, no items of any cash value, and no options for physical or occupational mobility. They were typically stuck right where they'd always been, working for the same landowner, now "free" to earn a wage but with no power to negotiate either salary or working conditions. Nor did they possess power to influence the governance under which they lived.

The post-war period we have now termed Reconstruction is quix-otically named. Yes, rebuilding of many of the buildings and other infrastructure destroyed in the war got underway. But for freed former slaves, their emergence into social and economic parity would need to wait for generations, and in significant ways is still underway. Jim Crow laws designed to keep the races separate in as many aspects of life as possible, and the terminology "separate but equal," emerged, although it never was equal.

While all this was going on nationally, in Virginia the political scene was being dominated by one Harry Flood Byrd. He was a descen-dent of one of the First Families of Virginia, including William Byrd II of Westover Plantation who founded Richmond and Robert "King" Carter, a colonial governor. Byrd became Virginia's 50th Governor in 1925 and then senator from 1933 until 1965. In the glow of a kinder historic light, he was known for his austere financial policies. But under the harsh glare of racial inequality, he was a determined segregationist whose thinking and strong-armed tactics permeated Virginia politics for decades, a period known as "massive resistance." Byrd's segregation-ist influence extended most insidiously in rural areas of the state.

Throughout the decades following the Civil War, blacks made inroads into American life and culture in countless areas, principally those where they had the most access, including sports, entertainment, religion, and education. By the 1930s and 1940s, prominent black law-yers emerged who began to use the inconsistencies of legal precedence to chip away at segregationist laws.

Among the legal challenges was the case of *Davis v. County School Board of Prince Edward County*. The R. R. Moton High School, named for Robert Russa Moton, a Farmville-born protégé of Dr. Booker T. Washington, was an all-black segregated high school in Farmville. Built in 1923 to house 180 students, by 1950 there were 477 students, and it was in deplorable shape due to chronic underfunding. In spite of the separate but equal mandate, the Prince Edward County Public School Board, all white at the time, purposefully ignored the needs of the black schools. It wasn't just overcrowded; there was neither a cafeteria nor a gymnasium. Teachers shared rest rooms with students. Many class-rooms had fewer desks than students and some had no blackboards.

The issue came to a head on April 23, 1951, when not parents nor teachers but students organized a strike. Led by a 16 year old named Barbara Rose Johns, a niece of civil rights leader Vernon Johns, stu-dents faked a call to the headmaster, claiming it was the police and summoning him into town while forging notes to all the teachers instructing them to bring their students to an assembly in the auditorium. Johns addressed her classmates and by the end of her speech, 450 students left the building and planted themselves in the lawns of the homes of the school board members. The student walkout lasted two weeks, at which point they resumed their attendance.

The goal of the students was to ensure better funding and thus better – but still segregated – facilities for themselves. Their modest demand was simply a new, adequate school. However, the protest had drawn national attention and players on the larger playing field had a loftier goal.

A month later, two NAACP lawyers filed suit to compel all the nation's schools to fully integrate. This case, *Davis v. County School Board of Prince Edward County*, was lost by the plaintiffs. They then appealed to the U. S. District Court where they lost again. Finally the case was appealed to the U. S. Supreme Court where it was consolidated into the landmark *Brown v. Board of Education* case in which the Supreme Court ruled that school segregation, and by inference all segregation, was illegal.

Brown was decided on May 17, 1954 (two months before I was born, it turns out). And everyone lived happily ever after. Wait. Wrong again.

Robert Russa Moton Museum

How can I explain the outrage felt by hundreds of thousands of white, racist Virginians? Nonplussed and unmoved by the supreme law of the land, they resisted integration as the Governor, Lindsay Almond, worked to end segregated schools throughout his state with varying levels of local cooperation. Back in Farmville in 1959, the Prince Edward County Board of Supervisors took a novel approach untried elsewhere: it simply ended all funding for their entire school system, forcing it to close immediately.

Without missing a beat, white parents banded together and formed the Prince Edward Foundation that founded several private schools, "segregation academies," where their kids moved forward with their educational careers unabated. Black kids faced starker choices. Where possible, black parents sent their kids to live with out-of-state relatives to be schooled there, or simply terminated their educations. Several benevolent organizations like the Quakers set up classroom environments to help as many black youth as possible.

At that point, Prince Edward was the only county in the state without a public school system. In fact, on March 18, 1963 U.S. attorney general Robert F. Kennedy said during a speech: "The only places on earth not to provide free public education are Communist China, North Vietnam, Sarawak, Singapore, British Honduras—and Prince Edward County, Virginia." Imagine the indignation and sorrow of a black child, a rising 9th grader, who had her high school experience ripped away! This group of students was called the "Lost Generation of Prince Edward County."

Later in 1963, Prince Edward County was ordered by federal courts to fund its school system and re-open its schools. This ended the era of Massive Resistance in Virginia.

But before I tell you more about *that* story, let's go for a bicycle ride.

IN THE EARLY YEARS OF PLOTTING RAILROADS, many cities actively courted the railroad companies. Farmville was one of them, offering a significant financial incentive to the South Side Rail Road to route through it, even though it necessitated the crossing of the Appomattox River, not once but twice, with one bridge just north of downtown Farmville and the other six miles east of town. The latter was named the High Bridge, built in 1854. The 21-span structure was one of the great engineering projects of the day.

At the time, C. O. Sanford, who surveyed for and engineered the bridge, declared, "There have been higher bridges not so long, and longer bridges not so high, but taking the length and height together, this is, perhaps the largest bridge in the world." So why call it the "High Bridge" and not the "Longest Bridge?" Or the "Largest Bridge?" Whatever.

It played a role in the Civil War and was ultimately replaced by a newer design in 1886. But as time went on, with it being phenomenally expensive to build and increasingly expensive to maintain, it, along with the entire line from near Burkeville to Pamplin, was abandoned by Norfolk Southern and donated to the State of Virginia for a state park.

So three blocks west of the Burkeville's major intersection, the rail splits, with one headed northwest to Farmville and then due west to Pamplin, and the other more directly west and then northwest over to Pamplin. It's the Farmville route that was abandoned.

Given the aspiration I had for a multi-modal experience on this journey, I decided to ride the trail on a bicycle, joined by my friend David Mullins, also from Blacksburg. We spent the better part of an hour shuttling cars around so we could ride point-to-point. We found a trailhead on the eastern end four or five miles northwest of Burkeville. The spot had little in the way of signage and no facilities of any kind. But hey, when you've gotta go, you've gotta go.

Dave is an avid backpacker, having done the "triple crown" of long-distance hikes, the Appalachian Trail, the Continental Divide Trail, and the Pacific Coast Trail, end to end. Clearly, he is more ambitious than me, motivated by challenges, and he strives to achieve landmark goals. So he headed eastward first to find where the trail actually petered-out, dutifully riding to the bitter beginning (as it were), just to say he'd done so. Meanwhile, I fiddled around with my bicycle and gear.

We got underway westward, riding the smooth, crushed gravel surface. It had rained heavily the night before, but the surface had been smoothed and it shed the water nicely so there were few puddles. There was nothing to see, really, as the trail meandered northward to the community of Rice. There we stopped for a few moments and chatted with the clerk who worked at the aged, tiny post office.

The clerk, Vince Taylor, told me Rice was a place where timber and lumber products were loaded onto the train. There was never passenger service. He said the trail had been opened in segments with the High Bridge itself being the most expensive retrofit and thus done last. "Since the bridge opened, that's been the focus of 90 percent of the visitors, at least the foot traffic. They park as close as they can and then walk to it, over it, and back. To me, the trail is like a town alley without the sheds and the garbage cans."

Taylor told us Rice boasted a convenience store nearby with great fried chicken, but no other commercial establishments. He said he used to work in Pamplin City and State Parks planners were working tirelessly to extend the trail that last mile into town.

His little post office served only 95 customers. I asked if the USPS was phasing out little offices. He said, "They really wanted to cut all of them out some time ago. But they got so much push-back that they had to go slowly. They got rid of many miniscule ones. The new postmaster general is female. She is intent on improving relationships between management, employees, and customers. My hope is that the shutting down of smaller post offices will fall between the cracks."

Back underway, we found alongside the trail an interpretive marker that told the woeful tale of one General Thomas Alfred Smyth. General Smyth suffered an unparalleled stroke of bad luck, in that he was the last Union general killed in the Civil War. He died at 4:00 a.m. on April 9, 1865, literally a few hours before Lee signed his surrender to Grant. Smyth had been shot through the mouth by a Confederate sniper two days earlier. The bullet shattered his cervical vertebra and paralyzed him, ultimately mortally wounding him.

Another twenty minutes of flat riding took us to the namesake landmark, the approach to the lengthy expanse of the High Bridge. The bridge loomed before us, arrow-straight and long. The landing had space for the current iteration of the bridge alongside the displaced bridge. We clippety-clopped across the wooden planks and rode across. There were three wider platforms, covered with tastefully designed pergolas, to pull off and take a gander. The first was directly over the Appomattox River, flowing swift and coffee-brown from our left to our right. The area around it was forested and much of it was swampy-wet, although the bridge deck was well above the canopy of trees. We took

High Bridge

some photos and continued to the next platform where we stopped again.

While resting there, a retired couple ambled by, both wearing heavy winter coats. The man told us, "We're traveling around the country. We have this nerd objective to visit every presidential grave site. We have very few left."

She said, "We're going to cover Harding, Harrison, and Hayes in Ohio. We've already done Garfield and McKinley."

They lived in Winchester, Virginia. Their plan was to stay at a reconditioned railroad car lodge that night. Seeing their winter coats made me shiver in the cool air.

Buzzards flew overhead. Some stopped on the bridge railing. Some excreted.

"We've done Nixon and Reagan in California," they boasted. He said, "Some graves are in really small towns. They range from elaborate tombs like Grant's or Lincoln's sarcophagus to Coolidge's tombstone. Teddy Roosevelt, my hero, is in a little private cemetery on Oyster Bay. It is locked, but the groundskeeper was there, and he let us in. It's the best way to learn of different eras of our history."

I asked who the last president who died was. Nobody knew, so she whipped out her smart phone and punched up Siri, the voice recognition queen and said, "Who was the last president that died?"

I quipped, "We have too much technology!"

(Answer: Gerald Ford. RIP.)

We rolled on another 5 miles or so towards Farmville. Arriving at the outskirts of town, we crossed a second bridge over that same Appomattox River. Of course, that made me wonder why, if the Appomattox River flowed west to east and the Norfolk & Western Railroad line essentially went east-west as well, why bother crossing it at all? Couldn't planners simply have paralleled it and without ever crossing it? Well, yes. And that's what they ultimately did. And that's why this section of track was finally abandoned.

The trail reached the outskirts of Farmville from the northeast, and there were more people using it as we got closer to town. Unlike most communities in the area, Farmville's Main Street ran generally north-south rather than east-west, and the trail crossed with a crosswalk at the grade level. There was a new park with several canopies, benches, and bike racks, and a rare feature most anywhere in America, a clean public rest room with real running water.

In the immediate area were several old buildings, which appeared to be former tobacco warehouses and factories. All were made of brick and were three to four stories high, and in seemingly good states of repair. There was a new bicycle shop at the intersection, clearly there to take advantage of the business generated by the trail.

DAVID AND I HEADED DUE WEST towards our final destination, about 16 miles away, according to a trail sign. We passed the old train station, a tan building with a high, steeply sloped slate roof. I peered inside and it looked as if it had been reconditioned as a meeting facility or conference room. Onward we pedaled.

The trail was flat, nearly straight, and frankly staggeringly, painfully boring. There were scrub woods, not particularly attractive, on both sides of the trail, but not close enough to offer any canopy. There was no wind. No sun. A slight drizzle. We rode and rode. After ten miles we saw another sign that said twelve more miles to go. After riding another eight miles, another sign said eight more to go. Dave pedaled a couple hundred yards in front of me for awhile, allowing me to catch up at Prospect. Then we rode into Elam. Did I mention it was boring? Finally, seven hours later, we arrived at our destination. (Note, I'm exaggerating; it really didn't take that long. It only seemed like it.) I'm surprised the High Bridge Trail Guide doesn't use the word "boring" for this section. "Attention: the trail from Farmville to the western terminus is resplendently boring. Use at your own peril. We are not interested in hearing about your experience."

We mounted the bicycles on the car and drove all the way back to retrieve the first one. Dave headed for home, and I drove into Farmville to meet with Bob Flippen, the park ranger. Should I tell him his trail was boring?

I HAD ARRANGED A MEETING WITH BOB at a fun and funky restaurant called Charley's Waterfront Café. Bob had been mentioned to me by a man named Howard Gregory of Appomattox, who was on my schedule to meet the following day.

Bob was late, so while I waited, I tapped into their Wi-Fi to learn that Farmville was a town of about 8000 people, formed in 1798 and incorporated in 1912. Most of the town was in Prince Edward County, south of the Appomattox River. But a portion of the town was across the river and in Cumberland County. So most residents who had business to do at the courthouse merely needed to go to downtown, whereas those across the river needed to go 18 miles north to Cumberland to theirs.

Farmville's two claims to fame were the hosting of hostile armies on the last days of the Civil War and a little kerfuffle regarding Civil Rights in the late 1950s that I alluded to earlier. More on those in a moment.

BOB FINALLY ARRIVED, dressed in a state park uniform. He worked for the Virginia Department of Conservation and Recreation, in the State Park division. He was assigned to the High Bridge Trail State Park.

It was before the dinner hour, so we had the large, nicely decorated dining room to ourselves. He introduced himself and promptly began his interpretive, being his normal line of work, telling me about his native area. "Farmville was comprised of fifteen acres in 1798, established as a town by the state legislature. The lot this building stands on was not part of the town. Judith Randolph, who gave the fifteen acres, retained this lot this building was on because she received an inspectorship of tobacco. It is the earliest tobacco warehouse in Farmville."

He showed me that the walls still had faded images of advertisements painted on them, dating back to the 1870s and 1880s. He said farmers would grow their tobacco and bring it in on carts during market days. The manufacturers employed brokers to go to the various warehouses throughout the area to make their purchases. They would grade the tobacco to the various different types.

"The advertisements on the wall are generally for the various dealers and retailers here in town. With the money they got paid for their tobacco, (advertisers) wanted them to come to their establishments to buy things. So they were actually advertising to the growers. Market days were typically big days for the retailers here in town."

About the new High Bridge Trail State Park, he said, "The last train ran on July 15, 2005, and (the corridor) was donated to the state on December 28, 2006. The final runs were just to pick up some rebar or pulpwood. One of the reasons they stopped using this line was because there wasn't enough business on it.

"I am not new in this area. I was born in West Germany, but I went to Cumberland High School and George Washington University. I came back to this area because of my love of history. My education is in anthropology, history, and political science."

He started working at the park as an AmeriCorps volunteer in 2011. "They liked me so much that they hired me two days after my service ended. I was like, 'Really? Does it actually pay anything?'" He was 56 years old and he said that the workload and the pay were such that ordinarily a person of his age would have declined. "I was really into it. I really was. I do what we call 'visitor experience.'"

"So I am not taking you from your job; I am your job," I boasted smugly, proud of myself.

"That's right. You pay taxes; they pay my wages. I'm good at this and you are getting your money's worth. Believe me, I'm conscientious about it."

Our conversation shifted to the rail line and the bridge. He told me the railroad was not supposed to have come here at all. "It came here because of what was called the South Side Rail Road. It was chartered in 1846 and construction started in 1849 running from City Point (on the James River downstream of Richmond) to Petersburg and then connected a series of county courthouses all the way to Lynchburg."

It traversed about 135 miles. It was not going to come to Farmville at all! It was actually planned to go through Hampton Sydney, which is about 8 miles south. A town called Worsham was at that time the county seat of Prince Edward County. The courthouse was not moved to Farmville until 1871.

"People in Farmville wanted this railroad so bad that they approached the railroad company with a financial incentive and said if they brought it to Farmville, they promised to band together and purchase $100,000 worth of railroad stock.

"There were only about 1,500 people then. The railroad took them at their word, but from what I can gather they had a devil of a time getting the money out of all of these people. Some of them probably paid upfront at $100 per share. But I think some of the others were paying over time at $2 per month."

The railroad made a significant detour to reach here. Farmville sits in a geological bowl or depression. In order to keep the real grade at a constant 1 percent to 2 percent, this necessitated building a huge bridge over the valley of the Appomattox River just downstream."

He explained the track layout engineers had to use a cut-and-fill technique to raise the grade above the level of the lower creeks and rivers.

"It took 1,000 men and 200 horses almost two-and-a-half years to build the original High Bridge. Think of this. Farmville only had a population of about 1,500, and now you have a construction project in a part of the country that public works of this magnitude are simply unheard of." He showed me a picture that he had in a scrapbook he'd brought along. It was taken looking westbound which is the same direction that we had just ridden it. "They estimated there were between 4 million and 7 million bricks made and placed to build the towers for this bridge. In my estimation, in its time, it is certainly one of the man-made wonders of the world. Undoubtedly. Period."

He went on to describe the contracts, the contractors, and various construction difficulties and cost overruns.

"We encounter a high caliber of individuals here. Healthy. History conscious. Friendly. I think part of that is because they are here because they want to be here. This isn't something that you can just ride up to and leave. You have to walk a mile to get to (the bridge). You are vested in it. It is a real pleasure to encounter these individuals."

"What has this transition from being a working bridge to being a nonworking bridge to now being a recreational facility meant to the community of Farmville?" I asked.

He said, "We were a railroad town basically watching empty cars going back west as the full cars were typically going east on the newer line to the south of us. I think they sent the empty cars this way because of the High Bridge. There was less weight and less wear-and-tear on the bridge. I think that is another reason they were glad to get rid of the line and all the cost of maintenance on it.

"Back in 1989, two kids got killed walking across the bridge. Lots of people walked across the bridge illegally, trespassing. For several years I lived at that brick house that you passed on the trail. I have walked across the bridge in the dark myself. I understood how to read the signal lights. The signal light had an amber light along with the red light and the green light. As long as it was amber, you were fine. When it turned green, that meant something was coming behind you. When it turned red, that meant something was coming towards you. As long as you were looking at that light and knew what to do, you could do it safely. There were also platforms where you could find safety.

"Anyway, we went from being a through community for the railroad to being a destination for recreation. Now all the hotels are filled on weekends. This place is packed. You see bicycles leaning on walls and railings up and down the street and you see people wearing bicycling tights. This trail specifically has really helped this restaurant. They have been rejuvenated because of this trail. I see what it has done for Farmville.

"We are America's Hometown. We are the perfect symbol of that. We have a nice Main Street. We have people who care. It is kind of like Mayberry RFD except perhaps a bit more sophisticated. This town is well-run and managed."

I said, "Now I'm going to ask about a dark chapter in Farmville's history. Would you care to comment on racial issues?"

"It's true," he admitted, ruefully. He knew I was talking about the Prince Edward County School system closing I spoke about at the beginning of this chapter.

I said, "There seems to have been a cloud over this town then. Is that cloud gone now?"

He said, "There are people who like to keep the cloud there. Let us move forward together. That is what I prefer. We all just want to live in peace and I believe it is happening more so. We are in a nice community here. The people here live together and when all that was going on, nobody was lynched. Nobody was hosed down by massive water hoses."

I challenged, "True. Nobody was physically assaulted. But it was still a profound divide. Am I being fair in saying that?"

He said, "Yes. I imagine when the schools were integrated, it was still tense. I am a few years too young for that. There was an electronics company that came to town in the 1960s. It made electrical components and switches. It was almost like Microsoft coming to Farmville today. People thought that no company in their right mind would ever come here because of the racial turmoil and strife that were here. But they did. I spoke with a newspaperman who said it was the first time that he had seen new people here."

I asked him what his best day was. He said, "I have had hundreds of best days. One best day was last Friday. We had an alternative spring break group. These were college kids who didn't go down to Florida to drink and smoke and party. They came to a state park and worked all week. They were from Georgetown University. I was so taken by them. They were genuinely interested. They asked great questions. They said they were there for the experience. We did all different things and when it ended, I took my hat off and said, 'Guys, I feel so humble by your presence.' I was looking at successful young people. They came to do something not for themselves but for other people, specifically for us. I said to them, 'I want you to know that it is true that when you do good things for people it comes back to you.' I saw a group of bright, shiny, happy people. I'm getting emotional about it."

I thought that was probably a really good place to conclude, but as I tried to wrap up, he said, "I love my job. I am here for the people who come to visit. I want people to come see me and ask me things. Engage me and I want to engage you. That is my job. I feel a certain sense of privilege as a Virginia historian."

I thanked Bob for his time and we departed, he bringing home a piece of pie for his wife. Nice guy!

I DROVE OVER to the former Moton School, now the Robert Russa Moton Museum, a National Historic Landmark. For some reason, I expected it to be a tiny building five miles outside of town on a dirt road lines with tarpaper shacks and emaciated goats tied to posts out front. Instead, the building, while certainly inadequate for the 450 or so students it had when the strike began, was not tiny. And it was only a mile or so from downtown, on a busy triangular intersection with a strip mall across the street hosting a Verizon store, a CVS Pharmacy, and a Kroger grocery store, and the ball fields of Longwood College behind it.

I wandered inside, hoping to perhaps meet someone who had experienced the closing of the school. Instead there was a self-guided tour brochure which I followed. As I walked from classroom to classroom, I heard the story of the civil rights movement and the struggles blacks faced in the era to have segregation abolished. It was moving and hopeful in tone, but I knew in my heart the struggle is ongoing.

I SWUNG WESTWARD AGAIN, this time towards Pamplin City, the village near the end of the bicycle trip I'd taken with Dave Mullins. I would soon learn that Pamplin City is known for its pipe manufacturing facility. Not water pipes or sewer pipes, but its smoking pipes. Seriously.

Never has the word "city" been used with such a sense of aspiration as it is in Pamplin City. What I found was a mere village, and a downtrodden one at that. There was a main street, one side only facing the railroad tracks, a short block long, without a single operational storefront. Most of the one- and two-story brick buildings were in a serious state of decay, with missing roofs, broken windows, and fallen walls. I doubt any of them had seen a customer or a working cash register in fewer than three or four decades. One, ironically with intact glass, had ghoulish figures on the windowsills. One was a particularly ghastly gargoyle with a gaping mouth and razor-sharp fangs. Vines were growing over most buildings and some had barricades in front of them and NO TRESPASSING signs on the entrances.

I wandered inside the only modern looking, occupied building I could find, which did triple duty as the post office, the town office, and a museum. It was the library at one time, but the county shut it down because the community was too small to support it. The "library" now consisted of a wooden cabinet on a post outside where people could loan or borrow books.

Pamplin City gargoyle

I found Mayor Billy Horton inside, who told me, "We are a city in name only. We only have two working businesses. Our downtown is a bit of a ghost town. The town got its start when the pipe factory opened. We had a clay smoking pipe factory here. This is what Pamplin is really known for. At one time the factory was the largest producer of pipes in the United States."

He explained that before cigarettes became popular, more people smoked pipes. "The building still stands but there is nothing in it. There is an archaeological society out of Maryland that actually owns the building now. They keep it preserved. A number of people out in the country would make their own molds and then bring them to the pipe factory. There was a house beside it that is no longer standing. We are still finding old discarded pipes around there."

He showed me a display of artifacts, of pipes that people had found and brought in.

"We are incorporated as a town. We have a town government, but I am both the mayor and the town manager. It pays a little bit of money, but not much. There are only about 220 people here."

I told him that I had ridden the High Bridge Trail.

He said, "Sooner or later it is going to end up terminating right here at the train depot. For the last half-mile or so, the trail will have to be on the road because this is still an active rail line. I am hoping that that will help our town.

"In your book, please tell people that we are up-and-coming. We will continue until we can make Pamplin the way it used to be. It is already a great place to live. I love this place."

My next stop was the historic town of Appomattox, the place where Robert E. Lee surrendered to Ulysses S. Grant effectively ending the Civil War.

Best I can tell, somewhere in the neighborhood of 75,000 books have been written about the American Civil War, or as some folks like to say, the War Between the States or even the War of Northern Aggression. All were written by people who know more about it than I do. So I'm not going to take a lot of your attention here to that essential American topic, but only enough to hopefully explain why Appomattox, Virginia, is at the top of every list of American wartime historic sites like Gettysburg, Pearl Harbor, Yorktown, and Antietam.

The War of Northern Aggression (hereinafter referred to as the "Civil War," because frankly I'm too lazy to type the longer name) began in the Charleston, South Carolina harbor when Confederate artillery fired on Fort Sumter. The battle lasted for a day, watched by large numbers of Charleston civilians in a celebratory mood. Four years of horror, death, and destruction ensued.

It may be worth arguing whether there is any justification in calling this the War of Northern Aggression when Southerners fired the first shots. But one thing is clear: with the Southern states purposefully splitting off to form a new nation, the goals in the war were much different. The North needed to win in order to restore the Union. The Confederates merely needed to not lose. They needed to draw out the war long enough that the Union would buckle under the stinging losses and simply give up and go home. Almost the entirety of the war was fought on Confederate soil, the terrible battles of Gettysburg and Antietam notwithstanding, so the Southern combatants may have felt they were defending their homeland, and thus easily mustered the requisite urgency to persevere. But I still have trouble envisioning the rationale of the poor farmer from Houghton, Michigan or fisherman from Burlington, Vermont, parting with his home, wife, and family to swelter and die in a Mississippi swamp just to bring those recalcitrant Southerners back into the fold. But thousands of them did. Honor and valor were more treasured attributes then, apparently.

Motives aside, the Civil War marched on. If the South had needed to win, it would have never been a contest, as given its resource disadvantage, it would have been impossible for them to truly defeat the Union. However, if the South could fight fiercely with bravery and resilience, there was a chance they could discourage the Federals into giving up. The longer the war dragged on, the more acute the Southern deficiencies became.

When Confederate General Robert E. Lee attempted, as a last gasp, to break the Union resolve by invading their territory in Maryland and Pennsylvania in July, 1863, and then failed, the proverbial handwriting was on the wall. The defeat at Gettysburg, and in particular the stunning massacre of Southern troops during Pickett's Charge, made Lee's surrender almost two years later at Appomattox inevitable.

Recall from our visit earlier to Petersburg that by April 2, 1865, Lee's army retreated westward and Richmond was overwhelmed by the Federals the following day. Lee was reeling!

The Battle of Sailor's Creek near Farmville was the last major engagement of the war, with nearly a quarter of Lee's remaining Army of Northern Virginia, nearly 7,700 troops, captured or lost. The retreating Confederates destroyed a portion of the High Bridge in a futile attempt to forestall the pursuing Federals.

Lee had hoped to re-supply and gain reinforcements with Gen. Joseph E. Johnston's Army of Tennessee at Amelia Court House, but Johnston never arrived. Lee's Army, arriving at Appomattox, was depleted, exhausted, starving, and without proper armaments.

Sensing the end, Grant sent a note to Lee on April 7, suggesting that it was time to surrender. Lee wrote back refusing to do so, but coyly asking for potential surrender terms. When Federals beat him to the depot at Appomattox, destroying three supply trains waiting there for him, Lee realized that further resistance would be futile.

By dawn on April 9, Lee's troops were still fighting, but by 8:00 a.m., Lee, with acknowledgement of most of his officers, decided that surrender was the only option. When Lee's letter arrived, Grant reputably had a splitting migraine headache. Grant's pain was evidently soothed by the news. My guess is that winning a four year long war is a better antidote for a migraine than Tylenol or Advil.

By 3:00 p.m. that afternoon, Lee sat opposite Grant in the home of Wilmer McLean. In one of those crazy ironies the Civil War produced,

McLean moved to Appomattox from Manassas Junction following the First Battle of Bull Run to escape the war!

Much has been made of the resplendence of Lee and the relative unkempt appearance of Grant. The two men had only met once before, serving the Army in Mexico, and Grant mentioned remembering Lee's imposing presence. Lee was six feet tall and sixteen years older at 59 than Grant at 43. Grant was five feet eight inches tall, with a deep-brown beard and hair. Lee's silver-grey hair and beard were nicely appointed by a clean grey Confederate General's uniform.

Grant acknowledged that the men who until that point Lee had commanded were now his countrymen, and as such made sure the terms of surrender were generous and without the spoils of victory so often seen in wars past. The men were allowed to keep their weapons which they would need back home, and simply disperse. The great American Civil War, which produced more total casualties than all previous wars put together, was over, ending at Appomattox, Virginia. And you were there!

THE NEXT MORNING, I connected by phone with Howard Gregory (the man who'd told me about Bob Flippen in Farmville) and he asked me to call on two people he thought could give me a good overview of Appomattox. The first was Marvin Hamlett, publisher of the weekly newspaper, the *Times Virginian*. The second was Wayne Phelps, a local businessman.

The *Times Virginian* was housed in a small brick building a few blocks from downtown. The moment I met Marvin Hamlett, he told me he was on a deadline (Aren't they always?) and could only spend a few moments with me.

I got right to the point. "What is it like to be in the town where the Civil War ended?"

"A lot of our economy relies on tourism and getting out-of-town visitors to come here," Hamlett said. "There are not a lot of jobs here in Appomattox."

"How is business?" I asked.

"Under George W. Bush, it was fantastic. Well, under the first part of his presidency. Towards the end, it got really bad. Not to blame him or anybody. It was just the timeframe of it."

And I am thinking to myself, "It got really bad?" It makes it sound as if Bush was a passive observer in the Great Recession, as if the worst economic disaster since the Great Depression dropped out of the sky. Fortunately, Hamlett continued before I said something that might have ended the conversation right then.

"The *Times Virginian* has been around for 124 years. I have been in journalism for 30 years and have been here at this paper for 18 years. Journalism has been my life.

"The industry is constantly evolving with technological advances. We have to stay on top of a whole lot of things we didn't used to have to stay on top of. We need to be Internet savvy. Social media. We are breaking stories now on the Internet rather than in our print product. We sell ads and sponsorships on the Internet, but we still consider the print product our bread and butter. People still want to carry the newspaper with them to the sofa. They still want to cut clippings of their nine kids and put them on the refrigerator.

"We print each week on Wednesday. We have a circulation of 4,000. Remarkably, it has been fairly constant. Many other newspapers have struggled to keep their print circulation at high levels. It is still relevant. The readers here have grown accustomed to getting their information through the newspaper. We have done a good job of providing that to them.

"The population of Appomattox County stayed constant for about 100 years when there were about 12,000 or 13,000 people here. In the last five years it has grown to perhaps 14,000 or 15,000. There are not a lot of jobs here. Many people commute to Lynchburg. The quality of life is still very strong. A lot of outskirts have seen major developments in new housing. Once people get our dirt in their shoes, they want to come back and live here."

I said, "General Robert E. Lee and General Ulysses S. Grant met here one April afternoon in 1865. People have been coming here to Appomattox ever since then to study history. Are tourists different than they were years ago?"

He said, "I think the Civil War gets less and less relevant with each passing generation. Many kids are fixated on video games and cell phones. I love history; I'm addicted to the History Channel."

I asked, "Is there a pride the people here feel in living in a town that changed the world?"

He said, "Yes, there is. But I'm amazed by the number of people who aren't even aware of it. When I go on trips, I tell people that I am from Appomattox, Virginia, and some people don't know where it is or haven't heard of it. I remind them that it is where the Civil War ended. Once I remind them of that, they remember the name. Some people wonder how to pronounce it. (Note: it's ap-poh-MAT-tix.)

"Appomattox is not viewed by most people as a destination. It is viewed as a stopover. They will stop here, tour the surrender grounds, and move on to Mount Vernon or Natural Bridge or Poplar Forest. Appomattox is working hard to make itself a destination. We have a new hotel opening. We are trying to create more attractions and make this more tourist friendly.

"Visitors are treated with incredible friendliness. Southern hospitality is still the lay of the land here. A man's word is still his bond. People are helpful. If you have a flat tire on the side of the road, five pickup trucks will stop to help you change the tire. That is just the way this area is."

I STUMBLED OUTSIDE into the still-cool morning air and drove the directions he'd given me a few blocks to the garage where I hoped to find Wayne Phelps. The building was deserted, but I called the cell phone number posted on the door and left a message for him. Meanwhile, I decided to explore town.

I drove towards downtown on Church Street. On my right was a stunning mansion, with a wrap-around front porch held by white columns and alternating, impricated horizontal shingle tiles painted in white, tan, and ochre, with a hexagonal turret room on the right.

Main Street was one block long with shops on one side and the historic train station, now a visitor's information center, on the other. The commercial buildings seemed mostly occupied, with art galleries, boutiques, bookstores, barber shops, and florists.

By the time I headed back to the Phelps Garage, I could see a light inside, giving me hope that Wayne had arrived. His building was one of those common old commercial garage buildings with a sloping tin roof, cinder block walls, and a smattering of old cars, tractors, heating oil tanks, farm devices, and cars – working and non-working – scattered about. My car's tires crunched as I drove across the tan gravel parking area. Inside the front door was a restored and working 1929 antique car.

FROM THE LOOK of his place and his southern demeanor, he seemed like the kind of guy who had been around almost since the Civil War ended. His office was cluttered and there was not an unused square inch of wall space. Walls were filled with framed photos of family, friends, customers, and cars. He said, "For many *yeahs* we ran a garage business. I still run a towing business and I am a land holder and businessman *heah* in town."

He spoke with a deep Southside Virginia drawl, slurring off the end of words that end in the letter "r", so the word "here" sounded like "*heah*," "car" sounded like "*cah*" and "farm" sounded like "*fahm*".

He was immediately bullish on his town, telling me that everybody supports small businesses. "When somebody goes into business, the community helps them, especially young people. That is the key to economic success in small-town USA.

"We just had a young lady who had been a waitress for *yeahs heah* and she just went into business with a little restaurant on Main Street. People have been *po-ing* in to *suppoht* her. She has roots in the county that go way back in the county and that helps a lot. Everybody is related to everybody.

"I was *bown* and raised *heah*. My family ties go back to the French and Indian *Wah*. We *weah* Albemarle County then. But I have got so many cousins around *heah* and they have been *suppottive* of my family, too. We first went into business in 1961.

He said, "I had *nevva* seen devastation from a *towanado* firsthand. I have lots of cousins that live in that area. *Evvabody powed* in with *effats* to make *evvathing* as available and helpful to the victims as they could."

I said, "Your community is known worldwide for something that happened here a long time ago."

He said, "*Surrendah*. Yes indeed. They ask me, 'What was the real cause?' They say, 'You come from a Southern family.' I say, 'It was basically states rights.'"

"What does that mean?" I queried. "I have heard it a million times, but not sure I ever fully understood it."

He said, "It means less control from the Federal *Govvament*. Slavery is often talked about but *theah weah* many slaves in the *Nawth* as well. Probably not as many as down *heah* but still a lot. In those days, there *weah* about 11,000 people in this county and a half of them *weah* blacks. Some of those blacks owned *theah* own people.

"My granddaddy was raised in the *aftamath* of the Civil *Wah*. He had some interesting stories to tell about things that happened. The one I remember best was about a Confederate Monument. Hurricane Hazel actually knocked it over. We raised money through a reenactment to have it *restoawed*. The first monument cost $3,000 which was a tremendous amount of money in 1905. We raised about $12,000 to have it *restoawed*.

"My grandfather attended the ceremony for that statue. Basically every county in the Confederacy had one. Grandfather said that at the ceremony, the most agonizing thing was to see those veterans, some of them being carried in carriages and in wheelchairs, and walking around with saber wounds and missing *ahms* and legs. That really had a profound effect on him.

"The turmoil that concurred after the Civil War with the destruction of property in the South was terrible. The South did not start getting *ovah* this destruction until perhaps the 1920s. That is when things started getting *bettah*. I deal with a lot of colored people because I sell them tombstones and so *fawth*. But I tell them like it is. We talk about the stuff a lot. I am a *Southernah*. It used to be that we wouldn't talk about it much but *ouah* blacks in this county have always worked with us in different ways." He spoke about his efforts to renew a war memorial, where he got lots of support from many black people but not as much from the white people. He said, "There was a City Councilman who is from up *nowath* and he went to talking against that *wah* memorial and I'm telling you the truth, it was really educational to watch those blacks go *aftah* him. Those blacks wanted that memorial. Those blacks *ah* still appreciative of not only me but what other people did with that. They had *moah* interest and they wanted that *wah* memorial more than some of the white folks.

"There *ah* always people who *ah* willing to stir things up and as long as they do, we will *nevva* be fully *ovah* it. I cannot help that I came from a family that owned slaves. What we can affect is what we do now."

I spoke for a moment about the legacy here, about the surrender and I asked him about the history of history. "How has the observance of what happened here in 1865 changed over time?"

He said his community has eschewed the potential for monetary gain from its historic legacy. "We *ah* proud of what happened *heah*. Most of the people *heah ah*. We have large reenactments and thousands of people come out. We made a good deal of money for *ouah* Historical Society."

I asked if people were still interested in history and were still coming as they once did. He said, "We *weah* at a peak just before the Sesquicentennial. People were interested in Civil War relics or really anything that had to do with the *wah*. Yes, people *ah* traveling all the time and will come to *ouah* museums because they *ah* really fully interested in it. Young people and old. A group of six people came from the VMI and they were looking at some of *ouah* memorials. They *weah* asking questions that needed to be answered about *ouah* history and about the statue. Things that you should be interested in as a patriot or an American.

"I love history. I am not a big fan of Robert E. Lee. That Pickett's

Chahge (at Gettysburg) was a *disastah*. I had some *ancestahs* killed at Pickett's *Chahge*. Lee was a great general, don't get me wrong, but he was too old *foah* being in the field. He should have been back in Richmond hanging out with President Davis. He had a lot of medical troubles, and by the end of the *wah* he was completely worn out. He thought his army was invincible and he could break the middle of the line (in Gettysburg). No man could have made that charge a mile across to the Union lines successfully. Half of the rebels *weah* killed."

I asked him about his family and whether he felt the future is bright.

He said, "I think so. My family has always been in some kind of business. One of my grandsons does not like school at all but he likes the businesses that we do. I hope maybe the future will be bright for him.

"It is tough now when you *ah stahting* out. But as I said, Appomattox is pretty good about helping anybody who wants to get ahead. If you do right and you treat these people right, you will have it. Around *heah*, word-of-mouth is as good as anything.

"I am passionate about promoting the history of Appomattox County and its people. That's my headline. That's what I'd like to be *remembahed fawh*, that I did everything I could to preserve and protect."

Howard Gregory arrived then and joined in our conversation. He was a stout man of about 65 I guessed, with that sturdy demeanor and booming voice of a lifetime officer of the law. He exchanged pleasantries with Wayne and we took a brief tour of the cluttered garage, spending extra time looking over the antiques.

Howard and I departed together, taking separate cars to the next stop, the Museum of the Confederacy, where Howard had arranged a meeting with Josie Butler, the education programs and interpretation manager at the museum.

I should note that the town of Appomattox and the restored historic village of Appomattox Court House are not the same place, with the former being three miles west of the latter. The museum was adjacent to the US-460 Bypass that formed a semi-circle on the north of town, separating downtown from the National Historic Park.

THE MUSEUM WAS IN A MODERN BRICK BUILDING with a long row of flag poles, each representing one of the Confederate States of America. There was a nice wood rail fence surrounding it.

Howard and I entered the museum and were directed into Josie's office where I introduced myself. I told her about my project and about how my reference era was the late 1960s, during the last running of the Powhatan Arrow. "Can you give me a sense of how the visitor experience might have changed in those nearly 50 years?"

She said, "Visitors have always come to Appomattox, particularly school groups. My mother worked at the national park when they were restoring it." She said that earlier, Route 24, the original Lynchburg to Richmond stagecoach road, still went right through it. Since then, the road had been re-routed and access was by a spur road leading to a parking lot. "Even then, they had school groups coming through constantly."

She told me that the current McLean House was a reconstruction of the original. "The McLean House had been torn down in the 1890s to be moved (in pieces for re-assembly) to the Chicago World Exposition. These days, we would call that a World's Fair. The country went into a depression in 1896, and the company putting the exhibition together went bankrupt. (The house) was left sitting in parts. A new plan was to take it to the new Smithsonian in Washington DC that was being developed. They could never raise money for that. So it was left sitting on the grounds in stacks of bricks and piles of windows and doors.

"Prior to World War II, in the 1930s, one of Franklin Roosevelt's programs was to clear the land and rebuild the McLean House. The plans were still there from the people who dismantled it. They were meticulous. Remember that they were planning to rebuild it back identically, just in another place. So they started clearing the land and they found the original hearth and the foundations and rebuilt the house on top of that.

"Then World War II got underway and all of the men were called away to fight. So again, plans to rebuild it were delayed. After World War II they started rebuilding it in earnest. By 1950 they had the dedication of the rebuilt, reconstructed McLean House. That is the building you see today. It is on the exact foundation. If you go into the basement, you will see the original hearth in the warming kitchen."

She explained that the Confederacy had many flags, some more controversial than others. "The Confederate flag that you see people waving today was the naval standard or the Army of Tennessee flag. It is not the Army of Northern Virginia's flag. That flag would never have been in this area. It was the Stars & Bars, the St. Andrews Cross flag. That was a square St. Andrews Cross, a red cross on a blue background.

"As part of my gallery tour when I take students through, we show them the first national flag. It has a broad red (horizontal) stripe, a broad white (horizontal) stripe, and a broad second red (horizontal) stripe. In the upper left-hand corner is a blue box with a circle of white stars. That was flown on buildings.

"That flag was easily confused on a battlefield with the Stars & Stripes. Men actually marched into the wrong lines because the flags were so confusing. So then they made a second national flag, a solid white background with the St. Andrews Cross in the upper left corner. That was also the Army of Northern Virginia battle flag. When you are in the midst of battle and you look up and you see a big white flag flying, you think they are surrendering. Battles stopped because of the confusion over this flag. So that didn't work.

"So then they took the second national flag and put a broad red (vertical) stripe down the edge of it and that became the third national flag. That was the national flag that was flying here when Lee surrendered."

I said, "The Stars & Bars, the archetype that is so controversial, that is the naval standard, correct?"

"Yes, that was the flag that was flown on ships. This is the flag (of the current controversy). We have a lot of battle flags on display here. Those flags were surrendered at Appomattox or captured at various battlefields. Those flags were never flown again. Those were flags that the men died for.

"The St. Andrews Cross flag came out of groups well after the war that had little or no meaning to the soldiers because they never had those flags. That is a 20th Century thing. And that became associated with white supremacy, with hate groups, and with pop culture like the (television show) Dukes of Hazzard. That is not the flag that the men fought for.

"We have outside all of the Confederate states' flags plus the flag of the United States. We do not fly any of the national flags, and we would certainly never fly a battle flag because battle flags were meant to lead men into battle.

"Older people ask why people would fight for slavery. 'Why would these people leave their country to fight against their country?' Robert E. Lee was a career military man. They ask why he would leave the military of the United States of America to fight against it. He offered his services to his state. You have got to put yourself back in the mindset of that era. Prior to the Civil War, United States of America, the term, is a plural term. The United States are. If people traveled and were asked where they came from, they would likely say 'New York' or 'Virginia' or 'Georgia'. 'I am a Marylander.' 'I am a South Carolinian.' Lee, and I suspect many others, were conflicted.

"Once Virginia left the Union, Lee said, 'I cannot raise arms against my state.' He offered his services to the state militia, and it was not necessarily accepted. Jefferson Davis brought him in as an advisor. He was not considered a good soldier or a good leader. He did not win those first few battles. It was not until after Joe Johnston was wounded at Seven Pines in 1862 that Lee ended up taking over because Davis had nobody else."

Howard said, "I hope, Michael, that you will help to get the truth out about the Confederacy. Some people think it is a bad word or the flag is a bad thing."

I said, "About the flag that gets taken down from state houses: I don't think anybody gets to decide what makes somebody else feel uncomfortable or fearful. As the inclusive, generous, and welcoming society we want to be, we should try to avoid those things. We all have black friends. If I was flying that flag in my front yard and those friends found it uncomfortable, I would want to take it down, whether it really meant the same thing to me as I think it means to them or not, or whether it has any historic relevancy or significance. From my standpoint, that flag belongs in museums. These are places where people like you can tell people what it really meant."

She said, "I had a difficult time with a teacher who told me that in terms of the presentation we were going to make to her students, there were certain things that she didn't want said. I told her, 'You are here at the Museum of the Confederacy in Appomattox. We will talk about things in historical perspectives. History is not something to be agreed with or disagreed with. It is what happened.'"

She told Howard and me the museum is privately owned, a 501(c)(3) organization. She said, "We have a homeschool group that is just coming in. It is their first time here. They are sixth graders and seventh graders. It is a group of 10 African-American Muslims. When I talked to their teacher, she told me that she wanted them to learn as much about the Civil War as we could possibly teach them, every aspect of it."

I talked about the fact that our United States of America has done a lot of really awful things in its history. That other countries have done awful things does not excuse our own. American history education has been largely whitewashed to eliminate all of the warts. In doing so, we have raised generations of children who are not interested in history because so much of what we are taught is a skewed version of the truth.

She said, "The Civil War is relevant largely because it was fought on our land. Also, because we lost. Appomattox is a tourist attraction. Visitors from all over the world come here. Decades ago, this was not a happy place for Southerners, not a place they wanted to visit. It represented loss: loss of a way of life, loss of a war. It was once proposed that at Appomattox we have a national peace center. The people here voted it down. This was back in the 1930s. Places like Yorktown are places of celebration for all Americans. We won our war of independence there. Appomattox, to many, is the place where we lost. It was not until the Centennial Anniversary in the 1960s that Appomattox became more accepted by both sides."

I noted, "If the signs around town said, 'This is where the Confederacy lost,' or 'This is where Grant defeated Lee,' or 'This is where Robert E. Lee gave up,' I don't think it would have been as widely accepted."

She said, "The flag walk outside is called the reunification walk. We want to position ourselves as a symbol of reunification."

JOSIE'S TOUR GROUP BECKONED, so Howard and I departed. Leaving his car, I drove him to the Appomattox Court House National Historic Park, only a couple of miles away. He got us in for free with his senior discount card, which as I understand cost a trifling $10 and lasts forever. This is the deal of the century; undoubtedly it will be discontinued before I get old enough for one.

The Historic Park is one of those simple yet excruciatingly poignant places that instantly helps visitors get lost in time. Only parts of it are original, as the two primary landmarks, the Court House and the McLean House where General Lee surrendered the Confederate Army of Northern Virginia to General Grant of the United States Army of the Potomac, have been rebuilt.

The Court House is situated in the center of a roundabout, slightly tear-dropped to the east, a cinder road without traffic, linking what was then the road from Richmond to Lynchburg. We met Ernie Price, Chief of Education and Visitor Services, who escorted us to the expansive porch spreading lengthwise across the two-story brick tavern, just to the north. The south-facing porch had several wooden benches where we took our repose to chat about his job and experiences. It was an absolutely lovely, bright, and crisp day. Price wore the government-release uniform of a National Park ranger.

Ernie said, "In the same realm of a Grand Canyon or Yosemite, this is a national park. The nomenclature is all over the map. You have National Seashores, National Parkways, and National Historic Parks like this one, in addition to the traditional National Parks. There are 407 units."

He was a younger man than me, perhaps in his 40s, with a gap in his front teeth and a pleasant demeanor. I asked him how he got involved.

He said, "I got started in 1987. I worked then as a seasonal (employee). I have been full-time since 1998. I have been around the country with the Park Service, but coincidentally I am here in Appomattox.

"I worked here as a seasonal when I was in college, and I fell in love with this particular park. I managed to get back here in 2008 in my current capacity and I have been here ever since."

"Why did you fall in love with it?" I asked.

He said, "The short answer is that it is big history and a small place and that appeals to me. I have worked in Washington, DC, and New York, and in Mississippi and all kinds of places. But I don't think there is a more pivotal moment in all of American history than what happened in 1865 at the spot where we are sitting right now. The name may not resonate within the National Park Service like a Yellowstone or Grand Canyon or even in an historical realm with a Gettysburg or an Independence Hall. But I do feel personally that one of the most pivotal moments in our nation's history occurred here. I think the nation that we all grew up in and struggle to know now, and its continual struggle, came out of the end of the Civil War.

Howard Gregory and Ernie Price

"The nation that existed prior to 1865 would be unrecognizable to us today. If you went back to the 1840s this would feel like another planet. The nation we recognize was born out of this event. There is no more iconic moment in place and time and what is represented by the end of the American Civil War than this. If you had to pin it down to one place, where that pivot occurred, it was right here. It is still relevant. It was not just about then as if you might say, 'Oh yeah, that was huge.' It is huge right now."

I told him that my wife, being from Ohio, never seemed to grasp the significance that most Southerners place on the Civil War. "I tell her that we are still living it. History is never really over. It is merely a precursor of what is to come afterwards. That's especially true of the Civil War to the former Confederacy."

He said "I'm not even really talking about reliving the war. It is that we still struggle with what the nation is, not just what happened then but the 80 years prior to it and the 150 years since then. What is the role of government? What is the role of the states? What is the role of Washington, DC? What are our responsibilities as citizens? It is not just about fighting the Civil War. It is still dealing with the questions brought about by the war and that are still unanswered. In the spring of 1861, it seemed that the answer to many of our nation's vexing questions was all-out bloodshed. The war effectively ended four years later in the spring of 1865, but the questions didn't stop. Our continuing struggle with it hasn't stopped."

I noted that although the impact of slavery is still open to debate, nobody thinks it had zero significance. "Even though black people were emancipated in 1865, it took 100 years before the civil rights movement attempted to gain full citizenship for all races. Racism is the original sin of the United States," I said, "and we are never going to get fully over it."

"We draw a very important distinction here, I certainly do," Ernie explained. "When I craft my language, which is what I do as an interpreter here, I talk about this moment. I don't try to tell you what the meaning is but provide opportunities for you to come to your own conclusions. There is an important distinction. I don't ever catch myself saying that on April 9, 1865, the black people of Appomattox County, Virginia, and of large chunks of the South, became free. There is an important distinction between emancipation and freedom. The promise of emancipation is not equal to freedom. That is what generations of people, black-and-white, would discover after 1865.

"However, the civil rights movement cannot begin until you have emancipation, making this an incredibly pivotal moment that is still relevant to us today. The things that Dr. (Martin Luther) King (Jr.) and so many others did were critical and fascinating to us as Americans today. But none of that could have happened unless this happened first.

"We are physically within the community of Appomattox. But I think philosophically and experientially it is still removed from the community fabric of Appomattox. See those people over there?" He pointed to a group of visitors. "There are perhaps a dozen people and I don't know where they are from. But I will bet you my lunch that none of them are from Virginia. You can walk to the parking lot and see license plates from all over the country.

"We get Virginians (as visitors), but not many and the Virginians that we get are probably not from Appomattox or the surrounding counties. I think the better observation is this: if I stop at the grocery store wearing this uniform after work and somebody asks me, 'Where do you work?' If I say that I work at 'The park,' the assumption would be that I work at Holiday Lake State Park where people go swimming in the summer. If I really want somebody to know where I work, I tell them that I work at the 'surrender grounds.' That is how people refer to it locally. I think that tells you something about the perspective of the local people and the Southern perspective. Nobody here calls this the 'victory grounds.'

"And I can also tell you that those of us who work here for the National Park Service do not feel it is our job to dictate what this place should mean. Sometimes a visitor will be here because he becomes aware that his great-great-grandfather might have been part of the surrender. It is not my job to tell him what to call it.

"You will call it what you call it based on what it means to you. But it is an internal struggle because as a National Park Service employee there is a certain objectivity that we strive for. I am here to talk about the whole story whether about the formally enslaved or General Grant or General Lee or whomever. I don't refer to this as the 'surrender grounds.' But I want the park to be part of the local fabric of the community. So sometimes I do refer to it as the surrender grounds. It depends on the circumstances and who I'm talking to."

I said, "It (the surrender) is what happened here. You cannot deny that. We are all capable of our own interpretations about history. We see what we want to see. But at the same time, what happened, happened."

"True," he said.

I asked him what his good days were all about.

He said, "Being able to sit here on this porch with you two right now will probably be the highlight of my day."

I said, "That's very kind."

He said, "It's the truth. Here we are in March and we have blue skies and green grass and trees are budding out. I'm talking with you about my love for this place. It doesn't get better than this.

"It is a good day when I go to the Visitor Center and talk to somebody who is researching, and they discover that their great-great-grandfather was actually here. We can pull out a map and say with some confidence that he was in the brigade that was lined up just to the west of the McLean House and would have fought out in that field on the morning of April 9th. There were some people in his great-great-grandfather's brigade that did not survive that day. For him to be able to walk out onto that spot to stand where his great-great-grandfather was when he realized that he had survived the war and he didn't know why, and he knew soldiers that didn't and could never make sense of it the rest of his life, that is very special.

"Unlike Gettysburg and more traditional battlefield parks where all the lines are laid out on a series of timed maps, we can't do that for a lot of the Confederates here. We can do that for a third of the Confederate army that fought here on the morning of the 9th, but the other two-thirds were back on the other side of the river and we don't know exactly, for example, where the 5th Florida camped. More than likely it is on private property now. But, we do have records from April 12th where there was a stacking of the arms ceremony which was right here in the center of the village. There was a whole division of Federal soldiers of about 5,000 guys lined up on this road and we know where each regiment was. So once again, when somebody comes in and their great-great-grandfather was in the 189th New York or the 155th Pennsylvania or the 20th Maine, we know where they were on the road. That person can go out and stand on that road and know that is exactly where their great-great-grandfather stood 151 years ago."

At this point, I must embarrassingly admit that in spite of the gravity of the moment and the veneration of Ernie's monologue, my mind wandered. I thought about those visitors who found it important to come to a place where an ancestor once stood. Or was thought to have once stood. This is the place, for example, where Sylvester Slobotnick of King of Prussia, Pennsylvania, would bring his longsuffering wife Anastasia and their three children, Sally, Sally, and Sally, so he could stand in the very place where his great-great-great-grandfather, Norbert McFitzgerald Sperlich of the 155th New York, alongside the other Union regiments, the 83rd New Jersey and the 55th New Zealand, stood on April 10, 1865, and try to impress upon his children how important it was to be there. Now I know what you're thinking, "Abraham, you're an idiot. New Zealand wasn't even a state in 1865. Now pay attention!"

Apparently my self-mirth, my lapse in attention span, and the glaze in my eyes, went unnoticed by my thoughtful host, as by the time I managed to redirect myself to him, he was continuing to speak uninterrupted.

"I think the events of the Centennial were a huge boost for a whole generation of people in the early and mid-60s where it really did crank up the interest. There was a resurgence at the 125th anniversary. We also saw a resurgence of interest when Ken Burns released his Civil War documentary. In fact, the early 1990s, and 1994 specifically, was the highest visitation this Park has seen since it existed. This was due specifically to the Ken Burns series. All of the years of the 1990s were big, but 1994 was the peak.

"I got here in 2008 and our numbers were running about half of what they had been in 1994. I can only speculate as to why visitation and interest ebbs and flows. But since 2008, visitation has crept back up. Almost every year since has gone over the prior year.

"Our own Sesquicentennial was in 2015, and we saw good numbers then. June and July are our busy months. If you are up 1 percent in July over the prior year that represents a lot of new people."

"How many people are here on really busy days?" I enquired.

"Certainly not a lot, compared with places like Disney World and Colonial Williamsburg. A good day for us is 500 or 600 people. In the early 1990s, we had days where a thousand people visited. Even with our living history talks, we may have had an audience of 80 to 100 people listening routinely. The porch would be full and people would be wrapped around that fence right there and the speaker would be standing in the middle. That would have been routine in the 1990s. Now, having 40 or 50 people for a living history talk is considered big."

I joked, "When Steven Spielberg comes out with his movie, *Appomattox*, you'll see a major resurgence of interest."

He laughed. "I think one of the magical things about working here is that people who are here right now holding these maps and walking around, they didn't stumble on this place. When they got up this morning, they knew they were coming to this place and they knew what they were coming to see. They might not have known the whole story and hopefully they will learn things while they are here, that the surrender wasn't actually in the courthouse building, that there is a village here, that there was fighting here and people were killed here. They will learn all that. But there is not an interstate highway within an hour of us in any direction.

"I tell my Park Service colleagues around the country, 'You will not beat this.' If you are an interpreter, people who come here are hanging on every word. They are intentional visitors; they want to be here, they mean to be here, they know why they are here, they want to learn more about it, and they want to hear the stories… You don't get that at Cold Harbor or Fredericksburg or Ford's Theater. I supervise people here who have only worked here and they're starting their careers and haven't been to other places before. I tell them they need to appreciate this.

"This is really special. It is rare to be an interpreter in a place like this. We are spoiled rotten. Visitors don't ask me where the bathrooms are. They don't ask me where the nearest metro station is. They ask me where the generals did this and that. Where did (General Joshua L.) Chamberlain and (General John B.) Gordon have that salute? If you study this for a living and you come to work and get those types of questions, it's fantastic. I have a lot of good days here.

"People talk about being here for April 9th, the anniversary. But climactically speaking, mid-March is probably more representative in accurately representing the landscape for April 9th when Lee and Grant were here. It is warmer now than it was 150 years ago and the onset of spring, the budding of the trees, and the greening of the grass is earlier now. When you think about what Lee and Grant and the soldiers back then would have seen, it would have been right about now. The landscape for the Lee and Grant meeting for the surrender was more like January than June. The trees were gray. They were empty (of leaves)." He pointed off in the distance and said, "When Grant was standing on that hill and Philip Sheridan pointed down the hill and said, 'General Lee awaits you in that house down there,' they can see it, plain as day. In June, you can't see it. During summer, three quarters of the village is obscured from sight by all of the leaves on the trees. You just see green. But on April 9, 1865, it was wide open just like it is right now.

"We have to remember that this was also a battlefield. Two hundred people died on the morning of the 9th. There were people who were mortally wounded here that would live for another few weeks.

"That is the thing about Appomattox. It is the last of everything. It is the last battle. It has the last shot fired. It has the last soldier killed."

I asked Ernie who his heroes were.

He said, "There are so many ways to evaluate that question. Militarily. Diplomatically. I think what Grant did in McLean's parlor that day was extraordinary. If you read the newspapers from 1864 and early 1865 and you start to get a feeling for what Grant's reputation was in the field at the time. He was considered the butcher. And yet you look at his conduct here and how he took Lincoln's words from the Second Inaugural Address, '…with malice towards none,' Grant put it into motion. They weren't just words anymore; they were actions. I think it is easy to look back and take that for granted. I think you have to give Grant credit. He didn't have to go that way."

I agreed, "The conciliation was astounding. Grant had been fighting Lee at that point for almost a year, both sides suffering unfathomable losses. And yet when they got here, in a moment, in the signing of the surrender papers, Grant turned into a human being. He seemed like a humanitarian. He let his enemies go home with their guns and their horses if they had them, and let them go back to their families and resume their lives as American citizens."

Ernie said, "This is what Lincoln ordered him to do, and Lincoln deserves credit for that tone of reconciliation. But it still was up to Grant to carry it out. When Lincoln met with Grant at City Point during the siege of Petersburg, neither one of them had ever heard of Appomattox. They knew that it was out there somewhere, but they had no idea when or where the surrender might happen. They knew that when the time came, Lincoln would not be there and was not going to set all of the terms and conditions of surrender. He gave Grant instructions on what he wanted the outcome to be, the tone. But it was up to Grant to articulate it in writing and in his actions and in the way he instructed his army commanders and division commanders to conduct themselves through all of this.

"Again, I think it is easy for all of us to look at the generous terms and to take (his magnanimity) for granted. Grant deserves a lot of credit.

"The thing that is so unfortunate for me when I think about this is that Grant's legacy does not benefit tremendously from this. For most people, Lincoln's assassination five days later is going to trump what happened here in the minds and memories of Americans. Instead of (remembering) Grant's favorable conduct and Lee's reception of that conduct here at Appomattox, Lincoln's assassination is the final stamp on how the Civil War ended.

"So a lot of this has gotten lost in the legacy of the war. When you go forward over the next 150-plus years it is really what happened here that should be more of our sense of motivation and understanding how to deal with each other even when we feel differently about certain political points. That is too bad, but that is part of what we can do here.

"We have the luxury of interpreting what happened here on April 8 through April 12, 1865. We know what happened on April 14 (at Ford's Theater) but that is not what happened here. This is a magnificent story with a magnificent legacy even if it is overshadowed by Lincoln's assassination. It still happened."

We all got quiet as we thought about what Ernie had said. Then I had one of those crazy notions to ask a question that may or may not have been appropriate. Per my usual, I was unable to hold myself back. So I simply blurted it out, "Is this place haunted? Have you ever felt a supernatural presence?"

After a pensive moment, Ernie the park ranger said, "I have certainly heard lots of people tell stories but I have not had that happen to me. But I am aware of people who claim to have had these moments.

Haunted… I guess there are a lot of ways to take that word. In another sense, I will say that I have. Every year it strikes me, it never fails… we are open December 24th but we are not open on December 25th. That is one of the three days of the year that we are closed. So when we leave here on the 24th, it is one of the few times when I leave this park, this village, that none of us are coming back the next day. It is almost dark because at five o'clock in the winter time it gets dark early. When I'm walking down that hill, I have always had this feeling that, however you think about it or feel about it or articulate it, 'For the next 36 to 48 hours, y'all can just have it back. We will just leave you alone for a day.'"

I found my eyes were moistening slightly and a big smile was growing over my face. I turned to Howard who was listing patiently this entire time and I said, "Can you see why I am having so much fun doing this?"

Howard whispered, "Amen."

I said, "That is a beautiful story, Ernie," finally exhibiting some sincere appreciation.

He concluded, "These were once people's houses. These were people's businesses. This was where children grew up, a long time ago. There is a footprint of what was probably a four year old child in a brick that was fired in 1819. It is a special brick for at least a few people who lived here, perhaps many more. This village existed a long time before the armies came here. It has its own history that may not be nationally significant like the surrender was. This was somebody's hometown. I don't ever forget that. We borrow this place from them, really. They certainly didn't want to be the place where General Lee surrendered. It became their fate."

I thanked him profusely for taking all this time to visit with Howard and me. As we departed, Ernie said, laughing, "Thank you for pulling me out of my office."

I FELT THE TUG of the road. So I dragged Howard away, took him back to his car, and after thanking him for his kind support departed Appomattox, headed again westward along the route of the Powhatan Arrow, thinking about war. Philosopher George Santayana made himself famous with lots of profound expressions. But the one most generally quoted is probably this, "Those who cannot remember the past are condemned to repeat it." True, I suppose, but every conflict is different. The Civil War was our nation's grandest catastrophe and most controversial and ambiguous event. I'm by no means an expert on it, but I've studied it all my life and still have no idea why it had to happen.

10:50 a.m.

Lynchburg

Mile 199.7

Built on seven hills. Virginia's fifth largest city. On a navigable stream, it was an early supply base for the pioneers to the West before the railway came. Large shoe manufacturing center. Three colleges: Sweetbriar, Randolph-Macon Women's College, and Lynchburg. The N. & W. passes the Elks National Home at Bedford, 24 miles west.

I lived in Lynchburg and I grew to hate it. I mean, not with a white-hot animus, but at least a simmering loathing. Let me explain.

During my senior year as a Mechanical Engineering student at Virginia Tech, many companies came to recruit new employees. I remember interviews with American Electric Power and General Motors. I was an average student in every way and I didn't do the research I should have done to properly prepare myself for these interviews. But a company called Babcock & Wilcox hired me anyway. Who knows what they saw? Maybe they needed engineers in the worst way, and I was the worst they could find. Those were boom times in electrical generation and in the economy overall, the mid-1970s.

Even back then, Babcock & Wilcox was a venerable company. It formed as a partnership between Stephen Wilcox and George Babcock as Babcock, Wilcox & Company in 1867 to manufacture Wilcox's designs for water tube steam boilers. The company became one of the world's foremost boiler manufacturers and had a number of innovations over the decades, eventually branching from the fossil-fuel boiler world into nuclear energy.

Engineering even in the 1970s was considered one of the most difficult curricula offered at Tech. The academic calendar was on the quarter system rather than the semester system, requiring successful completion of 204 hours to graduate. That meant we were in class 17 hours per week (17 hours * three quarters * four years), and we needed an overall grade point average of 2.0 ("C") out of 4.0 to gain a diploma. Courses were arcane subjects like "Thermodynamics," "Calculus with Linear Differential Equations," and "Kinematics and Dynamics of Machinery." Never before or after did I work as hard as during those four years. I still think of my diploma as my crowning achievement in life.

Upon graduation, I began my career in the city of Barberton, Ohio, adjacent to Akron. I spent the winter of 1976-1977 there and it was dreadful. I moved into an older house with two other B&W employees. I was a manufacturing engineering trainee at the boiler works, a fascinating place where enormous lathes and milling machines made parts and vessels for steam generation, mostly reactor vessels and related parts.

My roommates and I were not a good fit. They spent most of their free time chain-smoking cigarettes, drinking piss-poor beer, and playing cards. I wanted to ride bicycles and motorcycles, and explore. The house was poorly insulated and there were no gutters, so three foot long icicles grew in front of the windows and stayed there all winter. It was like an icy, smoky prison. I met few single women and had few dates. I wanted desperately to leave.

As it happened, B&W informed me that the job they were grooming me for in Barberton was not going to come to fruition. Would I like to interview for an opening at the Lynchburg Research Center in Virginia? Sure! I was lonesome for home and I got the transfer. I became a nuclear materials research engineer, primarily studying the performance of reactor vessel steels. My office was off Mount Athos Road five miles east of Lynchburg on a bend of the James River. I found a duplex apartment on the west side of the city. Life settled in. I was happy, mostly.

Recreationally, I did motorcycling, bicycling, and running. I did lots of hiking and backpacking in the neighboring Blue Ridge Mountains. I dated a few women, none seriously and none long.

Two years went by. Then three and then four. I felt stifled, restless, and started hating the place.

The work was challenging and interesting, but frankly I didn't feel that I was very good at it. And it scared me. The disaster – let's call it the incident – at the Three Mile Island plant occurred on March 28, 1979, and B&W had made the reactor. In the weeks that followed, I heard people I knew on public radio speaking to congressional hearings about our role in it, and I never wanted to be in that position myself. What if one of the reactors I'd been studying failed catastrophically? I began getting impatient for a new job and new locale.

In the summer of 1980, I took a three-month sabbatical and explored the Rocky Mountain and Pacific Coast states by car, my little Volkswagen Rabbit. I hiked the canyons of Utah, the mountains of California, and the forests of Oregon and Washington. I went skinny-dipping with five women I'd just met in the Olympic National Park in Washington, a situation I'd not been well-prepared for growing up in Dixie. I spent the next week in Seattle and loved it! I returned to Lynchburg and resumed the grind. I was immediately restless again.

Much of the problem was cultural. I was young, energetic, and progressive. Lynchburg was old, staid, and conservative, enveloped in religiosity.

That story dates back to the mid-1950s when a "particularly aggressive" (from Thomas Road Baptist Church's own description) man only in his early twenties, gathered 35 people in the Mountain View Elementary School for worship. Jerry Lamon Falwell, from that humble beginning, built a dynasty that brought millions to Jesus and changed the American political landscape forever.

From the original meeting, Falwell and his new followers found their first home at the former Donald Duck Bottling Company plant. Falwell had an instinctive understanding of the media, and his ambition led him from the beginning to move his ministry beyond the immediate congregation. Not a year from his first appearance on the pulpit, Falwell began videotaping the Old Time Gospel Hour, first on radio and then on television. Soon the nascent church extended its tentacles throughout the city and beyond.

Falwell's dynamic voice, rich with intonation and passion, brought an instant following to the young preacher. Falwell founded the Thomas Road Baptist Church in 1956, and by the end of the first decade, the congregation had occupied its third, even larger, sanctuary.

Falwell's ambition and devotion to Christ were boundless, and even his congregational and weekly television audiences weren't enough. In 1967 Falwell founded a private, parochial secondary school called the Lynchburg Christian Academy and four years later, Lynchburg Baptist College, both providing a unique educational system bound to Christ-devoted and activist learning. It is now Liberty University.

By the early 1970s, the Thomas Road Church was recognized as one of America's fastest growing churches.

It's often said that two things not to talk about in conversation with strangers are religion and politics. Reverend Jerry ignored the memo, confessing at one time "I was taught in bible college, religion and politics don't mix." Falwell, a deeply patriotic man, apparently perceived that America's morality was in decay and he needed to do something about it. By the late 1970s, Robert Grant, the Christian Voice's acting president, urged Falwell to found the Moral Majority, giving the so-called "New Christian Right" a national voice. By 1980, Falwell was a king-maker and the Moral Majority had chapters in 18 states. I saw presidential candidate Ronald Reagan's campaign jet fly into Lynchburg in 1980 to court Falwell and his hoards of followers.

At its zenith, the Moral Majority had over four million members and became one of the largest lobbying organizations in the United States. Just as quickly as it rose, Falwell and his directors by 1985 decided that its usefulness had been eclipsed, and it was folded into the Liberty Federation. In 1987, Falwell retired as its head. Falwell declared a dozen years later, "Our goal has been achieved… The religious right is solidly in place… and religious conservatives are now in for the duration."

We can and should argue long and hard about the value of Falwell's and the Moral Majority's influence on our nation. But we cannot deny the influence of religious conservatives today, as their strength and vociferousness counterweights the actions and goals of political progressives in every municipality across the country. And we cannot deny Falwell's influence on Lynchburg, both in terms of the economic impact and the heavy, moralistic, exclusionary tone that envelops the city like an autumn morning fog.

Nowadays, Liberty has over 15,000 on-campus students and 100,000 online students, making it the largest university, public or private, in the state and the largest evangelical Christian university in the world. Academic disciplines include music, law, osteopathic medicine, ministry, media, and divinity. The sports nickname is the Flames and the mascot is a construction crane. Okay, I'm joking about the construction crane, but there are always plenty of them around.

I STAYED IN LYNCHBURG for another year, but then packed all my belongings and headed to the West Coast for 10 years before returning to southwest Virginia. But to write this book, I returned to Lynchburg to explore in the same manner I looked at all the other Powhatan Arrow communities. By the time I dove into this project, it had been 35 years since I left Lynchburg. I faced my return with mixed emotions.

As I mentioned, my office was on the east end of town, and it wasn't long before my journey approached Mount Athos Road. I decided to make a detour and refresh that memory.

I left US-460 and headed northward on Mount Athos Road, quickly crossing under the bridge that once carried the Powhatan Arrow. To the west was the James River. In one place was a huge concrete pad, now derelict, clearly once the site of a building or factory. I located the complex where I used to work and to my surprise found it largely surrounded by a chain-link, razor-wire topped fence. There was a visitor's center, and all visitors were by signs demanded to go there. I parked my car and sidled inside.

There were a number of photos on the wall of the reception area of products and aerial shots of the facility. There was a kindly woman behind the desk where a trucker was standing to fill out forms. She had lots of dark hair and a set of front teeth that would make a gopher proud. She wore a name badge. It was a short name like "Su" or "El." Or "Esmeralda" or "Annamaybelline"; I can't remember.

I put on my most guileless, innocent smile and said, "Hello, Annamaybelline! My name is Michael and I used to work here. I was wondering if I could have a look around."

"No," she said succinctly, with an unyielding, authoritarian flair, exuding profound self-importance. "With the heightened security we have now, I can't let you in unless you have business here."

"My business is in rekindling old memories," I begged. "You see, Annamaybelline, I worked here in the 1970s and I'm a 'tourist,' not a 'terrorist.'" I smiled even more brightly. I searched for a crack in her brick-wall demeanor, hoping for a wavering in her intransigence. I figured the more times I called her Annamaybelline, the better my chances. "I worked in the 'Hot Cell,' Annamaybelline, in the research center."

"Nice try, Michael," she flashed those awesome teeth. "I'm sure you did. But unless you have an escort, this is as far as you're going to get today."

Hmmm. My brain did back-flips searching for a plausible retort, one that might produce more success. Then I shrugged, gave up, and retreated, honoring my patriotic duty to not get arrested for trespassing.

"Thanks anyway! Have a great day," I said as I left, thinking to myself, that the remnants of my memory would need to suffice for the duration. You can never go home.

(I will admit that I diabolically contemplated buying a drone and outfitting it with a video camera to fly overhead and take movies. I doubted doing so would produce a happy ending.)

ONE OF MY FRIENDS from the time I was living in Lynchburg was a guy named Larry Bailey. I had vague memories of knowing Larry far earlier because he was also a Christiansburg native. He had invited me over as a house guest and I went there next.

When I began working for B&W, I had not kept track of Larry and was surprised to find him working in the same building I was. We also lived close by on the west end of town, and we worked together on the east end of town, so we often carpooled to work. Larry was also a motorcycle rider and occasionally we would ride together. He called my Rabbit "hasenpfeffer," which of course is German for rabbit (actually, rabbit stew).

Larry is a glib, outspoken man, never shy to express an opinion. He can be testy at times, but he has a heart of gold and is one of my favorite people. He and his wife Paulette live in an A-frame home in the woods on the slope of Long Mountain between Concord, Rustburg, and Lynchburg, in rural Campbell County. Long Mountain isn't much of a mountain, really, a bit less than 1400 feet in elevation, but it is made up of rocks, different from the red clay I'd been traveling over since leaving Petersburg.

He was working in his garage/workshop when I arrived. He had recently retired from B&W and had grown a long pony tail, mostly grey, and added a few pounds to his midsection. He was cutting toys from wood for disabled children in a camp where he volunteered.

Larry had graduated from Christiansburg High School in 1966 and moved to Lynchburg in 1974. "Since we moved here, in a way Lynchburg has grown yet it has shrunk. Many of the industries that were here have folded up and gone to other countries. General Electric made mobile radio equipment, but they moved those jobs to Sweden. They made those old original cell phones that looked like suitcases. They closed their factory down. It is a huge building.

"Babcock & Wilcox has fragmented into several other companies. One of them was a French company called Framatome. The people I was working for got bought out. That company, in an agreement with the French government, became a company called Areva."

He said Areva continued to offer maintenance for commercial nuclear power plants for various electrical utilities.

I said, "Nuclear power plants are enormously complicated. Many plants in our country are 30 to 40 years old. It would sure seem to me that replacing old components would be a never-ending proposition."

He said, "They are complicated, but we continue to fix them because it is more economical for them to be upgraded and fixed than to be shut down. These plants are paid for, so all you have to do is maintenance on them. Maintenance is a lot cheaper than buying a new one."

He spoke about his city, "Lynchburg is a small relatively prosperous conservative Southern city. Lynchburg is going to be dragged into the 21st Century almost kicking and screaming. The city does not like change.

"One big change I can tell you about began in 1972 when Jerry Falwell started a school called Lynchburg Bible College. Before that, he was simply the pastor of a local church, the Thomas Road Baptist Church. Its primary purpose was to educate kids to be ministers. His first class had 14 students in the basement of his church. There was one professor. That is now Liberty University. Several years later, when General Electric left town, Falwell bought their building. Plus he bought most of the real estate on Candlers Mountain. At that point, he owned an enormous amount of property. As far as I know, even now he is doing construction, renovations, and expansions all debt free.

"The Falwells have a good base of people who support Liberty University. I'm sure the economic development people are very happy."

"But to everyone else, you included, even though you have self-professed as a conservative, does he have a bit of a heavy hand here?" I asked.

"Yes," he confessed. "Jerry Sr. did. It was his way or the highway. He was politically active through the church. That turned a lot of people off to him. Ultimately, he sort of backed off. When he passed away, his two sons took over for him. The two sons are Jonathan and Jerry Jr. Jonathan is the preacher at Thomas Road Baptist Church. Jerry Jr. is an attorney, and he is now the president of Liberty University. Jonathan also oversees the Liberty Christian Academy which is their private secondary school. They have principals just like other schools, but he is the guardian father. The two sons have brought the school and university into the 21st Century. They are relaxing many of Jerry Sr.'s mandates. In the early days, Jerry Sr. forbid the (students) from going to movies or dances. It was a strict life for them. That is gone away. Now the kids are active in public, in the community.

"The university has brought a lot of employment here. They have been actively building at the university for the last 10 or 12 years, and they currently have plans for another 10 or 12 years of new construction. Jerry Jr. just bought 75 percent of the River Ridge Mall. He will leave it in retail but will use it as a source of revenue. They will manage it. They have built a medical school. They have a law school. They have the only replica, right down to the woodwork, of the Supreme Court of the United States. That room is booked constantly. They put retired judges on the bench so that students and other lawyers can come here and practice."

I said, "You mentioned General Electric. They have completely moved away, correct?"

"Yes, they are gone. Craddock Terry Shoe Company used to be a big employer here. They are gone. Lynchburg Foundry built a huge plant down on Mount Athos Road near where we used to work. They are gone. They completely removed the building and all that is left is a huge concrete pad and lots of daisies."

I realized this must have been the concrete pad I'd seen earlier.

Larry continued, "There is still a large paper mill downtown on the (James) River. They do recycling and reprocessing of paper materials. As far as I know, there are no foundry operations still in town at all."

"So when you got here in 1974," I recapped, "the city was mostly industrial. It had shoe factories, foundries, and cell phone and electronics manufacturing. Lynchburg then is typical of the industrial transformation that has taken place in this country over the past couple of generations where major industries are moving overseas."

"Yes," he agreed, "but Lynchburg is still doing okay. Now our economy is based on service industries like education and health care. The two biggest employers are Centra Health and Liberty University. And both are booming. Health care is a big business now. Almost every doctor's office in the entire area is now affiliated with Centra Health. They have acquired all three hospitals and most of the independent doctors' offices throughout the region.

"The downtown is trying to make a comeback. We hear all the time about revitalization efforts. Main Street itself really hasn't changed much. Tenants in buildings come and go. There are still a couple of major banks downtown. There are buildings filled with lawyers. There are some loft apartments down there. There are some buildings that have been reconditioned into restaurants and upscale shopping. There is an art gallery or two. The train station has been turned into a really good restaurant, called the Depot Grill. Down on the riverfront is where most of the renovation is happening. The old headquarters for Craddock Terry is now an upscale hotel. They are trying hard to bring people back into downtown. We often have dinner at that restaurant."

I said, "When I lived here, we never went downtown."

He said, "In those days, you couldn't. Even now there are still areas where you have to be careful where you go. I see a slow, arduous transformation of gradually pushing the things that you don't want out of the downtown area."

"Do you think most people like Lynchburg?"

"Yeah. I think people like the small city part of it. You can go to Washington DC in 2-1/2 hours. You can go to Roanoke in an hour.

"The industry I was in, and I think this applies to many industries, is cyclical. We would see better times and worse times. My former employer provided me a good living. Of course, I earned everything they paid me. I did it well enough that I stayed there for 38 years. I think I got better at it, the more I did. I specialized on specific design issues and specific problems. I am a confident person. I know what I can do.

"I was raised by my grandfather who used to tell me that if there was a problem that needed to be solved, think about it and figure out how to do it. He taught me at an early age how to solve problems. When you design a piece of equipment that goes 40 feet underwater inside of a nuclear reactor and the equipment works perfectly, exactly the way you designed it to work, that is really satisfying.

"I would like our government to find a way to prevent all of our businesses from going offshore. I would like to see businesses here, American businesses, treated on an equal footing with businesses elsewhere. We are catering to foreign businesses. It is all driven by the bottom line, by the almighty dollar. We need to make it lucrative to do business here. Not China, Taiwan, India, or elsewhere. You've got to take care of your own first. All these businesses would not be leaving and going overseas if it were not advantageous for them."

I WAS EAGER TO VISIT DOWNTOWN for three reasons. First, the original route of the N&W, and thus the Powhatan Arrow, went right through alongside the James River. Second, I was eager to see the resuscitation of downtown that Larry had mentioned. Third, I was aware that in 2014 there was a derailment of a CSX train there.

So the next morning I headed west on US-460 and within a few miles found a new highway, US-29 Bypass, that I took north across the James River and then the old N&W tracks on the nearly half-mile long Monacan Bridge into Amherst County. Then I took the Amelon Expressway into Madison Heights and from there the 5th Street Bridge back across the James into downtown. I headed down towards the river, looking for anything that looked like a railroad crash site.

Railroads, avoiding hills wherever possible, took a more direct, more level route into downtown Lynchburg than the roads. The track followed a natural creek course from Concord towards the James. Then it crossed over Mount Athos Road and the James River to the Amherst County side, under the Monacan Bridge, then half-way back over the

James onto Percival Island and then from there into downtown Lynchburg. The Lynchburg Union Station, that served passengers on both the N&W and the C&O Railroads, was built before the turn of the 20th Century and demolished in the mid-1960s.

At that point, the tracks began ascending again through Hollins Mill tunnel and farther westward. When the line was built, the N&W maintained several facilities on Percival Island and called on several commercial customers downtown, notably the Lynchburg Foundry.

LYNCHBURG ALSO HOSTED the Southern Railway. The Norfolk & Western went from Norfolk to Cincinnati. The Southern Railroad went from Washington, DC, south into North Carolina. And the C&O went from Richmond to Charleston, West Virginia, and beyond. Lynchburg was a true railroad town!

Norfolk Southern had abandoned all of its rights of way through downtown and deeded most to the city to form a walking and bicycling trail. Percival Island is now owned by the city and is a city park. The only trains coming through downtown along the river were CSX, like the one that had crashed.

I found myself at The Depot Grill, the restaurant Larry had mentioned. I spoke with an employee who was taking a break outside. He looked to be in his thirties or forties and he wore a cook's apron. He was a manager. When I asked about the crash, he pointed directly to the north, not 100 yards away and said, "It was right there!"

From where we stood, there was a small linear parking area, then several sets of tracks, then a row of trees, and then the down-slope embankment to the river. "You can still see where some of those trees are charred," he pointed again. "It was a terrific fireball!"

The manager, Andrew Steger, told me he'd moved from Staunton, Virginia. The restaurant opened in May 2004.

"Business is fantastic," he told me, more interested in talking about his employer than the train crash. "Last year was the best year we have ever had, and the year before that was the best year we had ever had before that. Our owner is an experienced restaurateur. He hired a great management staff and he gives us plenty of freedom to do things that other restaurants, especially the chains, cannot do.

"We are a one-horse operation. So if we want to do fried mullet with hush puppies and collard greens this weekend, he will go, 'okay'. If we want to do (something, something, something)," he said with a faux French accent, "he will say, 'okay'. We can do anything as fancy as we would like.

"This area is considered the Downtown Riverfront area. For some reason, the other side of the expressway (farther to the east) is called the Lower Basin." He told me that you could drive there, but it necessitated the navigation of several cobblestone streets. "After you cross the railroad tracks, that road is called Concord Turnpike."

I envisioned it would have followed more closely the route of the Norfolk & Western rail line.

"This building is quite old," he continued. "I have heard 1911 and 1914 as when it was built. The building was built by Norfolk & Western as their freight depot. That is where the name Depot Grill comes from. For several decades, it sat abandoned." He showed me that his parking lot was laced with railroad tracks. He understood that the railroad still owned the rights of way. Every so often, a railroad employee would come into the restaurant saying they were running a train and they needed somebody to move their car because it was blocking the track. I noticed that in one area, the gap between the tracks had not been filled in and if you drove your car into it, you could never get it back out without a tow truck. This would be a hell of a fix for someone leaving the restaurant late in the evening after having too much to drink.

"There was a time period that I will call the shoe boom where manufacturing businesses in Lynchburg were going great guns. I think this was about the 1940s until the 1970s. (By the 2000s) this building was vacant."

The building was two stories tall, longer paralleling the tracks and the river than it was deep, with rows of windows on both floors. It had a typical look of an old freight depot. A long wheelchair ramp had been built up from the parking lot for ADA compatibility and there were decorative lamp posts outside.

Andrew described to me how the city, along with several visionary architects working in the early 2000s, had begun to take an interest in the redevelopment of downtown. "They were trying to make downtown not so bad (with crime). I moved here in 1997. It didn't take me long to realize that there was nothing happening here. They had a lot of nerve calling that street up there Commerce Street because there was really not a lot of commerce going on. There were a couple of restaurants, a jewelry store, a drugstore, and that was about all I can remember.

"It seemed like any restaurants would be open for a year or two, and then there would be something about tax evasion or serving alcohol to minors, at which point they would mysteriously shut down. The owner here was initially skeptical, but he took one look inside and went back to the restaurant he owned in Staunton and put a 'For sale' sign on it."

Andrew went to attend to a customer and I noticed that the dining room was fairly busy, given that it was a weekday. When he returned, he told me the city put an emphasis on downtown redevelopment. "Before that, there were lots of rats and hobos.

"When I first came down to give the downtown another chance, it was to attend the Rightmire Children's Museum, also known as Amazement Square. It is here near the Kanawha Canal Bridge. The people who own it have somehow managed to make the best children's museum I have ever seen. When I took my kids there, I had a chance to look more closely and I realized they were cleaning the place up a lot."

Children's Museum sculpture

Under Andrew's supervision, they began putting butcher paper on the table with crayons and came up with some cool furniture for the bar. "This is a great building. The building's foundation flares out at the bottom. The architecture isn't Charleston or New Orleans, but buildings down here really are unique. They are rock solid.

"When I started here in 2004, downtown had a few residences that would either be characterized as lofts or probably just rinky-dink apartments. There were not enough residents here to call it a neighborhood. As the years progressed, it became obvious that Lynchburg was serious about reinvesting in downtown and other (historic) places. It didn't take people long to think that some of these older buildings, as they came up for sale, were worth turning into apartments or lofts. That has been a trend that has gone on for quite awhile.

"Downtown has always had a strong Monday through Friday workforce. There are lots of people coming to work at eight o'clock in the morning and leaving from work at five o'clock in the afternoon. Singles. Professionals. Lawyers. Police and sheriffs departments. Bankers and jewelers. There are other retail venues. So there has always been an influx of people downtown. Now there are people living downtown as well. Now when I begin my shift at four o'clock in the afternoon, there seem to be an equal number of people who are coming home to downtown. We have people who live downtown and are commuting outward to some of the outside commercial areas.

"In the past, we were likely to be filled at lunchtime by the professional crowd working downtown. We have always had a strong lunch business. We get the mommies and the grandparents with kids.

"We are a casual dining room. I would not even say we were upscale casual. We run a single sample menu. So any hour that we are open, if you want to order a bacon cheddar burger, we will sell it to you at the same price. If you want to come here at lunch and have a ribeye steak, you can have that as well. A great crab-cake sandwich with a side order and a soft drink costs $15 or less. We have been told we do the best chicken tenders that anybody has ever had. We have great baby-back ribs. Everything is cooked literally in a boxcar."

Finally we got to the topic that led me into the restaurant in the first place, the derailment of the CSX train. He said, "I was coming to work and the manager I was relieving called and told me about the crash. Once I got here, I could see that the fire was across the parking lot towards the river. It was on the closest track to the river. From what I understand, it rained a lot for many days prior to the crash. As the train was going along the tracks, some of the foundation below the rail gave way and allowed the cars to fall off the track. Someone who witnessed it told us that it was moving at a slow speed.

"Three cars were in the river. I don't know how many actually came off the track. I also don't know why one of the cars exploded. We had some customers here at the time. We had staff working: waitresses and chefs. The smoke was dense and painful to breathe. It obviously was poisonous, noxious fumes." The first responders arrived quickly on the scene. "There was an alphabet soup of firefighters, paramedics, and rescue squad people here seemingly instantly. It is absolutely miraculous, but not a single person was killed or even injured. There were cars parked along there and not a single one got scratched. It was a massive fireball. I didn't see the initial explosion, but it was still burning when I got here. We had evacuated, but we knew that we needed to get inside to turn off our stoves and other equipment. It seemed like an eternity before they let us go back inside."

The restaurant was unable to open for regular business for several days. In the meantime the owner rented out space to the hordes of railroad officials and insurance people who needed a base of operations.

One of his employees walked by and heard us talking about the accident. She said she was there when the explosion happened. "It was incredible. Terrifying. The entire building was shaking. When the building started to shake I looked at the tracks and I saw this big explosion of orange flame. We immediately began to escort our customers out the back door and help them evacuate. All I could think about was getting our customers out of here and to safety. It was incredibly loud, even inside. I was expecting the glass to shatter. Those windows withstood all of the heat that was blasting at them." She showed me a picture on her cell phone of the explosion. "I have never seen anything in my life like it. Not one person got hurt. It was miraculous."

Andrew returned to our conversation and said, "Downtown Lynchburg is a really great renaissance of the arts, activities, restaurants, and loft apartments. It has a new Blackwater Creek (James River Heritage) biking trail. It has become a destination place. The infrastructure of downtown has provided a unique experience. Every town has their strip malls and chain restaurants. We probably have 20 unique businesses here in downtown. I'm optimistic. It's a happening place. My wife wants to get a loft and live down here. It's absolutely a lot different than it was, in as good a way as I could ever have imagined!"

ANDREW SENT ME UP THE HILL towards downtown to do some exploring, towards what he called the Bluff Walk. It was a bright, sunny day, with a brisk wind. I walked on the sidewalk on the street I'd taken to the restaurant and noticed it was over a nice arched stone bridge that an interpretive sign said was built for the James River and Kanawha Canal. It was probably built more than 170 years earlier. I began ascending through a park that had long, parallel ramps upwards to the next street. Everything was on a slope. There were several loft apartment buildings with lawn chairs and grills on balconies. I walked past the Craddock Terry Hotel, an upscale conversion of an old shoe company office building, with three rows of tall white-framed windows set beautifully in the brick façade and an enormous ruby pump (as in shoe pump) affixed to the side of the building. It was really quite lovely. There were almost no people around.

I strolled westward and back down to near the river level, passing still another old warehouse, this one freshly painted on the brick a bright red "Drink Coca-Cola" sign and a black "BOTTLING WORKS" sign below it. I hiked the Blackwater Creek Trail a mile westward, passing under several impressive highway bridges. On my right was the Blackwater Creek and on the left were vertical cliffs. I spoke with a blonde woman who was taking her brood for a walk, four mixed-race children. She spoke with an accent and said she was from Holland. She pushed a double-stroller to which she had affixed a running board where she could paddle her feet to provide propulsion. She said she and her husband had moved to Lynchburg a few years earlier. She commented on how she loved all the hills, different from her native pancake-flat Holland. Blackwater Creek was running swiftly and occasionally ducks and geese flew past. Homes and buildings sat atop the steep hill on the other side of the creek.

LYNCHBURG HAD ALWAYS BEEN a transportation hub. Its topography is complex and rugged, meaning that development of transportation corridors, commercial areas, and residential neighborhoods are more dictated by the availability of flat land than by much of a grid. On maps, Lynchburg's roads wander seemingly aimlessly, and the city sprawls significantly from the river's edge to the southwest for over 10 miles.

Great cities are where they are for many reasons. Those reasons can vary of course, from place to place. Cities such as New York, Pittsburgh, and Detroit are located on world-class harbors or major inland waterways. To the uninitiated, Virginia's capital and greatest city, Richmond, would seem to be in a curious location, mid-river in the James.

One of the most significant geographical features of the state of Virginia, as well as Maryland to the north and the Carolinas to the south is barely discernible on even the most detailed topographic maps. It is called the Fall Line, and it runs nearly directly north-south, separating the Coastal Plain in the east from the rolling Piedmont in the west. Delaney Ward touched on this when I spoke with him in Petersburg.

Each of the major east-flowing rivers in the state has its Fall Line port. The Potomac had old Alexandria. The Rappahannock had Fredericksburg. The Appomattox had Petersburg. And notably the James had Richmond. These cities were entrepôts, transshipment ports where merchandise was stored or traded or reloaded for exporting again.

Here's why the Fall Line was so important.

A wealth of rivers throughout the Commonwealth flow generally eastward and spill into the Chesapeake Bay. At this point in the earth's epochal history, sea level is such that the lower reaches of these rivers are tidal, meaning they are comprised mainly of seawater, they are brackish, they rise and fall with the tides, and they do not have sizeable flow. They support ocean-going vessels. Upstream, rivers have freshwater and uni-directional flow. They support vessels of a completely different design, being lower, often longer, and able to traverse moving water and rapids. The point in the southeastern United States where this happens is the Fall Line.

It is fairer and more accurate to say that Richmond is on the Fall Line than the Fall Line is in Richmond, because the Fall Line's presence is Richmond's reason for being.

Tobacco was the region's primary cash crop, the primary export crop, needing transport to overseas markets, with iron ore and furs also carried. Because ocean-going vessels that could come no farther upstream on the various rivers than the Fall Line, river-based boats were needed to provide conveyance from the interior Piedmont.

Their first option was the dugout canoes the English settlers copied from the Native Americans. Farmers in the James River watershed often lashed several canoes together for the journey to Richmond. Over time, the need for larger vessels and the paucity of the enormous trees needed to make the canoes gave birth to the ingenious replacement, the bateau, designed by brothers Anthony and Benjamin Rucker.

The word bateau is French for "boat." In translation to English, the spelling has varied and now encompasses "bateau" and "batoe" with plural spellings of "bateaus," "batoes," and "bateaux."

Eventually, bateaux were superseded as canals began to be built, in this case principally the James River and Kanawha Canal on the James. George Washington and others preached the advantages of canal travel, which offered greater capacities and speeds than river craft. Additionally, canal boats could carry passengers, something for which the bateaux were ill-suited.

The James River and Kanawha Canal route was surveyed by Washington, intended to extend all the way into current West Virginia southeast of today's Charleston. Construction got underway in 1785. But due to cost overruns and floods, sixty-five years later it had only been half-way completed, just shy of 200 miles, from Richmond through Lynchburg to Buchanan, in Botetourt County. Meanwhile, by 1815, the Erie Canal had linked New York with Buffalo on Lake Erie. New York's topography, linking the Hudson and Mohawk Rivers almost to the Great Lakes, made completion of the Erie Canal significantly less daunting than the mountains the James River and Kanawha Canal needed to cross. In fact, the Hudson and Mohawk valleys form the only near-level cut across the Appalachians north of Alabama. Had Virginia's mountains been less formidable, and had the James River and Kanawha Canal been completed contemporaneously with the Erie Canal, Richmond may have emerged as an even more populous and important city than it is now. Moreover, the lands planned to be served might have gained greater prosperity as their futures were to unfold.

In any event, even though at one time the James River Company was the largest corporation in the state, the James River and Kanawha Canal was never finished. The Civil War effort consumed all potential money and manpower both from its maintenance and its extension. During the war, the superiority of trains became clear. Still, the open portions of the canal continued in operation until 1877. Ironically, as flooding gave birth to the bateau, devastating floods in that year were the death knell for the canal. Its right-of-way was bought by the new Richmond and Allegheny Railroad, later to become the Chesapeake and Ohio Railroad, which is now part of CSX. The C&O disassembled much of the canal infrastructure and used the tow-path to place their rails and used the viaducts over the feeder streams for their bridges. This is the same C&O corridor that hosted the fiery crash.

The C&O filled in the canal terminus in Richmond, what was called the Great Turning Basin where cargo was transferred from river to ocean vessels, and used it for a railroad terminal. A century later in 1985, the C&O abandoned that site. When developers began excavation for construction of a convention center, they found remains of 30 sunken bateaux. Geologists and historians catalogued the area and saved as many bateaux as they could and took measurements and photos of the others for posterity. They found piles of other discarded junk, now historic treasures. For the few weeks before the bulldozers got back to work, Richmonders shared a trip into the past.

I WALKED UNTIL I FOUND and then went through the Hollins Mill Tunnel. It had a paved surface and overhead lights, and was on a curve to the left. It was cooler inside than outside and extensive amounts of water dripped from the ceiling. Nice!

There was a large interpretive sign at the entrance that explained that the tunnel had re-opened in 1999, following decades of planning by the city and the abandonment of the line in 1983. The sign featured a color photo of our favorite train, the Powhatan Arrow, streaming alongside the James River in a 1949 photo.

Hollins Mill Tunnel

My trail map showed me that there were creek crossings, railroad trestles, abandoned industrial buildings, and picnic areas in front of me, too far to walk. I turned around and went back through the tunnel and headed back to my car. I wished I'd brought my bicycle for this trip, it being infinitely more interesting than the High Bridge Trail I'd just done.

THAT NIGHT, I COULDN'T STAY with the Baileys because they were out of town doing volunteer work. So again I relied on the hosting service, Couchsurfing. I contacted host Kaleb Matson, whose profile photo on the Couchsurfing website had a pensive looking man smoking a pipe, playing a guitar, and wearing a zebra-striped hoodie. Not the most auspicious image. I envisioned a 40 year old Bohemian. What I found when I approached his door was quite different.

Kaleb and his wife Christina were instead in their late twenties. He was tall, pencil thin, with a golden-white mop of hair atop his head and almost none on the sides. She was small, dark-haired, and frankly adorable. I was instantly besotted by her. Their 3-1/2 year old blonde child named Esther flitted around. The apartment was the basement floor of a modest brick ranch home. The house had a wonderful smell of roasted wood that I'd associated with saunas, and indeed Kaleb told me that he'd installed a sauna as a link to his Finnish heritage.

The house was near the campus of Liberty University, and Kaleb in introducing himself, told me that he and Christina had both graduated there and had met and fallen in love while attending.

I offered to take everyone out for dinner, but when Kaleb asked Christina her preference, she said, "I'd rather stay home. I'll cook up something." So while he and I chatted and got acquainted, she sidled from refrigerator to cutting board to stove with the alacrity and élan of a gymnast.

He hinted about his self-excommunication from his Baptist faith after graduation from Liberty, but in a flash she said dinner was ready. I was treated to a delicious chicken and asparagus dish with a delectable sauce, a tomato salad, and fresh-baked biscuits that Christina pieced together with what seemed to be an astonishing ease.

As we chatted about my purpose for being in Lynchburg, Kaleb had an idea about someone I should meet. He made a couple of phone calls and after we'd finished putting the dishes away, he beckoned me into the passenger seat of his late-model sedan and spirited me off into the dark, drippy night. We drove on the aged Lynchburg Expressway towards downtown and then through it, finally crossing the river onto the north side into Madison Heights. Eventually Kaleb delivered me to the home of his friend, Rocco Nagy. For nine years of his life, Rocco had been a hobo. He had been in the Lynchburg area for over 10 years since those days.

Rocco said, "My dad was in the military and I am from Italy originally. I grew up here in North Carolina and Virginia."

I asked him how he got started riding the rails.

He said, "I was doing drugs and being a teenage idiot. When I was almost 18, my mother kicked me out of the house. I straightened up but I didn't know what to do. I always liked trains. So I just started hopping on trains. I got onto cars that were rideable and I just hid."

I asked him what was rideable.

He said, "Boxcars. Gondolas. Anything that is not exposed. Anything that has a cover. Flat cars were not good because they had no cover."

I said, "How do you actually do this? Where do you jump on a train?"

He said, "You go to the rail yards. To the sidings. Crossings. When I first started, I generally didn't know which way the train was going. I just knew what general direction. North. South. East or west.

"In the summertime, I would get on a train going north. It gets pretty technical in the East Coast because there is a spider web of routes, many of them short. Later on, I learned how to pick more direct shots. There are generally only three routes that go east to west. There is one in the middle, one up north, and one down south."

He said he got to know all of the major rail lines, and where they went. He even learned how to go to specific towns.

"When I first started, I just didn't know. I took the train wherever it went. Sometimes it would only be a couple of hours before it terminated. Sometimes it was days. That is how I started learning. I had nowhere to go. Everything I owned was in my backpack. I had a sleeping bag, water, and food. If it was colder, I would take thermal, a hoodie, and some socks, but you don't really pack that much. There were only so many things that I needed. Things are disposable and I could pick up things later that I needed. You can go to thrift stores and gospel missions to buy a coat in the winter. You can find stuff. Often times, people would give me stuff. Even in the summertime, when the train would crest over mountain ranges, it could get really cold."

He spoke with a gravelly, nasally voice and seemed to be suffering from a cold. He was wearing the clothes of a carpenter or a lumberjack. He would occasionally stop to spit into a tin can.

He said that certain types of doors were easier to open than others.

"Slide doors are what you want. They are common and they are usually open."

He explained that even when trains were moving, slack could be generated between cars and as they would slam into their couplings forward or backward, it could be jarring. "The couplings have springs in them and they can snap taut or gain some slack. You don't want to just stand. You want to lean against the wall. That way, you are not knocked over if it snaps.

"You need to be alert all the time. You can get messed up pretty bad if you're not careful." He said that many of the box cars are not comfortable. "If you are lying down, you will get bounced around and end up on a different side from where you started. You always go on high alert when the train stops. You don't want to get caught."

"Did you ever get caught?" I prodded.

"Oh yeah, several times."

"What happened then?" I inquired.

"Sometimes they gave me a warning and told me to get out of there. Sometimes they actually took me to jail. If I was arrested on a Friday, I wouldn't see the judge until Monday so I spent the whole weekend in jail. Sometimes they tried to give me a fine. What if I only had $5? I would say to them, 'I can work for you in the courthouse or in the jail and I can give you my $5 but that's all I've got.' How could I give them $175 if I didn't have it?

"There are a lot of people who say they (ride the rails), but they just do it once or twice for fun. Sometimes street kids will just do it to be cool. It was a drug for me. It was something I loved to do. I loved to be bumming around, camping, doing whatever. I wanted to be left alone. When I rode the trains, I felt like I didn't have anything to worry about. It was a cat and mouse thing, but I enjoyed it. If I didn't like a place, I would just leave. If I got tired of the weather, I would leave. If it was raining too many days, I would leave. Even then you didn't find too many people like me. I am 38 years old now. I was doing this from about age 18 until about age 27.

"I still love trains. But now it gets lonely. Most of the people I rode with are gone. Many of the old-timers are dead. I hung out with the Vietnam era guys. They were good people to me. I never had problems with them."

"Did you call yourself a hobo?" I asked.

He said, "The older guys would call themselves tramps. They learned from the people from the Depression era. I learned basic etiquette from them. It was jungle etiquette. I never told people I hopped trains. People thought I was a freak for putting a backpack on and traveling around and smelling like hell. Sometimes when people seemed sincere and honest I would talk to them. When you are on the fly, you are already moving and everything is in a rush. I hopped on while they were moving, typically 5 to 15 mph."

"How many trains do you think you hopped?" I asked.

"I don't know. A lot. Hundreds. I have been from Canada to Mexico and coast to coast. I have traveled hundreds of thousands of miles. (People) know that what I was doing was illegal and they didn't have any respect for it. I smelled bad and I had all kinds of weird clothes. I looked like a character out of Mad Max. There are lots of punk rock looking people now so I wouldn't stand out as much. Everybody has a tattoo now. The funny thing is that it wasn't even that long ago. It's not like I am 80 years old.

"I am pretty beat up now. It gets pretty haggard living that way as a lifestyle. It is really hard in the winter. I lived in abandoned places. I lived out in the woods. Sometimes I would get sick and have fevers.

"You take chances (on the road). You're going to run into bullshit. It is just inevitable. There is always some weird perv. If you're on the road, then you are homeless. That automatically makes you desperate. (People think) you will do anything.

"I have known some people who were drug addicts. Some were just pieces of crap. Usually whenever I got off the train, I was just looking for supplies or looking for a railroad yard to catch a different train. I wasn't paying attention to society; I didn't care to. I have never been particularly social anyway.

"I don't have any regrets. It was energetic. It was the freest, best time of my life. Some of the older guys, I don't have any idea how they are still alive to this day.

"There were times when I was just terrified. I have never been claustrophobic, but one time I was going east from Seattle and it goes through a really long tunnel, very slowly. Years later, it still scares me to think about it. I was in there, and I just felt terrified, alarms went off, I felt like my life was in danger, a must exit situation. I just felt like I couldn't focus. I was working on survival, on instinct, just reacting. I woke up out of my subconscious, and I moved from one car to another while this train was moving so slowly through the tunnel. There was a friend, and I woke him up. I could hear all the fans blowing air. It is ventilated, but it still smelled really bad of diesel fumes and I felt like I was going to be asphyxiated. You often don't sleep a lot when you are up on trains. So I was suffering from sleep deprivation, I'm sure. I often pushed myself really hard. I would get two hours of sleep here then another two hours there. And I would be up for 12 hours at a time. Months of this make you really weird.

"I decided I needed to kill myself in that tunnel because I did not want to die slowly. I had an idea that I was going to be suffering for a long time. Finally I convinced myself to snap out of it and to just think about the situation. I got a wet rag and put it over my face and convinced myself to just breathe slowly and deeply and to calm the hell down. It was a real panic attack. For years after that, I would wake up in the middle of the night and just go outside and take off running. It is post-traumatic syndrome from sleep deprivation.

"You pull into a city and you can't sleep because there are police looking for people on trains. I remember Atlanta in particular had security guards that would come out and look for us. You can't just sleep on a bench. So you look for places to hide where you can get some sleep. I would take baths whenever I could. Streams. Creeks. Ponds. Lakes. Rain. Whatever. Mostly I remember beautiful times.

"Sometimes there were town girls, and they were fascinated by tramps and travelers. I would tell them I wasn't going to stay there. I didn't really care to panhandle, but sometimes I would. Sometimes in the city I would just sit. For me, people watching is like television. Some of the people who were more social would invite me to a town where they knew about a party that was going on. There were always places to go. I could always end up meeting people. I think they were just curious. They would just come up and talk to me. I have tats, but I took all the piercings off a long time ago. You don't want that stuff on you if you end up in a fight. I kept my hair short. I don't like lice."

He wanted to know when my book would be done and graciously offered to help if I needed more information. He said, "I've always wanted to write a book, but I'm a horrible writer. I don't spell well. I just want to sit and explain my story to somebody one day. I'm starting to lose a lot of stuff now. There are things I'll always remember."

KALEB DROVE US BACK to his house, chatting about Rocco's stories. I was dead tired from the long day's activities, but I was achingly curious about Kaleb's and Christina's self-excommunication, and with the following being a working day, knew that if I wanted to hear about it, that evening was my only chance. Christina had put their daughter to bed, and she joined us in their small living room/kitchen. She seemed light as a feather and vaulted onto the sofa, playfully draping herself over Kaleb's long, outstretched legs.

Kaleb told me that he was one of 13 children, raised like the Dug-gers, from the television show *19 Kids and Counting*. "In fact we used to camp with them. We were part of the same homeschool network. I was born in New Hampshire and lived there until I was two. After that, I moved to Washington state and then to North Carolina until I came to college at Liberty University.

"My religion said that Paul the Apostle made tents to support his ministry. I got to an age where I felt that I needed to provide for myself, but I didn't want to spend my life pursuing a career or doing any world-ly things. I wanted to spend my life proselytizing and trying to save as many people from burning in hell as possible. So (in high school) I began to think about jobs that I could support myself while working the least to allow for most of my time to spend with my life's calling.

"I thought I would get a nursing degree because they only work 12 days per month. I could get a job anywhere. I could work in missions. Somebody in my homeschool program told me about Liberty and said they had a good nursing program. Before that I had never heard of it. I looked it up. Next week I was up here at an introductory program, and I ended up coming here. I had just turned 18."

Christina said, "I had a much smaller family, but I was also home-schooled in a conservative Christian environment. We were Baptist when I was younger, but became more nondenominational Christian as I got closer to the age where I left the house. It was not quite as strict."

Kaleb said, "We were raised in what was called an Apostolic Luther-an Church which is a Finnish cult of about 10,000 people. They felt that they were the only true Christians and the only ones going to heaven. My family left that cult when I was 10 and all of our family and friends said that we had left the one true faith and they could not greet us or associate with us any more. So at that point we had no community. It was that way until we joined the homeschool network and joined the Baptists. At that point we became worldly people. I went from the inner circle to the bigger tent, and now I have fully left Christianity. I don't know yet what the next cult will be that I will join and then leave."

Christina's story differed. "(My family was) never that conservative. Typical Baptists do not allow dancing or drinking. But we were fine with that kind of thing. We were less uptight and were fine with differ-ent kinds of music. I had a great childhood. I loved how flexible home-schooling was."

Both of them felt like they got good educations outside of the public school system. Statistically, he said homeschool kids are successful. "It was a great education." Kaleb told me that he graduated with a nursing degree at age 19. At 20 years old, he bought the house they lived in and put renters in it to pay his mortgage. He got a full-time nursing job.

She said, "I went to college when I was 16, and I was a pretty strong Christian at that point. I was doing the things that I should've been doing, like devotions and praying and having spiritual accountability with good friends and going to church regularly and being involved with my youth group. I did not drink under age, but I did lots of dancing. I was big into dancing."

"Those things were all sins," Kaleb said. "They were all evil."

"Premarital sex?" I asked.

Kaleb screamed, "Oh no! We were both virgins when we married. I had kissed one girl before. Nothing else. She and I never even touched each other in inappropriate places until we were married."

I squirmed in my chair a little bit, wondering whether I should have brought up such things. Sensing my discomfort, Kaleb said, "No worries Michael, you can ask anything you want. We are open books."

Reassured, I continued, "You have a child so obviously you have had intercourse at least once since you got married."

He said, "Oh yes, we love having sex."

Christina giggled childishly.

I asked if it was love at first sight. She said, "Oh no. He thought I was cute. It was an odd attraction for me. I thought he was interesting and crazy and he has a really big family. We were totally on the same page ideologically. We were both focused on what we wanted our lives to look like, and we both had our spiritual goals and purpose on track. That is what connected us at that time. We had four years of fun gallivanting around with our friends in college, and it was great. Finally after school, both of us decided to stay here in town and work. After I graduated and settled in, things finally clicked between us and we started dating. We were married in April after that, so we were dating for six months. We've been married six years now. We were very much tied ideologically.

"Our marriage was great. It was really blissful. We had no problems really. When we had our baby, Kaleb started to change. Obviously, having a baby changes things significantly, but that is when his big changes started happening religiously. I knew that he was stepping back spiritually. We weren't praying as much together and he wasn't initiating and we weren't doing the spiritual endeavors that we were doing before.

"Some of that I thought was because our community was getting a bit looser as people were graduating and moving on. People were getting married and having babies. We would do things like having Saturday morning breakfast with all of our friends who would come over and do Bible study. On Monday nights we were doing a house church, which is like a small group of worship time at Bible study. Sometimes this was here and sometimes at friends' houses. On Friday nights we would have dinner together and then we would all go out and evangelize on the streets. We were doing things all together all the time. Kaleb was beginning to withdraw from all of that. Many of our friends stayed (here in Lynchburg) and we loved that and that is why we stayed too."

He said, "For a year-and-a-half she knew that I was struggling with doubts. I was going to have to protect her from where my mind was going. I needed to go through this alone."

I asked Christina how she felt about that and she said, "I didn't like being kept out of the loop. I wanted to know what page he was on so we didn't just act like two ships in the night. I grew up in a nonconfrontational home. We didn't really talk about uncomfortable things and so, my tendency is to want to avoid difficult things. But the other side of me really likes to know what's going on even if it's going to be hurtful. We had kind of decided that we wanted to be honest even if it was going to hurt."

I asked him about the intellectual process that brought him to his conclusions. He said, "I was interested in the aspect of how a father relates to a child, how God reacts to his children. Like all babies, my little baby would be inconsolable at 4:00 a.m. and I was dead tired and I knew that I had to get up soon and go to work. I got extremely frustrated and upset with my kid, but I knew that I would never hurt her. I began to think about what we give mental assent to as far as what we believe as Christians. We believe that one day God is going to come back with fire in His eyes and swords in His hands and He's going to slay all those who don't believe in Him. These are Bible verses. There will be such a slaughter that there will be blood up to the eyeballs of horses. There will be rivers of blood from all the nonbelievers. This is in Revelation.

"Revelation is really violent. As Christians give mental assent to this idea, I thought about how it relates to me and my baby daughter and wondered at what point it would be okay for me as a father to inflict pain on her to cause her to suffer because of her rebellion. Would it ever be okay for me to take a nail and poke it into her spine and twist it? No. That would be barbaric and atrocious, unspeakably terrible. But when you think about what we say that our father, God, is going to do to most of creation is that one day He is going to come back with violence to all of those who do not believe in Him. After that fall is an eternity of torture, burning, and pain.

"I couldn't rationalize how Christians could give mental assent to this idea. I wondered if Christ was to come back, but this time instead of acting out in a redemptive way with death and resurrection to save humanity he is acting his future on promised wrath. Jesus picks people off the street and skewers them and roasts them over an open fire while they scream in pain and their flesh is burning. How many of us if we actually saw God doing what we say we think he is going to do could stomach his character? We would think he was a barbarian. This realization opened the Pandora's Box. I started reading and that led to more and more questions."

"Christina," I asked, "What were you feeling emotionally when you were watching what he was going through?"

"We still had a pretty good life. He tried really hard to be a good husband and a good dad. He was more patient with her than me, which impressed me. You could see his love for us and how he took care of us. It was a little bit disheartening because I felt that we were becoming more distant spiritually."

I asked, "Was your unhappiness due to the distance growing between you or were you most unhappy about the ramifications of his break from religion?"

She said, "It was the distance. I stopped feeling as close to him. We were talking about the most important thing that was going on in his life. I didn't know enough to think that he was going to totally de-convert. Doubt is one thing, but de-conversion is another."

Kaleb said, "Right now the church would call me an apostate. I was desperate not to lose my faith. I was dragged out of it kicking and screaming, intellectually. I couldn't deny what I was finding, but I was pursuing pastors and elders, crying out to God, praying that He would reveal Himself to me and save me from these doubts. We have the largest Christian university in the world almost across the street, and I pursued philosophy professors. As I was losing my faith I went to pastors to see if they could slap me around because I was having these doubts. To this day I have many friends who have PhDs in apologetics, the defense of the faith, and the justifications for believing. Philosophy professors. I had multiple, hour long conversations with professors and pastors to help me sort through this."

At that point, and I absolutely swear I'm not making this up, an enormous lightning bolt crashed outside, lighting up the back yard through the window where we sat, and the sound of thunder ricocheted around the room. We all got quiet for a moment. I thought about Revelation. Brimstone. Fire. Blood in the streets.

Christina said, "Once he really started wrestling with things, the depression got crazy. That really affected me. He would get black-out drunk almost every night. He was pulling away from us and was completely discontent. I was still very religious, and he was uncomfortable being around religion. I asked myself if I really wanted to be in this family. Do I want this life? Once we began to talk a bit more and I understood more, things got better. But when he began doubting, I was feeling really worthless. Until that point in our marriage, I was the best thing that ever happened to him. When he started having these doubts, he wanted to pull as far away from me as possible. I know he wanted only to pull away from religion, but I was still part of that. What are you supposed to think if your husband does not even want a family anymore? It angered me."

"So at that point," I summarized, "you (Christina) were angry and you (looking at Kaleb) were depressed."

"Right," he said. "Yes. I realized I'd built an entire world around religion and then I woke up in bed and realized I'd been duped and had been part of a cult that spews hate and spreads destructive stuff. All my relationships, my family, my friends and even my wife were all part of it. What was I to do? Everybody looked at me like I had four heads because I didn't believe it was true. Any time I talked about it, it caused pain. I got tired of inflicting pain."

"Christina," I asked, "When did the healing start for you?"

"August, last year. We didn't really start talking about things until about a year-and-half-ago. I had all that anger and frustration. He was definitely very reactionary. He was tactless in his debate. I am not a debater. I'm a feeler. So my defenses would be that 'I have felt God. I have experienced God.' Kaleb had hard-core evidence. I didn't know what to do with that. He was so rough! He was angry that I was fighting for a religion that he thought was destructive. He was getting fiery about it and attacking me as a person because that was part of me, and I felt destroyed all the time."

"Did you feel that destructiveness that Kaleb has been talking about in your religion and your religious upbringing?" I asked her.

"No," she replied. "In only the last six months did I start to transition to understand that the religion of my entire life wasn't that nurturing. I don't know what the switch was. I decided to not be so afraid and to try to listen to his arguments objectively. He started to be kinder and less heated. It was easier to talk to him."

He countered, "I was angry that I'd been duped my whole life. I was losing my friends and my family. They thought I was evil because I didn't believe what they did any more. It makes it hard to keep up friendships."

I said, "One problem that I have with many of my Christian friends is their overwhelming certitude. They know they're right! I'm never sure. I have lived my whole life in uncertainty, and I want to die not knowing all the answers. But with them, there's no avenue for discussion. There's no equivocation. I pursue reason. They're content with faith."

She said, "When I was willing to say maybe I'm not right, that changed things. He'd point at a particular verse in the Bible and ask me poignant questions like, 'Are you sure this is right?' whether it was condoning slavery or beating your slaves, atrocious things, and I couldn't say 'yes, I think they are right. In no context do I think that those things are okay.' When I was willing to admit that to myself, the snowball began to roll. That gave him some leeway, and he could back off a little bit. Our discussions got more level."

"Losing faith, for me," he asserted, "was more a process than a happening. It was like bleeding to death with a thousand paper cuts. When the Bible says you can beat a slave and it is okay, and if they die you need to pay 50 pence, that's not a good moral lesson. That's one cut. Then there's another. After a thousand more cuts, I found I'd bled to death.

Back to the matter at hand, I asked, "Do you think that the entire city of Lynchburg is in some state of conflict over this whole issue? There are a lot of really smart, technical people here. I'm not saying people who are filled with faith are not smart, but to me one of the marks of intelligence is curiosity and inquisitiveness. Is this community perpetually in a state of intellectual dis-ease?"

He said, "There is an aspect where the desire for knowledge is scandalous because you should not ask questions. You should trust in your faith. Your whole eternity, whether it is paradise or torture depends upon you maintaining the integrity of a belief set and those belief sets are very difficult to maintain if you actually look critically at facts."

I said, "To me as an outsider, both geographically and religiously, those belief sets strike me as extraordinarily arbitrary. Some of these beliefs don't seem to come from scripture."

He said, "The human mind has an incredible capacity to compartmentalize. There are many engineers in this town. They are analytic, but they apply a different standard of evidence where it comes to religion.

"The whole concept of faith is that we don't rely on empiricism or reason as an epistemology. We rely on faith. You believe in something not by sight or by evidence or whether it is reasonable, but you believe it by faith."

I asked, "Do either of you believe in a supreme being at this point in your life?"

He said, "I have no idea. Not really, no."

She said "I am much more agnostic about it now. I would not say that I am an atheist because I don't feel like I know enough to say that there isn't."

"Do either of you feel a sense of loss in giving up your religion?" I asked.

She said, "I am torn. An eternity in heaven would have been great. The notion that God would have really been looking out for you and that you really will be rewarded in heaven is comforting. But in another sense, no, because maybe it is a relief that all the terrible things around the world are not God just letting them slip through the cracks. It is nice knowing that I don't need to feel shame and guilt about all the things that I've always thought I needed to feel shame and guilt about."

I said, "The things that most of us cherish, things like charity, kindness, truthfulness, and all of the good things, in terms of those things, are you and he better or worse persons now?"

He said, "Oh, I definitely think we're better. It was an extreme sense of relief for me when I finally said, okay I am an agnostic. I felt like I could be moral for the first time. I felt like I didn't have to go around and justify the genocides in the Old Testament and do the mental gymnastics to figure out how it was okay to send most of the species to hell. It was really great for me to realize that I no longer had to hate gays. I never really wanted to. (Before,) I sort of felt that there was a religious obligation. Liberal (Christians) say, 'Well I don't want to condemn them or be mean to them, but I don't agree with their lifestyle and will figure out ways to tone it down a little bit.' But the truth of the matter is that if you take the Bible seriously, then God said he hates the workers of iniquity. So it is a righteous thing to hate people who sin."

I said, "So do you feel liberated?"

He said while she laughed, "Oh yes! There is so much relief that I feel over so many formerly stressful things. Imagine for a moment a Mormon sitting down to drink a cup of coffee. In their mind that cup of coffee, that caffeine, is evil and sinful, and it's going to offend the God of the universe and is going to send them to hell. When they take a sip of that because they have a desire for coffee, the psychological turmoil they go through and the stress and dissonance, shame and guilt is overwhelming. Now I feel like I can just relax."

I said, "You have been married for six years. What do you foresee six years from now in your relationship?"

She said, "Who the hell knows, but it sure is exciting!" she giggled again. "I hope we would still be together and we would have had lots of cool journeys together. I think what is cool about where we are now is that we can really talk about absolutely anything and be pretty okay with it. We are not being defensive. We are talking about things as if they are reasonable possibilities. We still may disagree, but it opens up a realm of possibilities of different experiences in our life that we might not have had before."

It had been a long and emotional day for me. I thanked them again for their amazing hospitality, openness, and candor, and fell into a blissful sleep in their little study, wondering how in the hell I'd get this story past my bevy of pedantic editors who would surely insist that such a personal bloodletting didn't belong in this, a book about trains. It rained hard all night.

I HAVE A LONG AND EXTENSIVE BACKGROUND of family history with a man named Chris Schieck who lives just outside of Lynchburg in the town of Forest, where Thomas Jefferson had a second home.

Chris grew up on Long Island in New York where his father was a good friend of Henry Abraham, my grandfather. Grandpa Henry was a train aficionado; he rode trains whenever and wherever he could and had a world-class O gauge layout in his large basement. Chris spent much time there learning about model railroading. Because our family trips to New York were infrequent due to the distance, Chris knew my grandfather better than I did.

Like my father before him and me afterwards, Chris went to Virginia Tech. He got a degree in Mechanical Engineering, graduating in 1966. We lived in Christiansburg, which was only eight miles from campus and so from time to time Chris would come over to visit with my dad and our family. I was only a child of ten or twelve back then. What I remember was the little handmade models that Chris would bring of things like tiny furnished buildings with removable roofs. He was a bright and clever guy, always smiling, with a distinctive voice and an infectious cackle. I remember his visits fondly. He and dad would play chess and chat and he'd stay for dinner, telling us about his schoolwork and his models. His creativity fueled my imagination.

After graduation, Chris got a job with the same Babcock & Wilcox

Company that a decade later would hire me and transfer me to Lynchburg. He and I worked for different divisions, so we saw each other only sporadically in those days from 1976 until 1981. I had not been back to Lynchburg to see him in over 30 years.

I recalled that he had built a working steam locomotive in his basement, something that completely fascinated me. I tracked down his contact information and made an appointment to visit at his house.

The ground was saturated from the prior night's rain, and the new day emerged cloudy, overcast, and cool. His front lawn shrubbery was budding, and a herd of six deer wandered away as I arrived, with only desultory interest in me. I could see that the entire back yard was a layout for his model railroad, which he called the Forest and Western Railroad. With him was a friend of his, Lee Hawkins, who also had an interest in railroading. We sat down to chat in the living room of Chris's brick ranch home.

Chris told me, "As you know from those old days visiting your father, I have always been interested in trains. I like the Norfolk & Western, and the Penn Central and Southern Railroad as well. I have been in this house for 42 years. My model railroading has expanded from the basement to the back yard.

"In addition to my Mechanical Engineering degree, I also have a Masters in Industrial Engineering from (Virginia) Tech. I started with Babcock & Wilcox in 1966 in the service department working on fossil boilers in the Midwest. I worked for them until (retirement in) 1996 when I was on the nuclear end of things, involved in licensing, here in Lynchburg.

"When they began the nuclear program, they drew people from the nuclear navy and the fossil fuel program. They put that together in the nuclear service department. I was a test program supervisor initially. I had an opportunity to move to Ohio, but I decided to stay in Lynchburg and to do so, I moved into the licensing department. I have been in Lynchburg ever since."

As we spoke, I heard remnants of his Long Island intonation. I interrupted him to chide him about it. He confessed, "I guess I still have a trace of that New York accent." He laughed heartily.

He and his wife raised three children in Lynchburg. All lived elsewhere.

"I got a Lionel (train) set when I was about four years old. That was about 70 years ago. From there it went to HO (scale), and I got into that in about 1954. Not long after that I saw a photograph in a model railroading magazine of a live steam engine. These are working models of steam locomotives and I decided I wanted one. I had never actually seen one and I didn't know anybody who had one. I didn't know how to build one. But I bought a lathe from Sears and Roebuck for about $160, which was a lot of money back then, and I decided that I was going to build a steam engine. I was 16 at the time. I got the money from delivering newspapers, cutting grass, and my allowance. I still have that lathe."

I said, "What I remember from my childhood Chris is you visiting and showing us little handmade models that you had made."

"I probably still have them, too," he clucked. "I have always enjoyed making things. When you are (working) in the world of licensing it is all paperwork. The company wanted me to actually feel the steel. So for me that meant coming home and working with my lathe and milling machine and learning how to do castings.

"I make up the patterns with wood. I start with the drawing, and then I machine or carve or somehow shape the wood to the image of what I want. Then I press that into sand. From that I pour molten metal to form castings. You get a piece that looks like your wood pattern.

"(For that locomotive) I had about 10 molds lined up. Each one was about 1 foot cubed. I took them over to the foundry and they showed me how to pour the molten metal into the molds. By the end of that day, I had all the brake shoes, all the wheels, and all the other parts that I needed. It was 1969. It took me 10 more years to actually get the steam locomotive running. The construction doesn't go very fast!

"The overall dimension of that locomotive is about 3 feet long and about 17 inches tall. It weighs about 250 pounds. It is a model of a Denver, South Park, and Pacific Railroad locomotive, originally built in 1882 by the Cooke Locomotive Works. It is a cute locomotive!

"I have always been interested in narrow-gauge trains which are (on a track width of) anything less than the standard gauge of 4 feet 8-1/2 inches. Narrow gauge locomotives were cheaper to build than standard gauge. The ties were shorter and the trains could take tighter curves. There are several different widths of narrow gauge locomotives. The most common was 3 feet gauge. Back in the 1880s, you could take a narrow gauge locomotive train all the way from Denver to Salt Lake City, and that was almost 500 miles.

"Years ago, all over Virginia, the area was dotted with narrow gauge railroads. The trestles were built for trains that were small and light. They were mostly made out of wood."

"So for you here," I asked, "Which came first, the locomotive or the track?"

He said, "The track was about 1978. My backyard operation was concurrent with a first run of the steam locomotive. I have a little 1950 Sears and Roebuck Craftsman transit. I went out into my backyard with it and a shovel and began to lay the course for the rail. Part of what is out there is the original loop. It was about 600 or 700 feet initially. Right now I have about 2,200 feet. You never get enough track," he laughed. "I continue to add passing sidings and more signals, but because of the topography, because my yard slopes off fairly quickly, there is limited room now to put in additional track.

"I now have about six locomotives in varying degrees of completion and operability. After the first one, I built another steam locomotive. It is a replica of a Maryland and Pennsylvania 10-wheeler. The prototype for that was built in 1904. It was built by the Baldwin Locomotive Works. I am currently building a British 0-6-0. It is a model of a Great Western Railway Paddington. It is extremely intricate. It is held together with some bolts as tiny as eyeglass screws.

"And then I have a couple of diesel locomotives which are battery powered. One was made in 1962 and is made out of wood. They are golf cart technology. They look like diesel locomotives, but there is only an electric motor inside."

"What do you know today about the construction of a live steam locomotive that you didn't know when you started?" I queried. "What are your greatest lessons?"

"My lessons are all learned by doing. I never took any shop classes. I made a lot of scrap that way. But I learned how to do things. My greatest lesson is that you have to start somewhere. And you have to not lose interest in what you are doing.

"I worked in an office, in a cubicle. I came home every evening and weekend and did this work. This is an interest that I have had all my life, at least all my life so far. Perseverance was never a problem for me. I get a lot of satisfaction out of it."

"Are your children interested in it?"

"Not a bit," he laughed. "They only hold the most passing interest in trains. I am interested both in trains and in modeling. The building aspect is most interesting to me.

"I enjoy running the train around the backyard, seeing the spark in a child, listening to his questions, and seeing his face. Some children really pick up on it. They ask really good questions. 'How does this work?' 'What does this do?' Some just ride around the backyard and then go off to do something else. When they ask me how something works, I tell them.

"I would love to share this (interest) with other people, but there are none. The only other live steam friends that I had are gone. One was from Richmond and he has died. A good friend over in Clifton Forge has also died. There was a guy up in Charlottesville with a steam engine and he is now gone. There are few people who are actually into making something. They are into video this and computer that, but if you watch O. Winston Link's video at the museum he talks about what young people do. That was shot about 15 years ago. He is right on target about how I feel. (Link) and I are two peas in a pod. I met Link several times, and we had good conversations. He was kind of crusty, but maybe I am a bit crusty too," he chuckled.

OUR CONVERSATION SHIFTED TO CHRIS' FRIEND Lee Hawkins, who grew up in Lynchburg. He attended E. C. Glass High School and then went to Bluefield Junior College in Bluefield, Virginia, riding back and forth on the Powhatan Arrow. He came back to Lynchburg and he worked for the *News and Daily Advance*, the local daily paper, in advertising. He became a linguist during the Vietnamese War, and he worked in Okinawa and in Thailand. "I finished my degree in accounting and business at Lynchburg College. I eventually became an accountant, a comptroller at Liberty University. Then from there, I went to Babcock & Wilcox. I started there in 1992, and I still work there today. I am an accounting supervisor. I'm past retirement age, but I like messing with figures.

"I grew up around railroads. My father worked for the Southern Railroad. Since dad worked for the railroad, we had free transportation. Often in the summertime, he would say to me, 'Lee, let's go take a train ride.' Mama would pack a lunch for us. We would walk to the station, and we would catch the train to Washington. There were men on board who would sell drinks, but they were too expensive. We would go to one or two of the museums at the Smithsonian. We would walk back to the Washington Street station and eat the lunch that mom packed for us. I would say to him, 'Dad, can I have a Coke?' And he would say 'Sure,' and he would reach into his pocket and grab a quarter. And then we would catch the train and ride back to Lynchburg. Our entire day's excursion for the two of us cost twenty-five cents.

"One of the reasons that I went to Bluefield College is that I could get free tickets each way. I rode the Powhatan Arrow a lot. It had a dome car, and I have ridden up there many times. One of the things I remember enjoying was a country club triple-decker sandwich that you could buy in the dining car. The train left Bluefield around six o'clock and around about seven o'clock it was coming down (upstream) the New River and I would get something to eat. The steward didn't like me because I didn't tip. I was just a college student. In the late 1960s, ridership really got thin.

"When I grew up, Lynchburg was mainly a factory town. There was one high school for the white kids and one for the black kids. It seemed like everybody knew each other. A lot of people worked for Craddock Terry Shoe Company. Lots of people worked for Lynchburg Foundry. It seemed like you could get a job if you knew someone who already worked in the factory. Your resume was who you were kin to."

ANOTHER MAN THAT CHRIS HAD INVITED, Tom Ledford, at that point joined in our conversation while Chris left to prepare his outdoor rail operation for our ride. Tom said, "I run Lynchburg's museum system which is a city agency. We have a general museum of Lynchburg history in the old courthouse downtown. It has everything about the city's founding and development. We have another site called Point of Honor. It is a restored house, built in 1815 for Patrick Henry's physician. It is architecturally one of the more unique buildings in Virginia. It has a semi-octagonal base. It is well-built. It has Flemish bond throughout, which is the way the bricks are laid in a long-short-long over short-long-short pattern. That gives you a diagonal diamond pattern both for strength and aesthetics. The house is owned by a foundation although it is administered by the city.

"Lynchburg was the only major city in Virginia prior to the Civil War that was not destroyed by the Union forces. It was never invaded or burned. At the outset of the war it was probably the fourth largest city in the state. Only fairly recently has it dropped down below places like Arlington and Norfolk.

"Lynchburg was at the crossing of the east-west route followed by your rail line at the James River and a north-south transportation corridor from Washington and Charlottesville down into the Carolinas. The east-west vector was predominant in the early days whereas the north-south vector is likely more important now.

"This was an excellent place to cross the river pretty much any time of year. There were shallows and shoals where the river could be easily crossed. In the 18th Century, a ferry was used to cross from one side to the other. Charles Lynch actually patented the ferry, but his son, John Lynch, was the ferry operator. John Lynch built the ferry and there was a toll house of some sort along with a tavern, and pretty soon there was a commercial nucleus where people could do trading.

"The town of New London was actually the political center. New London was probably 15 miles from the river crossing in Lynchburg. By the 1820s, it was eclipsed by Lynchburg economically. Lynchburg was incorporated as a city in 1852. When we go back to the earliest history, you will find Native Americans traveling by water whenever possible. They were using the James River for their circuit between the coast and the mountains."

He said before the English settlers arrived, the Native Americans had seasonal camps where they would gather socially and have ceremonies and harvest crops. "They didn't actually become agricultural until just before white settlers began arriving at Jamestown. Once they became agricultural, they stayed where the fields were located. Their (nomadic) movement slowed down. But when we think of the byways of Virginia, they go all the way back to the Native American trails. There are many references to buffaloes: Buffalo Creek. Buffalo Trail. Buffalo Mountain. There were many buffalo here. It was a major food source. Those trails initially utilized by the Indians later began to be utilized by the explorers and eventually became the highways.

"That is the template that sets all of the land transport in Virginia to the entire eastern seaboard. There is nothing unique about that.

"Trains arrived here in the 1850s. The Virginia and Tennessee railroad was originally conceived as the Lynchburg and New River railroad. The thought was that if they could reach the (New) River, then they could extend onward to Bristol and down to the Mississippi River and to New Orleans. The Virginia and Tennessee was remarkable, I always thought, because it took an original transportation medium, the canal, and went farther. (The railroad) didn't try to duplicate or compete with (the canal), but tried to extend it. The economic development of railroads in Virginia was retarded greatly by the General Assembly who had the right of charter. You couldn't have any business without their say so. Particularly when you had rights-of-way issues and eminent domain – not to mention funding – you were completely dependent upon the General Assembly for approval and funding.

"These are early forms of what we now call public-private partnerships. The state became heavily invested in the canals. The railroads were perceived by the canals as pernicious competitors and political power in the General Assembly adamantly and cleverly opposed the railroads. The Lynchburg and New River Railroad was an idea that dated back to 1828. The Baltimore and Ohio, which is the nation's first successful railroad project, began in 1825. So the Virginia people were right there on the ball.

"One school of thought was that the canal was the way to go. They were looking north to that Erie Canal and seeing how successful it was. And they thought the James River Canal and the Chesapeake Canal north on the Potomac River were sort of diminutive versions of the Erie Canal. What is different is that these canals were dramatically more difficult to build because of the rugged topography they needed to cross. Even the route from Richmond to Lynchburg required something like 20 canal locks. And at that point you were only really getting started into the Virginia mountains.

"Their ultimate goal was the Kanawha River in what was to become West Virginia, and that would have required a massive effort to cross the central Allegheny crest. Railroads were much cheaper to build and more capable of handling that unfriendly topography. Once they were built they were incredibly faster and could hold volumes more cargo. The rates for transport dropped, and effectively the canals were obsolete by 1860.

"There were two massive floods, one in 1870 and one in 1877, that doomed the canal forever. They scoured the James River basin and knocked out the canal. Believe it or not, the canal was rebuilt after both of them, and it continued to operate until 1880.

"After the Civil War, Lynchburg began to transition to a major industrial city. The foundries began operation because there were iron deposits all around. There was plenty of limestone. I think the first foundry was founded in the 1820s, but the major foundries that you think of today date to the 1880s. The iron industry started with blast furnaces that were built all over the place. They needed a water supply to power the bellows to blow air through the furnace to bring up the blast. Pig iron was then taken to forges like Buffalo Forge and Clifton Forge where it was hammered into wrought iron bars or rods or whatever was needed.

"Lynchburg became a trading center for iron and steel. By the turn of the 20th Century, Lynchburg was involved with trains, foundries, and tobacco. By the 1820s this was already a significant market for dark fired tobacco. It continued to be so and by 1880, Lynchburg was the largest tobacco market in the world. There was an enormous amount of money produced out of that. That money was being invested in other businesses such as the shoe industry, clothing industry, and iron industry. There was lots of manufacturing and much of it was agricultural machinery. For much of its history, Lynchburg has been prosperous.

"In the 1950s the Lynchburg Expressway was built and the city began to sprawl towards the west. By the late 1960s there were still lots of factories here, making shoes, clothing, and pharmaceuticals. The Craddock Terry Shoe Company had a decentralized operation with factories throughout the city and beyond, throughout Southside Virginia.

"Working-class people were making shoes, textiles, steel, or electronics. Many other people were supporting these people. When the major corporations, General Electric and Babcock & Wilcox, came here, they hired a lot of mid-level people. There is a significant legal and financial industry here, and healthcare has always been part of the mix. We have always had better than average health care.

"Today the economy is still relatively strong, although the mix has never been static. The (Great) Depression had its way with us and the reason we survived as well as we did is that we were already diversified. A much more recent sweep into technology has not happened here; contrast it with Blacksburg, Charlottesville, and Washington, because we do not have a technical university component."

Chris rejoined the conversation. I asked about Lynchburg's future.

Chris said, "I think the future is bright. Centra Health is our largest employer. They are stretching their tentacles all the way over to Farmville, Bedford, and down to Danville. Health care is an essential service and provides high quality employment. There is a company here called Griffin Pipe. They make pipe for water infrastructure. Much of the national infrastructure is dated and will need replacement in the coming years. We have Liberty University with its educational employment."

Tom added, "Many of the students in our universities end up moving away. Certainly the high school graduates, people like our children, do not think about moving back to Lynchburg."

I said, "Why is that?"

All in unison said there is the perception that there is nothing to do for younger adults. "Then why is everybody so bullish on the place?" I prodded. "You can't have a lasting economy if you can't attract young people."

Lee said, "We are a great family city. There is less interest here in young single people, but people do like to raise their families here."

Tom concurred, saying, "I moved here because I thought my kids could get a good education here and find a good quality of life. I think we need to see quality of life as an economic driver. We have good cable connections and high-speed Internet. You can be here and live this nice life and deal with anybody in the world remotely. We are on our way to making the place friendlier to young adults, particularly single ones. We have all been able to make good livings in Lynchburg in a multitude of ways."

Tom said that maintaining a clean, safe environment was essential. "If you have allowed your environment to degrade, you have sealed your fate. Nobody wants to move and set up a new business in a place where you can't drink the water or breathe the air."

This was an opinion I'd long shared, and I was pleased to have Tom articulate it so strongly. Recent events of widespread pollution in West Virginia, Colorado, and Michigan would surely impact economic development efforts in those communities for a decade or more. Populist notions of vilifying the EPA and our other environmental agencies are counterproductive.

Chris said, "As far as us old retired goats go it is a good place to live. We don't need those things that hold young people. The cost-of-living is low and the quality of life is high. Taxation is favorable."

AFTER LUNCH, WE WENT INTO THE BASEMENT to look over Chris' incredible indoor layout of HO scale trains. He was clearly meticulous with his record keeping and had route instructions for all the operators who worked on his exhibit days to keep the Forest and Western true to a working, albeit fictional, railroad. He had a jewel display case where hundreds of locomotives sat behind sliding glass doors. The various model buildings, trees, and even a river were wonderfully authentic and realistic.

We then toured his machine shop where his lathe, milling machine, welders, and hand-tools were stored. He had multiple shop tool cases and stacks of magazines and drawings packed into the tight space. Locomotives, both completed and under construction, sat on rails on elevated stands that were equipped with wheels to roll around. I was astounded at the incredible complexity of parts and assemblies that Chris fabricated.

We went outside and found a short train consisting of an electric locomotive, an engineer's car with padded seat, a bench car for passengers, a replica box car, a flat car, and a caboose. Chris sat on the engineer's car which had a removable control panel with speedometer mounted on a pivoting pole in front of him. Tom and Lee sat on the bench car and I sat cross-legged on the flat car. We pulled away from the "station" and passed the garage where the cars were stored out of the weather. We rolled merrily along on the 7-1/2 inch gauge track, soundlessly.

At one point, Chris looked behind and said, "Where is the caboose?" It was evidently not properly attached as it sat right where we left it! He laughed self-deprecatingly at his quality control failure.

The track wound around the yard, generally keeping to a contour so as to avoid significant climbing or descending, just like a real one. Whooo! Whooo!, as we crossed a pedestrian crossing. There were several replica crossing signs along the route, along with other yard ornaments, including a concrete alligator waiting in the rushes. The track made a near loop at one end, with much of it elevated up to four feet or so on a wooden trestle. It was fun, channeling my inner child.

We were going slow enough that I picked up a small fallen tree twig, perhaps a foot long and the thickness of a pencil, lying next to the track. Remembering how we'd put pennies on the track at the old station, I slipped the twig under my car's wheels, thinking it would snap as the wheel rolled over it. Instead, it simply derailed my car! I bumped along over a couple of ties and stopped as the train rolled on for a few feet without me until Engineer Schieck came to my rescue. He took the derailment in stride and said something about how these things happen sometimes. Of course, I neglected to confess to my immature transgression.

He deftly placed my car back on the track and we continued onward until it began raining, when we returned to the "station," and put everything away.

LEE HAD MENTIONED that he had a friend, Garland Harper, who worked for Amtrak, who could tell me about modern passenger railroading. So I dutifully backtracked into the heart of Lynchburg, following Lee as we drove our cars to the historic 1912 Kemper Street Station where Garland was the station master.

Our route took us near the center of the city, following increasingly narrower streets. We crossed a bridge over the railroad tracks and then wound ourselves down into the canyon where the Kemper Street Station is located. The last few hundred yards were on ancient cobblestones.

Inside, we found his friend, Garland. It was a quiet time since the arrival of the train from Washington was still several hours away, and for most of the time we were the only people there. Amtrak stations face long periods of stillness, punctuated by brief flurries of activities when trains arrive and depart.

Garland told me that he had had a lifelong interest in trains. "When I was a child, my father would take me to the rail yards in downtown Lynchburg. I watched them do the switching of cars. When I was in grade school, I was always hanging around the river taking photographs. I grew up on the campus of the Virginia Episcopal School and it was only a stone's throw above the river.

"I went to school at (The College of) William and Mary. Oftentimes coming home I would take the train from Williamsburg to Charlottesville and then catch the Southern Railway down to Lynchburg. It probably took two or three hours longer than driving or even taking a Greyhound bus. I think it cost $3.75 to go from Williamsburg to Charlottesville and another $1.64 to come down to Lynchburg.

"A few months after graduating from college in 1975, I got a job with Amtrak and I have been with them ever since. I credit hanging around the station in Williamsburg for breaking the ice for me to get the job. In those days, to make a reservation, customers called a toll-free number. Tickets were handwritten."

Eventually Garland obtained a job in Charlottesville. "It had me working there for three days a week and down here in Lynchburg the other two. I was working Saturday and Sunday nights. I have not had a weekend off in 40 years of working for the railroad.

"Both the Southern and the N&W built bypasses around Lynchburg. They called them cut-offs. They bypassed downtown because both of them had to navigate steep grades getting down there and back out again. All three railroads crossed in downtown Lynchburg at one time. It was a logjam. For a long time, it was thought that any city worth its stature had all of its rail lines come together at a central station, a union station, where passengers could move freely from one rail line to another.

"Now we have two trains here every day in both directions. We have a regional train that terminates here from the north. Then we have a long distance train, The Crescent, which continues all the way to Atlanta and New Orleans. So one train terminates and originates here and the other one passes through.

"When they added that regional train, they added a new position and I applied for that and got it. Since September 2009, I have been holding down the afternoon here five days a week. I do not have anything to pull me away. I enjoy being a flesh and blood interface between the system and the passengers.

"Business is good. If you come back here at eight o'clock tonight you will see a few hundred people get off a train that terminates here. Tonight it might be primarily students returning from break. There are about 300 getting off in Charlottesville and about 225 getting off here tonight.

"I am concerned about the low price of gas. I am one of the few that wants the price of gas to be back up at four dollars per gallon. It is too cheap right now!

"The infrastructure of American passenger rail is probably better than it was 20 or 30 years ago. It takes about 3-1/2 hours by train to get from here to Washington. If you try to go to downtown Washington by car, it can easily take 4-1/2 hours or longer. One of the reasons this train has done so well is there is no easy way to drive to Washington. Driving now between Charlottesville and Culpeper is hell, and once you get inside the Beltway, it really is awful.

"The success of this train has proven that people ride it if it is convenient. "When gas was $4 per gallon, there were people riding the train for the first time. Now, some people commute every week. Students go home during their breaks from school. They come up from Virginia Tech on the bus, and they come from Liberty University here to go northward.

"People in railroading complain that when (Congress) does transportation bills, the highways get a big chunk and the airlines get a big chunk for the airports, but the railroads are just an afterthought. Amtrak continually has to plead to Congress for funding. I don't think we should spend money willy-nilly on Disneyland-like rides, but I think we need to support trains as a good basic way to get from here to there.

"Our trains go up to 79 mph between here and Washington. North of Charlottesville, our train goes much faster than the cars. It is gratifying to me. An average round-trip fare is $90 from Lynchburg to Washington. If you buy a ticket in advance, you can get a $68 round-trip ticket from Lynchburg to Washington and back.

"For me, railroads are a hobby and an occupation, too. I have dozens of albums of pictures of trains coming through here."

LEE AND I WENT OUR SEPARATE WAYS, and I returned to Larry and Paulette Bailey's house, as they had returned from their trip. Larry invited me to attend a breakfast the following morning of retired Babcock & Wilcox engineers. Given that I'd been one myself, I decided to attend with him. So the next morning, we went to the west end of Lynchburg again, this time to the Timberlake area. We pulled into a small, locally owned café where we sat with three other men of the bifocal set in a corner wrap-around table. Soon another man joined us, making 6 of us, total.

I was introduced to each of them, but forgot most of the names almost as fast as I heard them. They were a kindly bunch, and they welcomed me graciously. One wore a baseball-style cap with the insignia of a nuclear submarine. Another had served in the Army in Vietnam.

Like so many engineers, they were loquacious and matter-of-fact, opinionated. We stayed away (mostly) from politics, but they weren't shy in talking about their erstwhile employer and its various mergers and acquisitions and the future of commercial nuclear power.

Our knees sat too closely at the over-crowded table. If you're a guy, have you ever had that mildly uncomfortable feeling of trying to maintain good, polite eye contact with a stranger while you speak to him, with your knees touching and your faces close enough to count his nose hairs?

The waitress was a perky young black-haired woman who seemed well-versed in the art of tip-enhancement by the liberal sprinkling of the word "honey" or its abbreviated "hon" with the older men. She had a nice, seen-it-all-even-though-I'm-only-35 look and a pleasant smile that worked well until she smiled too broadly, exposing some gaps where her molars were supposed to be.

I always sympathize with breakfast waitresses as there is a vast array of options that don't seem to exist at other meals. For example, eggs can be boiled (soft and hard), fried (over easy, over medium, over hard, sunny-side up or down), poached, deviled, and curried. There are frittatas, omelets, tortillas, burritos, and quiches. Potatoes are a breakfast favorite around here: boiled, hash-browned, home-fries, French fries, steak fries, potato waffles (waftos), wedges, and potato salad. Coffee at most places like this is regular or de-caffeinated, but fancier places have entire menus of options (lattes, cappuccinos, mochas, macchiatos). Meats are sausages (link and patties), ham (country, salted, boiled), and bacon. Breads are white, rye, wheat, pumpernickel (at your finer roadside cafes), sourdough, muffins (plain, fruited, or chocolate), French toast, rolls, and biscuits, and with a variety of heated or toasted options, along with an unlimited number of pancake and waffle offerings.

So breakfast waitresses are typically bombarded with detailed instructions on every aspect of food preparation. For example, "I'd like two eggs, over easy, lightly salted, with two link sausages, only pork!, white bread – no gluten!, de-caf coffee, and hash-browns. No, home fries. Did I say I wanted my three eggs over easy? No, make them poached. And cream." And then she has to carefully document this for everybody at the table. Not to mention what the cook goes through, especially considering that all six meals are due at the same moment.

At my favorite Mexican restaurant, by contrast, my dinner order might be, "I'll have the number seven combo. With a Dos Equis." Simple!

For some reason, waitresses, particularly perky ones, stimulate my latent snark gene, and I'm likely to emit something that I'll immediately regret, especially since she has the ready option to tamper with my food mere seconds before I put it in my mouth. Sometimes I'm tempted to simply say, "Bring me something that's been dead for less than a week," or "Bring me something that isn't white," but resist doing so fearing the consequences.

While I awaited my meal (an egg and sausage sandwich on rye with lettuce, tomato, and mayo, for the record), I listened to the guy in front of me talk about the lack of skills in the younger engineers. He reminded us that NASA engineers sent men to the moon and back working out calculations on slide rules, and kids today wouldn't even know what one was if you smacked them upside the head with one. My mind drifted as I listened and I played with the tiny jelly tubs, seeing how high I could stack them. I envisioned vast landfills filled with millions of tiny depleted jelly tubs.

I remembered listening to an engineer who worked at Boeing when I lived in Seattle back in the 1980s talk about a massive buy-out of jobs the company experienced during a downturn, and how so much of the company's institutional knowledge was sent packing, and how the company might never recover. Nowadays, I see that Boeing, employing vast pools of young engineers who wouldn't even know what a slide rule was if you smacked them upside the head with one, were building the lightest, sleekest, most fuel-efficient jetliners in the world. People seem to build expertise when necessary around the tools and technologies available to them. The next generation will be fine.

I AM A MOTORCYCLE ENTHUSIAST, and as much as I have enjoyed the trains and all the talk about trains here, when I had the chance to meet a collector of antique motorcycles, I could not resist. He was Larry's friend and his name was Paul Abbott.

Paul was a slight man, with a decided stutter in his movements. In his garage, he had a new Harley Davidson motorcycle. The antique motorcycles, he told me, were in a shed out back.

Paul was divorced and lived alone near New London in a house well off the beaten path, where no other homes were anywhere in sight. There was a cultivated field of rye in his backyard. We sat in a sunroom off the kitchen where I asked him about his hobby of motorcycling.

"I am interested in all things mechanical, but motorcycles are high on my list because I can afford them," he chuckled. "My dad was into steam engines. He had me in the cab of a full-size steam locomotive when I was three years old. I remember it vividly. It was a yard switching engine in Columbus, Ohio. He had lots of connections with railroad people. He went on excursions all over the country.

"The last one I rode with him was the 611 run back in the 1980s. That was the second rebirth and rebuild of the 611. Just last year was the third."

Larry added, "Paul and I went to see the 611 after it was reconditioned last year. I remember when I was a child, I would pack a lunch at my house in Christiansburg and go over to the train station and watch the trains go by. I would have been only eight or nine years old. This was at the end of the steam era, just before all of the other Class J locomotives got scrapped."

Paul was wearing a baseball cap that said on it, "21st Century Steam." He said, "I consider myself to be a chaser and an interested fan of old hardware. The 611 has fans everywhere.

"During the excursions in the 1980s, they did photo op runs. They went out to a place on the New River and they brought the train to a complete stop and let people get off that wanted to take pictures. And they backed up a ways and came to another stop. Then they poured on the steam as hard as they could, with that engine just smoking, and drove it by the photographers. Then they stopped again and backed up and picked everybody up again."

He said the attractions for him were the links to his youth and his father. He showed me a wonderful picture that he had taken of the 611 under full power, and he told me that his father was standing beside him when he took it. It was clearly a poignant moment for him. "We rode to Bluefield and back. It was early fall. In those days, they had coaches where you could open the windows. I remember the sights and smells and everything about it."

Paul said his father loved motorcycles, too. "When my dad got out of the Navy, he bought an Indian Four. (Note, it is an unusual motorcycle engine configuration with four cylinders running front to back rather than one side to the other. Indian, like rival Harley Davidson, was most famous for their V-twin engines, but from 1928 until 1942 Indian built the four-cylinder configuration as well.) I have some pictures of him on that in his Navy uniform. I don't remember ever riding that bike, but I do have a picture of me sitting on it and I was two or three years old."

We walked outside to the shed where he kept three of his antique motorcycles. One of them was an Indian Chief. Larry had helped him set up the shed which Larry had appropriately named the wigwam.

"Oh my," spilled from of my mouth as I first laid eyes on his bikes.

The 1955 Ariel Square Four captured my attention first. It was a 1,000cc motorcycle made in England.

"It is basically two 500cc engines," Paul explained, "one in front of the other, geared together at the crankshafts." Each gear has the same diameter as the spacing between the crankshafts. They are straight cut gears. There is then another gear that drives the clutch that transfers power to a four-speed gearbox.

He said, "It is an amazing motorcycle. It is fast and it is smooth." He tried to kick start it, but on that cool day, it was unwilling to start. I wished I could have heard it.

We then looked at the 1948 Indian Chief, a gorgeous motorcycle, fully restored. He said, "I bought it up in Pennsylvania and began restoring it about six years ago. It has been restored for about a year."

It had the oddest assortment of controls I had ever seen. It had a foot clutch on the left side. Where the throttle is on most motorcycles it had a spark advance. It had a hand shifter on the right side next to the gas tank. The left side had a twist throttle. It would scare the hell out of me to ever try to ride it. And I ride motorcycles a lot, typically around 15,000 miles a year.

1955 Ariel Square Four

The baby-blue paint was flawless and all of the leather and rubber parts were new. I asked him if it ran. He said, "Yes, but it is very hard to start." He said he needed someone larger to start it for him, but "I can start it when it is hot. I only weigh 150 pounds. I have ridden it only 8 miles. It is too pretty to ride. If anything ever happened to it, it would break my heart!"

I could have continued our visit and chat most of the day, but the (rail)road beckoned. So I thanked both men for their hospitality and candor, and off I went westward towards Bedford, only ten miles away.

In Bedford, like many towns in Virginia, if there was no Interstate highway nearby, VDOT kindly provided a limited-access bypass to speed travelers from one side to the other without the hassles of stop lights or commerce. This has effectively ruined most downtown commercial districts, as family-owned businesses have been supplanted by big-box stores that have gravitated to the open spaces where these bypasses diverged from the connecting highways. With the Walmart and Lowes hardware stores now outside the bypasses, there is a new necessity for traffic lights out on the connecting highways. So the downtowns have been decimated and the traffic has simply leapfrogged the interchanges with none of the hassles solved. And everybody needs a car for every trip, as these places are categorically pedestrian-hostile.

Someone once told me that Walmart spends a fortune locating new stores and Lowes spends a much smaller fortune finding where Walmart is going and then it builds there as well.

THE POWHATAN ARROW DID NOT STOP in Bedford, the county seat for Bedford County, situated roughly between Lynchburg and Roanoke. But I did.

I successfully navigated past all the outside-the-bypass traffic lights and then the inside-the-bypass lights and parked downtown. I wandered into the Bedford Museum & Genealogical Library on Main Street near the Bedford Court House where I met Jennifer Thomson, Educational Director.

She said that even though the distance trains didn't stop, Bedford did have a railroad station for local trains. Bedford's Liberty Station had regular service until around 1970. Behind her where we spoke were row upon row of labeled boxes of genealogy research, stacked textbook style like in a library.

She went on to explain that the original name for the community was Liberty, not Bedford. "Bedford County was formed in 1754. It was one of the westernmost counties, named after the fourth duke of Bedfordshire, John Russell. Our county seat was New London. It is between here and Lynchburg.

"In 1782, Campbell County split off taking Lynchburg with it. We needed a new county seat. They came here and established a town called Liberty. From the 1750s, when we were pro-crown, until the 1780s, when we were pro-America, we were thinking liberty. It was called Liberty from about 1782 until 1890. By then, we already had an east-west train route, the corridor you're studying. It was thought that we would get a north to south train route as well. At that point, it was renamed from Liberty to Bedford City to match the name of the County."

Virginia has an odd municipal governing structure where cities are completely independent with their own services, including schools, police, fire and rescue departments, and water and sewer services. However, towns are governmentally linked to their counties and share some resources. Most towns have their own police and fire departments, but always have county-wide schools. And it has no relevance to size. For example, Blacksburg is the largest town in the state at around 40,000 people, but the children attend Montgomery County Public Schools. Norton, far in western Virginia, is a city with 2500 people with their own school system.

Bedford City was incorporated with city status. Interestingly, in 1912, Bedford reverted to town status. Again, in its ongoing schizophrenia, in 1968 it again became a city and then in 2011 again became a town.

I asked her about the economy in the late 1960s, relative to today.

She said, "Bedford had more manufacturing in the late 1960s and the economy was stronger then. There were companies that made rubber, labels, clothing, and all sorts of things here.

"Bedford was literally placed here because it was in the center of the county. There was no other reason. There was already a road established, the original Lynchburg to Salem Turnpike. Its original route has not changed much, and it is now the corridor of US-460.

"The first courthouse is right across the street from where we are now. The second courthouse is still the site of our current courthouse. We are sitting in the 1895 Masonic Lodge. The Masons started here in 1813. They built this building in 1895."

She told me that while some people worked in Bedford, it was more of a bedroom community for people working to the east in Lynchburg or the west in Roanoke County. There were many retirees in the southern part of the county at Smith Mountain Lake. Like many other county seats, a sizable number of people in Bedford worked in government or in the legal profession.

She said there were some small shops downtown, but like many small towns, locally-owned retailers were struggling. I asked her if she felt the community was well-positioned to transition into a 2025 or 2035 economy. She said, "I hope so, but I don't know. It is hard to tell with so many downtown businesses struggling. Some of them are doing great. They have been there for a long time and they will weather the storm."

"Who is doing well?" I asked.

She said there was a jewelry store called Arthur's Jewelry. "They have been around for quite a while. They are doing great. Our coffee shop is struggling. We have had several coffee shops in town and they have all folded. One of the saddest things that has happened here is that our downtown hardware store closed. They were a staple for over 100 years. It still had an elevator that you had to pull with a rope. It was set up so a wagon could pull into the basement and unload. They had to close because of finances and competition. Truthfully, you may have saved fifteen cents on a furnace filter at Walmart. But the hardware store had people with knowledge and expertise. You probably can't even find a clerk at Walmart. The hardware store had antique and local stuff."

I departed and then wandered the downtown sidewalk past the courthouse that a metal historic marker informed me was built in 1930. It also contained much of the information about Liberty and New London that Jennifer had told me, concluding with, "Union General Hunter, with his army, passed here in 1864 on his way to Lynchburg, and re-passed on his retreat." So two things: one, writing historic markers must be excruciatingly difficult, with brevity being everything, and two, with places like Appomattox not far away; it really must be a stretch to make the passing through of a Union General and his army a matter of historic importance.

The courthouse was lovely, with the grand architectural style of the era. It had a white four-sided cupola atop it, held with a brick and masonry base, with each facet displaying an analogue clock. In a hollowed cylinder above that was a large bell, topped with a green copper crown.

The jewelry store Jennifer recommended was closed and had a sign saying, "Closed due to death in the family," and they would be open again the following day.

So I went to the old Liberty Train Station to see if I could speak with the owner, hoping I'd find as cordial a reception as I'd found at The Depot Grill back in Lynchburg. I arrived at the lunch hour. The owner wasn't in, and when the manager said he could only speak with me for a moment, I apologized sympathetically, left my card, and departed, again disappointed. However, while waiting for him I was able to learn that the station had housed several businesses since its abandonment by the railroad after passenger service was eliminated in 1971. It began operation as Liberty Station Restaurant in 2001, but when undergoing renovation in 2009, it caught fire and was almost completely destroyed. It was rebuilt and re-opened for business in 2010, architecturally much the same as the original. The interior was filled with railroad memorabilia, including an awesome neon representation of the Powhatan Arrow logo.

WHILE NOT AN ESPECIALLY NOTEWORTHY RAILROAD TOWN, Bedford did produce one of the industry's most influential recent characters, Stuart T. Saunders. A railroad executive, Saunders was a driving force in the creation of the Penn Central Transportation Company in the merger of the Pennsylvania and New York Central railroads. He served as its chairman when it was the largest railroad in the nation, from its inception in 1968.

However, his success may have sewn the seeds of failure, as the many years necessary to consummate the merger took a toll in both companies' morale and management structure. Additionally, Saunders' timing couldn't have been worse, as passenger service in those days was tanking, placing a financial burden on their profitable freight business. A mere two years later in 1970, Penn Central Transportation Company filed for bankruptcy. Its freight operations were taken over by Conrail and its passenger service by Amtrak.

As the railroad filed for bankruptcy, several of Saunders' officials were accused of insider trading, dumping their stock before the company folded. Although not directly implicated, it must have been an excruciating process for Saunders.

Prior to his leadership in the formation of the Penn Central, he served as president of Norfolk & Western from 1958 until 1963, where he oversaw the acquisition of the Virginian Railway and initiated negotiations with the Nickel Plate Road, the Wabash Railroad, and portions of the Pennsylvania Railroad, whose merger was completed the following year after his departure.

Saunders is a bit of a villain for our story, as he is responsible for the termination of N&W's use of steam as a motive force in favor of diesel. And he ordered the destruction of most of N&W's steam locomotives, including all of the Class Js. The 611 was the only one of the class to escape the cutting torch.

Saunders was born in McDowell County, West Virginia, farther down the line of my travels, but was raised in Bedford within sight of the tracks and graduated from Roanoke College and then Harvard Law School. He died in Richmond in February 1987 at age 78.

AFTER THAT, I MOTORED SOUTH from downtown towards the bypass to the National D-Day Memorial. Like the Museum of the Confederacy in Appomattox, its site seemed to have been selected for maximum vehicular access. I spoke with a kindly older woman volunteer at the guard shack about my project. She grabbed her walkie-talkie and called the Director of Site Operations, Jim McCann, and asked if he'd meet me. Getting his approval, she sent me to his office in a small building to the west of the circular drive that encircles the sprawling outdoor monument.

McCann escorted me to a covered pavilion where we sat on benches of metal picnic tables. There was a brisk wind from the northwest, the direction from where we could see the looming Peaks of Otter. It was a blissful setting. To the east, we could see the climactic, emblematic feature of the monument, the Overlord Arch, from where we sat.

He spoke with a pleasant accent-less voice. He told me that this became the National D-Day Memorial by writ of Congress in 1996. "It broke ground in November, 1997, and a dedication ceremony was held on Memorial Day in 2000 to dedicate the arch. It officially opened as the national monument on June 6, 2001. President George W. Bush and 15,000 or 20,000 people attended that day.

"They didn't collect any fees the first few months, and I think they had tens of thousands of visitors. I have been here since 2005. The original plan was to construct a modest monument in Roanoke because the founder, Bob Slaughter, was from Roanoke. He was in the second assault wave at Omaha Beach. He thought there needed to be a war memorial to D-Day. He and his buddies created the genesis of this idea. He formed the foundation as a LLC in Roanoke. They fully intended to build a monument on Mill Mountain or the Gainsboro area. Neither of those worked out.

"So why is the monument here? The answer you will hear is Bedford lost most of the men on that day. That is not how it happened at all.

"While (the founders) were unable to gain the land (in Roanoke) or make progress with that, the town of Bedford saw an opportunity. (Bedford) offered land, money, and services if they would move it here. And so they did. So it is not as romantic a story as people would like it to be.

"There were three companies that made up the first two waves at Omaha Beach, Dog Green sector. Those three companies hailed from Lynchburg, Bedford, and Roanoke. So where is the monument? It is in Bedford, equidistant from Lynchburg and Roanoke. These three communities suffered the highest losses as a group and you are now in the one that suffered the highest losses as a single community.

"I think that in the genesis of it they only wanted a plaque and a flag. Eventually they decided it needed to be something grander because it was a significant event in our history. The significance is partly that Bedford lost 19 men of Company A that was made up of about

180 men.

"Dating back to World War I, England formed companies out of communities. For example if the West Essex Fusiliers went over the top (of the trenches), an entire community of men could be lost. This was not going to happen again, or so we thought. But when World War II started and United States became involved, we were not prepared. So the United States looked to its National Guard units, and it used those to create the core of actual companies. Companies from all these towns around here formed up into a division and then in a battalion at Fort Meade, Maryland. Other communities through Virginia formed up letter companies and ended up fighting side-by-side.

"I didn't know a lot of that until I got here. Previously, I was a firefighter. I would go all the time on calls where older men might have COPD, and we would sit and talk for a few moments before we drove them to the hospital. They would say that they were there at Omaha Beach on D-Day. I always thought these guys just wanted us to think that. Years later, I learned that they were all telling the truth."

A crow flew overhead and cawed noisily.

"The 29th division landed primarily at Omaha beach. That is where all these men were. There were several other beaches that British, Canadian, and French (troops) landed as well as other Americans. (Our men) only made up a portion of the invading force. But the local guys were on the first wave at Omaha, tip of the spear. And they landed at the D1 draw which was one of the most heavily fortified areas. They had to cross an open beach for 300 yards where Germans were sitting on high ground shooting at them. Guys farther up the coast had a little more coverage. Our guys were at the worst place.

"I think Bob's initial plan was just to have a flag in the monument to honor those men from Company D, especially those that fought with him in Roanoke. What we see today is much grander. I think that it is even more grand than its title, the National D-Day Memorial. It is indeed the International D-Day Memorial. There are 12 flags flying. All that is required by the US government to have a National Memorial is that we list the names of the dead, and we fly the American flag.

"This gets to the part of why this monument is so much different than many others. The founders decided not to simply create a static monument but to create an educational center and to tell the story over and over again. So it is designed with the intent of taking visitors on the journey from England to Normandy to Paris. People don't always know that when they (plan to) come here. Once here, they realize that there is an intentionality in the story and in the design to tell that story.

"The Arch here is intended as a symbol of victory, but it is largely representative of the Arc de Triomphe in Paris. When you're out there in the plaza, you see five sections of concrete, representative of the five different invasion areas. Planning, invasion, and victory are the three stages represented here.

"Visitors go on the same journey as those people who participated in Operation Overlord. Some of the participants never got off the beach, but many of those men made it to Paris and beyond. We have a list of all the Allied soldiers, sailors, and airmen – not just American – who died.

"So we have gone beyond the national scope because the founders understood that we couldn't just tell the story about the Americans. Others paid the same price and we needed to include them, too. It is a local monument, a national monument, and an international monument.

"We are a private, nonprofit, 501(c)(3) educational foundation. It is not federally owned or operated. Our primary focus is educating people about the day and remembering the fallen. All of the money we generate through admissions, special events, gift store sales, and the like only amounts to about 25 percent to 28 percent. That means that every visit here is subsidized by somebody else, from corporate donations, grants, and private donations. We also have members who support us financially. We do different things to raise funds. We have many events and we work hard. We have 19 people on staff, mostly part time.

"When I first came to work here in 2005, the monument was only partially complete. It was built on borrowed money and the foundation went into bankruptcy right after it opened. I was working for the fire service in Lynchburg looking for a part-time job because I knew I was not going to get promoted and I needed a retirement job. So I came here and I had full hopes that this place would eventually emerge from bankruptcy and move on. I wanted to be here if something happened."

Within a couple of years, McCann had been promoted to Director. He said, "That changed my whole perspective. At that time there were still a lot of veterans who were working here, men who survived the invasion. In the years when we went from being bankrupt until we finished the monument, most of the veterans passed away. I only know of one man who is still alive. He is in his 90s and is still a volunteer here.

"The town of Bedford lost 20 men on the first day. In the span of 80 or so days from D-Day until the liberation of Paris, Bedford had 57 participants and 30 died. Lynchburg and Roanoke and many other cities lost their men as well."

I assumed that 57 men got on a train at the Liberty Station in downtown Bedford, likely pulled by one of the new and magnificent Class J locomotives that would ultimately pull the Powhatan Arrow for over 20 years, and went to Lynchburg and from there to Maryland and sailed to England. Over half of them never came back.

I told him about my recent visit to Appomattox Courthouse and he said, "The Park Service was not interested because nobody got killed here. (But) 30 guys from Bedford got killed over there. This is where we remember them.

"We have lots of foreign visitors. We have a memorial wall that was paid for by a French company, Areva, that is in the nuclear energy business with facilities in Lynchburg. That wall memorializes the French soldiers who died in the invasion. There are international dollars here. Bedford has a number of Sister Cities in France. People come from those cities to visit here all the time. We might have 50 of them at one time. For them it is more personal. Some of these people are in their 70s and 80s and were children then. They make a direct connection."

He told me that for many years he has been playing war games online. He was recently invited to Belgium to a tournament over there. The event was on November 14, and he knew that Armistice Day was on November 11. He went to four different ceremonies that day. He said, "They don't forget. Whenever anybody says that they don't appreciate us over there, I tell them that they don't know what they're talking about. (Europeans) remember a time when they needed somebody to help them. We were there for them. And we didn't stay. We gave them their countries back."

He mentioned that they were trying to build an education center to display thousands of artifacts. When he arrived, nobody was talking about building anything; they were just talking about getting out of debt. He said, "At some point we become the Civil War, too. You are a fool if you don't realize that. I have to give it a long-term perspective. Our goal here is to realize that D-Day was a pivotal moment not only in American history but in world history and for that reason, we just can't fail to remember it."

I asked what the memorial meant to the economy of Bedford.

He said, "I'm not from Bedford so I don't know. Bedford is still a pretty out-of-the-way place. We think and hope that if we were to build a more robust monument that invited visitors to stay here longer, it would help the economy here even more."

His foundation shares its plans with local town officials frequently. "If you bring 50,000 visitors here who stay for a day and spend some money having lunch, that is a lot of money. We know millions of dollars are added to the local economy."

I said, "From what I'm learning, heritage tourism is big right now and getting bigger. People in my generation are looking for authentic experiences. I personally am not interested in being entertained. I like experiential activities. Show me something real."

He agreed. "I don't just want to watch a movie. I want to participate. That is the most dynamic and lasting thing that people think about when they come here. The guide walks them through the invasion. They are not looking at it on the screen or reading about it in a book. They are going through the story. The beauty of that is that they have taken the time and in taking the trip will remember the story better. We are educating them not just in their head but physically.

"I believe in the providence of God. I think all of these came together at the right time and put it here, even though it was supposed to be in Roanoke. Even when I was still working for the fire department in Lynchburg, I had a feeling that this is where I wanted to be someday. When an ad popped up for a job here, it was the only one I filled out. To be hired a few days later was like having a sense of destiny about it I have had ever since. There was sort of a double destiny. If this had been placed in Roanoke that would've been too far away for me."

I THANKED JIM FOR HIS TIME and motored westward. A mostly clear sky gave me a magnificent look at the nearby Peaks of Otter, Bedford's imposing backdrop. There are three peaks, however, only two were visible from my vantage point. On the left was Sharp Top, at 3,862 feet elevation and on the right was Flat Top at 3,994, both eponymously named. Harkening Hill at 3,372 was hidden from view. Thomas Jefferson, in one of his worst scientific observations, wrote that, "The mountains of the Blue Ridge, and of these the Peaks of Otter, are thought to be of a greater height, measured from their base, than any others in our country, and perhaps in North America." He obviously never saw Mt. Rogers, later proven to be Virginia's highest peak, not to mention Mt. Rainier. Anyway, to his credit, he wrote a damn good *Declaration of Independence.*

ON MY WAY, I GOT A CALL on the cell phone, that through the miracle of modern technology came directly through the Ford C-Max's speakers. It was from Harry Leist, the owner with his family of the Liberty Station restaurant where I'd just been, who was kind enough to follow up. He told me more about the history of the building, indicating that it was built in 1890 and was used by the N&W until around 1971, and Amtrak for a few years afterwards. It sat vacant until 1989, when it was turned into a restaurant. It then had a series of owners until his family bought it in 2001 and they have run it since.

He told me, "We run a down-home restaurant with smiles and good food. We're mid-scale, in line with Outback Steak House restaurants." He said his wife did new decorating five times every year. They get lots of business at Christmas drawn to the Elks' Home nearby. "We're busy all the time."

I asked him about the neon Powhatan Arrow logo and he said he'd commissioned two of them custom-built by a neon artist in Richmond, taken from a cloth patch. They were the only two of their kind in existence. He was clearly a railroad fan.

He said the restaurant started the same summer as the D-Day Memorial, and many of his patrons visit there as well. "We had a group of Navy guys eat here who drove the Higgins Boats, the ones that dropped the soldiers on the beaches at Normandy. There were 40 or 50 of them in our back dining room having lunch. When they began walking out, everybody in the main dining room stood up and gave them a standing ovation. There weren't too many dry eyes in the house; it was something to see.

"Bedford is a small, quaint town, with nice people. It's a wonderful place to live. People come from 100 miles to eat with us. (Our restaurant) has grown tremendously. Bedford only has 6,200 people. We couldn't do this with only 6,200 people to draw from."

FROM BEDFORD, AGAIN US-460 closely follows the Norfolk & Western line. The town of Montvale is known for the two dozen or more gargantuan above-ground gasoline and diesel fuel tanks situated there, warehousing liquid fuels for the region. At the village of Blue Ridge, the track reaches its highest elevation so far of just over 1,300 feet before descending into the Roanoke Valley. There is a connector highway, Alternate US-220, which connects US-460 to Interstate 81, allowing long-distance westbound travelers to bypass the cities of Roanoke and Salem entirely. But I dutifully stayed on US-460, enduring twelve traffic lights, five of them red, before reaching downtown Roanoke, sacrificing my time and patience for the cause. You're welcome.

12:15 p.m.

Roanoke

Mile 252.3

Virginia's third largest city and the home of the Norfolk & Western. The road's general offices and extensive yards and shops are located here, where all N. & W. modern locomotives are built. N. & W. passenger station a model of functional beauty. City is industrial and retail center of Southwest Virginia, with structural steel, rayon, and printing the most important industries. Famous Hotel Roanoke over-looks the station. Hollins College nearby. N. & W. Shenandoah Valley and Winston-Salem lines converge here.

R oanoke and I have a complicated history. It's a Jewish thing.
My most vivid memories of Roanoke as a child were the weekly trips we made from my home in Christiansburg where I was born and raised. My parents, now in their late 80s, still live in the same house where I grew up. Each Sunday morning, Mom – more frequently than Dad who probably went fishing – piled my three siblings and me into the Buick Vista wagon, the land-yacht of an automobile we had back then, and we descended into hell.

Okay, I exaggerate, but sometimes it seemed like it. We were the kids from up the mountain. Poorer. Less refined. Less pedigreed. I was religiously conflicted and socially outcast.

There was a bright side to these repetitive trips down the mountain to the big city. Interstate 81 hadn't opened then, and the old route, part of the original Wilderness Road, and then and now the combined routes US-460 and US-11, was beautiful. It still is. And trains – long, black, coal-filled trains – were a frequent sight.

LIKE CREWE EARLIER ON MY JOURNEY and Bluefield to come, Roanoke was built by and for the Norfolk & Western. Nearby Salem was the first city in the Roanoke Valley, a broad plain surrounded by the Blue Ridge Mountains to the southeast and the Alleghenies to the northwest. Salem was founded in 1802, near where Andrew Lewis built a stockade fort in 1754. The area had always been a transportation corridor, with migrations along the Great Road or the Wilderness Road, now followed by US-11 and Interstate 81.

Ten miles east of Salem a town called Big Lick was established in 1852 and chartered in 1874. Named for the outcropping of salt at the Roanoke River, it was a natural location for a confluence of railroads, with our route coming from the east, the continuation of the Virginia and Tennessee continuing southwesterly to Bristol, the Shenandoah Valley Railroad to the northeast stretching from Hagerstown, Maryland, and ultimately a spur of the N&W south to Durham and Winston-Salem, North Carolina.

When the Clark firm acquired the remnants of Billy Mahone's AM&O and formed the Norfolk & Western, they appointed Frederick Kimball to head it up. He quickly realized the strategic importance of the little village at Big Lick and made it a center of operations. Grateful citizens wanted to re-name their community "Kimball" after him, but he modestly declined, suggesting the name "Roanoke" instead, after the river running through it.

The upstart city of Roanoke, ultimately chartered in 1884, grew so quickly that it became nicknamed "Magic City," and there are still establishments in the city that use that moniker. It literally (actually figuratively, using the traditional definition of the word) exploded, blossoming from 669 souls to over 16,000 between 1880 and 1890 censuses. Roanoke reached 90,000 people around 1950 and has hovered between there and 100,000 since. When the Powhatan Arrow made its first run, Roanoke was the only city between the endpoints of Norfolk and Cincinnati with more than 50,000 people.

Roanoke was not only the headquarters for the Norfolk & Western from the days of Frederick Kimball until its merger with Norfolk Southern and their subsequent re-location to Norfolk, but it was also a major operations and manufacturing center. Unlike many railway companies, the N&W built most of its own rolling stock, much of it at the Roanoke Shops. The Roanoke Machine Works was founded in 1881 and two years later was acquired by the N&W. The Roanoke Shops would grow to become the Roanoke Valley's major employer and would ultimately employ over 6,000 people working on four locomotives and

20 freight cars simultaneously.

The Roanoke Shops had a worldwide reputation for engineering and quality excellence, consistently upgrading technology and engineering expertise. In addition to our favorite Class J locomotives, it built the articulated Y5 and Y6 engines as well as the Class A, all for freight service. From 1927 until 1952, it built every locomotive the N&W used. At various times, the shop included a machine shop, foundry, carpentry, upholstery, and warehouse, providing new fabrication and repair services for the railroad.

ROANOKE WAS ALSO A STOP on the Virginian Railway, an N&W competitor from its inception in 1909 until they merged in 1959. The Virginian has its own history and avid following. I've mentioned it in passing, but here's its story.

William N. Page, an entrepreneur and civil engineer, built a small logging railroad in Fayette County, West Virginia, in 1896. He called it the Deepwater Railway. This landlocked railway needed concessions from either the Norfolk & Western or the Chesapeake & Ohio to transport its cargo to the sea. Those two railroads, which later he learned were colluding against him, refused to provide Page with acceptable rates to the coastal ports. So Page formed a partnership with Henry Huddleston Rogers, one of the world's richest industrialists who had extensive resource holdings in the West Virginia coalfields, and did what all good entrepreneurs did: they built their own! Together, they acquired, in some cases secretly, a right-of-way to Norfolk. Construction of a new railroad they named the Virginian Railway began around 1906.

The Norfolk & Western was comprised of several earlier railroads, some pre-dating the Civil War and the development of any of the coalfields. Those railroads moved commodities and people from town to town. Once the coalfields were opened up, N&W principally shifted to moving mostly coal and to a lesser extent other commodities, and of course for a while passengers. The Virginian was designed with a different focus, specifically to move coal from the mines to the markets.

With that singular focus, Page and Rogers purposefully avoided cities and towns, staying in more rural areas, principally to the south but parallel to the N&W. Roanoke was also a major Virginian Railway city, but primarily because it was a pinch-point channeling from the Piedmont into the mountains. The Virginian was able to use a more convenient entry point into the Roanoke Valley, the river course of the Roanoke River, avoiding the N&W's climb over Blue Ridge. Downtown

Roanoke's elevation is 930 feet, some 370 feet below the N&W's high point thus far at Blue Ridge. The Virginian bypassed downtown Lynchburg's rugged topography entirely.

From Roanoke to the West Virginia line at Glen Lyn, the Virginian and N&W tracks were never more than five miles apart. Interestingly, there is a long tunnel between Blacksburg and Christiansburg in Montgomery County crossing from the Eastern drainage of the Roanoke River to the western drainage of the New River, boring under today's current US-460 highway and bypass, generally unseen and unknown to most area residents.

The N&W tracks cross from the eastern to western side of the north-flowing New River just downstream of Radford, remaining on the west side to the West Virginia border. The Virginian tracks were on the east side of the river through the same gorge, crossing farther north near the border. Eventually the Virginian stretched 438 miles.

The N&W always enjoyed an outstanding reputation for quality, dependability, and profitability, but for much of the Virginian's existence, it was even better. Because it was more modern in design and construction, it had a straighter, more level track, and newer and more efficient locomotives. For a time it was called, "The Richest Little Railroad in the World." Almost exactly a half-century after its birth, the N&W in 1959 acquired its fierce competitor in a hostile take-over, incorporating its tracks and rolling stock. At that point N&W owned both sets of rails from Roanoke west. From my state map, it appears that much of the Virginian's line east of Brookneal (southeast of Lynchburg) to Norfolk has been abandoned.

In spite of the Virginian's almost singular focus on moving coal, it did offer limited passenger service from Roanoke to Charleston, West Virginia. Roanoke's circa 1909 Virginian Railway passenger terminal saw its last passengers in January, 1956, and suffered a fire in January, 2001, that nearly destroyed it. Renovation by the Roanoke Chapter of the National Railway Historical Society is underway and plans are to re-open it for a combination of public and private uses. It is historically significant, listed on the Virginia Landmarks Register and the National Register of Historic Places.

ROANOKE IS NOW A SMALL but cosmopolitan city. It has a pleasant, compact downtown with several skyscrapers, topped by the copper-topped, 320 foot Wells Fargo Tower. Roanoke's demographic composition is around 70 percent white, 25 percent black, and the rest a smattering of races from throughout the world.

Roanoke has a distinct visual landmark that has dominated the skyline since its construction in 1949, the five-pointed Roanoke Star (or Mill Mountain Star), the world's largest freestanding man-made star. It stands 1,000 vertical feet higher than downtown. Roanoke picked up a second nickname, "Star City of the South," then. It was funded by the Roanoke Merchant's Association as a way to inaugurate that year's Christmas shopping season. It was originally illuminated in all-white neon, but later would change to red for a day to indicate a traffic fatality. In 1976 as part of the bicentennial celebration, it was colored red, white, and blue, and was re-colored that way from September 2001 until 2007 to memorialize the attacks on 9/11. It is for Roanokers a beloved signature of their city and a welcome banner when they return home from their travels.

Roanoke's last N&W passenger station opened for service on April Fools Day in 1949, after a complete rebuild of the 1905 depot. It operated until all passenger service was terminated in 1971. It had an elevated concourse over the tracks with stairs leading down to the platforms between the rails. The concourse was demolished when passenger service ended.

At that point, N&W converted it into office spaces for its own employees. In 1992, NS donated the building to the Foundation for Downtown Roanoke. After renovation it was re-opened to the public in 2004, housing the O. Winston Link Museum and the Roanoke Valley Convention and Visitors Bureau.

Outside the station is the choke-point for rail traffic in all compass directions. A mile west of the old passenger terminal is the sorting yard where trains are broken up and then re-constituted for their various destinations. For 3 to 4 miles, NS operates a vast industrial complex where there are as many as 30 parallel rails used to provide for sorting operations. In railroad parlance, this is a "classification" yard.

I NEVER MET WINSTON LINK, but he's one of my heroes.

Ogle Winston Link, who drew an owl as part of his signature, was a visionary. Born in New York in 1914, Link recognized that steam locomotives, and particularly those of the Norfolk & Western Railway down in Virginia, were destined for the dust-bin of history, and he made it his personal quest to chronicle the decline. A half-century before I began my project, he embarked on his great work of preserving the legacy of this same region and its economy, lifestyle, and culture.

Link's younger brother called him, "smart, funny, and obsessive," and I'd love to have those words included in my obituary as well someday. Link earned an engineering degree from the Polytechnic Institute of Brooklyn. He was popular, being elected president of his class all four years. But his career path soon took him into photography, where his keen eye, his obsession for detail and quality, and his indefatigable nature soon put him in demand for commercial work.

War intervened on Link's occupation and pursuit of interests, as he was called to duty in 1942, to work at the Airborne Instruments Laboratory at Columbia University, helping his country find ways to use photography to find undersea submarines. At that time, he married a beautiful model, Marteal Oglesby. With steam trains whistling by his lab, he dreamed of ways to make better photographs than had been done prior, especially with the use of multiple flashbulbs for nighttime shots.

Once the war ended, Link pursued his own business as an independent freelance photographer, working for Texaco, Alcoa, Goodrich, and other corporate clients. Sadly, his singular obsession with his work doomed his marriage, and he was divorced by 1948. He should have stayed that way, it turned out.

On a work-related trip to Staunton, Virginia, in 1955, he stumbled upon the opening to the serious hobby that would consume the rest of his life. While photographing air conditioning units being manufactured for Westinghouse, he learned that the Norfolk & Western line in nearby Waynesboro presented an opportunity to photograph moving trains at night.

O. Winston Link Museum

Surreptitiously making several shots, he sent an apology to N&W management, confessing to his transgression but at the same time asking if they might allow him access on their property for future shots.

Link had the good fortune to find his letter in the hands of Robert Hall "Racehorse" Smith, president of the N&W from 1946 until 1958, who was an avid fan of steam locomotives. It is widely credited to Smith that the N&W ran steam locomotives as long as it did, although much of the justification was the extensive holdings of coal resources owned by the company. Smith gave his enthusiastic approval to Link to photograph and audio-record his pride-and-joy locomotives, although he granted Link no financial support.

Undaunted, Link began a five year project driving his 1952 Buick convertible towing a trailer with his photographic equipment on twenty trips from New York to Norfolk, Cincinnati, Hagerstown, Durham, and many places in between, chronicling the end of an era. Link is N&W's most notable "chaser."

There are a number of distinguishing characteristics of Link's work that makes it so iconic even today. Most of his shots were taken at night. Using black-and-white film, Link's images were stark and had high contrast and detail. Always the perfectionist, Link discovered that he obtained the best control over his subjects with artificial light, which he oversaw. Illustrative of his technical prowess, he was able to over-come the substantial technical challenges of firing dozens of one-shot flashbulbs while synchronizing the fast shutter openings he needed for freezing a rapidly moving train.

He came to realize that in addition to capturing the demise of steam, he was self-tasked with the quest of chronicling a rapidly van-ishing way of life. The largely Appalachian reach of the N&W took him into communities that were isolated from the rest of the country. Many of his shots include rural Virginians and West Virginians at work, at play, and at rest on front porches, at outdoor drive-in movie theaters, in living rooms and in country stores, while massive steam locomotives plied the rails in the background.

It is estimated that Link spent $150,000 or more of his own money in today's dollars. It seems almost incomprehensible today that the wit-ty, fast-talking New Yorker, making multiple forays into the Virginias, would be warmly accepted at many dinner tables and spare bedrooms by total strangers for the valuable work he was doing.

Link, typically working with only one assistant, arrived on scenes he wanted to capture, and spent hours lining up individual shots. Cam-eras were positioned. Flash bulb trees were placed. Cabling was strung. He benefited from excellent coordination from Racehorse Smith, who made sure his engineers had the locomotives at the right place and the right time. Link was also given access to multiple N&W facilities, roundhouses, stations, and shops. The work was mentally and physi-cally demanding, once involving crossing a river on a rope line to posi-tion his gear. It was not beyond him to light up an entire city block for a mere instant to take one photograph.

Link's scenes were both seemingly ancient and eternal. The scenes ranged from an old gravity-fed gas pump and a pot-bellied stove in a country store to cows led from a silo near Shawsville just as farmers do it today.

Tragically, while Link's Golden Years should have been his happiest, instead they were his most vexing. He made the worst decision in his life when in 1984 he married a real estate agent named Conchita Mendoza. He was 70 years old and she was 50. From that point on, in a story suitable for any soap opera, she inflicted upon him a series of unspeakable crimes, including but surely not limited to stealing $257,000 by forging his signature, liquidating his coin and stamp collections and other collectible gifts, and selling 2,400 of his photographs and profiting from them herself.

Conchita was a diabolical con artist. By 1993, she was indicted on criminal larceny and then convicted and imprisoned. After serving four-and-a-half years, she was released. Soon thereafter, she was convicted and imprisoned again.

Link died in 2001 at age 87. In 2004, the O. Winston Link Museum opened in the restored N&W passenger terminal just north of downtown Roanoke where the westbound Powhatan Arrow departed each day at 12:15 p.m.

The building is significant itself, as it was designed by one of the world's pre-eminent industrial designers, Raymond Loewy. The Link Museum has an exhibit dedicated to Loewy as well, although his noteworthiness seems to have paled by comparison with Link's. But let's give Loewy some love; if Frank Lloyd Wright is modern architecture's greatest domestic legend, Loewy is equally celebrated, or should be, for his legendary modern industrial designs. Loewy designed logos for Esso, Shell, BP, Nabisco, Lucky Strike cigarettes, Studebakers, Coca-Cola, and innumerable other products, as well as railroad stations from Roanoke to Pennsylvania. Chances are good there is a product in your house today whose packaging was designed by Raymond Loewy.

Bill Arnold for two decades has been an O. Winston Link Museum volunteer and was a personal friend of Link's. Originally from Radford, Bill worked in marketing for General Electric at the Salem facility. I had known Bill for several years. We sat together to discuss Link, the museum, and Bill's relationship with him.

Arnold said, "I have always been interested in trains." Bill was in his mid-eighties. He was a trim man with a kindly voice and lots of white hair. His wife of over 60 years, Ellen, did some paperwork in the next room while we spoke.

"My dad worked for the N&W at the Radford shop (46 miles to the west of Roanoke). I lived in a company house for seven years, in what we called 'back-track,' the other side of the tracks (from downtown). There were seven company houses including the superintendent's. I always loved trains.

"In the 1980s, my wife and I rode an excursion train to and from Norfolk and we decided we wanted to become involved in railroad preservation. We worked at the gift shop in the Virginia Transportation Museum in Roanoke's Wasena Park before it was flooded out there (in 1985) and it moved into the current building. Ellen did more volunteering than I did because I still had my day job. I became national director of the Roanoke Chapter of the National Railway Historical Society. I did that for several years.

"During our time at the museum, Winston Link would come into town to hawk his posters, books, and vinyl recordings. We handled the purchase and sale in the store of his things. Ellen used to say she played Winston's mother while assisting him with his poster and book signings, even though she was 15 years younger. Winston would come into town and invite me to lunch. He had a terrific memory about the places and subjects in his photos.

"He was divorced at that point. His relationship with Conchita was later. I knew her. She was charming and she realized the value of his work."

I had read the book *O. Winston Link, the Man and the Museum* to better know Link. I said, "Link was smart, active. He was charming. Was he modest? Did he envision an entire museum around his stuff?"

Bill replied, "Link said at least initially he took those shots motivated by preservation. He didn't think anybody wanted to see all those photos of black, smoky things. He wanted to preserve the steam locomotive, the people who worked on it, and the people who lived along the line. At some point, in his mind, his work transitioned from preservation to art. His friends began to understand the artistic value of what he had. He sold six prints to a museum in New York and that was the beginning of his understanding that people saw what he did as art.

"He was still a commercial photographer and had many loyal commercial customers. He was very successful, allowing him to do his work here.

"He told me that other cities wanted to do a museum of his stuff. He said, 'Those S.O.B.s aren't going to get it.' He wanted it in Roanoke and specifically in this building. It was his idea! It wasn't the city of Roanoke's idea. The knowledge of what he had and what he could do here was accepted (by the city government). A pitch was made to several influential individuals who got the ball rolling."

The building required extensive renovation to make it appear more like when it was a passenger station.

"Winston wanted the 1218 (locomotive) right outside, on a turntable. But the railroad wouldn't let that happen because there is a lot of ongoing (freight) service. People can still see lots of train activity. Winston always enjoyed a good relationship with N&W leadership. They appreciated what he did.

"I want people to understand the artistic value of what he was doing and the results that came from that. He was a true artist. He was a confident man, and he knew his work was great."

I added, "He had the vision, the motivation, and the skill. You can't accomplish what he did without all three."

Bill agreed. "He had some competitors who were doing the same thing, but they didn't have the engineering knowledge. He knew how to set up the camera and the bulbs. He knew when to push the button to open the shutter and fire the flashbulbs. Due to the technology at the time, at each location he only got one shot. And then he didn't know what he got until days later after the film was developed in the darkroom.

"He told me, 'Everybody, everywhere I go, wanted to help me.' He was a fast-talking New Yorker with a strong accent. And even though they never met him and never heard of him, they'd let him in. "The Link Museum opened in January 2004. Link was already known worldwide from his many exhibits. People still come from overseas to see this museum.

"Visitors say he's an artist; he'd love to hear that. He said once about Ansel Adams, 'What he photographs has been there a million years. It will still be there a million years from now. It doesn't move.' Link's subjects moved. He was cantankerous with a smile. He'd say, 'I told you it would be great!' He was confident with what he did. He was a character and a practical joker. If he was here right now, he'd say, 'Let's cut this out. I've talked enough.'"

So we did!

With Bill as my tour guide, we walked through the spacious lobby with its fabulous scale models of iconic trains including the 611 and its view of the tracks outside and then downstairs to the exhibits.

Everybody seems to have a favorite Link photograph. I have two. One is a daytime scene from Green Cove, Virginia on the spur long known as the Virginia Creeper that once plied the mountainous route from Abingdon to West Jefferson, North Carolina. On the right is the tiny, one-room station with the words "GREEN COVE" atop the door and in front of it a gaggle of people awaiting the arrival of a train, pictured head-on on the left, chugging uphill towards them. In the foreground is a white horse, tethered to a skid carrying small logs, with his head bowed, as if in reverence to the approaching iron horse looming. Today the Creeper's path has been converted into a rail-trail, my favorite!

The other is a scene from a drive-in theater in Iaeger, West Virginia, farther down my route. In the foreground, it showed a young couple in a convertible, snuggling towards the driver's side, heads together. On the back right was a massive steam locomotive whistling past, its stack pouring white smoke into the night sky. On the back left was a movie screen, ironically displaying a jet airplane.

My trip harkened one of my most indelible childhood memories. In 1963, my 3rd grade teacher, Mrs. Bane, took her entire class on a field trip to Roanoke by train. I don't recall whether it was the Powhatan Arrow – I suspect not given the time of day. But I remember the station with its overhanging walkways and stairs down to the tracks, now removed due to the discontinuation of passenger service in Roanoke.

BEFORE I LEFT THE LINK, my long-time friend Anne Piedmont who has lived in Roanoke for much of her life came by to visit with me and share some observations about her experience in the Magic City. We sat in the museum's lobby on one of those long, wooden, back-to-back benches that were so common in railroad stations in the past. Her dad worked during the latter part of his career for Norfolk & Western and then Norfolk Southern.

"So I have some railroad in me," she said, proudly. "We used to come to this building when my grandparents would take the train here to visit from Norfolk. I have a lot of history with, and I love, this building. I love that it's been preserved like this."

Anne was a business consultant, doing mostly quantitative research. So she knows the numbers. I asked how Roanoke had changed since the last running of the Powhatan Arrow.

She said, "We moved to New Jersey and moved back to Roanoke in 1979, so I was away when it ended. Roanoke has grown and changed in many positive ways. I was born in Roanoke Memorial Hospital. I lived in Aruba, New Jersey, North Carolina, Ohio, and in Danville. Now I am back in Roanoke and I can see the hospital out my living room window. Talk about going full circle!

"That's a draw for me. It feels familiar and safe. I walk to the same locally-owned grocery store I walked to as a child. It has been there since the 1930s. The old drug store now houses one of Roanoke's best restaurants. The 7-11 is still there as is the post office.

"The railroad is not the dominant employer it once was. It is sad, but it has not been a death knell for Roanoke the way the departure of other major employers has been for their cities.

"Health care has a future. We can't outsource it. I think the (medical) research aspect is very exciting. In its own way, Roanoke has always been an innovative city. There will be some great biomedical innovations that will come out of here. I think it's happening now.

"I love that we're turning our (marketing) attention to our natural beauty around us. We are drawing new corporations here, including the announcement of a new craft brewery opening up nearby. We have a healthy overall mix of tourism, education, research, retail, distribution, and manufacturing.

"We've always been a transportation hub. Even before the railroad, it was on the Great Wagon Road and before that on Native American hunting paths and before that on animal migration routes. There is no coincidence the railroad came here. This is what attracts companies here now; two-thirds of the population of the United States is within a day's drive.

"In the 1950s, this was the center of the regional universe when rail was king. If not for the Norfolk & Western, we'd still be Big Lick and Salem would be the commercial and population center of the valley.

"There is sustainability in diversity. I worked in Danville during the early to mid 1980s. This is when Dan River Mills had three shifts. It was busy; lots of traffic. In retrospect, if someone did an autopsy on a body and could see Stage 4 cancer, anybody could see that Danville's devotion to a single industry was sewing the seeds of its death already. They failed to realize it at the time and didn't have a back-up.

"I ended up being a numbers person. For 20 years I worked for the Roanoke Regional Partnership doing economic research and marketing. I like to think the numbers and words work with each other."

I asked Anne about her specific experience to communities facing similar challenges.

She said, "Start looking now. If you didn't start looking 20 years ago, you should have started 10 years ago. If you didn't start 10 years ago, start now. Get over 'it's all we've ever had.' Stop looking back and start looking forward.

"Roanoke learned only in recent terms that natural beauty is an economic driver." She talked about industrial cities that put their plants by the river, fencing them off from recreation. Cities like Pittsburgh and Detroit are now seeing their riverfronts being used for leisure activities. "I'm sure they ask themselves, 'Why didn't we think of this before?'"

WE PARTED WITH A HUG and I walked westward past the magnificent Tudorbethan style Hotel Roanoke. It was built by the new Norfolk & Western Railway in 1882 originally to house administrative workers to the new offices in the city. In 1989, Norfolk Southern deeded the Hotel to nearby Virginia Tech for $65,000, which closed it and liquidated its contents on a sale that lasted 17 days. By 1992, Tech decided to re-open it and mounted a campaign to do so. It reopened in 1995, and now operates it with an adjacent conference center. The rejuvenation and reopening of the Hotel Roanoke is considered one of the most important moments in the city's modern incarnation.

I TURNED SOUTH and walked over a lovely, glass and steel pedestrian bridge crossing the railroad tracks towards downtown Roanoke. The bridge was tastefully and helpfully equipped with a series of interpretive signs that told the Roanoke story much as I have done for you already. (Note: they misspelled "Raymond Loewy" as "Raymond Lowey." Somebody needs to fix this.) From there I saw the three sets of tracks diverging to the northeast, east, and south that Anne had mentioned. I also saw the new Taubman Museum of Art, a wildly futuristic building in flowing metal opened to considerable controversy, in 2008. Farther to the east, there was a sign for the Roanoke Shops.

Once steam locomotives were phased out, the locomotive fabrication ended. The N&W always sourced its diesel-electric locomotives from other vendors, although repairs and maintenance are done at the shops. The former car shop is now owned by a separate company, Freight Car America, that specializes in aluminum hopper cars, sold to the NS and customers throughout the world. Aluminum has replaced steel for hoppers, given its better corrosion resistance and lighter weight.

One of the great old stories about the Roanoke Shops is the famous whistle named "Old Gabriel," that blew several times per day to signify the beginning and ending of shifts. It was so loud that its voice could carry across the entire city. Copies were made and installed in various cities across the country, including one at Salt Lake City. Old Gabriel continues its unmistakable howl to this day.

I continued my walk across the bridge and then across Campbell Avenue into Roanoke's charming City Market. Popularly known as the Farmer's Market, it began in 1882, and is thought to be Virginia's oldest continuously operating open air market. Vendors, originally called "hucksters," were selling bright flowers, fruits, and vegetables. Very nice!

IT IS A STATEMENT OF CHANGING PRIORITIES that Roanoke is a city at all, much less the largest in Virginia west of Richmond. The plain upon which I was walking was found inferior to early settlers. There were scant habitations in the immediate area that is now downtown Roanoke even into the late 1870s, while nearby Salem was incorporated in 1802 and Christiansburg even earlier in 1792.

From prehistoric times, it was a gathering place for wildlife, large numbers of deer, buffalo, elk, and other mammals. So it was frequented by Native Americans who came to hunt. There is no record of any permanent settlement, but because of the travel corridor it provided, there was a constant exchange of people, providing social and economic cooperation and trade.

Prior to the time the nascent Norfolk & Western Railway chose to locate their headquarters there, the area that would become downtown Roanoke was a huge, salt-laden marsh. Trout Run, which now passes almost directly under Campbell Avenue, fed the swamp before it joined Lick Run. Both watercourses are now buried under pavement and brick. But in earlier times, when they would dry under hot summer weather, their banks would be encrusted white with salt. It was a better place to pass by than to settle.

The Europeans arrived around 1730, and seeing no permanent Native American settlement, instantly claimed the area as their own, naming it Long Lick. Because the Natives used the area for hunting and trade, the newcomers presented an obstacle that festered occasional violence. Transportation became increasingly important for the European settlers, as movement from the north, down from Philadelphia and the Shenandoah Valley, up from North Carolina, and east-west following the general path of the Powhatan Arrow, intersected there.

The salt deposits were not commercially viable, but wildlife was plentiful, so plentiful that in short order the area had been over-hunted. Meanwhile, the fickle nature of running water would wreak havoc on the emerging community. As early as 1749, a fatal flood swept through, killing four and destroying several homes. Additionally, the fetid nature of the swamp gave rise to multiple epidemics of diseases, illnesses cumulatively called "Big Lick Fever." Malaria and typhoid fever flourished.

Undeterred, plucky settlers stayed in the valley until the arrival of the N&W, at which point the swamps were drained and the streams were channeled into pipes underground. Campbell and Salem Avenues, the town's new main streets, were built over the marsh itself. During the year of the city's founding in 1882, a virulent epidemic of Big Lick

Fever swept through, prompting the city fathers to undergo an infra-structure development project to install fresh water and sewer pipes and treatment plants, along with hydrants and water fountains.

With modern city engineering, these obstacles no longer seem im-portant enough to discourage the emergence of a great city. But Trout Run is still under the downtown Roanoke. Occasionally during heavy rainfall events, it rears its head above the network of downtown streets, causing flooding into stores and shops and rendering the streets im-passible to vehicles and pedestrians. On a warming planet, storms are increasing in intensity and severity, so this flooding is likely to worsen. Nature bats last.

NOT A MILE AWAY to the west from the Link Museum sits the Virginia Museum of Transportation. Outside the museum is a 50 foot rocket, positioned upright for take-off.

The museum was founded in 1963 in Wasena Park. That museum was destroyed in 1985 during Roanoke's most devastating flood in modern history. It is now housed in a 1918 vintage N&W freight sta-tion that was donated to it. Initially, the Transportation Museum was called the Roanoke Transportation Museum. It was formed as a part-nership of the Norfolk & Western and the City of Roanoke. N&W had abandoned the freight station in 1964, and it became the perfect place for the re-located museum.

In 1976, the City helped form a non-profit corporation to operate it and in 1983, its name was changed to the Virginia Museum of Trans-portation. Today it is the official transportation museum of the Com-monwealth of Virginia.

The current facility has a large visitor parking lot, a 45,000 square foot building, and a 20,000 square foot covered pavilion where the most treasured locomotives are stored away from rainfall and snow. Indeed, while many forms of transportation are represented (although, I might add, notably not motorcycles), given Roanoke's rail heritage, the primary focus is on trains. Adding to the authenticity is the close proximity to NS's active rail lines; traffic outside on the rails is almost constant.

The museum boasts 2,500 objects with over 50 of them on rails: locomotives and rail cars. The spaciousness and 100 year old ambiance lends an authenticity and a relaxed atmosphere that is often absent from more contemporary venues.

I WALKED INTO THE SMALL LOBBY, paid my admission fee, and

entered the museum proper. I made a beeline for the outside exhibits, the trains.

And then, like a scene from a romance novel, there she was, basking in her historic and fabulous magnificence. Right before me, there was the 611, gleaming in glossy black, with her signature Tuscan red and burnt yellow horizontal stripe! Breathtaking!

I descended from the landing and walked around her, admiringly.

She shared a canopy with N&W's A-class 1218, the two representing the museum's most prized possessions. Both are the sole surviving specimens of their classes. Both locomotives were originally gifted to the City of Roanoke, but on the museum's 50th birthday in 2012, were officially given to the museum. The museum also currently houses the N&W's Y6A-class 2156. It is on loan until 2020 from the Museum of Transportation in St. Louis.

The 611 is sleeker, more rounded and feminine, compared with the busy, pipe-infused, industrial feel of the 1218 and 2156. The 611's nose is semi-spherical and pleasing. There is no discernable smokestack, just a flowing cowling, like the hair of a debonair aristocrat. Her front held a single, centrally mounted headlight, framed below with a polished silver horizontal handrail, appearing almost as if a face's smile. Below was a graceful prow, as polished and fine as the bow of a seagoing ship. The streamliner 611 is the graceful swan to the 1218 and 2156 ugly ducklings.

611 locomotive linkages

The 611's wheels are massive, in what rail fans call a 4-8-4 configuration, meaning 2 smaller wheels in the front, 4 larger driver wheels in the middle, and two smaller wheels in the back on each side. The drivers are 70 inches in diameter, almost 6 feet, gloss black, and linked together by massive unpainted "light weight" nickel alloy steel connecting rods.

Alongside the boiler was a walkway, painted on the outside in Tuscan red, and framed with another silver handrail above, to allow technicians to service the upper region of the boiler. The numbers "611" were painted in yellow inside the red stripe. Towards the back was the cab, where the engineer had a small window to the world ahead and a larger one to the side. And behind her was her tender, continuing the gloss black and Tuscan red motif and the words "NORFOLK AND WESTERN" painted boldly on her stripe.

These three iconic and monstrous engines make an indelible impression on visitors.

STANDING NEARBY I MET CHERI GEORGE, the queen of the steam excursion program. Nobody has been more influential or has worked harder in the "Fire Up 611!" program that began in 2014 to bring the iconic 611 back to life and resuscitate the Virginia Museum of Transportation's excursion program than Cheri. She was at the museum working with Scott Lindsay, the Chief Mechanical Officer who oversaw the mechanical aspects of the locomotive and is with it every mile it travels. She invited me into the cab of the 611, up its steep ladder rungs, where she sat in the fireman's seat and me in the engineer's seat, while Scott and his crew overhauled one of the steam pistons. I told her about my book and asked her about her interest.

"I fell in love with (steam locomotives) as a kid," she said. "When the steam engines came to town as part of the Southern Steam program, my brother would take me to see them. It was a public relations tool that the Southern Railway used. Back in the 1960s, the president of the Southern Railway contacted the Tennessee Valley Railroad Museum and asked if they could borrow a steam locomotive in order to go to specific cities with excursions to spread good will for the company. It was a smashing success! They operated for several years and expanded the cities they visited."

Cheri told me that aficionados such as she knew intimately the names, or in this case, the numbers, of all the remaining steam locomotives in the eastern United States. She said the Southern obtained for their excursions the 722, the 630, the 750, and 4501.

"Every year one of these engines came to town, I wanted to go see it. In the 1980s, the 611 was pulled out of the museum to be the N&W's representation of the program.

"The 611 is an iconic symbol, with grace, beauty, power, and speed." She said freight locomotives were more industrial in look and less ornate. "The 611 was purpose-built locomotive for the topography and schedule on which it needed to run.

"Businesses spend an enormous amount to get the public's attention. You will never get a bigger attention-getter than one of these engines steaming into town. It's not something you see every day; people stop in their tracks. That's what happened to me."

I asked her if she remembered seeing the 611 for the first time.

"I saw it in (Roanoke's) Wasena Park. It took a lot of imagination to think about what it would look like moving. When the 611 was restored for the program back in the 80s, it was such a beautiful thing to see going up the rails. It's beautiful to see static, sitting in a museum, but nothing like seeing it in motion. It left a tattoo in my heart! The 611 was steam on a different scale, comparing a prop airplane to a jetliner. It was modern steam. Large steam. Beautiful steam."

She told me that the earlier excursion program had both paid and volunteer help, managed by Norfolk Southern. "NS had five paid employees who'd travel with it: an engineer, a relief engineer, a fireman, a relief fireman, and a night watchman. They would occasionally allow a friend or family member to ride, help out, or wash. The 611 and the 1218 next to you," she pointed out the window behind me, "participated in that program.

"For four or five years I told the regular crew that they weren't cleaning it well; they were leaving (dirty) spots. This is a difficult engine to clean. It's not like washing a car.

"I chased the 611; I was there almost any time it was in Virginia. Lots of rail-fans chase. The crews see the same people over and over in the same cities. Richmond. Roanoke. Bluefield. Danville. The 1218 came to Richmond. I volunteered to help wash. Two of the regular crew agreed to sponsor me. I washed 1218 from coupler to coupler. I showed some aptitude. I did what I was told. I didn't talk too much 'rail-fan talk'. So they invited me to ride and fire a little bit. I'm not sure they envisioned it to go as far as it did. So I sat in the fireman's seat, and I began to learn to fire.

"It's not a skill that you learn by reading, and it is not something you learn in an hour. It's something you learn over time as you continue to do it. It's a balancing act. I knew the theories of combustion, and I studied how the engine worked. When I started firing, I made some mistakes. The person I was apprenticing under corrected my mistakes and told me what I did wrong. The next time there was a problem, I knew how to fix it. If you repetitively can't recover, then you're assumed to not have enough aptitude, and they won't let you stay in the seat.

"I graduated from college the same year the 611 was retired. All along, it was always a goal of mine to do whatever it took to get the 611 back on the rails again. Many of us never truly believed the engine would never run again. When the engine was prepared for display at the museum, it was well preserved, in position to be refurbished for use. When the opportunity arose again, it would be in the best shape possible. It was operational when it came back to the museum.

"For three decades, I've been intimately familiar with this machine. My degree was in public relations, and I hoped to parlay my education into something associated with this. But the timing was wrong and it didn't work out. Until now. It has come back around now in a big way.

"About five years ago, I asked Scott Lindsay what it would take to get her rolling again. Scott is a steam locomotive mechanical restoration contractor; he does this for a living. He estimated a half-million dollars. It was nothing!

"At that time, NS didn't embrace a steam excursion program. Putting a passenger train on the rails is disruptive to their normal freight operations. They still have a company to run. It requires a commitment from higher management. In the excursion program, they're inviting the general public into what is essentially an industrial operation. It's expensive. There can be liability. Nobody wants an injury."

She explained that in the next year, Norfolk Southern launched a program they called 21st Century Steam, featuring excursions along their rails throughout the East. It was a corporate-backed, employee reward program. It was the brainchild of the CEO, Wick Moorman. NS's program involved hiring contractors to run excursion trains on contract on a paid basis. They hired the Tennessee Valley Railroad Museum to bring a locomotive, the 4501, and their staff, to run it. They sold extra tickets to the general public. It was a money-maker for the museum, and it was popular.

"Not long after that, the Fort Wayne Railroad Historical Society came to participate with its own Nickel Plate locomotive, the 765. So they had two locomotives operating. Meanwhile, the 611 still sat immobilized in Roanoke. Its fan base, which had remained huge and vocal, wanted to see it run again. Wick Moorman attended a meeting in Chattanooga and was asked if the 611 could participate.

"There are only a handful of operational or close to operational locomotives. And of those, there are only three or four iconic locomotives around the country that are synonymous with their areas. You've got the Union Pacific 3985 and Union Pacific 844, both housed in Cheyenne, Wyoming. You've got the Southern Pacific 4449 in Portland, Oregon. And you've got Roanoke's own 611, right here under us. There are several others running at captive locations like the Cass Scenic Railroad in West Virginia and the Tweetsie in North Carolina. There are a couple of others, but only a handful that are truly famous.

"Mr. Moorman's response was that if there was an organized group to refurbish and operate the locomotive, he would be receptive. This museum has room for a static display, but not operational space or expertise. Preston Claytor and I are friends, and we learned that both of us were independently working on this. I had put together a business plan and Preston had his. A week before Christmas, 2012, I presented mine to Bev Fitzpatrick (who is the director of the Virginia Museum of Transportation (VMT)). Preston had done the same a week earlier. We finally got together and refined a cooperative plan. Mr. Moorman came here to the museum, and we presented it to him. He said if we raised the money and put together a viable business plan, he would allow us to participate in the 21st Century Steam program. It was full throttle after that!"

Preston Claytor is the son of Bob Claytor and is Jane Claytor Webster's younger brother.

"We knew the tremendous interest and support we'd get. There were some leaks to the public, and we finally decided to release a message. We adopted the name, 'Fire Up 611!' and the checks started flowing in. We received anywhere from $6.11 from kids to checks in the thousands; we received some checks for over $100,000! We got lots of media and fan attention.

"The 611 was towed to the shop in Spencer, North Carolina (where) disassembly and refurbishing got underway. The boiler remained on the frame, but almost everything else was disassembled and overhauled.

"Scott provided the expertise and he oversaw the work. Volunteers came from all over the country. Most did not have steam locomotive experience, but they loved the 611 and wanted to help. Interested volunteers applied online, and we selected the skills we needed. We invited them to Spencer and delivered safety training and background checks."

She went on and on with the incredible orchestration of getting the enormous project completed in under a year. Then the long-mothballed Norfolk & Western Class J 611 steamed back triumphantly to Roanoke amid a corridor of thousands of admiring, elated fans.

"I tracked over 10,000 volunteer hours. I spent over 3,000 hours myself. I sold my house in Atlanta and moved to an apartment in Spencer. I fired the 611 from Lynchburg to Roanoke when Mr. Moorman was on board. (In the earlier program) I fired for Preston's dad as well. So I've fired for two Norfolk Southern chairmen.

"I always thought I was the 611's biggest fan. But I came to realize that there are thousands of people who love this engine so much! Old men. Kids who weren't born the last time it ran. I met an old man who had worked at the East End Shops during original construction. He has tremendous pride for it.

"The story you're looking for isn't about me. It's not about a single person. This locomotive we're sitting on was designed and built by men from Roanoke before I was born. This is their story, their achievement.

"This machine and the 1218 behind you might be the best things this region has ever done. It was the most powerful 4-8-4 constructed in the United States. It did its job, and it did it well. There is a lot here for the people who were associated with it, and for their families, to be proud of. The men who designed and built it have come and gone. I'm part of the next wave. The kids who see it now will become the adults who perpetuate it. I am well-known for my work, but it's not about me. It's about the continuum.

"Today's kids are so engrossed (with electronics) it's hard to get a cell phone or computer screen out of their faces. If this locomotive steaming towards them doesn't make an impression, nothing will. I see a lot of potential for the next generation."

I noticed my eyes had moistened.

"I go to see and ride excursions all over the country," she continued. "When we steamed back into Roanoke in May (2015), it was unlike anything I'd ever seen. We had people come from Europe. People came from the U.K. From Australia. It is a symbol of steam power around the world. I was blown away by the crowds. I couldn't believe it!"

SCOTT LINDSAY, THE CHIEF MECHANICAL OFFICER, entered the cab and joined our conversation. Cheri introduced us, telling me Scott was a decades-long friend. She took a break, and I asked Scott for his side of the 611 restoration story. He told me, "The 611 is far too good a machine to sit here as a backdrop at this museum.

"I grew up in southern New Jersey," he said with only a mild accent. "My dad got me interested in steam locomotives as a kid, taking me on excursions from my earliest memory. I turned my interest into a career and then a corporation. I've been doing steam locomotive restoration, maintenance, operation, training, and consulting since 1977, full-time. My company is called Steam Operations Corporation. My customers are museums, private owners, or anybody who owns a locomotive. They may hire me to repair an operating locomotive. Sometimes it's cosmetic restoration of a static locomotive in a park. Sometimes I do full, ground-up restorations back to operational, compliant condition.

"In 1982, Norfolk Southern hired me in Birmingham to refurbish the 611. I had been working on a Chesapeake and Ohio 4-8-4, a similar locomotive. My first day working on the 611 was January 25, 1982. It turned out to be a long-term job that eventually turned into my own company. In 1994 when the program was discontinued, I was a contractor out of a contract. I got other contacts around the country. I've done over 50 contracts.

"I like steam for lots of reasons. I like the historical aspect, the advancement in technology from the late 1800s to the 611 era, and then to the end of steam, to the death of the best. Through that period, the country got larger. The demand for power got larger, and the locomotives got larger and more powerful.

"Steam is labor intensive, and requires lots of specialized craftspeople. Boilermakers. Pipe-fitters. Welders. That was true in both the manufacturing and the maintenance and operational sides. The total team package required many skills. When a steam locomotive came in for service, it was very labor- and time-intensive. Diesel is more plug-and-play. You do component change-out, which is fast and easy. Even when all the Class J locomotives were operational, they all had some different parts; you couldn't do one-for-one exchange.

"When one locomotive would be exchanged with another and would come into the shop, it would dump its ash, take on water, coal, sand, and lubrication, and have any mechanical repairs done. The A-class, Class J, and Y-class were noted for their 90-minute turn-around. This was amazing! Older engines with (higher maintenance requirements) took much longer to prepare for the next trip.

"Norfolk & Western had an edge over the other railways in designing, building, and maintaining their own locomotives. There is a huge library of drawings for these locomotives. A 1943 drawing may have been updated in 1945, 1948, 1949, '50, '52, and '57; they were constantly making subtle changes to make them better, either in quicker turn-around, longer life, or whatever their parameters were. They never relied on the status quo.

"What impresses me most about this machine is that it represents state-of-the-art in steam at the end of steam. The 611 represents the best of the best technology of the day. N&W got the best components and it represents the best of America when I think we were our best. After World War II, we were a designing, building, implementing, and doing country, not an information sharing, outsourcing country. We built things to last, things that could be rebuilt and rebuilt.

"This machine is 65 years old (in 2016). We are not building diesel locomotives today that will be running for 65 years. I'm one of a few people who have spent our working careers really focused on the 611 and on the 1218. The 611 is difficult (to maintain) due to the stream-lining. (Class J locomotives) were meant to run for a term of service with scheduled maintenance intervals, where they were torn down and rebuilt to run again. There was a class-based repair interval system, which was progressive. Some things were done every day. Some things were done weekly, monthly, and so on.

"We have a check-list after each run. When this locomotive moves, I'm on it. I have the overall responsibility for the locomotive. I'm the taskmaster. Safety is my number one responsibility, and I take that re-sponsibility seriously. We have a great team of 20-25 folks who helped with the restoration. I've pulled the best of the best from that group to form our road crew. The ultimate responsibility is mine.

"I have the type of personality that I'm never satisfied. If I need something done, even if a volunteer is to do it, they need to do it or get out. I'm an old-school guy. It's not about ego. We provide a service to bring a technology that is dead and unknown to 99.999 percent of the people to keep this country aware of where this country was and what it still could be. I'm legally responsible for this locomotive, and I don't want to wear an orange jumpsuit. If I lie on the (reporting) forms, I'm criminally responsible. It's not about ego or money; it's about responsi-bility. It can be fun, too. But the fun is in here," he tapped his chest.

"I've been doing this my whole life. Regardless of whether it's 3:00 a.m. or 3:00 p.m., when I drive steam locomotives through any town, there's always a crowd. The day we brought 611 back to Roanoke, the number of people we saw trackside between Spencer and Roanoke surpassed anything I'd ever seen anywhere. I heard guesstimates from 50,000 to 70,000. *Trains* magazine chased and they were live-streaming on the World Wide Web. People everywhere were watching the 611. This piece of machinery still has a worldwide appeal.

"Many of these people watching were younger people who had never seen a steam locomotive. They had no idea what they were going to see. It's loud! It's big! The wheels are monstrous. It's something they'll never forget."

I DESCENDED FROM THE CAB and wandered inside where I found Beverly Fitzpatrick, Jr., the executive director of the museum. I have known him for many years through my prior business connections.

Bev is a large, jovial man with an eager smile and a reassuring voice. He has one of those offices that is so cluttered with stuff that he can't even find a place to sign a piece of paper on his desk, and I never miss an opportunity to tease him about it. He is welcoming and enthusiastic about Roanoke, its railroad history, and the 611 locomotive.

"She is the queen," he said about the 611. "She has a following all over the world. Many men with high school educations or less created the finest steam engines in the world here (in Roanoke). Unless you understand this, you don't really grasp what she is.

"All of our locomotives, we called ladies. But this is particularly applicable to the Class J. One engineer would often say, 'If you treat her right, she will do more for you.' Some engineers were habitually able to get more out of her than others. They had an instinctive, intuitive sense of what needed to be done.

"The 611 is not a living, breathing thing like a human being. The locomotive alone is close to a half-million pounds. But it has a heart. It brings forth emotions in the people who see it. Nobody is used to putting emotion around a big piece of steel.

"The insurance company called me when I first started this job. They wanted to know what 611 was worth. I said, 'It depends on what you're looking at. If you want to know what she is worth in scrap value, we can calculate the number of pounds of cut scrap. And that will give you a number. Somebody else might say she is worth $10 million. It is all how you view her.' Anything that is completely irreplaceable, and the 611 is as irreplaceable as anything you can think of, cannot be valued (monetarily)."

This museum was partnering with several other museums and organizations to achieve mutually beneficial goals. Fitzpatrick particularly singled out the North Carolina Transportation Museum which has loaned the refurbishment facilities and Norfolk Southern that provided significant monetary and in-kind support.

He said, "If it was not for Norfolk Southern, the 611 would not be running at all. They helped with the restoration costs. They also let us run on their tracks. They tell us when and where we can run.

"Getting the 611 back under steam meant we met a considerable challenge. When I came to this organization in 2006, they didn't tell me at the time that the Virginia Museum of Transportation was, in effect, bankrupt. I was brought in for three weeks as a consultant. After that, they fired the executive director. They didn't tell me that until I went to the board meeting. And there they told me that I had been appointed his replacement. That was the first time I had been given the opportunity to look at finances.

"(Since then,) we have steadily been bringing the museum back into profitability. At that point, Wick Moorman came to us and said that the Norfolk Southern wanted to do a steam program. He sat in the same chair that you're sitting in right now and told me that he wanted me to be thinking about it. I said to myself, 'That means 611 might be able to run again!' Even then, we were barely breaking even. What has surprised me the most is perhaps that we had the intestinal fortitude to look beyond our means, take a huge risk, and put to the public the responsibility of funding the restoration of 611 not knowing what anybody would do.

"Back in 1981, (N&W) took full financial responsibility. This time, Wick basically said to us, 'You can use our rails, but we will not fund the restoration or operations.' At that point, we were a marginally profitable little transportation museum.

"When I started (the museum) had 12,000 visitors per year. By that time we had 50,000 visitors per year. We told the public, 'We are going to do this, but at the same we are totally dependent upon your support.' The 611 project is enormous relative to our overall business operations at the museum. The museum's budget now is around $900,000 per year. The 611 has two budgets, one for restoration and one for operations. Both of them are several million dollars."

The museum is raising money to build a new building to house the 611. They are negotiating with Norfolk Southern to obtain the land they need.

"Wick told us that we were going to get some help, but we never knew exactly what it was going to be. Ninety-four percent of the money we have raised for 611 came from outside of the Roanoke Valley. This says what this locomotive means to other people.

"There is no other museum in the Roanoke Valley that is bringing in a third of its attendees from out-of-state. We have an economic development engine here. There were over 3,000 room-nights purchased here in Roanoke Valley (hotels) last season attributed to the 611 steam program, rented by people coming to ride the excursions.

"(The 611) is better known around the world than the Mill Mountain Star. We think of ourselves as the Star City of the South. But Roanoke is synonymous with the 611. And the 1218. And the 2156. There are many people here in Roanoke who can't grasp that.

"I love this museum and this work. I'm not sure how long I physically can last. I'm 70 now, but I don't plan to retire any time soon. It's the most exciting time in the history of the museum."

He pointed towards the pavilion where I'd just been and said, "Last year for the first time in 53 years, we made real cash, and it's all because of *that* locomotive."

NOT LONG AFTER my visit with Cheri, Scott, and Bev, the transportation museum hosted a micro-excursion targeted at families and children. A diesel locomotive, one passenger car from the Powhatan Arrow, and two cabooses, made up the entire train. Five-foot long wooden bridges were placed from the platform into the cars to allow for passenger access. They were small and light enough to be hoisted back to the platform as the conductor bellowed, "All aboard!"

The passenger car resembled an airliner inside with two seats on each side of a center aisle, except it was twice as spacious. Seats were arranged with two pairs facing each other. They were tall with integral head-rests, upholstered in brown cloth. Windows were large, like a home picture window, with a sliding shade from the top. There was an overhead rack on both sides for luggage.

On the floor of the wide aisle of vinyl composition tile were special logos for the Powhatan Arrow, a mirrored forward-aft pattern of two triangles, on a black tile background with tan pinstriping, framed by Tuscan red tiles.

It wasn't much of a ride, only 15 minutes or so, but it was fun. And in a way, it was the first time I'd "ridden" the Powhatan Arrow in over 50 years. Returning to the museum, I ran into Dave Foster, a man I'd done some work for in an earlier occupation. He was a former NS employee where he worked for most of his career in marketing. Dave was a bushy-headed man with bright blue eyes. He had white curls of hair clumped atop his head and a white beard, tinged in red patina near his mouth from the ketchup of the hamburger he'd just eaten. He had a high voice, a native New England accent, and a friendly, purposeful demeanor. For many years, he's headed a non-profit special-interest group called Rail Solution, looking to solve many of our national and regional transportation issues using our rail infrastructure. We sat and talked on an outdoor, covered bench near the loading area for the little ride I'd just done.

"I'm from rural Connecticut, and I got a masters degree from the Wharton School at the University of Pennsylvania," he told me, munching on potato chips from a Lutz bag. "I got a job in 1972 with the Norfolk & Western. I worked in the Research Department."

Dave eventually moved into the coal marketing department, where his job involved negotiating siting agreements, which allowed a mine to lease some railroad-owned real estate with one or more tracks on it. "When there were changes in ownership, leases often needed renegotiation."

Eventually he became in charge of new business development,

working with new or expanding coal mines. Generally a specific coal mine has only one shipping option. "It is not axiomatic that any coal mine in the Pocahontas Coal Field has to ship with NS, but usually the closest railroad has a strong advantage at getting the business."

He spoke about what he called "unit trains," which are trains loaded with one commodity from origination to destination, then unloaded and returned for more. There is a marshaling yard in Norfolk where cars stay for days or weeks and act as moveable warehouses. It is common for the cars to be their own warehouses rather than putting the coal on the ground and returning the car for more. Some export facilities work that way. But not the NS facility at Lambert's Point.

He said, "Coal is not a fungible commodity. What that means is that each car load of coal is different and cannot be mixed carelessly. (By contrast,) when electricity goes into the grid, it instantly has no identity as to where it originated, as one power plant's volt is identical to any others'. Coal has an infinite number of specifications. Every coal deposit is different in composition. So the cars are used for warehousing to keep it separate before it goes into the hold of the vessel.

Dave Foster

"So a chunk of coal from the time it is mined to when it is burned can be a few days to many weeks. Large-scale consumers of coal tend to keep lots of inventory on the ground to protect themselves from strikes or shut-downs or major price fluctuations. The utilities have enormous stockpiles."

A unit train of coal may be destined for a utility plant. There is a rail line through Roanoke to the south that carries coal to the Duke Energy Belews Creek plant at Walnut Cove, North Carolina. The whole train would be coal for that one customer. It would be unloaded and would come back with the same cars that get re-loaded over and over. The utilities have a certain negotiated unload window of time, where they need to unload the cars and return them to the railroad for the return trip. The locomotives stay with it. It is returned essentially in the same configuration.

There are unit trains of wheat, corn, and other commodities where the train can move in a repetitive fashion.

"Coal was N&W's largest commodity and always represented a significant portion of its business. The overall percentage varied from year to year, not just because of fluctuations in the market, but in mergers with companies like the Wabash and the Nickel Plate which were diversified into other commodities and delivered to many places farther west.

"Most of the coal has gone east. Some has always gone to the Great Lakes ports at Sandusky (OH) and Gary (IN). The Southern Railroad had some coal mines they served, but they were not as vested in coal as the N&W. So when they merged, the percentage dropped more.

"As coal has been supplanted by natural gas (for power generation), the effects rippled through the economy. When there was a more robust market in export coal, there were jobs along the whole corridor. When (the market dropped) there were fewer people in all sorts of support roles like maintenance people and yard workers.

"Rail Solution is an advocacy group that tries to promulgate the economic, environmental, and energy advantages of rail. There are some compelling reasons why as much mid- to long-distance trade in this country should move by rail as possible. The railroads are not aggressive growth people. Rail market share doesn't grow. There is a risk that rail market share will decline and that's not good for our country. Our highways are clogged, more so than ever. The solution is not to build more highways. We're coming to realize that the impacts of doing that are unacceptable. That should give us some momentum to build on this.

"When we started (Rail Solution) in 2003, we were the flaky fringe of the advocacy world. Nobody was doing what we were doing. The environmental community has discovered rail, which has a relatively green reputation. That has helped with our advocacy. We still don't make much headway because the railroads don't seem too concerned and seem happy with what they're doing.

"For 50 years after the interstate highway system, the railroads were downsizing. They were shedding capacity. We need a consistent national effort to expand the rail capacity in this country if a meaningful amount of freight that is now on the highways can be diverted to rail.

"My vision would be that we would have a core national network of high-capacity, grade-separated, electrified rails, analogous to the Eisenhower highway network. It won't happen easily or quickly. The railroads themselves couldn't afford to do that. But with public funds, it could be done. The railroads spend billions of dollars each year. Lots of it is maintenance. Only perhaps a third could go to new capacity."

Makes sense to me. If the government can fund the Interstates, airports, and seaports, why not assist the railroad companies with expanding the rail network?

DAVE INTRODUCED ME to Skip Salmon, another volunteer working that day. Skip was dressed immaculately, wearing an old-fashioned conductor's three-piece suit and hat, his reading glasses dangling from his vest pocket. He was born and raised in Roanoke and began working for the railroad in 1962. His father was a railroad man, working on the cars at Shaffer's Crossing, the shop just to the west of us where locomotives were maintained and repaired. His granddad also worked for the railroad, running a crane car that picked up locomotives, cars, and materials that derailed.

"As a kid, I was able to go to the wreck and watch the salvage operations. Nowadays, they hire out those services, but in the old days they did it themselves. Until I was 14 or so, granddad would tell my dad where the wreck was and we'd go hang out on the bank. They'd let you do that sort of thing then.

"Dad helped me get a job at the railroad. The next January, I started as an electrician's apprentice at Shaffer's Crossing." He pointed to a diesel locomotive parked as an exhibit at the museum and said, "That's locomotive 521, and it pulled the Powhatan Arrow. I worked on it many times. The Arrow switched from steam to diesel in 1959, so when I started they were already fully converted to diesel.

"The apprentice program was for four years. About that time, they realized that the merger with the Nickel Plate and the Wabash was on the horizon. Norfolk & Western set it up that I could go to Virginia Tech and study electrical engineering. When I finished my engineering degree, I was promoted to supervisor. When I retired in 2004, I was electrical foreman in the Roanoke Shops.

"When you worked for the railroad, you got a pass to travel on their passenger trains. On several occasions, I got on the Pocahontas with my grandfather at 7:30 in the evening and by 7:30 the next morning, we'd be in Cincinnati. The old Crosley Field in Cincinnati is where the Reds used to play – you could see it and walk to it from the (Union) Station. We'd go to the ball game and then at 11:30 at night we'd get on the train and by 11:30 the next morning we'd be back in Roanoke. I loved to do that; those were favorite memories!

"The train was not only luxurious, but it was fast. The trip to Cincinnati from Roanoke, even with the stops, took less than twelve hours. I rode the trains a lot. There's nothing like sitting in a dining car early in the morning and having a waiter bring you a big plate of eggs and biscuits and gravy and coffee; it's fantastic. The plates were fine china. The utensils were real silver.

"I worked with a lot of the guys who actually built the Class J locomotives. They were on the cutting edge of the technology of the day. I've been to Europe and heard people talk favorably about the people in Roanoke. 'That's where they built those locomotives.'

"We had a tool shop in Roanoke that could make anything. I worked there for 25 of my 38 years of service. They made tools and dies for freight cars and steam engines. We had our own foundry. We had our own plating plant. Upholstery shop. Blacksmith shop. Woodworking. We did everything right there that we needed to build cars or locomotives. A lot of pride!

"If they made a part and it wasn't top quality, the best it could be made, the supervisor would reject it, and they'd have a little funeral to mourn the rejection of that piece before they'd put it into the scrap bin and ultimately recycle it. In my career, I saw them take parts of old coal hoppers and heat and beat them down to make new parts. Recycling is not new.

"I've got three sons. The lessons I learned at the railroad are lessons I've tried to pass on to them. Work ethic. When you start something, finish it. Be truthful. A lie takes forever to correct; sometimes you can never correct it.

"The N&W at one time had a (employee) magazine. They had a club for boys and girls and involved your whole family. The railroad is a closed shop; you have to belong to the union. One of the rules in the union book was that the son of a journeyman (which is someone who has finished their apprenticeship) has preference over the son of a non-journeyman. They reached out to your children. They knew if they hired your son to work where you did, he'd want to maintain the reputation of the family. I think it worked.

"At that time in history, I'm not getting religious or political, but people had a different attitude. Today, a lot of people's careers consist of working seven, eight, or nine different employers. When I hired on with the Norfolk & Western, I hired on for life. It was the same for most of the people I worked with. After 20 years of service, they'd give you a little silver pin for recognition. It was prized above anything you could get. After 30 years, you'd get a similar pin in gold. After 40 years, you'd be given a pin in gold with a sapphire in it. After 50 years, you'd get one in gold with a diamond in it. When my granddad died, he had that diamond pin, which at that time was probably worth $1,000, pinned to his lapel and when the casket was closed he was buried with it. Now that should tell you something about how people felt about working for the railroad.

"It was a lifetime commitment. It was part of their identity. You were recognized in the community as a railroad man. It was like being a police officer in that people knew that you were trustworthy, you were okay. It was like family. We looked after each other.

"When I die, I'll have my survivors put the N&W logo by my obituary!"

What an astounding testimonial for an employer!

THE MUSEUM COMPLEX also provided room in the basement for model railroaders to gather and build and maintain tracks. The model railroaders were also hosting an open house where the kids could come and have a look.

Sadly, I thought as I wandered around, most of the tables on which the track layouts sat were upwards of four feet from the floor, too tall for the children to see without stepping on a step-stool or being held by a parent. There were layouts of every scale, from the smallest Z scale increasingly larger through N, TT, HO, S, O, and G. They were in various stages of construction, some mostly completed and some still underway and not yet in operation.

I found myself in conversation with a man named Bill Oertly who told me that he had also retired from the Norfolk Southern. "Before that, I worked for the Association of American Railroads. I was a hazardous material compliance officer."

Like several of the men I met that day, he had grey-white hair and blue eyes. He had a bushy white mustache.

I suggested facetiously that I thought it might be a really good idea if hazardous materials were kept on the rails. He agreed, but added, "More importantly, it needs to be kept in the package!"

Bill was from Maryland, but had worked in the western states and in Richmond prior to joining the NS. He'd been in Roanoke for 11 ½ years. When he worked for the Association, he interacted with all the national railroads.

"Railroads are a common carrier, meaning they legally must take on any cargo they are capable of handling from any customer. Of course, if something is too big, too wide or too long, they can refuse it. Every section of track has a specification, classified from one to five, with the slowest allowable speed at class one and then upwards. There are certain requirements in terms of grade, curves, on bridges, flat land, that can all affect the class. There are lots of considerations.

"The weight limits of the cars are interesting. Four axle cars, a common car, can be rated for 50, 70, 100, or 125 tons capacity depending upon the design of the car structure and the bearings."

He explained that the most common bearing is 6-1/2 inches in diameter by 11 inches in length. They are permanently sealed with bearing grease inside. If an inspector sees grease on the wheel, he knows it has a bad bearing. All cars are routinely and carefully inspected.

On most cars, the bearing is outside of the wheel. Each car's two trucks hold the bearings and thus the wheels in place, under the "box" of the car where the material is stored. Each truck has an inverted U-shaped channel where the bearing assembly sits, held in place by the gravity weight of the car. If you jack the truck upwards, the wheels and axles will stay on the rails; they're not bolted on! Not only that, but the trucks aren't bolted to the car either, but are also held in place by gravity, resting on a center-pin so they can swivel as the car negotiates curves. There is a recess in the truck and the pin points downward into the recess. That holds it all together. In a wreck, the box can go one way, the truck another way, and the wheels still another way.

"People think of derailments of a big stack of cars piled up in a heap. Often, it's just one or two wheels on the ground."

Right on cue, a train whistle sounded and through the windows we saw a train rolling by on the tracks outside. It was a container train, with double-stacked cars. As we walked outside to have a look, Bill explained that the containers were designed to be loaded and unloaded using pin-loops at the top corners. "If you try to pick one of these containers up at the middle, they will break in half. They are 40 feet long. Those are going on a ship, overseas. There are also 45 foot, 48 foot, and 53 foot containers in regular use. And there are smaller 20 foot containers, always for overseas."

He also showed me something I'd never noticed, that some container cars, rather than having the truck wheels mounted a few feet inboard from the front and rear ends, can have the truck wheels actually between cars, with half the weight of mated cars resting on each truck. He called them articulated cars, with 2-platform, 3-platform, or 5-platform cars. The lower containers sit in "wells", and if each well is 50 feet long and there are 5 of them linked together, the total 5-platform car can be almost 300 feet long. That entire length acts as one car.

The containers are 8 feet, 8-1/2 feet or 9-1/2 feet tall. So at the extreme, a loaded rail car can be around 21 feet tall. Obviously, then, all clearances under bridges and tunnels must be taller, at least 22 feet.

He said a number of things could cause a derailment. "A broken wheel. A broken rail. Broken axle. Broken bearing. Improper train handling."

"If a wheel came off the rail right here," I continued, "would the engineer know about it?"

"Yes." He explained that every wheel has an air-brake. On an automobile brake, applying additional pressure to the brake fluid applies the brake. On a railroad, the brake system is pressurized all the time, upwards of 90 psi. If two adjacent cars separate, it will disengage the hose linkages and the pressure will drop immediately. The pressure in the system prevents braking, so if the pressure drops, the brakes will automatically apply themselves to all cars. Leakage of air from the hoses is also something inspectors look for.

The brake shoes actually apply directly to the outer diameter of the wheel, the same portion of the wheel that comes into contact with the rail. On passenger cars, there are disk brakes, but on these trains the pads press against the wheels. The engineer will use his air compressor to modulate pressure, incrementally applying brakes whenever he wants to decelerate. If you have an air-hose separation, the air pressure will drop forward and behind the separation, so the train will automatically apply brakes on all the cars and will come to a stop without any input from the engineer.

Sometimes heavier or longer trains can have locomotives at both ends. The locomotive at the back is unmanned and remotely operated from the front.

As with so many other people I met, I asked Bill what he found so appealing about trains. He echoed what I'd heard so many times before, "There are many things. Steam engines are really big and really noisy. Why are people interested in airplanes and automobiles? People get interested for various reasons. I was given a train set when I was 2 years old. My dad was an automobile mechanic. I was interested in all transportation. Railroads are so varied with so many considerations. It's fascinating to me. I'm a frustrated Mechanical Engineer. I couldn't handle the math.

"I just like machinery in general. I find the variety in appearance and operation of railroads to be fascinating. Even the rails are enormously complex. Steam locomotives are the ultimate expression. Internal combustion doesn't have the appeal.

"You may find that in the past, a fairly large percentage of railroaders were rail fans. They didn't go around taking pictures while working. It was still work. They had a job to do, with high responsibility. They cared about the business. Any business needs employees who care about it."

I thanked Bill and took my leave of the transportation museum, feeling happy with my fruitful conversations, my new knowledge, and my new friends in the brotherhood of train aficionados.

BACK UNDERWAY, I went a few miles out of my way to north Roanoke to call on Sam Rasoul. Sam represents the Roanoke area in the Virginia House of Delegates, and when he was elected in 2014 at age 32 was one of its youngest ever members. A son of Palestinian immigrants, he was the first and is still the only Muslim in the Virginia General Assembly. I wanted to ask him about his take on Roanoke's economy and diversity.

Rasoul had a small, nondescript windowless office in an office park. Behind him on the bookshelf were photos of his family and friends. He was tastefully attired with a dark shirt and tie.

I explained my project and said, "I see you as one of the new faces of Roanoke."

"I've seen quite a transition here," he said. He grew up in Roanoke, arriving with his family in 1984 when he was three. "We are historically a railroad town, but we now have the second most diverse economy in Virginia."

His grandparents arrived in Roanoke first, and his parents decided to move from Ohio to be closer to them. "My grandparents came to the States in the late 60s from Palestine. Sadly, Palestine is in a non-stop war. Ohio was a place people gravitated towards."

He told me that immigrant stories often involve one person arriving, scoping out a place, and if he finds it friendly invites others to come along. "They bring family members and build little communities and build businesses. I still have lots of family in Ohio and in Northern Virginia.

"Almost always location is based on economic decisions, that and family. We started in a one-bedroom apartment in downtown Roanoke. We lived the immigrant dream. Roanoke gave us opportunities and helped raise me."

He was educated in the Roanoke Valley, graduating from Roanoke College. I asked about his minority experience in Roanoke.

He said, "I was campaigning for US Congress a few years ago, unsuccessfully. With the last name 'Rasoul,' campaigning in western Virginia is interesting. I was knocking on doors in western Roanoke County. I went to a door and a young man in his early 20s came to the door. I introduced myself and told him I was running for Congress. I gave him my spiel. Lots of people were receptive to listening. I was selling myself on a ticket of (Barack) Obama (for President), (Mark) Warner (for Senate) and Rasoul (for Congress). He said, 'Well, I'll vote for you… but I'm not voting for Obama!' I asked why. He said, 'Because he's a Muslim.' And I chuckled and said, 'Obama is not a Muslim; he's a Christian. But I'm a Muslim.' Eventually, we learned that we had a lot in common. We were from the same generation and both from the valley.

"There's a lot of fear and ignorance out there. He must have thought all Muslims were terrorists. He had a lack of knowledge, and was reacting from that rather than from hatred.

"I'm the first Muslim elected for anything in Virginia. It's perplexing for a lot of folks. I am married with three kids and a small business owner. My story is a lot like everybody else's. We have more in common than in differences. If we all followed the Golden Rule, we'd all be better off.

"We used to think Roanoke was not good for young people. That has really changed. There's lots of development downtown, and we have a better ecosystem for young families. We enjoy our natural recreational resources. We don't have lots of traffic. It's appealing for those seeking quality of life. We have a great work/life balance. Millennials are interested in that. The career ambition that was there a decade or two ago has shifted to a focus on lifestyle. Everything goes with lifestyle.

"Roanoke has the best of many things.

"First, we have recreational resources. Hiking. Mountain biking. Kayaking. Sports. The Blue Ridge Parkway. Appalachian Trail. Explore Park. These things all coalesce around the Roanoke Valley. It's just a big playground.

"Second, we have low unemployment. There are thousands of open job positions for good-paying jobs with a median income of $39,500 annually. There is great growth of opportunity in the region.

"Third, we have access to great education. We have 13,000 people enrolled at Virginia Western Community College. We have the Virginia Tech Carilion School of Medicine. We have the Jefferson College offering bachelor and master's level degrees in nursing and occupational health. We have the traditional colleges at Roanoke College and Hollins University.

"Fourth, we have social activity.

"All those pieces weren't in place twenty years ago. I credit the private sector. There were many individuals in different ways that envisioned this. These were forward-thinking 'Gen-X-ers' who were tired of this talk. They began to rally different groups and laid the groundwork for the Millennials. The key was that citizens came together to meet these needs."

In 2015, there was a kerfuffle in Roanoke where the mayor said some unwelcoming things about refugees from the Middle East. I asked Sam about it.

He said, "Politicians say the darnedest things. No refugee has ever committed an act of terror in the United States. They are the most vetted individuals we have. We can't meet ignorance head-on, by quoting facts. We have to overwhelm people with love and compassion. We're all worried about terrorists. We're all worried about the rising cost of education for our children. We can all sit in our partisan camps barking facts, but that won't get anything done. It's not what we need.

"Roanoke is a good place for minorities. People are just now feeling relieved of the pressure to assimilate. I can be Palestinian. I can come here and be what I am. The city council is diverse, with an Arab American, a Jewish American, and several African Americans. They are young and old. That diversity is an economic driver, especially with an evolution of mindsets that we're seeing.

"My real job is a business consultant. Businesses look at the overall picture. They want to know if the community is inclusive. The world is evolving quickly, quicker than before. We need political leaders who are agile, ready to pivot on a dime. People stuck in their ways, Democratic or Republican, are an impediment.

"My name is Salam Rasoul. 'Salam' means peace. 'Rasoul' means messenger. My name means, 'messenger of peace.' In the 80s, I needed to be Sam. A five year old today in Roanoke could be Salam Rasoul. There are 50 languages spoken in Roanoke schools. This is a better place now.

"Everybody is looking for a purpose. The beautiful people of Roanoke gave me purpose, to be able to serve them. Regardless of all the craziness going on in the world, I won a primary and an election. There were people willing to let me have a chance. I think about the gravity of my obligation on a daily basis. I push my team pretty hard. There is not a day that goes by when we aren't trying to strategically figure out how to help people in three ways: We want to do community development. We want to impact public policy. And we want to change politics. We know it takes time, but we think there is a way to change public discourse."

WITH THE N&W HAVING ITS HEADQUARTERS there for nearly a century, Roanoke was certain to yield extraordinary insight to my process. And it did. But as so many times before, it was time to move westward.

The city of Salem is immediately adjacent to Roanoke and they share a long north-south border. Salem is an independent city of around 25,000 people and is actually older than Roanoke, founded 80 years earlier in 1802. Roanoke quickly grew larger, and Salem applied to the General Assembly of Virginia to shift from town to city status in 1967 to avoid being annexed by Roanoke. Salem is more conservative politically and less diverse demographically, with more than 90 percent of its residents being white, whereas as I mentioned earlier, only 70 percent of Roanoke's are. Salem is home of Roanoke College, and has a huge interest in sports. It is home of the minor league Salem Red Sox, and it annually hosts the Amos Alonzo Stagg Bowl, the NCAA Division III Football Championship game.

ADJACENT TO THE NORFOLK SOUTHERN tracks in Salem, hidden in a nondescript industrial building, I visited a company that builds locomotives. And railroad cars. Small ones.

Jim Humphrey owns Mountain Car Company, manufacturer of 1/8 scale railroad rolling stock (on 7 inch gauge track) like the ones in Chris Schieck's yard back in Forest.

"We design, manufacture, and sell throughout America and the world to hobbyists and light commercial customers," he told me as we sat in his office filled with railroad memorabilia. "We build replicas of diesel locomotives and the rolling stock. We are probably the largest manufacturer in the country doing this."

Another lifelong rail fan, Humphrey was a hobbyist from his childhood years. Long ago when the Virginia Transportation Museum was at Wasena Park in Roanoke, there was a 1/8 scale layout. Humphrey became involved in the new Blue Ridge Live Steamer Club, which ran locomotives like Chris' that burned coal and made steam to power them. He graduated from Virginia Tech in Business Management and started the company soon thereafter. "At the time I saw the stuff that was on the market, and I thought I could make it better and cheaper. And I've been banging my head against the wall ever since!

"We have nine employees. We do a variety of parts, kits, and assembled cars and locomotives. Our product designs are standardized to as great an extent as possible. Our train car designs are similar to each other. The parts are duplicated and the processes are similar. Even though the locomotives may look different on the outside, the chassis, engines, and other parts are similar underneath."

Mountain Car Company has a complete metal manufacturing plant, with CNC machining, welding, painting, and assembly. Many employees were skilled at several aspects, most learning on the job. Most have been with the company for many years; one has 17 years of experience. Sales are direct to the customer, with most of their advertising through the Internet. In years past, Jim attended many train meets, but with the Internet, he can be equally effective now without all the travel.

"Cost for our train cars averages around $1,500. Cost for our locomotives is around $15,000. It is an expensive hobby, but many people have expensive hobbies. A small track might be a 300 foot loop. A customer in Oregon has 200 acres and 35 miles of track. An average layout might be 3,500 feet of track on five acres. An entry level set-up with locomotive, a few cars, and 1,000 feet of track may cost around $30,000."

The trains are replicas of modern diesel locomotives rather than steam locomotives. They are exquisite and look surprisingly realistic. Each locomotive is powered by a two-cylinder gasoline engine that runs a hydraulic pump. It turns a sprocket, chained to all the locomotive's wheels. The locomotives are equipped with lights, a horn, and even speakers that emit locomotive sounds. Like the railroad companies themselves, most hobbyists found steam locomotives to be temperamental, inefficient, and expensive to maintain.

Jim said, "I haven't seen much of a bump (in sales) from the 611's return and the NS excursion program. Our business is national and international and the program is local. But there is great interest nationally in trains. The 611 program, which I'm all for and love, is targeted to people who like steam trains. People in my hobby like trains and ride-on trains and they're not particular one way or the other about the 611. It's apples and oranges to what we are.

"We're investing in ourselves to be able to produce better availability and quicker delivery times. We're helping customers get into it by making more product available now, rather than ordering and waiting. We're doing more pre-manufacturing and warehousing. Wait times are days or weeks instead of months and years.

"Business is growing," he beamed. "We had a tough time like everybody else in 2008 and 2009, but things have turned around. For me, the pleasure in this business is designing and manufacturing something that works well and looks good, and will stay that way for many, many years. There's a lot of satisfaction in putting out a neat product that people like. Even when I am long gone, this equipment will be around virtually forever."

WEST MAIN STREET IN SALEM is another one of those gawd-awful strip developments so prevalent on the edge of towns these days – a tangle of stop-lights and traffic. But it wasn't too many miles before I was back in the country again. Joining US-460 in this region is US-11, another of Virginia's most important and historic roads. It runs the length of the Great Valley of Virginia from West Virginia north of Winchester to Tennessee at Bristol, superimposing over the colonial era Wilderness Road and paralleling the much newer Interstate 81. From the Roanoke Valley to Christiansburg, they occupy the same stretch of mostly four-lane divided highway.

Just west of Salem in the Glenvar area, I called on another former Norfolk Southern executive, Chuck Wehrmeister. He lives in a rural area and owns several acres of land on which he has put a track similar to the layout Chris Schieck had. Before we went outside to take a look, Chuck told me, "I am interested in economic geography and in the business development of our nation," which of course coincided exactly with the purpose of my book.

He grew up in Toledo, Ohio, and went to Miami University of Ohio, eventually graduating with a degree major in International Studies with a minor in German. After working for the railroad during the summers, he was hired by the Norfolk & Western railroad starting as a management trainee.

The railroad transferred Chuck to Roanoke in 1971. He climbed the corporate ladder from being a trainee to an advanced trainee to an assistant to the trainmaster to trainmaster to assistant superintendent to superintendent to terminal superintendent to assistant vice president to vice president, a position from which he retired.

"Being on the railroad got into your blood. Norfolk Southern is a really good company, a family oriented company. Once Conrail was acquired, it became a large company and you needed to work hard in order to know people in the field.

"We were a strong engineering company. From the earliest days of the railroad, there was a tight link between railroad engineering and the military. Even when I was moving up in the company, it was somewhat militaristic. I like militaristic environments. As a kid, I always drew army tanks and battleships and such."

I joked with him, asking if people saluted each other as they walked down the hallways in the corporate office.

He said, "It was almost like that!" He explained that even today's railroad disciplinary procedures have the roots in the military. The culture of workers and supervisors is largely the result of the military history of the early days of the railroad.

"When I began working for the railroad, upper management seemed like gods to me. These people in the ivory towers, well, the workers never saw them. When I retired, I was in a position where 30 years earlier the entry-level workers would've seen me as a god. Over the years, the corporation modernized. It became less militaristic and more like most other large corporations.

"Roanoke had various neighborhoods of clustered workers. The Roanoke Shops were east of downtown, and all the workers lived in that area and into the separate town of Vinton. There was a neighbor-hood just north of the Hotel

Chuck Wehrmeister's model locomotive

Roanoke called Gainsboro. It was an African-American neighborhood. The well-to-do people lived towards downtown and to the south of Ro-anoke towards the slopes of Mill Mountain. Each neighborhood had its own shops and stores that catered specifically to those local residents."

He showed me an upright glass-fronted cabinet, filled with items he'd collected. "Your Powhatan Arrow was such a splash that it had its own chinaware and silver designed expressly for it." The china was all hand-painted, with lovely drawings of flowers and exotic birds. They were made at the Shenango China Company in Pennsylvania, and each piece had the signature Tuscan red strip around the rim. He had dinner plates, soup bowls, tea cups and saucers, gravy bowls, and other acces-sory pieces. The silverware was even more stunning. His collection had regular knives, forks, and spoons, plus soup ladles, water jugs, teapots, and more. There were salt and pepper shakers and bread bowls. Each piece was nicer than the one before. He said his collection was invalu-able.

I later learned that the dining car itself was ornately decorated, with the widespread use of the signature colors of Tuscan red, yellow, and gray. Draperies were of a two-tone horizontally striped gold mate-rial, matching the yellow ceiling. The kitchen was the most modern of the era, matching or exceeding the finest stationary restaurants, with ranges, steam tables, broilers, electric dish washers, garbage disposals, frozen food lockers, and cup and plate warmers. Servers were black men with black and white uniforms. What a treat it must have been to eat on the Powhatan Arrow's dining car!

Chuck said for early African-Americans employed by the railroad, there were only certain jobs that they could have, typically porters, cooks, and waiters.

We walked outside around his expansive layout, still under construction. He had several gasoline-powered diesel replica models like those Jim Humphrey's company made.

As I prepared to leave, he told me, "I have a guideline here from decades ago from the Norfolk & Western that says that in case of an injury, small amounts of alcohol may be administered. This seems to be in standard procedure all the way into the 1930s and 1940s. But it's no longer the case today. Times change."

CONTINUING WEST, US-460's corridor quickly becomes less urbanized and passes through the communities of Dixie Caverns, Elliston, and Shawsville, with the tracks running parallel, first on the left and then passing under the road to the right. Just off the road in Elliston is the venerable Big Spring Mill. I stopped to call on its owner, Bill Long.

Big Spring Mill has been in business with essentially the same business model for 165 years. It's one of two remaining commercial establishments in a community that once boasted three hotels and several stores. His factory nestles between the South Fork of the Roanoke River and the NS railroad tracks. To get there from the highway, the road turns to dirt and snakes under the trestle the road shares with the river, rushing with the spring freshet. The trestle has three lovely granite piers hoisting a steel structure, perhaps 20 feet over the river and 5 feet over the road. The river was green and swift.

I've known Bill for some time, years ago as a customer of the printing business I once owned and managed and more recently as a fellow Rotarian. He's now in his 85th year, but is still spry enough to use an upstairs office, filled with stacks of paperwork and memorabilia. He told me for his entire life he considered himself a miller, one of the world's oldest occupations.

He's a kindly man with a gentle manner, and I've always liked him. His company began operation in 1850, two years before the railroad arrived. Mills were always built with access to water power. He said, "We used running water from the river to power our mill. In the early days, there was also a sawmill. It was owned by another family initially. My family took over ownership in 1935. My grandfather and my great uncle ran a grocery store over in (the nearby community of) Ironto.

"We are in Montgomery County, and we may be one of the oldest companies still in operation. My theory is that in the early days, people hitched up a wagon and brought bags of grain for milling and whatever wood they wanted to have cut up to the mill. Most people had trees on their own places. But they needed to have the wood cut. The mill owners would grind the grain and saw the logs and send them home with flour and cut boards. So then they had food to eat and lumber to build with.

"To my knowledge, the mill was not attacked during the Civil War and probably remained operational.

"I was five years old when my family bought into this operation and so I have been bumming around this mill for my entire life. We moved into the mill-house in 1937. I married a local girl, and we have been together ever since.

"In our business, we grind grain to produce flour. We make also cornmeal and other types of meal both for human and animal consumption. Our customers are the grocery stores and the store chains. We buy the grain from the growers and the stores buy the end product."

I asked if he used stone grinding wheels anymore. He said, "No, we have in the past, but not now. We don't use water power anymore, either. One winter the river froze almost solid, and there was no flow to turn our turbine. And so we installed electric motors and have been using them ever since."

I asked him how his business model has changed over the years, especially since the 1960s, the time period of interest for my book. He said, "I don't know that there is a great deal of difference. As far as grinding is concerned, there is not any difference. We are doing it the same way we always have. I have a cleaning machine upstairs in the mill that was patented in 1894. It is now 120 years old, and we are still using it. It is one of the best machines I've got.

"Just like other businesses, we have had good and bad years. We have less competition now than we once did. There were once two mills in Christiansburg, but both are gone now. There were two in Floyd County. They are gone. There was one in Lafayette (another nearby community) and another on the (Roanoke/Montgomery) county line and there were some in Salem and Roanoke. The only one left is in Roanoke. And we are not directly competing with them. We typically mill for the housewife while they mill for industrial bakeries.

"In the 1940s, (Elliston) had three hotels. All of them are closed now. Visitors came by train. They stayed here and then got a wagon to

Allegheny Springs. They came to take the waters."

The central Appalachians were dotted with natural springs, including mineral springs and thermal springs. There was a thriving trade for at least 150 years of primarily wealthier coastal residents coming up into the mountains during the summer to get away from the stifling summer heat. In those days, without air-conditioning and with swarms of mosquitoes coming out of the swamps, life was excruciating in the summer. Resorts emerged to provide tourists a place to stay. Obviously, of course, poor people just stayed and dealt with it.

"We employ about 15 people. Since we are basically the only business in town, I think we are probably the largest employer."

I asked him if he thought the business model would carry the business through for another 100 years. He said he really didn't know, but they were milling flour just like it had always been done, "And we still use essentially the same equipment."

Bidding him goodbye, I thanked him for visiting with me and for his service to his community.

JUST BEYOND ELLISTON, the highway went through the community of Shawsville before ascending to Christiansburg. There was a long, flat valley the first few miles, and the railroad tracks hug the mountainsides on the right, slowly gaining elevation, more steadily and inexorably than the highway. So I had to look uphill to see the train ascending alongside me. In most communities, the train station is at the lower elevation in town, as it had been in Petersburg, Lynchburg, and Roanoke, but Shawsville's old depot is uphill from the town's old Main Street, cluttered with derelict buildings. The stretch of highway around Shawsville was always my favorite place on our weekly trips to Roanoke during my childhood. It was a great place to watch trains and wonder about the horrors that awaited me at the synagogue.

The highway followed another valley to the base of Christiansburg Mountain where the tracks disappeared to the right to go through the Montgomery Tunnel. I took a short detour on Den Hill Road to find it. The Montgomery Tunnel is actually two separate parallel tunnels, a "twin bore," with a length of 663 feet. Both tubes had been enlarged vertically to allow for passage of double-stacked container cars as part of a public-private partnership called the Heartland Corridor.

As with most of the train infrastructure on the Powhatan Arrow's line, the Montgomery Tunnel had been built to accommodate coal hoppers. The Arrow's locomotives and cars had been sized accordingly to fit that infrastructure. As container traffic increased, NS needed to use a circuitous route for double-stacked cars to avoid lower tunnels.

The Heartland Corridor project had begun in the 2000s to improve infrastructure along the corridor from Chicago to Columbus and then to Norfolk to facilitate carriage of stacked 9 feet 6 inch shipping containers. The rail route was the same as used by the Powhatan Arrow from Roanoke all the way to Portsmouth, Ohio. Originally estimated at $150 million, the final price tag exceeded $320 million. Roughly 2/3 was paid by federal grants and the remaining 1/3 by Norfolk Southern. Overall, 28 tunnels of cumulatively 30,000 linear feet had to be cleared and enlarged, with another 24 overhead obstructions removed or relocated.

In order to reach the required height, some tunnels required minor notching, some major notching, and some complete crown replacement. Others had their floors lowered.

This significant upgrade was completed in 2010. Only one of the two Montgomery Tunnels was done then; the other was completed in 2015.

Public-private partnerships like this are always political footballs, as our legislators grapple with the use of taxpayer money to essentially enhance the profitability of corporations. In this case, ensuring NS's competitiveness and the removal of untold numbers of containers and trucks from our highways were deemed significant enough to justify the public contribution.

Back on US-460, the highway climbed steeply until I reached the Christiansburg town limits and the intersection with Interstate 81.

Just before reaching Christiansburg, the Powhatan Arrow's tracks, a couple of miles away to my right, reached their highest elevation so far at 2065 feet. It was a considerable challenge for the Class J locomotives' operators to build heat and pressure in the boiler to power the train up the incline only to tamp everything down at Christiansburg's station a mile beyond the summit in the neighborhood of Cambria where the rails met a new watershed, that of the New River alongside Crab Creek.

12:59 p.m.

Christiansburg

Mile 284.9

Travelers begin to see the real mountains. 2,023 feet above sea level. Cattle and sheep-raising country. Virginia Polytechnic Institute is at Blacksburg on an N & W branch, nine miles west. Rail line for Bristol, Va. with connections for the Deep South leaves the main line at Walton (New River).

M y. Home. Town. Christiansburg.
  "What's it called?"
"Christiansburg," I tell them.
"No, seriously."
"Seriously. I'm not kidding. Around here, they're all Christians-burgs."

How can anybody write objectively about their home town? Highlight this whole chapter in an etherial, smoky haze and don't believe anything I've written. My view today is clouded in a mist of foggy memories, real and imagined.

"Progressive Small Town Living at its Best," the town boasts as its official motto, but if you ask me, it's only a statement of aspiration. What are the marks of a progressive community? It's racially diverse in its populace and its leadership. It is walkable and bikeable. It has sustainability initiatives. It has a viable downtown with locally-owned stores and shops, and with nightlife. It is safe and welcoming to all.

By most measures, Christiansburg is anything but progressive. The Town Council has seven members: one black man and the rest white men. No women or other ethnic minorities. The downtown core is dominated by the courthouse (It's the county seat of Montgomery County.), town offices, and related buildings, including a public safety building, town police office, law firms, and banks. There are few retailers and almost no night-life. The shopping core is now a vast, sprawling area of massive parking lots, strip malls, and an indoor mall three miles north of downtown, with traffic rivaling Charlotte's. There is only one mile of paved bicycle trails and almost no paved shoulders to allow safe bicycling. A former county planner once described Christiansburg as "pedestrian hell," without a single protected instant to cross any intersection in the town limits. If you Google "sustainability Christiansburg Virginia," you'll get a link to nearby Blacksburg.

Many of the towns and cities I'd visited had seen their share of sprawl retail development, but none had as totally bought into the car-based transportation monoculture as Christiansburg. The downtown I knew when growing up there for all intents and purposes had ceased to exist. Sure, some of the buildings still stood – many more had been razed and then paved into parking lots – but none offered the sense of community that once existed.

Christiansburg is an old community for the region, being founded in 1792, over 80 years before Roanoke. Happily, it has fared reasonably well economically since the days the Powhatan Arrow steamed last through. The population in those days was racing through 7,000 people and by the turn of the 21st Century reached 17,000, but is now estimated at over 22,000, commerce benefiting from the spill-over from nearby Virginia Tech in Blacksburg and the transportation network provided by the intersection of my companion US-460 and Interstate 81.

The Christiansburg Railroad Station is a mile away from downtown to the northeast in a separate community called Cambria. It was consolidated with Christiansburg in 1965. It was the only community on my route that had not one but two historic train stations still standing. I planned to visit both.

I'll be in trouble with the town fathers for writing this, but in my mind, it's a shame Christiansburg never embraced the idea of progressiveness, at least in the modern way of thinking. But through it the Powhatan Arrow once chugged, and thus, so too did I.

IN SPITE OF CHRISTIANSBURG'S DEVOTION to the mundane, to the franchises and corporate dominated establishments of retailing, some people continue to pursue their entrepreneurial spirit, seeing economic opportunities that other people pass by. Serial entrepreneur Marie March opened a new restaurant recently in a building that formerly housed a Waffle House at the east end of town where I-81 crosses over US-460. She named it the Fatback Soul Shack. The cuisine is a curious melding of Appalachian mountain cooking and African American soul food. Marie is a white chick; she's a bottle blonde.

I pulled into the spacious parking lot and wandered inside where a lengthy bar served individual diners and a small seating area had tables, both tall and regular. Marie agreed to join me for lunch, asking her cooks to bring a smorgasbord of food including frogs' legs, popcorn shrimp, pigs' feet, and pinto beans. She has a bright, ready smile and vibrant slate gray eyes. She has an infectious personality and everybody speaks fondly of her.

She chuckled and said, "Yeah. People are kind of shocked when they see the woman behind the curtain. We also own Due South BBQ down the street. My husband and I founded that. We came here for him to attend medical school. I couldn't find a job. We have always loved to cook pigs on a smoker. We used to do that tailgating when I went to Clemson University in South Carolina. We needed money really bad. We decided to take our hobby and open a restaurant."

They met a man in church who had a building that he offered to them at an affordable price. Due South has a small serving area and does a lot of takeout business. "The building only has about 1,700 square feet and last year we did $1.2 million in sales," she laughed heartily, modestly. "We were looking to open another Due South restaurant in Blacksburg. It is the real population center around here. But everything we could find (to house it) was too expensive. I knew what we could afford and we couldn't find anything."

The former Waffle House building was still in good condition and best of all, it was within a stone's throw from the Interstate 81 exit ramp. The Waffle House was in business from 1973 until 2013, so they had a good 40 year run.

Marie's new restaurant's menu included all sorts of items of Southern food. The decor was informal. The wooden tabletops had thick transparent polyurethane painted over the wood with whimsical stickers laminated within. Some of the booths had chair backs that were made from pick-up truck tailgates. A jackhammer was annoyingly pounding concrete outside, preparing for an addition already in the works.

She said, laughing, "My husband is from New Jersey. We feature traditional southern food. He doesn't have a clue."

I asked her if she had a secret to business success.

She said, "Buy low. Keep your overhead down. You have got to have a vision. You need to be highly creative. That is the most important thing. For a long time, we looked at good deals on used restaurant equipment. Now we have new equipment, but it has taken years for us to get to that point. When stuff would break down, we figured out how to fix it. You will not get anywhere without being thrifty."

Food appeared and I was ravenous. I began eating everything in front of me while she talked. I asked about her tolerance for risk.

She said, "It's not a lot of risk. It is just money, I guess. Money has not come real easy to me, but I read this article about Walt Disney and I felt like I was mentally a lot like him. The way he viewed money was that he was basically always bankrupt; he was always on the verge. He was always lining up the next thing to do with the money that he had coming in. That is how I view money. We keep everything moving and building and improving and making things better."

I picked up a little bony thing from the plate and asked, "What is this?"

"It's a frog leg."

"Do I put it in my mouth?"

She laughed and said, "Yes. It is pretty good, too."

So I did. And it was. I wondered where she was able to source quantities of frogs legs. What a frog farm looked like. How frogs were harvested. I didn't ask.

"That is a fried green tomato," she pointed. "Have some shrimp; they're good! That is homemade tartar sauce.

"When you were a poor hillbilly, you ate every part of the pig. We haven't added chitlins and hog maw to the menu just because those things smell so bad when you're cooking them. (Note: hog maw is the stomach of a pig, specifically the exterior muscular wall of the stomach organ. I had to look it up. I am a sorry excuse for a Southerner.) We are doing pretty good with what we have on the menu. Every southern thing that we had good recipes for, we threw on the menu. Almost everything here is homemade. We only use somebody else's product if theirs was better than what we could make ourselves. We try to buy from local suppliers.

"We pay our people $10-$12 per hour. My managers make between $50,000 and $60,000 per year. They get paid really well. This enables me to keep people on staff. We go as low as $8.75 per hour, but we try to pay well enough so that people can think of this as their career.

"I want people to make so much money that they can have everything they want. They may not live in a mansion in Hollywood, but as far as having a new vehicle or a nice place to live, I think the bare minimum for that here is $40,000-$50,000 per year.

"My husband and I have been married for 18 years. We have a lot of pride. We have been poor at times. We never reached out to our parents for handouts. It has been tough. We have learned how to value money. We want to reward those who are working the hardest. We try to keep the good vibes going in the kitchen. I let them play whatever music they want. I want them to have fun and I try not to be a dictator. There are so many franchises now, but I think people like to support family businesses. I really believe that."

"What has this community here in Christiansburg meant to you as a newcomer?" I queried.

"I was raised in Kingsport, Tennessee. It is about two hours' drive from here. It is still in Appalachia. I feel right at home here. There is lush vegetation with a mix of hardwoods and pines, and farming. Culturally it is exactly the same. My hometown was a college town and so there were lots of PhDs and really smart people. Just like here."

"Why do you think some communities are more successful than others?"

"That is really complex. Gosh, I tell you, it is so demographic. It is education and people having enough money to spend. We are in the restaurant industry. People have got to have enough money to go out and eat. We have universities (Virginia Tech in nearby Blacksburg and Radford University in Radford) that bring a lot of money. You have to start with the core industry that brings in money."

"Has this been a supportive community for you?"

"Hugely. Hugely. I cannot even begin to tell you..." she gushed.

I interrupted her and said, "What's this?"

She said, "It is a pig's foot."

I said, "Do I eat this?"

She just laughed at me and returned to her train of thought. "I don't know why but we feel extremely fortunate that people have taken us in and treated us like family. It has been that way since Day One."

I'm nobody's restaurant critic, but the shrimp was great. So were the fried green tomatoes. The pigs' feet? Might be useful to patch a hole in a pair of work boots.

CONVENIENTLY, MY OFFICE is in Christiansburg, in walking distance of Marie's restaurant. While I was home, I had a chance to suspend my travel and catch up on some business before continuing westward.

While there, I got a visit from Preston Claytor, younger brother of Jane Claytor Webster with whom I'd stayed with in Norfolk and son of the late Bob Claytor, who retired as CEO of the NS in 1987. Preston reminded me that he was 11 years younger than Jane. Bob was 38 years old when Preston was born, and was serving as Vice President of Norfolk & Western.

We sat around the glass table in my office, set in the Christiansburg Industrial Park, where Preston told me about growing up in a railroad family.

"When dad was promoted to executive Vice President of Law at N&W, he had his own office railroad car. I knew a lot about it because when dad had work to do in Washington, I would ride along with him in the car. It was a beautiful car inside and out. It had mahogany interior and painted walls. Norfolk Southern still has it.

"I grew up around the railroad. At that time, the headquarters was in Roanoke and that's where I grew up. During the summers I began working on the steam locomotives. In those days, they were no longer in regular service, but they were doing excursion work. It was the early 1970s. I started doing the most meaningless work, shoveling coal in the tender down to where the firemen could get his shovel under it. It is the best seat in the house, but it is also a lot of work when the coal pile gets low and you have to walk farther to reach it. When you are 14 years old, it is not hard to do. That would've been the Southern 4501 or the Southern 630.

"I really got an appreciation for steam locomotives. Dad told me I could do any job that I wanted at the railroad. But he wanted me to go to college first. I went to the Citadel and I graduated with a degree in business administration.

Preston Claytor

"The day I graduated from college in 1982, I got a job in Birmingham, Alabama working on the restoration of the 611 for Norfolk Southern, working for a subcontractor. It had been last used in regular service in 1959.

"Stuart Saunders was the president of Norfolk Southern then, and he hated steam locomotives. He was cutting them into scrap as quickly as he could. My father stayed in close contact with several people at the roundhouse. He told them that if they heard any rumors about scrapping the 611, to let him know first. He had his finger on the pulse."

I joked about whether he would steal it away in the dark of night, kidnapping it, and hiding it somewhere.

Preston said, "I don't think he would've done that, but I'm not sure what would have happened. My uncle Graham Claytor was personal friends with Stuart Saunders. Uncle Graham worked for a big law firm in Washington, and he probably spent 90 percent of his time working for the Southern Railway. He wrote to Saunders and told him that he needed to save the 611. I think Saunders decided that the best action was no action.

"By 1962, Saunders had moved on and was by then working for the Pennsylvania Railroad. That is when they formed the Roanoke Transportation Museum. At that point, Norfolk & Western decided to give the museum the 611 and some other steam locomotives. It sat there until 1981. Then it moved to Birmingham. That is when I worked on it. After that, it came back to Roanoke."

Preston explained that how you put up a locomotive for long-term storage is a vital aspect of how easy it is to put it back in service again years later. "If you leave sand in the sand dome, 20 years later it is more like asphalt and it is very difficult to remove."

Locomotives carry sand to drop onto the rails when extra traction is needed. There are many linear feet of pipes on every steam locomotive. If stored with water in them, they will rust. Scott Lindsay, whom I met in Roanoke, was meticulous when he put the 611 away after the excursion programs in 1995, with the idea that someday somebody would come back and restore it.

Preston continued, "I went out with the locomotive on the excursion runs in the fall of 1982. I was a fireman or a night watchman. I did whatever it took. In November, we took the locomotive back to Birmingham. I couldn't work for the Norfolk Southern because my father worked there. But he helped me with contacts to get a job at what is now CSX as a management trainee. I was an operating supervisor for 11 years. I lived in the Atlanta area and the Richmond area.

"After that, I was general manager of a short line railroad in Alaska. Then I went to work for my cousin Graham, and he sent me to South America. I was in business operations, working on acquisitions and business plans from 1996 until about 2000. This was not steam; it was just general railroading. I started a short line in British Columbia. In 2000, I became Vice President of Safety and Operating Practices, training conductors, engineers, and dispatchers. I had eight regional safety training managers who worked for me. This was all for RailAmerica." It was a holding company that owned and managed a number of different small railroads around the country and internationally. "Each one was like a little franchise. This was a real growth period for smaller railroad companies. The big railroads did not want to manage these little spur lines. I worked there until 2012."

With this background, Preston told me about the part he played on the most current iteration of the 611's appearance on the rails again. He said, "In 2010, the NS began to bring back limited steam operation using the Tennessee Valley Railroad Museum as their platform. It is in Chattanooga."

He described that with earlier excursion programs, the railroad managed the programs themselves. But in more recent years, they felt it was more appropriate for the museums to own the locomotives and to manage the excursion programs.

"I did a number of presentations. I asked my audiences, 'What is the purpose of the Goodyear blimp? It is not so they can make a few shekels putting a camera in it and filming a golf tournament. It is goodwill for Goodyear. What if Goodyear did not need to manage a blimp department, if they could subcontract that to a private company? If they could simply dial up a blimp museum and say, 'We would like to have a blimp for this event? Can you please show up with the blimp and the pilot?' That would be a lot easier and cheaper."

I said, "The difference it seems to me is that Goodyear does not own the air. Norfolk Southern owns these tracks. They would need to manage track operations."

He said, "That's true. But the museum needs to bring a certified locomotive and operators, their own engineer, firemen, and all of the logistics. NS simply reaps the public relations benefit. So in 2010, NS announced that they would run a limited program with the Tennessee Valley Railroad Museum. NS was buying and rebuilding coaches as part of that effort. 2010 was the 50th anniversary of the Tennessee Valley Railroad Museum. NS only allowed them to run 10 miles out of the museum in Chattanooga. This was the first time a steam locomotive had been on one of their main tracks since 1994. It was all part of the program they called '21st Century Steam.' I suspect that name was coined by the Norfolk Southern PR people.

"There were plans to take it farther, and in the coming years they did. Eventually these excursions went as far as Norfolk. Meanwhile, I was looking at the locomotive they were using. It was 100 years old. I felt that we needed the 611.

"My wife and I drove from Louisville to Chattanooga to a banquet where Norfolk Southern president Wick Moorman was going to speak. He promoted NS, as was his job. In the question-and-answer session, one guy asked him if he would consider getting the Southern 1401 out of the Smithsonian museum to operate. This is like asking if we are going to make the space shuttle fly again. That one was built in 1926. It is under cover, inside. It was the crème de la crème of the Southern Railway. Then Wick went on to say, 'While we are on the subject, The Virginia Museum of Transportation in Roanoke holds two of the crown jewels of the steam era, the 611 and the 1218. We would get that loco-motive out again if they could ever get their act together in Roanoke.' I was all ears. My skin tingled."

Preston described four interested parties in Roanoke: the Trans-portation Museum, the Winston Link Museum, the Norfolk & Western Historical Society, and the regional chapter of the National Railroad Historical Society. "Every one is different, with their own mission and own funding issues. They all compete when they all should work to-gether. But if they would (cooperate) we could do it. I went up to speak to Wick afterwards and I said, 'I can make those guys get their act together. We can do this, and we can make you proud.'"

I said, "There is a pretty damn bold thing to say! Did you have any doubt? Why were you so sure you could do that?"

"I don't know. When you say you're going to do something, then you go and do it," he said, matter-of-factly. "Wick's reaction was, 'I hope that you can.' At that point, I had my mission. Keep in mind that in 2007, the Virginia Museum of Transportation was bankrupt. It was only three years into the rebound."

He described to me an intricate legal issue that needed to be re-solved. Theoretically, the City of Roanoke owned the 611, given to them in 1960 before the transportation museum was even envisioned. But there was never a title like we have for an automobile.

He said, "If you search the archives for the *Roanoke Times* in that era, I am sure you'll find lots of information. But I don't know if there was ever an actual donation letter. They built the track for the city of Roanoke, drove it into Wasena Park, and parked it there. There was no covering; it was parked outdoors. When I was a kid, I used to play down there all the time, and it was just sitting there.

"Eventually, the Roanoke Parks and Recreation Department formed the Roanoke Transportation Museum. This later then became the Vir-ginia Museum of Transportation. From 1976 onward, the Transporta-tion Museum was its own entity. By 2012, the City Council of Roanoke finally decided to give the 611 and a 1218 to the Museum.

"Scott Lindsay and I began to talk to Bev Fitzpatrick. We learned that Norfolk Southern was willing to subsidize each trip and that the Museum could sell tickets on most of the cars and reap their own profits. It was a lucrative situation for the museum."

I mentioned my conversation with David Goode, the former CEO of Norfolk Southern who was the guy who canceled the steam excursion program in the first place. I asked Preston what he thought the conditions were that must have changed in order for Wick Moorman to decide to allow a steam program when David had canceled it.

He said, "I think probably Wick simply had a more personal interest in it. The (program) at Southern Railway was started by my uncle Graham and he had a personal interest in it. My father at Norfolk Southern had a personal interest in it. My father died in 1993. My uncle died in 1994. All of the champions of it were gone. The operating people were not big fans of it. David had all the other pressures of running this big corporation. The operating guys said they just needed to get rid of the excursions. So he did."

Preston described a program that had them doing trips all over the NS coverage area. They were running trips for the NRHS chapters, rather than promoting the NS Corporation.

"Wick is our hero. He said if we put it together, we could put it on his tracks. I put a business plan together to do that. Cheri gets as much credit as anyone. She has a heart of gold; I can't say enough about what she's done. It wouldn't have happened without her or without Scott. Wick ensured us that if we did our job well, we'd be monetarily successful."

I made a mental note to try my best to speak with Mr. Moorman and get his thoughts before my trip was done.

Preston continued, "This may be the most famous locomotive in the world, certainly the most popular in America. It is fine sitting in a museum, but it needed to be on the tracks. Good things would flow to the museum if she ran again."

I told him about the generosity NS had shown me in Norfolk.

Preston said, "They're a well-run company. They're good people. They keep the same structure and focus they had when N&W merged with Southern. Wick is a great guy, a real student of railroad history. He's similar to what my father was.

"We launched the 'Fire Up 611' program in 2013. We solicited money and began to look for a place to refurbish it. We put budgets together with proposed excursions and schedules. Potential profit was in the neighborhood of $30,000 to $50,000 per excursion. By June we had a big PR event and launched a big fund-raising effort. We weren't sure how much was enough. We needed to rebuild the locomotive, build a storage, educational, and preservation facility, and fund an endowment.

We targeted $5 million. That started the fund raising campaign.

"We needed $3.5 million to get it to move. But we moved it to Spencer even before we had the money. We went to businessmen and said, 'We want you to be part of it.' I gave lots of speeches at civic organizations. 'It's a good news story. Everybody needs to be part of it.'"

Preston said that because of a falling out he'd had with the museum leadership, he'd dropped out of the program, two weeks prior to the completion of the rebuild. "I've never seen it run, even now."

I said, "You should. It is an amazing, unmistakable thing. It is a complete adrenaline experience. The ground shakes. The air fills with sound. And that's before it has even come into sight."

He mused, "This locomotive meant so much to my father. He was a people-person. He liked being out on the railroad, not sitting in his office. He could get a better pulse on the company when out talking to people. He loved seeing happy faces.

"One other thing: my father was the first CEO of NS. He was succeeded by Arnold McKinnon. The office building you visited in Norfolk was named for him. David Goode was the next CEO. The office building in Atlanta is the Goode Building. Wick Moorman had the yard in Bellevue (Ohio) yard named for him. What has the Claytor name on it? Only the 611. NS placed a plaque on the side dedicating it to him in 1994. It's the only thing ever dedicated to him. It didn't belong there as it wasn't authentic, part of the original locomotive. I don't

N&W's Class J 611

Photo by John Singleton

know where it is now.

"The 611 is the family history. It is the NS's history. With the excursions, we had people who remembered (regular service in) the 1950s. We had a whole other group from (excursions in) the 80s and 90s. Now it has another group of fans. My wife has a picture of me from Spencer. I was in my office doing paperwork. Scott called me and told me to come over as they were going to move it under its own power. We were ready mechanically. We were only going to move it a few hundred feet. The picture of me is with my 611 hat on and I'm grinning from ear to ear. We finally did it! The 611 was alive again! I was as happy as I'd ever been." He smiled broadly.

Preston continued, "I know from reading one of your travelogues that for you, the 611 is only one small piece. But it's a good piece.

"I have one other story I want to tell you. This was in 1957 or 1958. Dad was head of the legal department then, but he rode the cab on a night run. There is a mountain on the way into Christiansburg. The engineer gave Dad the chance to fire. It was dark. The steam was up. They carried passengers, and they stopped at the station. Dad said, 'How'd I do?' The engineer joked, 'It's a good thing it's dark out there.' Dad was using too much coal, firing inefficiently. The guys who did it every day were really good at it."

As he departed, Preston showed me a steam whistle from the 611 that he had in a wooden box in the trunk of his car. He seemed like a proud father; he really did!

My mother often tells me how fascinated I was by trains, even as a child. She told me recently, "You took your first train ride when you were a baby. It was either Thanksgiving or Christmas the year you were born, 1954. You, David (my older brother), your dad, and I went to see your grandparents on Long Island. I think your second trip was with Grandmommy. I'm sure you went on the Powhatan Arrow from here to Petersburg where Aunt Gladys picked you up and took you to their house in Richmond. You and David spent several days away from us. You loved to go to Cambria and watch the trains. We did this almost every day."

My lifelong fascination with mechanical things led me to Virginia Tech, where I got my degree in 1976. Engineering was profoundly difficult for me, and to this day there's nothing in my life that gives me more pride than my Virginia Tech engineering diploma.

Broadly, Mechanical Engineering has two areas of study:

energy and motion. Motion takes in the study of linkages, bearings, gears, wheels, cams, and all manner of moving things associated with machinery and is academically termed kinematics. Energy's core is thermodynamics, the branch of science that deals with heat and its conversion into mechanical movement, and generally to a lesser degree electrical and chemical energy. Thermodynamics is more accurately thermo-statics, as it generally deals with steady-state science, whereas a subset is heat transfer, which is more accurately the movement of heat, say as what happens when a heat source like a lit candle is placed under one end of a metal rod.

Because of their massive size, power, and human-like characteristics, steam locomotives are irresistible to just about everybody, but to nobody more than mechanical engineers. The beauty of steam locomotives, from the perspective of Mechanical Engineering, is that they are dripping with real-world applications of both sides of the coin. Because of their exoskeleton nature, steam locomotives are captivating to watch. But there are also fascinating things going on inside.

I took several Thermodynamics courses which were excruciatingly difficult. The textbook was a printed sedative. Three pages, max, had me belching Zs. Terms like "latent heat of vaporization," "entropy," "absolute pressure," "enthalpy," and "dynamic viscosity" were bantered about as if every bar-hopping college junior should intrinsically know them. Just mastering the lexicon was an achievement for me.

By its nature, thermodynamics includes unhealthy doses of mathematics, especially calculus. The pairing of an entirely new vocabulary and intense math made that course of study one of the most difficult for virtually every student. Let me just say that if you could take all the math out of Thermo, people would find it fascinating, because it explains how lots of everyday things, essentially anything that gets hot, work. Cars. Laptop computers. Your wife when you forget to take out the trash. Etc.

So here, in the best layman's terms I can muster, is how a steam engine works, and how a steam locomotive can take a lump of coal and a gallon of water (actually, a greater quantity than that, but you get the gist), and propel a multi-car, multi-ton train down a long set of tracks.

It has been known for centuries that when water is boiled, steam is created, and the volumetric relationship is approximately 1,600 to one. In other words, if you were to boil off a cubic meter of water, it would expand to produce 1,600 cubic meters of steam. When I was a child, we had a whistling tea-pot that would alert us to the onset of boiling by sending the steam past a whistle-cap that would produce noise from the expanding gas. If you vent that steam to the atmosphere, you see the tell-tale vapor. But if you attempt to cap it, to prevent it from venting, enormous pressure will build. That pressure is what is used to move the locomotive.

So a steam locomotive has two basic assemblies. The first boils water and produces pressurized steam. The second uses that steam to move the wheels. The former is the thermodynamic part and the latter is the motion or kinematic part.

In order to boil water, of course you need a source of heat. That's where the coal comes in. Then you need a boiler. To visualize, let's section off the locomotive, from the wheels up, starting from the back into four sections: the cab, the firebox/combustion chamber, the boiler proper, and the smokebox.

The cab houses the operators (the engineer and fireman), and the controls. In front of the cab is the firebox, which of course is where the fire happens. It typically has a grating at the bottom and is hoop-shaped at the top. The fireman starts a fire with anything that will readily burn (e.g. yesterday's newspaper, one of my earlier books) and then shovels on some coal – I'll describe this process more carefully in a moment. The coal sits on the grates, generating immense heat, and then burns to ashes. The ashes produced during burning fall through the grating onto an ash-pan which is dumped during the maintenance process at the end of each run. New coal is fed into the fire box to keep the fire going, in older locomotives by simply shoveling it on and in modern locomotives by a mechanical stoker, typically an auger, from the tender.

Note here that "modern" means after about 1930. Since for all intents and purposes, nobody in the world has built steam locomotives for decades, the modern machines were frozen in time long ago, around 1945. (This is not strictly true: second-world and third-world countries were building locomotives based on earlier designs until 15 or 20 years ago, but true domestically.)

As the fire intensifies, the hot gasses rise. The firebox is below and the combustion chamber above a series of parallel pipes placed at perhaps a 25 degree angle from flat. Think of the combustion chamber as a "holding zone" where more burning occurs before the hot gasses make their way through the boiler proper. When we see black smoke, that's actually unburned coal in aerosol form (solid particles in a gas). The combustion chamber gives the powdered coal in the aerosol more time and space to fully burn so as not to waste the heat potential of the coal.

Heat rises, and the hot aerosol causes a natural draw of air from the bottom, through the grating and the burning coal and to the top of the

box. At this point, the gasses look for a way out and they find a series
of tubes (larger ones called flues), running nearly horizontally but with
a slight upward tilt through the boiler proper. The tubes span the gap
between two sheets of steel called flue sheets, front and back, to which
the tubes are sealed. Between those sheets is a horizontal cylinder
filled with water to a level above the uppermost tubes. After the gasses
transfer through the tubes, they are routed to the smokebox and then
upwards to the smoke stack for exhausting.

Meanwhile, the tubes, filled with combustion gasses, become quite
hot, in fact several hundred degrees. The pressure is regulated in the
boiler so the water in contact is too highly pressurized to boil at contact with the tubes, but instead it boils at the upper surface, producing
steam in the top of the horizontal chamber. Note that even the uppermost tubes are still fully submerged at all times, as they would be
weakened if allowed to be above the heat-transfer effect of the water.

There is also a pocket or "jacket" of water surrounding the firebox/
combustion chamber that cools the steel that encloses that area. The
sheet of steel separating the aerosol from the water is called the crown
sheet. Crown sheet ruptures are among the most horrific and violent of
failures in steam locomotives. High pressure steam is suddenly free to
expand. Water turns to steam at 212F, but if pressurized it remains liquid. If allowed access to the atmosphere, it will flash instantly to steam.
Even a small crown sheet failure will most likely cause fatal burns and
scalds to the crew. A large one may blow the boiler clean off the locomotive!

Steam rising from the surface of the water is collected at the top
of the boiler and channeled into a compartment called a steam dome,
which is cylindrical, standing on end, and typically only a foot high or
so. At this point, voilà!, we now have steam to use to power the wheels.
The steam dome has valves that allow the engineer to regulate the
transfer of this steam to the steam engines.

Through fixed pipes, known as dry-pipes, the steam is directed
from the steam dome vertically downward to the engines, in effect
transferring the engineering work from the thermodynamics guys to
the kinematics guys. A basic conventional (or typical, like the 611's)
steam engine is comprised of a horizontal cylinder, mounted rigidly in
front of the driving wheels (that is, the wheels that are powered by the
action of the engine) and a piston that reciprocates fore and aft within
it. Through an ingenious set of linkages controlling a chamber known
as the valve chest, the steam is first fed into the cylinder in front of the
piston, and then once the piston has made its full stroke, the steam is

re-routed to the back of the piston to return it to its original position.

So now we have a piston moving back and forth. Another series of linkages: the piston rod, the main rod, and the side rods, transfer this force to all the "driver" wheels. The remaining steam, now greatly diminished in pressure, joins the combustion gasses and is exhausted out the stack. Furthermore, the exhausting steam causes a draft that helps draw combustion gasses through the boiler's flues so more steam is continually produced.

We now have a moving locomotive. Meanwhile, there's lots of other stuff going on. Modern locomotives were equipped with turbo-generators that used steam to turn an electrical generator to provide electricity for appliances in the locomotive, such as cab lights and headlights.

Locomotives were also equipped with a reservoir called a "sand dome" to hold sand that was deposited on the track to improve traction when rainy or icy conditions made the rails slippery. Plus, they were equipped with headlights, whistles, and mechanical bell ringers. Other accessories, such as lubricators, injectors, feedwater pumps, air brake valves, air pumps, etc. were mounted in various locations on the exterior of the locomotive.

Locomotives also typically had additional wheels fore and aft of the drivers, the fore wheels (called pilot wheels) to help the locomotive stay on the tracks through the curves and both fore and aft (called trailing wheels) to carry some of the enormous load. An unloaded Class J locomotive weighs nearly a half-million pounds!

Every sliding or rotating junction required lubrication. Most of the fixed bearings and sliding surfaces were lubricated continuously through a pressurized oiling system integral to the locomotive. Parts that continually moved relative to the locomotive itself had to be lubricated by hand during servicing operations. Most modern locomotives had roller bearings on all wheels as well as the driving rods.

The piston cylinder, because of the intense heat under which it operated, required a specialty lubricant, a thick, heavy oil that did not emulsify under extreme heat and pressure. The other bearings required more conventional lubrication.

On the Class J locomotives, the piston shaft connected to the main driving rod which operated the pair of wheels second from the front. The other driving wheels, the pair ahead of this set and the two pairs behind it, were rigidly connected by dog-bone like connecting rods.

The main exhaust was through a smokestack located at the top front of the locomotive and was at the traditional spot where people expect plumes or puffs of black or white smoke to pour out. The main exhaust was of the flue gases from the coal fire. However, once the steam had almost fully relieved its enormous pressure in the cylinders, it was also routed through a nozzle below the smokestack. The nozzle acted as a venturi, accelerating the speed of the exhaust steam which created a pressure drop or suction which acted on the flue gases. This created a significant additional draft on the coal fire which helped it achieve a more efficient and hotter combustion. Black smoke coming out of the pipe was indicative of an inefficient, less than optimal fuel-air mixture and was undesirable, as Bob Claytor learned from the engineer running the 611 into Christiansburg.

On large modern locomotives like the Class J, a device called a stoker or auger transferred coal from the tender into the locomotive itself so the fireman didn't have to manually shovel it. This device was controlled by the firemen and was powered by its own small steam engine.

So here's how this works in real life, and you are at the controls:

You fill the tender with coal and water. The 611 has an extremely large fire-box, 109 sq-ft of grate area. You want a flat fire. You put a thin layer of coal on it, literally with a shovel, about 6 inches deep. You put some kindling in, wood soaked in petroleum. Then you light it. An enormous amount of smoke forms because there is no draft into the stack. You want to bring the temperature up slowly because it creates less thermal expansion shock in the steel – the 611's boiler literally grows two inches from cold to hot. It takes seven or eight hours before there is usable steam. There is no temperature gauge, but there is a steam gauge which you monitor. Once you get about 75 psi of steam, it creates its own draft. Until the fire is fully heated, thick black smoke comes out of the stack.

Then you start the auger, the mechanical stoker that will feed in more coal. There are steam jets that spray the coal to distribute it evenly in the fire-box. The fire box reaches 1700F to1900F. That's hot enough to melt steel, but the sheets are surrounded by water that is in direct contact with the metal to keep it from melting. By now you're making steam and can get underway. A water pump called an injector feeds new water into the boiler, via a pre-heater, to keep a consistent level in the boiler. The fire is so hot that it glows white, and you can't inspect it without sunglasses or goggles. You work to achieve 300 psi in the boiler before embarking on a trip with a heavy train.

The boiler is fired up 24 hours prior to a trip. If the engine stays hot for several weeks, someone will sit with it overnight for security and to keep the fire going.

Once underway, there is constant communication between the engineer and fireman. The throttle releases the steam to the cylinders. When you're going downhill, you need less steam pressure. If your pressure is too high, it's vented away via safety valves, which is wasteful. If there's an uphill grade coming up, you need to anticipate that and build more heat and pressure.

Auguring of coal is ongoing and requires constant attention. You listen to the stack. It makes distinct noises which can tell you how it's working. You listen to the water injector; it's a turbine so it whines. When you've lost rail adhesion, which happens sometimes on really steep grades, you feel and hear it and have to respond quickly.

Once a month, the locomotive would need to have its boiler inspected, and the fire was allowed to go out. Then the process began all over again.

I'D REALLY NEVER THOUGHT ABOUT IT, but not all of the Powhatan Arrow's passengers were alive. Richard "Dick" Horne is a railroad enthusiast and Chairman of the Board of a family business called Horne Funeral Services, a company that just about everybody in the Christiansburg area has at one time interacted with. Or will.

He spoke with me in his office on the second floor of his facility on North Franklin Street, not a mile from the N&W railroad tracks, escorting me down a hallway lined with train photos on the walls. He had a noticeable limp from a knee he destroyed while firefighting years earlier. He's a heavy man with a gentle manner.

"I grew up in the family business. It was founded in 1870 by a Mr. Leckie. They lived beside the old location on East Main downtown."

He described in detail all the businesses on that one side of one block of the street, the location of the current police department, circa around 1965, the era of the end of the Powhatan Arrow. In addition to the funeral home, there was a bank, grocery store, shoe store, dress shop, appliance store, florist, ABC store, jeweler, office supply store, and department store. "All of this is gone now," he told me. "We've been here at this location for almost 30 years."

He said that people often die somewhere other than where they are to be buried. If so, during the years of passenger service, the human remains would be shipped by rail. "If someone died in Cincinnati or Baltimore or New York, wherever, the cadaver would be embalmed and placed in a shipping case, a heavy wooden box. The remains weren't buried in them. We'd transfer the remains into caskets here.

"If a soldier died in the Korean War, for instance, his remains would be shipped back in the baggage car. We'd be hired by the family to pick up the box at the station and bring it back to have the body transferred to the casket. My family has always been community-minded."

I noted, "This is not a business that can be outsourced to China."

He chuckled and said, "No. Locally we are fortunate that we don't have conglomerate-owned funeral services. There is one in Roanoke. There are some nationally-based companies, but we don't have any here in Montgomery, Floyd, or Pulaski Counties. Our challenge is to stay ahead of that. We don't have trouble or arguments with competitors. We get along with all of them.

"This is not a real popular business. By the nature of it, people don't want to deal with dead people and the bereaved. People think there's lots of money in it, but there's not."

He talked fondly about the community feel that his hometown of Christiansburg used to have. "In my childhood there were mostly locally-owned and family-owned businesses. Most of them are gone now, sad to say. Decades ago, everybody knew everybody else. Families knew families. I knew everybody who ran businesses in town. I could walk from one end of Main Street to the other and walk into every store and I knew every owner. I knew the attorneys and judges in the courthouse and I called them by name.

"When we were downtown, I knew every policeman. Every minister. Every doctor. They were all friends. That was a better world, at least for me. If I ever moved from here, I'd move to a smaller place. And I'd walk up and down the street and try to meet everybody.

"Now I don't know lots of families we serve. Main Street is gone. Everybody is shopping at the (New River Valley) Mall and I don't know anybody I see there when I go."

I acknowledged that funerals are sad occasions, most of the time. "Are there some that affect you the most?"

"Yes. Children. Without a question. It isn't often, but it's too often. It's typically an accident or trauma, or a congenital disease. Some have been killed through abuse. I've buried children murdered by their families. I don't ever want to do that again."

"We all have an expiration date. How do you want to go?" I asked.

"I want to be buried. I have a plot picked out and paid for," he chuckled.

I LEFT THE FUNERAL CHAPEL and drove into downtown and walked that same stretch of Main Street from where Horne's Funeral service had moved.

In downtown Christiansburg is my dysphoria most acute. Christiansburg is often on lists of Virginia's most livable towns and best towns to raise a family. But it falls far short, in an opinion I share with Richard Horne, of the days of my youth in the 1960s.

I went to the center square at the intersection of Main and Franklin Streets, where three of four legs of a traffic circle still remain. There were two banks, an antique store, and the newly refurbished regional public safety building.

There is an historical marker commemorating the duel between Thomas Lewis and John McHenry in May, 1808, on that spot, which resulted in the deaths of both men. Of note was that Dr. John Floyd, later Governor of Virginia and the namesake of nearby Floyd County, was the attending physician. Imagine that job. "Yup, this one's dead. Yup, this one's dead, too."

Going east on Main, beside one of the banks was the headquarters of the town police department, with "19-WIMMER BUILDING-48" engraved above the second floor. Beyond that was an office building with mostly law firms in it. Then a parking lot. That was the whole block. The other buildings had long ago been razed. The streetscape was pleasant, with lollypop shaped trees and decorative streetlamps on a brick and concrete sidewalk. A newly-constructed majestic courthouse in brick, granite, glass, and concrete was across the street.

I sat on a wooden park bench to contemplate.

What were absent were pedestrians. There were no people, and it was the middle of the day. When I was a kid, it was a bustling place. Shoppers alternated between Roses 5¢ 10¢ 25¢ store on the north side of Main Street and Leggett's Department Store on the south. There was a movie house, the ratty old Palace Theater. Two drug stores. A photo shop. My father's printing company and the local bi-weekly newspaper. A furniture store. Hardware stores, antique stores, appliance stores, and banks. A stereo music store. Locally owned restaurants and bars. The schools were nearby and you could easily walk downtown after school. I'd see friends downtown and I'd know the clerks. It felt comfortable, safe. Stable. Enduring.

How could any community that jettisoned its downtown be a good place to raise a family? I longed for someone to walk past so I could share a cordial greeting. "Hello, sir! How's your day?" Nobody did.

So I drove into Cambria, where the railroad tracks were, looking for more activity.

My HUMBLE HOMETOWN is unique along the Powhatan Arrow's path in that it still has not one but two historic railroad stations. I've been talking a lot about the rails and the communities, but let's give the stations their due. Historically, when the track was laid through any town, it provided no benefit unless the trains stopped there. Other than the businesses they served through sidings, trains only stopped at the stations, making these buildings the focal point of their communities. From the earliest days, horses and buggies brought people to the stations where they arrived or departed, greeted friends, family members, and strangers, exchanged gossip, and learned about the outside world.

Arrivals and departures were always displayed prominently on signboards inside the station, along with a wall-clock. The stations were instantly transformed when trains arrived, as people and products scurried to and fro, embarking and disembarking. Mail was exchanged as were telegrams. The station agent acted as the station's conductor, directing all manner of activity, selling tickets, handling baggage, and in the winter keeping the pot-bellied stove stoked. In the smaller stations,

Christiansburg's 1867 station

he doubled as the telegraph officer. He handled interaction with the train's engineers and conductors and ensured safe access to passengers. Larger stations had a baggageman who took care of merchandise shipping. Some stations handled both passenger and merchandise in the same building, some separate.

In the earliest years of rail, neither shelter nor toilet facilities were provided; passengers simply stood by the track at designated locations and waited. Since there was no communication with the train, passengers got no notifications of late arrivals. Tickets were sold at hotels or any suitable business locations nearby. When shelters began to be provided, they were often built hastily of wood, and were vulnerable to fires started by sparks from the locomotives.

By the 1840s, stations of note were being built around the larger cities and throughout the 1850s, New York, Philadelphia, Baltimore, and Harrisburg had erected substantial, handsome stations. Eventually, brick and stone buildings were built, but the application of anything we could reasonably term as "architecture" typically didn't come into being in smaller communities until after the Civil War, often with a distinctive style of vast overhanging eaves and steep-pitched roofs.

Sometime around the arrival of the Virginia and Tennessee Railroad in Christiansburg, a small station was built. It was destroyed by Federal General George Crook the day after the Battle of Cloyd's Mountain in nearby Pulaski County in early May, 1864. Its replacement, now the older of Christiansburg's two stations, is in private hands, owned by Meghan Dorsett. Her home dates back to 1867, rebuilt under the direction of our old friend Billy Mahone after the Civil War. Its footprint is roughly in the pattern of an Egyptian sphinx, with the two "paws" being waiting rooms, one for men and the other for women, and the "head" being a control tower. The "body" was used as a freight area. It is painted yellow with a Tuscan red trim just like the Powhatan Arrow. The newer station, 300 yards to the east, was built in 1907.

Twin tracks are no more than 20 feet from the edge of the old building and when trains rumbled by, as they did frequently, it was too loud to carry on a conversation inside. In the "paws" of the building, Meghan runs a bookstore and a toy store.

Meghan and I sat in the old men's waiting room where she said, "The station started life as part of the Virginia and Tennessee Railroad, not the Norfolk & Western. It is designed as a Tuscan Italianate station. What is unusual about that is that while High Tuscan Italianate architecture was popular in residential structures from about 1860 to about 1875, it was quite uncommon in commercial structures. There are almost no commercial structures in the style of architecture throughout the southern United States. It is popular in New England and the north central states and out west and in California. But there are almost no commercial structures in the style of architecture throughout the southern United States.

"My mother was an architectural historian and I have a degree in design. The station is oriented towards the street rather than towards the tracks. If you look at it from the street you feel like you're looking at a house rather than a commercial structure. Billy Mahone's wife Otelia is generally credited with the design of these stations. She made most of the aesthetic decisions.

"Construction of the Virginia and Tennessee Railroad began prior to that in 1848. I believe they reached this area in about 1854. Then it continued onto Bristol. The station was constructed in 1857.

"By the time the Civil War broke out in 1861, only four years later, this rail line was extraordinarily strategically important to the Confederacy. It was literally the lifeline to Lee's Army of Northern Virginia."

Meghan produced a map showing all of the railroads in the United States at the onset of the Civil War. It showed a solid line running essentially from Norfolk to Christiansburg, exactly the same line as the Powhatan Arrow would later traverse, and then on to Bristol. None of the section northwest of Christiansburg at that time had been constructed. "After the war Mahone renamed his railroad the Atlantic, Mississippi, and Ohio Railroad, the AM&O. People often jokingly referred to it as the 'All Mine and Otelia's Railroad.'"

There was no line at that time coming down the Valley of Virginia from Winchester to Roanoke, paralleling current Interstate 81. A vast expanse of the central Appalachians had no trains cutting across. From Harpers Ferry in the north to Chattanooga in the south, it was impossible to cross the mountains by train. And by any other means, the trip would have been long, arduous, and treacherous.

Three lines crossed the Appalachian Mountains north of the Mason-Dixon Line, including the B&O from Baltimore to Wheeling. But essentially there were none from the northernmost tip of current Virginia all the way into southern Tennessee, a distance of approximately 250 miles. There were significantly more miles of railroad track in the Union states compared with the Confederacy.

Meghan said the disparity in rail mileage was only part of the problem. "Another one of the reasons that the South lost the Civil War is that all of the rails and trains north of the Mason Dixon and northwest of the Appalachians were of the same gauge. There were as many as four different gauges of track rail in the South. What that meant was at the intersection of two different gauges, all of the materials on one train needed to be offloaded and then reloaded onto another train to continue their journey. They had a lousy transportation system in the South!"

When the West Virginia statehood people began their effort to form a new state around about 1863, their efforts were centered in the far northwestern section of Virginia in Wheeling. You could take a train from Wheeling to Baltimore, but there was no direct way to take a train from Wheeling, Huntington, or Charleston to Richmond. This explains why, when the statehood movement got underway, the government in Richmond was helpless to stop it.

During the Civil War, there were really only two rail lines that connected Virginia with the rest of the Confederacy. One of them ran almost due south from Richmond down to the Atlantic coast. The other was the Virginia and Tennessee line. Early in the war, the Union Army secured the line directly south from Richmond. During a significant part of the War, only the Virginia and Tennessee was operational. This is why it was of such enormous strategic importance.

"Union commanders in 1864 sent General William Crook southward from the area that is now West Virginia with three strategic objectives.

"First, destroy the salt works in Saltville. Salt was used in the preservation of meat and in the production of gunpowder. Second, destroy the two supply depots, one at Dublin and the other here in Cambria. Third, destroy the bridge over the New River at Central Depot (later Radford).

"The armies engaged just north of Dublin at Cloyds Mountain. The Union commander, George Crook, lost 688 men, 10 percent of his force, and the Confederate commander, Albert Jenkins, lost 538, representing 23 percent of his."

The battle was one of the fiercest and most important in the war. The Confederates failed to stop the Union advancement, and Federal soldiers were able to accomplish all of their goals. With the Virginia and Tennessee essentially severed at that point, General Lee had no more supplies for his troops and this greatly hastened his surrender the following spring at Appomattox.

"Because of the naval blockade of southern ports, the only way to get supplies to Lee's army was from Tennessee, Alabama, and Mississippi via the Virginia and Tennessee Railroad line."

This area in southwest Virginia was considered the pinch point of the hourglass for the supplies. If the Union army destroyed the tracks in Salem or Lynchburg, the Confederates could still move their goods on adjacent roads. But this area had a poorly defined roadway system. When the Union Army figured that out, they focused all of their attention on severing the railroad line here. The only railroad bridge over the New River in the entire region was just outside of Central Depot.

"The station here in Cambria, which is actually the Christiansburg Station that was destroyed during that raid, is built exactly on the same location. I literally found the foundation of the older building while crawling underneath this building. The original building was about 4,000 square feet. This building is over 6,000 square feet. The Federals burned three or four warehouses, the mill, the telegraph station, post office, commissary, and this depot's predecessor. None of these would have been in this community more than seven or eight years after the arrival of the tracks in the first place.

"This building has two waiting rooms, one for men and one for women. The women needed to come through the men's waiting room to board the train. Presumably, any Negroes who traveled during that time period went through the freight area. When the Supreme Court decided in 1896 that blacks should be able to travel on all forms of public transportation and that the carriers needed to provide separate but equal accommodations for them, this particular station was no longer suitable. Therefore, the Norfolk & Western constructed a new station."

We were sitting on old metal chairs in the men's waiting room, nearest the tracks and on the left side of the building. She sent me across to the other waiting room which was on the right side of the building. It was a smaller room and it had more ornate trimmings around the doors and windows, suitable for the delicacies of the female rail patrons. When I returned, she continued, "It has a southern exposure, allowing it to stay warmer during the winter months because there was no heat in the building in those days. The eaves are wide enough in the building such that it stays cooler in the summer as well. Architects of that era knew about solar heating and cooling and employed techniques to make the building more comfortable, especially for the women.

"The women's waiting room is the side furthest from the track. Architects also apparently took into consideration keeping the women away from all the dirt, grime, and noise.

"This station has three main rooms: the men's waiting room, the women's waiting room, and the freight house. In the intersection between them was the ticket office. Upstairs in the tower were the trainmaster's office and the telegraph office." She showed me where a double door led from the men's waiting room directly outside to the landing where people could board the train.

Outside, she explained that on many occasions the railroad company had elevated the level of the rail. "The track has been raised 36 inches in the past 30 years since we have been here. It has created a headache for us because it has altered the rain water situation and floodwaters can surround the building that once would have drained away into the creek on the other side of the tracks.

"In the *Plessy v. Ferguson* case in 1896, the federal government affirmed that all public transportation needed to be accessible by blacks, however they did not mandate that these facilities be integrated. Therefore, companies like the Norfolk & Western were forced to provide facilities at each of their stations and on the trains themselves where blacks could be accommodated in what were supposedly equal facilities. N&W would have begun implementation of this law beginning in the eastern side of the state and working its way out here. The 'new' station was built here in Christiansburg in 1907. They essentially deemed that this particular building could not be properly and effectively segregated. Until then, this building had both a passenger component and a freight component. This freight depot was servicing all of Montgomery County, all of Floyd County and significant parts of Giles County. So they just decided to build a new passenger building and they left this building to service freight needs solely.

"The front end of this building then became the engineering office for this district which extended that time from here up to Bluefield. When we acquired the building, we found tons and tons of documents representing buildings all the way from here to Williamson, West Virginia.

"Prior to about 1880, the rail went westward through Central Depot (Radford) and Dublin eventually to Bristol. There was no spur at that point northward along the New River into West Virginia. Norfolk & Western built that northern spur into West Virginia in the 1880s following the New River on the west side. By 1907, the Virginian Railway built an entirely separate line westward from Roanoke through a large tunnel that now goes under US-460, and reached the river and paralleled it up the east side. Nowadays, these two railroads have merged and the Norfolk Southern controls the rails on both sides.

"The N&W left the New River near the West Virginia line and went through Bluefield, Welch, and Williamson, and of course is the route that you are following. This station was deaccessioned in 1964 and sold to a local wholesale company that used it as a warehouse. In about 1974, it was bought by a man who used it as a place to store fertilizer.

"On December 30, 1981, the fate of this building was altered dramatically. The official story is that an engineer was taking four pusher engines back to Radford. Legend has it that he stopped at the passenger station to get a cup of coffee, to sign some papers, and to wish his coworkers a Happy New Year. The unofficial story is that he had a girlfriend halfway up the hill on East Main St., and he wanted to see her before New Year's Day and before he went back to his wife in Radford.

"He apparently forgot to set the emergency brake on four locomotives. If you look out the window at the tracks, you might think that it is perfectly flat. In fact, there is a slight (downhill slope from) the passenger station. They began to roll downhill themselves. They were probably going about 10 or 12 mph by the time they slammed into two parked boxcars sitting on the siding on the street side of the freight-house.

"The boxcars jackknifed and derailed with one of them smashing into the side of this building. After the crash, the building was wrecked, there was no back wall, several walls were no longer plumb, and most of the windows were broken. It was truly a mess.

"My mother happened to be driving by one day when a demolition order was being attached to the front door. She said hell with that! She tracked down the owner and handed him an unsecured check for $17,000 and bought the building. Then she went back home that evening and told my father. By all reports, Dad nearly had heart failure.

"They sold their house in Giles County and bought another house up the hill from here. They built a building within a building, an apartment inside the warehouse of the freight house. They spent two years doing that and when it was finished, they moved in.

"This building is built to a much higher standard than virtually any building around here. This building was literally bumped off its foundation and we had to find contractors who could lift it back on and reset it back on the original blocks. The entire building is built out of American chestnut. After the chestnut blight that swept this area in the 1930s, there was no harvestable chestnut wood in this region.

"I have ten center-cut American chestnut beams under the floor of the freight house right now. These beams are about 7 inches by 11 inches by 40 feet long. The lumber in the building is worth far more than the building.

"We opened a bookstore here in the men's waiting room. The sole purpose was to raise enough money to provide for repainting of the structure, fix some of the siding, and restore two of the windows back to the original design."

She guessed that annual maintenance of the building was probably in the range of $6,000-$8,000. "We used to be able to keep up with that when the railroad charged us $680 annual rent for the land under the building. When (NS) raised the rent to more than $6,000, essentially they took away all of the maintenance funding. They can charge us anything they want because we have no choice. The building cannot be moved.

"It is pretty astounding to me how little recognition this station actually has. (But) every immigrant that arrived in Montgomery County from 1867 until 1907 came through this building. Every item that was carried into or out of this county from 1867 until about 1956 was shipped through this building. Every Model T automobile. Every Sears home. Every piano. Every farm implement. Every cooking set.

Every roll-top desk. Every wedding dress. And every soldier, airman, or seaman. They didn't want these people shipped through the passenger station. So from the Spanish American War to World War I through World War II, the Korean conflict and to the early days of the Vietnam War, they all left from here. For many of these people the last view in their lives of their loved ones was from the platform outside this depot. There was a point in World War II where the entire freight room, 110 feet long, was filled with flag-draped coffins.

"For lots of students at VPI, this was the place they met their girl-friends and future wives. The boys would come over from Blacksburg and the girls would come over from Radford. They would sit outside on the freight platform and they would court."

The depot was the center of what for decades was a thriving community. She pointed out the window to several buildings that are over 100 years old. "There was a teahouse, an inn, a hospital, a hotel, a grocery store, and many other locally owned businesses. There was even a brothel in the building adjacent to the hospital. Both were on the second floor. There was a door connecting the brothel with the hospital and during epidemics, they could open the door and have some of the patients recuperating in the beds in the brothel. It was one stop shopping," she chuckled. "You could get laid, get diagnosed, and get treated, without ever leaving the building.

"There was also a bar in town. During Prohibition, it was turned into a restaurant. But by all accounts, the food was awful. There was a service door between the restaurant and the pharmacy. You could go in and get a prescription for whatever nerve medicine you wanted, probably four or six doses per day and the waitress at the restaurant would put it on file at the pharmacy. Your medication would come in one ounce glasses. You would get your medication along with your lunch or dinner. I heard the stories from the daughter of the woman who ran the brothel.

"After we acquired the place, I was up in the attic looking at boxes and boxes of old records of time sheets and other transactions. I found records of large quantities of medicinals. The pharmacy didn't have room to store it. And so much of it was stored here at the depot. There were 128 medicinals, all shipped from the same Canadian distillery."

She noted that the grade into Cambria is the steepest on the Norfolk & Western line. It is where the rail crosses from the Roanoke River drainage to the New River drainage. The New River is a tributary of the Kanawha and ultimately the Ohio and the Mississippi; it's the Eastern Continental Divide.

We talked about the recent 611 steam locomotive excursion. She said they estimated that in the three days it ran past the station, once in each direction, over 2,800 people gathered to watch.

"For a long time, we did not value historical sites. Christiansburg is notoriously bad for this. They'd tear down an historic building before they'd look at it. Most municipalities in Virginia didn't have the infrastructure for preserving old structures. And generally the locals don't understand the urgency. So often, if preservation is going to happen, it is spurred by someone from the outside. It usually starts from people moving to a place. Specifically here, for a lot of people in Christiansburg, Cambria was a derelict old place. People stopped seeing what was special about it. They saw in this (depot) an old building that was falling down and should be torn apart. Christiansburg is becoming more mindful of historic preservation. The town leadership is becoming more responsive.

"Because of Virginia Tech, there are a lot of people here from outside the region. My mother saw in this building a rare Tuscan Italianate railroad station, and she wanted to save it. Nobody else around here – well, people around here might have known it had some significant historic significance – but nobody else knew of the Tuscan Italianate design and the rarity.

"For a long time, railroads were run by people who had a passion for railroads. Bob Claytor, who was CEO back when we were rehabbing this building, really liked trains. Now it's run by bean-counters who like bottom-lines and spreadsheets. My building pre-dates their corporation by 13 years. We can't move it. It's too wide to move, unless we took it apart piece by piece. There are only a few older buildings in town, but this may be the oldest non-residential structure.

"Cambria was the quintessential railroad town. Like any place, there are things that are good and things that are ugly. There was an active KKK here. There are stories of people on horseback harassing the African American families on the south side of the track, which was predominantly black."

Cambria was incorporated as a separate town in 1906. It consolidated with Christiansburg in 1964. "By the 1980s if you asked people here where they lived they'd say 'Christiansburg' and they didn't know Cambria even existed. We've spent 33 years selling the idea that Cambria still exists. Now it's all an historic district."

We toured the building together. She noted that "It's like living in a barn. We have wanted critters and unwanted critters, mostly mice and rats and an occasional skunk." She showed me the solid chestnut wood planking in the floor, ceiling rafters, and walls. "There is 110 feet of open length with no interior support. The roof has queen rod trusses, which is the most stable truss design ever created. It's just a great old building."

FROM DAVID GOODE IN NORFOLK to Cheri George and Bev Fitzpatrick in Roanoke to Preston Claytor in my office, I'd heard so many times about the contribution of former Norfolk Southern CEO Wick Moorman to the resuscitation of the 21st Century Steam program and getting the 611 back on the rails. So I asked these folks to help me find him, and I was able to do a telephone interview.

Moorman reminded me the NS had run a steam program a generation earlier, which had been discontinued during David Goode's tenure as CEO. "Graham Claytor at Southern (Railroad) and Bob Claytor at Norfolk & Western were responsible for it. Bob continued it (after the merger) at NS. It was effective for a long period of time. It was a big program; they were out almost every week. It had gotten somewhat tired. The operations people were tired, as it's not an easy task to manage. There were safety issues. David decided to end it.

"I was not part of that decision process. It was 25 years ago. NS gave the 1218 and 611 (locomotives) to Roanoke, put away in good shape with the idea they may get out again someday.

"I became CEO. I got letters and e-mails once a month at least from employees and rail fans to get the program going again. There is a lot of pride on the part of a lot of people at Norfolk Southern about the company. They see things that look good and present a good image, and they like it. I like it.

"Fast-forward to about five years ago and the genesis of the return of the steam program. There is a locomotive owned by the Tennessee Valley Railroad Museum (TVRM) in Chattanooga, the 4501. It was coming up on its 100th birthday.

"I came into (being CEO) believing that supporting the institutions that preserved the heritage of the combined company was important. We wanted them to continue to do good work in the preservation of NS and its predecessor companies. I had a conversation with our head of corporate communications. He thought from the standpoint of enhancing the image of the company, bringing back the steam program would be the best thing we could do.

"I thought about it. There is another successful program run by Union Pacific, one of the truly iconic companies. We were having employees ride on some of our business trips, our conductors and signal people and maintenance people. It was a good thing. I got comments that many had never even ridden a train. They wanted their families to be able to come along. Those trains were pulled by conventional diesel (locomotives).

"This combination of things came together. We came up with a plan to help the TVRM get their 4501 in running condition. We let them run fan trips to generate some revenue, but we would run employee trips. It followed logically that Roanoke would be interested; I expected that.

"When they came forward and said they'd like to get the 611 running again, that it would be great for the museum, great for Roanoke, and obviously great for NS, I agreed. It is the iconic locomotive of Norfolk & Western and one of two or three in North America. I decided we could help with capital if they would raise some money and manage the program. So it went forward."

NS had a valuable painting, and they decided to sell it. They made the Virginia Museum of Transportation and various other charities throughout the Roanoke Valley beneficiaries.

"From the founding days of N&W," Wick continued, "Roanoke has always been extremely important to us. NS is a large philanthropic benefactor in Norfolk now. We've focused to a great extent first on Norfolk and right behind it, Roanoke.

"With the fruition of the program, I've been very happy with it. It has gotten lots of positive reaction. I rode the 611 when it came back to Roanoke from Spencer. The crowds both in North Carolina and Virginia were stunning! They weren't just railfans. It was an event! They came out and saw the train and thought about NS and thought well of it; that's a great thing. These are communities where our employees live. Communities we serve. It's hard to create that kind of impression any other way.

"The prior steam program had run its course. In my time, several things came together. Previously, we owned the locomotives and rolling stock. We'd given it all away to various museums. It had been disbursed. We had some partners in TVRM and VMT that came forward. The museums were at a stage of maturity to where they were able to own, maintain, and run these locomotives. Call it serendipity. Timing is so much of it. Bev Fitzpatrick at the VMT got that museum back on its feet with his enthusiasm. Preston understands the steam program and has a passion for Roanoke and for the preservation of the heritage of his father and his uncle who were great men. You had me at CEO who always loved trains. We all felt it could be a good thing for the company.

"And it has been! For Roanoke having the 611 and the 2156 come back for a visit and with the 1218 in their VMT, it now has the three signature locomotives of Norfolk & Western locomotive classes. They were all built in Roanoke. That's really great! People will continue to come into that museum from all over the world to see them."

He said, modestly, "I had a lot of great people around, and we were able to make it happen. I wouldn't have said yes without this set of circumstances that enabled me to say yes. As chief executive officer of NS, I looked at circumstances and realized that by doing this we could benefit the city of Roanoke, the VMT, our employees, and the larger community, and that would be good for NS."

Wick was CEO from 2005 until 2015. I asked him during his ten years what accomplishments gave him the most pride. He said, "I tend to look back and see what I didn't get done, rather than what I did. I did very little on my own to be proud of. I had smart people working for me, doing things. We did lots of PR stuff. We survived and prospered. The company is owned by the shareholders and the stock was trading substantially higher when I left than when I got there; that's always a good thing. We improved the (corporate) culture in a positive ways. We kept the good things that made NS and N&W and Southern and Conrail successful companies, culturally. We were performance driven and accountable. We helped people feel more empowered to say what they thought and bring their good ideas forward. We ran a safe company for our employees and the communities we serve."

As I thanked him for his time in preparation to end the conversation, Wick said, "When we hang up, Google '*Wall Street Journal* and my name.'" And so I did. I found this headline, **Amtrak Names new CEO.** The article began, "Amtrak is naming Norfolk Southern Corp. veteran Charles "Wick" Moorman as its next chief executive as the national passenger railroad confronts big projects amid growing demand." How exciting! Congratulations, Wick Moorman!!!

FINALLY IT WAS TIME to renew my journey westward. From Christiansburg, the rail line went due west through the villages of Vicker and Walton. US-460 deviates away to the north to rejoin the corridor later in Giles County, so I needed to navigate a series of tiny, winding but familiar roads to stay close to the tracks. At Vicker there is an impressive coaling tower that looks like a massive tuning fork, tongs down. As the track approaches the New River, there is a wye, sending the left branch to Radford and on down to Bristol – the original Virginia and

Tennessee line – and my Powhatan Arrow line to the right branch, downstream towards West Virginia.

I took a side-trip into Radford to see famed railroad historian Bud Jeffries, who literally wrote the book on the N&W's steam era, a book entitled, *N&W Giant of Steam*. Bud, formally known as Colonel Lewis Ingles Jeffries, USA, Retired, is the official historian of the Virginia Transportation Museum. His home is on the family farm in west Radford, upstream on the New River from the wye.

Like Roanoke, Radford was a railroad town, head of the N&W's Radford Division. There were offices where workers managed operations for not only the main line, but spurs to Blacksburg and Galax, both which are now recreational trails (the Huckleberry and the New River Trails, respectively). As technology improved, fewer local operations were needed and tasks could be handled more centrally. Locomotives were assigned to specific divisions and the divisions were tasked with scheduling, refueling, inspections, and maintenance chores. Nowadays, all rolling stock is bar-coded and there are scanners adjacent to the tracks that scan each locomotive and car to monitor their locations. Everything is tracked by computers.

Bud's lineage is directly linked to Mary Draper Ingles whose famed escape from Indian captivity and return to the area in 1755 is still part of local lore.

Bud is a distinguished, learned man, quick-minded and articulate. In retirement, he runs the farm and was dressed as a farmer, with thread-bare jeans held by wide black suspenders and a tan flannel shirt with pockets bulging with his roving office. I approached his home walking the brick sidewalk and he met me atop the stairs to the porch of the "new" wing of the house, built in 1849. Rimming the yard was a freshly-painted white picket fence, also enclosing a 12 foot by 12 foot log structure, an old smoke house.

The house had a pine-like, museum-musty smell, with decades-old books on the mantle, ceiling-to-almost-floor windows with uneven glass, and finger-worn, old books scattered throughout. The room where we sat and talked had a massive fireplace rimmed by a white mantle. The room was painted in a deep red, reminiscent of the Tuscan red of the N&W. Our conversation was overseen by framed lithographs on the wall of Virginia Civil War legends Robert E. Lee and Thomas "Stonewall" Jackson.

Bud's admiration for the old Norfolk & Western Railway was boundless. He began our conversation by educating me on the history. "The N&W's predecessor line was laid from Norfolk to Bristol, built before the Civil War. Railroad companies in those days often had a single, linear track and the company was named after the termination points. For example, the Norfolk and Petersburg Railroad linked those two cities. The South Side Rail Road was between Petersburg and Lynchburg. And then the Virginia and Tennessee Railroad was between Lynchburg and Bristol. These were the lines that merged to become the Norfolk & Western."

His fingers played with white shocks of hair, gesturing over his head as we spoke, and often pushing his wire-rimmed glasses up the slope of his nose.

"(Radford) was an engine change point. One shift of workers and one locomotive would drive the train from Lynchburg to Radford and then another would pick it up and pull it to Bristol. It was about 100 miles each way. This line was completed in 1856."

Radford, originally Central Depot, was a city developed for and by the Virginia and Tennessee Railroad. "During the Civil War, the Union sent recognizance into the area that is now southern West Virginia. These men found significant deposits of easily-extracted coal. During the late 19th Century, the N&W constructed a new line downriver to West Virginia and into a spaghetti-bowl network of spur lines into hundreds of hollows where coal was extracted. That is the line down the New River that is still in operation today," and of course was the route of the Powhatan Arrow.

"In the N&W's first year of carrying coal, they only moved about 80,000 tons. Within a few years, they were moving millions of tons annually. The growth was dramatic. Initially, all the coal went east, either to connecting lines up the Shenandoah Valley or to ships at Norfolk. Around about 1890, a line was begun to the northwest to carry coal to the furnaces of the industrial cities of Ohio, Indiana, and Michigan. So the Ohio extension was built from the Bluefield/Pocahontas/Bramwell area into the valley of the Tug Fork of the Big Sandy River that separates West Virginia from Kentucky and to the Ohio River at Kenova."

Ironically, just after the line was completed in 1872, the Panic of 1873 bankrupted the company! From that the Norfolk & Western Railway was organized in 1883.

He continued, "They moved their first load of coal in 1883, but within five years, they'd already exceeded the capacity of the line. At that point, they began major renovations to handle additional trains. They straightened some track, lessened some grades, and added another parallel track along much of the distance. This allowed for almost continuous two-way operation. Most of this was done by 1891."

Scheduling and dispatching were primitive by today's standards. Then, an engineer would pick up an order to drive the train a certain distance. Unless updated at the other end, he would need to stop to get further orders. The physical locations of the various trains were monitored by hand on long chalk-boards.

Quickly, the N&W's primary business became the shipment of bituminous coal. By the turn of the 20th Century, 75 percent to 80 percent of the total tonnage was coal. As I had learned in Roanoke, from early on, the N&W was an active participant in the design and fabrication of its own locomotives. Because the grades were significant by railroad standards and because the trains were extremely long and heavy, the N&W needed the strongest, most powerful locomotives in the world.

A given train was typically only pulled 100 miles or so before a change of crew and a servicing of the locomotive. In some cases, for instance, a Y-class locomotive might move the train through the mountains from Williamson to Roanoke, whereupon a lighter A-class, more suitable for flatter, faster terrain, might drive it to Norfolk. It wasn't unheard of for a train to have upwards of 190 fully laden coal cars. A Y6 locomotive might drive it from Bluefield to Walton where another locomotive, a pusher, might drive it over the divide at Christiansburg and into the Roanoke Valley.

"Even though freight, and specifically coal, was almost always the primary business of the N&W, all railroads were inherently passenger-based from the beginning. They used the same rails, of course, but otherwise passenger service was completely different from freight service. The locomotives were faster. The cars were suited for people instead of stuff. The terminals were closer so the train had more stops. Frequently, freight trains would use passing sidings (parallel, short-distance tracks) to allow faster passenger trains to pass. As technology progressed, trains could go either direction.

"The peak usage of passengers on the N&W was in the 1920s. There were 10- to 12-million passengers per year throughout the N&W network. At that time, there were also many short-distance spur lines and many 'local' trains that would carry passengers to and from nearby towns. But then automobiles became more popular and by the Great Depression, usage dropped to perhaps 2-million annually. World War II brought another surge in usage, as five times as many passengers used the rail in 1944, the last full year of the war, as did in 1939 before it began. After the war, branch line usage dropped off dramatically and those lines began to close. The long distance lines stayed viable for another couple of decades."

Automobile travel in the corridor, especially through the mountains, wasn't easy. Cars were unreliable, roads were poor or non-existent, and the terrain was rugged. Improvements in automobiles and roads began to overwhelm passenger rail.

In the period of fifty years after World War II, many of the spur lines folded. The line that is now the New River Trail from Pulaski to Galax and Fries (locally called the Cripple Creek Extension) folded. The Virginia Creeper line from Abingdon to West Jefferson, North Carolina, folded (The Virginia portion is now the Virginia Creeper Trail.). The Huckleberry Line, from Christiansburg to Blacksburg near Virginia Tech, ran until 1958. The Huckleberry was originally built in 1902, as the Virginia Anthracite Coal and Rail Company from Christiansburg to the coal mines at Merrimac. Shortly thereafter, in 1904, it was extended into Blacksburg to allow passenger service for the cadets at VPI to access the main line in Christiansburg. Rumors abound about its naming, but my favorite story is that it was so slow, cadets would hop off the front car, pick some berries that lined the tracks, and then hop back on before the last car had gone by.

"During the Korean War, there was a slight bump upwards in ridership, but the downward trend continued afterwards. Back in the late 1930s, the premier train of the N&W was the Pocahontas. In April of 1946, they created your Powhatan Arrow to appeal to new, upscale passengers."

The Pocahontas, the Cavalier, and the Powhatan Arrow all went from Norfolk to Cincinnati, but had different departure times.

Bud Jeffries

There were also 'accommodation trains' that would meet these long-distance trains at various junctions and provide service to Winston Salem, Columbus, and other cities. In some cases, they'd switch entire cars from one train to another so passengers could stay on board.

"One of the special things about the Powhatan Arrow," Bud noted, "is that the scenic portion of the trip through the mountains of Virginia and West Virginia was done during the daylight. It was purposefully scheduled to take advantage of the scenery. This was a first class train. It was the best any railroad company could put on the rails at that time.

"The Norfolk & Western made money when other railroads didn't.

From 1946 until 1958, R. H. "Racehorse" Smith was the president of the company. Whenever there was a problem or a wreck, he would sit with his top manager to see how to prevent future occurrences. Many of their innovations were expensive, but they paid off in the long term.

"The new Class J locomotives came along in 1941 and 1942. They were always the locomotives assigned to the Powhatan Arrow, designed expressly for passenger service. Their 70 inch drivers were ideally suited to high speeds on difficult grades. They had good acceleration after slowing for curves to get back to cruising speed.

"Many railroad companies were looking for streamlining of their locomotives in that era. It has an aerodynamic effect. The Class J was sleek and beautiful, but it still looked like a steam engine. And the designers left the lower part of the locomotive uncovered so the wheels and linkages could still be seen and were easily maintained. If there's too much skirting, it's difficult to maintain what's underneath."

Bud explained the inherent necessity for frequent, regular maintenance, primarily lubrication. The Class J was designed to stretch out the lubrication schedule as long as possible. But still, each locomotive needed to be lubricated every 500 to 1,300 miles. All the Class J locomotives were based in Roanoke where special "lubritoriums" were built specifically for that purpose. These buildings were air-conditioned and equipped with a myriad of hoses to allow for assembly line servicing. "In twenty minutes the engine could be out and ready to go. No other railroad in America could do that. The Roanoke service area serviced 80 to 135 engines per day."

The N&W championed steam for many reasons, but principally due to their close relationship with the coal industry. Coal carriage was their primary business, so they were devoted to coal as a fuel. They wanted to promote the use of coal.

In spite of the power and maturity of the steam fleet, there were still many disadvantages relative to diesel. In the early days, diesel wasn't reliable or powerful. But eventually these attributes improved and steam's limitations became more evident and problematic. Virtually everything from the rail up differs between a steam locomotive and a diesel locomotive.

The main component is the diesel internal combustion engine, similar to a conventional automobile engine with pistons and cylinders, except the diesel fires from the heat of compression rather than a spark plug. The engine configuration is typically in-line, with long crankshafts. The crankshaft is connected to an electrical generator whose electricity is directly transferred to traction motors (electric motors) on the wheels.

Bud continued, "By 1939, General Motors had developed a diesel locomotive that was powerful and practical for moving freight. It could run circles round most steam locomotives used around the country, but it was still no match for the Norfolk & Western's! Through World War II and into the late 40s and 50s, N&W was still building steam locomotives that were competitive with diesel. In 1952, N&W did exhaustive comparison testing between the rival systems and arrived at a stand-off. But the handwriting was on the wall."

The disadvantages of steam vis-à-vis diesel were many and ultimately insuperable. Steam locomotives were more difficult and expensive to build and service. They were heavier, which meant greater stress on the tracks. They needed to pull their own tender carrying coal and water. Not all the wheels were "driven," and thus there could be slippage on the rail. There was longer start-up time (As Preston said, it takes hours to heat a cold boiler to the point where it produces usable steam, whereas a diesel starts instantly like a conventional automobile engine.). They required two operators, an engineer and a fireman, whereas diesel locomotives could be operated by a single person, generally possessing lesser skills. And each steam locomotive could only be operated singly by a given crew whereas several diesels could be linked together, run by a single operator, obtaining as much power as necessary.

Bud chuckled that a superintendent in the Radford shops once said, "One of the differences between steam and diesel locomotives is that when something went wrong on the steam, it took three minutes to figure out what was wrong and three days to fix it and on a diesel it took three days to figure out what was wrong and three minutes to fix it!"

Bud told me N&W explored several other options, including steam turbine locomotives and all-electric locomotives. But the winning system of diesel-electric emerged and the conversion got underway. "It was a hard decision for them! They had a tremendous investment in not just the stock itself, but the infrastructure of people who could design, build, operate, and maintain the steam locomotives. They hung on longer than any major railroad in the country. But eventually they faced insurmountable problems. For example, even though they designed and built their own locomotives in Roanoke, many of the parts were manufactured by outside suppliers. Things like brakes, safety valves, and turbo-generators became unavailable."

Our conversation returned to the Class J and its design. Bud said that the eight large "driver" wheels (four on each side) were on a rigid frame, unable to turn in the curves. The four front and four back wheels, smaller, were on a pivot mount and thus could turn. The wheelbase from the axle of the front drivers to the axle of the rear drivers was about 20 feet. So on curving track, there was some scraping, meaning wear on the track and wear on the wheels. This wasn't much of an issue on the main lines, but was problematic in the tighter rail yards.

The driving wheels were actually equipped with "tires" that had a service life of around 130,000 miles, meaning that they would need to be replaced about once a year. The tire is a hoop of steel with the flange that keeps the locomotive on the rail. The wheel itself is the large casting that bolts to the axle. To change a tire, the old one needed to be cut with a torch and a new one needed to be heated to expand to the point where it was large enough to slide over the wheel. When it cooled, it compressed onto the wheel and became an interference fit. But removal of a wheel was a complex, time-consuming job where the locomotive needed to be elevated, the linkages needed to be removed, and the wheel was then removed and re-tired.

Bud continued, "Until around July, 1958, the J locomotives pulled the Powhatan Arrow. Afterwards, the Powhatan Arrows were pulled by diesels."

Bud's family history is as dramatic as the railroad history about which he writes. "The home you're in was built by John Ingles," he said. "John was the youngest son of Mary Draper Ingles, who became legendary by her escape from Indians who had kidnapped her. She and her husband came here afterwards and she died and is buried here. They're my great-great-great-great grandparents. My mother's maiden name was Ingles. Their youngest son got the farm when he came of age. It was built in 1789-90 and is the oldest structure in the city of Radford.

"I'm the seventh generation on the farm and the sixth to live in the house. My parents came here to live when I was two years old so I was raised in this house. I took a career in the military and after they died in the late 80s, I came back to live here. I was in the Army for 27 years. I came back in 1991.

"This is still a working farm, right in the city of Radford. We have 119 head of cattle. The house is on the old Rock Road. It was the original thoroughfare around here. In 1847, when it was called the Southwest Turnpike, it was macadamized, meaning it was covered by crushed rock. That's how it became called the Rock Road. The Southwest Turnpike led all the way to New Orleans. Ingles Ferry crossed the river just down the hill from here. It was licensed in 1762 by William Ingles.

"I have always been interested in history. I grew up watching the

Norfolk & Western's trains. Steam (locomotives were) phased out when I was 16 or 17. I had the opportunity in the mid-1970s to interview a lot of the people. That led to my first book that was published in 1980. I called it *N&W: Giant of Steam.*

"I was never a railroad employee. But I'm now the official historian for the 611. When the 611 excursions were happening last summer (2015), I watched it every day. Other than the boiling of the water, on a steam locomotive you see, hear, feel, and smell about everything that's going on. The more coal you feed it, the more powerful it can be. You hear it, you see it, you smell it; it's a total sensory experience. There is a fascination that a diesel can't give you.

"Then of course another thing of interest was the N&W's reputation for designing and building these steam engines. They were the best that had ever been built, certainly the most productive.

"The steam engines were hallmarks of Roanoke. The 611 is one of the greatest examples of streamlined locomotives there is. It kindles the spirit. With the 611 immobilized for 20 years, bringing it back under steam was hugely exciting. When the 611 was first brought back to Roanoke under its own steam, I rode (behind) it from Lynchburg and there must have been 40,000 people lining the tracks. My goodness, they were everywhere!

"I'm 73 years old and I remember steam in revenue (generating) service. Most of those thousands of people had probably never seen a steam locomotive. People are fascinated."

THROUGH THIS AREA, the railroad track goes beside the New River. I wanted to add an on the water experience to my miles on bicycles, motorcycles, and cars. So I invited Blacksburg resident Greg Nelson and his girlfriend Emily Pyne to a canoe float. We chose a section of river that traverses the Radford Army Ammunition Plant. And we talked about pollution.

The RAAP was built by the U. S. Army in 1941, ten months before the Japanese attacked Pearl Harbor launching us into World War II. Locally referred to as the "Arsenal," "the Powder Plant," or sometimes "Hercules" after the contractor that operated it for the Army for many years, it has been a major employer for the region for 75 years. The Arsenal has seen tremendous swings in employment over the decades since, fluctuating as our country participates in and then withdraws from conflicts around the world. It has then been variously a good neighbor, employing thousands of local workers, and an awful one in the layoffs and downturns.

Additionally, it has emerged as one of the state's worst polluters, dumping and leeching countless tons of toxic heavy metals and other carcinogens into the river, air, and groundwater.

Greg is a PhD candidate at Virginia Tech who has based his doctoral dissertation on that pollution. He has been an active participant in the effort to force an end to it.

We picked a beautiful day to be on the river, with bright sunshine and clear skies. The temperature was warm and getting warmer as we drifted downstream, me J-stroking from the stern, big Greg in the front and Emily on a cushion amidship. The water was low, so I picked carefully over the ensuing ripples to avoid scraping the bottom.

We rounded a corner to the right and got our first glimpse of Arsenal property, which sat on both sides of the river on a huge oxbow bend to the east. An unmanned guard shack stood on a low tower on our right, accompanied by signs telling us we were in a government facility and not to land on shore. A flock of Canada geese floated near the right shore and on the left, five deer grazed in the low water. A great blue heron took flight as we approached. It was a scene of primordial tranquility and peace, belying the militaristic mission of the factory just beyond sight. As the river turned east, the N&W tracks crossed over the river on a graceful bridge and then vanished into a tunnel on the left, bypassing the oxbow entirely. There were several sets of ripples crossing the river which we navigated successfully, only once taking on water.

The river seemed clean enough, but I knew we were entering one of the most polluted places around. On the left, Greg showed me the infamous open burning area, where for decades the Arsenal has taken waste propellant and simply burned it on 16 elevated 6 by 18 foot metal "pans." We pulled up for a break on the opposite shoreline, not far from where a wake of black vultures sat, ominously. That was as close as I wanted to get. The shoreline I chose had mud so deep that my sandal sank 10 inches into the muck and I had to pull it out by hand.

Greg told me he grew up half a mile from the Arsenal and had long been concerned about the toxic plumes generated here. He said, "I study environmental justice and public policy.

"We know there has been a lot dumped into the river. Officials haven't ever fully assessed groundwater contamination. Off-site wells have not been tested. There is dinitrotoluene, trinitrotoluene which is TNT, perchlorate, lead, mercury, arsenic, and other explosives. Those deer are grazing on some of the most polluted soil at the site."

The open burning pans sat above the opposite shore just over the crest where we couldn't see them. Beyond that was a low, tree-covered hillside. There was no visible evidence of anything ominous.

"You can't see or smell the pollutants," Greg continued. "You have to have science and technology to see what's here. This has been operating for 75 years, so there are 75 years of soil deposition and layers of pollutants."

Three towns were in proximity: Radford, three miles to the southwest, Christiansburg, nine miles to the southeast, and Blacksburg, seven miles to the east. Virginia Tech's research farm at Kentland was less than a few hundred feet from Arsenal property.

"I have asked directly what they're burning," Greg continued. "They are permitted (by the state Department of Environmental Quality) to burn materials that contain lead, mercury, dinitrotoluene, nitrocellulose, and anything contaminated with explosives. They take these materials, put them on the pans, immerse them with diesel fuel, and set them on fire. They burn and then simmer for hours. They are permitted to burn 8,000 pounds per day. Before they had pans, they burned it right on the ground by the river. Thousands of people have wells that tap sub-surface water."

Though the government created the RAAP, the Army doesn't actually run the facility. That's subcontracted to private, for-profit companies, including over the years Hercules, Alliant Techsystems, and now BAE Systems, a British company.

Not only does the facility make ammunition for the Army, it also hosts several other private company tenants including those involved in commercial propellants, weaponry, and fireworks manufacturing, and painting. Greg said the Arsenal was set up in a remote area with river access, off the beaten path. But in the intervening years, the population of Montgomery County, Pulaski County, and the city of Radford, had approached 150,000 people. Nobody knows for sure, but all may be impacted by toxic, carcinogenic air pollution at some level.

"This open burning has been obsolete and illegal since 1980," Greg claimed, as he slathered on more sunscreen. "The military was given a special exemption. Alternative technologies have been developed, primarily in dealing with disposal of chemical weapons like mustard gas. These alternative technologies could be applied and used here. What we have here are recurring bonfires of hazardous wastes."

There is a facility planned to incinerate this stuff in a more environmentally appropriate way, but construction money has yet to be allocated.

"The Arsenal is here and they're polluting, but nobody's talking about it because they hire lots of people. It is the second-largest employer in Montgomery County.

"We have high levels of thyroid cancer in this region, consistent with endocrine disrupting chemicals. Much is unknown. I'd like to see an end to open burning. I'd like to see more openness to the public so they know what's going on. Even good employers need to be good corporate citizens. If corporations are people, as the Supreme Court has ruled, the people of the corporations need to be doing good."

Our last couple of miles on the river put us into a stiff headwind. I was tired and ready to be finished by the time we reached our endpoint.

DAYS LATER, I WAS ON THE ROAD AGAIN, this time on my Honda ST1300 motorcycle. I rode past the "McCoy Falls," a series of rapids in the New River where each summer hundreds of scantily-clad mostly college students raft and tube the river. Here, the river slices through two long ridge mountains, Brush and Gap, where the river's cutting action has still left ripples of rock in the water. Ironically named, the New River is actually one of the world's oldest, thought to be the second-oldest behind the Nile. These mountains were uplifted by tectonic forces after the river had set its course, with the river slicing through like a stationary knife with a layer cake rising through it.

From here to the West Virginia line is an area of intense scenic beauty, with impressive cliffs overhanging the railroad tracks and bountiful wildlife. At one point for a mile or so the road turned to gravel and narrowed to one lane for a couple of miles.

Remember the story about Mary Draper Ingles, Bud Jeffries' ancestor? Mary was captured by Shawnee Indians in 1755, and her dramatic escape from captivity in the Ohio River Valley and her long walk back to the New River Valley is legendary around here. Nobody I ever found has taken a greater interest in it than nonagenarian Jim Connell. He lives in Eggleston, just downriver from McCoy. Connell had only scant personal family history there. He selected Eggleston as the place to end his life journey specifically because of his infatuation with the Ingles story.

I followed his directions to the house which led me on a straight, dramatically downhill road paved only with loose gravel. His red pickup truck sat outside of a rustic log cabin structure that he had built for himself 20 years earlier.

The home was bordered by steep ravines dropping off from both sides of the road. It was surrounded by rich forests, where a pileated woodpecker hammered away at a tree before flying briskly away.

"I am from West Virginia originally, Huntington," Jim told me, reclining in a rich cloth upholstered chair. "I have been in Eggleston for 20 years. I moved here specifically to be close to the place that Mary Draper Ingles was found after her long walk home in 1755."

Connell had a rounded face, rimmed by a white beard and mustache. He had a passing resemblance to my own father, who was only four years younger.

"I worked for a Buick store for 55 years in Greensboro, North Carolina. I came to Eggleston after my fourth divorce. I was looking for something to occupy my time. My folks were Harmons. I had read in our Harmon family genealogy about Mary, but at the time it didn't impress me. I came here on an exploratory trip to Eggleston and to the Palisades. As time went on I began to get more curious and interested. The Palisades are impressive rock formations that overlook the village. I got up on top and I was afraid up there that the rocks were going to fall out from under me. There were buzzards flying down below me. They used to call the river Monongachatee, which is the 'River of death'. I don't know whether this is because a lot of people were killing each other or because a lot of people fell into the river and drowned.

"The stretch of river below the cliffs is one of the deepest in all of Virginia. I finally ended up buying the property where most historians think Mary Draper Ingles was rescued. I had no familial connection to this area other than the fact that my ancestor, Adam Harmon, was reputedly the guy who found Mary."

We talked about the Mary Draper Ingles story as he understood it. Her story began in 1732 when she was born in Philadelphia to immigrants from Donegal, Ireland. In 1748, she moved with her parents to what at that point was the westernmost frontier of English speaking settlements, to a community that became Drapers Meadow, now Blacksburg. When she was 20, she married a fellow settler named William "Will" Ingles. Three years later, in 1755, the Shawnee raided the village, killing several settlers and kidnapping others, including Mary and her two sons, Thomas who was four years old and George who was two years old at the time. They were taken to Big Bone Lick, Kentucky, where they were held in captivity.

Jim explained Mary befriended another captive woman who historians call the "Dutch woman." "I actually think she was German, or 'Deutsch,'" Jim claimed. These two women planned their escape together after about 65 days in captivity.

Jim continued, "I believe in coincidences. They escaped on September 26, 1755, which is my birthday. These two women walked together from Kentucky all the way back into Virginia. This trip, solely on foot, was thought to be about 600 miles, and they did this trip in 45 days. These women were following the Ohio River and the New River upstream. According to legends, Mary couldn't swim. So whenever they came to a tributary that was too deep to wade across, they needed to go upstream far enough to where it was shallow enough to cross it. So there were a lot of detours.

"These two women went through hell together. This was in the fall so it was getting colder every day. They must have been wet much of the time, crossing all of the streams. Nobody knows whether they had any shoes or if they did, what condition they were in. They were trying to subsist on roots and berries and any food they could find. Part of the legend is that they may have eaten some roots that were poisonous and they were hallucinating. I think there were days where they just laid on the ground vomiting. They had no shelter to escape from any harsh weather.

"I don't think anybody could do this trip today." He patted his round stomach which rested under a red flannel shirt and said, "People today are too overindulgent, including me. I think the hallucinations may have brought on additional paranoia. At one point, the Deutsch woman apparently became cannibalistic and Mary feared she might want to attack and then kill and eat her. Mary continued the trip on her own and was virtually a skeleton by the time she was ultimately found. All's well that ends well. She ended up being rescued and taken back to her husband and family. She must have had a strong yearning to be with Will.

"She had four more children with Will after returning home. Her family ultimately relocated to what is now Radford to where her descendent, Bud Jeffries who you met, now lives. That was in those days the last place for explorers to get provisions to move farther westward."

Mary's two sons remained captive. George died while with the Indians. But 13 years later, Thomas was ransomed and returned to his parents. I asked Jim why he found her story so compelling.

His eyes moistened. "When I think about what she went through, I still get choked up. Obviously, this was over two centuries ago, but I am a sentimental fool, and I have great empathy for what she endured. I was a male chauvinist for over 80 years. I always thought men were superior. But now I know that men, most men, could not do what she did. Men cannot carry babies.

"Even today, women are not recognized for their contributions. Women make less pay for the same work than men. It's not right! I was so busy having fun and I never paid any attention to it. Mary changed my way of thinking in a lot of respects. I like the outdoors, but I respect the power of nature. What that woman did really intrigued me.

"I have a unique ability that I want to tell you about. When I envision things, it is almost as if a movie screen is projected right in front of my face. I don't imagine things and I don't hear things. I see things as if they are in a movie. I think that is a very fortunate thing. After I moved to Eggleston and I acquired the property where Mary was rescued, I obtained a book called *Follow The River* which gives a day-by-day account of what she went through. I began each September to read one chapter of the book for each of the 45 day days it took her to make the trip home. I visualized what she was going through on this projection screen that I have. In 45 days, bingo, I was right where she wound up, just down the hill from my house, alongside the New River, in the shadow of the Palisades. I have done this almost every year for the last 20 years.

"I didn't do it this year. I'm 91 (years old). I'm not exactly like I was when I was a teenager," he shrugged, with resignation.

"I used to have an annual gathering at my place – I called it the Mary Draper Ingles Homecoming – for descendants and others interested in Mary. We've had up to 200 people there at the spot. Bud Jeffries' daughter, Jenny, is a queen. She's beautiful! She took on the character of Mary. I build a blind for her, and she emerged wearing nothing more than a quilt to wrap up in. She was practically naked. I take the role of Adam Harmon. For authenticity, she snags her legs so they're bleeding. She lived the part of her ancestor."

I asked about the acquisition of the land for the house. Jim said, "It's funny how different things influence you. I like trees. I live in a wooden house, surrounded by trees. I chose this spot because there is a beautiful oak tree there. I did some research. I wanted a log house, primarily. The house is astride the old road down the hill to Eggleston. The only reason I bought the property and built my house there was to be close to where Mary was rescued. Adam Harmon called the place 'Clover Nook.' So that's what I call it.

"My first love is Mary Draper Ingles. I feel like I've walked every step of the way with her. I envision the fine life she had with her family before the kidnapping. She was strong and had the fortitude to plan her escape and risk being captured again and killed. She and the Deutsch woman would often wander from the camp to pick berries and fruits. This one day, they just kept walking. The die was cast and the plan was made and they just kept going.

"They must have had a great sense of direction. I envision her studying the route as she was taken away, thinking that one day she'd need to re-trace it. I imagine that during those first days (of the escape), every step they must have been looking over their shoulders, thinking they were being tracked down. I don't think they even quit walking at night, at least for the first few days."

He admitted to me ruefully that there was meager local interest, especially among the young people and the school administrators, in the Mary Ingles story. "Can you imagine how I feel when I go to a school and try to interest them in teaching their students about Mary Ingles and I'm told they don't think her story applies? Regardless of how you feel about Mary Ingles, it's one hell of a story! I don't even like being interviewed about it. It's Mary's story, not mine."

I protested, "Mary isn't around. You've self-appointed yourself as her advocate, her publicist, her spokesman."

"I'm worn out," he claimed. "I've got a few lose marbles up here," he rapped the side of his head. "Bud Jeffries' son once told me that if it hadn't been for my ancestor, Adam Harmon, he would never have been born. I'd never thought of it, as I'd zeroed-in on Mary. But he's still right about that. Adam was about to go home to Radford. If he'd already left, she would have died."

He wiped some tears from his moistening eyes. "When I give out, I'm not sure who'll carry on. Mary's story needs to be kept alive. It's part of our heritage. Mary had strength. Courage. What makes Giles County special is the story of Mary Ingles. I would never have come here except for Mary Ingles.

"I'm a sentimental fool. I'm sitting here crying over that woman; she's 200 years dead. It's part of romance. It makes the world go around."

NOT TWO MILES from Jim's house I crossed the New River over a downsweeping concrete bridge that afforded an awe-inspiring view of the river and into the village of Eggleston.

Eggleston was in its heyday in the 1920s, 30s, and 40s. It once hosted a massive resort called Eggleston Springs and was also the railroad access point for Mountain Lake to the northeast, which still hosts a resort called Mountain Lake Lodge, at almost 4000 feet of elevation near the summit of Salt Pond Mountain.

Eggleston once boasted stockyards, grocery markets, a feed and seed store, a jewelry store, and even an ice cream parlor. When the railroad discontinued stops at its tiny station, the commercial operations in town gradually ceased operation, including the cornerstone Pyne

General Store.

Decades later, a local woman who had long before moved away came back and gave the Pyne Store building new life. Shaena Muldoon's Palisades Restaurant brings fine dining to a hidden, scenic location that requires several miles of curvy-road driving to access it from all directions. Now, other than a small machine shop and the post office, she runs the only businesses in town, including the restaurant, a gift shop, and various lodgings.

As Jim Connell had noted, the Palisades are a series of massive, dramatic limestone cliffs that face the river on the east side, forming spectacular views from the restaurant and from various vantage points in the village. It is common to see vultures and hawks soaring from their lofty perches in the cliff faces.

Coincidentally, it was my wedding anniversary, so I took my wife there for dinner. We ordered a pizza, homemade from their wood-fired indoor brick oven, but the menu featured such delicacies as pheasant breast seared with maraschino cherry gastrique, lime curd, sweet onion-potato gratin, spiced peas with cilantro and lamb skewers, hoppin' john, and Cajun trinity tzatziki. You get extra credit if you know what tzatziki is.

SHAENA IS A SLIGHT WOMAN with a quiet determination. After dinner, we sat and chatted about her entrepreneurial efforts. "I left (this area) after graduation from Giles High School. I went to college and then moved to South America. Then back to the States, then Spain, then back, then to Portugal, and even Antarctica for a few years.

"I was in DC when my brother bought this building. It was the W. M. Pyne General Store until 2000, the Walmart of its time. I came back to visit and my brother showed me the building. Moving back then was never a miniscule thought in my head, although I always thought I might move back after retirement. All my five siblings are very attached to Giles County and the farm."

The railroad track is directly behind the building, but the station is long gone. She had never owned a restaurant, although she'd worked in one. It took her four years of planning to open it. "From the instant of my decision, I re-geared everything in my life to do that. I walked in and said, 'Wow!' It was instantaneous. It was bizarre."

The kitchen was in the basement, the dining room was the main floor, and a conference room was upstairs. Her wait staff climbed the stairs dozens of times each evening.

She said, "I call this casual fine dining. More mid-scale. We have upscale quality food at mid-scale prices. It's a warm atmosphere. What's important to me is hiring people who are kind. That's what we want to portray here. We want customers to feel welcome. Some customers come in wearing flip-flops, others in nice suits and dresses.

"I thought it was time for everybody around the area to come and see how beautiful Giles is. It's gorgeous. Growing up, we had to go to Blacksburg to get things. So for us, going to Blacksburg was like going down the street. But for Blacksburg people to come out here was like an adventure. We have curvy roads, but that's what makes it special.

"We're on a continual climb in business. Our circle of customers comes from a wider and wider area and keeps growing. Our food is really good."

The ambiance was what you'd expect from an old general store: hardwood floor, brick walls with tall wooden shelves now filled with local antiques and knick-knacks, wooden tables and chairs, and a tin patterned ceiling. There was a small stage for live music. She had a gift shop in the adjoining building (where she sold my books!) and five houses on the street to renovate and turn into lodging. The old bank will be turned into lodging and a café. They also hand-made chocolate.

"I wouldn't have made it had the community not embraced me and welcomed me back. Not one of them believed it would be successful. They all admit to that. They came to support me.

"It is special here. I believe it helped (me) to move away and come back. People who never moved away may not have recognized (the potential). I am on the tourism board. We are passionate about what we do. We are turning mindsets that we don't need to focus solely on industry. Tourism is just as important and is cleaner and more sustainable. If we keep things intact, we can have a continuing, growing tourism industry.

"It's hard to be an entrepreneur. You have to have passion and dedication. Failure is not an option. Communities need to look at what communities have and need. If you make a go, you need to hang on. You want to give up every day, but you have to stick with it."

I said, "For years, lots of people drove by this building and let it go. You didn't."

"Lots of people told me they thought about buying it," she said. "I'm the one who did. This community did its part in making sure I was successful. Two neighbors came to eat every week to give me business. Others helped in so many ways. People helped me get the building ready. They painted. They mowed my lawn. They still tell everybody about us. They are proud it's here and it works. They helped get us to where we are, one dinner or beer at a time."

I RETRACED MY STEPS to US-460 on a curvy road, for a time alongside a dry section of Sinking Creek, a watercourse that for some of its 35-mile run to the New River is completely underground. I reached US-460 again and resumed my trek, passing through the town of Pembroke where a large, double-decker billboard presented a bizarre juxtaposition. Above, it boasted a white-on-black sign top that said, "God the Father... Making you an offer you shouldn't refuse," beside a bizarre drawing of two hands framing a cross with a dove flying below (for the Appalachian Christian Center). Below, it had another white-on-black sign that said "SOUTHERN "X" POSURE Gentlemen's Club, ahead 30 min.," alongside a washed out photo of a seductive blonde chewing provocatively on her index finger. I wondered which establishment was more popular.

Pembroke billboard

Onward, I crossed the New River again over a massive downsweeping, twin span near Ripplemead and pointed towards Pearisburg, the next stop of the Powhatan Arrow.

1:47 p.m.

Pearisburg

Mile 320.6

Some of the most striking scenery in the South is east and west of this community. The railroad parallels New River, which rises in North Carolina and flows northwest through deep gorges to its meeting with the Kanawha in West Virginia. Not far away is Mountain Lake, popular resort, 4,000 feet above sea level.

For my money, Giles County and its county seat, Pearisburg, has the most beautiful natural setting along the route of the Powhatan Arrow, at least the most stunning I'd seen so far. The county is roughly rectangular in shape, longer east to west, with the New River bifurcating it from south to north. The mountains in the area are generally linear, also east to west, and the river slices through leaving impressive "narrows" and river gaps. Vistas to and from the surrounding mountains: Walker, Sinking Creek, Johns Creek, Salt Pond, Butt, Peters, Wolf Creek, East River, Sugar Run, and Brushy, are postcard charming.

There are 37 miles of the New River within its borders, and the county in recent years has begun to see the river and other nearby natural wonders as economic development engines. In fact, Giles is the Southwest Virginia locality that has shown the largest increase in tourism business in the decade. There is one signature resort, the Mountain Lake Lodge, up Salt Pond Mountain from Pembroke, a frequent destination of tourists riding by train in the early part of the 20th Century. But most of the emerging beneficiaries of the burgeoning tourist trade today are more prosaic: restaurants, outfitters, country inns, and beds-and-breakfasts.

Conservation, tourism, and economic development professionals and citizens recognized their region's natural assets and mobilized to love and protect them. Fifteen years ago, activists formed an organization called "Renew the New" that annually sends a flotilla of canoes, kayaks, small boats, and rafts down the river to clean up after the carelessness of others. The first year they removed 350 tires and two tons of debris. Since then, they've removed nearly 3,000 tires and hundreds of tons of rubbish. All because people care.

Another improvement was to river access. There are now seven ramps and three more are planned. Signs have been posted naming the area the New River Water Trail. Ramps and parking lots have been paved and drinking water fountains and rest rooms have been built.

In Giles, through the initiative of primarily concerned citizens, a new economy is emerging. Sometimes it's not flash or bright lights that people seek in leisure activities. Not everybody wants to go to Dollywood or Busch Gardens. Sometimes people want a relaxing float down an ancient, peaceful river. If there's no garbage or oil slicks floating on it, they're more likely to come back.

Giles County has only around 17,000 people, roughly the same population for more than fifty years. Over 96 percent are white. The county seat, Pearisburg, was named for George Pearis, who in 1808 donated 50 acres for the development of the town that soon became the county seat. Modern US 460 bypassed the town to the north. I exited and rode Wenonah Avenue, past the 1960s era county high school, the Walmart Supercenter, and the expansive Birchlawn Cemetery into the intersection with Main Street, SR-100 in front of the courthouse. It was built in 1836 with bright red brick in the Federal style with two stories and a large octagonal copper-topped cupola at its apex. Mercifully, it avoided the raid of General George Crook on his path of destruction through the area in May, 1864.

I had learned that the train station was down by the New River, so I rode westward, crossed the bypass, and headed downhill. Not having an address to look for, I followed my nose to a cleared area almost directly under the US-460 bridge over the tracks and continuing over the river. I surmised this was the station's site, but there was no sign of it whatsoever. There were several maintenance vehicles belonging to Norfolk Southern parked there, but no activity and no standing structures. I parked my Honda and walked around for several minutes, fishing around my cranial cavity for some sort of inspiration or wisdom. Instead, I was just unhappy, sad that this part of Giles' history had vanished.

I retreated uphill and then rode over the bridge past the sprawling Celanese Acetate factory. Situated between Pearisburg and Narrows, it was by far Giles County's largest employer. I could see more than a dozen stacks emitting steam and could smell the unmistakably pungent stench of acetone. Peters Mountain to the north had a linear cut like a flesh wound where a gas pipeline had recently been laid to fuel Celanese's new boilers, formerly fueled by coal. It almost seemed as if the stacks were producing the low, overhanging clouds that clung to the nearby mountains like cotton candy on a wrinkled green shag carpet.

Giles County courthouse

NARROWS IS GILES' SECOND LARGEST COMMUNITY of around 2,000 people and is demographically over 98% white. It was named for the narrowing of the New River where the river sliced through the mountain just to the north of town.

On the east side of the river was Peters Mountain, which extended about fifty miles to the east-northeast into Allegheny County. On the west side of the river, the mountain was called East River Mountain. The border between Virginia and West Virginia was along it for much of its 50-mile reach westerly into Tazewell County. The cut formed by the river hosted both the route of the Powhatan Arrow and US-460.

The downtown area was situated on the western bank of the New River where Wolf Creek, running from the west with the base of East River Mountain on its north and Wolf Creek Mountain on its south, meets the New River. I rode across a new bridge over the river and found the old Narrows train terminal, which was squeezed between the river and the railroad tracks.

As I do more often than I should admit, I ignored several "No Trespassing" signs ("I'm sorry, officer! I assumed that sign only applies to literates...") and let myself inside. Like in Christiansburg's "new" station, NS had converted it into a maintenance shop for workers on the section of track in the area. There were schedules, company policies, and safety admonishments stapled to the painted walls. I called out, letting any occupant know I was in the building. An NS employee named Mike Shaw appeared. He was friendly, welcoming, and kind enough to take a few minutes from his work to visit with me. Mike was a slight man with a bulbish nose, a graying goatee, and blue eyes.

"I do maintenance on signals that apply to the railroad and to those that apply to vehicles," he said. "I also maintain the switches that move the rail so that the train can be transferred from one set of rails to another. My territory is from Kellysville, West Virginia, down to Pearisburg, Virginia. It is about 15 miles overall. I maintain five signals on the track and seven crossings. I do regular monthly, quarterly, and annual routine inspections. I check everything mechanically, electrically, and electronically."

He explained that each signal had sophisticated electrical systems that send current down the rails and can sense how far away the train is. The train itself literally acts as a conduit for an electrical signal to close the gap from one rail to the other. There is a pulse that goes down one track and comes back on the other. If there is a train present, it will connect that circuit. In doing so, it can gauge the distance and engage the signal.

He learned his job through a training program at NS, bringing prior electrical experience. He had been employed for 10 years. "It is a very good company to work for."

He spoke about the inherent dangers of being in proximity to a moving train. "If you go across a grade crossing and the gate is up, it's safe. As loud as a train can be, if it is going in a straight line and not around a curve or going up a hill, it is surprisingly quiet. If you are listening to music with headphones or talking on your cell phone, walking alongside the tracks is extremely dangerous. Those of us who work on this are accustomed to and trained for the dangers. But the general public does not know what to look for."

He said his father grew up in McDowell County in West Virginia. There were communities that were built literally right up to the side of the tracks. People walked on the tracks all the time, and many were hurt.

"Railroad tunnels are so narrow that the train will miss the wall but not by enough space to miss you if you are against the wall. Our maintenance people work inside these tunnels. Obviously, they stay in close communication with the dispatchers to make sure there are no trains in the area.

"When the dispatchers give us a piece of track, we can be sure we will not be in danger. I frequently check with the dispatcher to make sure that there is no trouble with any of the signals in my territory. An engineer driving the train may call the dispatcher and tell him about a burned-out light bulb or that perhaps he didn't receive a signal that he was supposed to. I want to be able to leave every signal and know that it is working properly and that the trains can operate in my territory safely.

"Bad days for me are when several pieces of equipment are not working properly at the same time. I have never had a situation that caused a wreck, but I have had situations where my equipment caused an engineer to stop his train.

"Right outside the station, there are two rails. In the old days, trains going east would be on one side and trains going west would be on the other. Now trains go both directions on either rail."

He said dispatchers have computers that show them everything that is going on in real time on every mile track. The mainline was all mile posted, meaning that signals were referenced by the mile, telling him exactly where problems were.

"I may work on a single crossing for an entire day. I may work on a single switch. In a 30-day time period, I am at every piece of equipment we have along my 15-mile section of rail at least once.

"The dispatchers are in Roanoke. They are the guys that literally send the electrical signals that move the switches that move the rails. They send the signals on the need of the train at a particular moment. The default setting on any switch is to point the train straight ahead. Once a switch moves, he gets feedback from the electronics within the switch.

"The switch mechanism is inside an enclosed box. When the switch has been activated and the rail has moved, there is a sensor that senses the completion of that movement and sends a signal back to Roanoke so that the dispatcher knows the switch has operated properly. If for some reason the dispatcher does not get confirmation, he will not let a train pass until that switch is fixed.

"It is horrible to have a derailment. Even if a train is moving at one mile per hour, it is really bad. Everything on the railroad is heavy. Just dropping off the rail is a major problem. Nothing good can come of it!" He laughed. "Any type of accident would cause me to have a really bad day. I have never witnessed nor been part of any serious accident since I've been here. I hope I never do."

I let him get back to work and walked outside into a bright, warming day, with the sun shimmering over the New.

ONE OF THE BENEFICIARIES of Giles' new tourism gains is Narrows' MacArthur Inn, a quarter-mile southwest of the station, on the edge of the tiny downtown.

It's a gorgeous two-story building, brick, with white-framed windows. It has a broad semicircular portico with four massive white columns with deep flutes, broad circular bases, and rosette and volute tops made of hand carved redwood.

MacArthur Inn

I don't know how anybody could not like Allen Neely, the owner and manager of the MacArthur, and the first face I saw when I walked inside. He has an incredibly expressive, distinctive visage, with a broad mustache that literally wins awards. He often plays with it, fluffing it out to the side when he speaks.

This historically valuable building was moments from the wrecking ball in 2008 before Allen committed to buying it. It sat vacant for years, and only at the last minute did he muster the foresight and the money to refurbish it, almost from the ground up. In doing so, he has single-handedly become an economic development engine for his hometown.

The MacArthur Inn opened in 1940, a cooperative venture between N&W and Celanese. Not long thereafter, the Japanese attacked Pearl Harbor and forced General Douglas MacArthur to evacuate the Philippines, at which he uttered those famous words, "I shall return." President Roosevelt suggested that they name this hotel after General MacArthur as a morale booster for him and his troops.

The Celanese plant began operation in 1939 primarily to supply essential polyester to the war effort. They needed a place to house some of their employees moving into the area.

The Inn has 28 guest rooms and it operated as a hotel until about

1968. "It closed when America lost its romance with old hotels," Allen told me, as we sat in the tile floor foyer. "For about six years after that an assisted living facility was managed here. It sat totally empty for almost 40 years after that.

"When I bought it, the roof had mostly caved in. Half of the ceilings were on the floor. Fifteen percent of the floors had fallen into the basement. The town wanted to tear it down. But it has such a rich history; I refused to let that happen."

He told me he worked most of his career as a general contractor, working primarily in commercial facilities. His customers were industrial and mining companies. He had contracts all over the country, but remained loyal to Narrows.

"The town posted the sale of this building. I mulled over it for about 30 days, trying to make a decision. I was working at Virginia Tech the day of the auction. It was supposed to start at 10:00 a.m. I kept looking at my watch as time was ticking by. It's a 30 minute drive. A couple of minutes before 9:30, I raced to my truck, and I just flew over here. I literally had to stop in the middle of the road. I jumped out and

Allen Neely

the auctioneer was already underway. I ran up the steps and put my bid in.

"I bought it for the cost of the back taxes, plus fines, interest, and penalties," he laughed, stroking his long mustache. "Then I put another half million dollars into it. It had already been robbed of all the electrical wires, which were outdated anyway. I had to individually work every room. I've spent three years so far refurbishing this building.

"Several businesses have opened up in Narrows since we did. I am getting ready to open up a coffee shop right across the street. It is ready to go and we are simply waiting for our permit.

"Our clientele includes people who are working in the area. I give them really good deals on rooms. I have rooms at different price ranges, from $45 on up to $140. Some work for Norfolk Southern or Celanese.

"We also have meals here in our dining room. And every week we have a bluegrass music jam. We will probably have 20 to 25 musicians here this week. And we serve a country meal. We do particularly well in the summertime. Occupancy is good except for December, January, and February.

"We are at the mouth of Wolf Creek where it enters the New River. So there are a lot of fishermen, kayakers, and canoeists in this area. The Appalachian Trail goes through Pearisburg. There is also a new trail called the Great Eastern Trail that comes right through Narrows. It runs from Alabama to New York State. The only place it intersects with the Appalachian Trail is at Sentinel Point above Narrows. Narrows is the only town in America where two major trails intersect. We host many hikers. We provide shuttles to and from the trailhead.

"There is a new network of trails in the Mill Creek Natural Area. Mill Creek has 800 feet of drop in 2,000 feet, creating a series of 22 waterfalls.

"Narrows is coming back. When I was a kid, on Saturdays you had to walk in the streets because the sidewalks were full. Now there are only about a dozen commercial establishments downtown. I hope to provide a boost to the economy."

He showed me a breakfront that housed several of his awards from mustache competitions. Among them was, "Mid-Atlantic Beard Championship, 2nd place East Coast." He called his a partial beard. "I always had a mustache and I just let it grow."

He said he'd had a big weekend in Hickory, North Carolina, the weekend before, winning a championship there. He was late getting home and his ex-wife called him, wondering where he was. He said he told her, "I've been house-hunting. She said, 'What do you mean?' I said, 'I got first place mustache, first place partial beard, first place best in show, won the arm-wrestling contest, and got laid!' I said, 'I think if I stay here another 24-hours, they're going to make me mayor,'" he chuckled.

I RODE BACK ACROSS THE BRIDGE and on the section of US-460 that went through the narrows. The westbound direction was curvy, high above the river, clutching the side of the steep mountain, with several overhanging cuts over the roadway. It's always a fun test for my motor-cycle's turning capabilities. There were two westbound lanes, but the big trucks take both lanes to stay clear of the encroaching rock walls. The two eastbound lanes were below, just above river level, superimposed on the grade of the abandoned line of the Virginian Railway. In former days, today's westbound lanes hosted both directions, a scary proposition indeed with oncoming trucks seeking clearance between each other, the rock walls, and the downside cliff face.

US-460 CROSSED THE RIVER for its third and final time as it approached the Glen Lyn Power Plant. This coal-fired electricity generating facility, owned by Appalachian Power Company (APCO), was built in 1919. APCO located it to have access to ample cooling river water and in proximity to the coalfields so as to procure ample fuel and return power to the mines.

The power plant was continually upgraded and improved with modern safety and pollution control equipment until a decade ago. Its boiler was finally extinguished in 2015, nearing its 100th year. Its aging infrastructure eventually doomed it. But its imposing structure and massive stacks still loomed over the river and highway. At the time of its shut-down, it was the oldest operating generator in APCO's grid.

Local citizens seemed determined to blame the EPA or the current administration for shutting it down, but like all engineered structures, it was simply at the end of its useful life. It was plumb wore out, as the expression goes.

IT'S NO MORE THAN A HALF-MILE from the power plant to the state line, where there was a cheery, colorful sign stretching over the four-lane highway that said, "Welcome to the Failed, Illegitimate State of WEST VIRGINIA." Actually, that's a bald-faced lie; it doesn't say that at all. The sign really says, "Welcome to WEST VIRGINIA, Wild and Wonderful." But both are accurate.

West Virginia is wild and wonderful. To a point. One of the great things about it is that its rugged landscape has discouraged travel and with years of diminishing population, many areas have reverted back to nature. These areas are as remote and secluded as any in the eastern part of the country. On the other hand, West Virginia's very formation involved some questionable aspects of constitutionality, and its current economic condition can accurately be described as a failure.

West Virginia was born of *Sturm und Drang* in one of the Civil War's most constitutionally ambiguous and hotly debated topics that emerged from our nation's most dire, complicated conflict. Should West Virginia have ever even been allowed to exist? Nobody is seriously talking about re-unifying the Virginias, removing one star from Old Glory, and making whole again what was a century-and-a-half ago put asunder. Nobody is saying that either state would again want to re-unify. But the interpretations of the split have never ceased to be debated and call into question the legitimacy of West Virginia.

Our story begins during the decades prior to the Civil War and is painted on a canvas of an incredibly intricate, forbidding geography.

As 13 British colonies formed on the east coast of what would become the United States of America, Virginia would become the largest, most populous, and most important. Centrally located, it encompassed all of what are now both Virginias, stretching from the coast to the west-flowing Ohio River. Prior to the mechanization of transportation, most commerce occurred on the rivers. Thus most of coastal, Piedmont, and Great Valley products flowed eastward to the great Atlantic ports of Richmond, Norfolk, and Alexandria while most Trans-Allegheny products flowed to the Ohio. Regional political differences emerged from one side of the mountains to the other, much as happened in eastern and western North Carolina and eastern and western Pennsylvania.

Completion of the Cumberland Road, or National Road, in 1811, the first improved highway (and literally the first "interstate" highway) in the emergent nation to receive federal funding, fostered significant trans-Alleghany growth along its corridor linking the Potomac Valley at Cumberland, Maryland, to the Ohio Valley in Wheeling, Virginia.

As railroads began emerging in the 1830s to 1850s, clearly showing their superiority in greater speeds and lower costs compared to both roads and canals, building of new routes became equally hyperactive. Baltimore, facing economic hardship relative to its rival New York, understood that to avoid stagnation, it needed its own conveyance inland. Lacking a major river, Baltimore embarked on the construction of a trans-Allegheny railroad, the Baltimore and Ohio, which reached Wheeling on January 1, 1853. Almost instantaneously, Wheeling's fortunes skyrocketed. Virtually every industrial or commercial concern along the corridor was dependent upon or tied to the railroad.

Wheeling was distant from Richmond and was culturally and economically removed. More importantly, Virginia's Richmond government was dominated by traditional Virginia culture and politics, of slave-owning plantations and farming economies and primarily English and African settlements.

Industrialists in Wheeling, connected politically and economically to the B&O, sought and in some cases received reforms and concessions from the government in Richmond that were better suited to their industrial rather than Eastern Virginia's traditional agricultural economy. Nevertheless, sectionalism across the state was festering.

Keep in mind that people throughout the fledgling nation were "state-centered" more than "nation-centered," and many of the people in the northwestern part of the state still considered themselves proud Virginians. And many of them owned slaves, the "peculiar institution" that was still legal prior to the war. So let's be clear that when a ragtag bunch of South Carolina radicals fired on the federal arsenal at Fort Sumter on April 12, 1861, most Virginians across the entire state were enthusiastic about secession and the budding Confederacy and were eager to join the fray.

In this era of constant, 24 hour news cycles and ongoing legisla-tures, it is difficult to fathom that Congress literally was not in session at the time and wouldn't be again until nearly 80 days later, forcing Lincoln as Commander in Chief to make executive decisions to protect his fracturing nation.

Virginia stretched from the sands of Virginia Beach in the east to Cumberland Gap in the west to Chester in the north (north of Weirton, West Virginia, scrunched between Ohio and Pennsylvania, within 80 miles of Lake Erie). Lincoln realized that with this northern exten-sion of Virginia nearly splitting his northeastern states of New York, Pennsylvania, and New England from the Midwestern states of Ohio, Indiana, Illinois, and the upper Midwest, it was imperative that the B&O, the transportation route through the area, must be protected. Baltimore, along with most of Maryland, was heavily Confederate lean-ing, and only by the occupation of federal troops was it prevented from seceding and joining the Confederacy.

Lincoln's first military order of the war was the mustering of 20,000 troops and deploying them into northwestern Virginia to protect the corridor of the B&O. They built a fortified screen, with many regiments doing nothing but protecting the railroad or rebuilding infrastructure on the occasions when the Confederate forces were able to reach and damage it.

Shortly thereafter, the Wheeling industrialists who had long clam-ored for additional reforms in the legislature in Richmond, called a meeting to talk about reforms they had wanted. Remember that Fort Sumter was fired upon on April 11. It was a mere 32 days later on May 13 when concerned citizens gathered in Wheeling and began discus-sion. In what came to be called the First Wheeling Convention (be-cause there was a second one a month later in June of that year), 429 delegates from 27 counties debated their fate. Note that an Ordinance of Secession had not yet been presented to Virginians for a vote and would not be until 10 days later. These folks were wasting no time!

Many of these representatives were chosen at makeshift public meetings and some came of their own volition, but none were legally elected representatives of anyone, so the legitimacy of everything they did was in question.

What exactly these men were meeting for and what they intended or had legal right to do was unclear. But they were nearly unanimous that the political and social differences between the northwestern part of the state and the rest of it were incompatible and unlikely to be reconciled. And again, we need to understand that the people of northwestern Virginia who didn't feel this way didn't attend the convention! So it was by no means representative.

They decided to petition Congress and the Lincoln administration to allow them not to form a new state, but instead to form an entirely separate government for Virginia, the entire state, as opposed to the secessionist government down in Richmond. They understood that constitutional restrictions forbid them from making a new state without the permission of the parent state, something the Richmond government would never do. So they instituted the "Restored Government of Virginia," and amazingly, Congress allowed this, admitting two new senators and two congressmen. So at this point, the state of Virginia, the whole state, was represented by one set of legislators in the U.S. Congress and another in the Congress of the Confederate States of America.

Lincoln was a savvy political strategist. He knew that even in the absence of the southern congressmen, he'd have a difficult time pursuing his agenda. So with all requisite consternation, deliberation, and the advice of his cabinet (which split 3-3), Lincoln consented to accepting this new delegation. And the new Virginia governor moved to Alexandria, although the legislature didn't.

Almost immediately after getting what they wanted through Congress, the Wheeling delegates petitioned for more. They arrogated for themselves the authority to form a new state. They considered several configurations of the state's boundaries, vis-à-vis the parent state, claiming and then rejecting and then claiming again a host of Virginia counties.

To validate their actions at least for appearances, they held elections. But they only held elections in counties controlled by the Union and most of the men (and only white men had the right to vote in those days) were already serving in the war. And no elections were held at all in the New River, Tug River, and Bluestone River Valleys. With so many eligible voters away fighting and with those voters who did vote facing intimidation at the polls, we can scarcely conclude that the results of the plebiscite were an accurate indication of public sentiment.

Again, the delegates had self-selected. Greatly overrepresented were attorneys and Methodist circuit riders. It's often called the Methodist Revolution. Most preachers rode circuit because the rugged Alleghenies weren't populated enough to permanently employ ministers or lawyers. These were the people who were well-known and had the financial wherewithal to travel to Wheeling.

News of the actions of self-appointed statemakers in Wheeling spread around the state and the nation. The government of Virginia aligned with the Confederacy was clearly apoplectic, but they had their hands full and there was nothing they could do about it. The people in the various border counties like Greenbrier, Mercer, Monroe, and others, places that were deeply devoted to the Confederacy, were similarly livid, so much so that the Greenbrier County's newspaper refused to use the term "West Virginia" for 20 years after the war. Yet they were similarly unempowered.

Many a man left his home in Pendleton, Mercer, or Jefferson County, fought a war on the side of his beloved Virginia and then returned home to find he now lived in a different state, a state ruled by a bunch of railroad executives of the B&O. And in some cases, he could be arrested for his service to the Confederacy!

As the war wound down and people became convinced the Union armies would prevail, the former Confederate states would be re-admitted, and the nation would become whole again, the West Virginia statemakers formed lumps in their collective throats, realizing a fatal mistake they'd made. In their quest for what may have been a defensible border, they proverbially bit off more than they could politically chew. Their original goal was to establish an Ohio Valley state with a modern industrial economy and constitution to foster it, along with a legislature filled with like-minded folks with the same aim. But what they got was a much larger state, filled with returning, angry Confederates from a couple of dozen counties of remote central Appalachia.

It took little time after the nation's reuniting for the Wheeling contingent, the victorious Unionist Republican statemakers, to understand this blunder, realizing that they were outnumbered and in fair elections destined to be politically dominated by the Democratic former Confederates. We can only speculate why the statemakers ripped away from Virginia the counties of Greenbrier, Monroe, Summers, and our subject counties of Mercer, McDowell, and Logan (Mingo at the time was part of Logan.). Perhaps it was for defense, not knowing the outcome of the war at the time. Perhaps it was to reward the Union sympathizers in those areas. Incidentally, from the Virginia counties that would become West Virginia, sympathies were almost uniformly split, with approximately 22,000–25,000 men fighting for each side.

Nevertheless, after the war ended, finding themselves in the minority, the Unionists mandated strict voting restrictions on the former Confederates, requiring a loyalty oath to vote or hold office.

For a couple of statewide election cycles, black men but not former white Confederates could vote. (It would take decades more for women to earn the right to vote.) Picture here a Confederate veteran from Mercer County, returning home from the war broken and angry, and realizing that his former slave could hold office and vote and he couldn't, unless he signed a loyalty oath to his former enemies. Well, that wasn't going to last! So when finally all white men could vote, the southern, Confederate-leaning counties began a domination of statewide politics that lasted for the next 30 years. When the loyalty requirement ended in 1870, enfranchising former Confederates, they rapidly began dismantling the statemakers' efforts. These former Confederates relegated the state-makers to the most obscure pages of the history books, so that only the most motivated learners would ever learn their names.

Both houses of the legislature instantly swept out the Republicans and replaced them with Democratic majorities. They called for a constitutional convention in Charleston in 1871, the last such meeting in West Virginia's history, and promptly undid the work of the statemakers. After attempting unsuccessfully to rejoin Virginia, they re-wrote their constitution to model the Virginia constitution the state-makers had so vehemently sought to leave behind. They made a number of changes, but most significant was the restoration of the property rights of alien non-residents, most of whom lived in Virginia. This left West Virginia woefully unprepared for the rapid industrialization and resource extraction that would begin almost immediately. By 1880, industrial operations spread like poxes across formerly forested and agrarian landscapes. Because the new constitution expressly honored absentee ownership, it had inadequate provisions for managing virulent exploitation by these extractive industries and preserving the unfathomable wealth so created for West Virginia and its people.

The next two governors of West Virginia were returning Confederates. Out of pure spite and vengeance, they burdened and impoverished their own new state with an equitable portion of Virginia's antebellum debt. Before the war, Virginia had borrowed $48 million, mostly from northern banks, to fund the development of canals, bridges, turnpikes, and railways. Much of this was destroyed by the Federals. When West

Virginia became a separate state, theoretically they owed an equitable share of it. However, the issue was hotly contested, primarily because most of what had been destroyed was in Virginia rather than West Virginia! The issue was understandably complex and not firmly resolved until a U.S. Supreme Court ruling in 1915, a full fifty years after the war ended. The Court mandated the amount to be $12 million, of which the final installment wasn't paid until 1939.

So there you have it, the unauthorized people's history of West Virginia.

Many history books present a more sanitized version. In this version, the reason for the split was that the malevolent slave-owning, agriculturally based, heavy-handed east-dominated government in Richmond didn't tax slave property fairly, instead placing the burden on the noble anti-slavery mountaineer of the west. That the men of the west were more categorically and universally more moral and just. That the dominant leadership of the east wanted not only to continue the peculiar institution of slavery over the Negro, but additionally put financial burdens on those furthest away from the traditional tobacco, cotton, and corn growers of the coast.

Each of us needs to select the version we find more compelling. All I can say is that if the true story is less like the former and more like the latter, it's no wonder so many kids can't stay awake in history class.

Anyway, welcome to West Virginia!

US-460 DIVERGED FROM THE RAILROAD TRACKS, so I left the superhighway and turned onto a smaller road, West Virginia SR-112, and wound downhill into the village of Oakvale. Alongside the road were a series of rock outcroppings where it was easy to see the laminar arrangements of the sedimentary rock.

Somewhere, I crossed the St. Clair fault. It should be on maps, because it demarcates a dramatic change in topography, culture, and economics. But it's not, at least on any in popular use. So I wasn't sure when I crossed over it. But things looked different, from the lay of the land to the abundance of commercial establishments servicing the coal industry.

Western Virginia from Front Royal to Galax to Cumberland Gap is a mountainous place, as is almost the entirety of West Virginia. These mountains are generally beloved and have shaped every aspect of the routes people have traveled, where and how residents work and live. Like so many other aspects of our natural world, since the arrival of European settlers these mountains have been frequently abused, sometimes destroyed entirely, and often assaulted in a variety of ways. These all relate back to their differential formation.

As I drove westward, along SR-112, the long, nearly uniform hulking ridge of East River Mountain dominated the southern skyline to my left. On the right were smaller, more corrugated, less regular and more jumbled contours. Both were clad in a dense carpet of greenery, but were of very different substance. Let's talk about how that came about.

We generally term a mountain as any mass of rock rising above the surrounding terrain. By international standards, even the grandest peaks of the great Appalachian chain running from Georgia and Alabama to Maine – Mount Mitchell in North Carolina, Mount Rogers in Virginia, Spruce Knob in West Virginia, Mount Washington in New Hampshire, and Mount Katahdin in Maine – are modest by comparison to those of the Rockies, Alps, and Himalayas. (West Virginia is significantly more uniformly mountainous than Virginia. However, Virginia's highest mountains are taller, with Mount Rogers' elevation of 5,729 exceeding Spruce Knob's 4,863.) Yet researchers today believe that at one point, ridges like East River Mountain once had Himalayan proportions. The "mountains" to the north weren't really mountains at all.

Other than volcanoes, the world's largest mountains are generally formed through continental collisions. Here's how that works.

Hundreds of years ago, as explorers and cartographers began lengthy journeys around the world, they began to notice that the eastern edge of the Americas resembled the western edge of Europe and Africa, as if two pieces of a jigsaw puzzle separated. Around fifty years ago, geologists developed the concepts of continental drift and plate tectonics. The idea that emerged, and is generally honored today, is that continents sit on "plates" and move about relative to one another, sliding like pancakes on a greased skillet. This movement is typically imperceptibly slow – picture the rate your fingernails grow – but with inexorability and incalculably powerful movement nonetheless. Sometimes they crash into one another. Where they do, mountains form, as the squeezed rock needs someplace to go and so it goes up. The Alps were formed as the boot of the Italian plate crashed northward into the central European plate. It's also how the Himalayas were formed, as the Indian plate crashed northward into Asia.

A billion years ago, this region was mainly flat, minding its own primordial business, covered with flat-lying sedimentary rocks. Then, with neither warning nor invitation, the plate we know as Africa smashed into it, giving rise to the eastern Appalachians, the mostly linear, folded mountains I'd traveled through since crossing the community of Blue Ridge east of Roanoke until the West Virginia border. These mountains were comprised of alternating layers of carbonates – limestones, sandstones, and siltstones – but folded with frequent exposures of limestone. Where the limestone was exposed or under a permeable layer, it has eroded, dissolved, or is dissolving. It's easy to spot where it's close to the surface, with the lush growth of eastern red cedar that favors it.

Much of this landscape is termed karst, meaning characterized by sinkholes, sinking caves, and springs, all associated with significant flows of underground water. The word is derived from a Slavic term meaning stony or barren and is widely used in this area regardless of the typically complete groundcover of trees, shrubs, and grasses. It is caused by the infiltration of precipitation into the soil that flows underground, with the weak acids in rainwater dissolving tiny fractures in the rock, widening into caves. Some caves in the region are extensive, and some in Giles County have been mapped for miles. Sinking creeks are prevalent, as surface streams reach "sinks" where they descend underground.

One of the reasons that groundwater pollution is so pernicious in the region is that sub-surface water systems can carry pollutants many miles from their source.

The action of crashing caused folding, producing long and immensely high ridges. Picture in your mind taking a throw rug that is lying flat on the floor and pushing one edge inward. It would create a series of ridges.

For whatever reason, the African plate became disillusioned with the American plate and reversed course, retreating back eastward where it belonged, or by that I mean where it is now. This motion is ongoing, and each millennia Africa is minutely farther away from us. This is why airline flights to Africa get more expensive all the time. (Not true! This is a joke!!)

As hundreds of millions of years went by, these immense mountains began to erode, sending streams of deposits over the flatter lands and alluvial planes to the north and west.

These flows of sediment rested successively on one another and began to build up, like layers in a cake. Global sea levels were rising and falling, alternatively leaving these low-lying areas immersed and then dry again. When sea levels were high, this mountain chain had water on both the east and west side, and in fact much of the continent was covered by ocean, including much of the Ohio and Mississippi River valleys. During the inundations, significant biological activity occurred, leaving unfathomable amounts of carboniferous material to rest and decay.

Successive flows buried the products of those biological activities and converted them over heat, pressure, and time, into fossil fuels, with layers of combustible rock covered by other non-mineral rock layers. The upthrusting of the ridges created the basin which would become the entire Allegheny or Appalachian Plateau. Coal, oil, and natural gas deposits developed in these layers of carboniferous materials on the stable platform below the towering peaks.

We live in a time today when the sea level is at or near its historic low with respect to the continents, leaving all of West Virginia well above sea level; in fact it has the highest average elevation in the East. There are areas of mountains in West Virginia that are similar in formation and construction to the Virginia ridge-line mountains. These are principally to the northeast, largely encapsulated by the Monongahela National Forest, stretching from Interstate 64 to the Maryland border. In southern West Virginia, I was entering an area of erosional mountains, really not mountains at all.

After all these successive flows of carboniferous and "regular" rocks from the high peaks to the southeast, erosion began to take over. As the area rose and became the Appalachian Plateau, drainage of abundant water began carving complex, irregular patterns of dendritic (like the veins of a leaf) streams and rivers. Eventually, the top of what was once the plateau was eroded, so there were no flat areas at all, merely deep carvings into multi-layered rock strata. Because of the convoluted nature of these "mountains," all travel through them was at the bases, in the valleys, locally called "hollows" (and locally pronounced as "hollers"). Whereas the traditional mountains to the southeast often have expansive valleys between them, the hollows are almost always narrow and framed by steep rises. As settlers encroached on these areas, first with trails, then with rudimentary roads, and finally in the late 1890s with our railroad tracks, they all clustered themselves deep below on any flat or reasonably flat areas adjacent to the streams. The entire region is susceptible to violent flooding.

In our area of study, the St. Clair fault traces the dividing line. Turns out, it can be a violent little bastard, and some of the Eastern United States' most severe earthquakes have occurred on it. In 1897, a magnitude 5.9 quake struck Giles County, with its epicenter near Narrows, causing the surface of the earth to roll in an undulating motion. Brick buildings were cracked and many chimneys were badly damaged throughout the region. It was felt as far away as Georgia, Indiana, and Pennsylvania. My research hasn't yielded the extent of the damage to any N&W facilities or track, then only in place for 15 years, but we can assume the new railroad company had some repairs to do.

We live in an era of heretofore unimaginable alteration of the national world: the oceans, fisheries, rivers, animal life, and landforms. Few places on earth are untouched by human hands. By the early 20th Century, almost the entirety of the region had been denuded. While much timberland has been reforested, it won't for several hundred years return to the grandeur and diversity of the primordial virgin forests, long after you and I are gone, assuming we leave it alone. I suffer considerable personal agony over this.

Similarly, largely predicated on the arrival of the railroad, the region has been extensively mined for coal. From the beginning, coal was mined almost exclusively underground. Men were sent inside the mountains with picks, shovels, and dynamite, removing the figurative "icing" while allowing the "cake" to remain in place to eventually collapse on the created voids.

In recent decades, however, mining has widely shifted to "surface" mining, also called "strip" mining or in the current lexicon, "mountaintop removal mining." This involves these steps:

- Clearing of all vegetation and topsoil
- Blasting the overlaying rock to fracture it
- Digging the fractured rock away with massive machines
- Dumping of the "overburden," which is industry-speak for the disturbed rock, into the valley below
- Removing the exposed coal
- Reclaiming the area, often by re-seeding with grasses and often non-native plants, utterly lacking in or able to support biodiversity

More than 500 mountains in the central Appalachians have been permanently destroyed in this manner and many people consider it to be the most environmentally destructive action humans have ever undertaken. Tragically, it's ongoing. It's astonishing to think that the overall elevation of an entire state has been effectively lowered, but indeed this has happened.

Other assaults on the landscape are groundwater pollution, linear clear-cuts for power lines and pipelines, and unchecked erosion from exposed soils.

The character of the people of these mountains has been shaped by this history.

No more than a couple of miles from the superhighway, I went past a new, modern elementary school and stopped to photograph a massive steel railroad trestle, parking the Honda in the paved access area for the community's fire department. The building was almost literally in the shadow of the bridge, except the bridge was to the north, and of course shadows go the other way.

Several of the firehouse bay doors were open, where I could see two firefighters being interviewed by a Bluefield newspaper reporter. I busied myself with photography. But when they were finished, I asked if I could fill my water bottle. The firefighters were in civilian clothes, a man and a woman who introduced themselves as brother and sister. Davina Clyburn was 42 and her brother, the fire chief, Victor Lester, was 37. Both were heavy-set – Davina was clearly the more loquacious and Victor the more circumspect. She had a round face; her hair was swept over her head and was streaked with dyed colors. She had blue eyes and a smile of pearl-necklace white teeth. We walked into their break room/kitchenette, where she pulled a bottle of water from the refrigerator and handed it to me. I introduced myself and asked about their work as firefighters in a rural community.

The fire department was comprised entirely of volunteers. Davina, who had

Norfolk Southern trestle in Oakvale and my Honda

been a volunteer for 18 years, was in the medical field, billing insurance companies. She had recently quit to fulfill a lifelong dream of becoming a cosmetologist. Victor, who made his living as a school custodian, was the fire department chief. The fire department had an annual budget of $65,000 to $70,000. Their latest fire truck cost them $287,000, which they bought in 2013.

"Our payments are $20,000 per year," Victor said. "Sometimes we can make a double payment and sometimes we can't, depending on our other expenses. We have five trucks and this is the only one we are paying for right now. The building cost $150,000 back in 2002, and it's paid for. We answer about 80 calls per year."

Davina said, "We do calls for car fires, car accidents, brushfires, house fires, and chimney fires. We are also called to do rescue squad work. If the rescue squad has to come from Princeton and can't get here quick enough we will initiate first aid.

"We are all certified in first aid. These certifications are necessary before you ever get onto a fire truck." She showed me a manual that all of their firefighters need to study in order to be certified. It was about an inch and a half thick and 9 inches by 12 inches overall. "When you lay your hands on a patient, you have to have all the same qualifications as a paid firefighter."

"So why do you do this?" I asked innocently.

"We do it for our community," she said. "Everything you send into someone else's life eventually comes back into your life. Good or bad. One day I might have an accident on a road down in Virginia or in the Carolinas and someone will be there to help me.

"We're finding that with the new generation coming up, this ethic is a dying thing. The new generation does not want to do anything for free. My son is 16 years old. We have taught him how to love his fellow man. We have taught him to not be so wrapped up in himself that he cannot go and help a person in need. We have taught him about community service, about not getting above his raisin.'"

I had heard that expression years earlier for the first time when I was working on my first book. I asked her specifically what she meant by it.

She said, "I don't want him to forget where he came from. We come from the West Virginia hills. My daddy worked on coal mining equipment. He worked on the electrical components of continuous miners for 42 years. Once we were old enough so that mom could go back to work, she became a cook in the local school. This is how my parents put food on the table for us.

"We had everything we needed," she continued. "We never wanted for nothing. We knew what it was like to sit down and talk as a family. If you owe a debt, you pay it. If you were raised on the side of the hill in a shack and you live in a mansion now, if you snub the people you grew up with, that is getting above your raisin.'"

"Were both of your parents involved in community service the way you are?" I inquired.

She said, "Honestly no. But dad and mom would not turn anybody in need away. They had no time for volunteering. They were working all the time. Daddy passed away a year ago; mom is still with us."

I asked if people were any different just across the border in Virginia. Where we sat was only two or three miles from the border. Davina said, "Not really. The people in Glen Lyn are very much like us. Down in Blacksburg and Christiansburg, people there are a bit different. The culture is different where you are. Don't get me wrong," she hesitated. "People there are more outgoing. You have more to do. Everything is a little more lively. When we look to go shopping or out to eat, we look more in your direction than towards Princeton or Bluefield. From Beckley north, that is really a different state. From Beckley down, we are the state's red-headed step child."

Victor said, "I don't think there are as many people here now as there were (when we grew up). The economy is not as good."

Davina said, "There are people moving in now that we don't know. Many of them are here to deal drugs. Drugs are terrible now, affecting even people that we know."

"You can tell when someone is dealing drugs," Victor said. "There will be a lot of traffic coming in and out, people parking their cars and going in for short stays at people's houses."

Davina said, "There are certain spots on the road at certain times of day, when people will come and park their cars. It is clear that they are buying and selling drugs. Many of them are from Virginia."

Victor said, "Not long ago I watched a black (GMC) Suburban pull up and stop at the parking lot just across from here. It had Virginia tags. It left and then came back. Another car pulled up. They pulled right up in front of me. I saw one guy pull out a wad of cash about like that," he said, spacing his thumb and index finger about 2 inches apart. "Another guy was holding a gun. The guy gave that wad of cash to another fella, and he gave back a tan paper sack. I'm sure it was filled with drugs."

"Can you tell when people are on drugs?" I asked.

She said, "We run car wrecks all the time. We have classes where we are taught to look for certain things. We need to be able to protect ourselves. Meth users have no teeth. Honest to goodness, their bone structure physically changes. Their face physically deteriorates. They have sores on their faces. They get what we call 'meth mouth,' which is a severe tooth decay and loss of teeth. It's horrible."

She explained to me that as bad as meth is itself, it is often laced with much more dangerous things, including rat poison. It can kill its users in any number of ways.

"Sometimes people will cook stuff in the back of their cars. We have to be careful when we attend to a car fire because there might be drugs involved. The car could literally blow itself up."

I asked what it takes to be a good fireman.

"Dedication," Victor said without hesitation.

"Absolutely," Davina agreed. "You have to have some ability to take risks. You have to take risks in a safe kind of way to where you are willing to put yourself out on the line to save a life. If you have a victim who has no chance of survival, you cannot allow yourself to be a hero by putting your family through the loss of you. If you come into a burning building and that room is fully involved (in fire), more than likely, the victims are already in eternity. There are firemen in this industry that would (enter anyway)."

I said, chuckling nervously, "Most people I know run out of burning buildings. You run in."

"It is a different ball game when you run into one," she said. "Even a building you have been inside before seems completely different when it is on fire. We recognize that every time we do this might be the last time. People are frantic, both those inside and outside. There is stuff all over the place. There may be pets. You have no idea what you are going to encounter. And we do it anyway. Any more, I don't even think about it.

"I do pray. When we get calls, I pray from the time I leave my house until I get here to the station. I pray that God gives us the knowledge and the ability to deal with what we have to deal with and to give us the mindset with whatever we may see to make our minds as mirrors to reflect the bad stuff as we do our jobs. It is much like what a soldier experiences. It is much like war and PTSD."

I asked about people migrating in or out of the area. She said most of the people moving in had grown up there and moved away and were now coming back. He said many of the new people without ties to the area were there to deal drugs. Most people who join the department are related to a current member. But they welcome anybody to join. "When someone has joined, but we've gotten a bad vibe, we don't let them stay," she said.

I asked the two of them about the worst traffic accident they can remember.

Victor said, "There was a multiple fatality car accident that was hard on me. Four dead kids on the curve up on the highway. The adults were probably drinking that night. They were likely going over 90 mph when they came around the curve. I was one of the first people up on that scene. One child was already dead. One was lying in the middle of the road. One was screaming, still in the car. I asked myself, 'What are you going to do?' There were so many people. It was a summer night, after 12:30 at night. Weather was not a factor and only one car involved. My mind just went crazy. It was about six years ago. Only one person survived."

"How do you guys deal with something like that?" I asked. "Do you just get up again the next day and do whatever needs to be done all over again?"

"You've just got to… cry," Davina said.

"You let it go, and then you go do it again," Victor agreed. "When you run one like that, you never forget it. It sticks in the back of your mind forever."

"It always walks behind you," Davina added. "They are like a little shadow. They don't bother you; they just walk behind you. They are always there. For a female doing this, it is a bit different. When I am on the scene, I am always all about getting the job done. But when I go home, I cry. In letting that emotion out, right then and there, I am putting it where it needs to go. Then I am fine.

"The one that got to me the worst was a girl that got killed when she flipped her Hyundai Tiburon on that same stretch of superhighway. She was a Virginia Tech student coming back from spring break. It was a white car.

"She drove her car off the road into the median. The drain channels are steeper than they look. They will send your car airborne like you will not believe. She was not wearing a seat belt. When her car rolled over, it threw her head into the sunroof and the glass shattered against her head. It rolled her around in her seat. The impact broke her back and when we got there, she was in a back-bend half-way outside her driver's side window. The car landed back on its wheels. She was already dead. The car flipped so fast that almost everything just rolled and set back down in its place. She had just been to Wendy's. She bought a baked potato with sour cream and chives on it. It was still sitting in the console between the front seats. She had took a bite and had set it back down. When she looked up she'd run off the road. I doubt it ever moved.

"Her purse came out of the car and flipped as it rolled. Everything came out. Lip gloss. Checkbook. Compact. There was a little teddy bear, about this big. No doubt she'd had that teddy bear since she was a kid – missing an eye, tattered and torn with a tail that had been re-sewed back on. This was about eight years ago. You never forget.

"It started to pour the rain. We had to wait for a Medical Examiner from Beckley. Two hours. The victim was still laying with her back broken, half-way out the car. We covered her with a sheet; we are big in the dignity of death. I'm setting there in the truck right behind her car. And I'm setting there and setting there and setting there. It was daytime. I said to my chief at the time who was sitting with me, 'I can't leave her stuff out there to get wet.' He said to me, 'Davina, you can't touch nothing.' I said, 'I am not letting her stuff get wet.' I said, 'I'm a momma and I can't let her stuff get wet. It's her purse. It's her personal stuff. Her mommy will want those.' I got out in the rain and I got her stuff. I was smart about it; I piled it in order by the way it came out of that purse. When I got to that teddy bear, I lost it; I just bawled. I stuck it down inside that purse and I zipped it and I got back up in that truck and I set it down. He said to me, 'You know, you're going to get in a lot of trouble for doing that. You know that the M.E. has to take pictures of that purse and its content where it landed.' I said, 'Let them fine me; I don't care. That dead girl is somebody's baby.'

"The M.E. got on scene, a female. The rain had stopped. I talked to her and told her about the purse and what I'd done. I took her to the truck and gave it to her. I laid the dead girl's personal items back on the ground where I'd gotten them so the M.E. could take pictures. The M.E. said to me, 'Davina, pack that girl's stuff back up. You're fine. Don't worry about that.'

"One more that got to me. I attended a motorcycle crash once. An older couple, husband and wife, were riding on the highway. They got a rear tire blow-out. They wasn't going very fast. He skinned up his knee a little bit. She was setting on the ground and I went over to her. She just kept setting there. I said to her, 'Honey, are you okay? I don't want to move you.' I sat down Indian style and laid her head on my folded legs. She had long hair. I was feeling her head; she had her helmet off. I had no (protective rubber) gloves but I said to myself, 'The Lord will take care of me.' I said to her, 'Are you hurting anywhere?' And she said, 'No.' She looked up at me, and these were her words, 'I'm not going to make it.' And I said, 'Oh, honey, yes you are! You're fine.' The rescue squad got there and took them off to the hospital.

"The next day, I spoke with one of the guys on rescue and I asked him about her. He said, 'She passed away this morning.' Maybe she was terminally ill; I don't know."

I said, "I want to die in a motorcycle crash going over a cliff at age 100."

She laughed, then quipped, "Please do it outside our coverage area."

I continued on my way with a heavy heart and moist eyes.

As I MENTIONED MOMENTS AGO when I crossed the state line, the work of the West Virginia statemakers was temporal, indeed, and their undoing would lay the groundwork for the miserable condition of West Virginia's current economy.

The new constitution, as I alluded, was completely unsuccessful in preserving the vast wealth of West Virginia's forests and minerals from the exploitation of outsiders. Sometimes called the "lawyer's constitution," it resulted in tax policies and land laws that were entirely favorable to large landowners.

Union spies, scouts, and opportunists were roaming around the central Appalachians during the war, seeking strategic advantages for Union armies, but for themselves as well. Even during the Civil War, they had an eye on what came afterwards, and the seemingly limitless resources of timber and coal that lay untouched in West Virginia's most remote counties naturally caught their attention. Working closely with the railroads, the N&W in the south, the C&O in the middle, and the B&O in the north, these opportunistic industrialists quickly worked to transfer vast holdings of mineral wealth to outsiders, bent on exploitation. They purchased vast areas of land and mineral resources, with many a hapless, often illiterate homesteader trading away multi-million dollar mineral rights for items as temporal and relatively valueless as a cow or a sewing machine.

West Virginia thus transformed from a largely poor agrarian economy to an industrialized one, but with the fruits of that industrialization migrating elsewhere. And it remains captive to that today. Almost a century-and-a-half later, more than two-thirds of all the non-public (principally national and state forest) land is owned by massive coal, oil, gas, and timber companies, and none of the top ten are headquartered in the state. Norfolk Southern, with 240,000 acres, is the second largest landowner (behind first place Heartwood Forestland Fund, headquartered in Chapel Hill, NC).

West Virginia's leaders in the intervening decades recognized this reality. The late senator Robert C. Byrd, arguably West Virginia's most influential politician of all time, noted, "(West Virginia) is a state whose rich resources have been largely owned and exploited by outside interests. Absentee owners, while living outside the state, wrested from the

West Virginia earth the wealth that made them rich – rich from the toil and sweat and blood and tears of the people in the hill country who worked out their lives, all too often, for a pittance."

Thus, West Virginia may be the most exploited state, essentially a resource colony for the rest of the country. This massive outflow of West Virginia's resources has filled the wallets of many extraordinarily rich corporations, trusts, and individuals, while impoverishing the state's communities and residents.

Today West Virginia is near the bottom of almost every positive index of national well-being: it ranked 49th of 50 states in the 2014 State New Economy Index and is 49th or 50th in entrepreneurial activity, workforce education, high-tech job creation, and higher education. West Virginia has among the nation's worst growth in Gross Domestic Product, and both population and jobs are on the decline losing employment in manufacturing, retail, construction, and education. The state's most populous city, the capital, Charleston, just dropped below 50,000 people.

West Virginia is the only state in the nation that has shrunk in population since the last census and the only one where more people died than were born. Wage growth is the worst in the country and overall income growth in the last 30 years is 1/3 the national average.

In a Gallup-Healthway study, West Virginians rated themselves the most miserable in the country for five years running. West Virginia is either 49th or 50th in 20 health categories, including cancer, diabetes, drug addiction, teeth loss, preventable hospitalizations, disabilities, and obesity. The life expectancy for an adult male is 16 years lower in McDowell County than in Northern Virginia. The counties surrounding McDowell are not much better.

And it's safe to say that the negative indicators are strengthening and the positive indicators, what few there are, are worsening. This is in a state geographically encircled by many of the nation's stronger economies. The seeds of this transfer of wealth away from the squatting locals and into the coffers of the nation's industrial elite were sewn during the aftermath of the Civil War. And people wonder why we're still obsessed with the war around here.

If that isn't the definition of a failed state, I don't know what is.

THE LITTLE, CURVY, TWO-LANE ROAD danced and weaved through Hardy, Ingleside, and Ada following the East River before reaching the edge of Bluefield. It rose and fell faster than the tracks, crossing at several places. I rode a spirited ride on my Honda and loved it. The road skirted under a magnificent, double-span highway bridge high above, carrying US-460, as our favorite road, the road we'd traveled for 350 miles, arched 100 or more feet above us from Princeton towards Bluefield.

I'm guessing you're thinking right now, especially if you're from West Virginia, that I've been overly harsh. There's a lot of truth to that. But at the same time, it's complicated. As difficult as life has been for West Virginians, there is a positive side, a side residents, visitors, and exiles never forget. Parts of the state are hauntingly beautiful. There are warm, generous, sincere people, folks who have made America a great and cherished land. These are folks who have been described as "salt of the earth" like Davina Clyburn and Victor Lester, who would in a heartbeat give anything they had for you, even their lives, whether they knew you beforehand or not. As is frequently said in West Virginia, "Tough times don't last, but tough people do."

2:45 p.m.

Bluefield

Mile 353.2

The highest city of its size east of the Rockies. Delights in nickname, "Air-Conditioned City." Lemonade free to all when temperature reaches 90. Hundreds of carloads of coal are marshaled here daily from the rich Pocahontas fields to the west and north. Bluefield College and Bluefield State College. Headquarters of the N. &. W. Western General Division.

At the city limits, I was greeted by a beautiful sign, engraved in gold on an oval brown plaque mounted on a stone base that said, "BLUEFIELD, WEST VIRGINIA, EST. 1889." Alongside, a thin metal pole held a small square sign that said "West Virginia Make It Shine Community."

Like Crewe and Roanoke before it, Bluefield was birthed by the railroad and has seen its fortunes rise and fall with it.

When Frederick Kimball gained control of the newly established Norfolk & Western Railroad in the late 1880s, he set his sights on the rich coalfields of southern West Virginia. His bulls-eye was 10 miles northwest of then Higginbotham Summit in a community to be named Pocahontas, the heart of the Pocahontas Coal Field, which Kimball called the "most spectacular find on the continent and indeed perhaps the entire planet." Higginbotham Summit was soon renamed Bluefield, by legend because of the fields of chicory that bloomed purple-blue in the springtime. It became the staging area for the local trains snaking up into the resource endowed, tight hollows of the region to prepare them for the long run to Norfolk. Bluefield had a rare (for the area) linear valley with a slight natural rise or "hump," in railroad lexicon, in the center, separating the watersheds of the East River from the Bluestone River, where gravity switching of cars could be employed.

318

Bluefield's "black gold rush" brought thousands of new people into the area and from a population of 1,800 in 1890 it blossomed to 10,000 by 1900. Bluefield's 10-story and 12-story buildings housed coal company headquarters, banks, and insurance companies and lower buildings along the tracks housed warehouses. In 1950, Bluefield, West Virginia's population hit its zenith at 21,500 residents, and since then the population has dropped at every census.

In 2016, Norfolk Southern announced that it was consolidating its Virginia and Pocahontas Divisions into a larger Pocahontas Division, headquartered in Roanoke. Many more people lost their jobs in Bluefield. By that time, the estimated population was around 10,500. Nearby Bluefield, VA's population has hovered between 5,000 and 6,000 since the mid-1960s and it remains Tazewell County's largest town.

I FOLLOWED MY LONGSTANDING PROPENSITY for walking into buildings where clearly visitors were not welcome, entering the imposing five-story building on Princeton Avenue that formerly housed the Norfolk Southern's Pocahontas Division. I was greeted by nobody. There was an interior ceramic wall framed lobby, with a locked glass door, and unstaffed with a phone on the wall. I picked up the receiver and dialed "0", not knowing who'd answer or what I'd say. It went something like this:

"Norfolk Southern Pocahontas Division," a male voice said.

"My name is Michael Abraham. I'm writing a book about the path of the Powhatan Arrow from Norfolk to Cincinnati. Is there anybody here I can talk with?"

"Where are you?"

I thought he'd know that. "I'm here in the lobby, in Bluefield."

"I don't think they staff anybody in that building any more, at least nobody you can talk with. I'm in Roanoke."

Stymied, I thanked him anyway and walked back outside to the bike, parked in the shadow of the building on Princeton Avenue and looked at the multiple parallel rows of rails across the street, filling the valley. I contemplated my next move.

As I stood eating a banana, a NS truck stopped nearby and a man exited and began walking to the door of the building. I intercepted him and asked if he'd speak to me. He was a slight man, seemingly a few years older than me, with a balding head and a salt-and-pepper beard. He seemed friendly, so I told him what I was doing and asked if we could chat. The interview that ensued was with us sitting on the three steps leading into the building.

His name was Tim Cox. He said, "I have been with the railroad for 29 years. I am 64 years old. I will probably work for another year-and-a-half and then I'll retire. Yep, I have spent most of my life in Bluefield. I do maintenance on the signals and the switches."

I told him I had met Mike Shaw down in Narrows and Tim said they did much the same work. I asked him about his city and how it has changed over the years. He said that decades earlier it was bustling, with significantly more activity than we were seeing on that day. "Right in front of you is the hump yard. It is where trains are made up. Gravity switching. They may bring in a train with 100 cars. They will want 25 cars to go south. They will want 25 cars to go north. They will want the other 50 cars to go on down to Norfolk. They will run it over the high point in the track, one car at a time, and push them down through the switches to join the train it needs to go on."

I asked him what speed they finally bumped into the stationary cars, connecting them. He said, "I don't really know. I hope it's not too fast. Along with that, you have an air operated braking system. It will clamp onto the wheels as they go by and if the car is moving too fast, it will slow it down."

I had him look across the valley as I was doing, both of us commenting on the things that we could see. They were perhaps a dozen sets of tracks just below us. Halfway across was a tall, concrete tube-like structure that I assumed was a coal loading facility or silo. Beyond that, on the hillside opposite the tracks were what I guessed to be two large cylindrical fuel tanks.

He said, "Yes those are fuel tanks. The tall structure was a coal loading tower. I don't think it has been used for anything in over 50 years. It was used to load the steam engines. At one time, the track to the west of us was electrified. Bluefield, when I was a kid, was really a hub. Princeton had the courthouse, but Bluefield had all of the activity, all of the business. Every day all the streets were busy with parked cars and traffic. I can remember coming over here as a kid to go to the doctor, and we would have to walk several blocks from where we could find a parking space. There was constant traffic instead of the one car we see going by at a time now. The valley where the tracks run was filled with smoke all the time, steam and diesel," he laughed heartily.

"At one point, the railroad employed one man per mile of track for maintenance. Now we have four in Bluefield and six in Kimball. That is for about 50 miles of track. So you have lost about 500 percent of your workforce.

"I don't think coal (mining in Appalachia) is officially over. The influx of natural gas into the market has hurt the coal business. That and the political situation. Natural gas has put a stranglehold on us right now. It is now plentiful and cheap. That has drawn the price of coal down along with it. And the fact that the politicians do not want us burning coal has helped to fuel that problem probably twice as fast as it would've been otherwise.

"Before I started with the railroad, I worked in coal mining for 15 years. Even if the political environment changed and we got new leadership in here that wanted to accentuate coal mining, it would probably be at least a year before you could ever open up another new mine." A single locomotive with a clanging bell rolled down the track in front of us. "I worked in deep mining. We needed to take an elevator shaft to get down to the seam. It was about 600 foot below the surface. One of my brothers-in-law worked in a mine it took three 600 foot elevator shafts to get down. It was so hot down there it wasn't funny. You could hear the methane gas spewing. When you were standing near the face, it sounded like a tire going flat all the time. If you turned the ventilation off and stopped feeding fresh air through the mine, you could be in an illegal situation with methane gas accumulation in five minutes or less time. We tried to keep everything under two percent methane. Over five percent,

Coal loading silo

it was a risk of explosion. The equipment had monitors and would automatically shut down if the methane concentration became too high."

Tim told me that he worked for notorious mine owner Don Blankenship, who had recently been convicted for illegal activities that resulted in the explosion in the Upper Big Branch mine in Raleigh County, WV, several years earlier. I asked him what it was like to work for Blankenship. Tim had never met Blankenship personally, but, "We were the only unionized mine that Blankenship had and he hated us for it. We run excellent coal."

I asked him what he meant by that. He said, "We had 150 men, and we produced 6,000 to 7,000 tons per shift."

"So by 'excellent coal' you mean not the quality but the amount?"

He said, "Right, it's the tonnage. It was metallurgical coal. Many of our contracts were with Japan. Japan figured out a way to use the coke twice and that cut our orders in two virtually overnight. We had a strike back in 1984 against Massey (Energy). They shut the door on the mine, and I lost my job. When I applied at the railroad, there were 200 of us vying for 30 jobs. It took about three months to run six of us through the training program in Atlanta. There were about 25 or 30 of us hired at that time. My expertise is in electrical stuff. I have learned all of my lessons the hard way. I got a job here because I was an electrician in the coal mines. And I learned that the hard way, too."

"Electricity down in the mines was anywhere from 250 V DC on up to 13,500 V AC, which you didn't want to play with. We had some guys who killed themselves doing things the dumb way. You don't want to stick a screwdriver in there to find out if the circuits are hot or not.

"Anyway, whenever you disturb a coal seam, it liberates methane gas. We were not trying to capture it; we were simply venting into the environment. Back then, and that was 30 years ago, we just blew it out of there with big fans. Nowadays, I think they pre-drill into the coal seam and leech off the gas before they ever begin to mine it.

"I enjoyed coal mining work. I would still be in the mines today if I could have stayed there. I have been in coal seams that were less than 30 inches thick where you were on your hands and knees all day long and your back was scratching against the roof. It wasn't too bad if it was dry; if it was wet it really got bad."

I told him about a story from several years earlier when I was working on an earlier book. I was in a mine in McDowell County, and I was talking to a young lanky kid as he took a break with his coworkers to visit with me. I was escorted in by their supervisor, and it was a family-owned mine. I told the kid that coal mining, in the view of most people, is the worst job on planet earth. He told me that he really enjoyed coal mining, that he enjoyed the camaraderie, the hard work, and the consistent temperature. And he enjoyed the money. Tim wasn't surprised.

He said, "I worked for 15 years in coal mining, and I don't think there was more than one or two years when work wasn't interrupted for a few weeks or more at least by labor strikes. Every two or three years we were almost guaranteed it would be a strike. We were off work for two or three months at a time. And there were better and worse times. It seemed like whenever we were in a war, they needed more coal to build our machinery. Whenever we were in peacetime, there were layoffs in the coal mines."

I asked him if people were talking about global warming. He said, "Oh yes, I have grandkids and they're being told about it all the time in school. I think there is global pollution, but I'm not sure if there is global warming. I have heard scientists on both sides. What I listen to mostly is conservative (commentators) and they say no, global warming isn't real. They compare a couple hundred scientists on our side to a few dozen on their side and it really comes down to who has the most money because they are the people who have the most influence. Anyway, regarding Bluefield, two of my three kids have already moved away. They live down in North Carolina. I don't think they will ever move back with their kids."

I asked him if he thought Bluefield today was a good place for children.

He said, "I don't think so now. West Virginia is one of the sickest states in the nation. We are one or two nationally in obesity. I think Mercer County is number one or number two in the state in terms of drugs, and I think the state is one of the top states in the country for addictive drugs. When I work over in Welch, I have to watch my step over there so that I don't step on needles. There are many other places around here like that, too. I work with a lot of guys who smoke pot. Pot is pretty benign, but I think it leads to other things that are worse. You start on one and then you try something else, and it just escalates.

"Drugs are terrible for the railroad. I had a supervisor tell me they were trying to hire two men and they had 200 applicants. They told the applicants when they came in the door that they were going to be subjected to a drug test. 100 of them left. I kid you not. After they took the drug test, 50 more were sent home. Then NS gave the rest of them a simple arithmetic test. It was the kind of test anybody who had a high school education should be able to pass. Two people ultimately qualified and were offered a job. One of those worked a single day and then quit, saying that he could make as much money on unemployment as he could make working. So ultimately they only got one good employee out of 200. The big shots down in Atlanta don't understand that. Really, I don't understand it either.

"I have worked since I was 15 years old. The mines were more tightly supervised. If one man didn't do his job, it quickly shut down everybody else. Of course, that was a different era. In one of the mines there were 750 people working at three shifts. We competed against each other to see which shift could be the most productive. There was even competition between supervisors."

I asked him if he thought the building behind us was going to close completely. He said, "From what I've been told, the big supervisor said they're going to keep it open. We had a big meeting about two weeks ago. They said we were going to be here. I have a section of track to maintain so it doesn't matter whether this building is staffed or not. Pretty much, my truck is my office. Most of the time, I work alone. I can call on the guys who work the track on both sides of me if I need some help with something."

I asked him if he had good days and bad days.

He laughed and said, "I have good and bad mornings. At my age, it takes me a while to loosen up. I have a bit of arthritis.

"For me, Bluefield is home. I like West Virginia. Back in the 1970s, you could work for a different coal mine every year if you wanted to. Everybody was hiring. All those jobs are gone. I don't know where you could get a job in a coal mine these days."

I asked him what he thought Bluefield would look like in another 20 years and he said, "I think just like it looks right now. There are re-tirees moving into this part of the state. Everything this side of Beckley is the red headed step child of the state."

I was stunned that I just heard Davina back in Oakvale say almost exactly the same thing. I wondered if it was in a brochure somewhere.

Tim continued, "About the only thing that is building up around here these days are retirement homes. I think the average age in this part of the county is probably in the late 50s. There are no young people; they're all leaving to get better jobs. You can get a job in the school system. You can get the job in a retirement community. I think the railroad is probably the third employer. There's nothing else."

A MUTUAL FRIEND put me in touch with Bluefield's Mayor Thomas Cole, whom I met in a new restaurant he owned in downtown Blue-field, a block or so from the NS building. He and his family were prominent business leaders and have been politically active for decades. His older brother was currently running for governor of West Virginia. The restaurant was called The Railyard, located on the main floor of a four-story brick building on Raleigh Street.

This was one of many of Tom's business ventures. The primary family business was in automobiles, and they were one of the largest automobile dealerships in the area. Tom was a tall, dapper man with a Yul Brynner haircut and a tightly trimmed goatee. He wore a suit jacket and tie.

"I am a second generation mayor of Bluefield," he said. "My father was mayor in the 1980s. He is the longest serving mayor in Bluefield's history, thirteen years. He was mayor during tough transitions for the city. He was William Paul Cole, Jr. My older brother is the third."

I asked him to describe his community.

"Bluefield is a casualty. In its heyday, we were an epicenter of activity. Prior to the global economy, we were headquarters for lots of corporations. There is no coal mined in Mercer County, but we serviced the mines. There was mining to the north and west of us. In the ramp-up of the industrial age, thousands of people were brought to the coal mining areas. The peak year here was in the 1950s. I was born in 1967. My entire life I have lived in a community in decline.

"I'm blessed. My family has been involved in this community and been successful. The car business has allowed our family to move into other opportunities. My family started in the baking business. That's what my father and grandfather did. I guess we trace our roots to the late 1800s when L. C. Cole arrived. He showed up in his covered wagon in what is now Bluefield, Virginia, and then was Graham, Virginia, and set up a grocery store.

"Bluefield was bigger and brighter and the streets were cleaner when I was a kid, even if they weren't. It's the way you remember things. We've always been a railroad town. That's been a driving factor of Bluefield's prosperity from the beginning. All the way into the 1980s, the national and world economy began to really take a toll.

"Downtown is still impressive. There are lots of big buildings. There are a lot of smaller communities on your route that were never the powerhouse that Bluefield was. We were little New York. It was a big deal for people in the surrounding areas to come to Bluefield. We'd have Christmas parades and people would be six people deep for as long as you could see watching it. We had every department store imaginable downtown. Big banks. Insurance companies. Coal and land companies. We were a hub of activity. Two parking garages. Two theaters. This was even into the 1970s.

"Around 1980, we got a mall, and the malls killed downtowns and Walmart killed the malls. All the department stores left. Sears. Montgomery Ward. Leggett. Cox's. All of them left. That took a huge piece of the retail segment of Bluefield. But we still had a fair amount of commercial (business). We started losing those, too. That was from the global economy, and the mergers, consolidations, and acquisitions. The need for brick and mortar (facilities) became less and less.

"We've continued to depend on coal and the railroad. We've always been the support center for coal mining operations. We were the gateway, both physically and economically. Lots of stuff was staged here.

Our coal industry has been decimated. There were a lot of factors. I'm not assessing blame. There is some hope for Southern West Virginia coal, the metallurgical coal, but it's expensive to get to. But what we used to know, it's not coming back.

"We are likely still dropping in population. We've lost a lot of people interested in the community and willing to participate. Our city board, five members, is all new, as of 2013. I'm one of five, the chairman who runs the board. We only get a $200/month stipend. Citizens are getting a good deal; we work really hard.

"I believe our economic development fate still lies with the railroad. We may have an opportunity with a bulk transfer terminal. Inland

Mural in Bluefield

customs. We're proceeding with a proposal to the railroad. Bluefield is on the Heartland Corridor, and there is a tremendous amount of freight that comes through here. We're 30 minutes from three separate Interstate systems. There's potential there.

"We know that (Bluefield) will never come back the way it was. There are a lot of communities that were once thriving communities that went into decline. But around here, there were not those of the size and breadth of Bluefield. Some were able to regenerate and give birth to arts, music, and eclectic tourism. Bluefield has a legacy cost of large buildings downtown. Others had two and three-story buildings; ours has eight and twelve. At one time, every office on every floor was full. Now they're empty and many are in disrepair.

"We had a classic old downtown hotel that a few years ago simply collapsed. The street was blocked for weeks while the debris was cleared. My great grandfather built the West Virginia Hotel, now utilized as a retirement home. It is difficult to do anything with an eight-story building that has few or no tenants, especially if it's 100 years old and has been vacant for thirty.

"It's not a popular thought, but we'll need to tear a lot of them down if they don't have an opportunity for a future life, even some of the historically significant ones. Infrastructure maintenance is a huge concern. Our storm-water system is over 100 years old in places. Some flows through terra-cotta pipe.

"We're still losing good jobs. The bakery my grandfather started finally closed down after several owners. Unceremoniously. They put a padlock on the gate and closed it. There were perhaps 100 jobs which you can't replace.

"We don't house big corporations. We're taking an active role in economic development, but it's tough. We've hired someone to focus on this. He has lots of local knowledge and years of experience. It's a risk, an investment of city resources to grow the base, to stop the base from eroding. Corporate America is at the root of all the problems this country has."

We discussed several national politicians, agreeing that most are in the pocket of big business. "I'm the most liberal Republican you'll find," he said.

Looking to wrap up, I asked, "Why is Bluefield a place that anybody would want to move to, visit, or start a company?"

"We all struggle with that. We ask ourselves that question every day. What can we do to make this a place people want to be? Our future lies with health care and potentially with the railroad. They've closed their office here, so it's pretty tough to put our eggs in that basket. But there are a lot of trains that still roll through Bluefield.

"There are people investing in this community. I'm one of them. I was tired of not having a place to go and listen to music and have a drink. When you're here (in the restaurant), you feel like you're in a more progressive area. Charlotte. New York. Asheville. I like to hear people smiling and laughing and having a cold beer. I don't want to sound arrogant, but I am proud and happy to have made it happen. Hopefully at some point it will be profitable. It was something we needed. When the hospital's CEO brings a prospective doctor to town, if he brings him here our chance of landing him goes up. If you're a 30-something doctor, this is an amenity you'd look for. We've brought some great music here that was never here before.

"We have the highest African American population in the state by percentage. If we have a jazz night, many of them will come. Selfishly, I wanted a place to go and have a good meal, a good beer, and hear some great music. But I love the fact that there are other people who are so happy!"

WHILE IN TOWN, I called on an old Virginia Tech classmate, Peter Richardson, who works in a law firm on the ground floor of the Law and Commerce Building right around the corner from Thomas Cole's restaurant. It's a 10-story building that was built in 1918, Bluefield's first modern office building. In the Neo Classical Revival style, it featured a bowling alley in the basement to provide recreation for area workers.

Pete got a degree in Mechanical Engineering with me, but rather than pursuing that as a career he went to law school and joined his father in their family firm. He's been working there ever since.

We exchanged pleasantries in his unadorned conference room with a window overlooking Federal Street, and I asked him about the change he'd seen during his life. He said, noting what we all recognize, "The economy has substantially changed since we got out of school. Back then, Bluefield was a regional center for wholesaling, retailing, and services. The world has changed in many ways from that arrangement. Bluefield has suffered as a result.

"People would use the Powhatan Arrow and local trains for shopping and recreation. Automobiles are much more prevalent than they were 60 years ago. A lot of activity does not stop here in Mercer County, but it goes to the south and the north.

"We used to have a number of companies on Bluefield Avenue (just to the west alongside the tracks) in the wholesale business, assisting the extraction (i.e., coal) business in McDowell County and elsewhere. There were a number of warehousing companies. Many are gone now. They ultimately became prey to other, larger, better capitalized companies from elsewhere: Roanoke, Charlotte, even Charleston.

"I do business law, but mostly commercial and banking. Business is good. I'm not putting together deals as much now as taking them apart. We're helping with deals on the downside rather than the upside.

"The economy has changed nationwide. I have two kids. Both went to colleges in other states and now live in other states. I'm living through the process and population shifts that others have. And I'm sensitive to the issue."

I asked if he knew when we graduated where Bluefield would be today, if he still would have come back to work his career there. He said, "Absolutely. I had the opportunity to sit at the same desk my grandfather sat and practice law in this building for 40 years. I practiced next to my father for 30 years. I lived in the same community as my in-laws and parents. So I wouldn't have changed a thing. I have many advantages. But I recognize lots of disadvantages, too."

I told him I'd just met with Tom Cole. Pete said about him, "He comes from a family that is well-entrenched here. They have a long history here, and they have made a substantial investment family-wide and personally to the community. If Bluefield does have a future, it will take people like Tom.

"There are still a few benefactors, but not as many as there used to be. I'm not sure how well their assistance is capitalized on. Tom is doing his part. Others are, too. It takes people to support themselves.

"There are changes in lots of industries, not just in Bluefield, in banking, insurance, telecommunications, and utilities. Lots of companies in these industries used to have regional offices here. Norfolk Southern used to have a regional office here. All of these things are slowly or quickly changing, mostly not for the better, at least locally. Things are different in communities like Bluefield that don't have the benefit of a large university to fuel the economy."

He said there were a lot of advantages to living in Charlotte or Atlanta. But they come with a cost. How you do that analysis, personally, dictates your decision. "I don't think I knew when I finished law school that Bluefield would be in a decline my entire working life, certainly not to the extent we've experienced. I was aware that Bluefield's population in the 1950s was significantly more than even in the late 70s.

"When we were in school in the early 1970s and the oil embargo was on, coal was doing fine. Our country was desperate for any source of BTUs. Since then it hasn't done as well. People have made and lost fortunes working in coal in different economic conditions. If you can't sell it for more than it costs you to produce it, you can't produce it for long. Now the industry is not only struggling with the EPA, it's also struggling with cheap natural gas. If you're looking for factors to blame, there are many to go around.

"The problem from the EPA is the uncertainty in the permitting process. Mines are extremely expensive. Even in good times, the payoff is long. When there's uncertainty and you've spent a pile of money to develop a mine and you've obtained your permit, with changes in political administrations, if the permit is revoked, you would be discouraged from ever making that decision again.

"So there are a lot of factors. It's an extremely challenging time, for a number of reasons."

WOULD YOU BELIEVE one of the most intelligent people in modern economic history was born and raised in West Virginia? Perhaps you've heard of him. His name was John Forbes Nash, Jr., and he was blessed with a beautiful, troubled mind.

Mathematician and economist John Nash was born here in 1928, the son of an electrical engineer and schoolteacher. During his career, he would revolutionize the arcane topics of game theory, real algebraic geometry, cryptography, computational hardness, and differential geometry that provided new insights into ways individuals and groups make complex but everyday decisions. He also suffered from mental illness including paranoid schizophrenia.

Growing up in bustling Bluefield with steam trains chugging through every day, child prodigy Nash devoured textbooks in Latin, math, chemistry, electronics, and generally any science he could get his hands on. His parents provided as much education for him as they could, but they realized that they had a genius on their hands and arranged for advanced courses in mathematics at the local community college while he was still in high school. He left Bluefield for good, attending Carnegie Institute of Technology on a full scholarship, majoring in chemical engineering, later chemistry, and then finally mathematics where he graduated with both a B.S. and M.S. in math at the age of 19!

His PhD dissertation, released in 1950 from Princeton (which he chose over Harvard because Princeton, New Jersey was closer to Bluefield than Boston), was 28 pages long, containing his thesis on non-cooperative games and definitions and properties of the Nash Equilibrium. Forty-four years later, that work won him a Nobel Prize in Economics.

Although I have no proof, I'm convinced young genius Nash made many trips on the Powhatan Arrow, likely from Bluefield to Roanoke where he'd transfer trains on his way to Princeton.

Nash was hired at MIT in 1951 and quickly distinguished himself for lots of bad reasons. One female acquaintance said he was "very brash, very boastful, very selfish, very egocentric." His colleagues did not like him especially, but they tolerated him because his mathematics was so brilliant."

While Nash's contributions to science were legendary, he struggled with his personal life. He impregnated a nurse he met when admitted to a mental hospital. But he refused to accept the child or have his name listed on the birth certificate. He was arrested for indecent exposure in what was deemed a homosexual relationship while still in his 20s. In 1957, he married Alicia Lopez-Harrison de Larde, an El Salvadoran physicist, but they divorced in 1963. Interestingly, they renewed their courtship in the 1990s and remarried in 2001.

At one point, Alicia had him committed to a psychiatric hospital. Upon his release, he moved to Europe, intending to renounce his citizenship. She followed and retrieved him, and they moved back to Princeton, where he secured another professorship and became legendary. His tenure there was marked by his brilliance and eccentricities, and he was dubbed "The Phantom of Fine Hall (its mathematics building)," for his late-night equation-bacchanalias on the building's blackboards.

There were more moves and psychiatric treatments in Nash's life story. But gradually his delusions diminished and he became more tolerable to collaborate with and be around. Author Sylvia Nasar's biography, *A Beautiful Mind*, published in 1998, made Nash an international celebrity.

In May, 2015, John and Alicia Nash were returning home to New Jersey from Norway where he'd been awarded an Abel Prize, when the taxi driver lost control of the cab in which they were riding and both were killed. I learned that his boyhood home was on Whitethorn Street, but regrettably I got my address wrong and couldn't find it. Still, it's a source of pride for Bluefielders to have produced such an incredible scholar.

THE STATE LINE IS CONVOLUTED in this area, to the point where Bluefield, Virginia, is actually west of Bluefield, West Virginia and the tracks go through the latter first. I know you don't believe me, so please have a look at a map. I swear it's true.

By this time, I had left US-460 for good and was now traveling on US-19 which was the main drag in both Bluefields. I crossed back into Virginia where a colorful sign with a red Northern Cardinal sitting on a dogwood branch framed the words, "Virginia Welcomes You."

BLUEFIELD, VIRGINIA WASN'T MUCH DIFFERENT from Bluefield, West Virginia, seemingly more of a continuation of the same strip of aged industrial buildings, car parts stores, fast food restaurants, tire stores, and hardware stores.

It turns out that Bluefield, Virginia was once named Graham, Virginia, and a number of businesses and the high school still bear that name. Here's that story.

As I mentioned earlier, Bluefield, West Virginia's ascension in the early 1900s was rapid, so rapid that its development reached the state line and compelled its neighbor, Graham, to match its rival. Named after Col. Thomas Graham, a Philadelphia capitalist, Graham had incorporated a few years before, in 1883, also along the Bluestone River in Tazewell County. By the late 1920s, bowing to the seemingly inevitable engulfing by Bluefield, Graham city fathers decided in an acrimonious election to rename their community, Bluefield, Virginia.

As fate would have it, a young Miss Emma Smith of Bluefield

became engaged to Mr. Lorenzo Wingo Yost of Graham, Virginia. So when the Chamber of Commerce decided to stage an elaborate ceremony they called, "The Marriage of the Bluefields," literally on the state line, Smith and Yost decided to marry as well at the same event.

The governor of Virginia was the best man and the governor of West Virginia gave away the bride. To this day, it is the largest gathering ever held in the region and the only time in the 20th Century when both governors were in Bluefield together. Smith was married with one foot on either side of the state line. When she took her vows the results of the election were certified and they cut the ribbon. Mr. Yost and Ms. Smith became husband and wife and Graham became Bluefield, Virginia.

By the 1960s Bluefield, Virginia, became relatively more prosperous. I've heard there are some folks there who want a divorce; they want to rename it back to Graham.

THE BLUESTONE RIVER RISES in Tazewell County on the northwest slopes of East River Mountain and flows east-northeasterly towards Bluefield, Virginia. There, it makes an abrupt turn northward and the N&W track joins it as they together slice against the grain through a series of minor ridges with numerous bends. The track frequently bridged from one side of the river to the other, at least a dozen times before the river arched northeasterly and the track northwesterly between Pocahontas to the west (in Virginia) and Bramwell to the east (in West Virginia). Confused yet? Along the way, the track and road snaked through the villages of Hales Bottom and Falls Mills, Virginia and then Yards, Nemours, and Wolfe, West Virginia. I crossed the state line still again into Virginia to visit Pocahontas, with Bramwell to follow.

DEATH IS NEVER EASY, even if one's legacy is tainted with a century-and-a-half of misery and despair. As I write this, in spite of what many hopeful politicians claim, Appalachian coal mining is in its last throes, a spiraling, inexorable spasm of extinction, and its demise is rippling through the economy from where the Norfolk & Western's main line entered the coalfields near Bluefield to where it emerged again near Ironton, and indeed along the entirety of the Powhatan Arrow's corridor.

In its better moods, coal employed hundreds of thousands of workers in the coalfields from Alabama to Pennsylvania. It produced hundreds of billions of dollars of wealth that have helped build many of our great national institutions. Its heat fired the boilers that electrified our nation and produced the steel that helped build it.

In its worse moods, coal killed prematurely hundreds of thousands of workers in those same coalfields, through explosions, pneumoconiosis (black lung), rock falls, and pollution. In the areas where coal deposits exist, it's hard to find a single sentence relating to the economy without the word "coal" in it. In many of the coal camps and towns of the central Appalachians, coal money built the schools, businesses, churches and ball fields, and in a cruel irony, coal even built the hospitals where its victims were treated. That fabric of a coal-base ecosystem continues to unravel before our eyes at a dizzying rate, leaving poverty, ruin, and death in its wake.

So coal has always been a fickle, capricious mistress, bestowing wealth, sustenance, and prosperity, yet coincidentally doling out misery, agony, and destruction. Those communities "blessed" with abundant resources of coal have benefited and suffered like few others in America, but more the latter. It is indisputable that there is a strong negative correlation between coal production and prosperity in a community. In other words, the more coal a community has produced, the poorer it has become, generally for two reasons. First, as with most extractive resources, most of the wealth generated has gone to the owners, typically distant. Second, the areas have been strapped with enormous costs in terms of sickness and pollution.

The rise of coal is part of the great fabric of America. Substantial deposits of coal in Appalachia, the "black diamond," the "rock that burns," were known about in colonial days, even on Thomas Jefferson's radar screen, referring to the abundance in his *Notes on Virginia*. Blacksmiths used trifling amounts of coal, when they could get it, in their hand-forges. But before the Industrial Revolution began to kick up steam (pardon the intentional pun), coal was a minor economic player.

Prior to the Civil War, larger foundries began emerging, notably for our subject area the Tredegar Iron Works alongside the James River in Richmond. Opened in 1837, the iron works was established to capitalize on the rapid expansion of the railroad industry. As I mentioned back in Suffolk, at least for the first century, you couldn't mine and carry coal without a railroad and you couldn't power a railroad without coal. And so the story went for decades. No coal mine could be opened throughout the mountains without access to the railroad. The coal deposits were widespread enough that almost anywhere the railroads went, mines could, and did, open.

But let's hold that thought for a moment and return to the era before the Tredegar. As early as the mid-1700s, deposits of coal had been found in the Richmond Basin coal field centered about 20 miles west of the city in Henrico, Goochland, Powhatan, and Chesterfield counties. Roads were chopped through the wilderness to carry coal in modest quantities in wagons into the city. By 1820, the Tuckahoe Canal connected the mines to the James River for transport. The invention of locomotives spurred the railroad industry into action and with it the insatiable demand for coal. The opening of the Tredegar Works coincided with the completion of the Tuckahoe and James River Railroad to bring coal to the new factory, and many other competing railroads followed, carrying coal behind primitive steam locomotives to foundries in Richmond and Petersburg.

As the Civil War ensued, the Union employed explorers and spies who scoured hidden areas of the border and southern states, looking for competitive combat advantages. What they found in far western Virginia, eastern Kentucky, and most of what would become West Virginia, were world-class coal seams of both thermal and metallurgical coal.

Some terminology is in order now: Thermal (or sometimes called steam coal) is the regular stuff. It is used in unfathomable quantities in America and across much of the developed world to fuel power plants that generate electricity. Metallurgical or "met" coal has a higher carbon content, lower volatile content, and lower moisture. It is used in the production of iron and steel. It is rarer and more valuable, and the central Appalachians are, or were, particularly endowed with it.

During the years following the Civil War, railway expansion exploded (not literally, but you know what I mean), as did all measure of industrial and municipal infrastructure. Steel was in enormous demand and coal mining was a thriving endeavor. These were the years that gave rise to the Norfolk & Western and crystallized their business model to being primarily a mover of coal. For decades, it seemed that the nation's appetite could never be sated.

After the arrival of the N&W in the 1880s, towns and coal camps sprung up in weeks, and thousands of workers began streaming in. Which brings us to Pocahontas, Virginia.

I ROLLED INTO POCAHONTAS with a feeling of trepidation. I'd been before several times, but not in recent years, starting with my exploratory journey for my first book, *The Spine of the Virginias*. I photographed a downtown building's façade, one of the most beautiful and intricate I'd ever seen. I featured it as a cameo on the cover. When we typically think of a façade, there's a building behind it, but in this case, most of the building had already collapsed into a heap. It was a wonderful structure with an old-world mix of whimsy and craftsmanship. But clearly, it was destined either for improvement or destruction; the status quo was temporal. What would I find now?

Pocahontas is one of western Virginia's most historic communities, with its rapid growth and a gradual, inexorable decline. In fact, Pocahontas was the specific goal of the nascent Norfolk & Western as it branched from the wye near Radford and headed northwesterly to the coalfields. The railroad reached town in 1882, and the rush was on!

I wandered the downtown, and my heart sank. The old country store, the grand façade, and all the buildings on that block had been razed, and only a grassy field was left, with one 3-story tower remnant of the store. Everything else was gone, all gone. On another block was a closed saloon with the words THE CRICKET painted in white on the brick outside. The building beside it was also vacant; it sported "1883 S. COHEN" near the ornate top.

I walked into the town office and spoke with a clerk who directed me to a nearby building where she said I'd find Tom Childress, the town's historian. Childress' office was in an older building by most standards, looking to have been built 60 to 80 years ago, but far newer than many in town. It was a three-story brick structure with an institutional look. I cracked open the aluminum and glass door and let myself inside. It was spookily vacant. I trudged up three flights of stairs and announced myself. I was in a central hallway surrounded by closed doors with clouded glass, all with "Friends of Coal" stickers on them. I heard a voice from behind a door imploring me to come in. I found Childress in a large, cluttered office, surrounded by books and piles of articles. He rose from his chair to meet me and offered his insight to his community.

He said, "I have the minimal qualifications to be an historian. I have a masters degree in History from East Tennessee State University. I am originally from this area. The only time I left was when I was in school and in the Army.

"I was a juvenile probation and parole officer. After I finished law school and did not pass the bar exam, I ended up teaching classes at Southwest Virginia Community College in history, government, and business law. I am grading papers right now for my last class."

I asked about the building we were in. He told me, "This is the former headquarters of the Pocahontas Fuel Company. They were the second largest producer of bituminous coal in the United States from the

1930s until the late 1950s. The building itself was built in 1942. It was abandoned by their successor in 2004. They gave it to an organization called Historic Pocahontas, a preservation and restoration organization that has been in existence since 1971. I am a member of the Board of Directors and the co-chair of the grants and properties committee. So we now own and manage this building."

He sunk low in his upholstered chair, his head resting in a slouch from his shoulders.

"We own other buildings as well. We own more property in Pocahontas than anyone. We have several tenants, but we do not charge any rent. A woman named Emma Yates ran a millinery shop from 1901 until the 1930s. The building now houses a library which has been named for her. We allow occupancy of these buildings by several nonprofit organizations. We are funded by contributions and a little bit from the Tazewell County Board of Supervisors."

I commented on the remoteness of the community, being at the far northeastern corner of the county. Perhaps 90 percent of Tazewell County is agricultural and rural. Pocahontas is industrial and urban.

He said, "Our community was founded in 1882. It was specifically created to extract the coal from the Pocahontas seam. By 1882, buildings were going up. The heyday here was from 1882 until 1929 when the stock market crashed and the Great Depression began. After 1929, this community was never what it was before."

Tom told me that during the heyday there was an opera house, taverns, and even a synagogue. Immigrants came from all over the world, many literally recruited off the boats at Ellis Island and put on trains to the coalfields.

I asked about the special façade. He said that was only one of several buildings along that block. They were all erected in the 1890s. "They never should have been torn down. I was part of a fight to protect them. Even though we owned the buildings, we lost that fight. We lost the old company store as well. The town of Pocahontas literally hired a contractor to come in the middle of the night and tear down those buildings."

He called the building an "iron-front," and said most of the buildings on the block were of the same construction. Even before the demolition, "The fronts of the iron-fronts were still standing. The buildings behind them were brick-and-mortar. But the roofs long ago collapsed."

For over 60 years, the St. Elizabeth's Catholic Church had an event they called the Hungarian Cabbage Roll. This was a dinner provided by the parishioners that attracted people from near and far, celebrating the diverse cultural history of the community. Tom said even it had been discontinued. Pocahontas still hosts an annual Miners Day, inviting all of the retired and still active coal miners to a free dinner and parade up and down the street.

"We have a famous and unique cemetery here. It was opened in 1884 after the explosion of the Pocahontas East mine that killed 114 miners. Keep in mind that this was only two years after the mine opened in the first place. It has 11-1/2 acres, and it is draped over a rocky, steep hillside. It documents how America developed from the 1880s into more modern times.

"There are many different designs for the tombstones and also a large number of stones that were inscribed in various languages of the deceased. There were Russians, Slovaks, Hungarians, Czechs, and Italians. There were a few Spaniards and a few French. All of these people came here to seek employment in the coal mines. We have a cemetery with 4,000 to 6,000 graves in a town with only 400 people. Our deceased people vastly outnumber our living.

Tom Childress

"Pocahontas has had some new people moving in in recent years. You can't explain the history to them. Many would be happy if all the old stuff got torn down. A few people still work in mining operations. Others work in service or retail, typically commuting to Bluefield, Princeton, or Tazewell.

"As I mentioned, initial decline was in 1929. But the great decline was in 1955 when the mine finally closed. But even then, Pocahontas remained the headquarters of the Pocahontas Fuel Company. They had a number of other mines. The first corporation involved in coal mines in the area was called the Southwest Virginia Improvement Company. This was primarily Philadelphia investors, many of the same investors that bought the remnants of Billy Mahone's railroad and named it the Norfolk & Western. The Pocahontas coalfield was the reason for the establishment of the Norfolk & Western Railroad. What I am saying is that the primary initial destination to bring the Norfolk & Western westward from Radford was Pocahontas. These people had interlocutory directories. What that means was that directors of one corporation may have been directors of related corporations. Bluefield was an afterthought.

"Afterwards, a railroad tunnel, the Coaldale Tunnel, was cut under Stone Ridge into McDowell County. Branches were built in all different directions to access coal mines in all the little hollows.

"The Southwest Virginia Improvement Company owned the mines and they mined the coal. On the West Virginia side, all of the land was owned by the Flat Top Land Company. They gave leases to entrepreneurs who actually ran the mines. The Flat Top Land Company eventually became part of the Norfolk & Western Railroad. The Southwest Virginia Improvement Company dissolved in about 1900, and the land was turned over to the Flat Top Land Company and the coal operations became Pocahontas Colliery. That is an old English name for a mining operation. Then it became Pocahontas Consolidated Colliery Inc., and in 1924 it became the Pocahontas Fuel Company. In 1958, it merged with Pittsburgh Consolidated and became Consolidation Coal Company which is now Consolidation Energy (or CONSOL). Even in the 1950s, there were still coal operations and the company was doing pretty good. But after 1958 when it became Consolidated Coal Company, the new company worked to make as much money as fast as they could. It was basically rape and run.

"I remember when the Powhatan Arrow started. I was in the first grade. I rode it many times when I was in the army. I rode it to Petersburg where I connected on the Seaboard Air Line Railroad down to South Carolina.

"I was always interested in trains. I remember my mother taking me to the train station in Bluefield to watch the Powhatan Arrow in the early 1950s. I remember the crowds. You had trouble moving around, there were so many people getting on and off. The station is not there anymore. For a while there was an Amtrak station, but even that is gone now."

IT'S ONLY THREE MILES along SR-120 from Pocahontas, Virginia to its more affluent sister town, Bramwell, West Virginia. On our way, let me tell you more about West Virginia's turbulent history.

No doubt about it, coal mining has produced incredible wealth for a small group of industrialists and investors over the last century-and-a-half. But it hasn't always been pretty and the costs have been extraordinary.

There is really no way to properly articulate the degree to which coal has affected the places where economically mineable resources have existed. Coal builds and destroys. From western Pennsylvania and southeastern Ohio into West Virginia, where 50 of 55 counties at one time had coal mines, to western Virginia and eastern Kentucky, no aspect of the social, economic, or cultural life has been written without the influence of coal.

Day One of this onslaught locally was March 12, 1883, when the first load of coal departed from Pocahontas on the newly arrived Norfolk & Western Railroad. The Coal Rush began immediately, as the demand for high-quality, low sulfur, low-smoke coal was insatiable. The smokeless burn of this region's coal was particularly valued by the Navy, as coal-fired ships didn't leave a 10 mile trail of smoke behind them as they steamed across the oceans.

Thousands of workers from across the country and around the world rushed into hastily built towns and coal camps. Wherever N&W stretched its tentacles, mines arose and communities emerged.

Poor workers came from the industrial cities of the North. As Tom mentioned, European immigrants were lured to the coalfields by recruiters who traveled to Hungary, Austria, Yugoslavia, and the Czech Republic to entice them to emigrate. Within moments of landing at Ellis Island, many were placed on trains headed for Bluefield, Bramwell, Pocahontas, and Welch. By the time they got off the train in their new land, they were already indebted to the mining companies. Blacks came from Mississippi, Alabama, Louisiana, and Georgia, lured away from miserable sharecropper work to jobs that paid them, for the amount of coal dug, the same as for the white men. It was extraordinary anywhere in America for blacks and whites to make the same money for the same work. Blacks in nearby McDowell prior to 1883, could be counted on the fingers of three or four hands; by 1910 over 30 percent of the population was black.

Every aspect of the economic system was rigidly controlled by the coal industry. Every man's paycheck had numerous deductions before he saw anything, and what he saw often wasn't U. S. currency. His wages were docked for equipment: his tools, helmet, and suit, rented to him at prices set by the industry. He lived in company-supplied housing for which he owed rent. And all the groceries and supplies he needed were only available in company stores, where the scrip he was paid – the local captive currency – could be spent. No on-line ordering from Amazon in those days! The company stores, having no competition, inflated their prices. As wages grew, so did prices, in absence of any moderating forces of competition.

Miners were paid strictly by the tonnage they produced, so again they were at the mercy of the mine owner. The checkweighman could alter the results of a miner's day of production as he saw fit, and favoritism and cheating were rampant. If the checkweighman determined that excessive rock, shale, slate, or other unusable materials were in the cart, the miner again could be docked his pay. Checkweighman were universally white, and if bigoted would often deliberately mis-measure the daily haulage of black miners.

If that wasn't enough, in its early years, coal mining was almost devoid of any safety precautions. Miners were often hurt or killed, and the carnage made mining one of the nation's most perilous occupations. Death statistics of the day were simply staggering. When miners died, their bereaved families were summarily evicted from company-owned houses, left to fend for themselves with no shelter and no breadwinner.

And of course nobody in control had much interest in clean drinking water. Hastily built towns had no sewer systems – most homes straight-piped their sewage to the creek, and many still do today. Electricity was controlled by the coal companies. School ball-fields were sponsored by the coal companies. Christmas parades were sponsored by the coal companies. You get the idea. Generally, if the companies wanted it to happen, it happened. Otherwise it didn't.

It says a lot to me about the quality of American workers and the desperation they felt in having and keeping their job that they would endure such conditions. These days, lots of workers will leave a company that doesn't have a Starbucks nearby. But I digress.

The industry has counted on that desperation continually. To this day it actively strives to keep out competing industries and restricts advancement opportunities for the workers, while feeding them a steady diet of poison water, polluted air, and decimated landscapes. The region is filled with imperiled homes and public buildings including schools that lay downstream of hastily constructed and poorly engineered impoundment dams that cumulatively hold trillions of gallons of wastewater. One dam collapsed in the hollow of Buffalo Creek in Logan County in 1972, unleashing 132,000,000 gallons of liquid sludge, killing 125 people, injuring 1121 more, and leaving 4,000 homeless. In an act of monumental callousness, the responsible company, Pittston Coal, referred to the disaster as "an act of God," and actively worked to deny survivors any benefits. God didn't build that dam.

As part of a worldwide trend, labor unions began to emerge as a force in mitigating the power of corporate moguls in the late 1800s. During the ensuing decades, thousands of strikes pitted the wills of workers and mine owners. Most strikes were short-lived and peaceable, and after concessions were made, miners returned to work. But the stakes were always high and tempers occasionally flared. By the turn of the 20th Century, most miners in Appalachia were represented by some brotherhood or labor organization, with the United Mine Workers of America, formed in 1890, being the most prominent and successful.

What did the miner want? Primarily, they sought the opportunity to meet, organize, and collectively bargain for better wages and working conditions. They wanted recognition of their constitutional rights to free speech and assembly. They wanted pay in currency rather than in scrip and alternatives to company-owned stores. They wanted accurate, verifiable scales for measuring their production, with union supervision to prevent cheating. Doesn't sound too unreasonable to me.

One of the most forceful and bellicose union leaders was Mary Harris "Mother" Jones. An Irishwoman thought to have been born around 1845, Jones was already in her golden years when she began her combative and sometimes profane verbal diatribes directed not only at coal mine owners but politicians as well. Mother Jones remains to this day a symbol of the plight of working people worldwide.

By 1902, workers in the Kanawha-New River Coalfield were organized, and almost as quickly the mine owners formed the Kanawha County Coal Operators Association. In spite of laws designed to protect miners' rights to unionize, the Operators Association began active harassment of organizers.

Tensions escalated, culminating in the massacre at Matewan and then the battle of Blair Mountain, which I'll tell you more about once we approach Matewan.

MOMENTS AFTER LEAVING POCAHONTAS, I entered West Virginia still again, leaving Virginia for the last time. I soon arrived in Bramwell, a fascinating village and one of my favorites anywhere. It sits on an oxbow bend in the Bluestone River and is only a few hundred yards from one end to the other. In the middle are a collection of mansions, about 20 of them, built for some of the richest and most successful people in the coal industry from the late 1890s. Pocahontas housed the workers while Bramwell housed the mine owners. Most of the larger communities and some of the smaller ones in the coalfields had wealthy residents and impressive homes. But because Bramwell was consistently upscale, it has enjoyed more loving care and there is less decay. Many of the homes are still valuable, although as I would learn, surprisingly affordable.

The same friend who put me in touch with Thomas Cole gave me contact information for Jackie Shahan, who with her husband owns one of Bramwell's most impressive homes.

Jackie was a small woman, unpretentious and chatty, with long, jet-black hair. She would never fit the image of what I envisioned as a mansion owner. But to call her house anything else would simply not be accurate.

The driveway snaked uphill between stone abutments. The house was grand, with multifaceted edges, stone walls and terra cotta roof tiling. I felt like I'd arrived at a movie set. I couldn't figure out which of the grand doors to approach.

Welcoming me inside, she escorted me into the kitchen filled with modern appliances and poured me a glass of flavored lemonade from a bottle in the refrigerator. We went outside to the front porch, overlooking the village, sat in high, upholstered chairs, and propped our legs on the stone railing. I asked how she came to own a mansion in West Virginia.

She said she was an army brat, growing up in Germany, Spain, and Texas. Her husband was, also. He had lived in Pakistan and many other places. "We didn't have any roots. But we've been here now thirty-one years. My husband is a radiologist and I was an X-ray tech. He was getting out of the military, and he found a job at the hospital in Bluefield, which he accepted before I'd even been here. That was 1984, maybe. We started looking for a home."

Long story short, they were looking in Bluefield, but found that this home was being sold at auction. Incredibly, they placed the winning bid at a mere $165,000! I was surprised that rather than being ecstatic that they'd bought such an incredible place at such a meager price, she expressed her reluctance.

"We didn't want to live in Bramwell. We wanted to live in Bluefield. It's only 15 minutes away, and there is no traffic. But it is a MANSION! I had no idea how to furnish it or take care of it. It felt like a lot of responsibility. We didn't even own furniture! I liked cities, and this was a tiny place. I was young. I'd always lived in basic, everyday houses. I was never looking for anything more. It was like, 'Wow! But what now?' I'm not an entertainer. I don't know how to decorate. I had no ideas or visions. We do our own yard work; I mow a lot of lawn!

"My favorite part is the view. It overlooks the village. It's an oasis. The (Bluestone) River is just below and beyond that is that fabulous church. It is peaceful and quiet.

"The house is huge. It has tons of personality and attention to detail. The artisans put their all into it. It cost $90,000 to build in 1912, and took three years to build. It has stone walls in the Tudor style and is reminiscent of the Biltmore (in Asheville, North Carolina). They spared no expense. It has a central vacuum system and walk-in closets which were rare at that time. All the closets have pull-out drawers and shelving. The third floor is a ballroom. There are dumb-waiters. There are gardeners' quarters, servants' quarters, a split-level peacock coop, and a barn."

She said it was built by a Colonel Thomas from Wales. He married the daughter of the mine owner and so he married into money, but was every bit a coal baron in his own right. He died only four years later and the house had three owners since. "It's a marvelous house. I'd never been in this type of setting before. We have 14 or 15 acres of land."

I asked if it was a good move.

"Absolutely! Absolutely! This is the most wonderful life. I love Bramwell. I love this house. I love this community. I love raising kids with my friends and their friends. They went to a local school in Bramwell early on, but they graduated from Bluefield High School."

"A good school?" I enquired.

"Yes. It's the same school John Nash went to. My oldest daughter went to Princeton so she had that connection. One of the kids she dated also went to Princeton. When you can graduate from high school in Bluefield, West Virginia, and go to Princeton, that's pretty good."

At this point, I'm thinking about her daughter potentially meeting someone at Princeton who would speak derisively to her about being from West Virginia, at which point she could retort, "Yup, I went to the same school as John Nash. Touché!"

She continued, "There's no economy really in Bramwell now. Everybody here is retired, came here with money, or works someplace else. We have schoolteachers. Magistrates. Ex-military. Musicians. Not a lot of original Bramwell people are still here."

It started to pour rain, dampening the air and splashing into the stone goldfish pond on the lawn in front of us.

"Bramwell is very progressive. We have seven or eight gay couples. That's nice. I was surprised I would care about my community. I was a military brat, constantly moving. Now I've been here over 30 years. It didn't occur to me that I'd ever have a community network. It's nice to plan and work and see ideas come to fruition. Pocahontas is deteriorating. It's a cautionary tale for us here (in Bramwell) to preserve what we have. They had something irreplaceable and much of it is gone."

"Do you feel a stigma about being a West Virginian?"

"Yes. But we live an independent life here. We forge deep friendships. I like West Virginians. We still travel a lot. My parents loved adventure. And we tagged along, all over the world. We've done that with our kids, too. That was important to us. Whenever we flew home and drove over the mountains and saw that sign that said, 'Welcome to West Virginia, Wild and Wonderful,' I always thought that my favorite thing was coming in and seeing these mountains. These mountains enclose you. As soon as I see these mountains, I always say, 'I'm home.' I feel like these mountains are like a big hug. They really hug you. This is the way it should be. I've got my mountains. I've got my trees. I'm home."

She took me for a tour of her home. There were delightful surprises at every turn, with beautiful artwork, antique furniture, and whimsy throughout. The grand staircase elevated from the foyer and then split in two with a magnificent stained glass window set in front and a conical crystal glass chandelier above. Strains of Joe Cocker played in my mind's ear, singing "Luxury You Can Afford."

You, too, can own a mansion in Bramwell. I'll surely miss Blacksburg, but I want to move to Bramwell, West Virginia. And live in a mansion. One potentially positive part of the economic development puzzle in the coalfields is the low cost of housing. The international economy is spawning countless new jobs that can be done anywhere in the world there is a laptop computer and good Internet service. You can own a mansion in southern West Virginia for half the cost of a bungalow in Seattle or San Jose. And there's no traffic.

Leaving Bramwell, I drove a mile or so to the intersection with US-52 and turned left, heading west. I crossed over Coaldale Mountain that leads into McDowell County. The Mercer/McDowell county line is actually near the base of the mountain on the west side.

THERE IS A PALPABLE SENSE OF DESCENDING as one enters McDowell (pronounced "MAC-dal" by the locals), as if its entirety, or at least the portions where people live, is within the crevices of a deeply corrugated landscape. I can't remember ever seeing an outdoor photograph of anything in McDowell – a home, church, tipple, or train – that didn't have a wall of forested mountainsides behind it. Familiarity means nothing. I'd made repeated trips to McDowell County in recent years, and the impressions were as vexing, as wrenching on this trip as they'd ever been.

Neither words nor photos, neither qualitative nor quantitative analyses, can adequately describe the reality that is contemporary McDowell.

Created as part of Virginia by the state legislature in 1858 from Tazewell County, McDowell was a remote, largely inaccessible place even as late as the 1880s when that year's census counted 3,074 people. The coming of the N&W railroad changed everything. By 1910 population neared 50,000 people and by 1950 almost 100,000, at which time it was West Virginia's fourth most populous county.

Those people were scrunched into topography where perhaps only 6 to 8 percent of its land area was flat enough to support habitation. Parts of Keystone, Welch, and Gary were astonishingly dense, with homes clinging to hillsides like fungi on a decaying tree trunk. After 65 years of unsteady but hard decline, McDowell now boasts fewer than 20,000. This represents one of the nation's largest diasporas. But in this context, numbers mean nothing either, at least to how being there makes you feel.

The railroad and the mines were predominant, taking the most valuable land. If there was a flat area and the railroad needed it for a siding, station, or other use, it got first dibs. The mines used land for outside storage of coal and equipment. What was left was allocated to the community. Wide spots got schools or retail stores. Less wide spots got churches, which were and still are everywhere. Smaller spots got single or multi-family homes. McDowell was built during an era when architecture mattered, so many structures were well-built and pleasing to the eye, lending an even more macabre feel as they now succumb to the inexorable march of natural reclamation.

Besides the buildings' walls and roofs that are routinely collapsing, the remnants of massive conveyers still loom overhead in places, occasionally flaking off pieces of steel as spears that plummet to the ground below. Industry in general and the coal industry in particular have historically not been conscientious in cleaning up their messes. Whenever a coal operator folded, there was no civic group or governmental agency left behind to clean up the detritus and residue, often persistently toxic and pernicious.

So through every hollow I drove, there was the ubiquitous creek, often decorated with massive quantities of rubbish, the road, never more than two lanes and often less, sometimes unpaved, and the railroad track, often looming overhead, and typically with innumerable bridges, trestles, and tunnels to attempt to give it a straighter path than the landscape would normally allow. Even on the slower routes, there was too much visual stimulation for the brain to process. An abandoned church here. A decrepit, formerly attractive house on the hillside there. Impressive stone staircase and archway there. Patch of daffodils there. Hulk of a car chassis here. Massive train trestle overhead, with rumbling diesel locomotives there.

McDowell has no bad drivers; they're all long dead. This is not the place for inattention as driving demands utmost focus. There were people around, walking on sidewalks (Yes, these towns were built when pedestrians still mattered, too.), standing in front of cars with opened hoods, emerging from convenience stores, but they were uniformly sullen and laconic. Don't bother waving a friendly wave; nobody waves back. Over half the adult population was on some form of government assistance. People were listless; the passage of time was inconsequential.

There were no golf courses, few tennis or basketball courts or bicycle trails. With the exception of four-wheeling, seemingly nobody recreated, or at least nobody recreated outdoors and in public view.

Abandoned school

When we think of the ghost towns of the Wild West, they're always unoccupied, with creaking doors, empty water towers, and blowing tumbleweed. McDowell's towns are still inhabited, albeit with only 20 percent of the people they were built for. More houses were unoccupied than occupied, and the former were in a vast array of disintegration, from mild to extreme. Some looked occupied, or at least only recently vacated, but had widows that were broken or missing entirely. Others had fallen roofs or exposed skeletal beams. Others were burned-out shells. Some had trees growing inside. The official flower of McDowell County is the glass shard.

Back to the statistics: While the oil embargo of the 1970s gave a momentary boost to McDowell, within another decade the economy there was in full-fledged collapse. The domestic steel industry, a major consumer of McDowell's valuable metallurgical coal, also declined.

The Appalachian coalfields in the 1980s lost 70,000 mining jobs, but no county was more dramatically impacted than McDowell. By decade's end, almost 40 percent of the County's residents were under the poverty line and the worst was yet to come. When U.S. Steel ceased all operations in the County, personal income plummeted over 60 percent in a single year, effectively destroying the value of any real estate. Thousands of homes were worthless overnight and personal equity simply evaporated. The ripple of misery became a torrent. The public school system lost funding and teachers began leaving. Academic standards plummeted. Poverty rates skyrocketed and hundreds of students arrived at school each day hungry, malnourished, or literally starving.

Due to poor nutrition, drug abuse, obesity, mental illness, smoking, and accidents, life expectancy according to recent data is the lowest in the country, with males living just over 63 years, a full 13 years fewer than the national average.

If all this wasn't enough, because of McDowell's rugged topography and tight hollows (and certainly to an undeterminable degree because of the poor water retention capabilities of strip-mined mountains), it is uniquely susceptible to devastating floods. And on July 8, 2001, and May 2, 2002, they came. After many disasters such as Hurricane Sandy in New York and New Jersey and the Loma Prieta earthquake near San Francisco (that we remember as the World Series Earthquake), rebuilding efforts were underway immediately. However in McDowell, after these floods destroyed everything in their paths, more buildings were abandoned and more people departed.

Two aspects of the environment give McDowell a uniquely cloistered feel. First is the physical confinement of the landscape. If Montana is Big Sky Country, McDowell is Little Sky. Hundreds of homes throughout the County don't feel the sun's warming rays for months at a time in the winter, obscured by enveloping mountains. Second is the astonishing fecundity of nature, where trees, shrubs, and vines grow with breathtaking rapidity, quickly overwhelming those abandoned structures. The ebony soil is richly fertile and produces great garden crops. But necessarily the gardens are small and of little commercial value. On an earlier visit, a man showed me a bushel basket of the largest potatoes I'd ever seen that he'd grown in his back yard garden.

Many communities across the country from the ghettos of Detroit or Camden to the industrial wastelands of Gary or Flint or the silver mining towns of the high Rockies have suffered. But there's no place I'd ever seen that matched the forlornness of McDowell. My mind reeled with curiosity over the lives, the loves, and the losses hidden behind all the crumbling walls.

As you might imagine, various charity organizations have poured their hearts, money, and sweat equity into McDowell in attempts to alleviate the suffering, bringing food, clothing, toiletries, and other necessities to families in need. The reality is that these well-meaning efforts are fingers in a leaking dike before a rising sea of misery.

The best of McDowell's human capital was also the first to leave. The brightest and most capable of the County's offspring fled long ago and those less intellectually gifted, emotionally or physically handicapped, or, to their credit, emotionally attached, stayed behind or in isolated cases even returned.

There were no physical neutron bombs that dropped on McDowell, but in places it feels like it. If you have a pulse or a shred of empathy, you will never come fully home from your first trip to McDowell.

While production has dropped substantially from the heyday, some coal is still being extracted. However, the employment necessary to provide that production has plummeted. Four major factors kicked in to leave the descendents of miners brought to the coalfields from the 1890s until the 1950s superfluous and economically stranded. Assigning relative value or impact to each is not fruitful, as they all played a significant part.

First, starting in the 1950s and 1960s, mines became mechanized. No longer did a man use pick-axes, shovels, explosives, and his back to liberate coal from its eternal resting place and load it into an awaiting bucket for transfer to the coal hopper waiting outside. New machines did that work. And even primitive, rudimentary, continuous mining machines could do the work of 40 men.

Second, as it is with all extractive resources, the industry took the low-hanging fruit, extracting the best quality, easiest to access minerals first. The Pocahontas Coal seam was vast in reach, in places 13 feet thick, and thought to be the richest coal seam in the world. It is mostly depleted now, its ash remaining behind the foundry or power plant where it was burned, its heat and light long dissipated into the universal void, and its greenhouse-gas by-products now in the atmosphere. Miners are now extracting seams that are thinner, deeper, and of lower quality and thus more expensive to reach and less competitive. Other mining areas worldwide are now more profitable.

Third, underground mining gave way to "surface" mining, now variously referred to as "strip-mining" or most descriptively, "mountaintop removal mining," as we've already discussed.

Fourth, with concerns about pollution and global warming, the world's industrial consumers looked for cleaner fuels that emitted fewer heat-trapping gasses and toxic chemicals into the atmosphere.

These factors are irreversible. Employment can't and won't rebound, regardless of shifting political winds. For politicians to say otherwise is disingenuous and irresponsible.

On their way to brighter futures elsewhere, McDowell's economic refugees simply drove away, abandoning their mortgages and homes that had zero value and often many of their belongings as well. Some bothered to lock their doors upon departure, some didn't; it mattered not. Today there are literally thousands of abandoned structures throughout McDowell County: homes, coal tipples, stores, schools, and churches. This excess infrastructure is difficult to rationalize as it becomes more visceral than cerebral. The cerebral says that the coal industry, in the heyday of labor-intensive, pick-and-shovel mining that reached its apex, brought hundreds of thousands of workers into the hidden hollows of central Appalachia. The visceral, the end result (Does anybody know the difference between an "end result" and a "result?"), is that significant portions of the Appalachian coalfield region today are almost post-apocalyptic in their poverty, decrepitude, and decay.

SHORTLY THEREAFTER AS I MOTORED ON, near the town of Switchback, the railroad tracks appeared coming from Barlow Hollow on the left, destined to parallel the highway until Welch. There was a stunning railroad trestle in masonry and steel that crossed over the highway and reminded me why I was there.

A few miles later, near the town of Northfork, traffic came to a standstill as highway workers were working farther up the road. I used the opportunity to explore a bit. There was a small pullover area on the right side of the road, then an embankment to the Elkhorn Creek, and on the opposite bank a set of tracks. On the left was a small business district, and I walked into a restaurant called "Shupester's The Dinner Bucket," dedicated to the miners of the region. I struck up a conversation with two waitresses, telling them about my project. The younger waitress looked eerily like one of my college classmates. The older woman wore an apron. She was the cook and the younger sister of the restaurant owner. There were only three or four customers sitting at tables, and so both women had ample time to visit with me.

The waitress told me that generally their customers fell into one of three categories. Some folks came to ride the Hatfield and McCoy trail on their four-wheelers and motorcycles. Some came to watch the trains. Others were locals, just having a meal out. She said there were trains every 15 minutes, "Especially around nine o'clock when you're trying to watch a movie, they are back-to-back."

The owner's and cook's surname was Shupe – I assumed "Shupester" was his nickname. The cook told me, "This is my brother's restaurant. He lives upstairs. He's always wanted to (own a restaurant).

He worked for Kroger for 46 years."

I asked about the history of the building. The cook said, "It was a drug store many years ago. It became a discount store. It had flea markets. My brother bought the building in 2012. In the beginning, business was good. The coal mines continue to close down. They closed the Walmart near Welch. We didn't want to have to rely on the four-wheelers, but now we do."

I asked about the four-wheeling season. She said, "They arrive from February until November. There are resorts that have cabins and motel rooms. There are lots of businesses now tied to them. They come in by the truckload. Some come every month.

"There are only a few mines still mining now. We wanted to rely on the local people to make this restaurant work. If you've got no job, you don't have no money."

"I remember twenty years ago," the waitress said, "Everywhere you went, you saw black faces (of the coal miners). Men looked like they had eyeliner on. Now it's rare."

A black man finished his meal and bused his own dishes, carrying them to the bar. He paid his tab and left, the waitress saying, "See you later, Red."

I asked if they knew McDowell County was the poorest in the state. The cook said, "I don't know. It makes me hot when they say that. They put it out there that it is. But we're still here."

By the time I got outside, the roadblock was gone, and I was able to strap on my helmet and continue.

MY NEXT DESTINATION WAS KEYSTONE, only a few miles away. Let's not mince words: Keystone was a whore-town, the Sodom and Gomorrah of West Virginia. It had one of the most notorious red-light districts in the nation for decades. "Cinder Bottom" was known by everybody in the region and everybody around there mentions it. That, and the collapse of the Keystone Bank, made Keystone one of the most infamous communities in the coalfields.

Keystone was named after Pennsylvania, the "Keystone State," as many of the town's founders were from there.

As I mentioned, blacks in massive numbers had immigrated from the depths of the post-Confederate South searching for gainful employment and the same opportunities as whites. Because labor was so much in demand in the coalfields, this was largely attainable. Empowered blacks participated in politics, locally and state-wide, in school boards, and in law enforcement. It was unheard of in that era for a black policeman to arrest a white man, but it happened in Keystone many times. Black children went to modern schools, funded by the state, just as the white kids did. In 1916, a black man was elected to the state House of Delegates and by 2008, of the 24 blacks ever elected to statewide government, 12 were from McDowell.

Locals often refer to their county as "The Free State of McDowell," coined by Matthew T. Whittico, a newspaperman from Keystone in the 1920s. Keystone was considered to be its capital. Whittico published the *McDowell Times*, the longest running Negro newspaper in West Virginia.

Cinder Bottom, the "International Whorehouse District of the Coalfields," satisfied the sexual needs of thousands of coal workers, mostly new immigrants, as they sought carnal pleasures after the toilsome and dangerous work deep within the earth. It got its name from the two feet deep layer of cinders placed there, residue from nearby coke ovens. Whorehouses were painted different bright colors, and the brothels were surrounded by gambling joints, restaurants, burlesque shows, and barber shops. Although the sex trade was concentrated in Cinder Bottom, prostitution could be found all over town.

Keystone has always been approximately 80 percent black. But Cinder Bottom catered to both blacks and whites, even if the customer base and the cocottes themselves often were self-segregated to individual brothels. Authorities long knew of the activities there, but for decades never made attempts to shut it down. It was generally acknowledged that massive investments locally and the national economy in general were tied to production in the coalfields, production that could only persist on the backs of thousands of miners who wouldn't have endured without the occasional entertainment provided by the call-girls.

By the late 1960s, the decline in coal mining employment and the increase in community respectability doomed the prostitution business, and Cinder Bottom ceased to exist as a provider of entertainment.

I WALKED INTO THE FORMER KEYSTONE BANK building, not knowing what I'd find. The sign outside said "Keystone City Hall," and I assumed there would be a mayor or city manager. I found several people, including Vondelere Scott.

Vondelere was a huge African American woman who sat with her arms folded high over her breasts. Her hair was swept back in a bun with a white scrunchie. After telling her about my interest, she said, "At one point, Keystone had 5,000 people. Now there are less than 300." She sat directly in front of the built-in bank vault's open door.

"There were stores all up and down through here. There's a convenience store and a hardware store now. The hardware store used to be the company store. There was a men's clothing store. A laundromat. A movie theater. A furniture store. Drug stores, one white and one black."

I asked her if she knew any of the women that worked in the brothels. She said, "Yes, but they are going to say they didn't. They won't even admit it to me. Why did they turn to being prostitutes? It had to be a reason. Some to feed their families. Some may have enjoyed it. If you enjoy it, you might as well get paid for it. There was no color in Keystone. Everybody got along fine. It's still that way. This is a good place for whites and blacks, if you want to live here."

I asked about the Keystone Bank. She yelled for a woman in the other room. "Nita!"

Juanita McKinney joined us. She was a white woman with long, wavy blond hair. She had manicured nails and a thin gold necklace. She told me that she'd worked for the Keystone Bank and lost her job when it was closed by the U.S. Office of the Comptroller of the Currency in 1999. "Greed," she said, succinctly.

The bank opened in 1904. A man named Knox McConnell arrived from Pittsburgh to take over the bank in 1977. It drew deposits from around the region and the country, energetically marketing sub-prime home-equity loans and providing excellent interest rates.

He brought two women with him, Billie Jean Cherry and Terry Lee Church, and was apparently romantically linked to Cherry, although they never married. He employed an all female staff that he called "Knox's foxes" and set a stated goal to become the number one banker in the country.

McConnell's efforts boosted assets from $17 million to $1 billion in 20 years. But when he died of a heart attack in 1997 at age 69, things began to unravel. Under suspicion of fraud, investigators arrived and recovered 370 boxes of bank records that were literally buried in a 100 foot-long trench on property belonging to Church, then the bank's senior executive vice president. Cherry later was convicted of embezzlement and died in prison.

Going to Keystone may have made sense for an aggressive businessman like McConnell in the 1940s. But by the late 1970s, the community was already deep in decline. We can only guess that he had his reasons, given what he may have intended to do even before he arrived. He put "Time Tried, Panic Tested," on a sign outside, but the panic that ensued after his death would kill the bank as well.

McKinney told me, "They ran a bank and a mortgage department.

The bank was fine. The mortgage side was where they were stealing. They underwrote loans. They booked loans that didn't actually exist. Then they were milking from the top.

"Every year the regulators came in and did an audit. The eight years I worked here, they came more and more often. I worked for a short time in the mortgage department, but most of the time I was a bookkeeper in the checking account department of the bank. I knew something wasn't right, but I didn't know what until afterwards. That's why I'm not in jail."

"I'll tell you how good it was (before it collapsed)," Vondelere said. "The city of Keystone was getting $400,000 a year in B&O (business and occupational) tax from the bank."

Nita agreed. "When the Keystone Bank was operational and that hardware store and Heilig Meyers were open and the mines and the tipple were running, this was a booming town."

Nita McKinney

Heilig Meyers was a retail furniture store chain founded by Lithuanian immigrants, J. M. Meyers and W. A. Heilig in 1913 in North Carolina. At one point it was the largest furniture retailer in the country with over 1,000 stores. It filed for bankruptcy in 2000. The colorful green sign is still on the now-empty building in Keystone, just a few doors away from the bank.

Nita continued, "I lost not only my job but my retirement, everything. Devastating. There were lots of women, 100 or more, who worked here and at the other branches. Mr. McConnell and Terry and Billie did good things for this community. I'm sure they were doing things wrong internally. It cost us all a way of living. I had to start over from scratch. When the bank folded, I was 25 years old, making $22.50 per hour. I started (two years after I graduated from high school) and worked for the bank until it closed in 1999. It was a good wage then for a high school graduate. It's unheard of even today, 16 years later. After the bank closed, I got a job at Lowes over in Bluefield, Virginia, making minimum wage. And I had to commute. I've never had another job as good as at the bank.

"I own a plumbing place now. I am a master plumber. But I'm also the city manager. It's a volunteer job. It's great being here. These people are family to me. You'll not go anywhere and find people no more friendlier than we are or will help you if we can. There's no doubt in my mind. I love it here. I was born and raised here and I am blessed to be here. My husband is foreman on a strip job mine in Mercer County and I'm able to do what I do because of him. McDowell is the friendliest, down to earth, best place in the world.

"I wish it could prosper again, to be what it once was. There is nothing else here (but coal). Here's what's sad; there have been people coming in and stripping this place, made their millions here, run their coal trucks through our town, they've made their mess, and they've left us. Coal has come out of these mountains and made outsiders rich. That's not right."

"Are you angry?" I asked.

"No. Not really. It's sad, but what are you going to do? You smile and go on. Make each day new. Do what you can do to help and what you can to make it look good. That's what we're trying to do. If you go around being mad all the time, what are you going to have? Nothing! It is what it is. But it is what you make it. We do our best; that's all you can do. It's hard here. But you roll with it and keep going.

"My husband makes $150,000 per year. We're blessed. When they reclaim a mine, it's beautiful. It looks like a golf course. They get reclamation awards."

Vondelere said, "This is a good place to call home. People are welcome."

Nita agreed, "We don't see color here. We're all family."

I departed, thinking to myself about Nita's husband's $150,000 per year salary blowing mountains to smithereens and how complicated things are in West Virginia.

ALL ALONG US-52 were homes, churches, schools, and stores in various states of decay. The best homes invariably had metal roofs, which apparently were cheaper than traditional asphalt tile roofs. Many buildings were complete ruins, with collapsed walls and roofs. There were lots of abandoned vehicles, some decades old. There were remnants of a formerly robust industrial economy, including old trucks, old mining equipment, and large tires. There were many stone walls and sidewalks, placed in an era when stonework was common. There was almost no new construction of any kind. In the towns, most of the buildings were brick, of two- and three-story, some occupied and some not. Traffic was moderate with occasional coal trucks roaring by and lots of other commercial vehicles, mostly from utility companies.

DAN CLARK AND HIS WIFE, ELISSE, bought a derelict building sandwiched between the N&W tracks, US-52, and the Elkhorn Creek, and turned it into a bed and breakfast, filling it with flowers and eccentric artwork. I had met them on a prior trip through the area and stopped to say hello. After ringing the doorbell and as I waited for one of them to arrive, I noticed an ornate mezuzah affixed to the entrance door of their Elkhorn Inn. Dan welcomed me inside, telling me Elisse wasn't feeling well. He and I sat in the dining room where two long parallel dining tables welcomed visitors amidst the smell of fine herbs.

As with my theme, I asked Dan how he'd gotten to McDowell County and happened to open the inn. He said, "I was here on a FEMA assignment for six months, working on assessments on buildings after the flood of 2002. I worked in logistics. This building was vacant at the time. It was owned by Ms. Cherry at the Keystone Bank, but (after her arrest) the federal government obtained it. It was derelict.

"Originally it was built in 1922 as the Empire Coal and Coke Company's Miner's Clubhouse. It replaced another building built in 1910 that burned down. So they made this one out of brick and concrete. There is no wood in the building other than the trim. The concrete is 18 inches thick. The flood was huge; this building had five feet of water in it. People who lived here at the time were trapped on the second floor. About 20 homes here in Landgraff washed away in the flood.

"I seen the building and made an offer to the government and bought it for $10,000. I had $10,000 in the bank, and I wrote them a check. It's 90 feet by 40 feet and three stories. I put 240 sheets of drywall on the first floor. I had to re-wire, re-plumb it and paint it, with the intention of turning into a bed and breakfast.

"We thought our market would be four-wheelers, but it turned out to be train photographers. And trout fishermen. The Elkhorn produces the largest trout in West Virginia. They are 18 inches to 20 inches long. Trout Unlimited rates it as the second or third best trout stream in the United States, and nobody knows about it."

A train rumbled by and drowned out our conversation; it was that close. It was only three locomotives and one car, apparently shuttling the locomotives for service nearby.

"In 2008," he continued, "the economy collapsed, and business hasn't been as good. From the beginning until 2008, we were growing about 10 percent each year. 2008 was our best year as the collapse was late in the year. We've come back. We have interesting, different people. Film crews. Railroad fans. Historical people. We have had several people come looking for fathers' or grandfathers' homes. They're researching how life was.

"We have 12 rooms, a capacity of 24 people. Our occupancy is about 50 percent on the weekends. We thought we'd have more."

A house cat jumped on the table and Dan picked her up and set her on the floor. A dog emerged from the hallway, and Dan took him outside. While he was gone, I noticed the ornate chandeliers and stained glass in the room. There was fine artwork, large and small, and high stacks of magazines on every flat surface on the room's perimeter furniture.

When Dan returned, I asked him about his lessons learned from starting a business in one of the nation's poorest places. He thought for several moments and said, "The surprising part is that there's high unemployment, and you'd think you'd find people willing to work. You can't. There is no work ethic. When people are in a cycle of poverty and you live in it and you accept that level that you're living on because you make it every day with food on the table, there's no incentive to do better. Try to find somebody to cut grass at the first of the month; you can't. That's when the government checks come. If people have three meals a day and a roof over their head, they're surviving off other people's money. One kid came in and worked a couple of days. Then he took off. He was surprised that anybody wanted him to work a full 40 hours a week. That is common. I now have a core group of people to work for me.

"Not many people move here; most move away. Most of the new businesses in the county and the area are started by people from some-place else. People here don't see the opportunities. I came from New York and thought I could make something here. (Prior to that,) others just drove by. To do something, you have to take a risk. It can be scary if you're not predisposed."

I asked about his social life. He said, sipping his coffee, "Our social life is limited. Most people have their social life on weekends. We work every weekend. So we don't get out like we'd like to. We have to go to Bluefield for a social life."

I mentioned that I had noticed the Elkhorn Creek was a milky-grey color, and asked him about it.

Dan said, "It's just because of all the rain we've had. It's a clear, pretty creek, usually. It's clear and fast-running. After the 2002 flood, they dredged it. They went down about four feet. We don't live in fear whenever we have heavy rain. When a hurricane stops over the moun-tains, and it rains 18 inches in 24 hours, you're going to have a flood. I don't expect 14 years of work to wash away in an afternoon. But if it did, I'd just start over.

"McDowell County has been kicked around for decades. It was once one of the richest counties in the state. As a country, we've lost our industrial base to China, Mexico, and everywhere else. As this goes on, we'll see what's happening in McDowell County happening in other places. Chicago. Detroit. What are you going to do to employ the people?

"The positive things that could happen in this county will happen slow. Next year they'll bring an elk herd in. If we can make West Virginia the hunting state of the East like Colorado is in the West, we could make enough money in 60 days from a lot of these people coming in to survive through the year. We'd be filled every day during that time. The restaurants would be filled. About our only viable growth industry is tourism.

"West Virginia lost about 60 percent of its population in the 70s. People come back to visit to explore their roots. Some people come back to stay where they came from. Not a lot, but a few. You can buy a mansion here for $50,000 if you can find one. There aren't many habitable houses left that you can buy, ready to live in. They all need work."

IT WAS ONLY A FEW MILES farther west to Kimball where I stopped to see Clara Thompson, administrator at the Kimball World War I Memorial. I met her years earlier when I wrote my first book. The Kimball Memorial was the first built in the United States to honor the sacrifices of the African American soldiers and seamen of World War I and today is the only one left. Over 400,000 African Americans volunteered to serve in combat, with 50,000 serving overseas. An incredible 1,500 black McDowell Countians volunteered.

The War Memorial was designed in the classic Greek style with four massive columns in yellowish sandstone against a building with the same construction material. Dedicated in 1928, it housed an auditorium, meeting rooms, library, and trophy room, and was a focal point for the black community for decades. As the decades went by, the population diminished and like so many other buildings in the county, it deteriorated. A fire in 1991, suspected to be arson, left nothing more than the outer shell. A dedicated community effort obtained funding through state and federal sources, and the museum reopened for lectures, special events, and discourse on improving relations between citizens from all races.

Whenever I've seen her, Clara is beautifully dressed with countless rings, bracelets, and earrings. She always greets me with a warm hug. She grew up in nearby Gary. "Once the mines started shutting down," she said, "we had to relocate. My dad brought us here. It's only ten miles or so, as the crow flies. Dad was a coal miner. He came from Jackson, Georgia. Lord, it was many a blue moon ago! It was approximately 1932.

"He came to McDowell because coal mining was booming. He heard about it, looking for better things, better jobs. Mom was from Springton, West Virginia, which is 20 miles east of here. They met and married here. This was one of the most equal places in the country for blacks.

"Everybody was here, living together. Poles. Hungarians. Blacks. People talk about segregation and the (bad) things that happened to blacks across America. I can't relate. I didn't experience that.

"We had segregated schools. We had the best thing going in the world. When we integrated, the black schools were closed. Our schools were better. Our teachers made sure we were there for the right reasons. If a student wasn't performing, teachers jumped on them. Now parents jump all over the teachers."

Former Walmart parking lot

She said that segregation brought to black people an ethic where they didn't need to do as well as the whites, but even better. Teachers knew their kids better get it. "The way things were at that time, they knew education was the key to making us successful. McDowell County has produced some fantastic people.

"The civil rights movement was happening away from me. I went to a black, segregated school. A segregated church. At work, my father worked with white men.

"It was just the way it was. The town had sections where different people lived. But we played together. It was prosperous because of the mining. We never went hungry and there were 15 of us, 9 boys and 6 girls. I was number 12. We had two bedrooms, one for the boys and one for the girls. The older ones were already left and gone.

"We had only an outdoor toilet, one seat. It was shared with our neighbor; we used one side and they used the other. We had indoor water, but an outdoor toilet. We had a tin tub for a bath. Now you take a shower every day. We bathed once a week. Other times we just washed off. You didn't stink and you didn't go hungry and you weren't dirty. The water was clean enough. My dad walked to work from where we lived.

"My other neighbors had lots of kids, too. They took the Bible seriously. 'Be fruitful and multiply.'"

I asked her where the museum's visitors came from. "Listen, most of our visitors come from the eastern United States, but the furthest away visitors were from Australia. They love it! They think that West Virginia is the most beautiful state in the world. We have tour buses. They are looking for roadside markers. When they see an actual building, they are amazed.

"There are lots of buildings that are falling in. People comment on that. I say that the people in Charleston don't care. They need a charity county. It's terrible. I tell people not to listen to the lies. I tell people that McDowell County is one of the best places in the world. Every city has its slum areas. We have the best people! They are not selfish. They're loving. There are some bad ones; there are bad ones everywhere. I'm telling you, it's the people!

"There are no places in this county I wouldn't go alone. The floods took things. Things can be replaced. I went to really remote places. I found excellent folks. Excellent people."

I GAVE CLARA A PARTING HUG and motored on towards Welch. On my left I drove past a vast parking lot and a recently closed Walmart store. The ubiquitous Walmart sign was painted a funereal black. Walmart destroys jobs when it arrives as locally-owned stores can't compete. And Walmart destroys more jobs when it departs. In this case, 140 jobs were lost in early 2016 when their store, as one of 269 under-performing locations across the country nationally and internationally, shuttered their doors. What is a resident to think when their county can no longer even support a Walmart? The closest remaining Walmart was back in Bluefield, nearly an hour away.

This Walmart was a major donor to the Five Loaves and Two Fishes Food Bank, donating over 90,000 pounds of food annually. Now that's gone as well. That food served over half the entire county's population.

On I rode into Welch for my rendezvous with Delegate Clif Moore, McDowell.

3:50 p.m.

Welch

Mile 387.4

Surrounded by mountains of fine Bituminous Coal. Seat of the largest coal-producing county in the nation. In this area many branches reach out to coal operations. Some tipples may be seen from the train. Distribution point for mine supplies and petroleum products. (Tug Fork of Big Sandy River)

About the same time I met Clara Thompson years earlier, I met Clif Moore, representative to the House of Delegates in West Virginia from McDowell. He frequents the modern public library in downtown Welch, where I planned to meet him again.

I parked my motorcycle across the street where the meter accepted no money. One of the nice things about towns in decline is that there is seldom a problem finding street parking. And it's typically cheap or free.

Like the rest of McDowell County, of which Welch is the county seat, Welch's population had steadily plummeted since its apex in 1950, when 6,600 people crammed tightly into its steep crevices. Welch was named after Isaiah Welch, a former Confederate Army captain and surveyor who planned a city at the confluence of the Tug Fork of the Big Sandy River and the Elkhorn Creek, to serve as a center of commerce and law. The junction provided some level ground upon which to build a town, but not much. Steep mountains surround it on every side and tightly confine it. Houses and stores hug the roads that emanate like tendrils from the downtown hub, and long stone stairways arch upwards from the sidewalks. Even now many large homes and significant buildings are built on steep slopes surrounding the tiny, compact downtown.

Welch has been marked by a violent history, including its worst year, 1921. On March 2 of that year, the City Council met to discuss the impeachment of Mayor J. H. Whitt. Unhappy about it, Whitt arrived and caused a ruckus, overturning the table where they sat. When the City Council asked Sherriff William Johnson Tabor to investigate Whitt, Whitt shot and killed Tabor who was only 28 at the time. Whitt was arrested and put on trial in September, then acquitted by a technicality, and then he vanished.

Meanwhile, on August 1, Matewan Police Chief Sid Hatfield and friend Ed Chambers were assassinated on the steps leading to the McDowell County Courthouse by employees of the Baldwin-Felts Detective Agency, following a shootout in Matewan in May of the prior year. I'll tell you that story when we get to Matewan.

Welch soon became a bustling place, self-proclaiming as "The Heart of the Nation's Coal Bin," as cosmopolitan as any domestic city outside New York. As small and geographically confined as Welch was, in its heyday, it was the trading center for the county's nearly 100,000 people. Like most of McDowell County, its population was amazingly diverse, especially compared with non-coal producing areas of Appalachia. Money flowed like wine and Welch was teeming with activity and prosperity, beyond comprehension of anyone visiting these days.

In its heyday, Welch had two ballrooms and had tea dances once a week. It had two top theaters with excellent stages for vaudeville. Culturally it had everything, from the ballet to symphonies. The theaters were highly supported, and the greatest names in entertainment came to Welch. The city built the nation's first multi-story parking garage in 1941, and it still stands today, a three-story white concrete structure near the Tug Fork River. Take *that* San Francisco!

Then like the opening of trap doors on a coal hopper, the bottom fell out. Welch was already in decline when John F. Kennedy visited in 1960, noting that McDowell was getting more surplus food packages than any county in the country.

When Chloe and Alderson Muncy and their 13 children of nearby Paynesville became the first recipients of Food Stamps as part of Kennedy's "War on Poverty," Welch became a poster child of Appalachian poverty.

Beyond that and the floods, nothing much has happened in Welch since then to draw anybody's attention, other than the 2006 lawsuit by the ACLU against the police chief when he prevented rescuers from attending to a gay man suffering from cardiac arrest.

On a more positive note, renowned artist, Tom Acosta, of nearby Kimball has painted several magnificent, colorful murals celebrating local history around town, on buildings and water towers.

I walked into the library and found Clif who was reading a two-week old *Wall Street Journal*. He reminds me of a younger Bill Cosby, minus the alleged sexual misconduct of course. He's bespectacled, with a graying beard and curls of dark hair dropping to his shoulders.

We exchanged greetings and got to work, as I told him about the current project. He told me years earlier that McDowell County was at the top of every negative state category and the bottom of every positive one. I wanted to know how that had changed in the meantime.

"I want to be the most optimistic person you ever talk to," he claimed. "But at the same time I want to be truthful as well. On the horizon I've always had something to look forward to. I don't have that (now). I'm afraid of where we're going to be in five years; it scares the hell out of me. We don't have anything that we can point to that says this might be the turnaround that might spur something else and then something else.

"I was born in Gary. I am a young 67 years old. I left here to go to college in 1971 and I came back in 1992 for good. I was gone for 21 years. I was first elected in 2004. I took the seat in the House of Delegates in 2005. I will have been in office for 12 years next January.

"McDowell County has seen a precipitous loss. My House of Delegates seat today includes most of the county. Back in the heyday, there were six or seven delegates from McDowell County alone. My district continues to get larger geographically with each redistricting process because there are fewer people here, and it is a fixed number of people that I am supposed to represent.

"The population began to decline in 1950, but in the meantime, it began to level off. In 2001, we had a terrible flood. In 2002, we had an even more horrific flood."

I asked him to describe the floods.

He said, "Oh my God! If those floods had occurred at night when people were asleep we could have lost 8,000 to 10,000 people. They were that violent. They were that mean. They were that disruptive.

"After the first one, we all got our heads together and said, 'Let's rebuild because we know this will never happen again.' Almost a year to the day, it happened again. It was in May. It was not a winter thaw. There was no predictability. It (resulted from) a tremendous downpour of rain. We have had tremendous removal of timber, both in mountaintop removal mining and in traditional timbering."

When surface mining is done, it removes the ability of the soil to absorb rainfall. This allows for more rapid run off and thus more severe flooding. Timbering does much the same thing.

Clif continued, "We just got rain, on top of rain, on top of rain. It is almost like surfing on an ocean wave, the water rises so fast. There is a trestle here in town. The road dips underneath it and the train tracks are on the top. There was so much water that the top of the trestle was underwater. It was like a waterfall.

"The library we are sitting in was completely flooded under 4 feet of water. This building shares offices with City Hall. Those offices were all flooded. This happened twice.

"After the first one, we were almost complete with the physical recovery, but we were also dealing with the mental and emotional aspects. As I recall, nobody died as a direct result of the flooding, primarily because it occurred during the day. As we were undergoing the economic, physical, and emotional recovery of the 2001 flood, we got another the next year. People couldn't go back to flooded areas. There was no place for the displaced people to live! Many moved to Princeton or Bluefield and other places. Some had residual thoughts they might come back when there was some degree of normalcy until the 2002 flood, which was more violent and disruptive than 2001.

"Serious floods destroy everything in their path. We went up to one of the hollows where everything was washed away. There was a train trestle at the entrance to the hollow, and everything piled up against the pillars. Semi-trucks and trailers. Houses. Trees. In one hollow, everything was destroyed except one little white church that sat (above the water). Everything beside it, everything before it, everything after it: GONE. I can't explain that. It was phenomenal to me.

"Every time it rains really hard for more than 10 or 15 minutes, people begin to panic. We are traumatized not only economically but by nature.

"I recently read an article in the *New York Times* or the *Wall Street Journal*. It was chronicling life expectancy for every socio-economic strata of society. Everybody's life expectancy had crept up a bit except female Caucasians. They were looking at a place in Oklahoma that sounded just like McDowell. They interviewed a young lady who talked about all the dreams she had, all the things she wanted to be, and for various reasons she didn't make it. She died of cirrhosis. All of the definitions that fit her so well apply to McDowell.

"Our young people, even the good ones, the smart ones who have their hearts in the right place, they have the rug pulled out from under them. I've never been a Walmart fan; I never shopped there. But when they came a few years ago, some people told me to go because a lot of my constituents worked and shopped there. So I started to go there to shop. That was a bright spot. But I'm willing to bet you that 90 percent of the people working at Walmart were asking in the back of their heads, 'When will this rug be pulled out from under me?' And then it was.

"We people in McDowell, Michael, we know how to deal with failure. I'm not sure we remember how to deal with success. Lots of people have never had it."

"I can only be so harsh about this place," I told him, "because I don't live here. You're living here and you're dealing with it, doing the best you can. But when I tell people about McDowell, I tell them it is the place where charitable, social assistance programs go to die."

He sighed. "I'm not sure I disagree with that. It pisses me off when I see a church group come to help. It tells me we are at the mercy of someone or something else. It says we can't take care of ourselves. Church groups don't go to prosperous areas.

"We don't have the emotional or economic stability to dream. Somewhere in the back of our minds, we know that great dream will turn into a nightmare, no matter how hard we work. So the philosophy is, 'Why try? It will only work for a couple of months or a couple of years. Then I will be back where I was before. Or worse. So to deal with that, I close myself off to those social and economic factors that define McDowell. Or I leave.' If you close yourself off, you may still be here geographically, but not from an involvement standpoint. You're not here from a vision standpoint. You're not here from a working standpoint to make things different. When we've had all those disappointments stacked on top of each other, year after year after year, we've lost hope.

"The day that really crystallized was in May of 2001. The second flood began to trigger the whole thing again, a year later. Now, we are inextricably intertwined in poverty, hopelessness, and despair. I do not know how to get us out of it. I thought at one point that I had some of the answers, but I don't think so now. I am just speaking for me as an individual, not for everyone, but I don't have a clue as to what to do, and how to resurrect, revitalize, and stabilize this community.

"I work in the state government, and the state government is helpful to a point. If we go to the state government with a package, a proposal, and we say 'This is our package,' we may get help with it. Probably on a per capita basis we have built more water systems than any county in the state over the last 15 years. We have gotten federal and state money for water systems and sewer systems.

"The lifeblood for economies like ours is roads. Highways. We don't have any. We have perhaps a total of three miles of three-lane roads. We do not have any four-lane highways. There has been one (the King Coal Highway) planned for years, but it has not yet reached this county. We don't have a community college or any higher education here, either. We do not have an airport, other than a small municipal field. We do not have a port facility. And now we do not have passenger rail. We have almost no flat land. Much of the flat land that we do have is susceptible to flooding.

"We have a population of people who have worked here and stayed here all their lives. I left here and came back. I came back because I wanted to. Now we have young people who cannot wait to graduate and get out. We have another group that has no skills, cannot be marketed, cannot get a job, and they are here, trapped.

"People have always left communities where they grew up. I left mine. You left yours. They have their own reasons. They have economic reasons or educational opportunities or sometimes they just simply want to go somewhere else. But when people started leaving because of the loss of jobs, because of the flooding and other issues, that layer of people who stayed became thinner and thinner. When people have left Blacksburg and Christiansburg, you had layers of other people coming in to take their place. When our older people die off, we have no younger people moving here to replace them."

AT CLIF'S INVITATION, an elderly man named Claude Banner joined in our conversation. He was in his early nineties. He had earned a Mechanical Engineering degree from Virginia Tech as I had. He was a handsome, vital, white-haired man. I asked him what the area looked like back in the heyday.

He said, "You had houses set on all the sides of these hills and everywhere. The wider spots were typically set aside for commercial structures, and the houses went up the hillsides.

"During World War II, there were over 5,000 people in Gary Hollow. The coal companies provided housing all over the place. Out back, each house had an outhouse and a coal bin beside it. You could talk to your neighbor every morning while you were doing your business. In 1956, US Steel built a water system. They owned all the mines."

I asked, "It was not a municipality that built it?"

Clif jumped in, "The coal companies were the municipalities."

Mr. Banner agreed, "The companies even provided local security. They were the local police department. They knew everything that went on. Some actually had arresting powers and carried pistols. In the earliest days, (the companies) provided the schools. They provided and ran the stores. Every community had a company store. I got paid by check rather than in scrip so I could shop anywhere I wanted. But there were no stores that weren't owned by the company. The bank in Gary went bankrupt in the 1930s."

Clif said, "As a kid, I remember being amazed going to the company store on Saturday morning in Welch and seeing people in native dress and hearing a whole assortment of foreign languages, including Greek, Hungarian, and Russian. When you walked through the towns you could smell food from different cuisines. It was a real melting pot."

Mr. Banner added, "This applied to the whole county. There were enough Jewish people that they had their own stores, and there was a synagogue here in Welch. It is gone now. The Greeks and Italians had a bunch of restaurants.

"Gary had its own power plant. It was probably only $25 (per month) for your rent, water, and electricity. I think maybe you had to pay a little bit for a ton of coal for your heating and cooking. We had coal burning kitchen stoves. So the whole house smelled like coal all the time.

"Back in those days, we had jobs, we had many stores, we had schools, we had transportation, including buses, cars, and trains. There was entertainment. We had pool halls. Welch in particular being the county seat had everything. Gary is only 6 miles away. They had consolidated bus lines between the towns.

"Eventually, people got their own cars and stopped riding the trains. As people stopped riding trains, there became fewer of them and then you had to have a car because the trains did not come often enough to suit you. Finally they didn't need the buses any more."

I told them that a friend of mine who lived over in War (a community in the southern part of McDowell County) once said to me that if McDowell County hadn't had any coal mining reserves, the population would probably have maxed out at around 5,000 or 10,000 people. So instead of spiking up to 100,000 and now back down under 20,000 it probably would have been stable.

Clif said, "Absolutely. I agree with that."

I said, "McDowell County today seems to be a typical example of all extractive resource regions. When that resource is first exploited, owners bring in a lot of people from other places to reach the resource. The extraction eventually reaches a maximum, and then employment plummets, leaving thousands of people with no jobs and lots of health and pollution problems. And the profits go elsewhere."

Mr. Banner said, "Our late Senator Robert Byrd once said, 'When McDowell County runs out of coal, it will eventually become a national forest.' We still have coal here. We still have what I call gopher mines, small family owned mines. What we don't have any more are the large-scale corporate operations."

Our conversation shifted to the public school system. Clif told me that the entire state of West Virginia has a public school teacher shortage. He said the starting salary was about $30,000. "It is not enough, but in addition, we cannot provide quality of life for these people. After they finish their workday, what is there to do after that? There is no place to go out and have a nice meal. From here, you literally have to drive over an hour to Beckley or Bluefield to find a nice restaurant where you can have a glass of wine with your meal.

"The housing standards here are not that great. There are no longer any recreational or entertainment opportunities. How do we attract people? We do not have outlets to let off steam. We do not have outlets to reverse those trends of negativity and health outcomes."

"The middle class is either leaving or has already gone," Banner agreed. "There are thousands of people on welfare or some type of government assistance. Manufacturing companies are not going to come and provide jobs because they would need to truck in the raw materials and truck out the finished products, and we do not have good roads."

I asked both of them if a miracle could happen what it might look like.

Clif said, "Let's fantasize and say that maybe tomorrow Toyota wants to come here to McDowell County and put in a car manufacturing plant. They want to hire 500 people. We do not have a trained and educated workforce to take advantage of those jobs.

"You always used to hear around here, 'We will be down for a couple of years, but then coal will come back.' I think people are generally resigned to the fact that it is never going to come back again the way it once was," Delegate Clif Moore concluded ruefully.

I WALKED OUTSIDE TO MY MOTORCYCLE to grab a water bottle. (Note: I always bring my own water to McDowell County. You never know.) While I was standing beside it, a man drove by slowly and leaned out of the window of his car and spoke to me in a friendly way. I noticed that his car had a sticker on the back indicating that it had been purchased from a major dealership near my office in Christiansburg. He happened to pull in at the library, and we continued our conversation. It turned out that he was a recently retired coal miner, and I asked him if I could get some of his thoughts about his career. He graciously agreed to tell me about it as we returned to the table and chairs I'd shared with Clif Moore and Claude Banner.

The coal miner's name was Tom Morsi.

He said, "My grandparents were immigrants from Italy. They settled in Gary Hollow in the 1920s. I grew up in Gary, and I graduated from Gary High School in 1976. I am 60 years old."

I asked, "What age do people retire from coal mining?"

He said, "If they're lucky, 55 or 56. It takes a toll on a man's body. I have had two knee replacements. I worked in deep coal, working in seams from 48 inches to 60 inches thick. It was probably the greatest coal seam in this country, the Pocahontas 4 seam. It is all through here. The 1970s were the boom era."

Tom Morsi

In terms of production, Morsi was correct. However, in terms of employment, due to the mechanization I'd mentioned earlier, the highest numbers were a quarter-century earlier.

"A coal miner today," Morsi continued, "if he is lucky enough to have a job, averages an annual salary of about $70,000. This is not including his benefits. Working in any other job here would pay next to nothing. You would be lucky to make minimum-wage.

"I have been retired for two years. In these last two years, I have seen one of the greatest downfalls since the 1980s to the city of Welch. There are some hospital jobs and some prison jobs. Many people here cannot even get a prison job because they cannot pass a drug test. Their cut-off age is around 35; you can't be older. I think they assume that you need the stamina of a younger person."

He said he had two children. "I worked long enough to get them through college. One went to West Virginia University. The other went to Bluefield State College. Both of them work for the Department of Human and Health Services for the State of West Virginia. One of them is here in Welch and one lives in Charleston. The one here works in child protective services."

I asked flippantly, heartlessly, "Is he busy?"

Tom shrugged. "This county had 425 cases of child neglect last month."

Tom described some of his volunteer work to feed people and to help them with their heating and electric bills and to weatherize their houses. He said because of government funding cutbacks, "We no longer have the funding to do this. There is great need for us to do this. The problem with McDowell County is that there is no infrastructure. We have to drive 43 miles to get to the nearest interstate or four-lane road. We have to go to Bluefield, Princeton, Beckley, or Grundy. We are the most geographically isolated community in all of West Virginia. I always say that the state line, from the perspective of the people in Charleston, stops at Beckley."

That sure sounded familiar.

He continued, "We are number one in obesity. We are number one in drug overdose deaths. We have the lowest life expectancy for a male of anywhere in the country. It is only 64 years old. We have the highest unemployment per capita in the country. We are at the bottom. This is as low as it goes. I was fortunate to work all the years that I did. It was a blessing to work 36 years. But it has deteriorated me."

I said, "Tom, most of the people in this country go to work with the expectation that they will come home safely and without overall weakening of their health, day after day, year after year. They have the expectation that their job is not going to kill them. You don't have that here, do you?"

He said, "I have been diagnosed with second stage silicosis. This comes from breathing fine particles of silica from rock."

Silicosis is a type of pneumoconiosis as are black lung and asbestosis. Silicosis is marked by scarring of the upper lobes of the lungs and is incurable. Victims literally die of inability to breathe. Overall, the worst cases of pneumoconiosis have quadrupled since the 1980s in the coalfields of Virginia, West Virginia, and Kentucky.

Clif said, "There's a promise the companies made. They tell you that if you work for them for so many years, you will get retirement benefits. Companies today, not just in coal mining but across the spectrum, are not keeping that promise. So even when a person like Tom may work for that company for 40 years and not get hurt and not die from black lung, he works to retirement and then does not get the retirement benefits that the company has promised him. They say to him, 'I am not paying you, brother.'"

Tom said, "This is what big coal companies like Massey (Energy) and Alpha (Natural Resources) and Arch (Coal) have done. The company that I worked for was bought out by another company and the new company, they laid off the entire workforce. They only hired back

40 percent. And they told them that they wanted them to sign another contract. The workers voted on a contract, and it was rejected. When the miners came back to work a couple of days later, they had been locked out."

I asked, innocently, "How do you get up every day?"

Clif and Tom echoed simultaneously, "You have to."

Tom said, "McDowell County people are resilient people. Times are going to be tough. We have to be tougher than the times. We have got to keep going. The reason that we stay here is that we love it here. We were born and raised here. Our parents were born and raised here."

Clif Moore continued, "People who work in modern coal mines are electricians, job planners, supply technicians, and machinery operators. People need a whole different skill set from traditional coal mining."

Tom said, "We had fiber optics underground. We were Internet ready inside of our coal mines. We had Wi-fi underground. We had laptop computers in the mines. It is not picks and shovels anymore. When I started in 1975, it was different. There was none of this. I worked in the coal mines for almost 40 years and I was continuously required to upgrade my skills. Every decade changed. I am a lucky man in the sense that I had a 38 year run and came out without too serious health problems. I can breathe. I can walk across the room. But I got out at a good time.

"A guy like me who is perhaps 15 or 20 years younger than I am is in bad shape. He has no promise of a health care when he retires. The only thing he is working right now for is his paycheck. If his company closes down, he loses it. His healthcare is only guaranteed for three months after he loses his job. It used to be guaranteed for one year.

"John L. Lewis was the greatest mine labor leader the country has ever known. He got miners cradle-to-grave healthcare coverage. Now we don't have that. These companies are filing bankruptcies. Bankruptcy courts are giving the CEOs million-dollar bonuses while leaving the workers, the ones who worked six days a week, 10 to 12 hours a day, without healthcare."

Clif said, "There is nobody to march for better conditions anymore. There are not enough miners now. Somebody did a study and they were talking to miners who were sick and had been injured and couldn't walk. They asked them if they had it to do all over again if they would go back to the mines. Eighty-five percent of them said 'Yes.' They said they didn't know any other way and that (mining) provided pathways to healthcare, education, economic opportunities, housing, and vacations."

I told him that I had met a miner years earlier, a black man who told me that he'd been in the military and there were terrible racial problems, but none in the coal mines.

Tommy said, "It is a buddy system. You are watching my back, and I am watching yours. That is the way it has always been in coal mining. Really, that is the way the whole world should work. We are all here together for one reason.

"U.S. Steel Corporation purposefully integrated their coal camps. They were a model system of the way housing should be. We were Italian immigrants. We were Polish immigrants. We were black. We were white. We were Irish. Everybody melded. It was a true melting pot of people in Gary Hollow. Everybody got along. We didn't have trouble. Everybody looked out for each other. I would like to see a return to that, like it was in the 1970s when everybody had a job. When you look at this town today, we don't have anything."

Clif said, "We had seven car dealerships right here in Welch!"

I said to Tommy, "And you went to Christiansburg to buy your last car."

He said, "Yes, I had to go to Christiansburg to buy my last car." It is 100 miles away, a two-hour drive.

As I was ready to depart, Tommy said, "I love this library. It is the greatest asset this county has right now."

I WENT FOR A CLOCKWISE WALK through town. Almost all the buildings were made of brick, mostly two and three stories. A small café was open, as were some beauty salons and banks. Many other buildings had offices for magistrates, lawyers, child protective services, and other professionals associated with county business. A mortuary. Insurance agencies. The architecture was wonderful, remnants of a bygone era. There was a magnificent school looming almost overhead on the hillside to the southeast, a four-story grey stone structure.

I walked towards the confluence of the Elkhorn and the Tug, past a modern movie theater showing first-run movies. I turned right on McDowell Street past the aforementioned parking garage. There were only a handful of vehicles in it. I passed several buildings with "For Rent" signs on them, in various states of decay. I stopped to repose at the Martha Moore Riverfront Park, a small park with a series of concrete landings and planters, leading down to the Tug Fork River, which was only 50 feet across or so. The park was part one of the beautification efforts of the namesake late mayor. Alongside the park on the side of a five story building was a stunning Acosta mural, the state's largest, of a street scene from the era of prosperity.

The Tug Fork of the Big Sandy River was a small, placid stream, belying its notorious position as one of America's most storied, violent watercourses. The Tug Fork's headwaters rise near the Virginia/West Virginia border, with its Dry Fork extending into Tazewell County, Virginia. From its initial elevation of around 2,450 feet, it travels northwesterly for 126 miles, where the lower 90 forms the border between West Virginia and Kentucky to Louisa where it is joined by the Levisa Fork. From there, the Big Sandy continues to the Ohio at Kenova.

McDowell County courthouse

For the N&W, it was the most natural route from the main line along the New River to the Ohio, picking up the Elkhorn Creek tributary just this side of the Coaldale Tunnel and following all the way to the mouth. But the Tug has exemplified the rugged, troubled nature of coalfield Appalachia both geographically and culturally, so the N&W's route would not be easy.

The upper reaches of the Tug Fork slice through bands of sedimentary, coal-bearing strata, producing V-shaped, steep sided valleys, with high hogback ridges looming overhead. In McDowell, the ridges are 1,200 to 1,500 feet above, less so but still up to 1,000 downstream in Mingo. The river drops 1,875 feet in the upper 26 miles, producing a series of falls, rapids, and swift-moving water.

Because of its daunting geography, it was one of the last places in the Virginias to be populated, and it remained sparse until the N&W arrived. At that point, thousands of people almost overnight hyperpopulated the region. Construction filled every flat piece of land and many that weren't flat. The remoteness, ruggedness, and pressures of overcrowding and burgeoning industrialization spawned a culture of tension and violence typified by the nation's most notorious feud, the Hatfields and McCoys, but there were many other disagreements that produced intimidation and violence over the decades.

While to N&W's favor, the Tug River generally ran northwesterly, detailed maps show multiple curves and bends, all testing the skill and verve of those who engineered and built the rail line. Multiple bridges and tunnels were needed to allow the track to stay a safe distance vertically above the normal elevation of the river (to avoid the all too frequent floods) but still maintain proximity. In many places I would find, including just west of Welch, the river was simply too rugged for highway engineers who moved US-52 towards and away from the river repeatedly.

By the way, by legend the Tug River is thought to have been named during the disastrous Sandy Creek expedition led by Major Andrew Lewis in 1756, when his men, nearly starving at a point near the head-waters, were forced to boil and eat their buffalo hide boot strings, called "tugs."

I CONTINUED ON AROUND the block, past more vacant buildings. One had several antique cars parked inside. Garage space is abundantly affordable here. I rounded the corner and found another Acosta mural, this one mirroring the look down the same street, with 1920-era cars ambling down the street. The words "19 WELCH DAILY NEWS 27" were engraved in metal over the eave of a brick building.

Then I passed the magnificent Romanesque Revival style court-house, built in 1893 and still in use today, and the long branched stair-way leading to it from Wyoming Street. I climbed half-way up, pictur-ing in my mind where Sid Hatfield and his friend Ed Chambers may have stood until their bodies were riddled with bullets and tumbled towards the street on a bloody day in August, 1921. I wandered back to my Honda, packed my stuff, hopped aboard, and was westbound again.

Long ago, as I mentioned, highway planners plotting the route of US-52 were apparently intimidated by the sinuous route the Tug Fork and the N&W line took leaving Welch. Instead, they took it on a more direct route that made a modest climb just south of town, and then turned west towards Iaeger.

I decided it was my duty to you, my dear reader, to stick as closely to the rail line as possible. This led me to SR-7, arguably the curviest road I've ever ridden. Not being a geographer, I have no quantitative measurement of such things, but I'm guessing this 15-mile stretch of pavement follows the Tug's most perilous canyon.

How curvy was it? For most of the 3 miles from Welch to the first tiny community, Capels, I followed a large tractor-trailer coal-hauling rig. He was blitzing along at a good clip, given the size of his vehicle, and for at least 90 percent of the time was taking at least part of the oncoming lane. On the tighter curves, he was leaving his back tires off the pavement and on the gravel shoulders… on the LEFT side of the road! What I'm saying is that his trailer completely blocked the oncoming lane. Again and again. I'm guessing this driver made this route multiple times each day, every working day. Surely the life expectancy of an underground miner would be longer than a truck driver frequenting this road!

In spite of his purposeful pace, he was no match for me on my Honda ST1300. But although I'm sure he knew I was behind him, he seemed entirely disinclined to pull over or slow down to let me pass. There were no legal passing zones. So I matched his speed from behind, testing my patience. Fortunately it was a gorgeous day, with bright sunshine and the pink blossoms of the redbud shrubs everywhere lining the road.

I could see the railroad and the river to my left, but without room for it on the narrow channel below, the road gained and lost elevation, contouring around the hillsides. Whenever a side hollow joined the main hollow from the right, the road swooped "inland" towards it, maintaining the fixed elevation, and then back out again. My movement on the bike was acceleration, upshift, deceleration, downshift, lean and turn, then acceleration again. Over and over again.

Tired of breathing his dust, I simply pulled over in Capels and took some photos of that tiny community, of its most prominent structure, a two-story white-painted cinder-block building with a cross and "Royal Kingdom Ministries" painted on the side. I photographed a building on the slope above, what appeared to be a duplex house, with the left half in total disrepair and literally crumbling and the right half with a reasonably new coat of yellow paint and an intact roof; for all I could tell it may have still been inhabited.

I got back on the bike and within only a few miles had already caught the truck. Mind you I stopped, removed my helmet, opened the saddlebag and retrieved my iPad, took some photos, replaced the iPad, put my helmet back on, and still caught the truck in only a few miles. As I said, he was no match for my Honda.

At one point, the entire canyon curved to the left, opening up a vast view of the road ahead of us. In the distance, I could see a similar oncoming truck, presumably taking up an equal amount of roadway. There was no possibility for these two vehicles to get by one another in a curve. So "my" truck, clearly understanding that, finally slowed to a crawl on a straight stretch to await the cooperation he'd need from the other driver to get past one another. This was the break I needed and I quickly zoomed past him (on a double-yellow line, of course), before the two trucks would come together. I never saw him again.

At the end of this expanse, the ridge of the mountain came to an end and my road curved about 150-degrees around it to the right. The rails couldn't make such a sharp turn, so it tunneled under the road, under the mountain, and emerged under me again on the other side. The road dropped back down to track level and crossed the tracks in Davy. Three miles later, as the river made a series of massive S curves, the rails and the road made use of tunnels to straighten their course. The roadway tunnel was primitive, with only exposed rock overhead at the entrance and inside.

Finally I arrived in Roderfield and it was only a short distance to the T intersection with US-52 (which, by the way, was unmarked). The whole distance from Welch by this route was about 15 miles, but there was no way my speed (brisk!) could have ever matched that of the Powhatan Arrow. Best I could count, the N&W tracks employed nine tunnels in this section and the roadway used one. And yet, as with most of McDowell County, most habitable places still hosted dwellings, again with some in use and some decrepit. Imagine commuting on this road!

I turned right on US-52 west and continued towards Iaeger.

ONE OF WINSTON LINK'S MOST RENOWNED IMAGES was shot near Iaeger in a tiny village called Sandy Huff. The photo has been called "Hot Shot Eastbound." In the foreground, we see the back of sweethearts on a date at a drive-in movie, she with dark bobbed hair above a low neckline tightly crowding him, their heads leaned together. These were actually hand-picked "models," Willie Allen and Dorothy Christian, which Link placed in his own convertible. I found nothing to confirm or disconfirm whether they were indeed romantically linked or even acquainted with one another before captured for eternity by Link's film.

Mid-image are all the other cars, and the lot was packed, and all were pointed towards the movie screen showing a 1950s era fighter jet. In the right-side background, a locomotive streamed by, its steam showering the night sky with white smoke. This was an N&W Class A locomotive No. 1242 built in Roanoke in 1949-1950.

Link reputedly used 80 flash bulbs, fired simultaneously. The on-screen image was from the 1955 movie "Battle Taxi," but the cynic in me leads me to believe that Link's image wasn't real, but was instead placed there by some technique from that era's version of Photoshop, as surely the 80 bulbs would have overwhelmed the projector's image and

Link's film would have shown nothing but a blank screen.

Nothing shown in that image was destined to persevere, not the locomotive, the jet, the cars, nor the theater. Because of the unique imagery, setting, and temporal nature of the shot, this may be Link's most desirable and iconic photograph, a true masterpiece. So I searched for the setting.

Just shy of the town of Iaeger, I found Sandy Huff Branch Road, a dead-end, but paved street to the north. Just over a steel and concrete bridge over the Tug Fork, I turned left into what I suspected was my destination. I was on somebody's paved driveway, with a beautiful two-story house where the screen once stood and beside another smaller home with a three-door garage. As I stopped to take a photo, orienting myself as Link did, one of the garage doors opened and a red Nissan emerged. I spoke with the woman driver who bore a striking resemblance to Aunt Bea Taylor from the Andy Griffith Show. Beside her sat a girl licking a huge lollypop. The woman seemed to already know why I was there. "We get people coming by from time to time to see where the Link photo was taken. It's neat to live in a place so marked in history."

Iaeger and Tug Fork

DOWNTOWN IAEGER was on the other side of the Tug. So the scene that presented itself was a row of commercial buildings seen from the back, clinging to the embankment. Some of the foundations of those buildings reached down to the water's edge, some began higher up the slope. The tallest was four stories with masonry bases and brick upper stories. All were in advanced states of deterioration.

I rode over a bridge over the Tug and into downtown. I passed a nice but clearly underutilized playground with a tennis court and a basketball court, along with some playground equipment. Nobody was there. Beyond that were a series of decaying, mostly abandoned buildings. Several had pigeons flying into and from missing or broken upstairs windows. Some had sloping painted exterior walls where adjacent buildings had once stood, etching their ghost images into the brick.

There was an eerie silence and nobody around. I tarried for only moments and then rode on.

JUST BEYOND DOWNTOWN, again highway engineers decided the path of the railroad following the Tug Fork was simply too rugged for the road. So as the rail stayed westward alongside the river, the road angled due north, ascending out of the Tug River watershed and cresting into the Little Huff Creek watershed, a tributary of the Guyandotte River. The road briefly caught the corner of Wyoming County before reaching Mingo County, or "Bloody Mingo," as it is often called, and not because of any profusion of phlebotomists.

Mingo is West Virginia's newest county, formed from Logan County in 1895 over a legal issue regarding a still. An illegal moonshiner was found guilty in a Logan County Court, but he argued that his still was actually in Lincoln County. Again he was convicted, but the legislature decided that Logan was simply too sprawling for the efficient application of justice. The county was then established and named after the nearby Mingo Indians. Suffice it to say Mingo hasn't always been a happy place.

NOT TO BE OUTDONE by McDowell's misery, a devastating flood hit the area upstream of Gilbert in May, 2009. I visited the area a few weeks later, and remember a scene of destruction, mud, dust, and filth. I remembered a hardware and lumber store that was both a victim and a beneficiary of the assault. Downstream of it were endless piles of rubbish from its own yard. Meanwhile a steady stream of customers pulled away with newly delivered and bought packages of plywood and other building materials. I remember seeing many cracked or totally destroyed bridges across to private homes, stranding their occupants. House trailers were wrapped around trees and truck bodies were swept into the creek. The road was still buckled in several places then, and I felt guilty as if my presence was hindering recovery efforts. I was eager to return all these years later and see what recovery had ensued.

On this trip, I tried vainly to find that same lumber store, but couldn't. Perhaps it had been converted to another purpose. Perhaps it had been torn down.

I REACHED GILBERT, a town at the mouth of Gilbert Creek where it joins the Guyandotte. Gilbert seemed larger and moderately more affluent than Iaeger and Welch, but equally as geographically confined with commercial establishments and homes placed only where flat land would allow. There were a number of fast food joints, both national chains and locally-owned stores, plus hardware and auto parts stores. There were lots of ATVs (all terrain vehicles) on Central Avenue, the main street, as by local ordinance they were legal to ride on public roads without license tags in many communities.

There were a number of small hotels, cottages, and inns, mostly seeming to cater to the ATV tourists. I stopped at one called the Devil Anse Trail House to ask about it, and there I met the proprietress, Nancy Hatfield. She introduced herself as a descendant of old Devil Anse himself, one of the two primary antagonists of the legendary Hatfield and McCoy feud. Telling me how busy she was, I begged a brief conversation and got more than my money's worth. We sat on lawn chairs on the bottom porch of a two-story, four room rustic wooden lodge.

She had long, blonde hair and green eyes, covered by dark shades. She wore a bright, sleeveless blouse. I told her about my book and asked about her life and community.

She said, "I am Devil Anse Hatfield's great-great-granddaughter. He died long before I was born, so I never met him."

"What does it feel like to be in the infamous Hatfield family?" I asked, assuming she'd well up with familial pride.

She said, "Drama. All the time. We are simply militaristic people."

I said, "Your family was involved in the most notorious feud in our nation's history."

She yelled, "It is still a feud! It is still going on. I could write a book about this. You wouldn't believe what I can tell you."

Nancy told me she was 68 years old. I complimented her on how good she looked.

She said in her staccato voice, "I stay busy. I never sit down. You don't want to hear about my life. My daddy was just like Devil Anse. I lived a hellacious life. I loved my daddy, but he had a mean temper. My siblings, we said we lived with Devil Anse. It was like he never died.

"This is bloody Mingo County. We have had a lot of odd things happen. There has been a lot of people killed.

"I loved my childhood. I was raised in a hollow like Loretta Lynn. It was about 12 miles from here. The first house, daddy caught on fire with the plastic curtains in the kitchen. Daddy got in the mining business and made some money and then we got a nicer home, but in the meantime we had to live in a feed shack. Daddy went broke three or four times. He worked really hard and finally he made it; he got big in the coal industry.

"I am the oldest of six children. My youngest sister is 18 years younger. My mother is still alive; she is 88 years old. Daddy didn't live long. He was only 62 when he died. I have already outlived him. He was not a drinker. Neither am I. I'm glad. I might have liked it. You never know. I am so glad that I could never drink.

"I have been in every kind of business. I have sold gold. I have sold produce. I would take the fruit off my grandmother's trees straight into town and sell it. I have always tried to make money. I guess I am just aggressive. I have been successful. Without God, I wouldn't be anything. God has been good to me.

"Drugs have destroyed the world. It is so sad. Most of it is Oxycontin. You can blame the doctors and the pharmaceutical companies for getting everybody addicted to it. They knew it was addictive. Heroin is in every medicine you take for pain. But I am stronger than that. I know what the Devil is trying to do. I am not stupid.

"Daddy was a lovely person. He was funny. You would have loved him. Everybody loved my daddy. He hired so many people in the coal mines. Ain't nobody didn't love my daddy. He would give you the shirt off his back. If you needed money, he would hand you $50. That was the way he was.

"Daddy never wanted us to leave the house. He wanted to control everything we did. He wouldn't let me spend the night with any of my friends. The Hatfields are clannish. We like to have our kids right with us. I am so clannish it is

Nancy Hatfield

scary. I am protective. I have one daughter. She is my life. My granddaughter had meningitis, and we almost lost her. I have seen what God can do. I saw it with my own eyes. Her doctor was a Christian woman, and she never give up."

I asked her about the cottage where we were sitting.

She told me, "It has four rooms. We rent primarily to ATV riders. We are filled most weekends during the season. There is a new section of the trail that has just been opened. The new section goes right by Devil Anse's graveyard. It has brought a lot of people here.

"The hospitality business here is only a six-month business. People don't come in the winter. And we are only reliably filled on the weekends." She quoted her room rentals, which seemed reasonable. She added, "I have to make it at that. I don't have any other choice. Nobody has any money today. The economy is bad.

"I have people come from all over. I have many customers from Canada and some even from Australia. I get customers all the time from New York, New Jersey, Virginia, and Ohio. Canadians in particular love it here. People are interested in our heritage. It is amazing. I see people from all over the world.

"We have lots of recurring business. People come back. They want to live here. They love it here. It's beautiful. Look at it! Where else could you find this? I'm blessed to be here.

"I lived in Florida for 21 years. I would come back here for the summers. I am back here permanently now, about 15 years now. I love it here. This is my roots. I will never leave again. I didn't like it there. It's not home. People there are not like us. Nobody is like us. They are not as giving as we are. They are not as caring."

I said, "You say people here are giving, but there's still a lot of violence. How do you resolve that in your mind?"

She said, "I hate it. I hate violence. But if you make me mad, I am just like Devil Anse. I am dangerous. I am a Christian woman, but if you come at me with a gun, you are going to die. Would you defend yourself?"

I admitted, "I don't own a gun. I've never been in a situation in my life that I thought would have had a better outcome if I'd brandished a gun. I think a determined person can kill me if they want, no matter what weaponry I have. Are you packing now?"

"Not right now. But I do when I travel. I have never pulled it."

So I was thinking that she carries a weapon when she travels, but she lives in "Bloody Mingo." When I expressed this, she said, "I'm not afraid. I leave my doors unlocked. Nobody will bother you here. People on drugs may break into your house. If you're in a store, you can tell if somebody is on drugs. By the way they talk. By their eyes. Eyes give away everything. I have Devil Anse's eyes. They're green." She pulled her dark sunglasses down her nose so I could see them.

"I like my hollow. Ben's Creek. Wharncliffe. There ain't nothing I didn't do when I was little. We stayed outside. We stayed in the mountains. We had so much fun. We hunted mayapple and redroot. They're used medicinally.

"The economy is worse than when the recession started. Coal mining has been decimated. Forty-five hundred people have left West Virginia. It's sad. We need factories. We don't have a highway. We don't have technology. Coal brought poverty and misery, even when it was up.

"All five siblings of mine are workers. We've all (been successful). Daddy didn't want us to ever leave. He wanted to control us. I love daddy. He was a mess. He bought me a Corvette when I was 16. You don't know what I've seen in my lifetime! I can laugh about it now. At the time it was frustrating. My first husband was as mean as my daddy. My current husband was a coal miner. He's a good man.

"It's a hard life. You don't know how hard coal mining is. It has killed a lot of people here. Black lung. Cancer from smoking. Drugs. I don't smoke or do drugs and I don't drink. I don't eat sugar. I eat right and take vitamins. I grow my own tomatoes.

"This is one of the safest places I could live in the world. I'm not afraid to come out at night. If I fall down, someone will pick me up.

"You'd love my mother. She's a Hatfield, too, descendent from Devil Anse. He had 13 children. Nancy was his mother and his daughter, so that's why I'm Nancy. I am a real Hatfield. Being a Hatfield sometimes is no fun. There is drama every day in my family. I'll fight until I die."

As our conversation ended, I couldn't help but think how crazy it would be to ghost-write her biography!

Nancy walked away and I donned my motorcycling garb and attempted to raise the bike from the sidestand. My Honda ST-1300 is big and heavy. It was leaned so far over on the gravel that I couldn't pick it up vertically while standing over it. I could get it vertical from beside, but not while astride, and if I got it vertical then I couldn't get back on. I solved the problem by finding a rectangular piece of wood in a firewood bin and propping the kickstand on it, then hopping aboard and riding off. I'm sure Nancy wondered when she came back how and why a piece of firewood was in the middle of her parking area!

LET ME GIVE YOU SOME BACKGROUND on Devil Anse Hatfield and the family feud Nancy was talking about.

There's an old expression that says, "Good fences make good neighbors." In this regard, the Tug Fork of the Big Sandy River is a piss-poor fence. Mingo County (part of Logan County, back then), West Virginia on the northeast and Pike County of the southwest were the primary scenes from the nation's most notorious feud, almost a figure of speech for what a family feud is. The Hatfields and the McCoys. The mental images run wild.

There are many events and names. And there are causes. Both sides were given ample reason for their grievances. I prefer to think they just didn't like each other. Take age-old hostilities. Mix in a healthy dose of isolation. Jealousy. Pressures of industrialization and outside money and influence. Love interest. Out of wedlock pregnancy. Pretty soon you've got on your hands a cultural maelstrom painted in a patina of vitriol and bloodshed.

Where this animus began is a story too old to pinpoint. The Hatfields, on the West Virginia side mostly, originated from England, descendent from Ephraim Hatfield, born around 1765. The McCoys, on the Kentucky side, originated from Ireland, when William McCoy, that family's patriarch, was born around 1750. That alone may have gotten the clans off to a bad start. English/Irish hatred is centuries old.

Both antagonists, Randolph "Ole Ran'l" McCoy, son of William, and William Anderson "Devil Anse" Hatfield, son of Ephraim, were born prior to the Civil War.

The Civil War pitted brother against brother, neighbor against neighbor. Especially on the border regions, a plethora of constitutional ambiguities and spiteful, malicious behavior, along with the knowledge that those caught in the middle were helpless from attacks from both sides, hardened men and provided ample provocation for vengeance.

Here's a brief view of what transpired over the course of the feud.

Interestingly, both antagonists sided with the Confederacy, as did most of their neighbors in this tangled, rugged, hyper-rural geography. Devil Anse was founder of a Confederate guerrilla unit he named "The Logan Wildcats." One of Old Ran'l's brothers, Asa Harmon McCoy, died in the war, reputably at Devil Anse's hand. Later it was learned that Devil Anse was home ill at the time and instead the killing was likely instigated by Anse's uncle Jim Vance instead. Nevertheless, seeds of discord were sewn, but things were pretty quiet for another 20 years.

Keep in mind that given the large families on both sides and the relative isolation, in spite of the feud there was considerable intermingling and intermarriage. The Hatfields were more prosperous and politically connected. But even Devil Anse – entrepreneurial like Nancy – hired McCoys as employees in his various business operations, principally timbering.

Nothing about this historic event is particularly clear-cut. For example, Vance made it known that the Logan Wildcats were determined to kill Asa Harmon McCoy, and did so in a most brutal fashion, tracking down the slave who helped him hide in a cave and murdering him there. But nobody seems to know why they bothered.

Honor is honor, and that set off a chain-reaction of recrimination and retaliation, but not until 13 years later did violence again erupt. In this case, it involved ownership of a pig! Swine were allowed to free-range the forests, with owners keeping track of whose was whose by slicing notches into the pigs' ears. When this particular pig, whose name isn't in the literature, but I'd like to call him, "Tug," if you catch my drift, was claimed by Ran'l. The matter went to the Justice of the Peace who happened to be Devil Anse's brother, "Preacher Anse." Some things you just can't make up. Any guesses how Preacher Anse ruled on the matter? If you said, "Hatfields," you would be correct! His decision was largely predicated by the word of Bill Staten, who in fact was related to both families. Shortly thereafter, Staten was killed under mysterious circumstances by Sam and Paris McCoy, who were acquitted in court on grounds that Staten acted first.

So far with our stressors, we have war and a pig. Next up: romance. Johnson "Johnse" Hatfield, son of Devil Anse, took to courting Roseanna McCoy who left her family to live with the Hatfields. When that romance ended, she returned to Kentucky. But upon reconciliation, Johnse, on one of his trips across the Tug to see her, was arrested for bootlegging. Roseanna rode horseback through the night to enlist the help of her lover's father, Devil Anse, who set off to a successful rescue of Johnse. To repay her for the favor she'd done to him, Johnse, after impregnating her, left her for her cousin Nancy and they wed in 1881. Roseanna's baby died at age 8 months from the measles.

What a tangled web we weave!

The following year, Tolbert, Pharmer, and Bud McCoy, three of Roseanna's younger brothers, found themselves in a fistfight and then a knife-fight with Devil Anse's brother Ellison. The brothers stabbed Ellison 26 times and then, just for spite, shot him. The brothers were led off to trial in Pike County's seat, Pikeville. But vigilante Devil Anse intercepted the constables and kidnapped the brothers, dragging them back across the Tug into West Virginia where their bodies were sprayed with 50 gunshots.

About then, things started to get tense, culminating in the New Year's Night Massacre of 1888, where Ran'l McCoy's home was surrounded by Hatfields. Ran'l managed to escape but not before two of his children and his wife Alifair were murdered. Soon thereafter, nine members of the Hatfield family were captured in West Virginia and taken by avengers back to Kentucky to stand trial for Alifair's murder. All were found guilty and one was executed by hanging while the others were given life imprisonment sentences.

Court cases and land disputes rambled on for another decade or two. By the time the feud eventually simmered, a dozen people from both families had perished.

Decades later, entrepreneurs had set up dinner shows and other themed ventures to entertain tourists to the area. These days, progress being what it is, there are audio CDs with self-guided driving tours, Tour Apps for your iPhone and iPad, and GPS coordinates of historical sites. At a joint family re-union in 2000, 5,000 people attended and three years later, the families got together to declare an official truce. Signed by more than sixty descendents and the governors of West Virginia and Kentucky, June 14, 2003 became Hatfield and McCoy Reconciliation Day. Since then, every June a festival is hosted in Matewan, Williamson, and Pikeville to commemorate the reconciliation, with motorcycle tours, pancake breakfasts, dancing, foot-races, and craft events.

If these folks can find peace, can't we all?

JUST A FEW MILES AWAY TO THE WEST but inaccessible by road, a terrible calamity occurred. In 1956, there was a fatal crash of the Powhatan Arrow's sister train, the Pocahontas, pulled by the 611 near a little community called Cedar. In a way, the 611 owes its life to what happened there.

Let's head back together, shall we, 60 years or so. The Tug Fork valley between Iaeger and Matewan in winter has always been a frigid, remote region. That time of year, the trees that cloak the neighboring hills and hollows are completely shorn, bereft of the overpowering greenery that cloaks them in the summertime. It's a hushed, desolate place, where nature reigns and the human hand is barely felt, except notably when a train rumbles by. There are few habitations and almost no artificial light.

It's the last place in the world a man would want to die. But die there 62 year old Walter Willard did.

Willard was the engineer on the 611 on that icy-cold January night, January 23rd to be exact, when he took his last, painful breath. The moon, resplendent, one day before full, rose above the eastern horizon as Willard took controls of the magnificent 611 in Bluefield for his run to Williamson. Willard was given the signal by the station crew to get underway, and as he eased the throttle, the great locomotive, hitched to a tender and 11 cars, slowly rolled forward.

I'm guessing movement and the Arctic-cold evening air made him feel better, as he felt a bit feverish. As the train followed the track first westward and then arched northward toward Bramwell, he caught a glimpse of the moon, shining brightly for an instant before being hidden by encroaching, enveloping Mercer County hillsides.

It would be the last time he'd ever see it.

Willard hadn't felt well for a couple of weeks and had complained to his wife about tightness in his chest. He also had some pain in his arms and strangely in his gums. He attributed the arm pain to the exertion he'd gotten a few days before while helping his neighbor shovel some new-fallen snow. He considered calling in sick, but he was proud of his 15 years of perfect attendance; the last day he missed was when his wife had fallen and broken her leg, and he took her to the hospital in Bluefield from their home in rural Giles County, across the border in Virginia. Although not a young man any more, he felt vital enough to not even be considering retirement. Besides, he felt he had a special privilege in operating the finest piece of machinery his beloved employer had ever produced.

He skillfully guided the great locomotive through the Coaldale Tunnel into McDowell County and reached Northfork at 12:02 a.m. With nobody scheduled to de-train and nobody waiting to board, he eased forward and by the time he stopped in Welch at 12:28 a.m. was back on schedule. This was his last planned stop. Ever.

He drove past the Sandy Huff Branch Road where Winston Link would come later that same year to take his famous drive-in movie scene. He drove through Iaeger, Mohawk, and War Eagle, and then into Bloody Mingo County. Imperceptibly to the passengers on board, the train began accelerating and near the little town of Cedar, the 611 jumped the tracks and derailed, tumbling down the embankment towards the Tug Fork's ice-water. Her tender and four other cars jumped the rails as well.

Only fate can explain how nobody was killed other than Willard himself. It is unknown whether Willard's fatal heart attack occurred before he allowed his locomotive to achieve too high a speed through the many curves or whether it occurred during the crash. Nevertheless, forensic coroners listed the cause of death on his death certificate not scalding, as originally thought, but coronary thrombosis. Hauntingly to everyone on board, Willard, evidently anticipating the end, had reached for the rope to blow the black behemoth's whistle, and even in death he never let go. The sound only dissipated into the cold night hours later as the boiler finally relinquished its accumulated steam.

Thirty-two staff and passengers were injured, some severely. They included the postal workers on the mail car, the first occupied car to leave the track, plus station hands and baggagemen. Hurt paying passengers were businessmen, a mother and daughter returning to their home in Colorado, and two professional dancers.

Accounts from the day don't give much information on the rescue efforts for the injured, although it must have been some time before rescue personnel were summoned, arrived on site, and victims evacuated and treated. Walter Willard was buried at the Pleasant Hill United Methodist Church cemetery a few miles south of Pearisburg in Giles County. Willard was not an organ donor – transplantation was rare in those days – but his death gave new life, in a manner of speaking.

Grainy black and white photos of the crash taken from the Kentucky side across the river showed a scene of utter terror, the front vehicles strewn in awkward angles like a race-horse's broken leg. To the left was the massive hulk of the 611, laying on her port side at a terrible angle down the embankment. Her fore slid less far than her aft, with the fore only 15 feet below the tracks and the aft another 20 feet farther down, only 15 feet above the river. The tender was fully upside down, with her aft resting in the river, altering the water flow. The next car, the mail car, laid almost upright, pointed directly downslope, her fore reaching the river and her aft only feet from the track. Other cars in the view were still upright but off the track, listing comically.

It was the best thing that ever happened to the 611. Seriously.

As I mentioned earlier on my travels, the 611 was one of 14 Class J locomotives built by the N&W during the tenure of Robert "Racehorse" Smith (Vice President of Operations 1941-1946 and President 1946-1958), who was determined that his railroad company would use the coal it made money hauling.

After the crash, two massive cranes were brought into place and the crippled 611 was lifted back onto the tracks. It is a credit to her design and construction that she was robust enough to have only suffered superficial damage. She was towed back to the Roanoke shops for repair. While there, the N&W took the opportunity to upfit her with the latest technology and repaint her. She emerged as good as new, better really, and within a few months was hauling passengers again.

Two years later, Racehorse Smith retired and Stuart Saunders, his successor whose story I told back in Bedford, felt not an ounce of nostalgia about steam. He had a company to run and stockholders to satisfy, and diesel locomotives were simply superior in every operational sense. Sure, a diesel would never match steam for pure power or even longevity. But they were cheaper and easier to fuel, easier to operate, and much easier to maintain. The transition Saunders ordered wouldn't be glacial, it would be immediate. Saunders' directives came so quickly that the company needed to lease hundreds of diesels from other railroads until their own stock could be ordered and delivered. Saunders ordered that the entire fleet of steam locomotives be sent to the scrapyard.

Our friends Winston Link and Bob Claytor must have been horrified!

As I mentioned when we met Mr. Link back in Roanoke, he had been undertaking his photographic journey along the N&W's lines from early 1955 until March, 1960. I doubt he had the same cordial relationship with the corporate-minded Stuart Saunders that he'd enjoyed with Racehorse Smith. But mustering all their persuasive powers, Link, Claytor, and several other rail aficionados convinced Saunders, perhaps reluctantly for all we know, to spare at least one Class J locomotive from the wrecking torch. The others died in short order, relegated to piles of scrap steel. The 611 was spared.

I'm sure you realize some of the story I've told you of poor Walter Willard was embellished. Details remain controversial to this day and through anecdotal accounts of that terrible night, I have heard that this story may be significantly false. A competing, entirely plausible account is that the Pocahontas was behind schedule and Willard may have been purposefully speeding, going 60 mph in a 35 mph zone, causing his own train to wreck. Otherwise, why would his fireman not have intervened to save the train? N&W may have hidden that information from the media, fearing the public relations nightmare.

In any event, the 611 was selected for survival. Was it because she had undergone renovation following the crash and was in better shape than the others? Did she at the time have the cleanest service record and would be the last to need maintenance again? The former is a more romantic version, and I'm sticking with it, verifiable or not.

Six years later in 1962, the N&W, under much fanfare, donated the newly refurbished 611 to the city of Roanoke, making her the centerpiece of the Roanoke Transportation Museum, later the Virginia Museum of Transportation, which was created almost specifically for her. The museum has owned her ever since. Without the renewed excursion series in 2015 and my observation of the tremendous interest it generated, this book would never have been written. So the late Walter Willard, unknowingly and unwittingly, gave his life not only to the survival of 611, but to the Virginia Museum of Transportation and ultimately to this book. We all owe him a debt of gratitude, and may he always rest in the peace of knowing that his death resulted in great joy to railfans worldwide.

NOT TWO MILES DOWNRIVER from Cedar is another equally tiny and isolated community called Vulcan that you've also never heard of, unless you have a fabulous memory for 40 year old trivia. It's safe to say that almost nobody in America had heard of it until 1977 when it made national, in fact international, news for its budding partnership with the USSR.

Like all the communities in the area, by the mid-1970s Vulcan was experiencing hard times. Vulcan was worse off than most because in spite of the state map showing a bridge over the Tug Fork from the accessible Kentucky side, the West Virginia Department of Transportation never bothered to build one. The only ingress or egress was a cable suspension bridge, suitable only for pedestrians and marginally at that. It had been built by the coal company and when they left, all maintenance ceased. Although boards were missing and crossing it was a life-or-death experience with every crossing, children needed to use it to access school buses on the other side.

Worse yet, the bridge was separated from the approximately 20 habitations by the railroad tracks, and there was no crossing signal. So children were forced to cross the pair of tracks without supervision. Often, a parked train blocked their way, so they literally had to crawl under it. One boy lost part of his leg doing so.

The N&W had an access road solely on the West Virginia side, but it forbade anybody under the threat of fine or prosecution from using it. N&W maintained that it was not its responsibility to provide vehicular access options for the citizenry. And the state maintained that it didn't have the money, at least as it prioritized its always-lengthy list of statewide needs, to build a proper bridge.

Not getting help from either N&W or their own state, plucky residents wrote to the Soviet and East German Embassies in Washington and appealed for foreign aid from them.

Now mind you, this was during the heart of the Cold War. The Kremlin, seeing an opportunity to shame its foe, dispatched journalists to the remote Tug Fork valley who interviewed the residents and broadcast their plight to the world. In doing so, they gave Vulcan the mouthpiece they'd long lacked, and for a few weeks they were the talk of the nation.

Suitably embarrassed by the notoriety their insouciance had produced, chastised state officials promptly committed $1.3 million and a new one-lane bridge was hastily planned and built.

Not far west of Gilbert, the highway left Gilbert Creek for Horsepen Creek, and then ascended again, cresting another mountaintop, this time from the Guyandotte watershed back to the Tug Fork.

Near the summit, I took a new, modern spur road for a mile or so and entered the King Coal Highway.

You may recall back in Welch, Delegate Clif Moore mentioned that one of the impediments to McDowell County's economic advancement was the lack of any four-lane roads. Someday that might change. In the 1970s, plans were devised for a new, limited access road between Bluefield and Williamson, the brainchild of the Greater Bluefield Chamber of Commerce, seeking a faster way to Huntington. The old two-lane U. S. 52 I'd been following since leaving Bluefield snakes through highly mountainous terrain and through 35 communities, frustrating motorists with typical overall average speeds of no more than 30 mph. Over 90 percent of the route functions at a level below common highway standards. Coal-hauling trucks, difficult curves, school buses, and steep grades test the verve of every driver, regardless of vehicle. Ambulances are hindered and products move slowly from suppliers to consumers.

In March of 1999, the West Virginia Legislature established The King Coal Highway Authority to oversee design and construction, with the goal of reducing the travel time on the 100 mile corridor from 150 to 87 minutes. The planned road would be a high-speed four-lane divided highway, just below interstate standards. McDowell County would have nine interchanges and Mingo another five.

At the time of my journey, however, only a small segment near Bluefield and a 12 mile stretch between Gilbert and Matewan, the "Red Jacket" (named for a nearby community) had actually been built, the portion I was now riding. I was immediately struck by the enormous difference in look and feel it had to the older route. While old US-52 snaked through a succession of deep valleys, the King Coal Highway skirted the rooftop of the region. In cities, we talk about "surface" streets and "elevated" highways, with the latter typically being perhaps 15 to 30 feet above the former. In this case, the King Coal was upwards of 1,500 feet above!

Much of the road was built upon a mountaintop removal mine, and the landscape had a windswept, foreboding, otherworldly feel, with stunning distant views of the surrounding mountains, none much higher than any other. In places, the road had significant dips and bumps, as the compaction necessary for roads is greater than for reclamation sites and the work had not been done properly for the current usage.

There were no habitations or commercial establishments on this road whatsoever, but surprisingly near the middle of it, to the left, was a newly constructed school, the Mingo Central High School. It was a large, modern brick building. It had all the wrong feel for me. I'm a big proponent of community schools, where kids can walk or ride a bicycle to school. This one, isolated on a ridgetop, would require a car or bus ride for every trip. This was the only high school serving the entire, vast county, and some students' commutes would take over an hour.

Somehow I was equally less than sanguine about this road's obvious improvement to the area's transportation network. Perhaps it will provide a needed economic boost. But it felt to me like too little too late, bringing its benefits at a significant cost for a rapidly diminishing population. This twelve-mile section alone cost $65 million, with much of the additional cost borne by a coal company that contracted with the state to leave a right-of-way for the highway after destroying the mountain during mining. Otherwise, it takes an estimated $28 to $30 million per mile to continue construction in that topography, an amount the state of West Virginia may never find. And the road had almost no traffic on it.

Admittedly, prior to complete construction of the planned highway, through-traffic might still seek other options; the short completed stretch alone would provide little benefit to travelers. Would it ever be completed, and if it was would it actually spur development in another, emerging era? Hard to predict.

The King Coal Highway descended to a gap and there came to an abrupt stop at a T intersection seemingly in the middle of nowhere. A sign pointed left to Matewan and right to Delbarton, and following my quest to return to the Powhatan Arrow's corridor, I selected the former. The road descended sharply at up to 10 percent grades through massive cuts in sedimentary rock with man-made cliffs looming overhead on both sides of the road. I reached the bottom and returned to a smaller, older, more confined West Virginia road again with habitation alongside and entered the town of Matewan, one of the state's most interesting and storied places.

MATEWAN IS A TINY VILLAGE with fewer than 500 people, roughly half its zenith in 1950, laden with American industrial strife. It sits on a flood plain of the Tug Fork of the Big Sandy River, penned in by steep mountains on the east and the river on the west. The town was named for Matteawan in upstate New York, hometown of the N&W civil engineer, Erskine Hazard, who laid it out in 1890 and drew its first map. Interestingly, Matteawan no longer exists by that name, and local residents of the West Virginia version changed the spelling and pronunciation to the current incarnation.

The Tug has a propensity for horrific flooding, and in 1974, the Army Corps of Engineers deemed that Matewan had the most severe flooding vulnerability in the nation. So they constructed a concrete floodwall on the bank of the river to prevent floodwaters from reaching the town. It has massive, sliding steel doors that could shut across the access roads in four places and the railroad in two more. The concrete section was tastefully decorated in raised-relief images of the town's rich history, the Hatfield McCoy feud and the Matewan Massacre. I had a protective feeling crossing through the open gates of the floodwall into the tiny town.

REMEMBER A GUY NAMED SID HATFIELD, who was ruthlessly gunned down on the stairway of the McDowell County Courthouse back in Welch? Here's the prelude to that story, dating back to the terrible spring of 1920.

Early on as coal mining brought thousands of peole into the Appalachian coalfields, miners increasingly joined unions to bolster their rights against the abuses of the coal companies. And as they did, mine owners fought them every step of the way. Many coal companies, in collaboration with the N&W, employed the Baldwin-Felts Detective Agency to protect their interests and throttle union organizing in the coalfields. By 1919, Mingo and Logan Counties represented the largest non-unionized coal mining region in the Appalachians. "Bloody Mingo," seemed to be the most likely place, given its history in personal and familial strife, to host a skirmish between locals and outsiders. Was this indeed a struggle between traditional, culturally insular, and backward people fending off onslaughts from overbearing corporate goliaths? Or was it a mere fist-fight that got out of hand?

It's hard for me in the modern era not to take sides in this; I'm increasingly drawn to the plight of the miners. See what you think.

The agency known as Baldwin-Felts was founded just prior to the turn of the 20th Century by William Gibbony Baldwin, as the Baldwin Detective Agency. A native of Tazewell County, Virginia, Baldwin studied dentistry but a fan of detective novels in his youth, he found his calling as a detective. Securing a lucrative contract with the N&W, he moved to Roanoke and later to Bluefield in 1910.

Originating from Galax, Virginia, where there is still a large park named for him that annually hosts one of the largest conventions of old time music, Thomas Lafayette Felts was educated as a lawyer. He joined the Baldwin Detective Agency in 1900, bringing to it his legal expertise. He eventually became a partner.

The new company's primary focus was investigative work into robberies, forgeries, train wrecks, assaults, and other related offenses relating to and in protection of railroad and mining operations. It acted as guards for cash transfers and payroll employees. It also took in investigative work for state and federal law enforcement agencies.

The agency made a national name for itself when detectives found and brought to justice several fugitives of the 1912 massacre at the Carroll County Courthouse in Hillsville, Virginia, including Floyd Allen, who was eventually tried and hanged. Less than a decade later, the Baldwin-Felts Agency would be back in the national news.

As unionization efforts got underway, organizers and new union members were often harassed and evicted from company houses. On May 19, 1920, Lee and Albert Felts, brothers of Thomas Felts, along with 11 other agents, banded together in downtown Matewan and walked to the neighborhood of Stone Mountain Coal Company's camp, just outside the town, and began evicting miners and their families. Their first victim was a miner's wife and her children, thrown with their belongings into the street in a steady rain. Her husband was not home and her eviction was done at gunpoint.

Naturally furious, witnesses ran into town and informed the mayor, Cabell Testerman, and the sheriff, Sid Hatfield, about the abuse. Hatfield's grandfather, Jeremiah Hatfield, was a half-brother to Valentine Hatfield who was grandfather of "Devil Anse" Hatfield. Sid Hatfield, nicknamed "Smiling Sid" because of gold caps on several of his front teeth, was an ardent supporter of miners' rights, as was Testerman.

When the Baldwin-Felts men arrived back in town to take the train back to Bluefield, Hatfield, Testerman, and a gang of newly deputized miners now lurking from windows, doorways, and rooftops, confronted them. Shots rang out. Moments later, the two Felts brothers were dead, along with five others. Mayor Testerman was mortally wounded and two miners were also killed.

History will decide whether Felts and their men were unfeeling, brutal, jack-booted agents of industrial capitalism and whether Testerman and Hatfield were the self-anointed mountain saviors. Like all historiography, the story morphs over time as new observers emerge to retell it.

Your mind will reel when I tell you that Hatfield, not two weeks after the massacre, married Cabell Testerman's widow, Testerman's second wife, Jessie Lee Maynard. Did Hatfield actually kill Testerman in a lust move towards Testerman's wife? Or did Hatfield do the right thing by the martyred Testerman, marrying his widow in order to provide for her and her young son Jackson? You make the call. In any event, their marriage would be almost as short as their courtship. Meanwhile, Hatfield acquired Testerman's jewelry store and converted it into a gun shop, presumably to help arm the miners.

Initially, the miners considered the massacre a victory for them, as casualties were higher among the detectives. Union efforts to recruit and organize improved. A miners' strike on July 1 saw significant violence and bloodshed, with company mining equipment and railroad cars and locomotives destroyed.

In spite of gains by the miners, the coal companies, in their power over the state government, generally maintained the upper hand. Revenge would be swift and bloody.

Company owners convinced local law enforcement to arraign and charge Sid Hatfield for the deaths of the two Felts brothers. Hatfield and 22 others were brought to trial. Hatfield, ever the showman, talked eagerly to reporters, bolstering his own reputation. By the time charges were ultimately dropped, Hatfield was a legend. Yet he knew he was still in danger from the Baldwin-Felts thugs who yearned for revenge.

On August 1, 1921, fourteen months after the Matewan incident, Hatfield accompanied his friend and deputy, Edward Chambers, along with their wives, to court in Welch at the McDowell County Courthouse, where Chambers was to go on trial for unrelated conspiracy charges. There, as the Hatfield contingent ascended the steep steps of the courthouse lawn, they were assassinated by Baldwin-Felts' men. In a hail of gunfire, Hatfield and Chambers were mortally wounded, tumbling down the stone stairs as pools of their own blood drained from their multiple hits. Against Chambers' wife's tearful protestations, one of the murderers followed Chambers' body as he tumbled, firing again into his skull at point-blank range.

None of the Baldwin-Felts men were ever convicted of the attack, claiming self-defense even though the Hatfield contingent never fired a shot and indeed were unarmed. Jessie Lee Maynard Testerman Hatfield lived another 55 years, eventually passing away in 1976 at age 82.

I parked the Honda at Matewan's nice visitor center, a reconstruction of the old train station. It was a long, narrow building with yellow painted wood walls and a rust-red roof. It had a gravel parking area, and again I had to search for a place to park the bike where I could get it off the side-stand when it was time to depart. I walked inside and spoke with the attendant, a young black man named Juan Joyce and an older black man named Thomas Moore who seemed to be his friend. I asked about the high school I'd just passed.

Moore said, "Mingo Central is the only high school now. All the kids get bussed up there from Williamson, Matewan, Gilbert, and Delbarton, our four main communities. Williamson is the largest of the four. They go from the 9th to the 12th grade up there, with middle schools in the communities. Fog is a terrible problem, worst in the fall. Drivers really have to take their time."

Restored Matewan train station

The elevation at the school is 2,200 feet, well above nearby Matewan's 700 feet.

I asked if he'd been through any of the floods. Moore said, "Yes, I was here in 1977. Oh, man, almost all Matewan was covered with water. My house is up the hill and out of the flood. It really hurt the area because so many people left. The flood wall may have been too late. My kids graduated from school. My three all left; there was nothing here for them.

"I was an underground (mine) supervisor, 29 years on the job. I'm feeling effects of coal dust, but they turn you down on black lung (benefits). Something is causing my chest to burn. I'm short-winded. My father was a miner, too. My mother got his black lung (benefits) until she died. Rightfully so.

"There are no activities here for kids to enjoy. Matewan is good for retired people. We don't even have a major grocery store in Mingo County. We go to Kentucky. Kentucky is more successful. Their politicians put more money back into their state. (Here,) they put it back into their pocket."

The men sent me into town with some ideas of places to visit.

I WANDERED TOWARDS the small downtown and on my way, a man who was standing on his porch at a nice, older home greeted me. I told him about my project, and he agreed to speak with me about his hometown. His name was Paul Phillips. We sat on two upholstered porch chairs with his two modern bicycles chained together behind us.

Paul told me he had grown up in Matewan, but left for college at West Virginia University 40 years earlier and had just moved back. I asked him about the town, what it was like when he left.

He said, "It's much more livable now. The river's been cleaned up. There's less coal dust. But the economy is trashed. I lived in Charleston for 17 years and came back regularly. I grew up in this house."

I asked about the 1977 flood. He said he was in Charleston then, but his parents still lived in Matewan. His mother was a banker and his father ran the seed store. When the water rose, his mother was out of town but his dad was at home. "He knew the water was rising, but you can't stop it so he went upstairs and went to bed. In the middle of the night, dad got out of bed and the water was up around his ankles on the second floor. Somebody came by in a boat and took him away through a second floor window. This water was 14 inches higher than the second floor. It's crazy to comprehend. The water was 10 feet above where we're sitting now.

"Everything in the house was ruined. Another house floated down and hit the porch, moving the roof over a bit. That was the main structural damage to the house. Another house floated down and landed in the back yard. I came down the next day and the water had receded. We just started cleaning up. People put ruined stuff in piles by the street. Some houses completely got washed away, at least two of them behind us."

I asked if the labor history was part of his life. He said his dad knew a man kicked out of his home during the mine wars. His dad was born in 1915 and remembered the shootout in town. "He was five years old. He said he saw a flatbed railroad car pulled by town with a machine gun on it, shooting up the hillside to intimidate people. I don't know if anybody got killed.

"I've been to 30 different countries and worked in 15 or so. I tell people that I'm from Matewan in Bloody Mingo County, West Virginia. I never go into the story of the mine wars. People overseas don't relate to the Hatfields and McCoys. I keep trying to get friends to visit, but it's hard to get them here.

"It's fun living here now because I can go into the mountains or into the river. I can bicycle the main roads. When I grew up, this was the main street. There was one coal truck after another in both directions. The coal trains would rumble through. More coal dust. It was totally unlivable by current standards. Nowadays, nobody would stand for it.

"When you have extractive industries, a lot of stuff is destroyed. Oil wells. Coal mines. I know this; I am an environmental engineer and a petroleum engineer.

"There's a half-mile walking trail on the other side of the wall. Lots of people are overweight, diabetic, and smoke all the time. People don't try to get much exercise. People like motorized things. They take their four-wheelers up into the mountains. But you can walk into the mountains, too. It's a lot more effort, but it's healthier."

I asked him if he was the only avid bicyclist in Matewan.

He said, "I haven't met any others. I understand there are some in Williamson. Every ride I've done, and I've only been back two months, has been alone.

"There is more and more tourism around. It doesn't pay like coal mining. And it's seasonal. But it's growing. It's pretty here. Scenic. My cousins in California can't believe how lush and green it is here."

PAUL SUGGESTED I ALSO SPEAK with Robert McCoy, an insurance man who had an office on the other end of town. So I wandered along

Matewan flood wall

Mate Street, past several small stores, one with a window display that said "Hatfield/McCoy Fued [sic], 1865-1890" along with photos and sketches of the antagonists. All the buildings had matching pine-green awnings. It was quaint. And very quiet.

Robert McCoy's business was called Liberty Insurance. He had a nine foot tall green Statue of Liberty outside, so it was easy to find. He did tax services and sold insurance. He grew up in Matewan and had run the business for over 30 years, seeing many changes in the local economy. He was born in 1946 and his formative years were in the 1950s.

"There were lots of people working in the valley in those days. By today's standards, they weren't that prosperous. Most didn't own a car. Lots of them walked to work, to the mines or the company stores. The town was a viable place with department stores, food stores, a theater, and beer joints. Very seldom did they leave to shop somewhere else.

"Many of my family members were involved in the massacre, what we call the Battle of Matewan. The feud was a problem back in the 1890s. I'm distantly related to Ran'l McCoy, but none of my family members participated. There are still lots of McCoys around. Most people know about the feud because of Hollywood. It wasn't talked about much. The Hatfields were long looking over their shoulders. There were still hard feelings into the 1950s."

McCoy was a huge man, with a mop of graying hair atop his head. "The railroad was a big part of the community. We had service here, four per day, to Norfolk and Cincinnati. We went to Williamson to the movies or for the dentist or piano lessons. It was like a bus, it stopped so often."

I asked about his business.

"It's pretty awful right now. It has been in decline for three years, badly. My best years were in the late 1970s and 1980s. This is the worst. It's never been like this. There have been lots of ups and downs, strikes, recessions, but there was always a pot of gold at the end of the rainbow. Now it's pretty hopeless. Dentists and doctors have lost lots of patients. I expect it to go even further down, like Welch or Iaeger.

"People who work on the Internet can work anywhere in the world. So we might have some hope there, if we had better service. Some miners have prospered up to $70,000 and $100,000, if you have a job. A home here can be had for $100,000 or less.

"Long ago, every house in the valley had hot water heating or steam heating with coal. The air would burn your eyes in the wintertime. The railroad always fascinated me. I would watch the Powhatan Arrow as it came through town, all black and maroon. The cooks were in their whites and the chefs' hats. The other trains were like that, too, but not like the Powhatan Arrow. I loved the steam trains. They were wonderful pieces of equipment."

I WALKED BACK TO THE CENTER of the town and turned right on Phillips Street, not 100 feet long, to find a series of interpretative signs documenting the location of the 1920 shootout. In the edge of the brick wall of one building were a couple of metal slugs placed in the bullet holes from that event. It was all pretty eerie.

Back aboard the bike, I headed west again, past another floodwall gate. Highway SR-49 from town to Williamson was pretty, with several splendid homes and some modern stores. There was one nine story apartment building, much grander that I expected to see. There was a nice riverside golf course, something I wouldn't have thought the area could support.

5:35 p.m.

Williamson

Mile 452.8

Railway division point with extensive yards and shops. A vast volume of coal is weighed and dispatched from here. Spurs from mines in Kentucky, across the river, converge at Williamson. East and west of Williamson the main line threads its way over numerous streams rolling to join the Ohio.

I arrived in Williamson under overcast skies.
  Williamson, like Bluefield, was established by the N&W as an aggregator rail yard town, handling traffic headed westward to the steel mills and power plants of the Great Lakes as Bluefield performed similar work for traffic headed to Norfolk.

Williamson is Mingo County's seat and largest city. Its population has risen and fallen dramatically. Incorporated in 1892, the city reached 9,410 people by 1930 but dropped to around 3,000 now in the city proper. It was believed to have been named in honor of Wallace Williamson or his father Benjamin Williamson, a wealthy family that once owned the land upon which the city now sits.

Like Matewan, Williamson is also protected from flooding by a massive wall with a series of movable gates across road and railroad tracks. It has two noteworthy buildings, the Coal House and the Mountaineer Hotel.

The Coal House is a single-story downtown office building built of coal masonry, with blocks dressed as stone. The question naturally arises as to whether a building constructed almost entirely of a flammable rock might ever burn. In fact, in October 2010, it did catch fire. Inexplicably, the fire did extensive damage to the interior, but minimal damage to the structure. Go figure. Although named the Coal House, it has indeed never been a residential structure. It was build for and still houses the Tug Valley Chamber of Commerce.

The other is the Historic Mountaineer Hotel, a massive 5-story building originally with 116 rooms, all named for famous Americans who have stayed there.

These two buildings are alongside each other on Second Street, and I planned to visit the former and stay in the latter.

THE SIGNIFICANCE OF THE MATEWAN MASSACRE was huge. Sid Hatfield became an instant hero to the miners, a stark symbol of resistance and triumph over the unconquerable Baldwin-Felts Agency and its men. The months to follow became increasingly tense, and hostilities often gave way to violence, mayhem, and death. Hatfield's assassination on the courthouse steps in Welch only exacerbated the tension, which came to a head three weeks later on August 25, 1921, opening date for the largest labor uprising in American history, the Battle of Blair Mountain.

The Matewan Massacre was on May 19, 1920, and by the fall of 1920, skirmishes between miners and company men, principally Baldwin-Felts agents, were common in the coal camps along the Tug River Valley. The governor of West Virginia imposed martial law, arresting hundreds of miners without charging them or granting them representation. Company agents could act without repercussion while minor acts of disobedience could lead to a miner's arrest.

Hatfield's murder in Welch was the spark that brought thousands of armed miners together in a massive resistance. On August 7, 1921, the United Mine Workers union organized a rally in Charleston. UMW leaders presented a petition of miners' demands to the Governor, Ephraim Morgan, who dismissed them. The miners decided to march to Mingo County to end martial law. They needed to cross Blair Mountain in Logan County where Sheriff Don Chafin, a lawman who unlike Hatfield supported the mining companies, waited for them.

The anti-union Chafin was backed by the Logan County Coal Operators Association, waging an active campaign to prevent union organizers from making inroads into Logan County. He and his deputies beat, harassed, and arrested those suspected of working towards unionization, employing additional staff to do the job, paid with funds directly from the association. Chafin pieced together an army of around 2,000 men, braced for the confrontation. Estimates of 10,000 armed coal miners faced-off against them. Chafin's men, although outnumbered, had better weapons and more strategic locations. Chafin employed private airplanes to drop bombs against the miners, the first and only example of bombs ever dropped on American citizens on American soil. For an event that happened less than 100 years ago in an American state, we have painfully little knowledge of the exact casualties. Death estimates range from 50 to 100 on the miners' side and 10 to 30 of Chafin's men.

The arrival of federal troops on September 2ND signaled the end of the battle, with miners scurrying home after leaving hidden caches of their weapons scattered about the woods on Blair Mountain. Collectors scour the steep slopes with metal detectors to this day.

So who won? Clearly the battle was an overwhelming victory for Chafin and the coal mine owners. Miners had been routed and union membership dropped precipitously. However, national awareness of the plight of the miners was heightened dramatically and the union's loss in West Virginia helped strengthen other unions across the country. Mining employment rose during World War II, as the production of energy and steel was vital to the war effort. Afterwards, the long, slow, painful demise of the Appalachian coal industry began.

In the steep hollows of Appalachia, coal has always been difficult, dangerous, and expensive to mine. More accessible seams in Illinois, Wyoming, and elsewhere gained a competitive advantage. The very industry that brought hundreds of thousands of workers into the coalfields pulled the figurative rug out from under them, and the exodus was massive.

Because the coal industry took an active role in impeding the access to other employers, and because of the general remoteness and imposing nature of the geography, there were then and remain today painfully few other employment options. What's left now are the few remaining coal miners, the people who live off the income produced by the coal miners, the scavengers who live off the remaining spoils of a former economy, and the drug dealers and welfare recipients. And the few who cater to the tourists, who look for adventure on two- or four-wheeled off-road vehicles, return to the home of their youth to see parents or lost friends, seek to experience or understand the history, or the photographers or writers looking for poverty porn to shoot or write about.

WHAT DO JOHN F. KENNEDY, June Carter Cash, Conway Twitty, Henry Ford, Adolph Rupp, and Soupy Sales have in common? They all stayed overnight in the Historic Mountaineer Hotel. And now they all have a room named after them.

After a long day's ride, I pulled into the parking garage across

Second Avenue from the hotel. It was nearly vacant, but notably there was a dust-encrusted DeLorean automobile parked just inside. Huge chunks of the ceiling had fallen and left gaping holes where I could see the exposed wooden structure. I hoped nothing would fall on the Honda overnight.

I met the manager, Edna Thompson, and got my room key. We arranged to meet after dinner when she could take a break and tell me about the hotel.

The lobby was grand, marvelous in an old-world way, with a mezzanine above and huge crystal chandeliers hanging. There were display cases of the city's history and railroad memorabilia. Two large leather chairs sat opposite a table with a huge chess set where the kings were ten inches tall. There were mirrors everywhere, lending greater spaciousness and light. I felt like Cary Grant.

I CHECKED INTO MY ROOM (named, incidentally, the Tex Beneke & Orchestra room) and put on some fresh clothes. I wandered to the Coal House where I met Natalie Taylor, the young executive director of the Chamber of Commerce. It began pouring rain outside.

I said to start the conversation, flippantly, "I thought coal disintegrates when it gets wet. Is that true?"

She said, "We put a coating of black paint and varnish on it every two years. That helps to seal it. But water does seep in through our windows."

A clap of thunder boomed overhead.

"The building was built in 1933. It is comprised of 65 tons of locally mined

Historic Mountaineer Hotel

coal. It was actually a community project. Most of the labor and materials were donated. It has always been the Chamber of Commerce building. It was built as a tribute to coal in the 1930s. We are part of the billion-dollar coalfield. The idea came from the manager at the railroad.

"I grew up here in Williamson. There has been a decline for most of my life, but especially during the last 10 years. There are more stores closing and most of my friends have left. I have a few friends who are teachers, but there are not a lot of jobs here so most people have to leave to find work. I have a marketing degree from Marshall University and I consider myself lucky to have found a job in my field. This was pretty much the only fit for that here.

"I am an only child, and so I wanted to stay. My father has a family-owned business but it is coal-related, so it is not doing well. He does mostly electrical repair on mining equipment. I think at the highest level, he had 28 employees and now he only has five. It is not good.

"I turned 30 last year. I will probably stick around. My husband started a tire recycling business. It has been hard, but I feel that his business has potential. He could create some jobs. He was also recently elected to the job of County Commissioner for Mingo County. He has his work cut out for him. There is not a lot of money to work with because the coal severance tax income is down."

I asked her about her impression about the downturn of coal.

She said, "EPA regulations have been tough. It is not the only

The Coal House

reason, but it has pretty much put a stop to any new mines coming in. They have imposed many new regulations both at the power plants and at the mines. Coal is not popular anymore. Nobody wants to breathe coal dust. Strangely, people like mining, and they would go back to doing it if they could."

About her job at the Chamber she said, "I am the Executive Director and the only employee. We have taken more of a tourism-related role. The Hatfield and McCoy miniseries put us back on the map. So we are pushing the tourism aspect. But we do not have a big budget. We don't have money for billboards and brochures. We just try to make sure that when we do get tourists here that they have a good experience.

"We have about 100 members of the Chamber. That is not too bad for this area. We have had members in the past that couldn't afford to stay in it, but now this year businesses are actually just closing. It is kind of crappy."

I said, "Let me recap. Businesses are closing. Coal mining is dying. Tourism people are coming here to explore your fairly disreputable past."

She said laughing, "I can work with that, though. Kevin Costner did the miniseries, and he is a fairly attractive and reputable actor. That helps to put that face to Devil Anse rather than this backward hillbilly with a beard."

I asked her if she puts a positive spin on the Hatfield and McCoy feud.

She said, "People whenever they come in already seem to have their minds made up about which side they like. It is like picking a favorite team." Thunder continued to rumble outside. Rain pelted the sidewalk outside the glass door. She continued, "Most people who come here are just passing through. They just happen to find us. Nobody sets their GPS to Williamson. You'd be surprised about the people who come here. They always compliment us on the people. They say everybody is so friendly. It seems like people from New York or Maryland must not be that friendly. We pretty much talk to everybody. That is the number one feedback that we get.

"Our top attraction is the Hatfield and McCoy feud. We do have some people who just want to see the Coal House. We have a lot of people who used to live here, and they come back to visit.

"We do not have great cell telephone coverage here. We only have one source. I drop a lot of calls. There are some places in the county that do not have any coverage at all.

"We are a railroad town, and railroad operations are not what they once were. There are still a few railroad jobs here. These are probably the best jobs. We have some lawyers, doctors, nurses, and teachers as well, but there are no really specialized jobs otherwise."

I asked if she thought the decline would continue.

She said, "There are some bright spots in the community that I hope will get brighter. We have a health and wellness center. They are doing some good things. People here are generally unhealthy. In addition to black lung, there are high incidences of diabetes. A lot of people eat too much fast food.

"Our biggest annual event here is the Hatfield and McCoy Marathon. It brought in 1,000 runners. That is a lot for this town, and it is our best event of the year. I would hope that those bright spots would grow. Maybe my kids, if I have them, can get a job. I don't make a lot of money. I could make more elsewhere, I'm sure. But this is home. That is about all you can say about it."

WHEN THE RAIN STOPPED, I wandered outside and walked the wet streets of downtown. I walked westward on Harvey Street through one of Williamson's largest flood gates and over the bridge into Kentucky, taking photos of the Tug Fork River and the floodwall, even grander and more massive than Matewan's. Williamson had been nearly de- stroyed in the 1977 flood, where waters were 20 feet deep in the street and people were stranded on the third floor of the Mountaineer Hotel. After another severe flood in 1984, the Army Corps of Engineers com- pleted the wall in 1991. The gates had only been used twice since, once in 2002 and again in 2003. The wall had multiple column-like features rather than a smooth surface, apparently to break the force of the rush- ing water.

The sun was bright on the wall and large puddles filled the streets with the just-fallen rain water. The roads only had a few cars, and it

Street sculpture

was clear that the city had tremendous excess infrastructure, being built for far more people than populated it now. Near the underpass where downtown linked to US-52 under the train tracks, a halo of water gurgled up from a drowned manhole cover. City Hall was in the old railroad station, but it was closed by the time I sat out the rainstorm.

I RETRACED MY STEPS BACK TO SECOND AVENUE and found an open door through which I felt compelled to walk. It was to the Williamson Health and Wellness Center. Inside I met Darren McCormick, a former mayor of William- son. He told me, "In the last 18 months, there have been over 19,000 jobs lost in coal mining nationally. There is a lot of metallurgical coal here. China is not building anything right now, so they don't have a need for cheap steel. There are many market factors involved. It is not just the shrinking availability of the resource. Employment in the coal industry has declined since the 1950s due to mechanization and modern mining methods. The railroads originally came through here for timbering, prior to coal. They put railroads up the various valleys and hollows where they could not float out the logs.

These mountains were all clear-cut.

"I became mayor in 2005. We have been doing community development training, leadership training, and things like that. In 2007 we were designated as a Blueprint Community and from that we spent 18 months in broad-based teaching of strategic planning and community development planning. From that, we got a strategic plan. From this work emerged a program called 'Sustainable Williamson.' We started getting some press about the effort around 2012."

In 2014, Williamson was one of six communities around the country to receive the Robert Wood Johnson Foundation Culture of Health Prize for Innovative Efforts to Improve Health.

"We have to reinvent our economy," he continued. "We are a mono-based economy. We are here because of coal and lumber. Timber is still here, but it is a small percentage of the local economy. Coal is on the decline. Tourism is growing because of the Hatfield and McCoy Trail system. Our system of trails is so big that (riders) can spend many days exploring."

"Is there anything else doing well?" I asked.

He said, "We are trying to reinvent a local economy based around agriculture. West Virginia spends $7 billion each year on food and $6 billion of that is imported. The highest point in the county is under 2,400 feet. We are about 750 feet here. It can be warm and humid here.

"We have a declining population. The users for city resources and government services will have to pay more per subscriber. The state's whole budget was based on the coal industry. We are looking anywhere we can for assets.

"A number of these old buildings downtown have upstairs floors that are not being used. We can renovate them and make apartments and then cash flow the bottom floor as a potential storefront. There are all kinds of apartments that you can rent for $350 you don't want to live in. (People) might be willing to pay $600 or $700 for a clean livable apartment. There are professional people like doctors and lawyers who have temporary business to do in town and can rent these apartments.

"We do a lot of support for entrepreneurship development. People have to think differently. For a long time they have had a 'job' mentality. West Virginia used to export tons of tomatoes and potatoes. There was an agriculture economy. Williamson was a retail center. Food was gathered here and then wholesale companies ran these foods to the various coal communities. There were farmers who grew (crops) either in the river bottoms or on the mountain tops. There is no in-between. But the elevation on the mountain tops is low enough that they can be farmed."

He said the clinic gets a federal subsidy for healthcare. This is because they were providing for anyone, regardless of whether insured or not. But they still generate patient services income. "That gives us opportunity to intervene in the community. We are trying to reestablish soil on post-mine use lands for food crop production. We are strategically planning mining reclamation for honey production and things like that. We are holding sustainability workshops to educate people. We have an energy independence day. We have a solar house."

I asked, "What do you know today that you wish you had known when you started 11 years ago?"

"A lot of wealth has been sucked out of here. There was no plan to take the wealth created here to keep and use it here. A lot of money in severance taxes was taken and invested elsewhere in the more populous places in the state. We are overdue to invest in infrastructure in this community.

"We do a lot of things at this clinic based upon healthy living and community intervention for healthy eating and active living. Our approach is holistic, more about the economic and mental well-being. I am a walking demographic. I smoke. And now I contribute to the running of a health clinic. I've quit smoking seven times."

I HAD BROUGHT SOME FOOD along for dinner, so I returned to the hotel and ate in my room, catching up on some correspondence. My room was lovely, with a massive king-sized bed, bedecked with eleven (count 'em, ELEVEN!) pillows, and plenty of space. It was $70/night, half what a similar room would have cost at most equivalent hotels.

After eating, I took the elevator back to the lobby and found Edna Thompson. We sat at a wrap-around upholstered booth and talked about the hotel.

Edna was a wisp of a woman, with flowing blonde hair and blue eyes. She wore an ankle-length skirt. She said, "The hotel was built for passenger train service. The community recognized that when people stopped on the train, they did not have a place to stay. So they sold stock to raise enough money to build it.

"It was built in 1925. It is now owned by a man named Mark Mitchell, a local attorney. He bought it in 1996, and he has been restoring it. Every day of its 90-plus years it has been an operational hotel. Even during a flood of 1997, it continued to operate because people were stuck here."

I asked about living inside a flood wall.

She said, "I was with someone today from Kansas, and they said that it was kind of like living inside a prison. I don't think of it that way. There are murals painted on it. It's okay. The alternative is worse.

"My family is from here, but I grew up in Columbus, Ohio. Growing up here, people learn reading, writing, and Route 23. (Note: US Route 23 runs from Jacksonville, Florida to Mackinaw City, Michigan through the center of Ohio in Columbus and on to Detroit.) Thousands of people moved from here to Cincinnati, Columbus, and Detroit. My parents moved out because there were no jobs. I moved back when I was in high school and I graduated from high school here. Then I went away to college and came back again.

"For many years, railroad workers would ride the train down from Portsmouth, Ohio, and finish their shift here and spend the night in the hotel. The railroad would call them when their train came back, and they would get back on and ride it back to Portsmouth.

"It is a big hotel. I think it started out with about 125 rooms. But in the 1960s, they started combining some rooms. Now we have 50 rentable rooms."

She said the owner had put a lot of money into the hotel, including refurbishing the lobby and adding new fixtures like the crystal chandeliers. "All of the rooms are named after famous people who have stayed here. Williamson was a big, important town. Many prominent people have stayed here. People who come often request rooms by name. They'll want to stay in the Roy Rogers room or the Loretta Lynn suite. There is a lot of history here. We want to preserve what we can.

"We've had tons of people who come and remember being here when they were young. The first black couple that was ever allowed to stay here after segregation ended were said to have gotten up on the registration table and danced, they were so happy to be able to stay at the Mountaineer. I think it was in the 1960s. Everything was segregated. I think we're still fighting it. There's still a lot of injustice.

"We like it here. The Internet opens the whole world. Amazon delivers everything. It's still a small town. It's safe. I know everybody. It's still a hometown. From the outside, it may look dead but it's not. Not everybody can live in a small town, but not everybody can live in New York City, either. People make their own entertainment here. There's lots of music.

"We have people working here for sustainable energy to give us another industry. Those people are doing well. There are solar panels on the roof of the hotel. But it's hard. The coal community doesn't like to hear anything but coal. Coal isn't coming back. They've cut off the tops of the mountains and destroyed the water and killed lots of people.

Why do we want them back? You know the story here. I don't think there's anything I can tell you that you don't know.

"This is a good place to work. A good place to live. We like it. I talk to lots of people who are visitors. They talk about the friendliness. We have good people."

I GOT A GREAT NIGHT'S SLEEP and awoke early. I carried my motorcycle panniers back to the parking garage where blissfully nothing had fallen from the ceiling and got underway again. US-52 instantly crossed the Tug River into Kentucky and then almost as quickly re-entered Wild and Wonderful West Virginia.

Finally once again on a four-lane highway, I couldn't get out of my mind an idea I'd heard only weeks before that seemed to have the real potential to revitalize one of the nation's poorest economies: a modern edition of the Federal Government's Homestead Acts.

In the midst of the Civil War, President Lincoln recognized that the security and welfare of the nation could be enhanced if thousands of citizens could be persuaded to take up residency in the yawning expanse of the American Great Plains. The first such act was signed in 1862, eligible to any adult who had never taken up arms against the United States Government (specifically excluding Confederates). The 1866 version explicitly targeted immigrants, women, and African Americans. Various provisions were applied, but the gist was that if someone was willing to move to the foreboding prairies of the Dakotas or Montana and live for a time, the government would give them the land. For free.

By the time the various Homestead Acts had run their course, 1,600,000 Americans received a share of 270,000,000 acres of public land, nearly 10 percent the entire acreage of the country.

Much later on and closer to our area of study, by the 1960s, notable politicians like John F. Kennedy and Lyndon B. Johnson traveled the hollows of Kentucky, Virginia, and West Virginia, examining for themselves the abject poverty of the coalfields. Kennedy died in November, 1963, but by the following January in his first State of the Union address, Johnson introduced legislation designed to alleviate the penury and coined the term "The War on Poverty." Soon programs like VISTA, Head Start, TRIO, and Job Corps began appearing in the hollows. Presidents Reagan, Bush, and Clinton presided over and in some cases fostered an ideological shift away from the government's role in education, nutrition, and health care as poverty alleviation strategies, and Clinton signed legislation to "end welfare as we know it."

While it is undeniable that these programs helped many, their relative success or failure is in the eye of the beholder, and I will leave you to draw your own conclusions. I will say, and I don't mean to be harsh, that the area was one of the poorest in the nation when the programs began and one of the poorest in the nation when they ended. Perhaps another option is called for.

Thus, a new Homestead Act.

There's something about ownership of your own property that provides an inherent incentive to make something of it. As we have learned, much of the land throughout the coalfields is owned by the Federal government, the single largest landowner in Appalachia, and by absentee coal, oil, gas, timber, and railroad companies. Many of those coal companies are in trouble financially; some are in bankruptcy. Even many people who own their home don't own the land upon which it sits.

What if we gave much of this land to new homesteaders?

Remember how coal and timber barons swept through the Appalachians after the Civil War and purchased mineral and timbering rights for a fraction of their worth? Perhaps it is time to give it back to those already there and those willing to move there, for farming, livestock production, sustainable forestry, gardens, and homes. With those bankrupt companies looking for cash, the Federal government could buy vast acreages for a pittance and give

Williamson flood wall and Tug River

it to those willing to stay and work there. While food programs like Food Stamps (now SNAP) are gone when the meal is over, this might provide an enduring solution to poverty. It may provide a beginning for budding entrepreneurs from inside and outside Appalachia looking for a way to enter the economy with minimal up-front investment, to build a sustainable economy in a time of uncertainty. The scourges of alcoholism, drug addiction, and obesity could all be addressed if not solved by landowners working their own fields for their own gain and eating fresh, farm-to-table foods.

Homesteaders by nature are risk-takers, and their entrepreneurial zeal would likely soon produce fruit orchards, crop gardens, meat growing and rendering facilities, and milk production. Carefully managed forests will yield exceptional hardwoods and give rebirth to custom furniture, musical instrument, and building products industries. Restored woodlands and water features would attract hikers, bicyclists, horseback riders, canoeists, and others long neglected in the coalfields, not to mention birds and other wildlife.

It's undeniable that when people own something, they take better care of it. When a cadre of newcomers arrives with dreams, plans, ideas, and aspirations, they bring with them a new sense of both stewardship and hope, things that are sorely absent now. It may be the only thing that will.

FOR THE FIRST SIX MILES or so, US-52 shared the highway with US-119, the road to Charleston. US-119 was a modern four-lane road, but US-52 quickly exited, and back to the more typical two-lane mountain highway I returned.

Around Kermit, it began to rain. I stopped at a convenience store to get some gas and put on my rain suit. But I've learned from past experience it is impossible to keep dry when riding a motorcycle in a hard rain. I've been wet before and I've been cold before, and I've been cold and wet before. Wet is tolerable. Cold is tolerable. Wet and cold is intolerable. Fortunately, it was a reasonable 70F on my bike's dashboard thermometer. I was only wet.

The only community of any note on this stretch of road is Crum, some 25 miles north of Williamson. It was made infamous by fellow writer and motorcyclist Lee Maynard in his eponymous novel, released to acclaim and scorn in 1988. Maynard's bacchanalia of insults disguised as a fictionalized account of life there in the 1950s managed to piss off everybody in the village (with 182 people in the 2010 census), and earn Maynard widespread animus. On its re-release in 2001, the book was banned by Tamarack, the state run artisan center, due to its lurid sexual content and scathing portrayal of West Virginia. This action ironically increased sales and turned it into a cult classic. (Note to the folks at Tamarack: Please ban this book.)

Not content to earn the loathing of merely his own state, Maynard described neighboring Kentucky as "a mysterious land of pig f*ckers,"[1] although he actually used the letter "u" where I have an asterisk. (Hey,

---

1   *Crum: the novel.* Vandalia Press, Morgantown, WV, 2001.

my mother might read this book.) I didn't stop in Crum.

Farther on, the topography became mellower and less forbidding, and the highway gradually became straighter with wider shoulders, and thus allowed for faster speeds. It also had fewer cars and trucks on it although it would have easily supported more. I was able to quicken my pace, and I had more room to pass slower vehicles.

It is an item of amazing historic significance in the struggle of working people to gain a rightful share of their slice of the American dream that almost exactly 60 years after the battle of Blair Mountain, their quest was effectively destroyed by one Ronald Reagan.

Prior to his ascension to the Governorship of California and then the Presidency of the United States, Reagan had served as President of the Screen Actors Guild, leading a walkout in 1952. At that time, nearly a third of the entire national workforce held a membership in a labor union and labor strikes was a frequent feature on the nation's newspaper headlines. From the days of New Deal legislation, the rights of labor unions to exist and workers to join them was unquestioned, and the union's right to collectively bargain and if necessary to strike for better wages, working conditions, and concessions, was commonly exercised.

Nevertheless, although federal workers, like their civilian counterparts, were allowed to unionize, strikes were considered illegal. Between 1962 and 1981, there were 39 illegal strikes anyway. A legal literalist, Reagan, the former union champion, would have none of that.

Nationally, air traffic controllers were represented by PATCO, the Professional Air Traffic Controllers Organization. Striking for wages in August, 1981, PATCO demanded a 32-hour work week and a $10,000 annual raise. Reagan had sought and obtained PATCO's endorsement for his presidential run against Jimmy Carter. Reagan wrote to PATCO's president during the campaign that he recognized the "deplorable state" of our nation's air traffic control systems, with assurances that he would be an ally in their needs for better equipment, pay, and overall public safety.

On August 3, 1981, when 13,000 PATCO members decided to strike to achieve Reagan's promises, he reneged and summarily threatened to fire them. Ten percent returned to work, but Reagan fired the rest, additionally imposing on them a punitive lifetime ban from federal service. It took until 1993 for President Clinton to lift the ban.

Reagan's move was risky both politically and for the security of the nation. Had a serious air disaster occurred while scab controllers were on the job, Reagan may have been excoriated. And the costs to the air traffic control network to pre-strike levels far exceeded the amount PATCO had demanded. Reagan, to say the least, got lucky.

No airplanes crashed. Our international challengers were impressed by the pugnaciousness of the new president. Most perniciously, no other unions called upon their members to join in brotherhood with striking PATCO members.

The union movement, from that moment on, was emasculated. Over the next 30 years, the number of union members participating in walkouts plummeted to almost zero. Productivity gains were impressive during that period, but without the representation of unions and the bargaining power they once provided, almost all income gains went to management and ownership rather than to the workers.

Obviously, the evisceration of the unions hasn't been the sole factor in the vast yawning gap of income inequality we're seeing today. But it is undeniably a major factor. We can think of August, 1981 as the month when working people stopped being compensated proportionately for the productivity and profit gains they fostered.

THERE WAS A BYPASS of the town of Prichard, where I'd found in my research there was an intermodal terminal for transferring containers from trucks to rail and back. It was out of sight from the bypass and I had an appointment to keep in Kenova, so I didn't explore it. But it did get me thinking about the way products and commodities are moving around our country and world, and about how that's evolving.

It's hard to say where the NS's history truly began, given all the reorganizations, mergers, and acquisitions that have occurred. It's even harder to say definitively where it's going. As they say, predicting is difficult, especially the future. But that won't stop me from embarrassing myself by giving it a shot.

Automation has already had significant impact on the national and worldwide economy. I believe the automation of transportation is coming soon, and it will change *everything*.

Remember that the Norfolk & Western made most of its profits hauling stuff, principally coal. Its primary, arterial route linking Norfolk and Cincinnati that I was following, was mated with a myriad of capillaries extending through the twisting hollows of the West Virginia, Virginia, and Kentucky coalfields. Those capillaries joined the main line in several locations where smaller local trains carried the coal to Bluefield and Williamson and were gathered into longer trains for the long run eastward to Lambert's Point for export shipment or westward to Cincinnati, Columbus, and beyond, to the power plants and found-ries of the Midwest. Passenger revenue never exceeded five percent of the company's overall income.

By the late 1960s, Norfolk & Western was weaning itself from passenger service, relying solely on freight. The stuff that wasn't being moved by rail was typically moved by trucks. But prior to the develop-ment of the Interstate Highway system in the late 1950s and through the 1960s, trucking was hampered by poor roads and choking in-ner city traffic, whereas railroads typically breezed right through on dedicated rights-of-way. That changed dramatically as the Interstates became fully implemented, and trucking boomed across the country.

In nature and in the economy, every change in the environment has winners and losers. For example, consider Hurricane Katrina's impact on the Gulf Coast and New Orleans. There were thousands of losers for every winner, but rubbish removers, building salvage operators, and insurance adjusters did extremely well. Another example is digital pho-tography, which seemingly overnight almost destroyed every company devoted to traditional film-based photography like Kodak and Fuji, but benefited companies like Canon, Nikon, and Olympus, at least initially, until hand-held computers and cell phones became equipped with internal cameras. I took the photos in this book with an iPad.

To the case in point, our nation's decision to fund, build, and imple-ment the Interstate Highway system grandly benefited the trucking and related industries, to the detriment of the railroad industry.

Trucking had many advantages. Because a dedicated driver and truck stays with the load from origination to destination, trucking for a specific customer's load is most immediate. Manufacturing companies began relying on just-in-time inventory management, as only the parts that were needed at any moment were typically in the plant, and what was needed tomorrow was already en-route, scheduled to arrive tomor-row. In earlier eras, a manufacturer might order from a vendor several months' supply of sub-assemblies, and then would warehouse them on-site for use when needed. Just-in-time allowed manufacturers to re-duce inventory costs. Similarly, retailers kept fewer items on-site, with deliveries of some items, particularly perishable items, arriving daily. These days, most grocery stores receive orders of milk, bread, eggs, and produce every day.

Nevertheless, trucking has never been suitable for long-distance haulage of heavy commodities, notably coal. When a shipper has a large volume of heavy freight, railroads are optimum. With minimal stops, slight elevation variability, and the high rolling efficiency of steel

wheels on steel rails, railroads are the most efficient form of land transportation ever devised. One train can easily haul the weight equivalen-
cy of 300 to 400 trucks, and do so with two engineers rather than 300
or 400 truck drivers.

One of the most significant developments in haulage transport in
recent decades has been containerized shipment. Intermodal shipment means any type of shipment by one or more conveyances, without handling of the freight itself. In the 1950s, the U.S. Department of
Defense established standard specifications for intermodal containers
that allowed them to be easily and efficiently loaded to and from ships
and then onto railroads and trucks. By the 1960s, the use of containers
increased steadily and technologies emerged at seaports and land terminals for transferring them. Ships, truck bodies, and train cars were
specifically designed to convey them. By the mid-1980s, rail car manufacturers had engineered double-stacked configurations which could
then carry twice as many containers per train. Seaports were massively
retrofitted with enormous cranes capable of unloading and re-loading
specially-designed ships in as little as ten to twelve hours. It is without
exaggeration that the national fleet of rail cars and especially containers
on trucks became the nation's new warehouses.

Improvements in railroad technologies and the demise of passenger
service meant that many smaller towns on the Powhatan Arrow corridor were no longer as viable. Railroad operations were consolidated
into the larger cities. Smaller towns found their fortunes intertwined
with the Interstate highways. In other words, towns that had Interstate
access were more likely to thrive than those that didn't. A vast array of
retail and service companies appeared at virtually every Interstate highway exit, principally hotels, convenience and fuel stores, and fast food
restaurants. Inner cities atrophied.

Meanwhile, significant railroad employment shifted to the trucking
industry, which is now huge. There are almost 9 million people employed in some aspect of the trucking industry, including 3.5 million
professional drivers, operating 15 million trucks of which 2 million are
tractor trailers. Many of these drivers are the customers for all those
hotels, convenience stores, and fast food restaurants. In over half our
states, the most common job is truck driver. For now, the employment
picture is rosy, with a lingering shortage of qualified drivers in the labor
pool.

Imagine all that vanishing virtually overnight.

Self-driving trucks are surely in our near future. Automation will, I
believe, reach full implementation in a few years. Lacking clairvoyance,

humans are incapable of fully predicting the ultimate outcome. But necessarily, changes will be of immense proportions.

In what only a few years ago may have seemed like a pipe dream, driverless vehicles are already on our roads, boasting safety statistics beyond human drivers. On May 6, 2015, a self-driving truck drove across Nevada, employing ordinary radar and cameras. Because of their relative universality, trucks on interstate highways will likely become driverless in a few years; if you're 60 or younger today, you may see it in your lifetime.

Just as automation let one machine mine as much coal as 40 miners, driverless trucks have enormous advantages. They don't drink alcohol or smoke weed. They don't fiddle with their cellular telephones. They don't get tired and their "eyes" never blink. They don't sneeze. They can work 24 hours a day, 7 days a week, without a break, and don't take vacations. Best of all from the trucking companies' perspective: they don't need to get paid. They don't need health insurance. And they don't call in sick.

It's hard not to conclude that truck driving, as a significant employer in America, has a limited future. Beyond trucks, buses may also become automated. And then commercial airplanes. Why would we want a UPS airplane to fly from Memphis to Los Angeles with anybody on board if computers can do the piloting safely? The likely outcome is that we'll have millions of unemployed pilots. And truck drivers. And bus drivers. And taxi drivers. Anyone whose livelihood is earned behind a steering wheel is likely at risk.

Even prior to fully driverless trucks, the technology is already available that will allow one driver to drive his truck while several more are "linked" electronically in platoons, following closely behind. Trucks closely drafting each other can save 5-10 percent of their fuel by reducing wind resistance, while requiring fewer drivers.

The loss of truck driving jobs is analogous to the loss of coal mining jobs four or five generations ago. As machines replaced people in the mines, fewer workers were needed. Communities that relied on coal mining jobs suffered, and we can expect that communities that rely on truck drivers will shrivel similarly. This will usher in massive economic and social disruption.

This scenario has played out before and will continue at an even more rapid pace. Let's go back and re-consider all those shipping containers. The efficiencies of transportation of goods via containers has allowed for the cost-effective manufacturing of virtually every consumer device to be globally away from the consumer. First to go were electronic devices, which in the 1960s and 1970s began to migrate from American factories into initially Japan, then Korea, Taiwan, and Singapore. The migration continues now into China, Vietnam, and Malaysia, and now includes a plethora of consumer products. Almost every item in my office was made overseas, from my computer to the monitor to the printer to even the desk chair. A battery-powered clock hangs on my wall that ticks away the seconds; it was made in China.

Manufacturing is Darwinian, evolving to allow for the survival of the fittest. Fine furniture making was heavily concentrated in early days of our republic in New England, where there were plenty of hardwood forests and ample water power. Then it went to the upper Midwest, then to central Virginia and North Carolina, then to the Far East, and likely soon to Africa, always in search of cheaper labor and costs of living.

Many displaced furniture workers were forced to take jobs at any income level they could find, dropping 50 percent to 70 percent or more from skilled factory work. This diminished wages throughout the employment ecosystem, as workers become dependent upon any income source they could find. Support businesses suffered the loss of their economic underpinning.

Retailing was once dominated by local, family-run stores. Now, we have mega-stores like Walmart, which are able to claim benefits of scale in buying, especially from distant suppliers, and to provide fewer total workers. Even these stores are now facing increasing competition from on-line companies, pioneered by Amazon, which even further reduce the labor force by shipping directly to consumers from enormous automated warehouses. It is easy to envision a day when you order a product on the Internet that is delivered a day later, manufactured by machines in Taiwan, shipped to our shores in a container, unloaded by a robot and delivered to an airplane, flown by an automated pilot to a nearby city, unloaded by still another robot into a self-driven truck to your town and then flown to your doorstep by a drone. That day might be sooner than any of us want to think. How will consumers generate the money to buy that product, given that millions of jobs have vanished? And how will various communities fare?

And its not just drivers and retail workers. Diagnostic apps will replace hundreds of thousands of health care workers. Food service jobs. Construction. Logistics. Management. Education. Farming and food production. Some experts estimate that upwards of 47% of all jobs in the country face extinction due to automation within the next two decades.

In 1952, when General Motors was our nation's largest employer, its president Charles Erwin Wilson told a congressional committee that, "What is good for the country is good for General Motors, and what's good for General Motors is good for the country," implying that the fates of the national economy and the company were inextricably linked. Their full-time workers earned an hourly wage of around $50 in today's dollars. Walmart is now the nation's largest employer, with 2.1 million employees. Walmart now pays its average full-time worker around $9 and fully a third work fewer than 28 hours and therefore don't qualify for benefits. Walmart generates annual profits of around $16 billion, yet thousands of their employees qualify for federal assistance, so taxpayers are making up the difference. Walmart, with all other major employers, constantly looks to automate as many functions as possible.

In short, human labor is, as animal labor was 100 years ago, becoming increasingly unnecessary. Where will those people reap income to provide for themselves and fuel consumer purchasing?

The upshot of this ongoing disruption of our national labor force is that jobs are eliminated and with it the money that used to circulate through our communities. More of our essentially finite capital is increasingly concentrated at the top of the economic food chain, widening wealth inequality. Because our wealthiest citizens typically consume proportionately at rates far less than everybody else (For example, a man buys only a few pairs of shoes every year whether he makes $10,000 or $10,000,000.), the movement of money slows and the economy languishes.

So what happens when we have a country of people who still must consume to live, but have no means for income? When computers take our jobs, as happens more every day, what will we do? We have seen enormous disruptions in the economy of the corridor of the Powhatan Arrow in the half-century since the last run. The technological innovations that wrought those disruptions have only accelerated, and we should expect that the disruptions over the next half-century will be even more dramatic. How will Petersburg do? Pearisburg? Portsmouth? Time will tell.

As I reached the outskirts of Kenova, the rain stopped. To my left was an enormous industrial operation, a refinery for Ashland Oil Company. A fiery flame shot skyward as waste byproduct hydrocarbon gases were flared off. I had clearly entered a new economic region, less of coal and more of oil, chemicals, and agriculture.

7:17 p.m.

Kenova

Mile 525.8

Manufacturing town and shipping point, where three states meet: Kentucky, Ohio, and West Virginia. The route crosses the Ohio River into Ohio and parallels it through Ironton and other industrial towns. (Ohio River)

Kenova, West Virginia was incorporated in 1894, its name a portmanteau using the "ken" from Kentucky, the "o" from Ohio, and the "va" from West Virginia. Seems like it should have been Kenowva! From there, a bridge over the Ohio River put N&Ws trains into Ohio for continuation into Cincinnati, Columbus, Cleveland, and throughout the Midwest. Kenova is on the south bank of the Ohio, with the mouth of the Big Sandy River immediately to the west, where the three states join at the mouth of the Big Sandy.

The rail that carried the Powhatan Arrow comes up from the south. Instead of heading directly across the Ohio, it curves eastward for about three miles, then due north over the Ohio, and then both the Ohio and the rail turn northward towards Ironton, Ohio.

TIM HENSLEY IS UNDOUBTEDLY Kenova's most ardent rail fan and is the author of several books, including the recent, *N&W 611 – Three Times A Lady*, about the three incarnations of the 611 locomotive, co-authored with Ken Miller.

I called on him at his 1907 Victorian home in a quiet neighborhood of parallel streets just west of downtown Kenova. His home doubles as a bed and breakfast, "The Trainmaster's House," where each room is themed to either a railroad or to the nearby Marshall University Thundering Herd. We sat in the parlor room in the back of the main floor, surrounded by memorabilia, notably dozens of railmen's lanterns.

Tim got a journalism degree at Marshall. "My neighbor was Willis Cook, PR Manager for C&O in Huntington. He nurtured me and taught me photography. I hung out in his office. It was walking distance from Marshall to the station. I got interested in the railroad. N&W had steam until I was eleven. I worked for the *Williamson Daily News* and a weekly for awhile. I worked for Congressman (Nick) Rahall for three years. I started to look at things in the context of money. Mom had a terminal illness, and I needed a job. I hired on as a brakeman. Within less than two years, I'd been promoted to engineer, which was unheard of.

"I started doing project work and writing about safety. So I was both on the train and behind a typewriter. I had a hankering to use my education and work experience. I got in with the Brotherhood of Locomotive Engineers. I worked for them as an editor and public relations person in Cleveland, commuting there from 1984 until 1986. It was a five-hour drive.

"The brotherhood was not just a union, but a fraternal organization. Then CSX came and offered me a position. I traveled as a feature writer all over the eastern United States. I became regional manager of corporate communication. Then I became Director of State relations for West Virginia and resident Vice President. Then I went to Amtrak and became a locomotive engineer on their Cardinal for my last 13 years of my career.

"I love both being on the train and writing. I pride myself as a wordsmith. I retired after a serious car accident. I worked three days a week and made $60,000 more a year for Amtrak than as a vice president for CSX.

"I bought this house in 1984 and have lived here off and on since then. I have two daughters and grandchildren. I have three rooms to rent. I write and publish now."

I asked about his interest in 611. He said his father would bring him down to see it come through town every evening. "I grew up with my school near a switch yard, so I got to watch operations.

"I've been in a family of railroad people, dating back to the steam days. Ken Miller and I are partners. We probably have the finest private collection of N&W materials in the country. We've collected for years. Photos. Files. Short lines. Coal roads. Country roads. The Appalachian coal area."

He has amassed the N&W's finest lantern collection from seven different manufacturers. He has torches and oilers as well.

"Ken and I talked about (writing the book) for a long time. We had it all lined out. I have another 10 or 15 books all planned out.

"I'm interested in the steam era. If I could have picked an era to be born, it would have been 1870 and been working on the railroad by 1890, and then finished my career by 1950. I'm interested in lots of things. Railroads. Appalachian culture. Coal. Timbering. My area.

Tim Hensley

"Huntington (West Virginia) was once a bustling place. It peaked out around 86,000 people. There are around 50,000 now. It's a metropolitan area of 340,000 now, including Ashland (KY) and Ironton (OH). What we've lost (in jobs) in Huntington has been offset by the gains at Marshall and in the medical industry. There are several medical centers and hospitals in Huntington now. It's similar now to Roanoke. Huntington has a 4 year medical college now.

"Ironton has faired worse economically than the rest of the region. It had a large steel and iron industry. That's all gone. They had a large coke plant. Ashland lost the headquarters of Ashland Oil. Portsmouth was a major steel center. This is the Ruhr of America. It was the industrial empire."

The Ruhr is a river of 135 miles in west-central Germany that formed that country's primary industrial center from around the turn of the 20th Century until World War II, and thus was a frequent target of Allied bombing.

I added, "This was also chemical alley. There was lots of cancer."

He agreed, "At one time, the fog and pollution all the way to Charleston was bad. But with air quality standards, it's not so bad now. People live healthier lives, or they can. I'm a young 66 now. I walk 2-3 miles every day. I'm still sore from the accident, but I'm able to sit up and take nourishment," he chuckled.

"The downgrowth of coal has happened within the last two or three years. Yes, (everyone) knew it was coming, but nobody projected the bottom would drop out as quickly as it did. This is due to the low price of natural gas. That is really what has accelerated the demise of coal.

"Part of it is also due to the slow down in the Chinese economy. I have been to China before, and I shot 7,000 images of Chinese people, places, and trains. That was the last place in the world where they used steam locomotives.

"At one point, Huntington was the busiest inland port in the nation in terms of overall tonnage. There were five coal terminals here. Now we only have one."

OUR CONVERSATION SWITCHED TO passenger rail in America. He opined, "We should have brought high speed rail into this country years ago. For many reasons, we didn't. All the systems in Europe that everybody loves are nationalized, socialized. Locks and dams here are subsidized. Interstates are subsidized. The railroads get some assistance, as NS did with the Heartland Corridor expansion of the tunnels to allow for double-stacking of containers on the rail cars. But generally (railroad companies) have to fund expansion on their own."

We spoke about the possibility of completing a major highway, between Kenova and Bluefield, to encompass the King Coal Highway I'd ridden the day before. It was projected to be part of an Interstate 73 stretching from Detroit to Myrtle Beach. He said, "All of West Virginia's highways feed into Charleston. This has hurt Huntington and other places like southern West Virginia. I'm an advocate of completing this. It's time to stop worrying and focusing on Morgantown, Clarksburg, Fairmont, and the Eastern Panhandle. The state needs to focus on southern West Virginia."

"If you could wave a magic wand over my corridor from Bluefield to Kenova, is that the best idea you can see?" I asked.

"Yeah. I'm not sure what else we could do. We can't replicate the War on Poverty; it didn't work well. Companies move factories here and find the people have a good work ethic; they have good mechanical skills and work well with their hands. They show up on time. The strength is in the people."

I said, "I've heard that, but I've heard the opposite, too."

"You have to pay people something," he said. "You have to provide benefits. If you pay a pittance, you may not get good help."

He had offered to take me on tour around town, so we loaded up in his SUV and went for drive. "We are equidistant between Huntington and Ashland. Kenova was less of a commercial center than Huntington because Huntington got a much earlier start. Kenova wasn't even a city until N&W arrived. We had a station, but it no longer is standing."

We drove thorough downtown, and he showed me captions for murals that he'd written for their Main Street Project. One featured Mary Draper Ingles, Bud Jeffries' ancestor, who walked through on her way back to Eggleston, Virginia. We crossed under the stanchions for the bridge that the N&W line took to approach the cross over the Ohio River.

The CSX line ran at ground level, east to west. The N&W ran over it to gain elevation to cross the Ohio River and still leave elevational room for river traffic underneath. The old station, he told me, served both lines and was thus on two levels. "More coal tonnage has passed over this place than anywhere in the world. There were about 30 trains through here every day."

Right on cue, a CSX train pulled towards us, with two navy blue, yellow, and grey diesel locomotives pulling a long, mixed train from the west. Its engineer gave us a nice horn honk, responding to my wave.

Moments later, Tim pointed to a track area and said, "The depot was just over there. At that time, all the passenger trains stopped for just a few minutes, and the car inspectors went over them and flipped the journals and put oil in them and all that." He

Tracks in Kenova

pointed to the former location of several signal towers, maintenance shops, and a roundhouse also gone now. There were railroad tracks going every-which-way.

Back in his car, he showed me neighborhoods where many of the railroad workers lived. He said some were only worth $35,000 to $40,000 now. "My house is appraised at $168,000. If it was in California, it would sell for $500,000. Housing costs are manageable."

He worked for CSX, but seemed partial to N&W. When I asked him about it, he agreed. "The N&W was the greatest of steam railroads. They had an *esprit de corps* that few railroads could equal. Their employees were proud. They were treated well and fair. Growing up with steam trains running by cemented my enthusiasm for the N&W."

The scene was of an industrial, working class community, decades past prime. He took me to a residential neighborhood on a bluff above the city to the south. We looked directly north to the Ohio River and across into the state of Ohio, but also to our right to Huntington and left to Ashland. Clouds were low and heavy grey, but vegetation was lush and green. Directly in front of us was a steel girder bridge that once carried the Powhatan Arrow across the river. "That bridge was of the top 10 targets of the Germans in World War II," he claimed.

We drove back down to the riverside, and he showed me the industrial heart of the city, with several current and former port facilities. He showed me the massive floodwall, "It was three feet higher than the crest of the 1937 flood."

It was time for me to follow the way across the river into Ohio myself.

THE RAILROAD BRIDGE TIM had shown me was three miles upstream on the Ohio River from the mouth of the Big Sandy, but the highway crossing was even farther east, on the edge of the city of Huntington. It was a two-lane metal truss bridge, painted in green, and the low Jersey-barriers provided a nice view upstream to the tree-lined banks and the broad river, where a barge was being pushed downstream on the milk-coffee colored water.

A small, cheerful sign said, "Welcome to Ohio, Where nothing much has ever happened." Actually, that's a bald-faced lie; it doesn't say that at all. The sign really says, "Welcome to Ohio, So much to discover." But both are accurate. I do seem to have issues reading state welcome signs.

Anyway, while Ohio can't boast the Civil War battle history of Virginia or the distinct extractive industry and labor war character of West Virginia, it is one of our most populous, industrialized, and influential states. In fairness, while Ohio only saw isolated skirmishes during the Civil War, it produced many of the Union's most capable and aggressive generals, including Ulysses Grant, Philip Sheridan, William T. Sherman, and most influential politicians, including Secretary of War Edwin Stanton and Secretary of the Treasury Salmon Chase.

Formed in 1803, Ohio is the 17th state to join the Union, one of the earliest after the original thirteen colonies. Seven of our U. S. Presidents were born in Ohio, second only to Virginia's eight, although the former's Harrison, McKinley, Taft, and Harding can't hold a candle to the latter's Washington, Jefferson, Madison, and Monroe. But hey, numbers count for something, eh? The state is actually named for the river, not vice versa, and it originates from the Iroquois word ohi-yo, meaning "great river." Clever, those Iroquois.

As the first state carved out of the federal domain west of the Ohio River, Ohio is well known as the birthplace of the Public Land Survey System prescribed in the Land Ordinance of 1785 and the Northwest Ordinance of 1787, both parts of U.S. organic law that predate the Constitution. While much of the state is subdivided into discrete districts composed of rectilinear surveys and populated by 640-acre square sections, most of the area between the Scioto and Little Miami rivers – a significant portion of southwestern Ohio – is part of the 1794 Virginia Military District, set aside as bounty land for Virginia veterans of the Revolution.

Virginia had colonial-era claims on parts of the Northwest Territory, ceding this area to the United States to appease less-endowed states in order to ratify the Articles of Confederation. The land in this district was instead surveyed by the traditional metes and bounds system beloved of drunken surveyors and litigious small-town barristers throughout the original colonies. Virginia continued to issue veterans bounty warrants in this district until Ohio became a state in 1803. The result has been a distinctive southern character to this part of Ohio, also partly because of the influence of Kentucky, a mysterious land of pig f*ckers, just across the river.

Prior to emancipation, this region became known as a hotbed of abolitionist sentiment, with many stops on the Underground Railroad. Part of the reason was that by laws enumerated in the Northwest Ordinance, Virginians could not import their servant chattels into the Northwest Territory. Thus the region became a haven for abolitionist and anti-slavery Virginians in exile from the mother state.

The area I'd just entered was called the Hanging Rock region. From its inception, Ohio was an industrialized state and Hanging Rock was important in that. Hanging Rock had lots of iron ore, some coal deposits, with more across the river in West Virginia, and a massive river, everything necessary for iron production.

My now familiar US-52 became straighter, often with four lanes, and in places marked with a 70 mph speed limit, the highest I'd seen on my journey. It felt refreshing, liberating. The rains moderated and the cloud cover had lifted.

7:32 p.m.

Ironton

Mile 537.2

Industrial city established in the early days when ore deposits were found nearby. Now has several manu-facturing chemical plants.

The Ohio Department of Transportation was kind enough to build a bypass for Highway US-52 around the northeast of Ironton. The highway hugged the base of low mountains and the city occupied the plain between it and the Ohio River.

I exited into town to find a small, pleasant river community of around 11,000 kind souls, and no doubt a smattering of cantankerous curmudgeons, but I couldn't be sure. Like McDowell County in West Virginia, the town's population apex was in 1950, but the diminishment was nowhere near as steep, falling from around 16,000 then to 11,000 now.

As had become my habit, I wandered towards the river area where the railroad tracks always seemed to be. Near the river was another concrete flood wall, over which spanned a huge bridge across the Ohio, this one an elegant truss bridge painted in light blue. I found an old train station, which, like those in Bedford and Lynchburg, had been converted into a restaurant. It was another lovely building, with brick and column construction, the columns and trim in crème color taste-fully offsetting the red brick. Red three-dimensional letters spelled THE DEPOT above the front entrance. There was a brick paved street in front of it, with multiple vacant parking spaces and scant traffic. The inside had lots of dark hardwood trim, white-tablecloths, and etched glass panels of several of the area's traditional railroad logos, including the circular "N&W RY" and the stallion of Norfolk Southern.

STEPHANIE RICHENDOLLAR WAS THE BAR MANAGER of the Depot

426

Restaurant. She said it was converted in the late 1970s or early 1980s, but she hadn't been there that whole time and didn't know. It had been owned by multiple owners. "The current owners have owned it for two years.

"The owners are Asians. Business is really good. The steel mills are mostly shut down. Armco still has a mill. There's Kentucky Electric Steel on the other side of the pond," her term for the Ohio River.

"There are still many chemical plants. We call this Cancer Alley. You will find more strains of cancer here than just about anywhere in the United States. I grew up in Kentucky, on the other side of the pond. I don't have cancer, but my brother does. He works for Marathon."

"Why don't you move away?" I enquired, as one naturally would.

"It's home. They're going to frack us to death next. It's not so much gas here, but more up in the coalfields to-wards Eastern Kentucky. We do more iron mining here.

"We used to be a nasty, dirty old coal, chemical and industrial town. We've cleaned up from that. I credit our city government. We have a new mayor, Ms. Keith, and she's doing a good job."

She suggested I speak to Joe Unger, the owner of Unger's Shoe Store. "It is one

Depot Restaurant

of the old authentic shoe stores. They sell Florsheim shoes. They still measure your feet."

So I TOOK HER ADVICE and walked to Unger's Shoe Store. It had navy blue lettering on the side of the building with "Unger's" in a script font and "SHOES" below. It was just as she described, with tastefully arranged window displays of gifts and shoes. I walked inside and asked a clerk if I could speak with Joe. She said he was out of the store and wouldn't be back for a while. I was tempted to buy a pair of shoes, even though I didn't need any, just to support the store.

Instead, I walked outside and crossed Third Street to City Hall, deciding to try my luck with seeing the mayor. I noticed several lamp posts had cloth signs printed with photos of prominent city citizens' photos and a brief resume of their accomplishments. There were USA flags all around and flowers in hanging baskets.

INSIDE CITY HALL was a large atrium lobby rimmed with city offices. There was a yellow, diamond-shaped sign about 10 feet above the floor with black lettering that said, "1937 HIGH WATER MARK" with a waved horizontal line on it. Katrina Keith's office was on the third floor, accessible by elevator.

I told the mayor's assistant what I was up to and after a brief wait, was ushered into the mayor's office. Keith was a youthful looking woman with a mop of jet-black hair, a pearl-white teeth smile, and designer eyeglasses. About her recent electoral victory, I expressed both my congratulations and condolences. She chuckled, agreeing, "It depends upon the day!"

I asked about her city and her personal history. She was born and raised in Ironton, and had been there most of her life, graduating from O. U. (Ohio University) Southern, also in Ironton. "After college, I got a job in Ashland, Kentucky, with the Chamber of Commerce, and I then went into the Main Street organization, a downtown revitalization group. Then I went to Junior Achievement and then into Hospice of Huntington. So I did a lot in the non-profit sector. Finally I got a job with the mayor here in Ironton thirteen years ago.

Mayor Katrina Keith

"The mayor is a paying position and a full-time job. I'm also the city manager. We have seven council members. I served for that mayor for four years, and for the next mayor I worked in workers' compensation. After that, I heard the call to run. My husband and I prayed about it. I had three opponents, two of them previous mayors, and I got the most votes, but not enough for a win. So we had a run-off special election two weeks later, and I won that. It was a nervous time. It was amazing."

I asked about the city's challenges.

"We were established in 1849 by John Campbell and were named for the iron deposits nearby. Our riverfront was lined with iron furnaces. We were instrumental in World War I and World War II because the iron that built the ships came from here. There was money here hand-over-fist during those times. When the manufacturing industry went overseas, that killed our economy. The peak era was the 1950s. That was the last of the boom times, well before I was born. This community has been in decline my entire life.

"I was raised around a whole generation of people who remembered when. But I had nothing personally to go on. My generation didn't know about the old times. We had nothing holding us captive. Older folks said, 'We did it this way then.' We were like, 'It's a new day. Let's do it this way now.'

"By the late 1960s and early 70s, we hit rock-bottom. Government aid came in to help people. We were never able to really get back on our feet, but government aid stayed. Only twenty percent of our residents are taxable, while everybody else is either a child, a retiree, or on public assistance. So we keep getting weaker and weaker as a city government. We've lost much of our population."

I said, "You don't look depressed."

She chimed, "I'm upbeat. It's a new day."

"You said that twice. What does that mean to you?"

"It is a new era for me. I'm a true believer in my faith. I believe in destiny. I believe we're all called to something. I believe I'm called to this position. When I ran, I realized this new economy doesn't offer us much. I ran on (revitalization and utilization of) the riverfront. We have the beautiful Ohio River sitting next to those railroad tracks you're following. The floodwall protects us from flooding. The river doesn't bring much tourism now, but we're developing our riverfront. We're developing a marina. We've raised some of the riverfront for upscale housing to promote the beautiful view. Nearby we'll develop commercial properties like a hotel or restaurant. We're calling ourselves the 'Southern Coast.'"

She said Ironton is known for sports. It has an historic stadium, legacy of their former pro football team, the Ironton Tanks. The stadium was recently renovated with donations from concerned and motivated parties. I asked if she thought her city was unique in that regard.

"Absolutely! Our people, our civic clubs, know there is no big money here any more. We're not Columbus, where we can just buy anything we want. We have to look outside the box for solutions to get things done." She mentioned several events and initiatives undertaken by local citizens.

"Old timers still remember devastating floods. We're fortunate to now have the flood wall. We credit the Army Corps of Engineers.

"We are a community that refuses to die. We have a skill set you won't find in larger metropolitan areas. We'd love to have a new industry bring jobs, quality jobs. But we're used to having one big employer hiring 300 or 500 people and then having them go away taking the whole city down.

Ironton City Hall

"I'll be frank. We're in Lawrence County. It represents a socialized environment, in that we take other counties' tax dollars to subsidize our existence. If you can give me a house and you will pay for it and my rent and phone and day care and my college education and utilities, what's my incentive to go to work? There are limited high-paying jobs. If you pay all that for me, I'll dumb down my wants and take it and give nothing back. There will be no tax dollars to come to the city to pay for police, fire protection, roads, health, water, sanitation, and sewer. It cripples the city. We need entrepreneurs to pull us out of that. But there need to be incentives.

"Handing people everything dumbs-down mankind. I know because I was once there. I was raised in this environment, in government assistance, with a child during a divorce and going to college. My only option was public assistance. I would have stayed there."

"But you didn't stay there. Why not?" I prodded.

"Because I wasn't taught that way," she asserted. "Our city has a whole generation of people taught that way. I don't want to point fingers because people are full of ideas. But their parents' and grandparents' economy was ripped out from under them. Even if the jobs came back, we might not have the motivated workers because they didn't grow up with it. We don't have a deeply ingrained historic culture of entrepreneurship. For decades, industrialists brought jobs to us. Then they took them away. We need to learn how to make new ones ourselves.

"We are experiencing a shift here. Before, depression set in. We played the blame game. 'It's somebody else's fault.' 'It's industry's fault.' 'It's the government's fault.' We did that for years. Come back in a few years and see if there's a difference. We have a growing culture of ownership. We've been kicked down for decades. We're getting over that. It's time to get back up."

BACK ON HIGHWAY US-52, my thoughts returned again to transportation, and in this case our highways. When we were back in Williamson, I talked about driverless trucks and all the way back in Petersburg I touched on driverless cars. Let me discuss cars further because it is undeniable that the changes worldwide and along the corridor of the Powhatan Arrow will be massive and inestimable.

Automated or driverless cars are already a reality and are being refined by Tesla, GM, Google, Toyota, and others. There's some humor that needs to attend to this eventuality, as we might quip that if Microsoft designed your car like they did their software, the car would crash frequently requiring that you re-start to continue, that on spontaneous occasions all the gauges would freeze and you'd need to open the trunk, change radio stations, and stomp the parking brake in order to make them work again, you could only carry one passenger without a multiuse license, and you'd push the "start" button to turn it off.

All kidding aside, there will be several more years of testing and refinement, then gradual introduction into the market, and then significant and perhaps eventual total penetration. These will be phased in as technologies evolve, but I'm more convinced every day these innovations will become widespread realities at dizzying rates, leaving massive carnage (pardon the pun) and providing unfathomable disruption and opportunities.

First, cars will have automation for specific function, as in cruise control and automated parking. Almost all cars now have the former and some the latter features. Second would be combined driver/computer functions, where a driver is still needed but on some highways, the cruise control would also include steering. Third would be self-driving cars that only rely on the driver for specific functions such as navigating gravel roads or off-road. Fourth is complete self-driving automation, where you enter your car, give a voice command and tell it where you want to go, and then do whatever you want, including sightseeing, working or playing on your computer, or even falling asleep.

Will we feel relaxed enough to truly fall asleep while our car drives us somewhere? I don't see any reason why not; we fall asleep regularly on airplanes. We sit in a chair 7 miles above the surface of the earth breezing along at 600 miles per hour and most of us have enough sangfroid about that miracle to snooze. So why not cars?

As modest a lifestyle improvement as allowing everybody in the car to doze, I'm guessing the ramifications of a complete change-over to self-driving cars will radically transform virtually every aspect of our lives, from our cities, our schools, offices, stores, homes, and even the roads themselves.

It's hard to know where to start, but let's first consider the design of these cars themselves. Cars evolved from horse-drawn carriages and were called horseless carriages, defined by the removal of a characteristic, the same as driverless cars. But initially they still resembled the horse-drawn predecessors. When driverless cars emerge, they'll be like human-driven cars, but will soon diverge and become their own entities, looking, feeling, and acting differently. For one thing, they'll likely be mostly or fully electric. Electric drivetrains are more compact and powerful than conventional gas or diesel versions, and thus can fit literally between the drive wheels, leaving more room for passengers and luggage. Electric cars produce maximum torque at all speeds and capture some otherwise lost energy in regenerative braking. Alternative, "sky-based" energy, primarily solar and wind, will continue to drop in price and replace traditional fossil-fuel "ground-based" energy like coal, oil, and natural gas. Like the Powhatan Arrow that had somebody else driving it, driverless cars may have rear-facing seats or even seats in a circle or around a table.

Automobile utilization in America is now only 5 to 7 percent, meaning that most cars are only doing anything useful for just over an hour each day. It is likely that millions of Americans will decide they don't need a car at all, as one can merely be summoned to take them where they want to go. These folks won't have the costs or maintenance responsibilities of ownership. Ride-sharing companies like Uber – what we currently call "taxis" – will multiply to capture that emerging market. Consider that most of what you pay to ride a taxi goes to the driver, and that if the car doesn't have one, the cost will plummet. People justify the vast expense of a personal vehicle because of the instant access and mobility. You can already summon a vehicle now on your Smartphone or tablet computer that will arrive in short order. So if rides are cheap and readily available, why have your own car?

My point here is that while it stands to reason and is easy to conclude that people will own and use self-driving cars much the same way they own and use driven cars now, that's unlikely to be true.

Increasingly, if more families don't need a car or as many cars, houses won't need garages. All those industries that cater to private car ownership will diminish or be eliminated. Cars will be sold in fleets to the ride-sharing companies, so we won't have the need for nearly as many car salespeople or dealerships. There will be no rental car companies and fewer mechanics, car washes, valets, insurance companies, and loan companies.

Driverless cars will also reduce the need for massive parking lots and garages at shopping centers, schools, and workplaces, because the car will simply drop you off and go to the next customer. As these fleets of cars owned by the car-sharing services return to "home bases" after busy daylight hours, massive parking lots will emerge at those places rather than at individual destinations. That will revolutionize how we use immeasurable amounts of land currently paved for temporary storage of cars.

Because cars are in more constant use, overall utilization will increase, further reducing fuel consumption and pollution. It is possible that fleets of self-driving cars will be on the road servicing clients at 25 percent or even 50 percent. This would be utterly transformational for the entire auto industry. The dealerships will become superfluous because manufacturers will sell to the services rather than everyday consumers. Sales overall will drop because fewer cars, traveling more miles, will be needed. Today's $20 trillion worldwide asset capitalization in conventional cars, with only a miniscule utilization rate, makes little sense to continue if this alternative exists. Young people may never bother to learn to drive, get a license, or own a car. Already some developed countries have reached their zenith in per-capita car ownership.

It's a good thing, and I suspect an absolute necessity, that cars become more fuel efficient because petroleum is still the primary energy supply, and we're consuming it rapaciously. World crude oil consumption is around 86 million barrels per day, or 35 billion barrels a year. Numbers like these are impossible for me to wrap my head around. But oil is an extractive resource. The earth isn't making any more of it (which is not strictly true, but it is for all intents and purposes, as the earth is only making petroleum at about one one-millionth the rate it is extracted). In spite of a recent uptick in production due to a boom in fracking which allows previously unreachable resources to be tapped, eventually production must peak and enter terminal decline. Just as coal replaced wood, oil largely replaced coal, and natural gas is replacing both, we have moved from poorer to richer energy resources. But all of these are earth-bound and limited (except wood, which re-generates, but again not at the speed we'll require). I can't help but think that our transportation fuels will become increasingly expensive.

The value in auto manufacturing will shift towards "software" from "hardware." In the same way esteemed companies like Kodak and Fuji failed to transition from film to digital photography and Blockbuster failed to transition from cassette movies to on-line streaming, unless they possess requisite corporate resourcefulness and agility, GM, Ford, and Toyota might lose out to Tesla, Uber, Google, and other emerging automakers.

I mentioned auto insurance, which is a $200 billion market now. It will virtually collapse under the new model. Collision repair shops and car-parts aftermarket firms will struggle to retain their footing. No more traffic court, because nobody will be speeding or reckless driving. And all those damn lawyers who feast on your misfortune will need to find other avenues for lawsuits.

Because the new generation of cars will crash less often, the long quest automakers have been on since the 1960s to make cars safer will diminish in importance. Combining reduced emphasis on heavy safety features with advancements in material sciences, cars will be much lighter in weight, again boosting mileage efficiencies.

There are many other benefits as well. A car that drives itself will dramatically increase the mobility of our elderly. Additionally, children and adults who are disabled to the point where they cannot drive will also gain mobility. Plus, if you're leaving a bar and you're plastered, a driverless car can deliver you home safely (although with regards to negotiating the front steps, you're on your own).

Automated cars can accurately gauge stopping distances and the safe spacing between cars and like automated trucks will be able to platoon on the highways, linked to one another electronically at optimum safe distances based upon speed, weather, and roadway condition. This will increase highway capacity and reduce congestion, pollution, and fuel costs, as vehicles will essentially be drafting one another. Self-driving vehicles will self-select routes for maximum efficiency based upon regional traffic, as they'll all be communicating with each other, monitoring possible congestion and other problems. And they'll communicate and cooperate with other transportation options such as trains, airplanes, and even hyper-local solutions such as scooters and e-bikes to get travelers that last mile or two.

Computers aren't perfect, of course, and accidents will happen. But I venture to claim that they'll happen with much less regularity and severity than with human drivers. Today, over 90 percent of accidents are caused by human error, mostly by the evil trio of distraction, speeding, and impairment due to alcohol or drugs.

Sounds pretty rosy, eh? Downsides…

System failures could produce a tangle of liability issues. Will your car be programmed to make good ethical decisions? If you're being driven in a driverless car on a country road and it moves to the left to get around a bicycle rider and then a deer runs across the road, it has a decision to make. It can swerve off the road endangering the bicyclist. It can hit the deer and potentially endanger you. Or it can swerve into the oncoming lane, endangering you and the oncoming vehicle. Who is legally responsible for the outcome? As I mentioned with attempted humor, above, what happens with system failures? Today if my computer dies, I lose files; if my car's computer fails I may die.

Speaking of bicycles, there are concerns about the continuing viability of this and other antiquated forms of transportation like motorcycling and I daresay walking, should we transition to a fleet of automated cars. Will communities and state governments still invest in pedestrian, transit, and bicycle improvements? For people at the lower end of the economic scale who cannot afford a car or taxi services, will their needs be met? If self-driving cars become common, will there be reduced transit services for poorer people?

There are privacy concerns. You'll pay for your ride electronically, and now *The Man* will always know where you've been. This is consistent with a steady degradation of privacy we're already suffering in the Internet age. (For one of my earlier books, a novel, I was doing research on pregnancy and the midwifery, as one of my characters was studying to be a midwife. For weeks, I received on-line advertisements for pregnancy products.)

There are security and terrorism concerns. Driverless cars could be used for bomb delivery, drug transfers, or other criminal activity. These cars could be used as mobile offices and even venues for sexual trysts.

As our legislatures are now scrambling to devise legislation for drones to keep them away from airplanes and prevent accidents, those same legislatures will soon be tasked with devising laws to regulate driverless vehicles. In the transition phase, what if human drivers attempt to join autonomous vehicle platoons? Will speed limits change and will autonomous vehicles be allowed different speeds than human-driven vehicles? In mountainous areas, what if one car in a platoon lacks sufficient power to keep up?

Once self-driving cars become commonplace, will ordinary human-driven cars be banned? Will I still be allowed to ride my motorcycle? Will we quickly accept robot-driven vehicles and prefer them to human-driven? With the driverless cars on the road now, drivers sharing the road with them are sometimes bothered by their timidity and over-sensitivity towards safety.

I mentioned that strategies like platooning that will reduce congestion. But if the elderly, young, and disabled now have complete mobility, will there be more trips and more congestion? We don't know how this will all play out. Like any other massive change in the way we do things, we simply cannot predict whether we'll see rosy or dark outcomes.

Our transition from passenger rail and transit to private automobiles was rapid, driven by the automobile's real and perceived advantages, especially the freedom of mobility. You could go where you wanted when you wanted, rather than having to await the train's arrival and the inconvenience of transfers. But that freedom has eroded to the point of becoming illusory. In car commercials on television we see happy, fit young people, typically with the smiling male sporting a 3-day old beard and the woman in tight, revealing sportswear, with surfboards or skis on the roof rack, motoring happily to some pristine beach or mountain. But the everyday driving experience for most of us, especially in crowded urban areas, is significantly different, with endless waits at traffic lights and long periods of immobility on the freeways. If the driverless revolution plays out correctly, our future may find us wondering why we ever tolerated the massive time-inefficiencies, money, and carnage of personal ownership of human-driven vehicles. If all goes well and I stay healthy, I expect to see that day, and view my former cars longingly with the same fond nostalgia that I now hold for the great steam locomotives like 611.

And with those thoughts, I rode towards Portsmouth.

8:10 p.m.

Portsmouth

Mile 568.3

Steel, shoes, stoves, and brick. Flourishing industrial center where the Scioto River joins the Ohio. N. & W. maintains one of the largest single railroad yards in the world here. Seat of fertile, rolling Scioto County. Founded in 1803, it was among the earliest permanent settlements in the area. Here the N&W's lines to Cincinnati and Columbus diverge. (Scioto River)

As kind as Ohio's Department of Transportation had been to me (and thousands of other motorists) back in Ironton, there was no similar bypass provided around Portsmouth. So US-52 becomes a city street, with intolerable numbers of traffic lights. The road splits in two in nearby New Boston, with Gallia Street handling westbound traffic and Rhodes Avenue carrying eastbound. A massive railroad switching terminal lay to the south along the banks of the Ohio.

The lanes of the highway converged then diverged again in Portsmouth proper, now Robinson Avenue and 11th Street. Construction of underground utility lines made going even slower. I took Chillicothe Street southbound to the center of the old city and found street parking across from the elaborate Columbia Music Hall. I then wandered around on foot.

Pleasantly, I noticed there were murals seemingly everywhere! Portsmouth's floodwall alone has 2,000 linear feet of murals, painted by artist Robert Dafford over 15 years. Panels tell the story of Portsmouth's history, including Shawnee war Chief Tecumseh and famous Americans such as baseball coach and innovator Branch Rickey, painter Clarence Holbrook Carter, and singer/actor Roy Rogers, who grew up nearby.

I walked to the west on 2ⁿᵈ Street, past many fine older buildings, some in good repair and some crumbling. There were several vacant lots, presumably once occupied by buildings that had long been razed. I headed over to the Scioto County Visitors Center on Jefferson Street.

PORTSMOUTH WAS ESTABLISHED at the confluence of the Scioto River (which incidentally is pronounced "sy-oh-tah," as I was frequently informed) and the Ohio River. The original town was called Alexandria, named after the city in Virginia, but after repeated flooding, it was relocated slightly to the east on higher ground and renamed Portsmouth (which, ironically, is also the name of a Virginia city).

Portsmouth's location was fortuitous as an industrial site, and it grew quickly as a shipping and meat packing center. When the Ohio and Erie Canal opened in 1832, its growth further accelerated, as Portsmouth was the end of the 308 mile long canal that connected the Great Lakes to the Ohio River via Cleveland, Akron, and the agricultural and manufacturing heartland of the state. The last lock is still visible from the Ohio River.

The state of Ohio provided the shortest distance between the slave-owning states and freedom in Canada. So Portsmouth was a hotbed of the Underground Railroad. Abolitionists helped to ferry slaves across the river. Slaves could still be captured in Ohio and taken back to their owners for ransom. Slave catchers and dogs roamed the area looking for them. So slaves took to the Scioto River where the dogs would lose their scent. Thousands of slaves used the Scioto for travel.

By the end of the 19ᵗʰ Century, Portsmouth was one of the premier Ohio River cities between Pittsburgh and Cincinnati. Industries of prominence included shoe, brick, and steel making. At its peak, 16 shoe factories and over 100 manufacturing companies called Portsmouth home. Today there is one shoe factory remaining; it only makes shoelaces.

Foreign competition and nation-wide restructuring of manufacturing hit Portsmouth hard. Population peaked in the 1930 census at around 42,000 people, and today its population is just below half that. All of the attendant miseries of a city in decline are afflicting Portsmouth, with high levels of unemployment, crime, and epidemics of drug abuse. The transportation network that made Portsmouth so successful and prominent in the early years became a scourge, as it became a distribution and trafficking center for drugs. Drug rehab facilities treat patients at five times the national average.

The former train station was on the corner of Chillicothe and 16ᵗʰ

Streets and was long ago torn down. Today a jail stands there.

On a more positive note, there were many lovely old buildings, the murals I mentioned, especially on the floodwall, and the two-tower cable stayed Ulysses S. Grant Bridge over the Ohio. Like many of the cities I'd visited, the current largest employer is the local hospital. Portsmouth is also home to a college, Shawnee State University, which has a campus alongside the Ohio River.

I MET JOE PRATT, Executive Director of Main Street Portsmouth, in his office. He told me that Portsmouth's history is of engineering and industry. "We saw a decline of both those things in the mid-20th Century."

He was a young man with a round face. He said, "'Main Street' is a national organization that breaks down by state and is overseen by the states. They work on four approaches: promotions, organization, design, and business. Our goal is to get the downtown thriving. We want to be a resource for new business. We help them navigate through taxes, regulations, and construction. We help current businesses to promote with social media campaigns to pull people to downtown. We do design elements from the river to 10th Street and from Gay Street to Alexandria. That's our boundary." He dug out a map to show me the region they covered.

"We're having a renaissance right now because we're seeing small business owners buying properties. They're seeing that in ten years there won't be more of them to turn into what they want to do with them. There are many impressive buildings that are largely empty now.

"We're placing park benches and flowers on the sidewalks. We're spending money on public art. We have a deal with the city to get $50,000 per year, spending $15,000 on office expenses and salaries. We give $25,000 as small business grants. We put money into our design fund. We have several endowments, used for things like flowers and public spaces.

"People started looking at downtown in a different light. Craft breweries are in. Shopping 'small' is more popular with the younger generation. When I was a kid in school, I hung out downtown with the small shop owners. I knew the shops and I knew the buildings were huge and mostly vacant. They boarded up the rest and couldn't afford to upkeep it. People now are investing in these buildings and developing from the top floors down. They'll renovate the fourth floor first, opening it for residential apartments. It's the most valuable because it has the best views. Then they'll install the elevator and renovate the third floor. The income provides money for the lower floors for even smaller apartments. They can spend the time and money on the first floor to develop it for retail. People like living in these places.

"Most of what we do is connected to preservation. I've only been here for a few months. I was a newspaper reporter before that. Before I leave this job, I want to be able to drive down Chillicothe and 2nd Streets and see that not only are there benches and flowers everywhere, but I want to see pride in the area. I want to see every building filled."

ADAM PHILLIPS SHARES OFFICE SPACE in the same building, and he is the Asset & Site Development Manager of the Southern Ohio Port Authority. He joined our conversation. He said, "We're a development agency, working with businesses, existing and new ones, to work through regulations and incentives. I grew up in New Boston, just to the east.

"I am too young to know about the heyday. I remember the New Boston Coke Plant that provided coke for the steel mill. New Boston's air was awful and it smelled really bad. I grew up accustomed to it. I'm 27 years old.

"I went to Shawnee State (University) and got undergraduate degrees in history and international relations. I delved into asset mapping and economic development. I went to Washington, DC, to present to the Appalachian Regional Commission about different assets and how to leverage them. I got my masters at Ohio University in Athens; it's the oldest university in Ohio, founded in 1803. My degree is in political science with a concentration in public policy and political organizing."

mural

"So what are your community's assets?" I asked.

"Rail, river, and natural gas," he said, noting that they were listed on his business card. "In the region we have unparalleled access to the Ohio River. The port of Portsmouth provides us that access. We have two Class 1 railroads, CSX and NS. We have two transcontinental natural gas (pipe)lines. They transport billions of cubic feet of natural gas.

"Plus, the natural gas sourced here in southern Ohio has become the cheapest in the world. Most of the fracking is done east of us. We take advantage of the downstream byproducts of natural gas. Companies that use lots of gas like glass manufacturers can benefit. Also, chemicals and plastics."

I said, "You've always had those things, at least the river and the railroads. This led to a rapid rise in this city's fortunes a century ago. Why will they make a difference again?"

He replied, "Transportation is always a part of our past, but also a way to position ourselves to move forward into the future. Highways in major urban centers are becoming congested, costing industries greatly. We have uncongested highways and our highway infrastructure is only getting better. We have a bypass planned. We're relatively uncongested."

My thought swept to those interminable traffic lights I'd just endured, thinking the new road could come none too soon.

Adam continued, "We want to leverage that asset while we can. As congestion gets worse, we want to take full advantage of it. We have both river and rail, too. When the Panama Canal expands, we expect more freight on the river through our area. They'll pass through larger ships that can come to East Coast ports. We may see a 17 percent to 30 percent increase in shipping to East Coast ports rather than West Coast ports.

"NS's Heartland Corridor, which allows double-stacking of containers, goes from Chicago to Norfolk, passing right through here. We're where the Corridor intersects the Ohio River. We have tremendous opportunities to make investments in multi-modal transportation. If you need to move freight from rail to river, this is a good place.

"We entered the America's Best Communities competition. It was a small town revitalization initiative. It had four major corporate sponsors. They invited towns to submit their economic development strategies. Four hundred communities applied. We made it to the top 50. We were given $50,000 to devise a plan, and we invested that in a plan to enhance river access for recreation. That plan got us to the top 15. We got another $25,000 for that. We have a riverfront plan now.

"Our city is embattled. But there is a lot of optimism. We've seen a massive decline, but it's a tale of two cities. I hear the stories of drug addiction and poverty. But that's not my story. I didn't grow up rich; my dad worked at a hardware store and my mother worked at a nursing home. I took on a lot of student debt to get my degrees. But there were always opportunities for me. I never took drugs. What made me different? There is a duality. Some people are energized and passionate about the community, and others aren't. You have to write your own story."

I CALLED ON TERRY OCKERMAN, a man Joe Pratt told me about, who has found entrepreneurial opportunities in two abandoned downtown buildings. He developed "The Lofts," in a former furniture store building downtown, and then a coffee shop named Coffee @ The Lofts, located in a renovated metal office building next door.

A native of Lucasville, ten or so miles north of Portsmouth, he worked construction and retail most of his career. He returned to Portsmouth to purchase the building. "I didn't come into Portsmouth a lot growing up, but it was *the* place, like going to Cincinnati or Columbus now. It was busy, vibrant, especially with retail downtown.

"That changed for most communities on either side of the (Ohio) River over recent decades, with the outsourcing and off-shoring of manufacturing. What happened to us is the same as what happened to many other communities up and down the river.

"The building was about 100 years old. It had always been a furniture store. I had been exposed to some loft living in Cincinnati. I saw that as a trend. (After we bought it,) we first started shoring up the infrastructure, the roof, plumbing, and electrical, with the idea of developing the upper floor for loft housing. It had been empty for several years and there was some water damage. We built apartments on the fourth floor. Without advertising, we leased up the first one, then the second and third. People said we couldn't do lifestyle housing in a Rust Belt city. But it now has 14 units and all are occupied and we have a waiting list. We are about 50 percent empty nesters and 50 percent professionals.

"We started at the top and worked down to not be working over top of people with construction noise and mess. We opened the coffee shop a couple of years ago. Coffee shops are popular. We do specialty coffees, plus fast casual fare with sandwiches and soups. We're selling better wine, bourbon, and scotch. We even sell cigars. Business is building up.

"I think in ten or twenty years, people will trend to smaller cities. It's more cost effective to live in smaller cities. We'll see a trend towards a focus on lifestyle. Millennials are more concerned with lifestyle than money. We won't see the steel mills or shoe factories come back. These were things we were known for. Smaller cities have people in the 25 to 35 age range, people who have finished their degrees.

"People raised here have deep roots here. It takes a lot to drag them away. If they can make a decent living, they'll stay, rather than putting up with higher costs of living in bigger cities, further away from their families. With technology you can be anywhere in the world simultaneously."

I LEFT PORTSMOUTH and headed due west over the Scioto River and my long-term companion US-52, turning northward on SR-73 paralleling the river. The rail of the Powhatan Arrow stayed on the east side for a few miles, and then crossed on a 1,000 foot long bridge over to my side where it came into view again.

This stretch of rail between Portsmouth and Cincinnati was colloquially known as the Peavine, not a specific name for this section only, as there are others with the same nickname nationally, but more an indicator of its sinuous, short-line, narrow gauge character.

This roughly 100-mile run into our terminus has its own unique history, apart from the section of track I'd been following for the first 575 or so miles.

The Peavine was originally built as a narrow 3 foot 0 inch gauge line, smaller than the standard gauge of 4 foot 8-1/2 inch. In the 19th Century, narrow gauge lines were popular for short-run, specialized trains. In fact, by the late 1870s, about 35 percent of U.S. railroad mileage was narrow gauge. This was the result of the painful recognition that, despite nearly universal interest in modern transportation, railroads were incredibly expensive propositions. The major railroads had by this point cartelized to some extent and certainly did not welcome new competition. Most projected railroads never came to fruition. The Panic of 1873 underscored the precarious nature of industrial investment.

American railroads often borrowed from British experience in engineering. Engineering journals at the time showed that railroads could be built less expensively on a narrow gauge than the standard gauge. The tare weight, the unladen weight of a train before it carried any revenue traffic, whether freight or passenger, was less with narrow gauge stock in both the locomotive and the rail cars. Lighter trains allowed for lighter rails and lighter, smaller locomotives. Greater operating efficiencies could be realized.

Indeed, this cost saving philosophy was extended to the basic routing as well; narrow gauge alignments often hugged the terrain, favoring following the contours of the land rather than indulging in expensive grading. Cost projections showed that a narrow gauge railroad could be constructed for about one-half to three-fifths the cost of a comparable standard gauge railroad.

The peak of this movement in the United States coincided with the Centennial Exposition in Philadelphia, where manufacturers displayed the latest in railroad equipment and rolling stock.

The railroad that was to become the Peavine was a result of a confluence of a low-cost railroad-building movement that peaked in the 1870s and the interests of businessmen in both Cincinnati and the Portsmouth-Ironton area, primarily coal and iron interests who wanted to connect with Cincinnati-served markets by rail.

It was chartered in 1876 as the Cincinnati, Batavia, & Williamsburg and, as ambitions grew, renamed almost immediately to the Cincinnati and Eastern (or I've also seen simply Cincinnati Eastern). From Cincinnati, it extended eastward in fits and starts, reaching Batavia in October of that year and Winchester in August of 1877, a distance of 46 miles, and by 1882, the nascent village of Peebles. The railroad was extended fitfully, alternating short extensions and completions with periodic receiverships.

Nevertheless, in 1884 it was completed to Portsmouth with the predecessor to that 1,000 foot bridge over the Scioto River. Completion of the projected route did not immediately translate to profitability.

The Cincinnati and Eastern found itself at the center of the narrow gauge movement in 1878 when a national narrow gauge convention was held in Cincinnati, with Major John Byrne of the C&E as one of the convention's organizers. Indeed Cincinnati could be said to be the center of the movement at that point, as the most extensive system of interconnecting narrow gauge lines was found in the Midwest, between Philadelphia and St. Louis, with Cincinnati hosting five different three-foot gauge lines by itself.

The narrow gauge movement was short-lived. Ultimately the lack of interchangeability doomed narrow gauge lines, as did safety concerns with the growing perception of narrow gauge being synonymous with an underbuilt physical plant. Lurid press coverage of railroad disasters probably peaked during this period as well, and collapsed trestles that were often built to avoid more costly fills were blamed for many fatal accidents.

Beginning in 1884, the Cincinnati and Eastern made efforts to convert to standard gauge, but this did not happen until the line was sold to the Ohio & North Western Railroad in 1887. This line too foundered and was reorganized as the Cincinnati, Portsmouth, and Virginia in 1890. It was in this incarnation when it was consolidated into the N&W in 1901.

The N&W, being the quality-conscious company they were, engaged in a program of steady upgrades to what was, for them, a hilly, curvy line, atypical to their well-engineered alignments. However, it was never double-tracked, so sidings were frequent to allow for trains to pass one another in opposite directions.

Certainly for a traveler on the Powhatan Arrow, the Peavine represented an impediment to a swift arrival in Cincinnati due to speed restrictions on the line. Although the Powhatan Arrow's timetable doesn't indicate such, it and many of the other long-distance trains functioned as locals between Portsmouth and Cincinnati, with scheduled stops at Peebles, Winchester, and Sardinia. According to the timetable, the last 100 miles took two-and-a-half hours, far below the typical operating speeds the Powhatan Arrow was capable of.

The rail line got progressively curvier as it approached Cincinnati. The first third of the route, from Portsmouth to just east of Peebles, followed the gently ascending gradient of Scioto Brush Creek, thus passing westward out of the unglaciated Allegheny Plateau and into the rolling glacial till plains of Ohio's bluegrass region. It is this zone, progressing westward into Cincinnati, that most betrayed the Peavine's narrow gauge heritage.

That bridge over the Scioto was the most capital-intensive feature of the line. It was built by American Bridge Company in 1913. Ironically, this valley-spanning bridge is now the most deficient structure on the line and is reputed to be the reason that Norfolk Southern railbanked the Peavine in 2004. The western portion of the line has been leased to a small railroad operator to serve industries in Batavia and Winchester. Currently NS traffic that once traversed this line to Cincinnati now goes from Portsmouth to Columbus and thence to Cincinnati, which is a significant detour for a system that is supposed to be as efficient as the Heartland Corridor.

So my chance at seeing a train running down the Peavine on the rest of the trip into Cincinnati would be as rare as a black man's face behind a hood at a KKK rally.

SR-73 would be my new companion for the next 35 miles or so, where I made a slight detour onto Duck Run near McDermott.

I HAVE TO TELL YOU I was swept over by a warm, fuzzy, mom-God-apple-pie feeling when I stopped at the boyhood home of one Leonard Franklin Slye, a youngster who would grow to become a cultural icon of grace, honesty, and talent. Roy Rogers, as young Slye would soon become known, was that and so much more. With his hand-made boots, his bandannas, his fine white Stetson hat, his immaculate white rhinestone tasseled shirts and wide leather belts, Rogers was what every growing boy in America wanted to be. He had a gun, a guitar, a horse, and a fine woman, and all the musical ability God could bestow upon a man, the epitome of what an American man and cowboy could be. Yet this image of the West was born not in Tucson, El Paso, or Amarillo, but in ironically in the heart of Cincinnati and raised outside of tiny Lucasville, Ohio, just north of Portsmouth.

Rogers' sterling behavior seemed to be no act; he lived his life outside the public eye with the same honesty, decency, and humility as we saw on camera. He held a strong religious faith and sincere caring for the less fortunate. Every episode of his television shows and his movies had moralistic overtones and his unwavering goodness and strength of character were resolute (unless you count having three wives suspect,

Roy Rogers birthplace

although in fairness, after his divorce from Lucille Ascolese after three years of marriage, his second wife Grace Wilkins died of complications after birthing their son Roy Jr. ("Dusty"). Rogers married Dale Evans in 1947 and remained her constant companion until he died in 1998.).

The King of the Cowboys was born on November 5, 1911 in a building later torn down to make way for Riverfront Stadium (later Cinergy Field, demolished in 2002 giving way to the Cincinnati Reds' current home, the Great American Ball Park). His father, mother, and three sisters eked out a meager life for themselves on the farm, where childhood agreed with young Len Slye, riding Babe, the old racehorse his father bought for him, and doing farm chores. The family and their few neighbors made their own entertainment with music. Len applied his musical talent to the mandolin, guitar, yodeling (which apparently was popular in those days... seriously) and vocals, and was soon appearing on local, then regional radio stations.

Rogers made his first film appearance in the height of the Great Depression in 1935, but his talent and handsome look ensured that he would find steady employment thenceforth.

Roy also adapted well to horsemanship, and shared a close companionship with a golden palomino/thoroughbred mix colt foaled in California in 1934. At the time named "Golden Cloud," Rogers acquired him, renamed him "Trigger," and a lifetime partnership ensued. Trigger was so sensitive to Roy's touch that Roy never used his spurs or a whip to produce just the movements he wanted. Trigger remained a stallion his entire life and died in 1965.

Roy's other primary relationship was born Lucille Wood Smith, renamed Frances Octavia Smith as an infant and then Dale Evans. (If there's a connection in these disparate names, I have no idea what it is.) She already had a singing career when she adapted her moniker, and was thrice-married before hitching with Roy in 1947. Dale was strong-willed, intelligent, beautiful, and talented. After Roy's prior succession of leading ladies, from the moment he and Dale were paired on the set of *The Cowboy and the Senorita*, they were inseparable both on- and off-stage. Everybody embraced them and their careers blossomed. She outlived him and died at age 88 in 2001.

Roy had a gaggle of sidekicks, including Smiley Burdette, Raymond Hatton, Gabby Hayes, and William (Hopalong Cassidy) Boyd. By the 1950s, movies were giving way to television, but Roy, Dale, and Trigger were as picturesque on the small-screen as they'd been before on the big-screen. *The Roy Rogers Show* appeared on December 30, 1951 on NBC, and millions of people tuned in each Sunday night. Dale, as talented a songwriter as a singer, penned *Happy Trails*, the theme song that became synonymous with the couple for the rest of their lives.

There is so much more to the Roy, Dale, and Trigger story, but the wholesome, forthright, mid-America image millions of viewers received makes a strong statement of the character of the area of southern Ohio traversed by the Powhatan Arrow.

The home itself was in private hands so I didn't approach it. But there was a nice, colorful, cast metal roadside marker that said "BOYHOOD HOME OF ROY ROGERS, The King of the Cowboys," erected in 2000. The house was up a gentle rise and surrounded by foliage, so it was difficult for me to see. It was, however, surprisingly small. I thought I'd find a *Bonanza*'s Ponderosa replica or something equally grandiose, and I was suitably disappointed. Still, I envisioned a child growing up in that house these days, going to grade school proudly proclaiming to new friends, "I live in the house where Roy Rogers grew up," only to vacant stares of befuddlement.

THE ENSUING MILES OF SR-73 were scenic and not dissimilar to the area around Southwest Virginia I'd traversed earlier, albeit with smaller hills and gentler topography. I emerged onto a larger road, US-32, the "Appalachian Highway," presumably not for the section I was on, but for where eastbound traffic would be going. It would deliver me to the outskirts of Cincinnati.

MEA CULPA. I APOLOGIZE to the people of Otway, Peebles, Sardinia, Batavia, and the many other small towns along the road into Cincinnati, because I didn't stop in any one of them. There are several reasons. For one, US-32 was a major Interstate-quality road that didn't lend itself to stops. For another, the N&W acquired rather than built the Peavine, and the company had less influence in the development of those communities. For another, the track was generally not seen from the road – out of sight, out of mind! And I confess to the bias of familiarity I had with the Virginias, envisioning tiny towns of southern Ohio to be somehow less interesting… less *worthy*. If I'm wrong, then again I apologize. Lastly, I was frankly road-weary, eager to get into the city and finalize my journey.

US-32 had little traffic when I joined it, increasing steadily until I reached I-275, Cincinnati's beltway, at Mount Carmel. I realized that with over 2 million people, not only was Cincinnati the largest metropolitan city of my journey, but the only one with what we might characterize as suburbs. I could feel my blood pressure rise.

10:45 p.m.

Cincinnati

Mile 676.6

The Norfolk & Western reaches its most westerly point at the Queen City's beautiful Union Terminal. City of over half a million. A truly metropolitan center, Cincinnati not only has diversified major industries, but looks with pride on its museums, symphony, educational facilities, parks, observatory, and its baseball team.

Cincinnati is the bed-bug capital of the nation. I know this because my chiropractor told me. Several times. "If you go there," he intoned, as I told him about the book I envisioned, "There are some good haz-mat suits you can wear. It will cost you somewhere between $12,000 and $20,000 to rid your house of them once you bring them home."

So I thank you for buying my book, as by now I'll be needing the money. I told him I was not dissuaded (scratch, scratch) and was indeed fully committed to the project regardless (scratch, scratch).

On a more serious note, welcome to Cincinnati, the Queen City of the West. Settled in 1788, it was, arguably, the most important transmontaine U.S. city for the first half of the 19th Century. It was almost certainly the first truly American city, in that it completely postdated the Colonial Era and was thus liberated from the influence of the Mother Country. It was long Ohio's most important city, and between 1825 and 1870, it was the most industrialized city west of the Appalachians. Those dates bracket a span of years that represent, with the former, the year that Cincinnati overtook Baltimore as the leading meat packing city in the nation, and the latter the year that the iron industry came to rival the meat packing industry. By 1870, Ohio's other large cities surged to equal it in importance.

450

Cincinnati grew because it was ideally located on the Midwest United States' first superhighway, the Ohio River, at the mouth of the navigable Licking River that drained a sizable portion of the most fertile region the new nation had yet known. Interestingly, the Licking River flows northward and reaches the Ohio from the opposite, Kentucky, shore.

Cincy has always had transportation as its economic foundation. The first steamboat arrived in 1811. Portsmouth was the southern terminus of the Ohio and Erie Canal, but Cincinnati had its own canal, the Miami and Erie, completed in 1825. The first railroad arrived in 1836, astonishingly a mere five years after the Best Friend of Charleston exploded.

Interestingly, Cincinnati's rapid growth and commercial importance had little to do with railroads, which tended more to strengthen its economic competitors. It emerged as a river city, one that had more commercial connection with Louisville, St. Louis, and New Orleans than any city on the eastern seaboard. Still, it was its role as a transportation nexus that pushed its growth. It served as a gateway to German immigration into the fertile prairies of northern and western Ohio and Indiana, an ethnic heritage that is preserved in neighborhoods such as Over-the-Rhine and traditional industries such as brewing. Enough Germans lived in Cincinnati that the city had a German-language newspaper until World War I.

Germans have always been industrious people, and Cincinnati's economic strength has been a constant throughout the city's history. Almost from the time I left Christiansburg, I'd traveled through a region in decline. That ended abruptly at Cincinnati's beltway.

Did I mention Cincinnatians like baseball? And trains?

IT WAS LATE IN THE DAY when I carefully navigated my way through the center of the city to the west end where I found my lodging for the night, another Couchsurfing host, an enormous, kindly young man named Mark Kinne. He lived in a stately old home with high ceilings and magnificent leaded-glass windows on 8th Street, a city arterial. Mark had two other Couchsurfing guests that night as well, touring motorcycle riders from England. In arranging my stay, I had offered to treat Mark to dinner, so the four of us went to a restaurant called the Incline Public House. 8th Street points directly east towards the city where it abruptly ends near the edge of a bluff where the restaurant is located, with a commanding view towards downtown.

In the foreground below was the Mill Creek valley, running from left to right towards its confluence with the Ohio River. The 8TH Street Viaduct ran directly from the base of the hill away towards downtown. At the far end, a railroad trestle ran perpendicular to it, crossing the river to the right on a steel truss bridge. In the distance was downtown, with the football and baseball stadiums alongside the river that ran from the distant right towards us and then around a bend out of sight over my right shoulder. Downtown had several skyscrapers in the customary glass and steel cladding, with the tallest, the Great American Tower, predominant. At its top was a metal girder structure inspired by the tiara of Diana, Princess of Wales, fitting for the Queen City.

To the left of the viaduct I saw for the first time the back of the half-dome of the Union Station, my ultimate destination and my proverbial "Point B", with a sprawl of railroad tracks and cars just this side of it. I decided, given that the Powhatan Arrow terminated at the station, that my travels would as well. I would purposefully bypass it until I had a chance to explore the city and its relationship to the Powhatan Arrow.

IN THE LATE 19TH CENTURY, Cincinnati had a series of inclined planes, which were the primary public transportation devices over the city's hills. Most would literally take the accompanying streetcar, put it on a moveable platform, and with cables, winch the platform to a higher elevation and then release the streetcar.

The earliest in the city was the Mount Auburn Inclined Plane, opened for business in 1872. It ran 900 feet from the head of Main Street to the crest of Mount Auburn, an elevation gain of 312 feet. Seventeen years later, a car was inadvertently released at the head of the incline and it crashed to the bottom with many lives lost.

The incline where we dined was called the Price Hill Inclined Plane. It opened in 1875 ascending 350 vertical feet over 800 linear feet. Reputedly, in its heyday, it created a backlog at the bottom as cars awaited their turn to ascend. By 1943, traffic had diminished to the point where it was finally shut down.

After hearing about Cincinnati's unique German-influenced cuisine, I bought a Reuben sandwich for myself, and found the corned beef to be thick and flavorful. The view behind where I sat at the railing was fantastic, and I appreciated the opportunity to meet new people and share stories of our travels.

Countering that pleasure was my assigned bed, a hide-a-bed minisofa with no sheets, no pillow, and no blanket. Hey, it was free! And likely sans bed-bugs!

THE NEXT DAY, I began my exploration of the city. My first appointment was with Harry Black, the City Manager. One of the best pieces of advice I ever got was from my mother, who often said, "It never hurts to ask – the worst they can say is 'no.'" So I got in touch with his office and his administrative assistant made an appointment for me.

I was breathless with excitement and anticipation by merely approaching City Hall. WHAT a magnificent building! Cincinnati City Hall was a four-story building with a nine story clock tower, mostly constructed of tan, ochre, and brown stone and topped with a red roof. It was constructed in 1888 and is now a national historic landmark. It was designed by architect Samuel Hannaford, a protégé of H. H. Richardson, arguably the most influential American architect of the era. Stone and marble came from Missouri, Ohio, Wisconsin, Indiana, Italy, and Tennessee and granite columns were brought in from Vermont. It had an elaborate, appealing texture, and through an optical trick called forced perspective, its smaller windows at the top made it look even grander. I can't imagine any American city doing anything as grandiose nowadays.

Once inside and through the requisite metal detectors, I could see the intricate stained glass panels, the ornate wallpapers, and the marble staircases. The ceilings must have been 16 feet high. I was enthralled!

I waited briefly in the lobby, then in the manager's outer office, before being ushered in to see Mr. Black. I told him about my project and where I was from, and he immediately told me of his Virginia roots.

He was born and raised in Baltimore, but "My mother is from Virginia, from Northampton County on the Eastern Shore. It's just across the Chesapeake Bay Bridge Tunnel from Norfolk. My mother's side of the family emanates from there. I traced my family history to about 1830, based on oral interviews with my grandparents.

"My great-great-grandmother was a freed slave in Northampton County, prior to the Civil War. I don't know how she gained her freedom. When Lincoln signed the Emancipation Proclamation, interestingly, it only freed slaves in states and parts of states that had rebelled against the Union. In states and parts of states that hadn't rebelled against the Union, they were allowed to continue slavery. The Eastern Shore didn't rebel against the Union, so there slavery was allowed to continue. My great-great-grandmother actually took a band of slaves across the bay to get them freed."

My mind spun at this story. I reiterated what I'd heard, that a free black woman from a slave state in a region that hadn't rebelled, took slaves *BACK* to the rebellious region so there they would have become free.

"The Union captured and occupied Norfolk early on," he said, hinting that she may have taken them there. "They had to because of the naval strategic importance. It's fascinating stuff."

Cincinnati City Hall

He had close-cropped, graying hair and an intensity that made me think he'd remember every word of our conversation forever. He had a deep, gentle voice and a thoughtful manner. I liked him immediately.

"There is tremendous history throughout Virginia," he continued. He pointed at his Virginia State University diploma on the wall, with his University of Virginia Master's Degree in Public Administration diploma beside it. He was clearly as much a student of history and culture as I.

Our conversation shifted to the subject at hand. "Cincinnati has tremendous railroad history. The B&O Railroad terminated here. Camden Yards in Baltimore was the eastern terminus and we have the identical set of warehouses here.

"Our city government actually owns the Chattanooga Choo-Choo. We have an outside partner to manage it, but they are accountable to us."

He asked about my book and my quest, and I said, "I have but one question for you, sir: What are the economic challenges and opportunities your city faces and how are you addressing them?"

"Impressive question," he said. "Cincinnati was significantly impacted by the recession (of 2008) like many other communities. We began to turn the corner around 3 to 3-1/2 years ago. We're growing. People are moving back into the city. The population is increasing. From an economic standpoint, we have tremendous commerce. We've got nine Fortune 500 companies here. We have another twenty Fortune 1,000 companies here. We have lots of new businesses, start-ups, and small businesses. The city is healthy. We have a vibrant arts scene, food and beverage scene, and beds and meds (hospital and medical) scene.

"But everything is cyclical. Our key is to make certain that we leverage to the maximum extent possible this current positive economic window, a productive one, for the next down cycle. We need to be as strong as we can be.

"We're dealing with challenges of poverty and public safety. We do a good job, not perfect, in keeping the city safe. We're doing better than a lot of other cities. We need to deal with poverty, which is further aggravated by the digital, global economy. Things are moving faster, and people are getting left behind. We've got to find ways to allow everybody to participate in the evolving, digital economy. Too many people are not on that train. We need to find ways to get them on that train because if we don't, we won't be able to be as successful as we need to be, nor as sustainable in our success.

"I can only address this in a way that has a structural impact that moves the needle. Our policy makers are in a better position to do this. My city council and elected officials define policy, and I implement it. I surely make recommendations, but I execute policies and run the day-to-day operations. I undertake studies to get information to suggest better policy. Poverty is a result of a myriad of disparities. Health disparities. Educational disparities. Technological disparities. Income disparities. And they're only getting worse. There's no other way to say it.

"So we've got to figure out the quantum effect strategies because what we're doing today is helpful, but it's not moving the (poverty) needle. We're not changing things on a structural standpoint.

"We're a second-tier city, bumping against the ceiling to top-tier cities. We're more successful than most in our tier. Cincinnati and Cincinnatians punch way above their weight class. I liken Cincinnati to Evander Holyfield, who was a small heavyweight, but a champion. He had a big heart. That's Cincinnati.

"I've only been here two years, but I see this in the history, ingrained in the overall fabric of the city. There is always a can-do, never step away from a challenge mentality. That is my mentality, too. I feel at home here.

"We have regional and bus transit. We are launching a street car, the first new rail component to our overall public transportation network. A big challenge, a good challenge, is to accelerate our efforts to become what is a 'smart city.' Transportation is part of that process. We're not really focused on one mode, its multiple integrated modes. This used to be a huge railroad center."

I interrupted, "With all due respect, your Amtrak service sucks. I tried to use it for a trip here..."

He snapped, "That's indicative of passenger rail interstate and intercontinental travel across America now. The Boston to (Washington) DC Northeast Corridor accounts for more than 40 percent of Amtrak's total revenue. It subsidizes everywhere else. Rail travel has dissipated. It's unfortunate, but it's reality."

I asked if there were any warts, any continual thorns in his side.

"Cincinnati continues to struggle with race relations. I think it will still be a long time until we evolve to the next version: Human Being 2.0. It's an undercurrent. It's not obvious. It is part of almost every conversation on any subject matter.

"Cincy is a jewel of a city. Even from a design standpoint, it is stunning. The river is beautiful."

"If I come see you again in ten years," I asked, "what will you boast to me that you got done?"

"I have introduced here with varying levels of success a performance management program where everything is about transparency, accountability, and results. We have initiated a creative and innovative infrastructure enhancement program. We'll be doubling our street repaving efforts. Road rehab. Maintenance. We're modernizing our city's fleet of vehicles. We're basically re-tooling the city government. My goal for ten years is to do all the things that makes Cincinnati viewed as the best managed city in America. That's my Number 1 goal."

I EMERGED FROM CITY HALL and called a company across town, the Verdin Company, which I'd heard about. I knew they were an old company, manufacturer of ornamental clocks and bells. During the state's bicentennial they literally carried a mobile foundry and cast ceremonial bells in every county in the state. Their head of marketing, Bob Santoro, agreed to meet with me.

I found him in a temporary office, as Verdin had been forced out of their office by a recent fire. We we sat opposite one another at a fold-up table, surrounded by boxes.

Bob said that Verdin was founded in 1842, making it the oldest privately held manufacturing company in Ohio still run by descendents of the founders. "We are in our sixth generation in the Verdin family. The president is fifth generation, Jim Verdin." There were several other Verdin family members in key positions. "Our seventh generation is on the way.

"We make custom clocks and bells. We also make electronic bells for churches and organizations that can't afford real cast bronze bells in a tower. These make the sounds of bells (through loudspeakers). We launched a line of organs, manufactured to our specifications in Europe. We now combine bell sounds with organ sounds, which is very majestic and beautiful.

"We take lots of pride in innovation. The family is from Alsace, France. They were iron forgers in the clock business. Our first installation is in St. Mary's church, just down the road from here. While our technicians were in the towers, they realized that lots of bells needed repair, so they got into making custom bell equipment like yokes, clappers, and pins.

"Nowadays, our typical customers are churches, universities, towns and government municipalities, cities, small businesses. About 80 percent of what we do is funded by donated dollars, beneficiaries. In this age of the Internet, they'll Google us and find us. We have reps and service techs all over the country to install, repair, and service our products.

"We don't release our annual sales publicly, but we employ nearly 100 people and manufacture literally thousands of bells. A large bell of 36 to 42 inches might weigh 1,000 to 1,800 pounds and a 48 bell carillon might sell for a million dollars, depending upon how much installation and other work we do."

Bob was a native Ohioan who came to Cincinnati from Columbus for another job. But he spoke fondly of his new home. "It's a great community. I used to be in banking. Cincinnati has one of the largest family-owned business numbers than any other city in the country, as opposed to corporate or publicly owned companies.

"People love living here. Lots of people who grow

Bob Santoro and Verdin bell

up here never leave. I raised my kids here. I've lived in all three major Ohio 'C' cities: Columbus, Cleveland, and Cincinnati. Cincinnati has a special appeal. Friendly, good people. Good work ethic. That's why businesses do well here. Family-owned businesses support their communities. Cincinnati goes back to German pork heritage. There are lots of pigs around here."

He said the company started on Broadway and 2nd Street, moving to the current neighborhood later on. As the company grew, it opened a series of manufacturing locations to the east of town. The current office location in a neighborhood called "Over-the-Rhine." It is thought to be the largest urban historic district in the country, named by the German immigrants about their pedestrian commute over the Miami and Erie Canal bridges, with the canal being nicknamed the Rhine after the river in Germany.

He looked at his watch and said, "I've got time to give you a brief tour of the factory before my next meeting. Would you like that?"

"I won't turn that down!"

Moments later, we were in his car, weaving through the neighborhoods on the east side of the city on Kellogg Avenue, my old companion US-52, for several miles paralleling the Ohio River. We parked between two large, industrial buildings and entered one of them to find a technician piecing together a post clock with four faces, each one approximately 42 inches in diameter. In this one was an electric motor in the center with a gearbox radiating four rods to drive each of the four pairs of hands identically. Bob said the cost would be $25,000 to $30,000 for this clock. There were many others nearby in various stages of manufacturing and assembly. The building had a large overhead rolling crane and concrete floors with high-bay lights overhead.

The parallel building had most of the bell manufacturing. He showed me the forms in which the bells were sand-cast. Bells were coarse-tuned by their size and profile, then fine-tuned for specific notes by close machining on the inside. "A smaller bell might ring in 'C' and a larger in the note of 'A'. In a multi-bell carillon, the bells must be tuned to each other."

He said they have certain product offerings, but "Everything is custom, made by hand. We don't cast 28 bells and wait for someone to buy them. Everything is made to order.

"Lead time is three to six months for an order. We have a foundry for casting. We do fiberglass work. We have a machine shop and a fabrication shop. We train people on the job." He said they did some business overseas, but most of their products were shipped to domestic customers.

"Our bells will sound the same forever and last forever. The clappers and springs may need maintenance over time." He posed for me alongside a large, Liberty-bell like bell. He showed me that every bell needed to be installed in its frame and then tested, then disassembled and packaged for shipping. We went into a mezzanine office where an electrical technician was programming electronic touch-screen carillons that play multiple tunes making bell sounds, with thousands of songs programmed in.

On our way back to his office, he spoke about his company's resiliency. "The recession impacted everybody. But by having various products serve different markets, we were able to get through that and keep the talent and craftsmanship we have. The church market did well. When economic times are tough, people donate to churches. Churches had the opportunity to use that money. City and municipal markets didn't do well. Colleges and universities and other private donor organizations hung in there.

"We are an innovative company. We innovate in the product area and on the (manufacturing) floor area. (Our staff) is constantly innovating."

He spoke about the event that brought me to him in the first place, the casting of a ceremonial bell on location in each of Ohio's counties for the state bicentennial. "That had never before been done. When Jim looked into doing this, he had to come up with a way to engineer it so it could be done successfully and safely. The state of Ohio funded it as part of their celebration. We cast 88 bells on site. It's (one thing when) you're casting in a factory, but casting outside when it's windy, rainy, and sometimes cold, is a real challenge.

"My best days are making and shipping projects that provide tribute to our veterans. The community brings (our bells and clocks) to the town or cemetery through their efforts. Most people don't even know what they've bought until they see and hear it. Until then, it doesn't mean anything. What we make is the centerpiece of almost every overall project. It is for the past, the present, and the future."

CINCINNATI IS IN A PART OF OHIO known as the Symmes Tract. In 1802 New Jersey judge John Cleves Symmes purchased 330,000 acres bordering west of the Virginia Military District on behalf of the Miami Company, a syndicate he assembled for this purpose. Judge Symmes had been a significant financier of the revolution and held numerous certificates of indebtedness guaranteed by the federal government and proposed to exchange them for Ohio land.

This area was largely comprised of land enclosed between the Great Miami and Little Miami Rivers and the Ohio River; the northern boundary was somewhat fixed by the Greenville Treaty line. Though the Miami River Survey was subject to the Public Lands Survey System, Symmes' surveyors made numerous and consistent errors, including a faulty baseline, no correction of magnetic north to true north, and the survey and sale of land outside the purchase boundary.

The survey was executed so badly that after the Symmes purchase, the federal government ceased to sell unsurveyed tracts. The government land offices thereafter established a standard level of survey control that met the minimum qualities of a legally defensible survey, with corners becoming points fixed by law. To this day no field records have been found of this survey, save what was recorded at the courthouses of the 23 counties encompassed by this tract. The land that encompassed most of today's Cincinnati was part of this tract.

I FOUND DURING MY TRAVELS that I was always comfortable in the smaller towns wandering around on my own. But as in Norfolk where Jane Claytor Webster was so helpful in guiding me around, I felt that a tour-guide in Cincinnati would be beneficial. So I put out a plea through social media. A classmate from engineering school at Virginia Tech who spent part of his career in Cincinnati put me in touch with a friend of his, who coincidentally also went to engineering school at Virginia Tech a few years earlier.

John Burchnall had recently retired from a career at Procter & Gamble. With his Civil Engineering degrees, both bachelor's and master's, he initially worked on the design of manufacturing facilities, then transitioned to the design of affordable products, manufacturing equipment and supply chains for what has become the world's largest consumer products company. From a young age, he was always interested in trains and was an avid model railroader and rail fan, building friendships with many others sharing similar interests.

I arranged to meet him in a gorgeous home of a friend of his, Gerry Albers, who had literally designed and built his Tudor near-mansion in an intercity neighborhood around the plans he had for his track layout. Gerry wore a tan baseball-style cap and black T-shirt, both with the circular "VGN" logo of the Virginian Railroad. The entire basement of the house was devoted to his HO scale model railroad layout and operation. In this scale, one real foot is equal to about 1/8 inches, so a six foot tall man is modeled at ¾ inch and a locomotive like the 611 is 2.5 inches tall.

Gerry said like many boys of his era, he started with a Lionel train set when he was six. As a teen, he got interested in girls and cars and his interest in model trains went dormant. After raising his family, he got back into it. "I've always had a feeling and love of railroads and model railroads. It's in some people's DNA. I fell in love with the Virginian Railway when I was white-water rafting on the New River in West Virginia. I saw these awesome trestles and several still had little plaques that said 'Virginian Railway' and I started investigating it. It is just the right size to model."

Gerry's layout replicates in miniature a 60 mile stretch of the Virginian in central West Virginia, the "Deepwater District." He was an electrical engineer by trade, in engineering and teaching. "But now, this is a full-time job!" he laughed.

"Think of this basement area as a theater. What you see is the stage. But there is an off-stage left, off-stage right, and backstage. There are multiple hidden 'staging yards' that you don't see underneath and behind what you do. You have actors, and here they are the operators. The props are the trains. It's a 4-D (dimensional) art form, 3-D but the trains move. When you put on a play, what we call an operating session, we have multiple actors who get scripts, what we call train orders, and they direct activity. Everything is minute-by-minute time-lined. We compress 12 scale hours to 4 hours of operation. So our 'play' lasts 4 hours. We're only limited by how long people are willing to stand!

"The terrain the Virginian traversed in West Virginia was fascinating. I loved mountain railroading and coal hauling. I built the hills tall enough so you can't see across to the other side. So it's not child-friendly; it's too tall. The base level is around 41 inches."

I looked at the nearest portion of the layout. It was amazingly realistic, modeling not just the trains and the track, but also buildings, cars, people, billboards, mountains, creeks and rivers. The cars were even dirtied to become more lifelike. The perimeter walls behind the layouts were painted as if in continuations of the physical scenes. It was unfathomable how much time must have been invested. Gerry and ten or twelve guys had spent thousands of man-hours on it over 14 years. The locomotives were controlled wirelessly, electronically. The switches were thrown in a nearby control room, also electronically. "During our operating sessions, nobody physically touches anything on the layout, including the trains."

I asked both men about the choice of HO scale.

John said, "It's popular because you can have a decent empire in an average basement. This is a giant empire in a giant basement."

Gerry said an artist friend painted the backdrop. "You've got to do the backdrop first, before the layout, because otherwise you can't get to it. It's coordinated with the layout in the foreground. So you've got to

plan the entire thing first. I spent 2-1/2 years designing it on a com-
puter-aided design program before we ever started building. The artist
dictated the horizon line and I went from there."

John said, "In model railroading, we don't do the proportions
exactly. The hillsides are steeper on the model than in reality. These 60
miles of real track are scaled to 360 feet of track. We do selected compression of lots of features. We also don't make track straight or parallel from the edges, because curved track looks longer. We work with illusions."

Gerry added, "Our start-
ing and ending points in
real life are Deepwater in the
Kanawha River in the north
to Elmore near Mullins in
the south. I'm modeling the
summer of 1959, the year the
N&W took over the Virgin-
ian Railway. I'm modeling
five different railroad (companies)."

Gerry Albers and Allen McClelland

Gerry does workshops
on computer-aided-design, electronics, operations, and other aspects
of model railroading. "I've been building this for 14 years. It's more
fun than I ever envisioned. We go from operating session to operating
session. I have 35 guys who operate this railroad. We spend a few days
afterward repairing things and getting things back in order. Then we
prepare for the next session. We're always innovating. I have a to-do list
that's pages long."

He said his operating sessions were complex and intricate. "What
holds people's interest? Operating! We're modeling not a set of railroads
but a transportation system. I am the trainmaster, the director of the
play. What keeps my interest is the orchestration. That's what I love."

I asked Gerry about his monetary investment.

He said, "I don't know. I don't want to know."

John quipped, "A house to a model railroader is a basement with a
roof over it."

I ALSO SPOKE WITH ALLEN MCCLELLAND, who was working on
Gerry's layout at the time. McClelland was an elderly man who walked
with a bend in his back. He wore round wire-rimmed glasses and wide

tan suspenders. He was a legendary model railroader, having developed a number of cutting edge technologies over the years. He'd been retired for seventeen years. He was in marketing and graphic arts during his career. "I built my first model trains in about 1947-48. The fellowship is something I enjoy. I like creating things. Cincinnati has lots of enthusiastic people in railroading and model railroading. This is a family thing for me, with my son and grandson interested.

"I rode your Powhatan Arrow twice. The first was around 1957 or 1958. It had more cars and services then, but by the mid-1960s, there were only a few cars. The last time was just for fun. The Class J locomotives were part of the reason for riding it. I was once on a train when Winston Link was taking photos of it."

John said about him, "Allen is humble, but he invented many techniques in model railroading. He ascribes to the 'good enough' philosophy where things look visually good but don't take the hobbyist forever to build. Everything looks pristine and nice, with just enough but not too much detail."

Gerry rejoined our group as we looked over a portion of the layout. I asked about the next generation. He said, "There are young people getting into it."

John added, "We have active Boy Scout programs. There are young adults interested in photographing trains."

Gerry said, "I bring kids in to operate the railroad. I give kids the throttle. I want kids involved."

John said, "I started (model railroading) at 3-1/2 years old and have stayed in it all the way through. Kids these days have more distractions. Young adults are finding careers are tougher nowadays, and they're working longer hours. When they get closer to retirement age, they have disposable income. Older guys have more time and money. It's a lifetime hobby and it's extremely diverse. There are so many skills necessary to build and operate a model railroad."

Just like the real thing, I thought.

JOHN OFFERED TO BEGIN OUR TOUR of his city. He took me to the Mill Creek industrial area northwest of downtown stretching northward for several miles. We crossed under several railroad bridges, with each one he pointed out the particular railroad company. Many appeared to be in dire need of maintenance, with cracked concrete and rusting metal. We drove past the sprawling plant of Procter & Gamble, his former employer. The creek itself in that area was confined by steep banks, often concrete lined, to mitigate damage from flooding.

We were getting hungry, so John suggested one of Cincinnati's regional specialties: chili, served in a most peculiar way. He took me to one of the many Skyline Chili restaurants in the city.

On our way, near the riverfront, John spotted a slow-moving locomotive pulling a few cars, and he recognized it as being a new, experimental model. He excitedly parked his mini-van and ran with his camera closer to the track to attempt to get a photo, much like an avid bird-watcher will stop his car in the middle of a highway to better view a perched hawk.

Skyline Chili was founded in Cincinnati in 1949 by Nicholas Lambrinides, who had immigrated to Cincinnati from Greece. He opened his first store on Price Hill near the intersection of Quebec and Glenway Avenues and named it after the panoramic view of the city. Skyline now has over 100 locations, dominating rival chili parlors like Gold Star Chili and Camp Washington Chili, who serve a similar product.

The taste is unique and although the recipe is a closely guarded secret, many people believe it has cinnamon and chocolate in it. As peculiar as that is, it is served over – you won't believe this – spaghetti noodles. It is served "3-way" with finely grated cheddar cheese, "4-way" with cheese and either beans and onions, or "5-way" with both beans and onions. I'm convinced the quantitative aspect relates to the flatulential potential for the following morning. Given that I was a guest at someone's house overnight, I limited mine to "3-way" but it was more than enough food to be my primary meal of the day. Their other signature dish is called a cheese coney, a stubby hot dog topped with their chili, cheese, and onions.

Our waitress was a big, friendly woman who said she'd been with the company in that same location for 37 years. She loved working for Skyline and enjoyed her repeat business and seeing her young customers turning into parents and bringing their kids.

We then crossed the Ohio River south into Kentucky, a mysterious land of pig f*ckers (I'm sorry! I can't help myself!), to take in the view of Cincinnati. There were several bridges crossing the Ohio, both for railroads and motor vehicles. The views were grand, with the two stadiums, predominate. The Great American Ball Park hosted the Reds Major League Baseball team. Paul Brown Stadium hosted the National Football League Bengals team. Incidentally, I have never been able to figure out why a team from Ohio named itself after a region of India. It'd be like calling your team the Miami Siberians. Or the Minneapolis Sumatrans. The Green Bay Turkestanians. This is fun!

Anyway, that night we decided to attend a game, as the Reds were in town playing the Chicago Cubs. The Reds were one of Major League Baseball's most storied franchises, and are thought to be the first professional team in the country, dating back to the Cincinnati Red Stockings of 1881. Arguably their greatest team, and widely considered the finest baseball team ever assembled, became known as the Big Red Machine. Under the management of George "Sparky" Anderson, they featured stars Joe Morgan, Dave Concepcion, Johnny Bench, Tony Perez, Pete Rose, Ken Griffey, Cesar Geronimo, and George Foster. The 1975 team won 108 games. The Reds of 1975 and 1976 were a juggernaut, the last National League team to repeat as champions. Many fans of the era can still name their starting lineup, as I'm sure could any opposing pitcher who ever faced them.

In recent years the Reds had been less successful. We arrived at the stadium early, armed with the knowledge that they were the worst team in the Central Division and the Cubs were the best. As more fans filed into the stadium, it was clear that the Cubs' blue-clad fans would rival the Reds' red-shirted fans for sheer numbers and would exceed them in enthusiasm. Still, it was a warm, clear evening with lovely views of stern-wheeled riverboats and barges plying the Ohio River. Had the loudspeaker system not been an order of magnitude louder than necessary, it would have been an entirely pleasant experience.

The game started off as poorly as possible for the home team, with the Cubs' lead-off hitter sending a ball into the outfield bleachers for a home run. Chicago scored again in the 5th inning to give the visitors a 2-0 lead. Until the time the Reds got on the scoreboard with a bases-empty homer in the bottom of the 8th, they'd only had one hit! We were tired and surmised the game's outcome was likely decided at that point, so we headed home. But by the bottom of the 9th, the Reds were only down one, and to prove us wrong they miraculously scored a run to tie the game, sending it into extra innings.

It was not until I checked the news the following morning did I learn that five more scoreless innings went by until the game ended. The Cubs scored a run on a single snapping the tie, and then in the same inning got a grand slam for good measure. With the Reds still unable to muster much offense, the game ended in the 15th inning, 7-2, the longest game of the year. Although the game didn't turn out as hoped by the Reds' faithful, the Reds pitchers threw more than 11 strikeouts, qualifying John, me, and everybody there to a free pizza at LaRosa's, a local chain of pizzerias.

THE NEXT MORNING I MET up with John Burchnall again, he still eager to show me more of Cincinnati's amazing model railroad layouts. John was a founding member of the Eastern Loggers Model Railroad Club back in 1980. The club's layout was located in the basement of his house. It was oriented on a huge rectangular set of tables, about ten by twenty feet overall, with the built portion of the layout on the perimeter. It included a series of industrial areas, including a large sawmill complex, a wood chemical plant, a tannery, a gunpowder mill, and two smaller rural sawmills. The detail was amazingly realistic, with the yard at the sawmill complex populated by many stacks of cut wood, each of the thousands of pieces of wood about the size of a toothpick. John told me that the friend who cut the wood on a full size table saw ended up with more sawdust than usable pieces.

Like Gerry's layout, the number of man-hours here would be incalculable. I asked John about the fascination and dedication it must have taken him and his friends.

"If you have a nice, scenic model railroad and you've got a beautiful train going through it, it looks awesome! I'm also passionate about photography, and have been so since high school. Photography of model railroading is totally different than real trains. Both are fun.

"I run bus tours to layouts, and I know how long it takes most people to look at a complex layout. Most will only spend 15 to 20 minutes looking at it before they get bored and walk out of the room. If you start asking the owner about things, really take an interest, and get stories like you're doing, you'll get a better experience."

JOHN THEN TOOK ME TO a unique tourist attraction, the American Sign Museum. It may be the only museum of its kind in the country to display the artistry and craftsmanship of historic signs, reflecting the history, commerce, technology, and culture of our communities. The venue was a large industrial building where even the parking lot was part of the exhibit, displaying signs too large to fit inside.

Shell. McDonalds. Howard Johnsons. Phillips 66, Gulf, Holiday Inn, Kentucky Fried Chicken. These were some of the most famous, notable companies whose historic signs were represented. There was a huge "Big Boy Hamburger" figure, hawking a rich, double-cheeseburger and flashing a big-cheeked smile. Lesser names were Kelly Springfield Tires, Dolly Madison Ice Cream, and Emerson Television and Radio. All were brightly lit, some with conventional incandescent lighting and some with neon. Imagine the place's electric bill! All this was the brainchild of Tod Swormstedt, the founder.

After our tourist tour, including a live exhibit of neon tubing being formed and bent, I sought Tod to get his thoughts. He was sitting at his desk whose backdrop was shelving containing thousands of archival issues of magazines for the sign-making industry.

Tod had long grey hair, tied back in a pony tail. He said, "I worked on a trade magazine called *Signs of the Times* for about 28 years. It's a business-to-business magazine for sign makers. It began in 1906 and my great-grandfather was editor of the first issue. It was always here in Cincinnati and it's been in my family since early on. There were articles on the craft, like how to do gold leaf. We'd do cost comparisons on pricing across the country. Advertisers sold equipment, tools, and such. I started in 1974 or 1975. I took over in 1981, spending time in sign shops. I've always been interested in history.

"I expanded the company to Europe and South America. Then to Asia. I always liked new projects. There was not a public sign museum anywhere in the country. I thought about what I'd like to do when I don't grow up, and I had the idea to start a sign museum. I called some mentors and asked about the idea. Everybody said 'Go for it.' My family was supportive. I used the magazine originally to announce it, and in January, 1999, I stopped working on the magazine and started working on the museum full time.

"I started looking for sign stuff. I found a box in a safe that contained tools and samples from a man who did gold leaf. There was a letter inside addressed from the owner to my grandfather who said, and I'm going to paraphrase, 'I'm getting up in years and nobody in my family wants to follow my footsteps, so I'm sending you my sample kit because you'll know what to do with it.' It was locked up, hidden in the vault. It was one of the sparks that made me decide I needed to do this.

"So we incorporated and applied for not-for-profit status. We had a soft opening at a trade show. And we started getting donations and materials."

He said he tried to open the museum in Los Angeles or New York, then Chicago, and finally Las Vegas, a mecca for signs. But none worked out. Then Memphis. And then St. Louis. They didn't work out, either. So he found himself and his nascent museum back in Cincinnati. His original museum was only 4,500 square feet. It was there for six years. He found the current building in 2009, which had served a variety of industries over the decades. The museum expanded to 20,000 square feet, with an option on another 20,000.

"The old building had only me on staff. Here, we are seeing over 11,000 people, but we do lots of events as well. We do corporate events, weddings, and other gatherings."

I asked, "What do you know today that you wish you'd known in 1999?"

"Every time I hit a 'What the hell am I doing?' moment, something very cool would happen until the next down-time. I got incredible support from some sign companies. One company owner in another state donated $30,000, but has donated close to $3,000,000 since. He's a believer in the museum.

"Different people on our team have different contributions to make. My contribution is the grand vision. I work with detail in the exhibits as well. When I saw this building and toured the inside, I did the layout on a piece of paper with a pencil. When I started looking at the building, I knew that I could only do 20,000 square-feet of exhibits with the money that I had. I thought about traffic flow. As I envisioned more levels of detail, it just started making more sense. It was laying itself out in my head. I think I did really well for the money that I had."

"What do you hear your visitor say that brings you the greatest pleasure?" I asked.

He said, "I hear people talk about how these signs conjure up good memories from people's past. I hear different things from the general public than I hear from people in the sign industry. When I hear this stuff, sometimes it makes me tear up. I don't tend to dwell on it, but in the moment it is really cool.

"I used to question why I left my job. I was making six figures as publisher of nine or ten magazines. But I was wearing a suit every day and managing people. I didn't want to manage people; I wanted to do projects. I want to envision things in my head and make them real."

"What's the most valuable piece here?" I inquired.

"We have a vintage McDonalds sign that we've got over $30,000 in. We had to buy it, take it down, get it here, and refurbish it. It was a production sign and hundreds were made. But it's too big for collectors. It weighs two tons.

"This is nostalgic for a lot of people. But there is an artistic and craftsmanship component to it. I wanted not so much to help people with their memories, but to tell the story of the sign industry. These people are going by the wayside. Most sign guys, mostly men, had to know a lot of stuff. They needed to know how to design, paint, install, sell, and then collect the money. The downfall was most often from the business side. They were mainly of the stereotype of the artistic side and not so business-oriented. But these people had rich stories to tell. I wanted to do oral history, but I didn't have time and money.

I said, "I feel like this is what I'm trying to do with this book. I'm trying to honor the skill, dedication, and passion of the railroaders."

"Yes, I'm honoring the legacy of the sign guys. We're the heartland of America. There were some real characters. Lots were itinerant sign painters. The stereotype was a guy with a pint bottle in his back pocket whose hands shook like crazy until you put a brush in his hand and then he could draw a perfect line, like pinstriping on a car. He was as steady as a rock."

BY VIRTUE OF OUR BASEBALL GAME attendance the prior evening, John and I were each due a free pizza at LaRosa's Pizzeria. They have over 60 locations throughout the Cincinnati and Dayton region, and in customer repeat business, they exceed the chains of Pizza Hut, Papa John's, and Domino's. Their signature pie has a thin crust with a sweet, thick sauce whose recipe was devised by the founder's aunt.

It's a given that I speak with just about everybody, and on our way into the store I struck up a conversation with Antwan Campbell, an employee who was returning from a delivery, wearing a green LaRosa shirt and a pinned badge that denoted him as a manager. "I've been here 19 years. It's a good company. Crazy sometimes. Easy sometimes. I love Reds season when I get people coming in from all over the place. I work first shift, 9:30 until 5:00 p.m."

"How many pizzas go out of here in a day?"

"Maybe over 1,000. We don't hand spin, but we have them panned up and ready to go out the door. We prepare the crust ahead of time and then when we get the order we add the sauce and the toppings. We can (prepare) a pick-up order in 10 to 15 minutes. The pies are in the oven for only 5 to 6 minutes. One oven we have is kept at 650 degrees.

"People like the sauce, the sweetness, more than other places. It's our recipe. We have one location that makes the sauce for all the stores. We opened the first restaurant in 1954. We strive to do our best. We want to make sure everybody is loving pizza here in Cincinnati! Yep! Enjoy your day, man!"

It was a great little pie, and with my root beer the tab was $1.95 plus tax, with the free pizza.

TRAVEL ON THE INTERSTATE HIGHWAYS these days is, I imagine, nothing like the developers envisioned. For most of us these days, for varying levels of our life depending upon where we live, travel is dangerous and nerve-wracking with interminable traffic jams.

We made decisions as a nation to make automobile travel convenient and predominant, and thus people started traveling more by car. And shippers started shipping more by truck. Be careful what you wish for, as it may eventually overwhelm you.

As we discussed early in our journey together back in Norfolk, as global climate change presents an unparalleled challenge to our future, so too may an impending energy crisis.

I spoke earlier about self-driving cars and the potential they have for reducing energy consumption through things like platooning, ride sharing, and optimization of trip planning. There's a good chance we'll need those savings, as the energy that has fueled our explosive growth in population, travel, and commercial activity, seems destined to wane in the near future.

Let's start this conversation about 200 years ago, when the Best Friend of Charleston started steaming along the track in South Carolina.

Since the time humans emerged on planet earth (from evolution or divine placement, take your pick), there were never more than 1 billion of us until around 1820. Since then, human population has bloomed to around 7.4 billion. Just since the 611 was taken from active service, growth has been astounding, up dramatically from a mere 3 billion in 1960. What has happened to allow this phenomenal irruption – a sudden upsurge in numbers – to occur?

Energy is defined as the capacity of a system to do work. More pointedly, it is usable heat or power. When you have lots of energy at your disposal, you can do lots of work: plant, harvest, process, package, and distribute crops, build skyscrapers and superhighways, transport the products of a modern society, and drive your daughter to soccer practice.

Conversely, when you have less energy, you can do less work. Energy can neither be manufactured nor engineered. In thermodynamics we learn energy can neither be created nor destroyed, only concentrated or dispersed. The concentrated stuff is what we're after. Once we "use" it, it is dispersed. No amount of engineering talent or fantastic inventions will make more energy; we can only consume what nature has given us. We can waste it, use it efficiently, or bank it for later use. But we can't make more of it.

All life on earth is dependent upon energy. Prior to the 19th Century, mankind reaped the energy of the sun, in the form of grown crops, wind to propel ships, hydropower from dammed water to turn machinery, and the like. There were never more than a billion people supported this way. Afterwards, mankind began the extraction and use of the fossil fuel endowment literally always buried beneath our feet, and the population bonanza I mentioned ensued.

Energy and technology are not the same thing, not interchangeable or substitutable. If you run out of one (energy), you can't just plug in the other (technology). Jetliners have fabulous technology, but without the energy contained in liquid fuels, they are immobile hulks on the runway.

Oil is the most valuable energy source human beings have ever found. It provides nearly 40 percent of global energy needs today, including 98 percent of what we use for transportation. It's historically been abundant and cheap. When you look on a street or a farm field or in the air and see something moving, it is invariably powered by oil. A gallon of gasoline contains the energy equivalent of over two months of hard human labor, yet we purchase it for less than half the national hourly minimum wage. A personal pan pizza at LaRosa's costs twice as much.

Like a spoiled rich kid with daddy's credit card, since oil's first commercial extraction 150 years ago we have engineered countless systems around us to consume it in an insatiable, profligate way. We have re-engineered our transportation systems and our communities around the notion we will always have $20/barrel oil, spreading out everything we need to access. We think nothing of 40 mile commutes, 300 mile trips to a dance competition for the kids, or 600 mile trips to watch a football game or (in my case) research a book. Imagine a society where people drive cars to a gym to get a workout!

Additionally, we have found literally thousands of uses for oil other than energy. There's oil in fabrics, pharmaceuticals, plastics, synthetic rubber, and household and industrial chemicals. If you look at any aspect of your material world, you will see ample inputs of oil. Oil is amazing stuff.

When you consume a fixed resource at a growing rate, at some point you will not be able to produce more each year than the year before. If extraction of the earth's wells is plotted over time, it resembles the famous statistical bell-shaped curve, with accelerating consumption, peak, and then decline. During the decline, every year sees the production of less than the year before. This is inevitable, irrevocable, and inarguable.

Energy is not like every other resource. It is a precursor to other resources because without energy, other resources are out of reach.

The gathering predicament begins not when we run out, but instead as we pass the all-time production peak and begin a downward arc of depletion. We continue to find new and better extraction technologies (e.g. "fracking"), but peaking is inevitable eventually.

Once we reach the maximum of extraction, the point where, for the first time in the history of industrialized civilization, there is LESS oil available to the world's consumers than they are able to consume, the impact may be extreme. Historically, energy consumption and our country's economic health have been inextricably linked. If energy availability diminishes, will economic activity follow?

One potential outcome is major increases in the cost of all transportation, but especially air travel, increasing costs for heating and cooling, food, and nearly everything else, and thus major changes in the American lifestyle and all automobile dependent activities.

Cornucopians and so-called "free-market" economists waggishly proclaim, "The Stone Age didn't end because we ran out of stone. We went on to something better!" Will we this time? Nobody can really know.

Yes, there are other energy sources, including principally those land-based (e.g. coal, nuclear, and natural gas) and sky-based (wind and solar). Volumes can and have been written about these alternatives, but the short version is that the former are fraught with environmental problems and the latter are largely insufficient, at least with today's technologies, especially with regards to transportation. Scientists and engineers are exploring an array of amazing new technologies like thermal depolymerization, solar nanotechnology, space based solar arrays, and such. These fantastic new technologies are still perhaps decades from working systems, if ever.

Draw your own conclusions. Will these sources, individually or collectively, come to our rescue and provide anywhere near the per-capita supply we now consume? Societies and communities that better anticipate and prepare for this situation will fare better than others. Getting this right will have profound repercussions.

RAIL TRAVEL IS THE MOST EFFICIENT WAY to move lots of heavy stuff around on land. River craft provide an efficient way to move heavy stuff on water. If an energy shortage scenario plays out, Kenova, Ironton, and Portsmouth may show new life. Cincinnati faces a mixed bag, given the asset of its Ohio River and widespread rail connection, but its liability of expansive, inefficient suburbs. We may see a resurgence of smaller cities and towns, especially those with proximity to rails, rivers, and food production. Farming may become the predominant industry it once was and always should have remained, because three percent of the population will no longer be able to provide food for the other 97 percent as happens now.

Nowadays, massive trucking fleets move things around the country and cargo 747s fly fruits, vegetables, and even roses for Valentine's Day around the world. Alternative liquid fuels like biodiesel won't be able to ramp up to the scale to keep them flying and driving, meaning we'll need to move more stuff by rail and barge.

Some cities like Las Vegas, Phoenix, and Salt Lake City, increasingly parched by rising temperatures and unsupported by the rest of the country due to diminishing shipments of food and other supplies, and without the energy to run their air conditioners, will simply wither away. Other Sun Belt cities that have seen expansive growth since the running of the Powhatan Arrow, notably Orlando, Dallas, Phoenix, Los Angeles, Houston, and Atlanta, suffer from extreme energy dependency, with vast suburbs and sprawl, shoddy construction of homes and commercial spaces, and devotion to Interstates as their sole transportation option. They have the potential to fail spectacularly.

We've been working as a tacit understanding that cheap, available energy and increasing transportation is a reliable, eternal constant. We may be forced by the vicissitudes of the future to return to smaller cities and towns, walk-able and bike-able, connected by waterways and railroads. We'll eat locally grown and sourced food, adjusting to the seasons, living with greater personal interconnectedness and on a slower, more human pace. As difficult as this transition seems, there may be more winners after all.

FINALLY, I FELT IT WAS TIME to put a wrap on my journey. It was time to see the Cincinnati Union Station.

Given that this long pilgrimage was coming to an end, I was thrown into reflection about what I'd seen, heard, and learned. In no particular order:

• I met dozens and dozens of people along the way, and I can say with candor and honesty that I liked every one of them. I met rich people, poor people, and many in between. If you watch the evening news, you'll find an America that is violent, bigoted, and dangerous. Maybe it's out there somewhere, but I never found it. I went to lots of places other people seem wary about, escorted and unescorted, and I had not a tense moment anywhere. There is not a single person, including Junior the panhandler in Petersburg, who I wouldn't want to see again. (In a way, I perversely hope he really did have cancer, as at least he wasn't lying to me. Yes, if I saw him again, I'd give him another $5.00.)

I was treated with extraordinary kindness and generosity everywhere I went.

•   I saw slivers of anger and fear, but what I saw more often was everyday people going about the business of living, laughing, crying, raising kids, and doing the best they could, often in the face of considerable odds. People are frustrated and disillusioned by their governments, but regardless, there is an amazing resiliency and optimism out there. I'll leave it to the demographers and sociologists to decide whether it's innate or cultural. Most people I met just want to have another safe, happy, and productive day, and a future they can look forward to for themselves and their children. They seemed to internalize great joy in helping me do the same.

•   Economies are Darwinian, survival of the fittest. There is efficiency and productivity in uniformity, but there is resiliency and sustainability in diversity, which ultimately is more vital. Everybody I've ever met in economic development says they'd rather have ten companies emerge or come to town with 20 jobs each than one with 200. The reason is that the former better adapts to changing environments.

•   Automation has and will continue to destroy jobs on an unprecedented scale. While over the past 35 years, manufacturers in America have shed about 7 million jobs, our factories are actually making more stuff than ever before, twice as much as in 1984 with one-third fewer workers. Because the penetration of information technology into every part of the economy is not a passing phase but an escalating trend, it is hard to see how this employment will be replaced. Solutions such as increasing minimum wages and universal basic incomes (that pay people a stipend even if they don't work) are seldom advocated by either side of the political spectrum. No government or major political party shows any sign of comprehending the scale of this issue.

•   As with the strength in diversity of commerce, communities benefit from racial, ethnic, and sexual identity diversity, as different backgrounds spawn creativity in innovation and problem solving. Generally, for example, there is a positive correlation between how a community treats its immigrant and gay and lesbian populations and the strength and resiliency of its economy.

•   When people are fearful and angry, it is most often because their economic opportunities have been yanked out from under them. Compared with 50 and 60 years ago, our middle class is markedly smaller and shrinking each year. The time of the Powhatan Arrow was the time of our nation's greatest economic prosperity. I don't want to get too nostalgic about that era because we still had significant problems, especially pervasive racism and segregation. But everyone, ultimately, benefits from a strong middle class. And it didn't just happen; it was the result of numerous policy and legislative choices. We were a country that invested in itself, in infrastructure and education, in the Interstate Highway System, in the space program, in the G.I. Bill, and in Social Security. We do so now to a lesser degree.

• And we didn't hesitate to impose upon our wealthiest citizens a higher than proportional share of the cost. Today's economy has increasing wealth and power at the top of the food chain, where millions of Americans still inexplicably subscribe to a supply-side "trickle down" theory (cutting taxes on the rich and allowing the wealthiest members of society to keep more earnings in the hope that it would eventually reach the rest of us) that has never proven to actually occur. Rich people don't create jobs; consumers create jobs because they create demand for products and services, and they do this when they have money to spend. The era of our greatest prosperity coincided with the era of the highest marginal taxation rates on the wealthy, as that money was invested in the economy, eventually benefiting everybody, even the wealthy.

• The places that put all their proverbial eggs in one economic basket fifty or one hundred years ago – especially extractive industries – are those most likely to be struggling now. The nature of economies based on extractive industries is predictable and often tragic. The pattern plays out again and again. The owners of the resource make fortunes, while the miners, unless organized and unionized, make poor wages and incur terribly dangerous working conditions, the land is ravaged, and when the resource wanes as they all eventually do, the communities fall into deep decline. You can bank on it.

• We need to see quality of life as an economic driver. When you allow your water, land, or air to degrade, you bankrupt your future forever. Sacrificing pollution for commerce is a false argument, doomed to failure.

• Pay homage to reality. Beware of charlatan politicians who make promises they cannot fulfill.

• Global climate change is real and is already underway. Coastal areas are being flooded more often and more severely. This will put unpredictable but massive stress on those areas, places that now house significant segments of our population. And there will be stronger inland storms, with more direct storm damage and more risk of flooding. Affected communities ignore this reality at considerable peril.

• We face a looming crisis in energy availability that has the potential to derail economic progress essentially forever.

The people, communities, and societies that properly assess these risks and the opportunities they present will fare better in the future than those that don't. It's that simple.

JOHN BURCHNALL AND I TURNED into the Union Terminal complex from Western Avenue, and there it was, making me feel like Dorothy seeing for the first time the magnificence of Oz! The grand plaza entry looking westbound to the edifice was reminiscent of approaching the Taj Mahal, a vast promenade with the inbound roadway on the right and the outbound on the left, separated by a central reservation planted with grass, flowers, and shrubs.

The station loomed ahead, its front with a great semi-circular roofline, reminiscent of Yosemite's Half Dome, inlaid with hundreds of glass windows and in the top center with a huge dial clock. It pointed east, with the great façade facing the city, framed by that long concourse.

Spilling down from the building was a green-painted fountain waterfall, now dry during refurbishment, but I learned it was normally lit at night to great effect with a beautiful light show. The lighting poles lining the circular driveway were in the same carefully sculpted limestone as the building itself. When it was built, buses, taxicabs, and private cars were segregated on multiple levels, giving each separate treatment. On the columns framing the semi-circle were bas-relief images, carved in multiple blocks of Indiana limestone, one a female form representing transportation and the other a male form representing commerce. It was clear that the hand of an artist touched every square inch of the structure. The building was not only architecturally pleasing, but suitably proportioned for a city of Cincinnati's size and importance, imprinting an indelible image on the first-time traveler. It remains one of the classic Art Deco masterpieces ever constructed anywhere in the world.

We walked inside to find an equally impressive interior. The large open semi-circular main concourse had a diameter of 180 feet, with a massive, arched ceiling 106 feet above, painted in bands of bright colors swooping from end to end. A horizontal band containing a pair of giant rectangular murals of Cincinnati history swept across the circular wall above the base of stores and various other entry rooms. The murals were not painted but were mosaics made from thousands of ceramic color-impregnated tiles, each smaller than a nickel. The concourse had a richness of light and color enhanced by the abundance of natural light streaming through the great eastern panel of windows, actually parallel panels with five walkways sandwiched between them.

Not to be outdone by the exterior and the grand concourse, lesser rooms such as lavatories, dining halls, a theater, bookstore, barber shop, and retail stores were imbued with extraordinary panache and elegance exemplary of the era. I went into the men's room not so much that I needed to urinate, but just to see it.

Saying we don't build things like this any more seems self-evident to the point of being trite. It was truly an amazing structure!

The author at Union Terminal

Through his connections, John finagled a tour for me in what was called Tower A, the main switching and dispatching office for the passenger terminal. This room was accessed only through a maze of staircases and hallways, and I was told we were the last visitors allowed into it until a site wide refurbishment program was complete about two-and-a-half years hence. We were met by a friend of John's named Jim Edmonston, an expert on the Union Terminal.

Jim was a tall man, older than me, distinguished in his sport shirt, eyeglasses, and grey hair. He told me that Cincinnati was once home to seven different railroads. "We had the B&O (Baltimore and Ohio), C&O (Chesapeake and Ohio), New York Central, Pensy (Pennsylvania), L&N (Louisville and Nashville), Southern, and your N&W. They all had passenger service and they all came into this station. Before it was built, they all had their own stations spread throughout the city. If you had to transfer, you had to take a cab from one to another, especially burdensome during bad weather."

By 1928, Cincinnati was already hosting 108 inbound and 108 outbound trains every day, representing an average of 1,100 passenger cars and tens of thousands of travelers.

"(The railroads) all got together with the city to build this," Jim continued. "They had a political situation to determine which railroad would become predominant. The money came, pooled from the railroads, pro-rated by their use. The station opened for business in 1933, during the height of the Great Depression.

"All the trains were pulled by steam engines. The first diesels arrived in the late 1930s. There was a roundhouse over there," he pointed out of the expansive windows that wrapped around three of the room's walls. He sat on a long, Formica-topped desk with dozens of drawers below. In the center of the room, rectangular other than the yard-facing window wall which had a semi-circular center portion, was a rectangular pattern on the floor where the massive banks of track and signal switch levers once sat. Hanging on posts on the station side of the room was a vast illuminated track-plan of the entire passenger yard. The rail plan was reminiscent of one of those expandable blood vessel stents that is thin on both ends and thicker in the middle. The center area had a lattice of over 20 parallel tracks under the station's former concourse.

Counter to what I'd assumed, Jim told me the Powhatan Arrow actually came into the station down the Mill Creek Valley from the north, not from the south from the Ohio River edge. Trains arriving from Norfolk went through the small city of Norwood, located within the northeast portion of Cincinnati, then farther to the west to due north, then southbound through the station area. There was a rail loop between there and the river where the train could be turned around for the return trip. So the Arrow never saw the Ohio River again after leaving the north shore at Portsmouth.

The Mill Creek Valley, prior to the arrival of railroads, hosted the Miami and Erie Canal. Even prior to its completion in 1845, Cincinnati provided the junction of three transportation corridors, the east-west Ohio River and the north-south Mill Creek and Licking Creek on the Kentucky side. The railroads often followed the corridors of the canals and ultimately displaced them.

Cincinnati benefitted from this, starting, as I mentioned earlier, as a pork packing location. The tallow rendered from them was used for making candles and soap, and from these local byproduct resources household products juggernaut Procter & Gamble emerged. Technology evolved, companies evolved or failed, and Cincinnati's economy thrived. Bernie Kroger opened a grocery store here in 1883 that grew to become the nation's largest supermarket chain and second-largest general retailer in the country. In 1899, the American Rolling Mill Company formed and ARMCO, now AK Steel, is one of the nation's premier steel making companies. Household products. Machinery. Food. Medical equipment. All of these thrived in Cincinnati at least partially due to the transportation mix.

John pointed out the window to one of the trains going over the Ohio River Bridge to the south. Like all the others I could see, it carried freight cars only. There was a crane-like machine working up and down one of the stationery trains, loading double-stacked containers on low-slung cars. There was activity as far as the eye could see. But there were no passenger trains at all; Cincinnati only gets six per week now via Amtrak, three eastbound and three westbound. And frankly, as City Manager Harry Black and I discussed, the service is awful, with the eastbound departure that would bring a train closest to me in Virginia leaving Cincinnati at 3:00 a.m., and then only every other day. John said it was often hours late.

I kept looking outside the window, mesmerized. I became transfixed, my eyes darting from place to place, like watching the activity in a massive ant farm. I became light-headed, aware of sounds around me and voices behind me, but unable to react or process. I felt somnolent, road-weary and disoriented. I sat on the radiator below the massive windows to steady myself, hearing Jim and John as they continued to talk, but not listening. Words danced around the room like molecules, like balls in a Powerball machine.

Derailment. Excursion. Tractive Effort. Words from my journey populated my mind's dictionary. Thermal efficiency. Corduroy. Hobo. Feud. Coal. Images of people I never met flashed before my eyes. Billy Mahone. Winston Link. Bob Claytor. Sid Hatfield. Walter Willard. I became bewildered and the hairs on my arms and neck prickled. My eyes refused to focus.

I turned back to my company of new friends, and all looked mysteriously decades younger. Inexplicably, a massive switch lever board materialized before me. The track board's lights flickered hypnotically. People, mostly men wearing dark pants, shined dress shoes, white shirts with pencils in them, and thin dark ties, were scurrying about the room, barking commands at each other. I looked at the back of my hands and the aging spots and wrinkles began to disappear as if salved by some unseen balm. I brushed back my hair from my forehead, hair that hadn't grown there for decades.

I looked outside again and saw the roof of a large covered concourse below me. People scampered to and fro, formally dressed men wearing fedora hats and neckties and women wearing overcoats covering long dresses and high-heeled shoes. It became darker and a nearly full moon's reflection glowed from the numerous parallel rows of railroad tracks. Locomotives spewed steam and ashes to the sky and a low cloud of pollution hung over Mill Creek Valley. I listened. Watched. Listened some more, hearing but not responding or processing.

A massive locomotive, resplendent in its bright ebony shine and flowing, feminine form appeared from the north, chuffing as it decelerated towards the concourse. A mass of white steam puffed from its roof, shining off the moonlight and obscuring the string of cars behind it.

A loudspeaker barked, "Announcing the Norfolk & Western's Powhatan Arrow, now arriving from Norfolk, Lynchburg, Roanoke, Bluefield, Williamson, and Portsmouth on Track Number Four." I shook with excitement and curiosity, and rubbed my wide, disbelieving eyes. The Powhatan Arrow! I'd finally caught the Powhatan Arrow! There it was! I was giddy with excitement and self-satisfaction.

Then one of the guys mentioned my name and in a flash my daydream flickered. My fantasy was shattered, my hallucination vanquished. The crowd of people vanished from the concourse below, as did the concourse itself. The sky lightened outside. The control room returned to how it was when I arrived, and my small company of new friends continued to talk about their love of railroads. I sat stunned and slightly embarrassed, like a child caught daydreaming in class.

Change is part of the basic nature of everything. Yearning for stasis, for eternal stability, is futile and angst-producing. Resisting change is like asking the child not to grow. Or old men not to pass away. Or a river not to flow.

About the author

Michael Abraham

Photo by Jane Claytor Webster

Michael Abraham was born, raised, and educated in southwest Virginia. He graduated from Virginia Tech with a degree in Mechanical Engineering.

He has one adult daughter and currently he lives in Blacksburg with his wife, two dogs and four motorcycles.

He loves hearing from readers.

E-mail <michael@mabrahamauthor.com>